Top Cow Productions Presents...

Created by Stjepan Sejic

Published by Top Cow Productions, Inc.
Los Angeles

Top Cow Productions Presents...

Sunstone

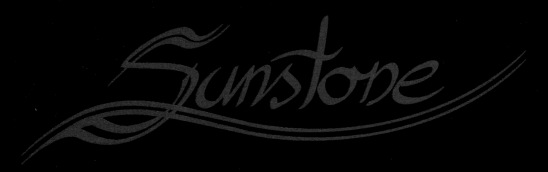

Stjepan Sejic
Creator, Artist, and Writer

Stjepan Sejic
Cover Art and Logo Design

Ryan Cady
Editor

Tricia Ramos
Production

For Top Cow Productions, Inc.
Marc Silvestri - CEO
Matt Hawkins - President and COO
Ashley Victoria Robinson - Editor
Elena Salcedo - Director of Operations
Henry Barajas - Operations Coordinator
Vincent Valentine - Production Artist
Dylan Gray - Marketing Director

To find the comic shop nearest you, call:
1-888-COMICBOOK

Want more info? Check out:
www.topcow.com
for news & exclusive Top Cow merchandise!

IMAGE COMICS, INC.
Robert Kirkman—Chief Operating Officer
Erik Larsen—Chief Financial Officer
Todd McFarlane—President
Marc Silvestri—Chief Executive Officer
Jim Valentino—Vice-President

Eric Stephenson—Publisher
Corey Murphy—Director of Sales
Jeff Boison—Director of Publishing Planning & Book Trade Sales
Chris Ross—Director of Digital Sales
Kat Salazar—Director of PR & Marketing
Branwyn Bigglestone—Controller
Susan Korpela—Accounts Manager
Drew Gill—Art Director
Brett Warnock—Production Manager
Meredith Wallace—Print Manager
Briah Skelly—Publicist
Aly Hoffman— Conventions & Events Coordinator
Sasha Head—Sales & Marketing Production Designer
David Brothers—Branding Manager
Melissa Gifford—Content Manager
Erika Schnatz—Production Artist
Ryan Brewer—Production Artist
Shanna Matuszak—Production Artist
Tricia Ramos—Production Artist
Vincent Kukua—Production Artist
Jeff Stang—Direct Market Sales Representative
Emilio Bautista—Digital Sales Associate
Leanna Caunter—Accounting Assistant
Chloe Ramos-Peterson—Library Market Sales Representative
IMAGECOMICS.COM

Sunstone, Volume 5.

First Printing. January 2017. Published by Image Comics, Inc. Office of publication: 270 NW Vaughn St., Suite 780, Portland, OR 97210. Printed in the USA. For information regarding the CPSIA on this printed material call: 203-595-3636 and provide reference #RICH–702021. ISBN: 978-1-63215-724-9

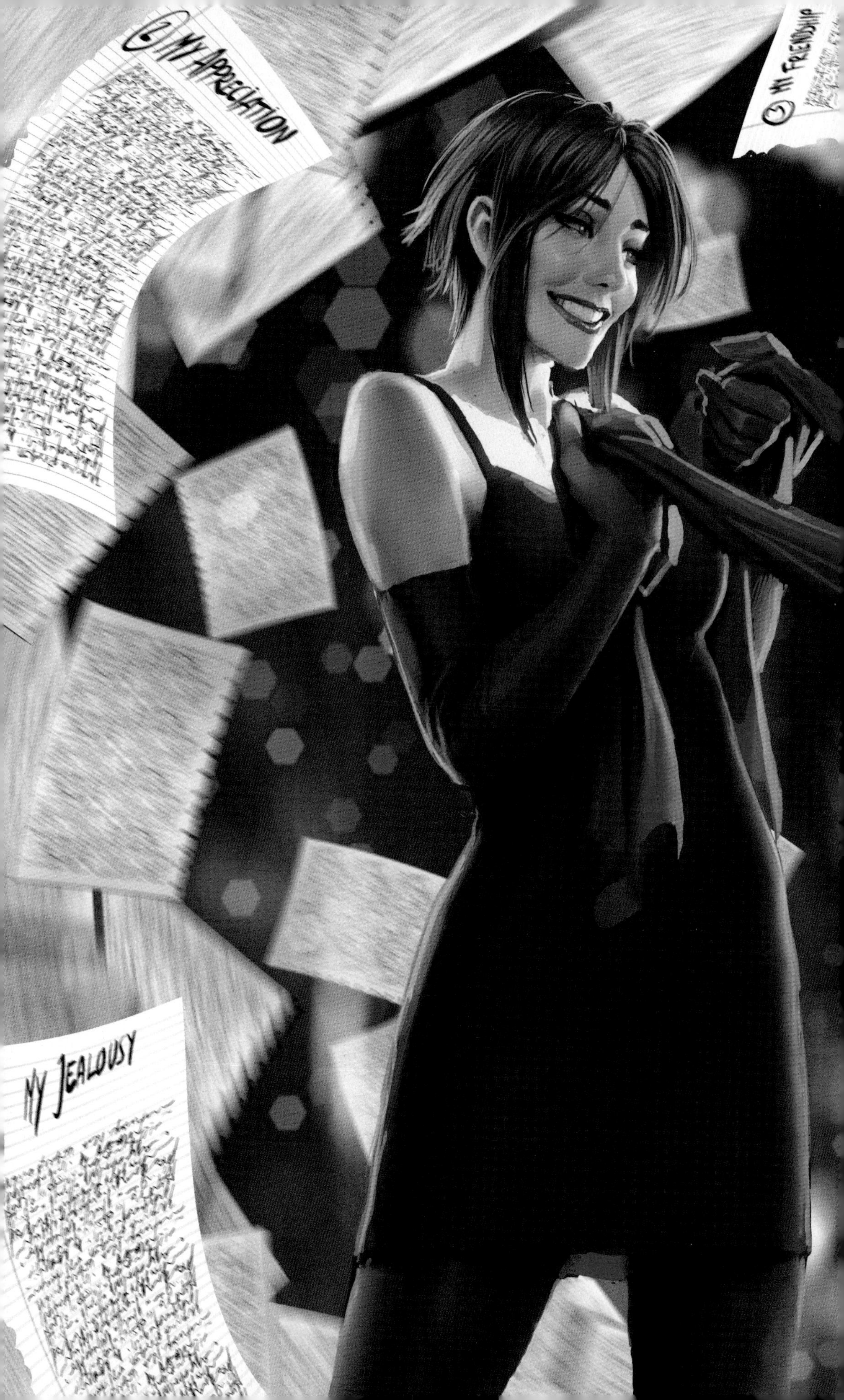

MY APPRECIATION
MY FRIENDSHIP
MY JEALOUSY

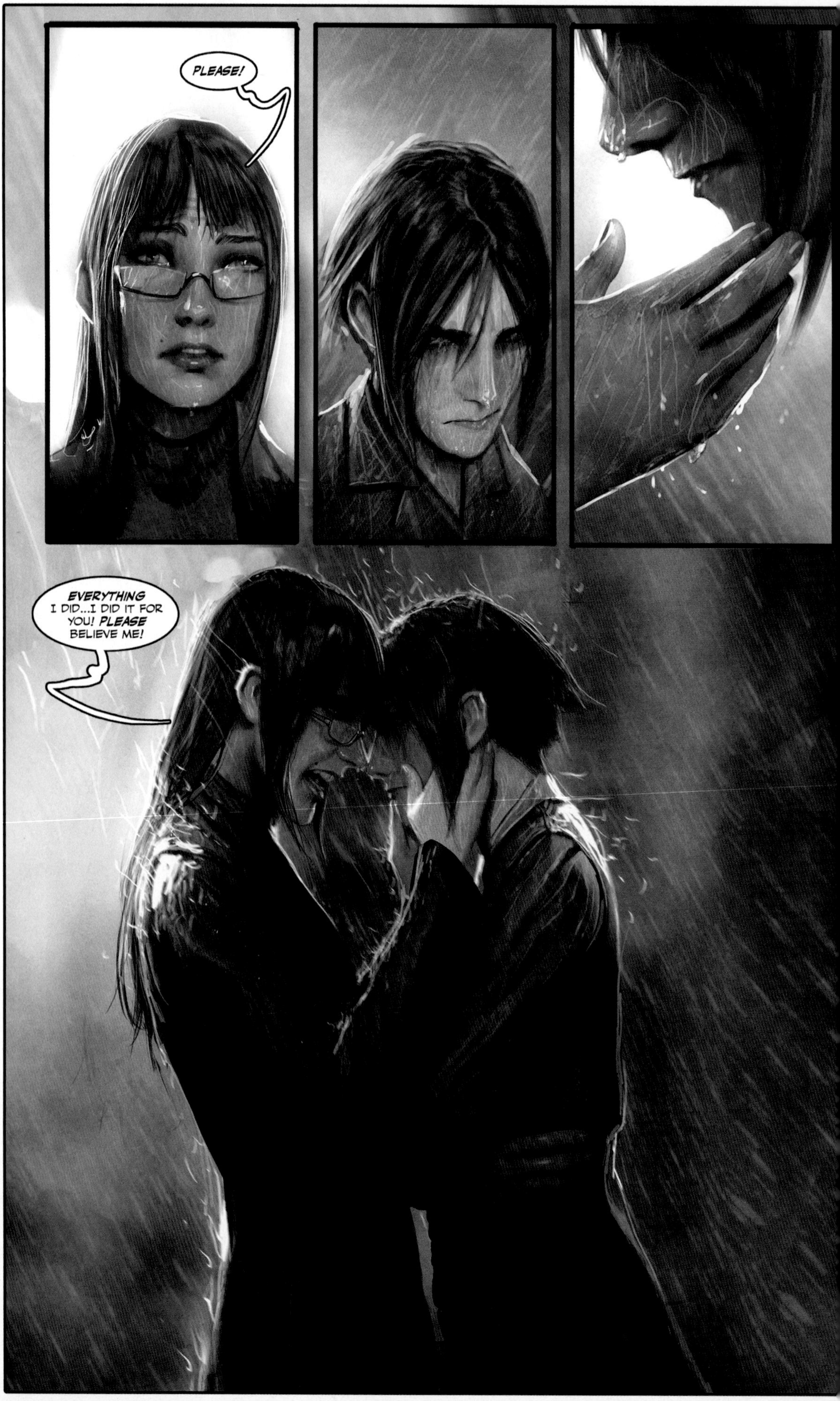
PLEASE!
EVERYTHING I DID...I DID IT FOR YOU! PLEASE BELIEVE ME!

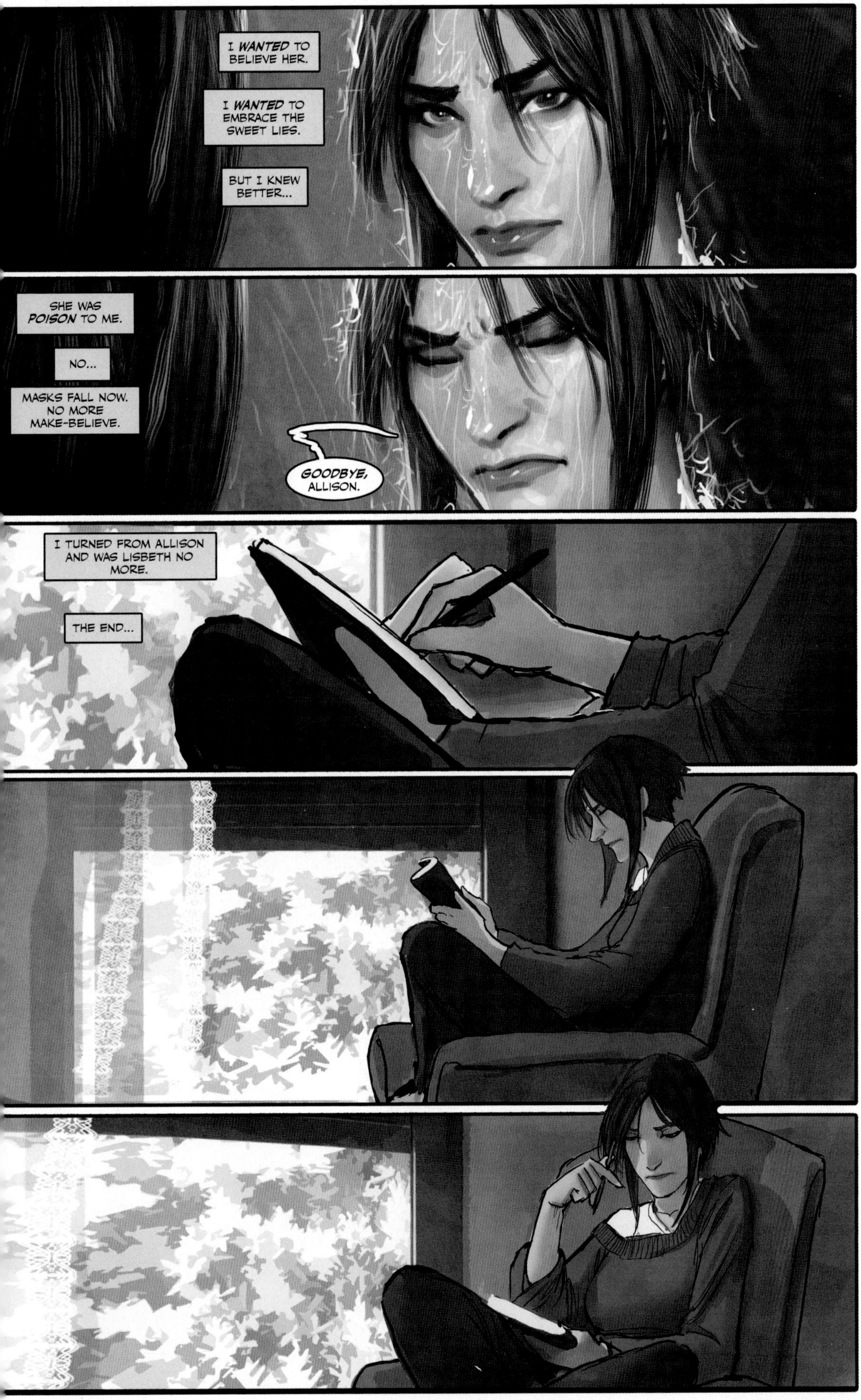
I WANTED TO BELIEVE HER.
I WANTED TO EMBRACE THE SWEET LIES.
BUT I KNEW BETTER...
SHE WAS POISON TO ME.
NO...
MASKS FALL NOW. NO MORE MAKE-BELIEVE.
GOODBYE, ALLISON.
I TURNED FROM ALLISON AND WAS LISBETH NO MORE.
THE END...

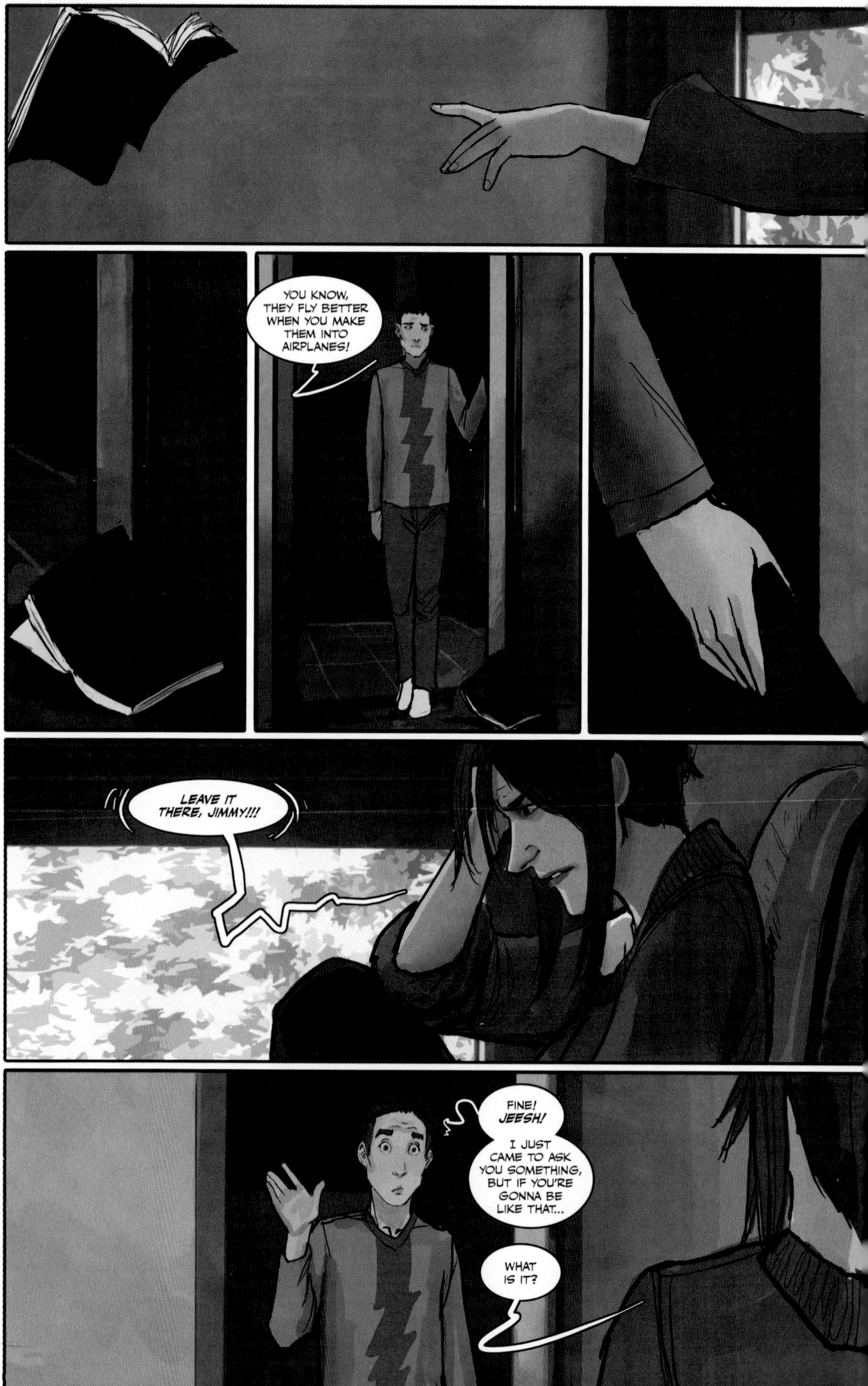
YOU KNOW, THEY FLY BETTER WHEN YOU MAKE THEM INTO AIRPLANES!
LEAVE IT THERE, JIMMY!!!
FINE! JEESH!
I JUST CAME TO ASK YOU SOMETHING, BUT IF YOU'RE GONNA BE LIKE THAT...
WHAT IS IT?

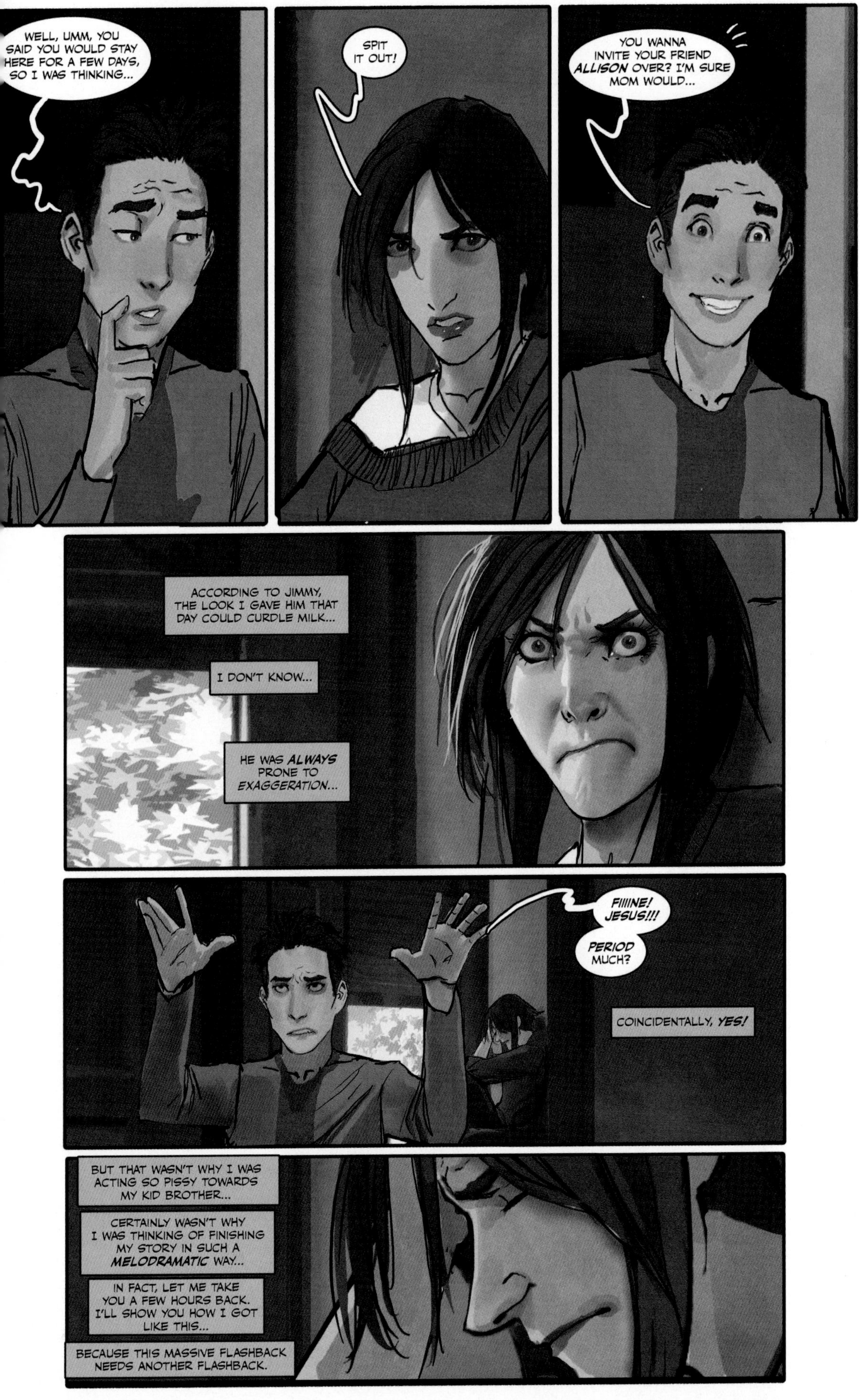
WELL, UMM, YOU SAID YOU WOULD STAY HERE FOR A FEW DAYS, SO I WAS THINKING...
SPIT IT OUT!
YOU WANNA INVITE YOUR FRIEND ALLISON OVER? I'M SURE MOM WOULD...
ACCORDING TO JIMMY, THE LOOK I GAVE HIM THAT DAY COULD CURDLE MILK...
I DON'T KNOW...
HE WAS ALWAYS PRONE TO EXAGGERATION...
FIIIINE! JESUS!!!
PERIOD MUCH?
COINCIDENTALLY, YES!
BUT THAT WASN'T WHY I WAS ACTING SO PISSY TOWARDS MY KID BROTHER...
CERTAINLY WASN'T WHY I WAS THINKING OF FINISHING MY STORY IN SUCH A MELODRAMATIC WAY...
IN FACT, LET ME TAKE YOU A FEW HOURS BACK. I'LL SHOW YOU HOW I GOT LIKE THIS...
BECAUSE THIS MASSIVE FLASHBACK NEEDS ANOTHER FLASHBACK.

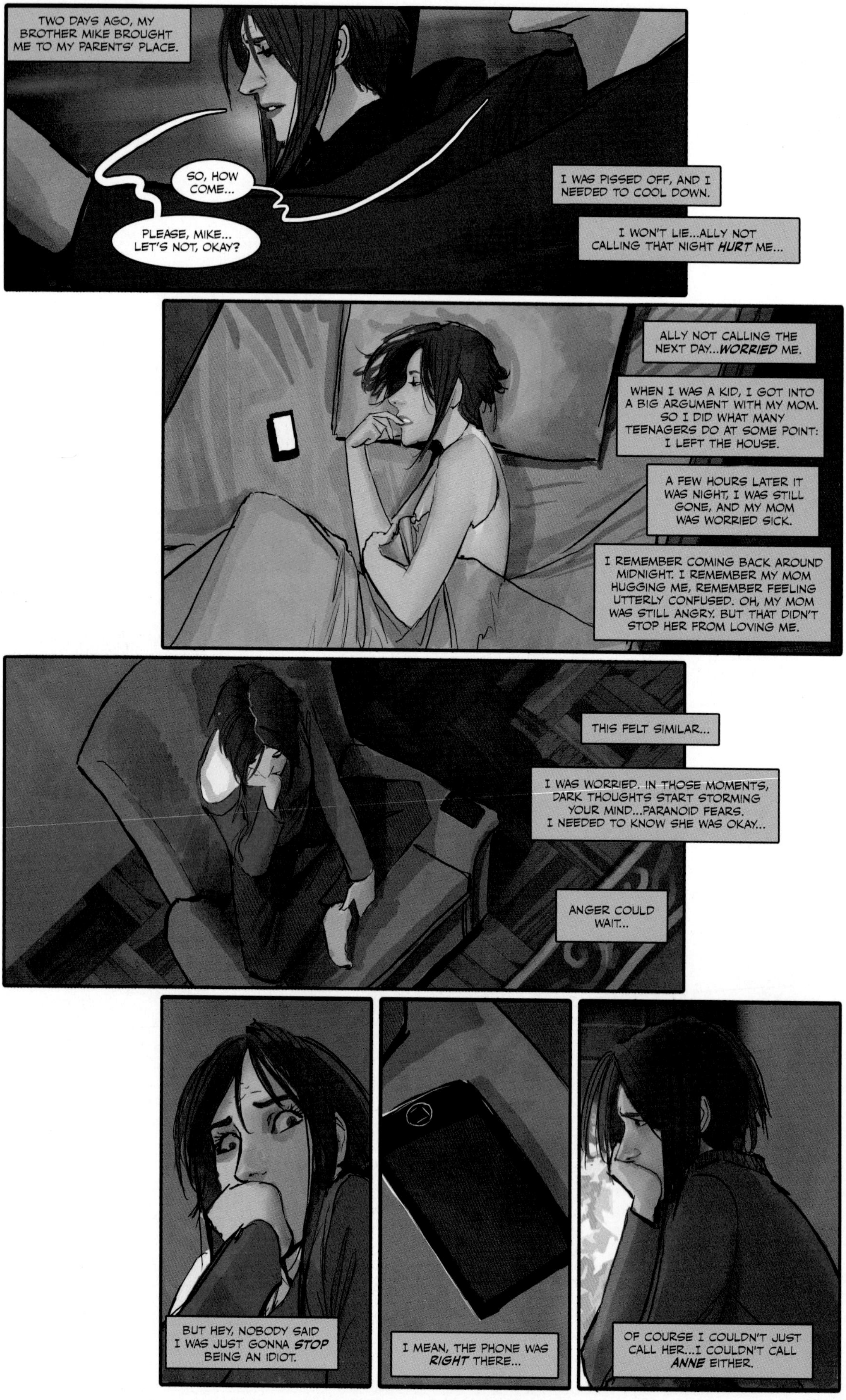
TWO DAYS AGO, MY BROTHER MIKE BROUGHT ME TO MY PARENTS' PLACE.
SO, HOW COME...
PLEASE, MIKE... LET'S NOT, OKAY?
I WAS PISSED OFF, AND I NEEDED TO COOL DOWN.
I WON'T LIE...ALLY NOT CALLING THAT NIGHT *HURT* ME...
ALLY NOT CALLING THE NEXT DAY...*WORRIED* ME.
WHEN I WAS A KID, I GOT INTO A BIG ARGUMENT WITH MY MOM. SO I DID WHAT MANY TEENAGERS DO AT SOME POINT: I LEFT THE HOUSE.
A FEW HOURS LATER IT WAS NIGHT, I WAS STILL GONE, AND MY MOM WAS WORRIED SICK.
I REMEMBER COMING BACK AROUND MIDNIGHT. I REMEMBER MY MOM HUGGING ME, REMEMBER FEELING UTTERLY CONFUSED. OH, MY MOM WAS STILL ANGRY. BUT THAT DIDN'T STOP HER FROM LOVING ME.
THIS FELT SIMILAR...
I WAS WORRIED. IN THOSE MOMENTS, DARK THOUGHTS START STORMING YOUR MIND...PARANOID FEARS. I NEEDED TO KNOW SHE WAS OKAY...
ANGER COULD WAIT...
BUT HEY, NOBODY SAID I WAS JUST GONNA *STOP* BEING AN IDIOT.
I MEAN, THE PHONE WAS *RIGHT* THERE...
OF COURSE I COULDN'T JUST CALL HER...I COULDN'T CALL *ANNE* EITHER.

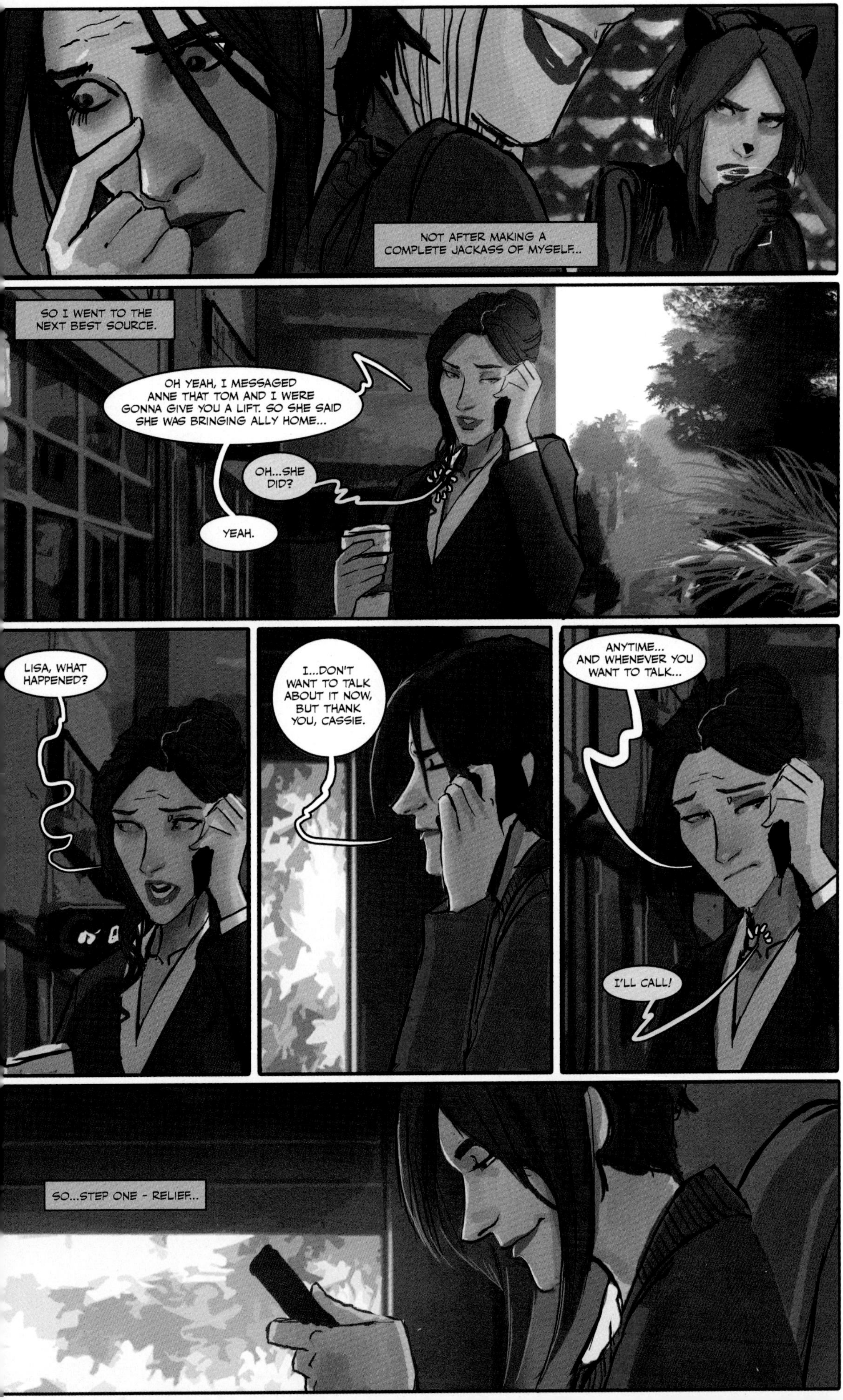
NOT AFTER MAKING A COMPLETE JACKASS OF MYSELF...
SO I WENT TO THE NEXT BEST SOURCE.
OH YEAH, I MESSAGED ANNE THAT TOM AND I WERE GONNA GIVE YOU A LIFT. SO SHE SAID SHE WAS BRINGING ALLY HOME...
OH...SHE DID?
YEAH.
LISA, WHAT HAPPENED?
I...DON'T WANT TO TALK ABOUT IT NOW, BUT THANK YOU, CASSIE.
ANYTIME... AND WHENEVER YOU WANT TO TALK...
I'LL CALL!
SO...STEP ONE - RELIEF...

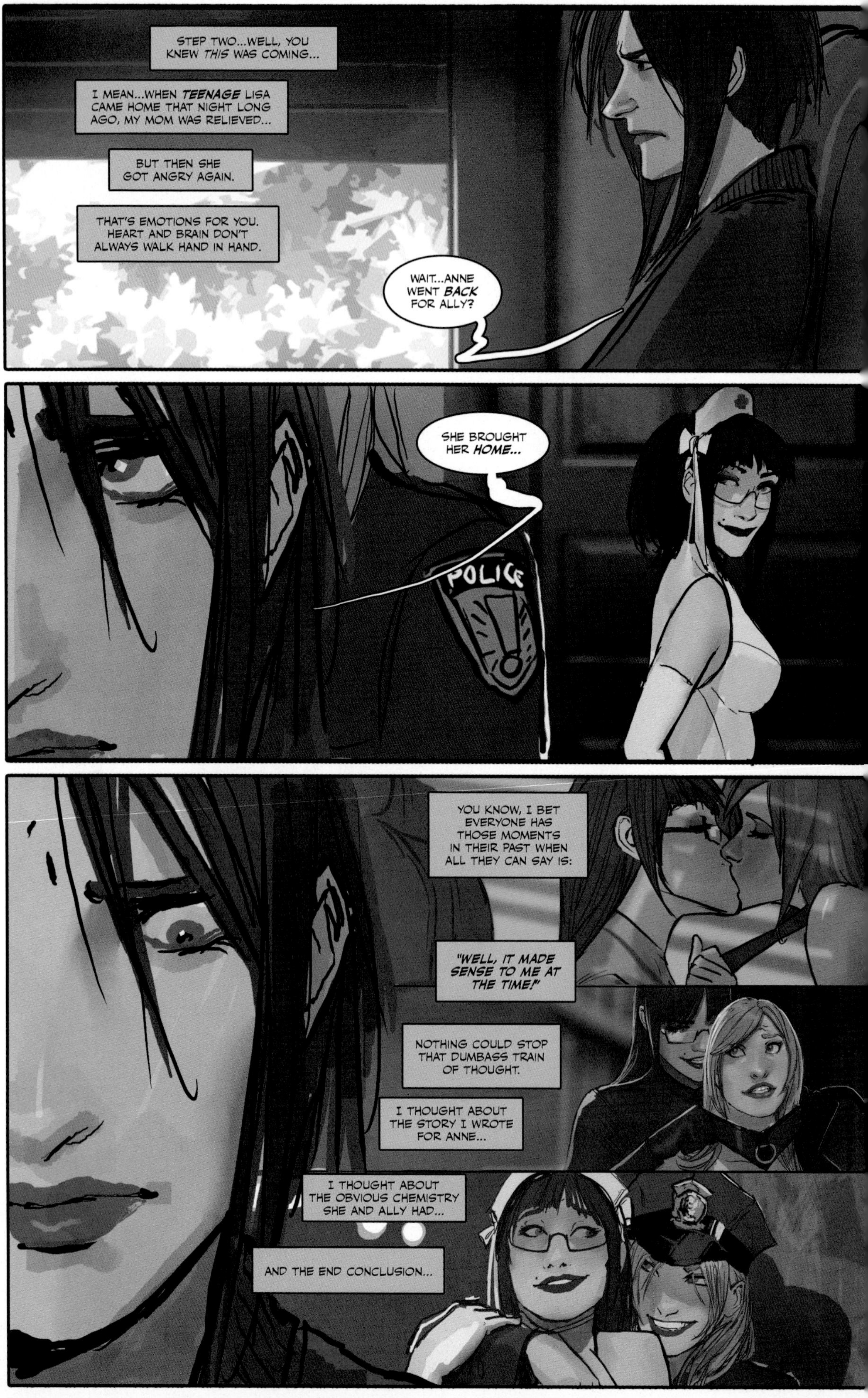
STEP TWO...WELL, YOU KNEW *THIS* WAS COMING...
I MEAN...WHEN ***TEENAGE*** LISA CAME HOME THAT NIGHT LONG AGO, MY MOM WAS RELIEVED...
BUT THEN SHE GOT ANGRY AGAIN.
THAT'S EMOTIONS FOR YOU. HEART AND BRAIN DON'T ALWAYS WALK HAND IN HAND.
WAIT...ANNE WENT ***BACK*** FOR ALLY?
SHE BROUGHT HER ***HOME...***
POLICE
YOU KNOW, I BET EVERYONE HAS THOSE MOMENTS IN THEIR PAST WHEN ALL THEY CAN SAY IS:
"WELL, IT MADE SENSE TO ME AT THE TIME!"
NOTHING COULD STOP THAT DUMBASS TRAIN OF THOUGHT.
I THOUGHT ABOUT THE STORY I WROTE FOR ANNE...
I THOUGHT ABOUT THE OBVIOUS CHEMISTRY SHE AND ALLY HAD...
AND THE END CONCLUSION...

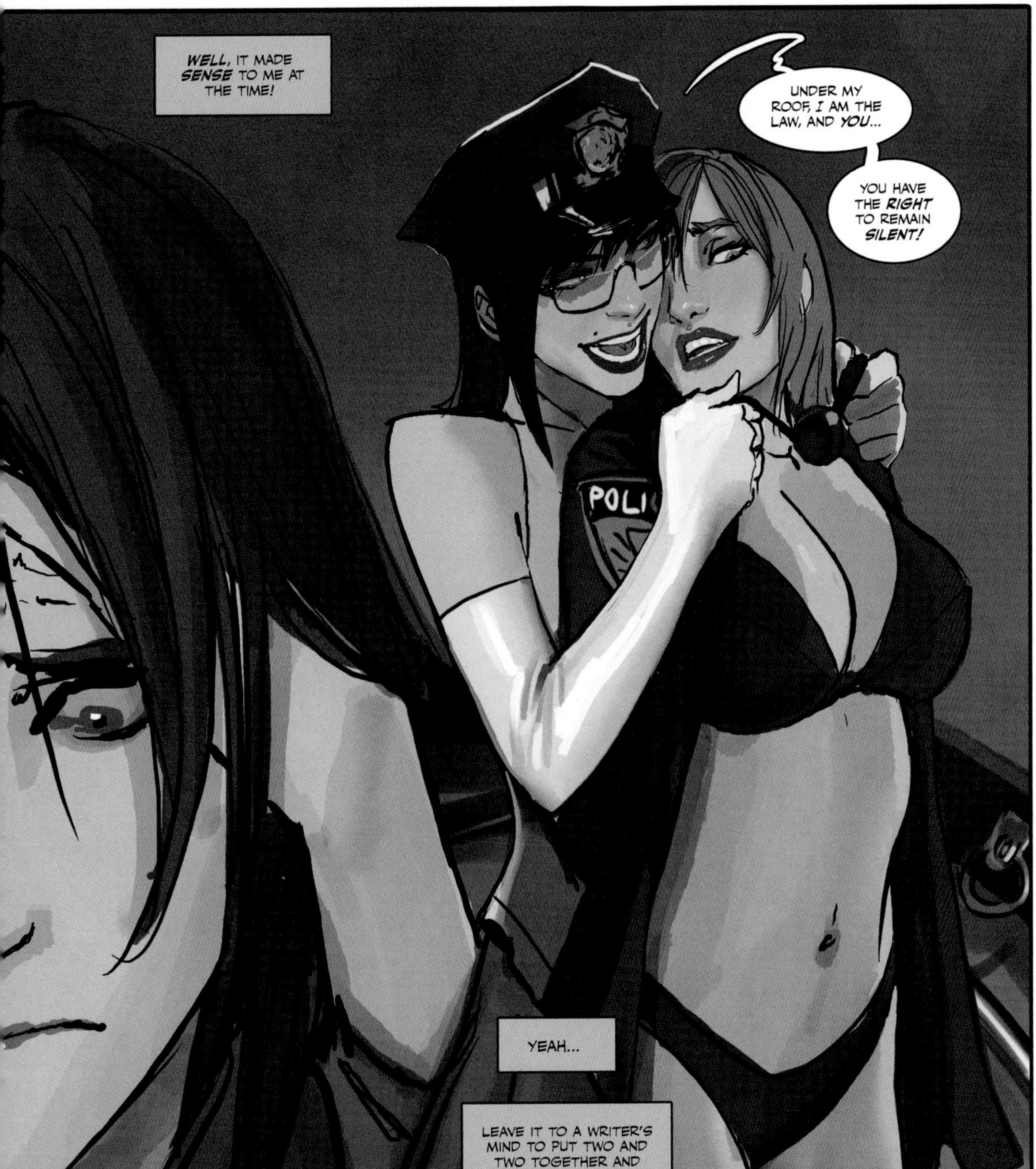
WELL, IT MADE SENSE TO ME AT THE TIME!
UNDER MY ROOF, I AM THE LAW, AND YOU...
YOU HAVE THE RIGHT TO REMAIN SILENT!
POLI
YEAH...
LEAVE IT TO A WRITER'S MIND TO PUT TWO AND TWO TOGETHER AND COME UP WITH 69.

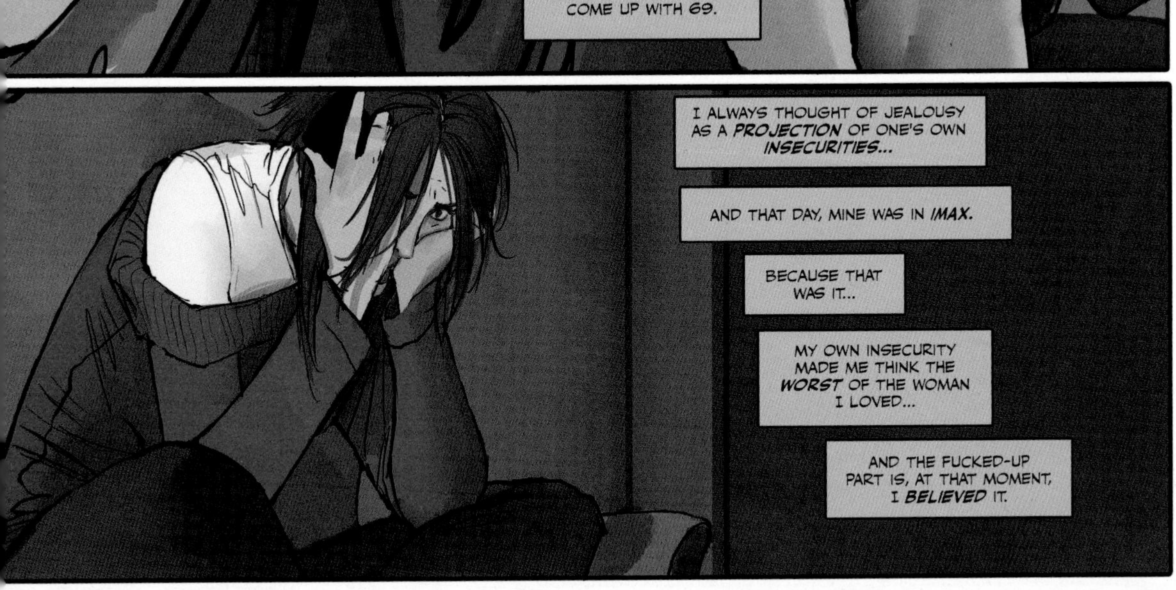
I ALWAYS THOUGHT OF JEALOUSY AS A PROJECTION OF ONE'S OWN INSECURITIES...
AND THAT DAY, MINE WAS IN IMAX.
BECAUSE THAT WAS IT...
MY OWN INSECURITY MADE ME THINK THE WORST OF THE WOMAN I LOVED...
AND THE FUCKED-UP PART IS, AT THAT MOMENT, I BELIEVED IT.

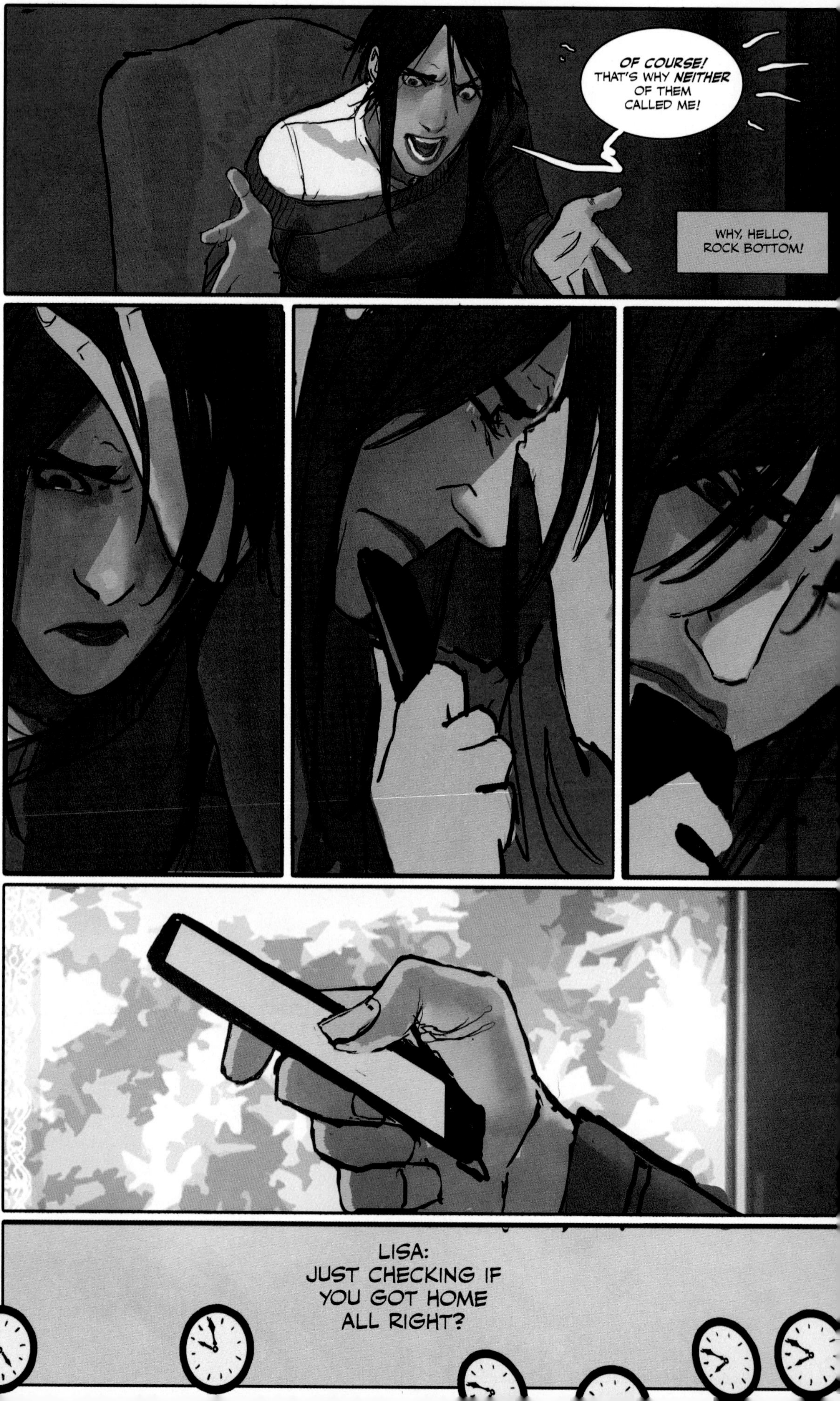
OF COURSE! THAT'S WHY NEITHER OF THEM CALLED ME!
WHY, HELLO, ROCK BOTTOM!
LISA: JUST CHECKING IF YOU GOT HOME ALL RIGHT?

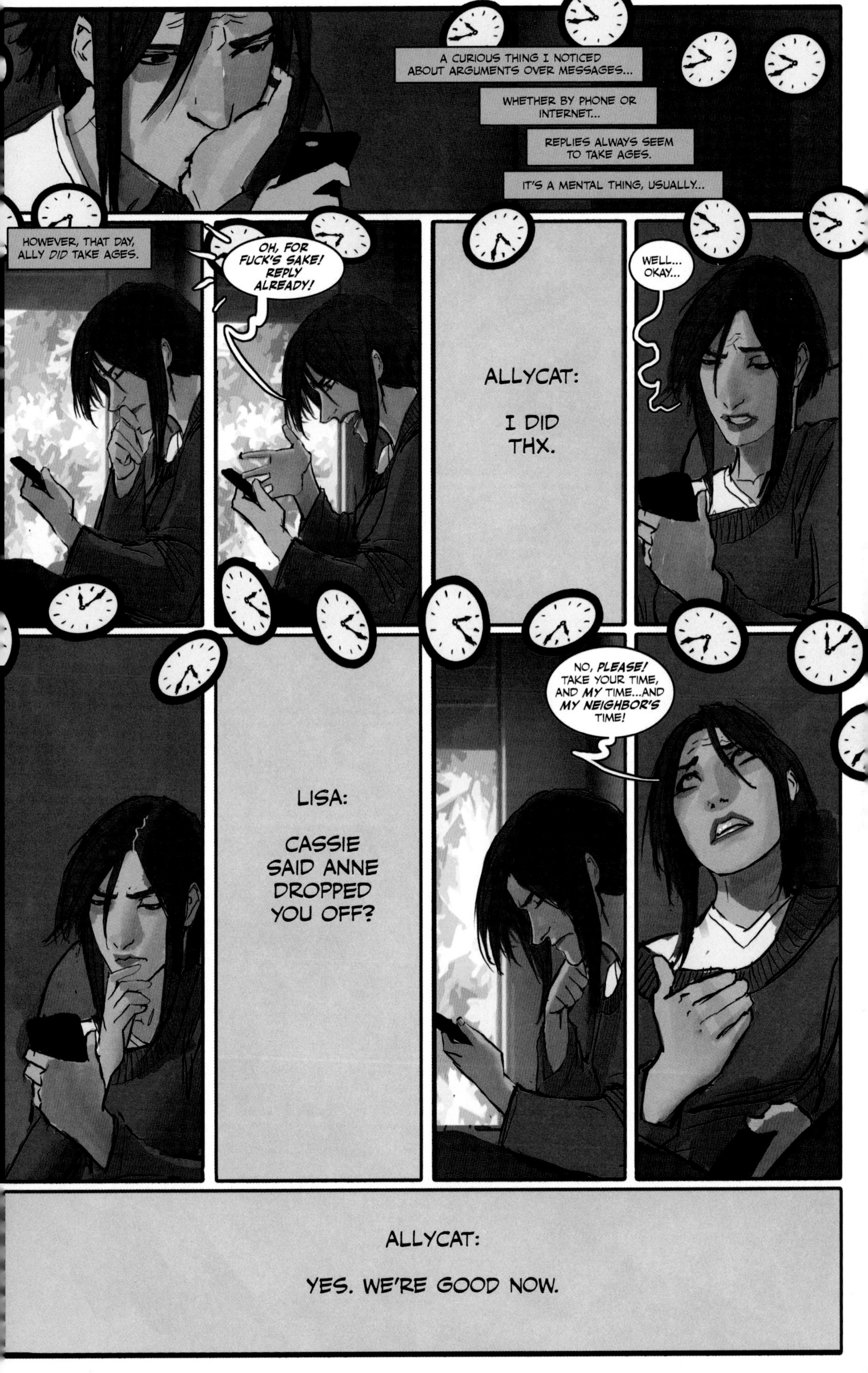

A CURIOUS THING I NOTICED ABOUT ARGUMENTS OVER MESSAGES...
WHETHER BY PHONE OR INTERNET...
REPLIES ALWAYS SEEM TO TAKE AGES.
IT'S A MENTAL THING, USUALLY...
HOWEVER, THAT DAY, ALLY DID TAKE AGES.
OH, FOR FUCK'S SAKE! REPLY ALREADY!
ALLYCAT:
I DID THX.
WELL... OKAY...
LISA:
CASSIE SAID ANNE DROPPED YOU OFF?
NO, PLEASE! TAKE YOUR TIME, AND MY TIME...AND MY NEIGHBOR'S TIME!
ALLYCAT:
YES. WE'RE GOOD NOW.

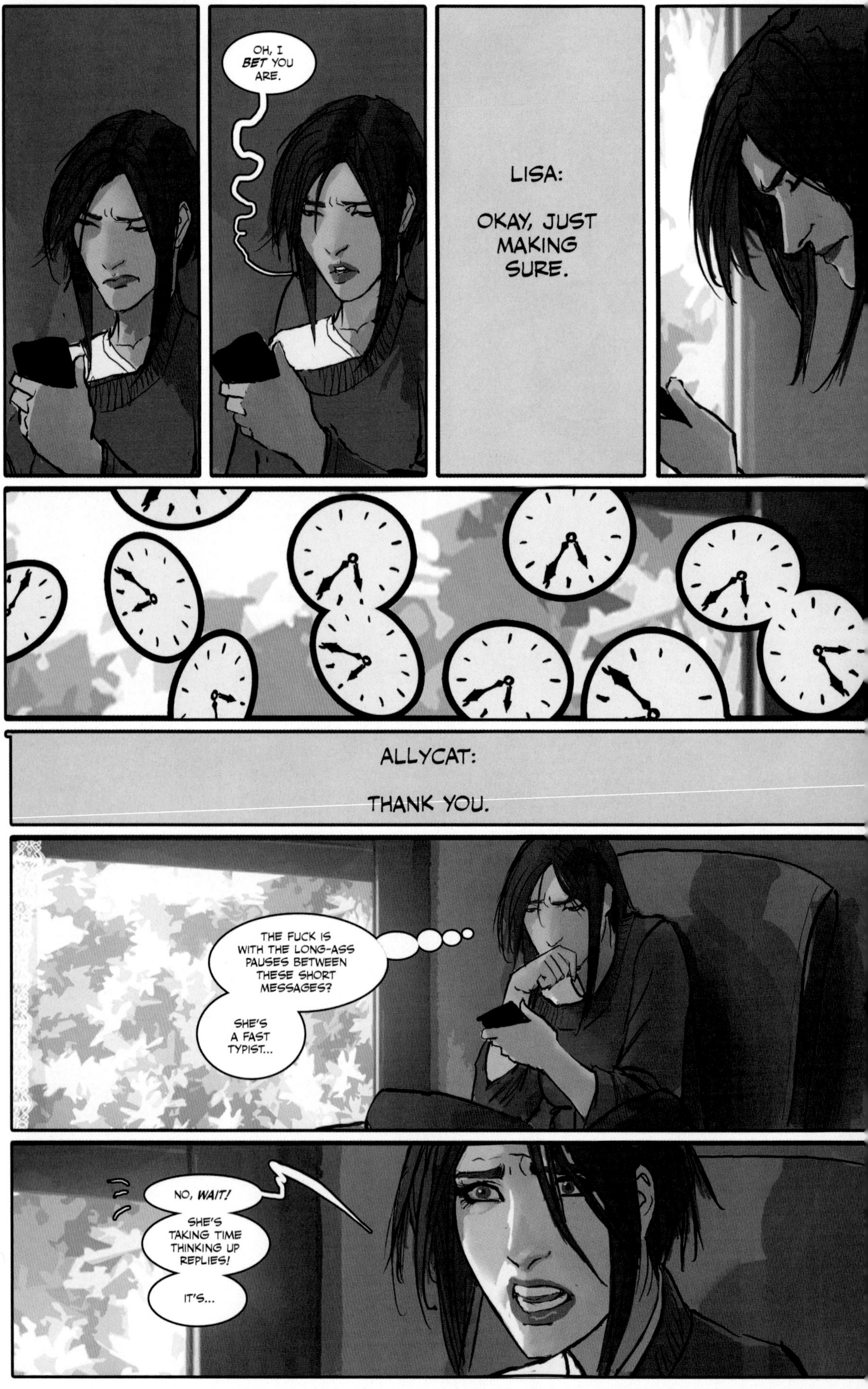

OH, I *BET* YOU ARE.
LISA:
OKAY, JUST MAKING SURE.
ALLYCAT:
THANK YOU.
THE FUCK IS WITH THE LONG-ASS PAUSES BETWEEN THESE SHORT MESSAGES?
SHE'S A FAST TYPIST...
NO, *WAIT!*
SHE'S TAKING TIME THINKING UP REPLIES!
IT'S...

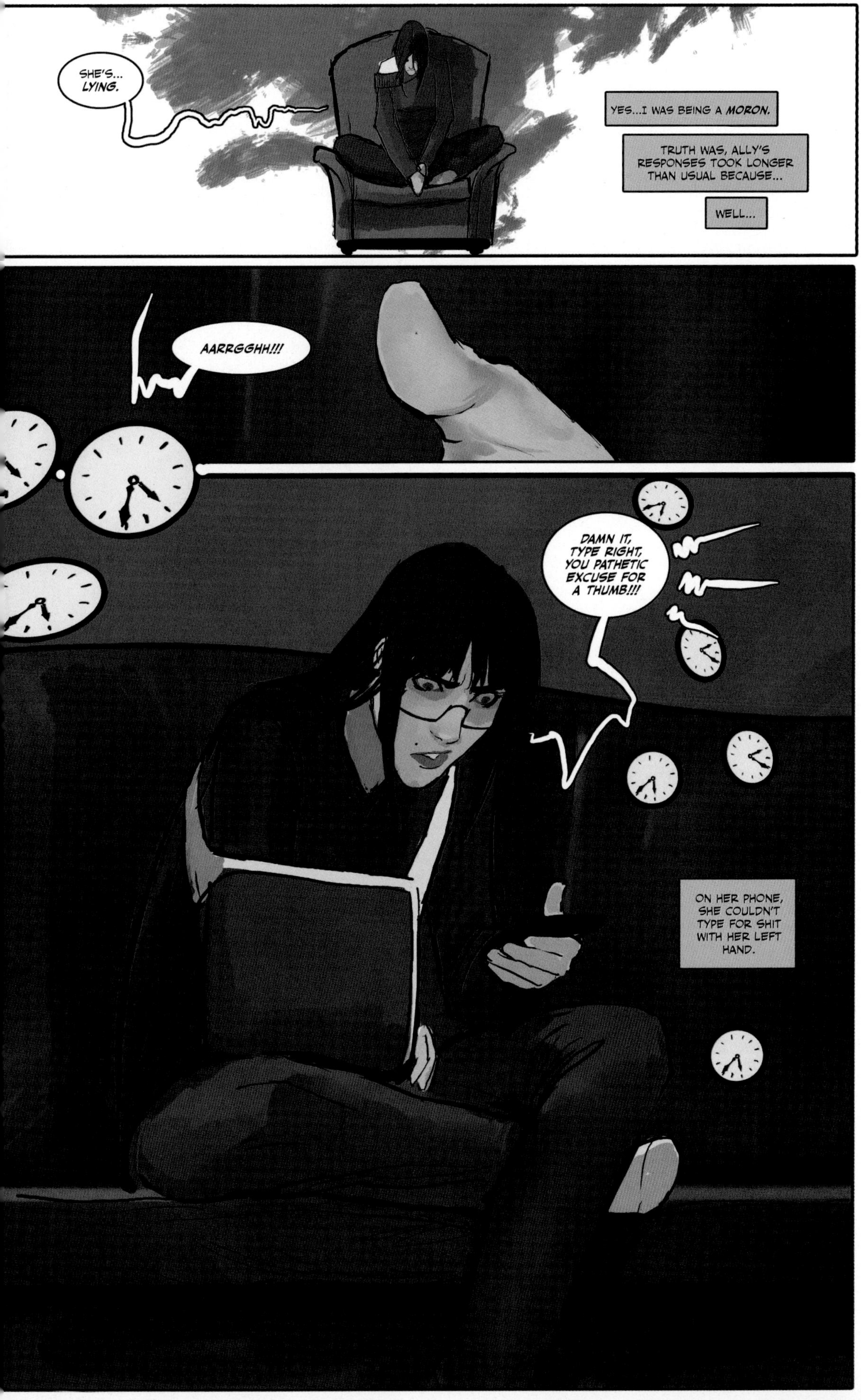
SHE'S... LYING.
YES...I WAS BEING A MORON.
TRUTH WAS, ALLY'S RESPONSES TOOK LONGER THAN USUAL BECAUSE...
WELL...
AARRGGHH!!!
DAMN IT, TYPE RIGHT, YOU PATHETIC EXCUSE FOR A THUMB!!!
ON HER PHONE, SHE COULDN'T TYPE FOR SHIT WITH HER LEFT HAND.

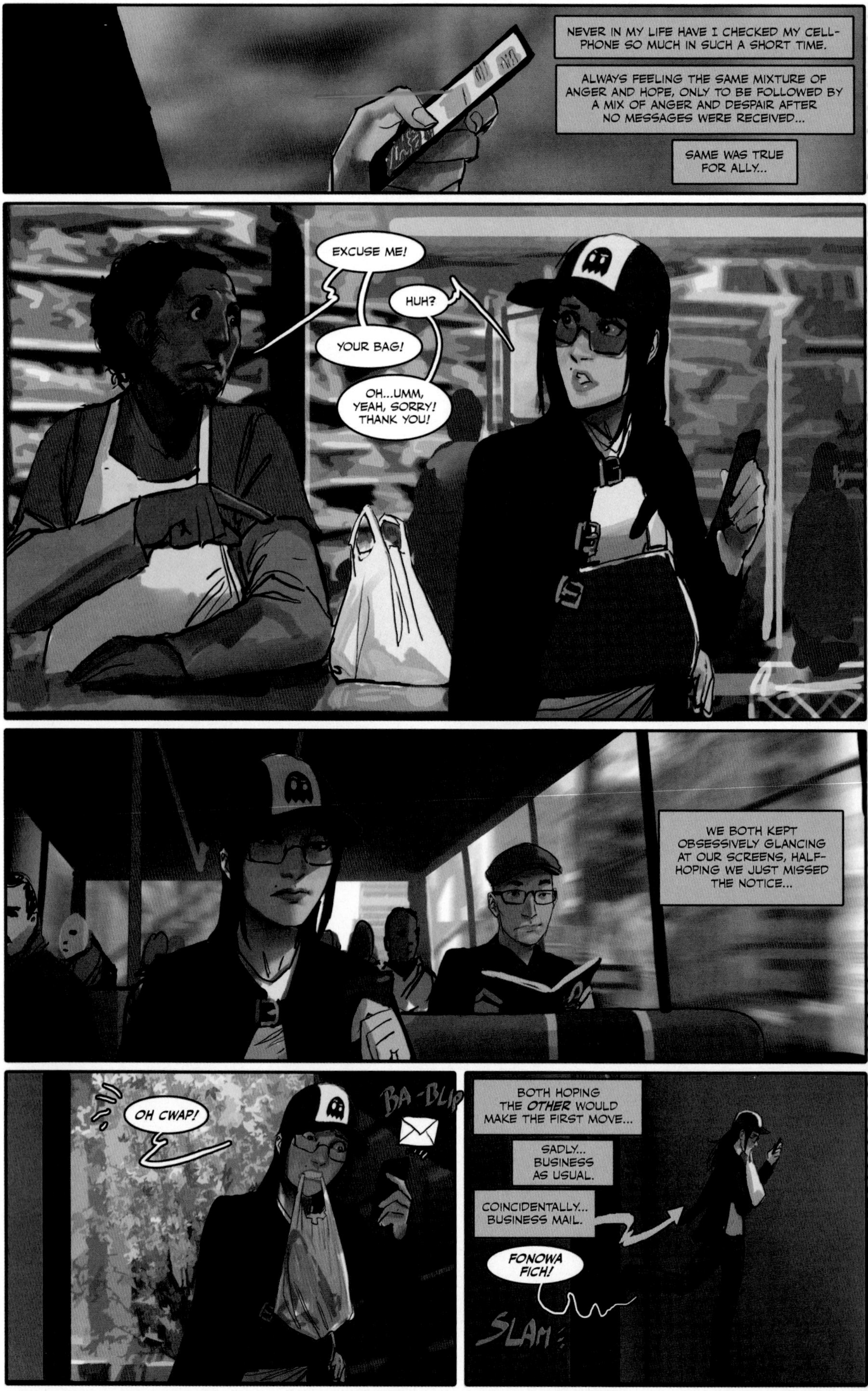

NEVER IN MY LIFE HAVE I CHECKED MY CELL-PHONE SO MUCH IN SUCH A SHORT TIME.
ALWAYS FEELING THE SAME MIXTURE OF ANGER AND HOPE, ONLY TO BE FOLLOWED BY A MIX OF ANGER AND DESPAIR AFTER NO MESSAGES WERE RECEIVED...
SAME WAS TRUE FOR ALLY...
EXCUSE ME!
HUH?
YOUR BAG!
OH...UMM, YEAH, SORRY! THANK YOU!
WE BOTH KEPT OBSESSIVELY GLANCING AT OUR SCREENS, HALF-HOPING WE JUST MISSED THE NOTICE...
OH CWAP!
BA-BLIP
BOTH HOPING THE *OTHER* WOULD MAKE THE FIRST MOVE...
SADLY... BUSINESS AS USUAL.
COINCIDENTALLY... BUSINESS MAIL.
FONOWA FICH!
SLAM

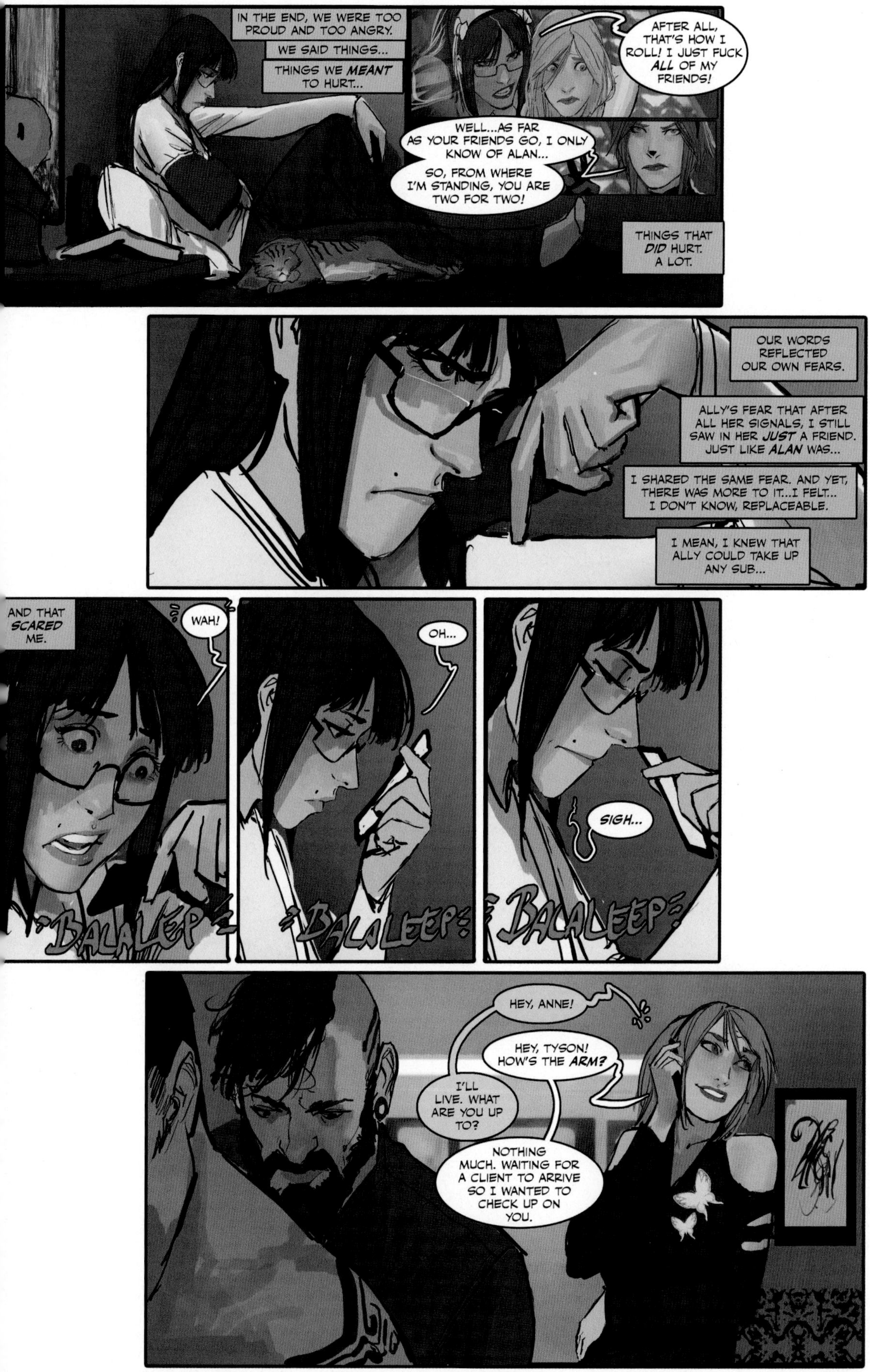
IN THE END, WE WERE TOO PROUD AND TOO ANGRY.
WE SAID THINGS...
THINGS WE *MEANT* TO HURT...
AFTER ALL, THAT'S HOW I ROLL! I JUST FUCK *ALL* OF MY FRIENDS!
WELL...AS FAR AS YOUR FRIENDS GO, I ONLY KNOW OF ALAN...
SO, FROM WHERE I'M STANDING, YOU ARE TWO FOR TWO!
THINGS THAT *DID* HURT. A LOT.
OUR WORDS REFLECTED OUR OWN FEARS.
ALLY'S FEAR THAT AFTER ALL HER SIGNALS, I STILL SAW IN HER *JUST* A FRIEND. JUST LIKE *ALAN* WAS...
I SHARED THE SAME FEAR. AND YET, THERE WAS MORE TO IT...I FELT... I DON'T KNOW, REPLACEABLE.
I MEAN, I KNEW THAT ALLY COULD TAKE UP ANY SUB...
AND THAT *SCARED* ME.
WAH!
BALALEEP
OH...
BALALEEP
SIGH...
BALALEEP
HEY, ANNE!
HEY, TYSON! HOW'S THE *ARM?*
I'LL LIVE. WHAT ARE YOU UP TO?
NOTHING MUCH. WAITING FOR A CLIENT TO ARRIVE SO I WANTED TO CHECK UP ON YOU.

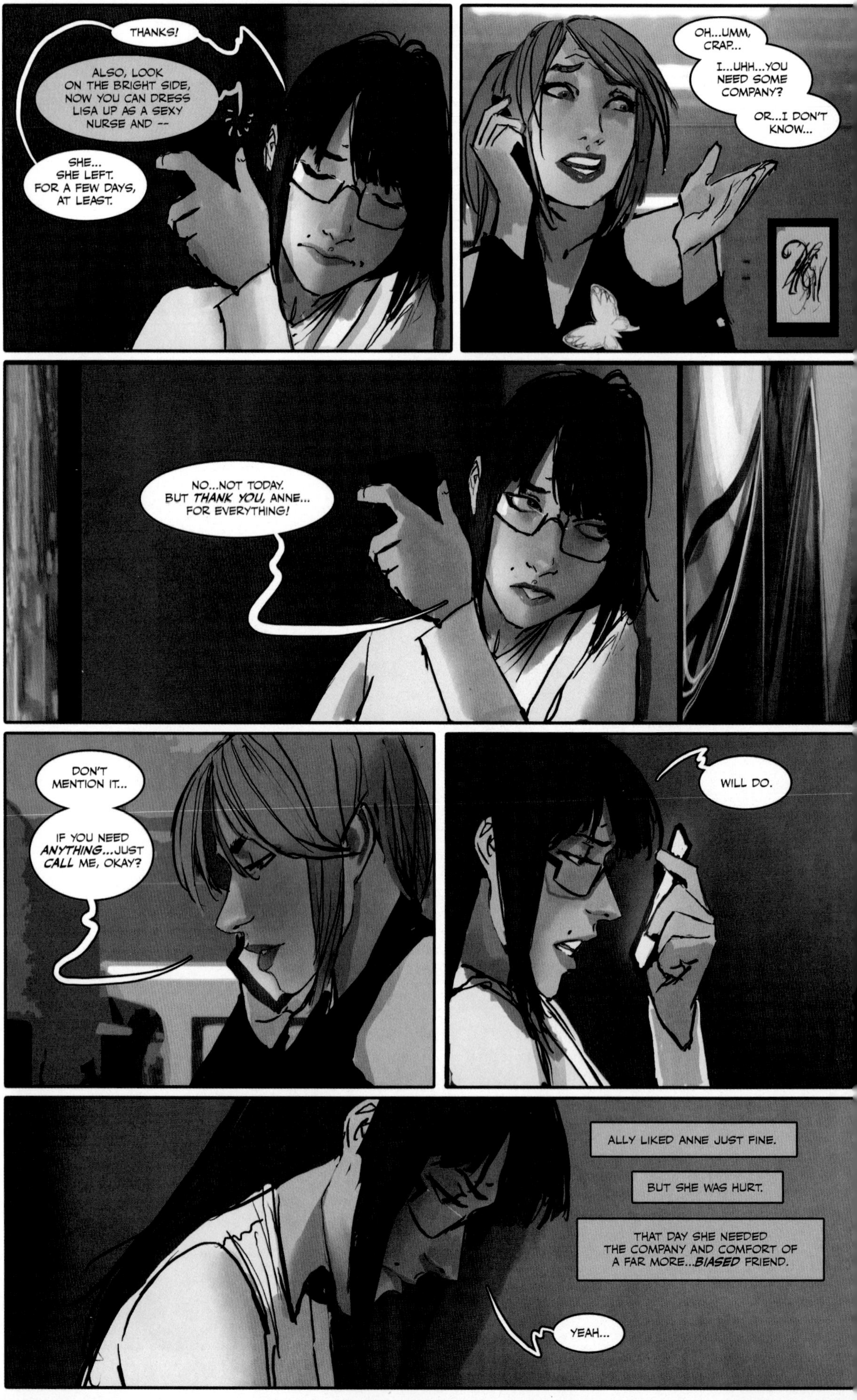
THANKS!
ALSO, LOOK ON THE BRIGHT SIDE, NOW YOU CAN DRESS LISA UP AS A SEXY NURSE AND --
SHE... SHE LEFT. FOR A FEW DAYS, AT LEAST.
OH...UMM, CRAP...
I...UHH...YOU NEED SOME COMPANY?
OR...I DON'T KNOW...
NO...NOT TODAY. BUT THANK YOU, ANNE... FOR EVERYTHING!
DON'T MENTION IT...
IF YOU NEED ANYTHING...JUST CALL ME, OKAY?
WILL DO.
ALLY LIKED ANNE JUST FINE.
BUT SHE WAS HURT.
THAT DAY SHE NEEDED THE COMPANY AND COMFORT OF A FAR MORE...BIASED FRIEND.
YEAH...

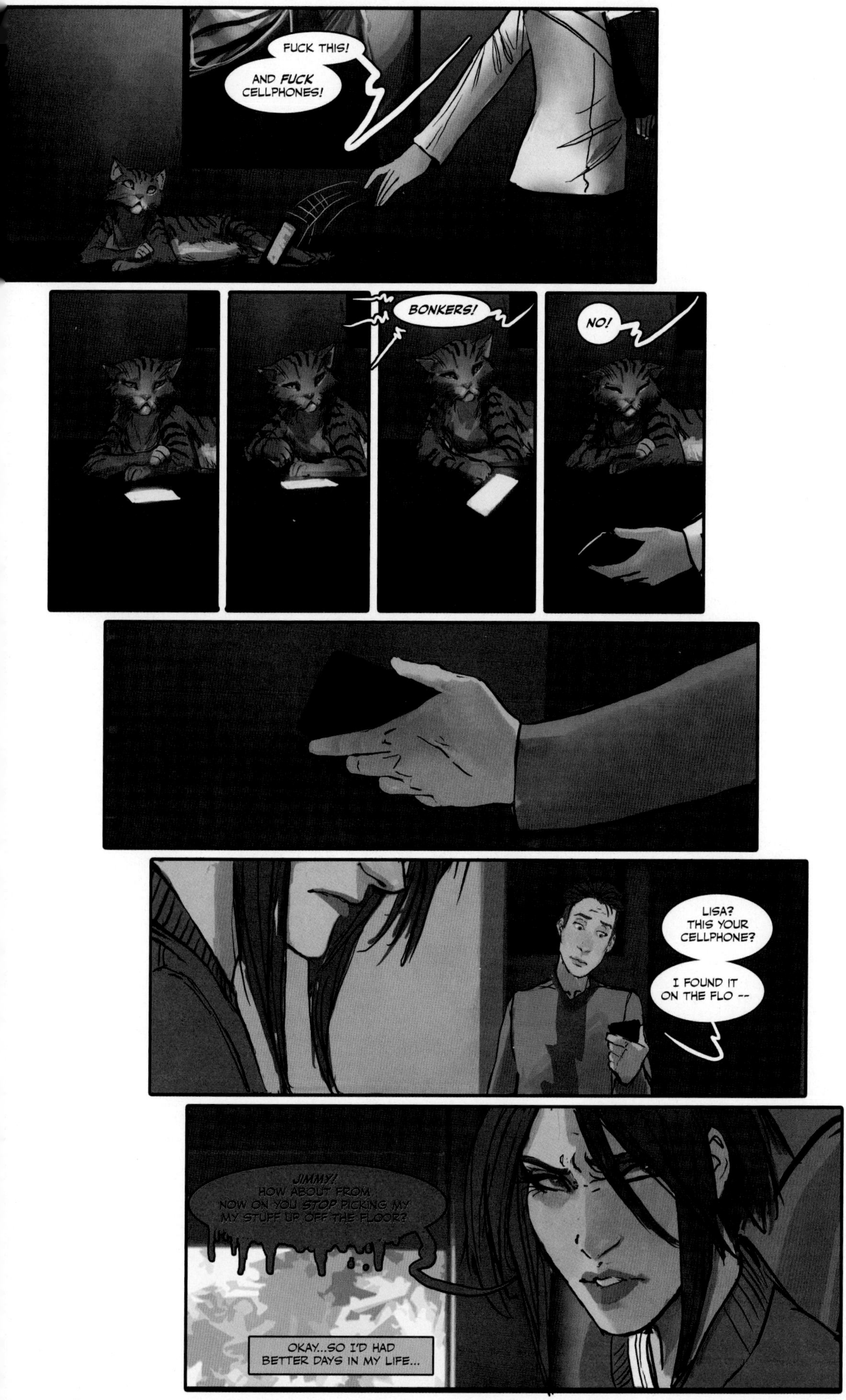
FUCK THIS!
AND FUCK CELLPHONES!
BONKERS!
NO!
LISA? THIS YOUR CELLPHONE?
I FOUND IT ON THE FLO --
JIMMY! HOW ABOUT FROM NOW ON YOU STOP PICKING MY MY STUFF UP OFF THE FLOOR?
OKAY...SO I'D HAD BETTER DAYS IN MY LIFE...

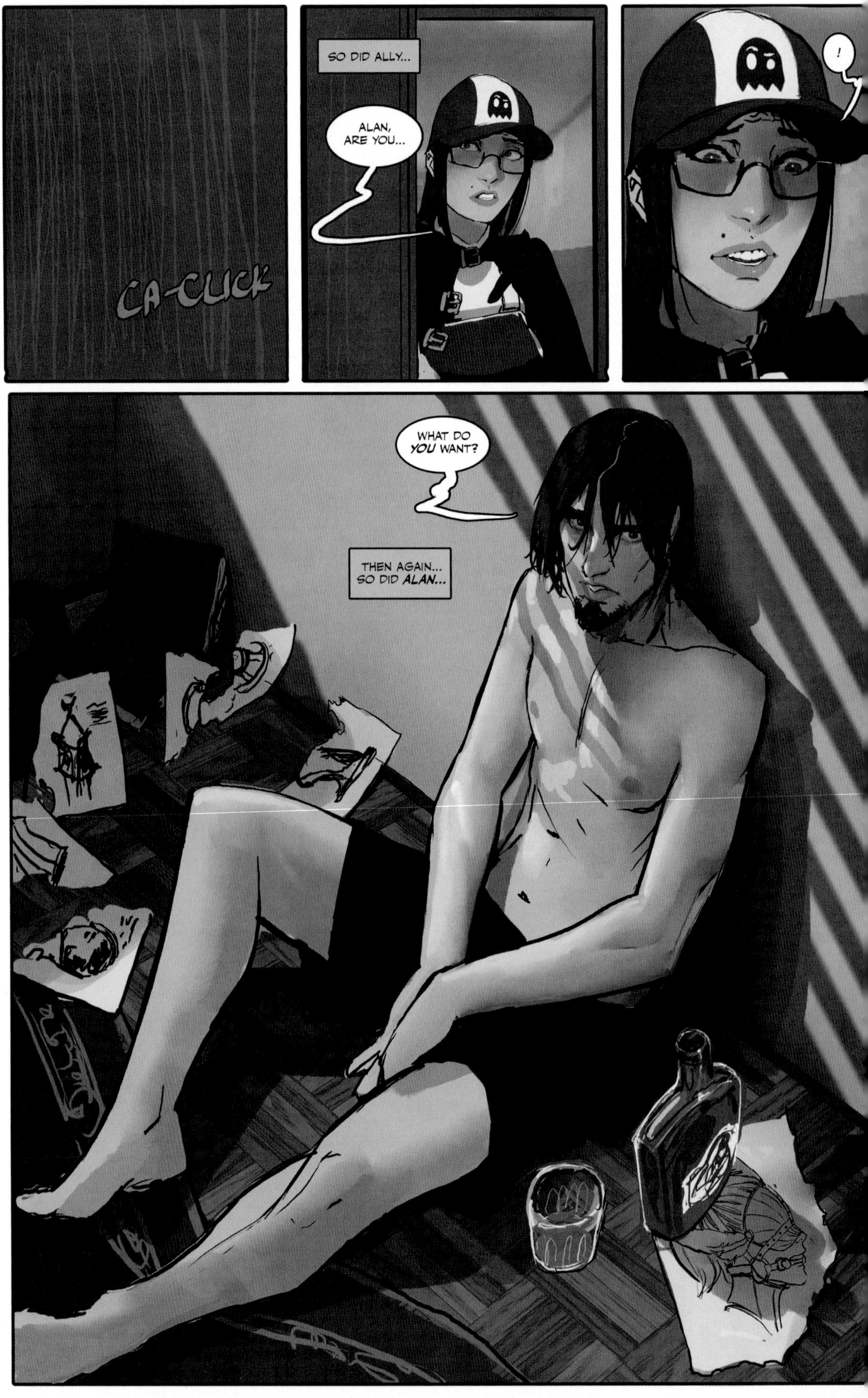
CA-CLICK
SO DID ALLY...
ALAN, ARE YOU...
!
WHAT DO *YOU* WANT?
THEN AGAIN... SO DID *ALAN*...

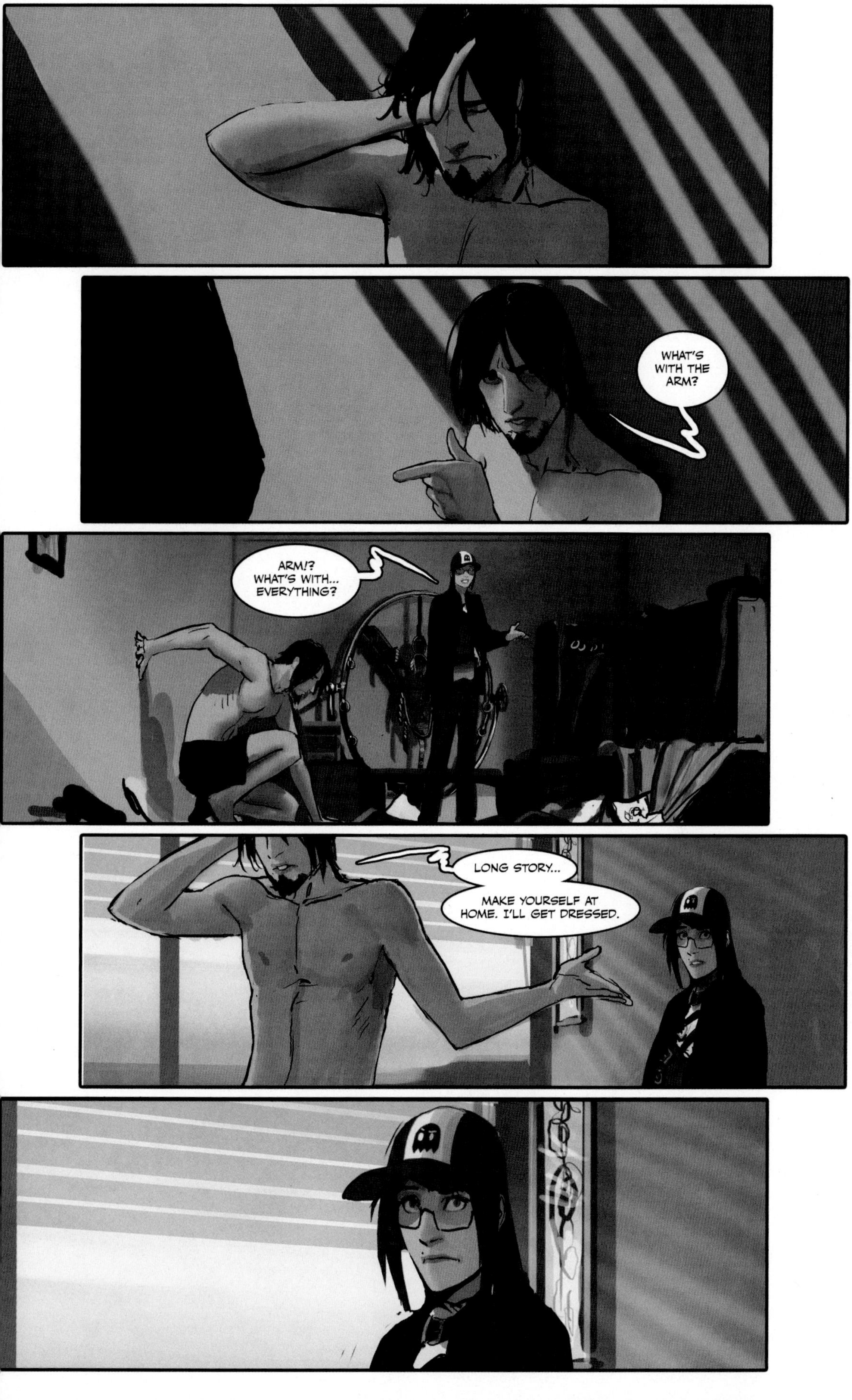
WHAT'S WITH THE ARM?
ARM!? WHAT'S WITH... EVERYTHING?
LONG STORY...
MAKE YOURSELF AT HOME. I'LL GET DRESSED.

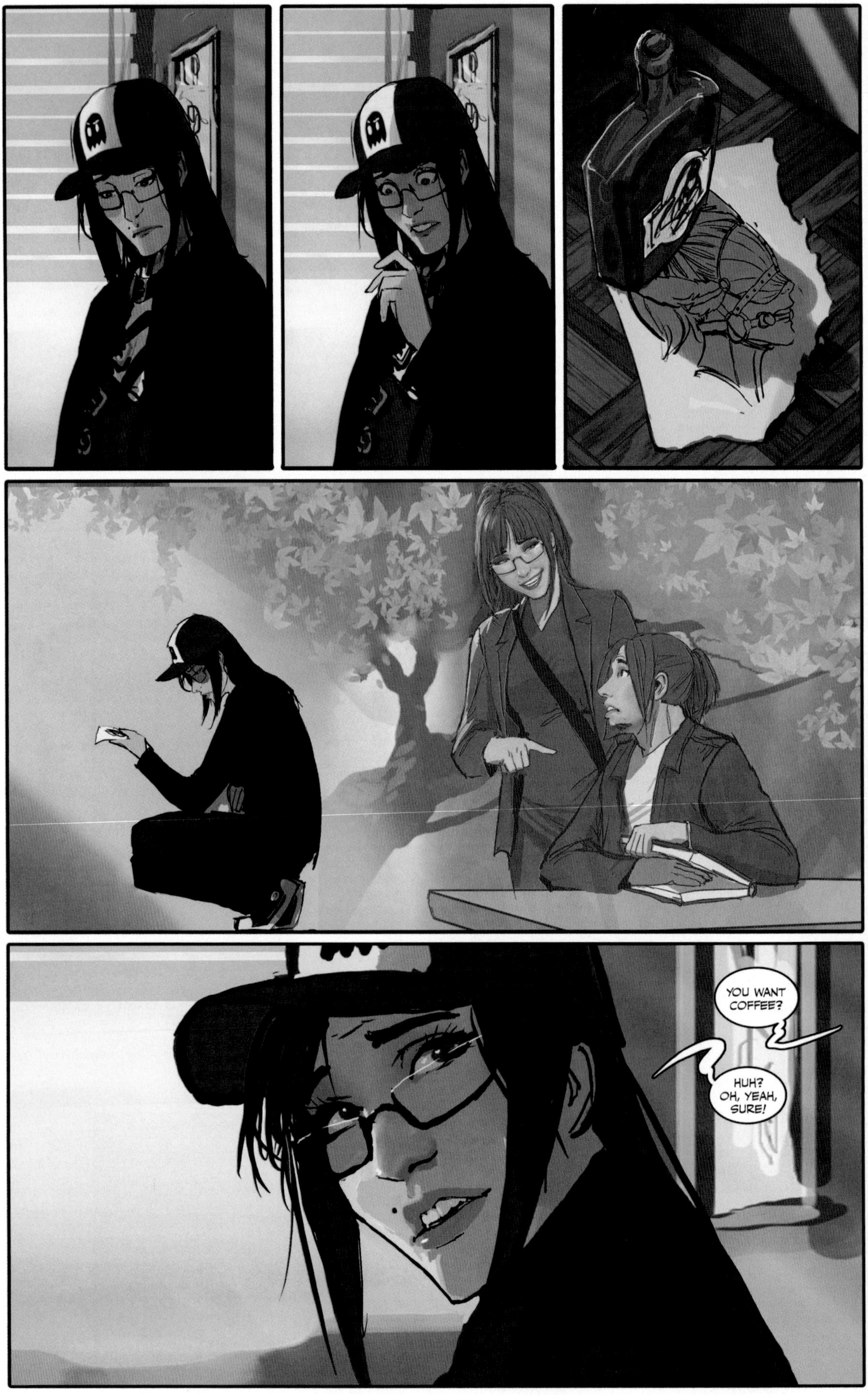
YOU WANT COFFEE?
HUH? OH, YEAH, SURE!

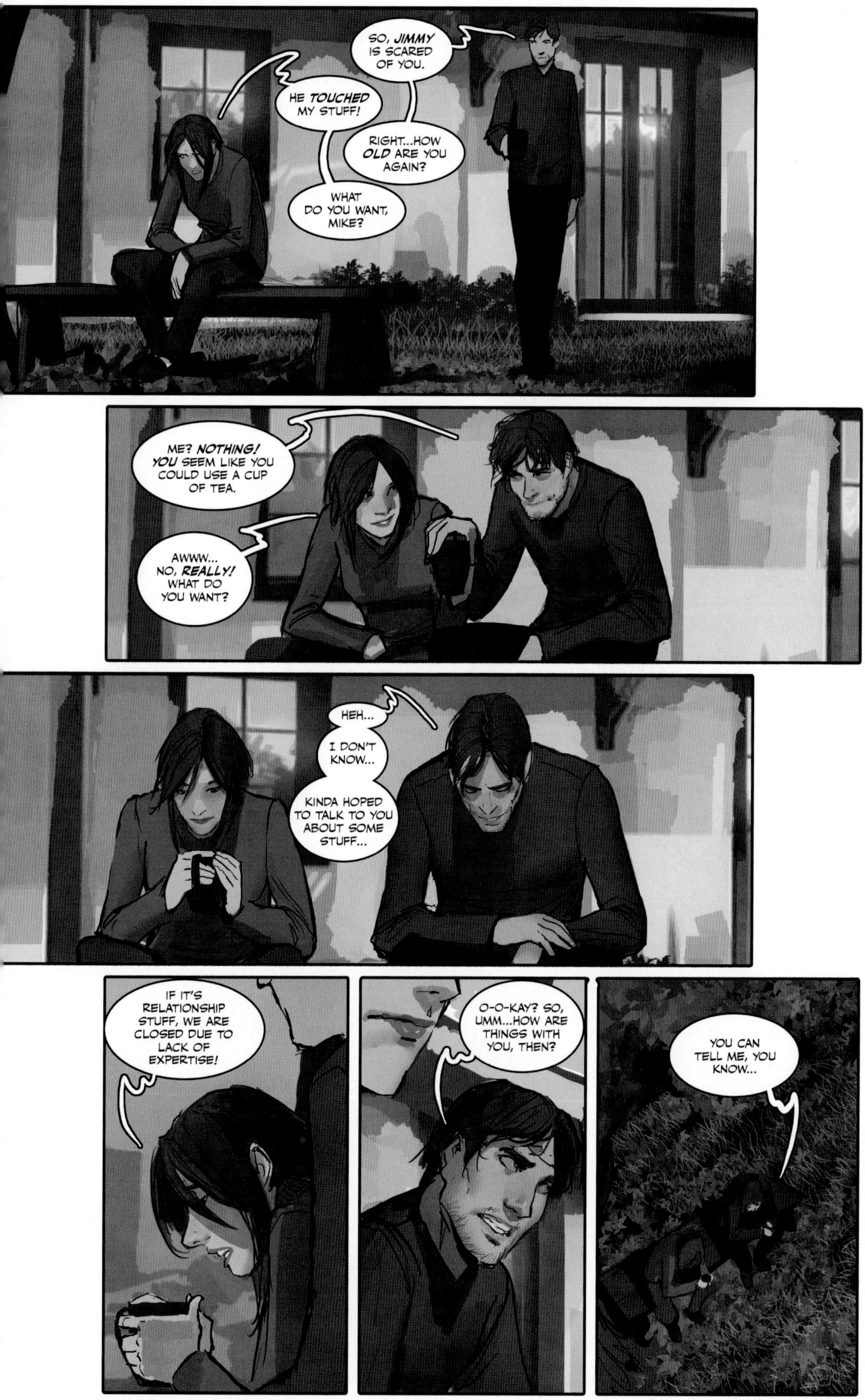
SO, JIMMY IS SCARED OF YOU.
HE TOUCHED MY STUFF!
RIGHT...HOW OLD ARE YOU AGAIN?
WHAT DO YOU WANT, MIKE?
ME? NOTHING! YOU SEEM LIKE YOU COULD USE A CUP OF TEA.
AWWW... NO, REALLY! WHAT DO YOU WANT?
HEH...
I DON'T KNOW...
KINDA HOPED TO TALK TO YOU ABOUT SOME STUFF...
IF IT'S RELATIONSHIP STUFF, WE ARE CLOSED DUE TO LACK OF EXPERTISE!
O-O-KAY? SO, UMM...HOW ARE THINGS WITH YOU, THEN?
YOU CAN TELL ME, YOU KNOW...

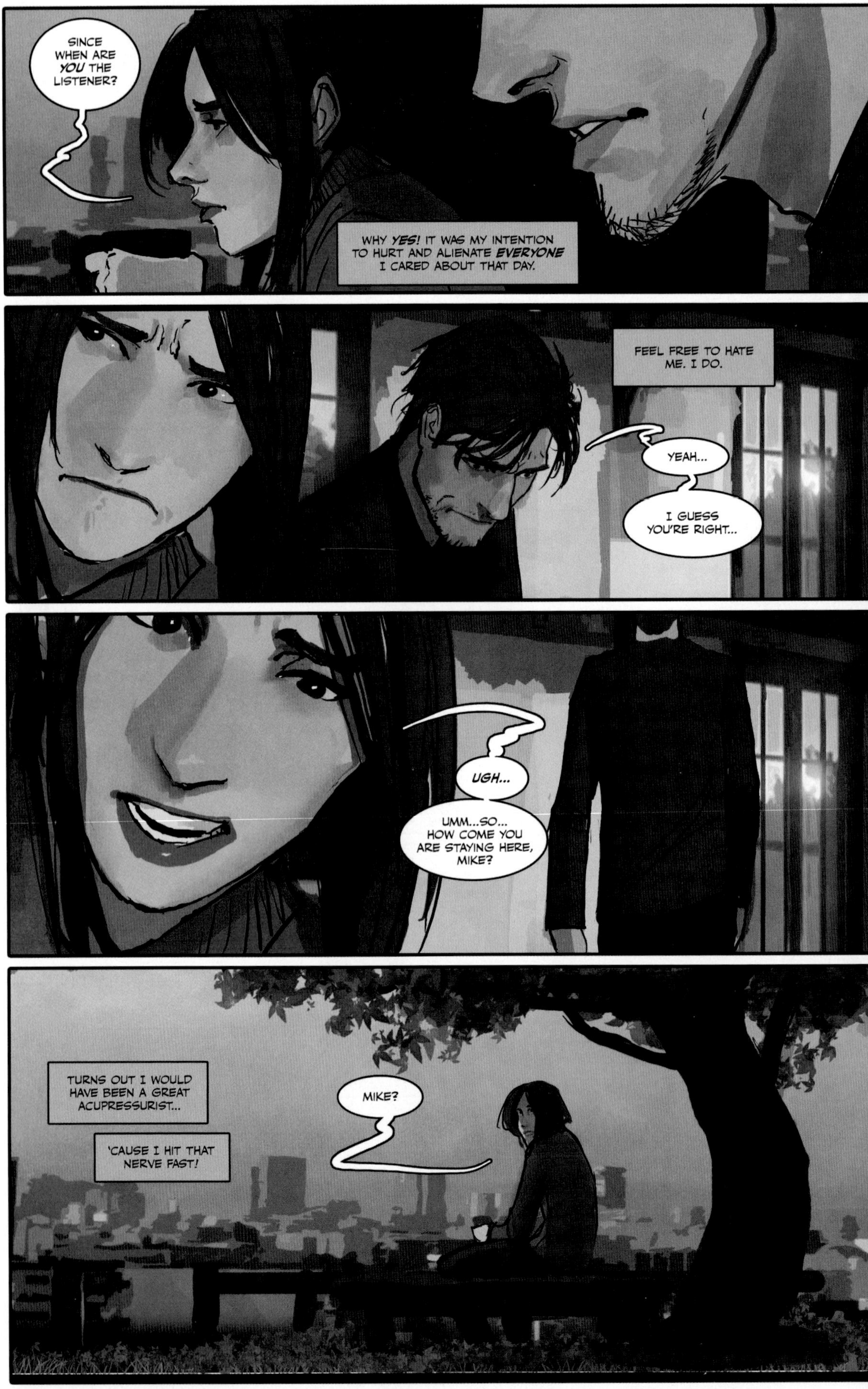
SINCE WHEN ARE *YOU* THE LISTENER?
WHY *YES!* IT WAS MY INTENTION TO HURT AND ALIENATE *EVERYONE* I CARED ABOUT THAT DAY.
FEEL FREE TO HATE ME. I DO.
YEAH...
I GUESS YOU'RE RIGHT...
UGH...
UMM...SO... HOW COME YOU ARE STAYING HERE, MIKE?
TURNS OUT I WOULD HAVE BEEN A GREAT ACUPRESSURIST...
'CAUSE I HIT THAT NERVE FAST!
MIKE?

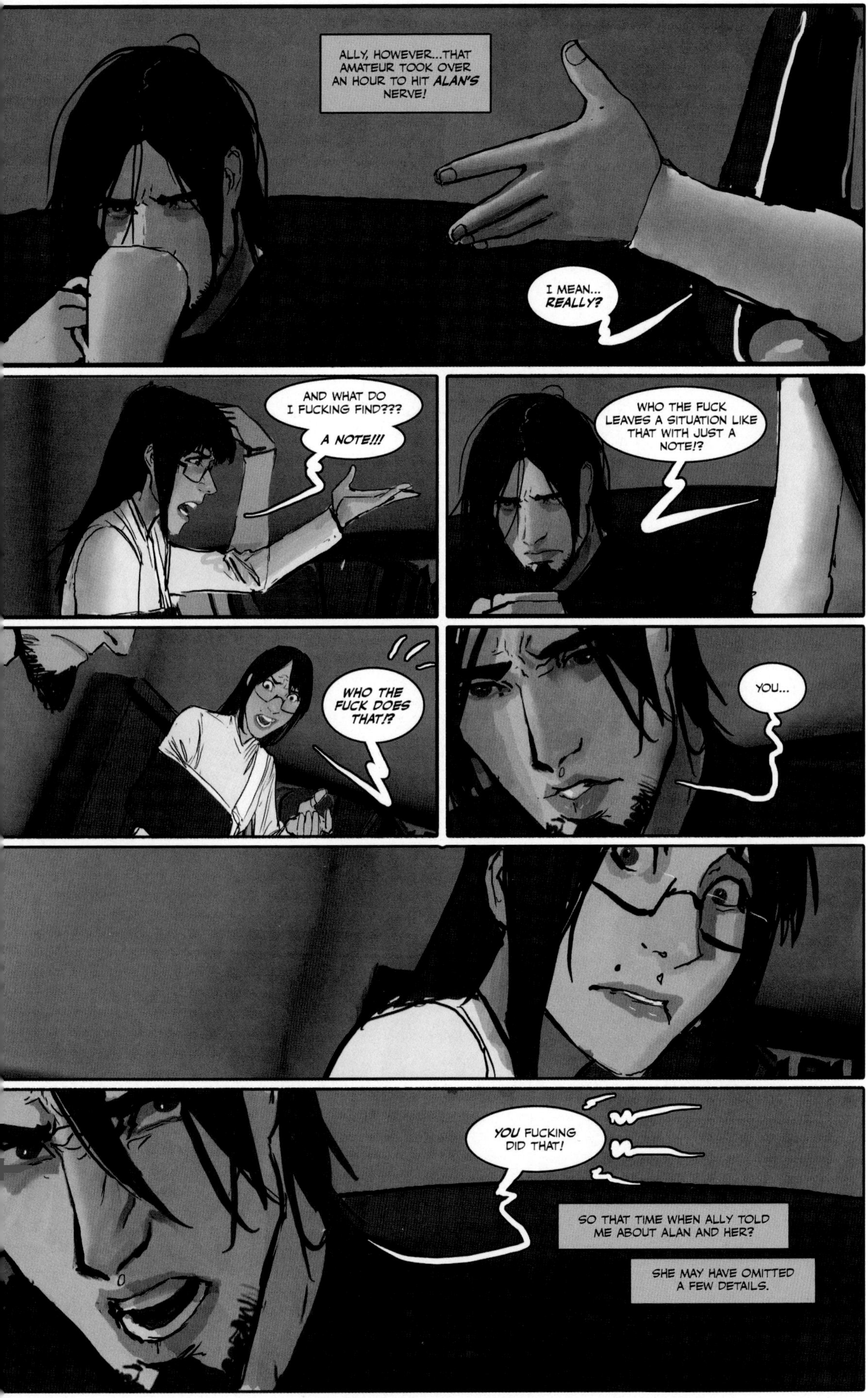
ALLY, HOWEVER...THAT AMATEUR TOOK OVER AN HOUR TO HIT ALAN'S NERVE!
I MEAN... REALLY?
AND WHAT DO I FUCKING FIND???
A NOTE!!!
WHO THE FUCK LEAVES A SITUATION LIKE THAT WITH JUST A NOTE!?
WHO THE FUCK DOES THAT!?
YOU...
YOU FUCKING DID THAT!
SO THAT TIME WHEN ALLY TOLD ME ABOUT ALAN AND HER?
SHE MAY HAVE OMITTED A FEW DETAILS.

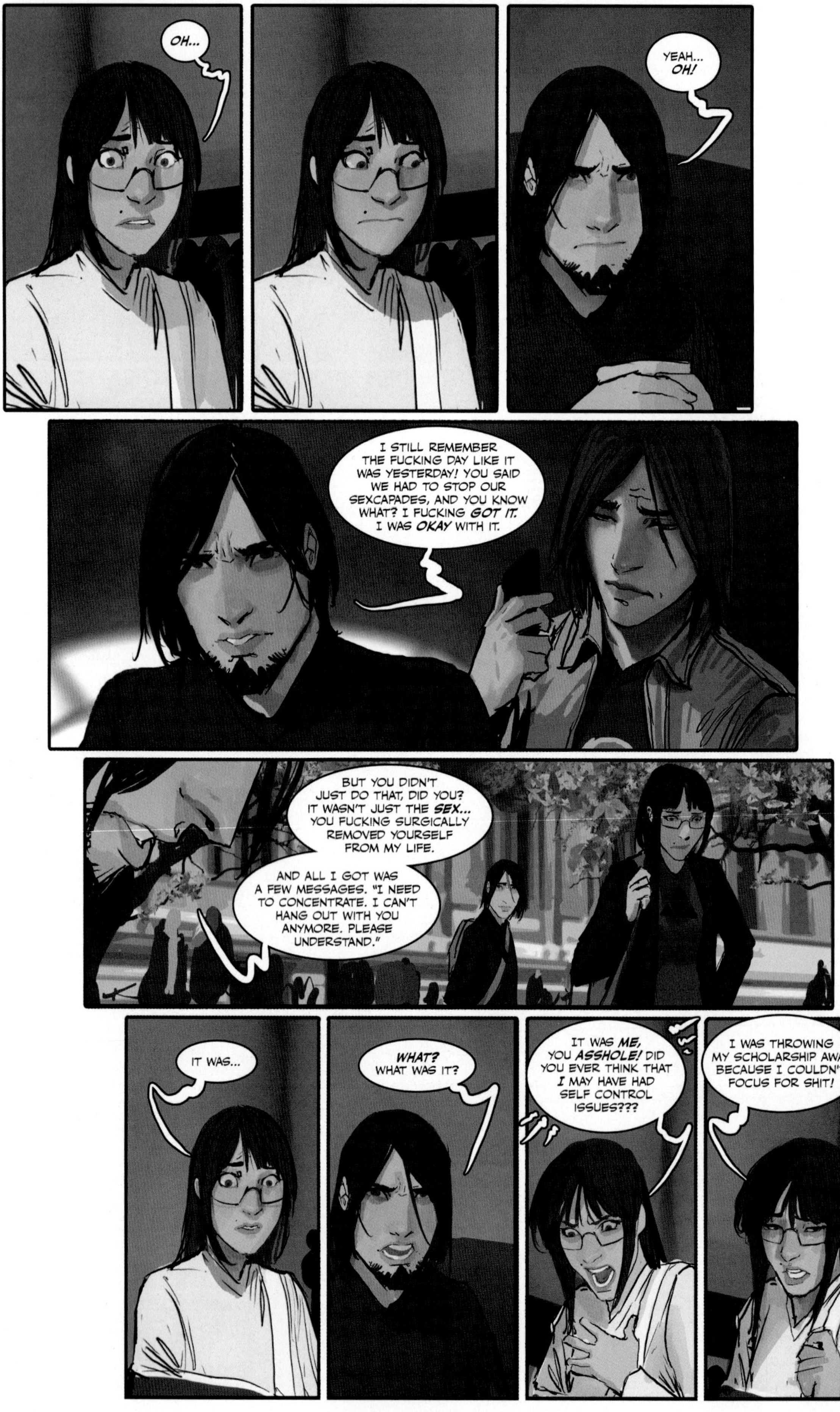
OH...
YEAH... OH!
I STILL REMEMBER THE FUCKING DAY LIKE IT WAS YESTERDAY! YOU SAID WE HAD TO STOP OUR SEXCAPADES, AND YOU KNOW WHAT? I FUCKING GOT IT. I WAS OKAY WITH IT.
BUT YOU DIDN'T JUST DO THAT, DID YOU? IT WASN'T JUST THE SEX... YOU FUCKING SURGICALLY REMOVED YOURSELF FROM MY LIFE.
AND ALL I GOT WAS A FEW MESSAGES. "I NEED TO CONCENTRATE. I CAN'T HANG OUT WITH YOU ANYMORE. PLEASE UNDERSTAND."
IT WAS...
WHAT? WHAT WAS IT?
IT WAS ME, YOU ASSHOLE! DID YOU EVER THINK THAT I MAY HAVE HAD SELF CONTROL ISSUES???
I WAS THROWING MY SCHOLARSHIP AWAY BECAUSE I COULDN'T FOCUS FOR SHIT!

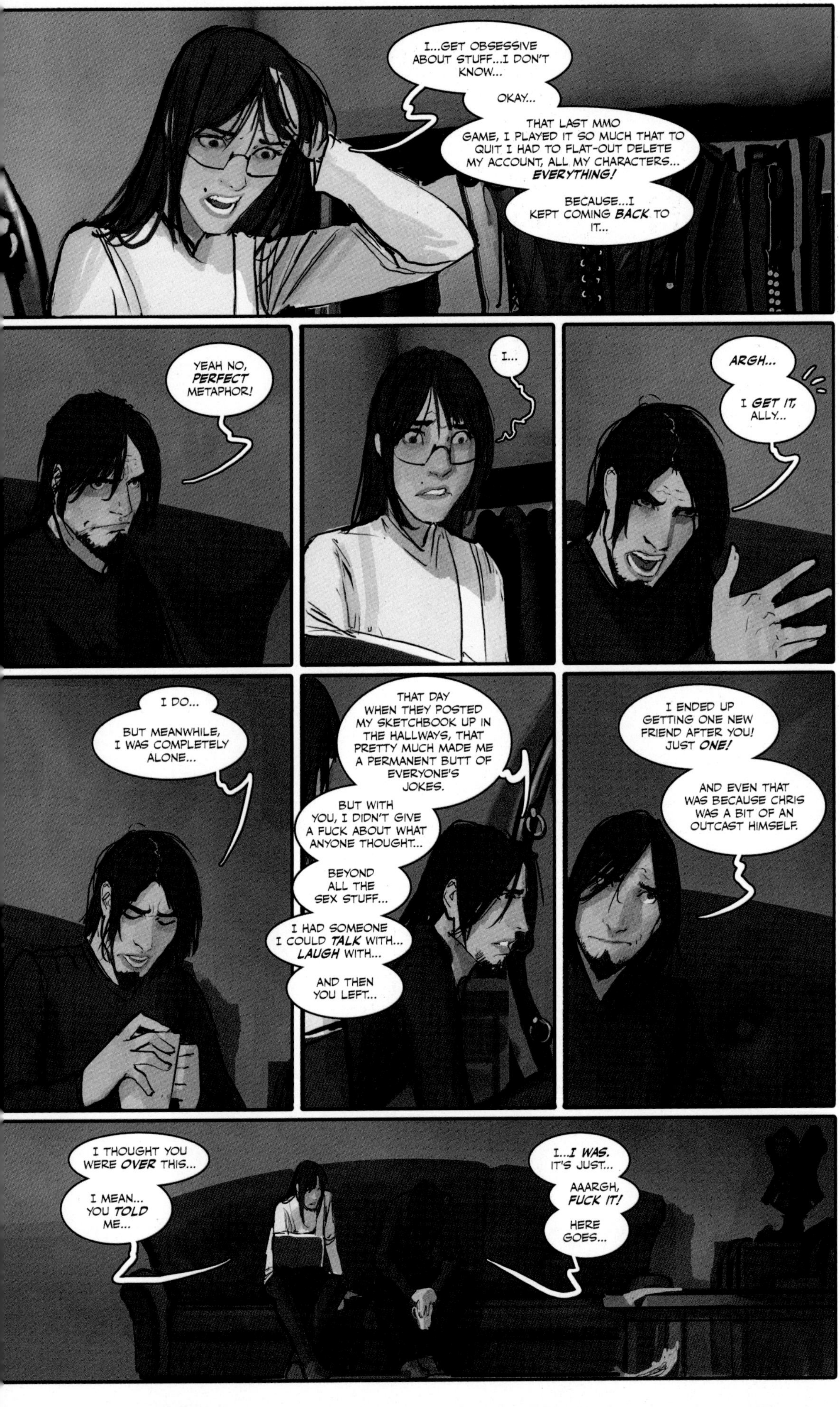
I...GET OBSESSIVE ABOUT STUFF...I DON'T KNOW...
OKAY...
THAT LAST MMO GAME, I PLAYED IT SO MUCH THAT TO QUIT I HAD TO FLAT-OUT DELETE MY ACCOUNT, ALL MY CHARACTERS... *EVERYTHING!*
BECAUSE...I KEPT COMING *BACK* TO IT...
YEAH NO, *PERFECT* METAPHOR!
I...
ARGH...
I *GET IT,* ALLY...
I DO...
BUT MEANWHILE, I WAS COMPLETELY ALONE...
THAT DAY WHEN THEY POSTED MY SKETCHBOOK UP IN THE HALLWAYS, THAT PRETTY MUCH MADE ME A PERMANENT BUTT OF EVERYONE'S JOKES.
BUT WITH YOU, I DIDN'T GIVE A FUCK ABOUT WHAT ANYONE THOUGHT...
BEYOND ALL THE SEX STUFF...
I HAD SOMEONE I COULD *TALK* WITH... *LAUGH* WITH...
AND THEN YOU LEFT...
I ENDED UP GETTING ONE NEW FRIEND AFTER YOU! JUST *ONE!*
AND EVEN THAT WAS BECAUSE CHRIS WAS A BIT OF AN OUTCAST HIMSELF.
I THOUGHT YOU WERE *OVER* THIS...
I MEAN... YOU *TOLD* ME...
I...*I WAS.* IT'S JUST...
AAARGH, *FUCK IT!*
HERE GOES...

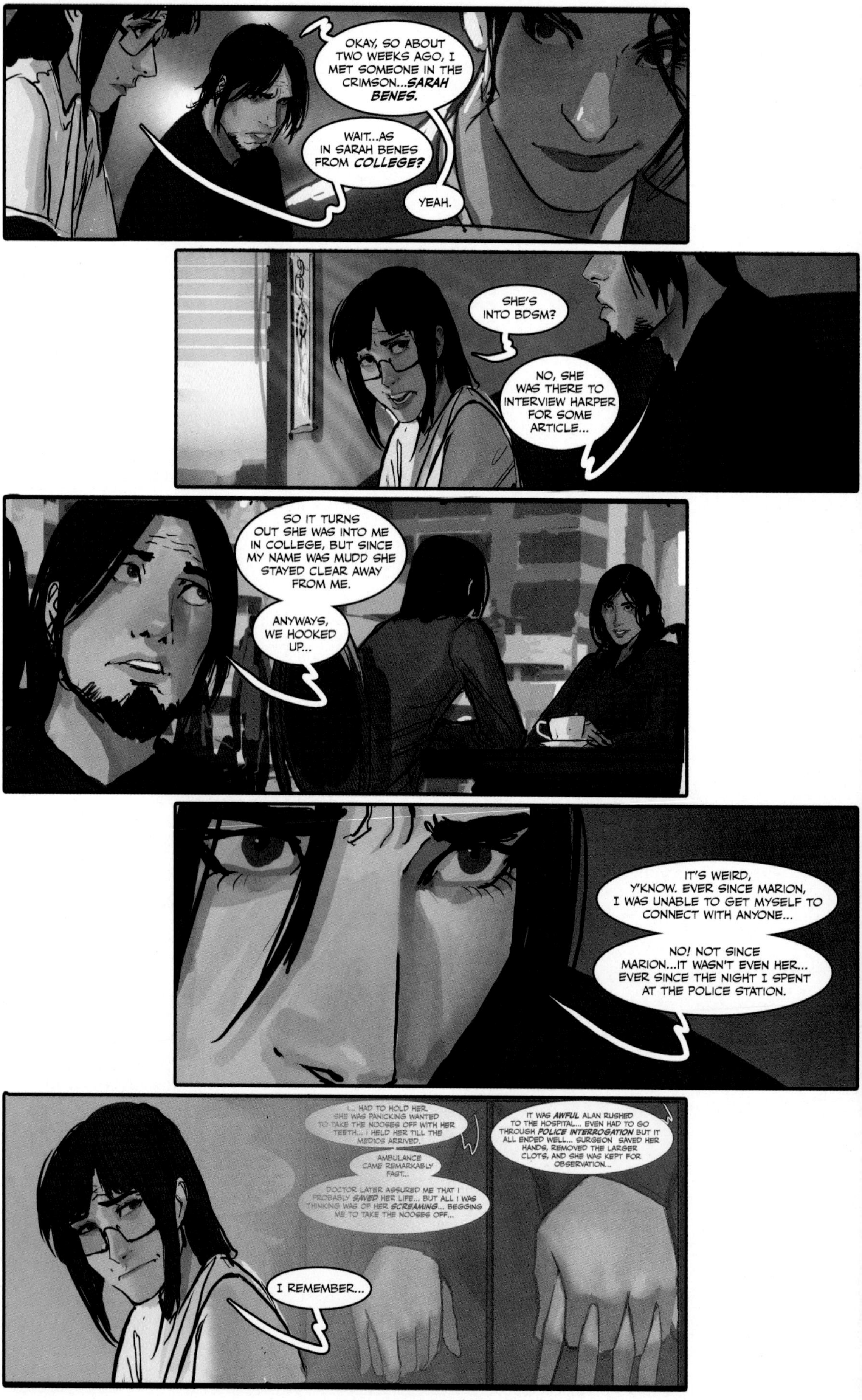
OKAY, SO ABOUT TWO WEEKS AGO, I MET SOMEONE IN THE CRIMSON...*SARAH BENES.*
WAIT...AS IN SARAH BENES FROM *COLLEGE?*
YEAH.
SHE'S INTO BDSM?
NO, SHE WAS THERE TO INTERVIEW HARPER FOR SOME ARTICLE...
SO IT TURNS OUT SHE WAS INTO ME IN COLLEGE, BUT SINCE MY NAME WAS MUDD SHE STAYED CLEAR AWAY FROM ME.
ANYWAYS, WE HOOKED UP...
IT'S WEIRD, Y'KNOW. EVER SINCE MARION, I WAS UNABLE TO GET MYSELF TO CONNECT WITH ANYONE...
NO*!* NOT SINCE MARION...IT WASN'T EVEN HER... EVER SINCE THE NIGHT I SPENT AT THE POLICE STATION.
I... HAD TO HOLD HER. SHE WAS PANICKING WANTED TO TAKE THE NOOSES OFF WITH HER TEETH... I HELD HER TILL THE MEDICS ARRIVED.
AMBULANCE CAME REMARKABLY FAST...
DOCTOR LATER ASSURED ME THAT I PROBABLY *SAVED* HER LIFE... BUT ALL I WAS THINKING WAS OF HER *SCREAMING*... BEGGING ME TO TAKE THE NOOSES OFF...
I REMEMBER...
IT WAS *AWFUL* ALAN RUSHED TO THE HOSPITAL... EVEN HAD TO GO THROUGH *POLICE INTERROGATION* BUT IT ALL ENDED WELL... SURGEON SAVED HER HANDS, REMOVED THE LARGER CLOTS, AND SHE WAS KEPT FOR OBSERVATION...

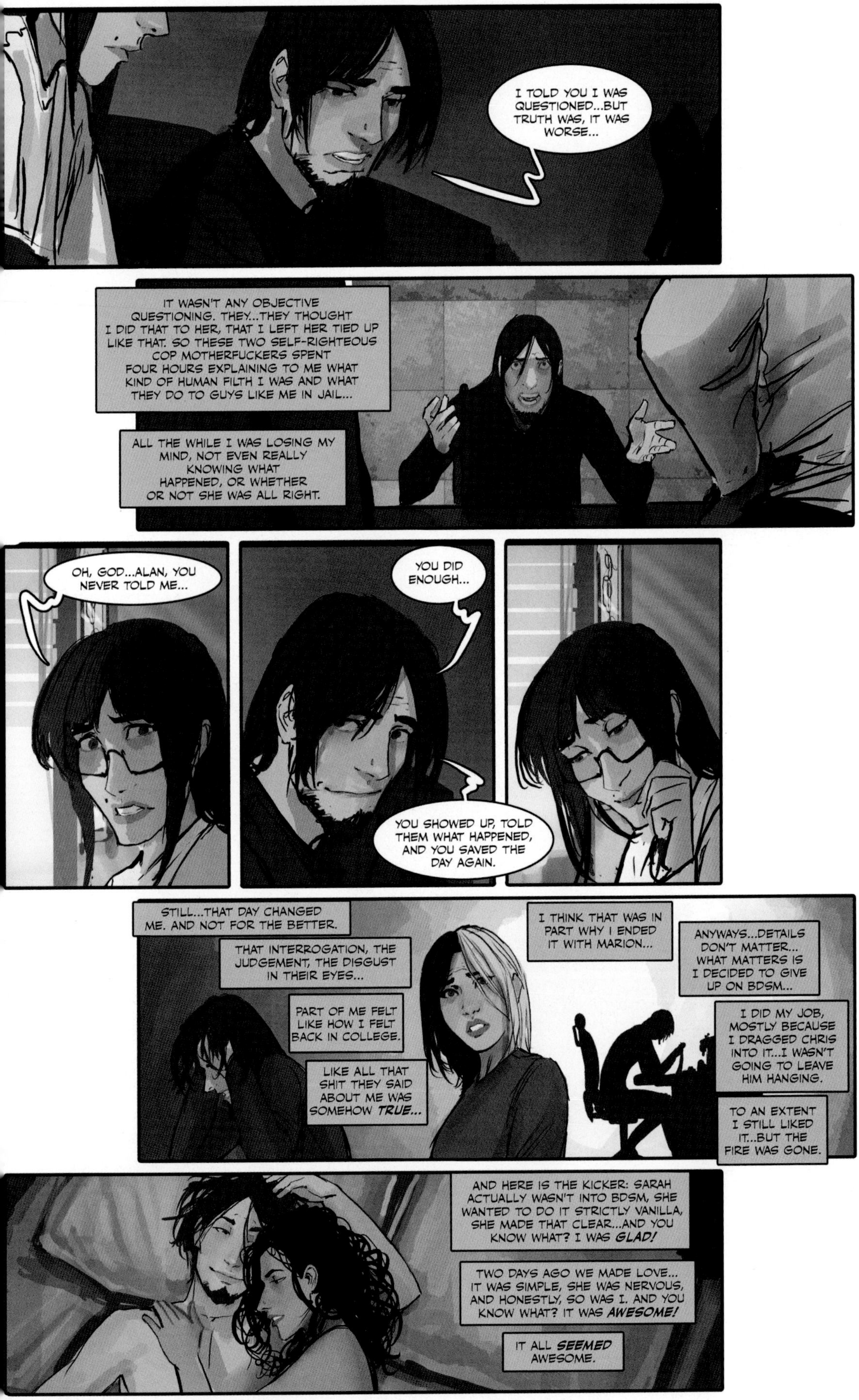
I TOLD YOU I WAS QUESTIONED...BUT TRUTH WAS, IT WAS WORSE...
IT WASN'T ANY OBJECTIVE QUESTIONING. THEY...THEY THOUGHT I DID THAT TO HER, THAT I LEFT HER TIED UP LIKE THAT. SO THESE TWO SELF-RIGHTEOUS COP MOTHERFUCKERS SPENT FOUR HOURS EXPLAINING TO ME WHAT KIND OF HUMAN FILTH I WAS AND WHAT THEY DO TO GUYS LIKE ME IN JAIL...
ALL THE WHILE I WAS LOSING MY MIND, NOT EVEN REALLY KNOWING WHAT HAPPENED, OR WHETHER OR NOT SHE WAS ALL RIGHT.
OH, GOD...ALAN, YOU NEVER TOLD ME...
YOU DID ENOUGH...
YOU SHOWED UP, TOLD THEM WHAT HAPPENED, AND YOU SAVED THE DAY AGAIN.
STILL...THAT DAY CHANGED ME. AND NOT FOR THE BETTER.
THAT INTERROGATION, THE JUDGEMENT, THE DISGUST IN THEIR EYES...
PART OF ME FELT LIKE HOW I FELT BACK IN COLLEGE.
LIKE ALL THAT SHIT THEY SAID ABOUT ME WAS SOMEHOW *TRUE...*
I THINK THAT WAS IN PART WHY I ENDED IT WITH MARION...
ANYWAYS...DETAILS DON'T MATTER... WHAT MATTERS IS I DECIDED TO GIVE UP ON BDSM...
I DID MY JOB, MOSTLY BECAUSE I DRAGGED CHRIS INTO IT...I WASN'T GOING TO LEAVE HIM HANGING.
TO AN EXTENT I STILL LIKED IT...BUT THE FIRE WAS GONE.
AND HERE IS THE KICKER: SARAH ACTUALLY WASN'T INTO BDSM, SHE WANTED TO DO IT STRICTLY VANILLA, SHE MADE THAT CLEAR...AND YOU KNOW WHAT? I WAS *GLAD!*
TWO DAYS AGO WE MADE LOVE... IT WAS SIMPLE, SHE WAS NERVOUS, AND HONESTLY, SO WAS I. AND YOU KNOW WHAT? IT WAS *AWESOME!*
IT ALL *SEEMED* AWESOME.

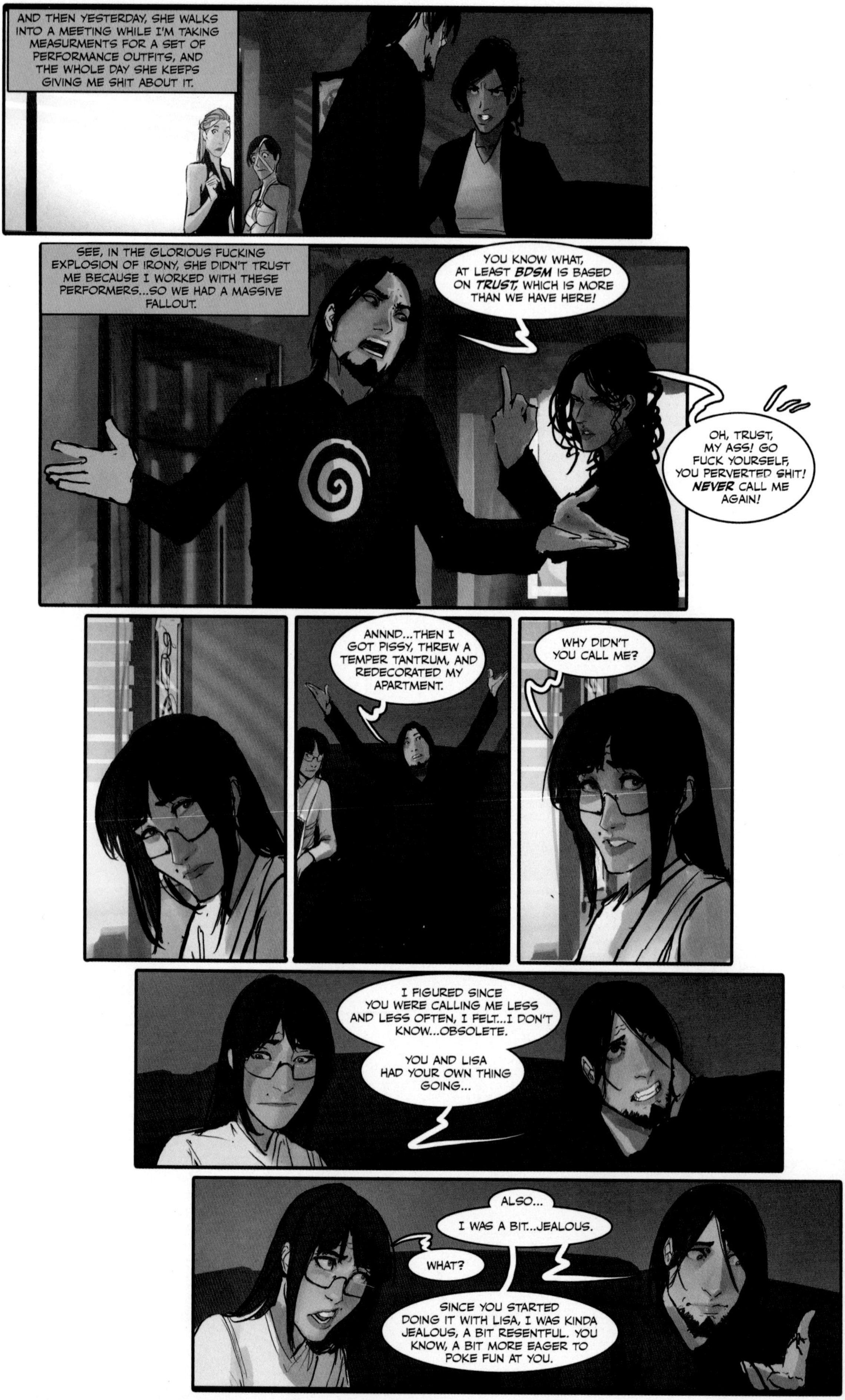
AND THEN YESTERDAY, SHE WALKS INTO A MEETING WHILE I'M TAKING MEASURMENTS FOR A SET OF PERFORMANCE OUTFITS, AND THE WHOLE DAY SHE KEEPS GIVING ME SHIT ABOUT IT.
SEE, IN THE GLORIOUS FUCKING EXPLOSION OF IRONY, SHE DIDN'T TRUST ME BECAUSE I WORKED WITH THESE PERFORMERS...SO WE HAD A MASSIVE FALLOUT.
YOU KNOW WHAT, AT LEAST BDSM IS BASED ON TRUST, WHICH IS MORE THAN WE HAVE HERE!
OH, TRUST, MY ASS! GO FUCK YOURSELF, YOU PERVERTED SHIT! NEVER CALL ME AGAIN!
ANNND...THEN I GOT PISSY, THREW A TEMPER TANTRUM, AND REDECORATED MY APARTMENT.
WHY DIDN'T YOU CALL ME?
I FIGURED SINCE YOU WERE CALLING ME LESS AND LESS OFTEN, I FELT...I DON'T KNOW...OBSOLETE.
YOU AND LISA HAD YOUR OWN THING GOING...
ALSO...
I WAS A BIT...JEALOUS.
WHAT?
SINCE YOU STARTED DOING IT WITH LISA, I WAS KINDA JEALOUS, A BIT RESENTFUL. YOU KNOW, A BIT MORE EAGER TO POKE FUN AT YOU.

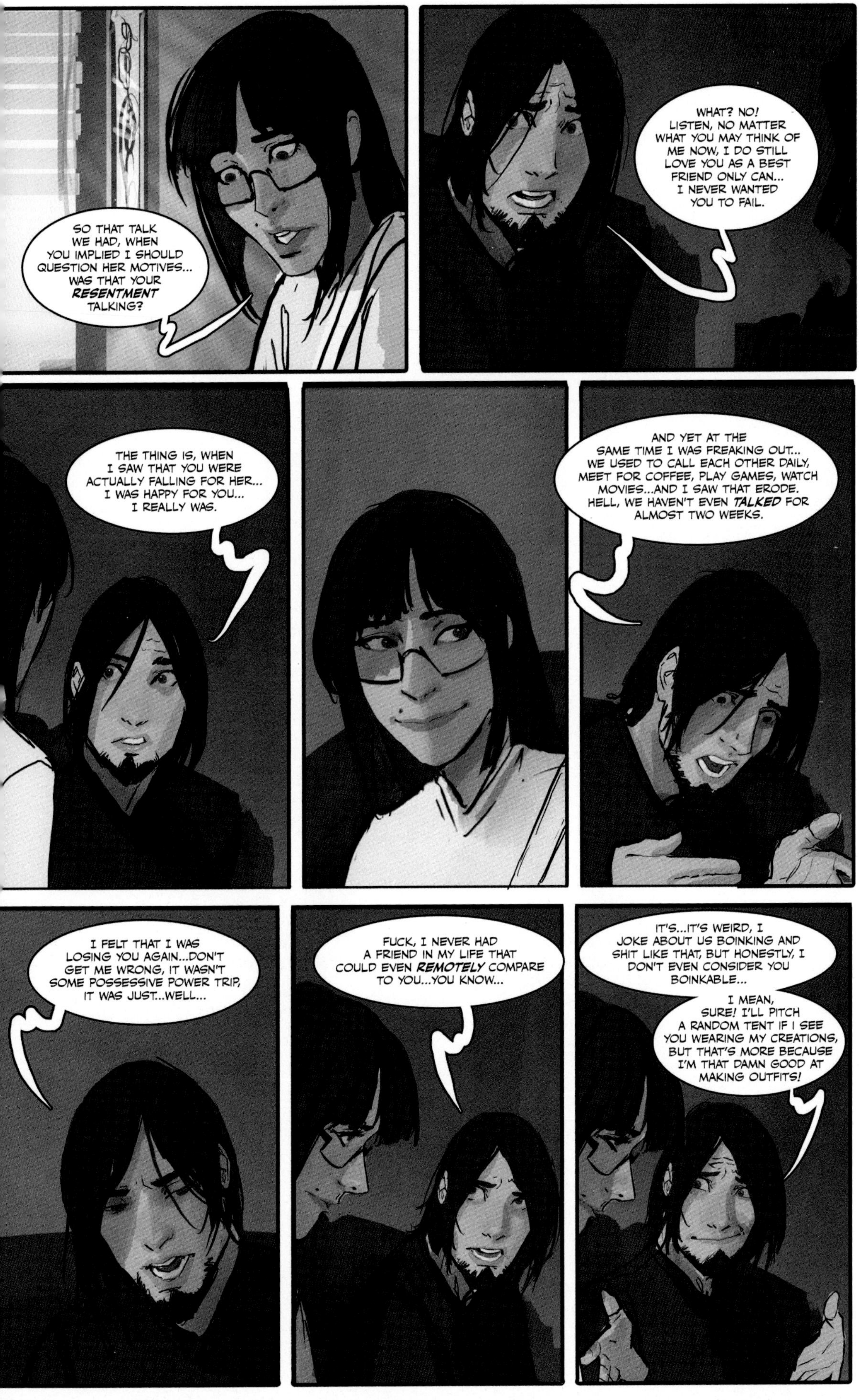
SO THAT TALK WE HAD, WHEN YOU IMPLIED I SHOULD QUESTION HER MOTIVES... WAS THAT YOUR RESENTMENT TALKING?
WHAT? NO! LISTEN, NO MATTER WHAT YOU MAY THINK OF ME NOW, I DO STILL LOVE YOU AS A BEST FRIEND ONLY CAN... I NEVER WANTED YOU TO FAIL.
THE THING IS, WHEN I SAW THAT YOU WERE ACTUALLY FALLING FOR HER... I WAS HAPPY FOR YOU... I REALLY WAS.
AND YET AT THE SAME TIME I WAS FREAKING OUT... WE USED TO CALL EACH OTHER DAILY, MEET FOR COFFEE, PLAY GAMES, WATCH MOVIES...AND I SAW THAT ERODE. HELL, WE HAVEN'T EVEN TALKED FOR ALMOST TWO WEEKS.
I FELT THAT I WAS LOSING YOU AGAIN...DON'T GET ME WRONG, IT WASN'T SOME POSSESSIVE POWER TRIP, IT WAS JUST...WELL...
FUCK, I NEVER HAD A FRIEND IN MY LIFE THAT COULD EVEN REMOTELY COMPARE TO YOU...YOU KNOW...
IT'S...IT'S WEIRD, I JOKE ABOUT US BOINKING AND SHIT LIKE THAT, BUT HONESTLY, I DON'T EVEN CONSIDER YOU BOINKABLE...
I MEAN, SURE! I'LL PITCH A RANDOM TENT IF I SEE YOU WEARING MY CREATIONS, BUT THAT'S MORE BECAUSE I'M THAT DAMN GOOD AT MAKING OUTFITS!

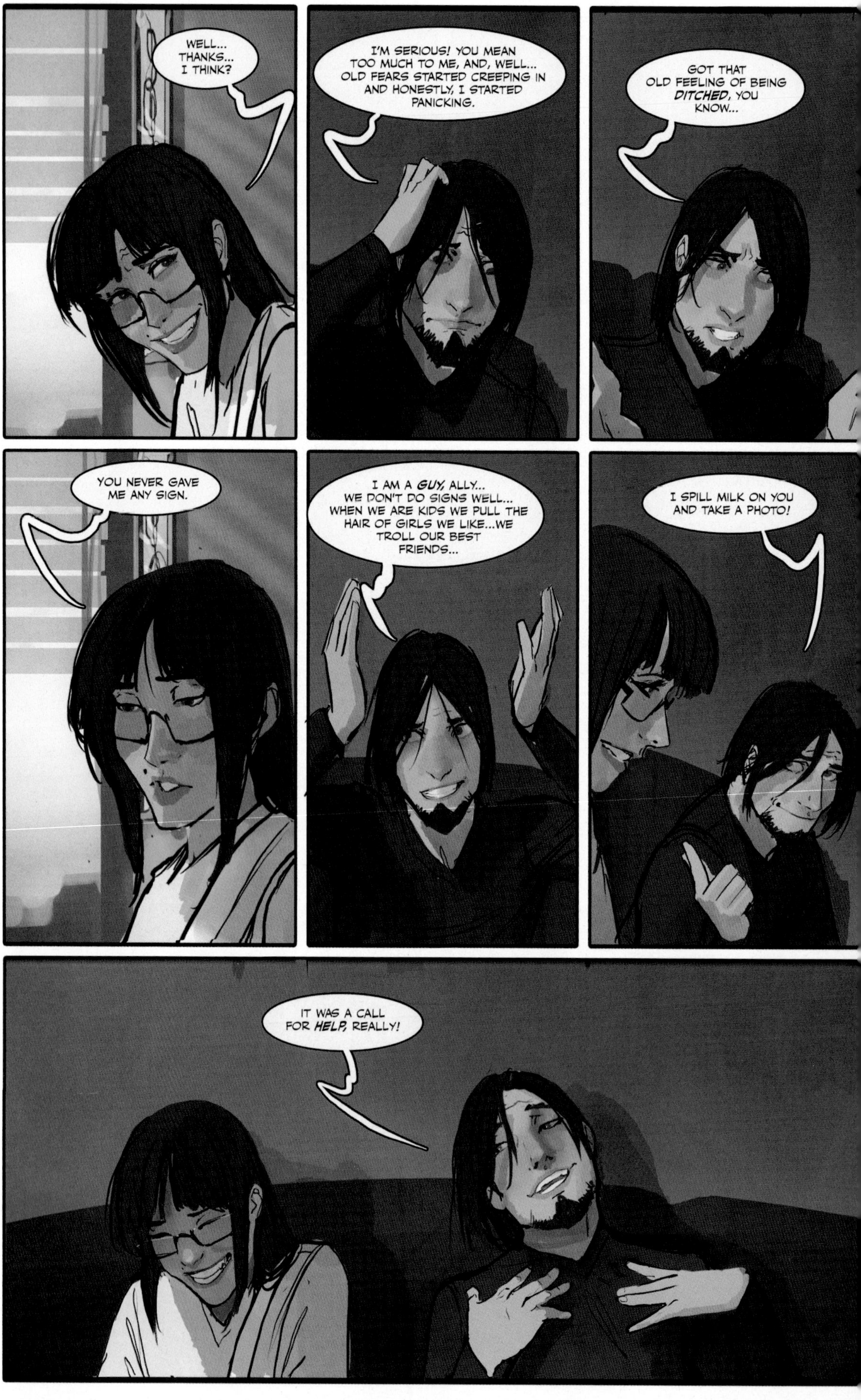
WELL... THANKS... I THINK?
I'M SERIOUS! YOU MEAN TOO MUCH TO ME, AND, WELL... OLD FEARS STARTED CREEPING IN AND HONESTLY, I STARTED PANICKING.
GOT THAT OLD FEELING OF BEING DITCHED, YOU KNOW...
YOU NEVER GAVE ME ANY SIGN.
I AM A GUY, ALLY... WE DON'T DO SIGNS WELL... WHEN WE ARE KIDS WE PULL THE HAIR OF GIRLS WE LIKE...WE TROLL OUR BEST FRIENDS...
I SPILL MILK ON YOU AND TAKE A PHOTO!
IT WAS A CALL FOR HELP, REALLY!

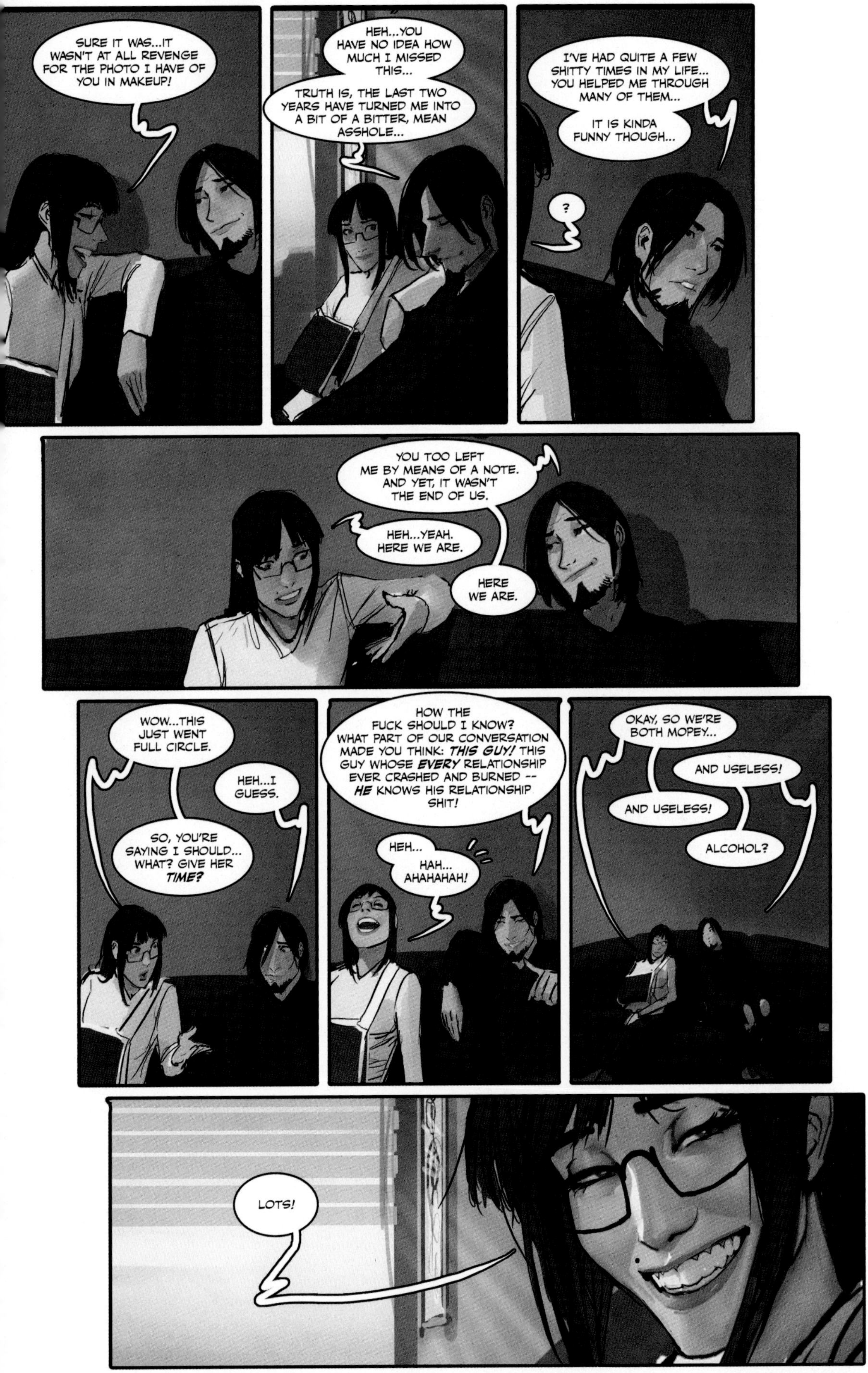
SURE IT WAS...IT WASN'T AT ALL REVENGE FOR THE PHOTO I HAVE OF YOU IN MAKEUP!
HEH...YOU HAVE NO IDEA HOW MUCH I MISSED THIS...
TRUTH IS, THE LAST TWO YEARS HAVE TURNED ME INTO A BIT OF A BITTER, MEAN ASSHOLE...
I'VE HAD QUITE A FEW SHITTY TIMES IN MY LIFE... YOU HELPED ME THROUGH MANY OF THEM...
IT IS KINDA FUNNY THOUGH...
?
YOU TOO LEFT ME BY MEANS OF A NOTE. AND YET, IT WASN'T THE END OF US.
HEH...YEAH. HERE WE ARE.
HERE WE ARE.
WOW...THIS JUST WENT FULL CIRCLE.
HEH...I GUESS.
SO, YOU'RE SAYING I SHOULD... WHAT? GIVE HER *TIME?*
HOW THE FUCK SHOULD I KNOW? WHAT PART OF OUR CONVERSATION MADE YOU THINK: *THIS GUY!* THIS GUY WHOSE *EVERY* RELATIONSHIP EVER CRASHED AND BURNED -- *HE* KNOWS HIS RELATIONSHIP SHIT!
HEH...
HAH... AHAHAHAH!
OKAY, SO WE'RE BOTH MOPEY...
AND USELESS!
AND USELESS!
ALCOHOL?
LOTS!

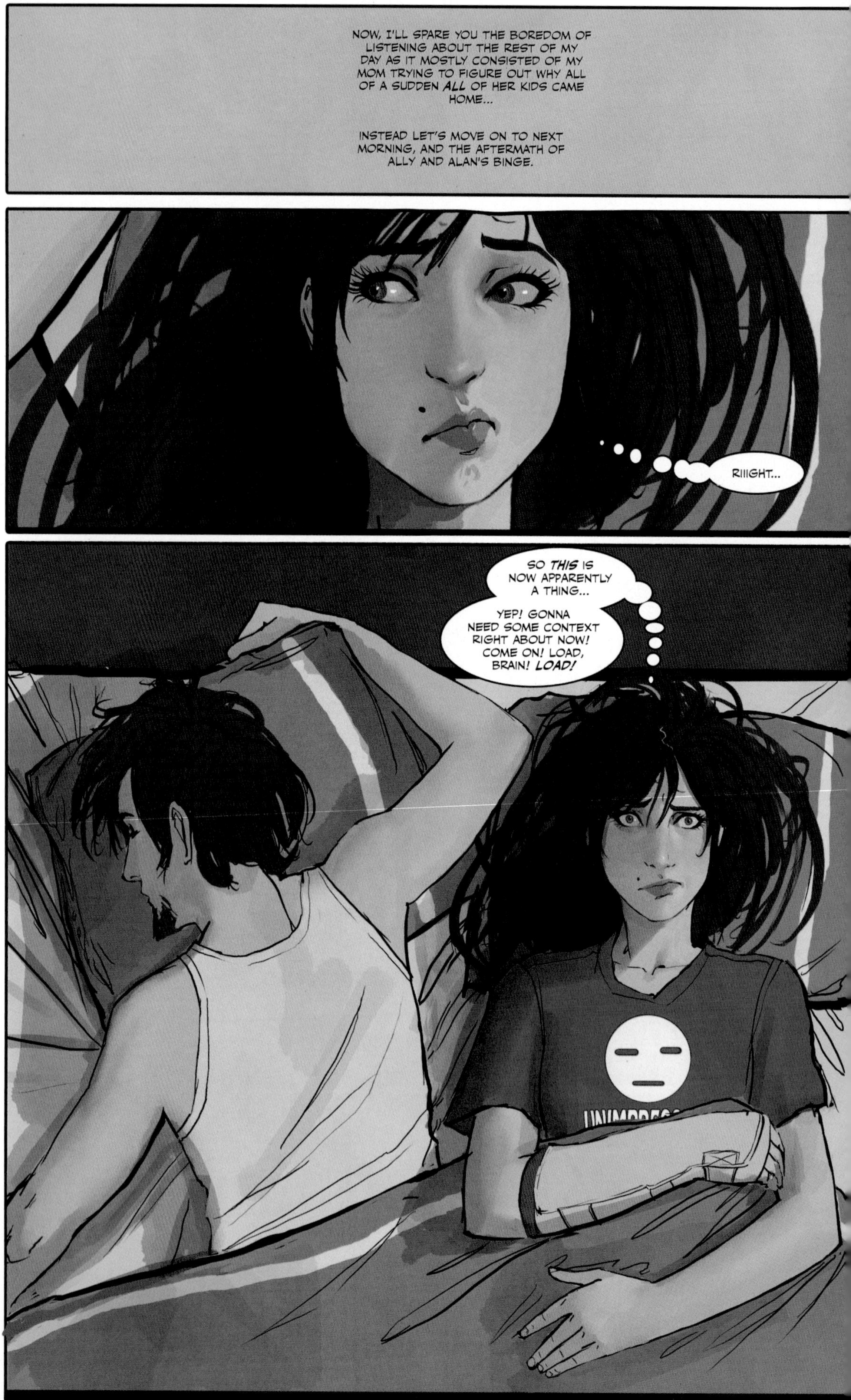
NOW, I'LL SPARE YOU THE BOREDOM OF LISTENING ABOUT THE REST OF MY DAY AS IT MOSTLY CONSISTED OF MY MOM TRYING TO FIGURE OUT WHY ALL OF A SUDDEN *ALL* OF HER KIDS CAME HOME...
INSTEAD LET'S MOVE ON TO NEXT MORNING, AND THE AFTERMATH OF ALLY AND ALAN'S BINGE.
RIIIGHT...
SO *THIS* IS NOW APPARENTLY A THING...
YEP! GONNA NEED SOME CONTEXT RIGHT ABOUT NOW! COME ON! LOAD, BRAIN! *LOAD!*

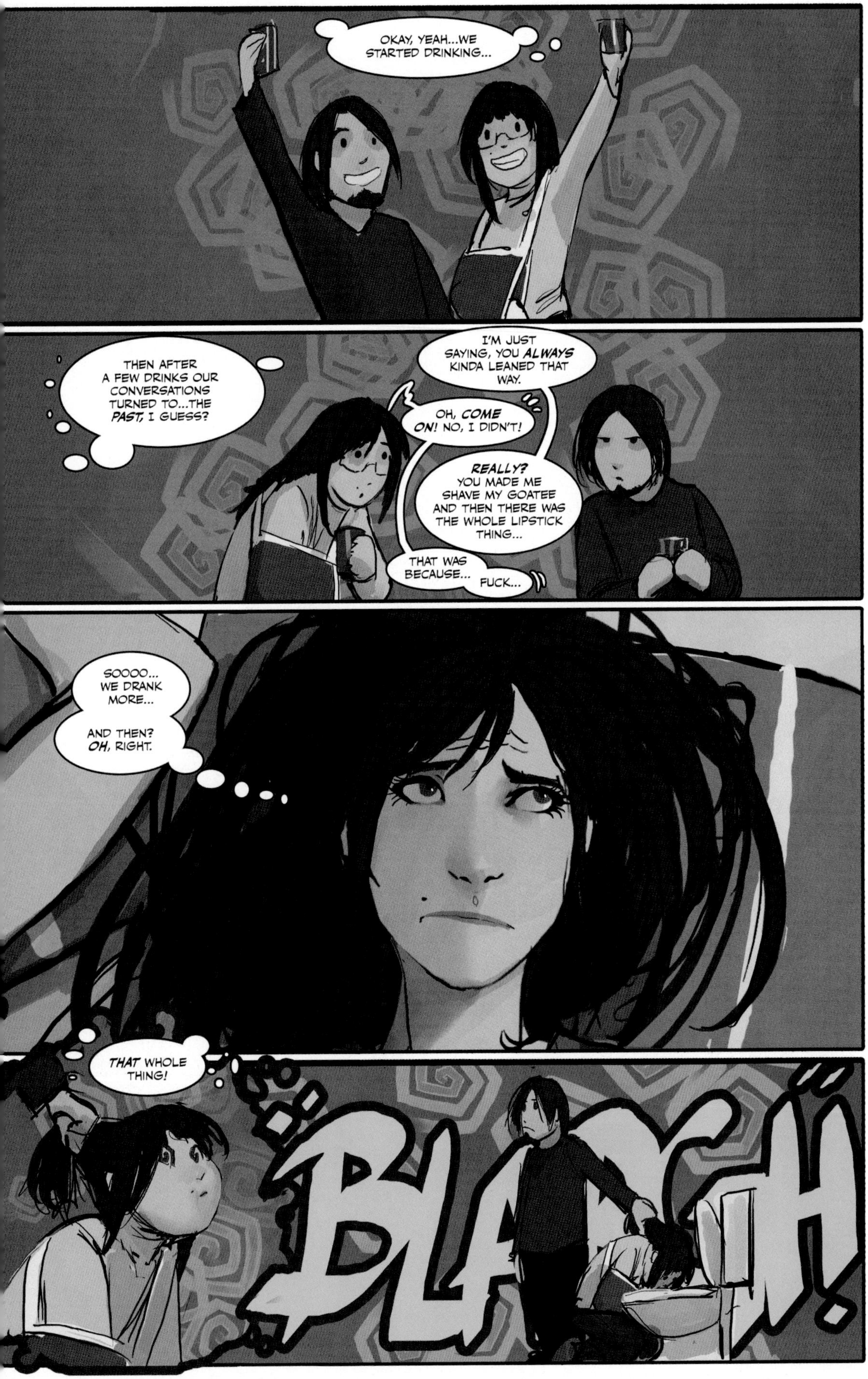
OKAY, YEAH...WE STARTED DRINKING...
THEN AFTER A FEW DRINKS OUR CONVERSATIONS TURNED TO...THE *PAST*, I GUESS?
I'M JUST SAYING, YOU *ALWAYS* KINDA LEANED THAT WAY.
OH, *COME ON*! NO, I DIDN'T!
REALLY? YOU MADE ME SHAVE MY GOATEE AND THEN THERE WAS THE WHOLE LIPSTICK THING...
THAT WAS BECAUSE...
FUCK...
SOOOO... WE DRANK MORE...
AND THEN? *OH*, RIGHT.
THAT WHOLE THING!

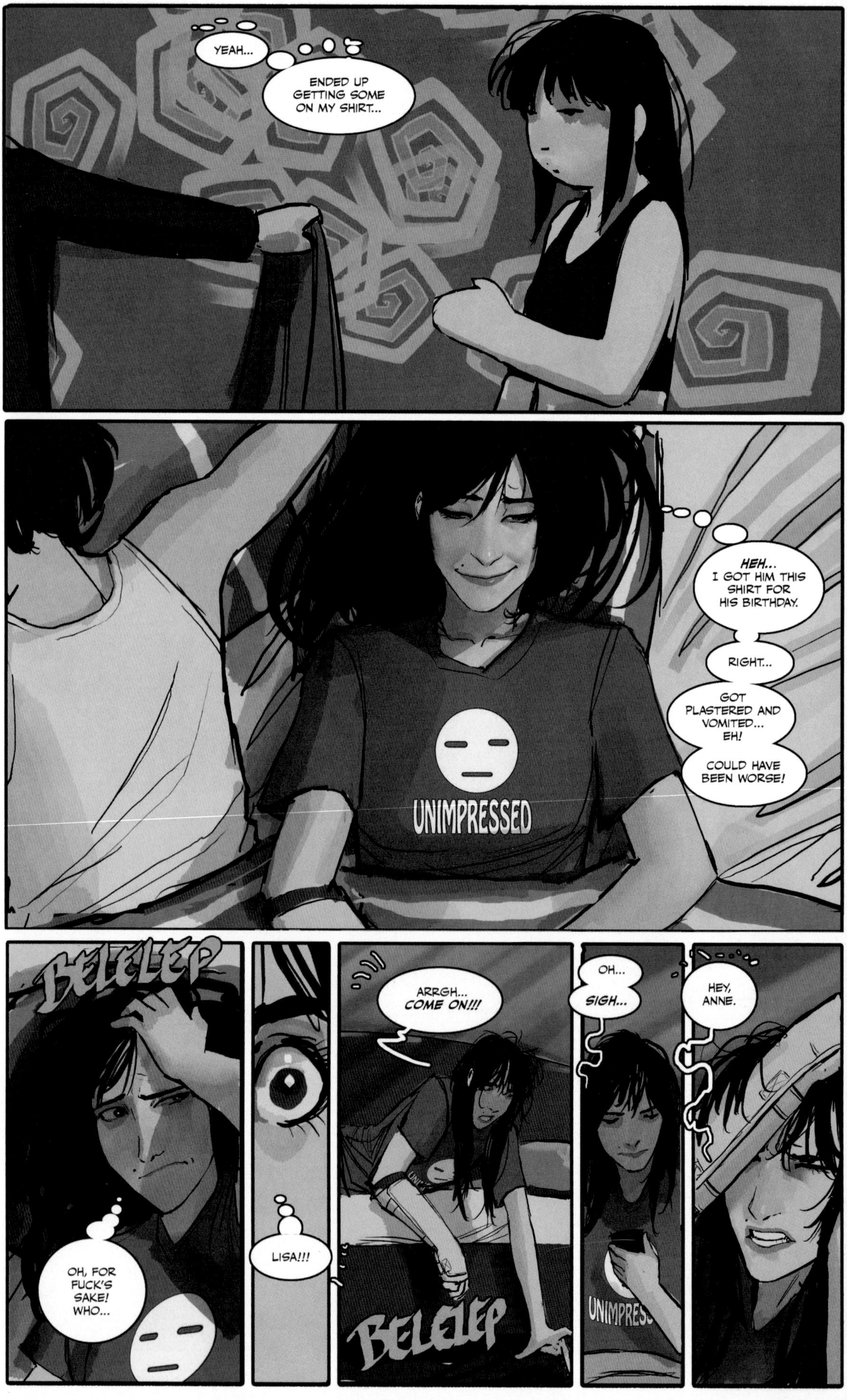
YEAH...
ENDED UP GETTING SOME ON MY SHIRT...
HEH... I GOT HIM THIS SHIRT FOR HIS BIRTHDAY.
RIGHT...
GOT PLASTERED AND VOMITED... EH!
COULD HAVE BEEN WORSE!
UNIMPRESSED
BELELEP
OH, FOR FUCK'S SAKE! WHO...
LISA!!!
ARRGH... COME ON!!!
BELELEP
OH...
SIGH...
UNIMPRESS
HEY, ANNE.

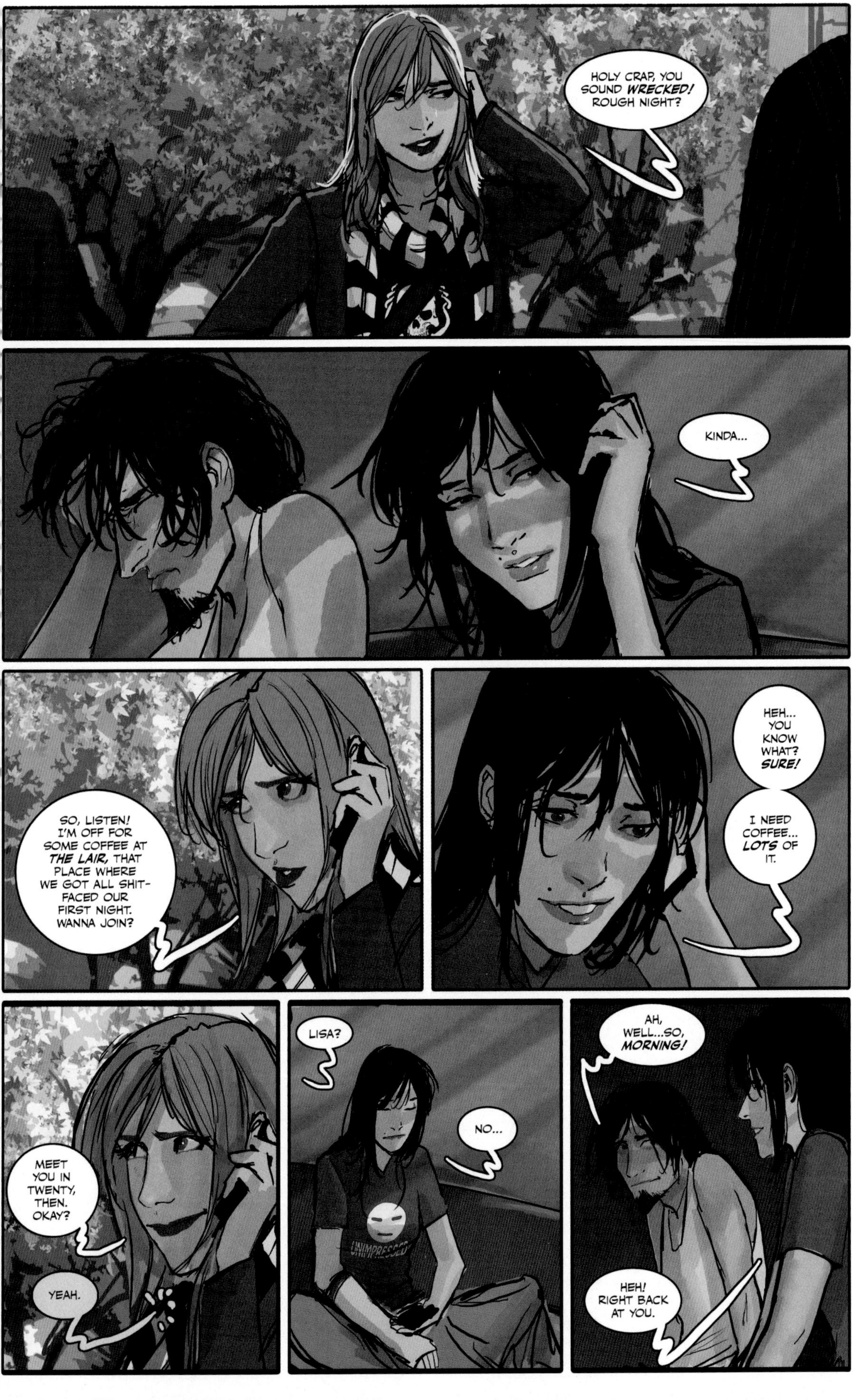
HOLY CRAP, YOU SOUND *WRECKED!* ROUGH NIGHT?
KINDA...
SO, LISTEN! I'M OFF FOR SOME COFFEE AT *THE LAIR,* THAT PLACE WHERE WE GOT ALL SHIT-FACED OUR FIRST NIGHT. WANNA JOIN?
HEH... YOU KNOW WHAT? *SURE!*
I NEED COFFEE... *LOTS* OF IT.
MEET YOU IN TWENTY, THEN. OKAY?
YEAH.
LISA?
NO...
AH, WELL...SO, *MORNING!*
HEH! RIGHT BACK AT YOU.

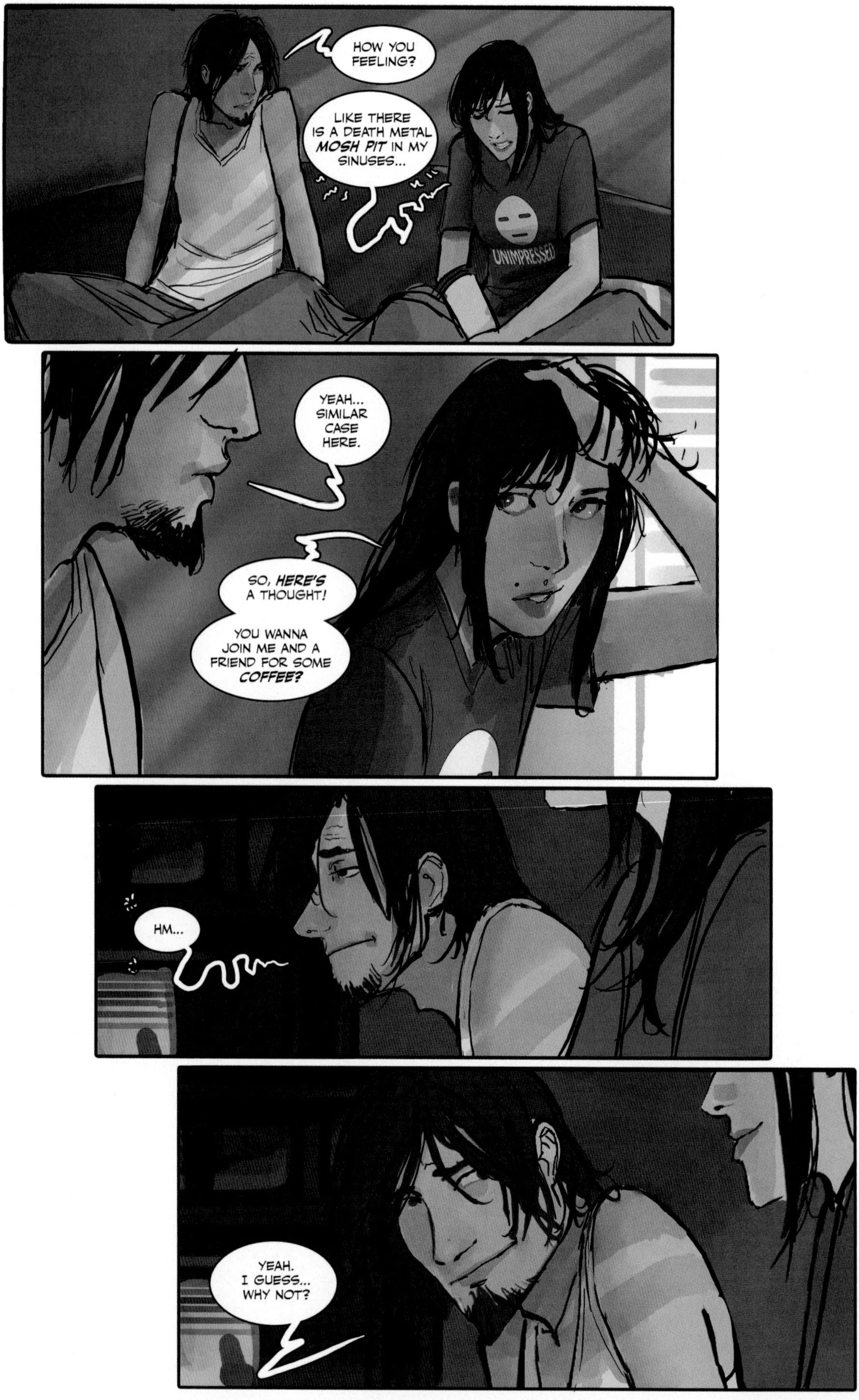
HOW YOU FEELING?
LIKE THERE IS A DEATH METAL *MOSH PIT* IN MY SINUSES...
UNIMPRESSED
YEAH... SIMILAR CASE HERE.
SO, *HERE'S* A THOUGHT!
YOU WANNA JOIN ME AND A FRIEND FOR SOME *COFFEE?*
HM...
YEAH. I GUESS... WHY NOT?

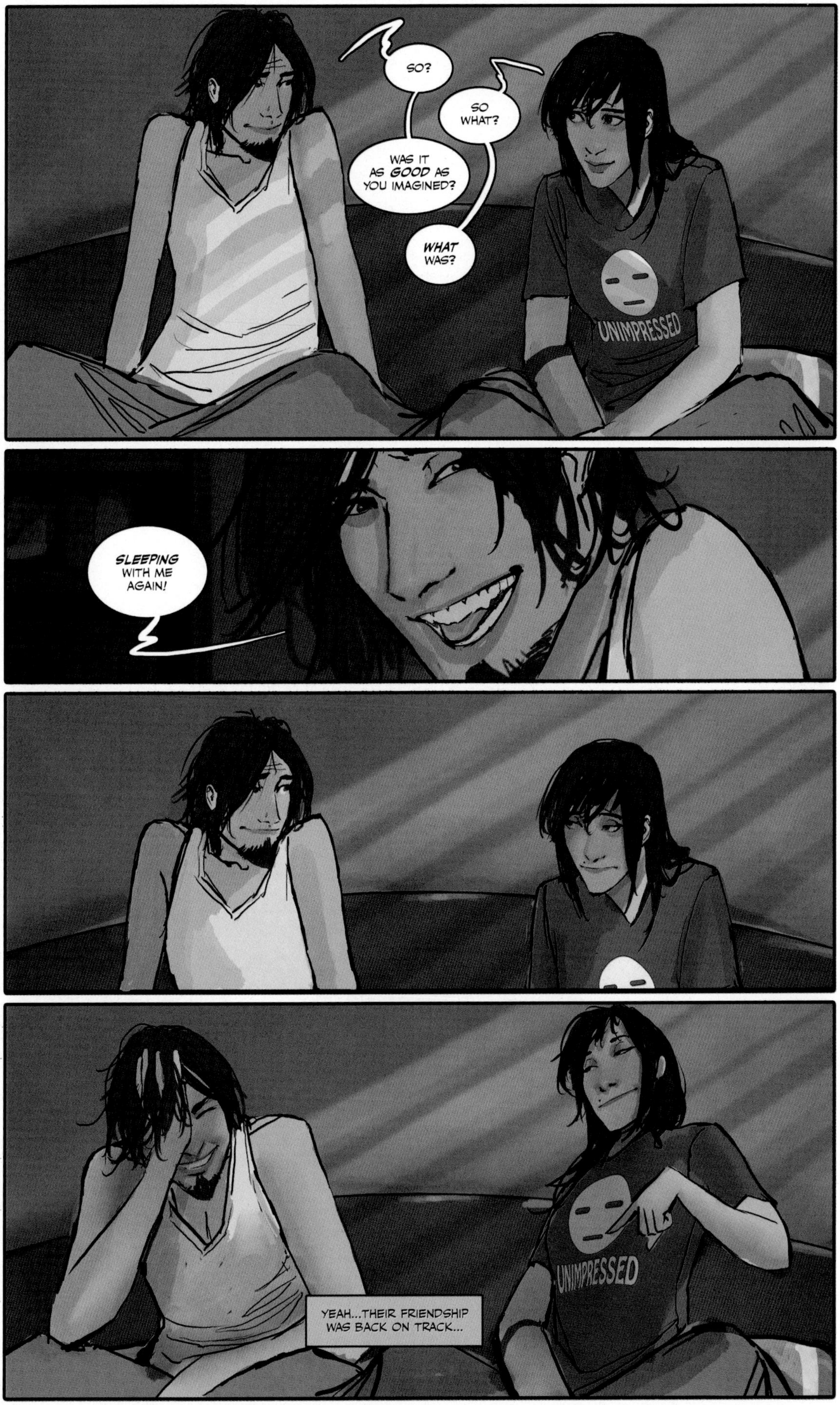
SO?
SO WHAT?
WAS IT AS *GOOD* AS YOU IMAGINED?
WHAT WAS?
UNIMPRESSED
SLEEPING WITH ME AGAIN!
UNIMPRESSED
YEAH...THEIR FRIENDSHIP WAS BACK ON TRACK...

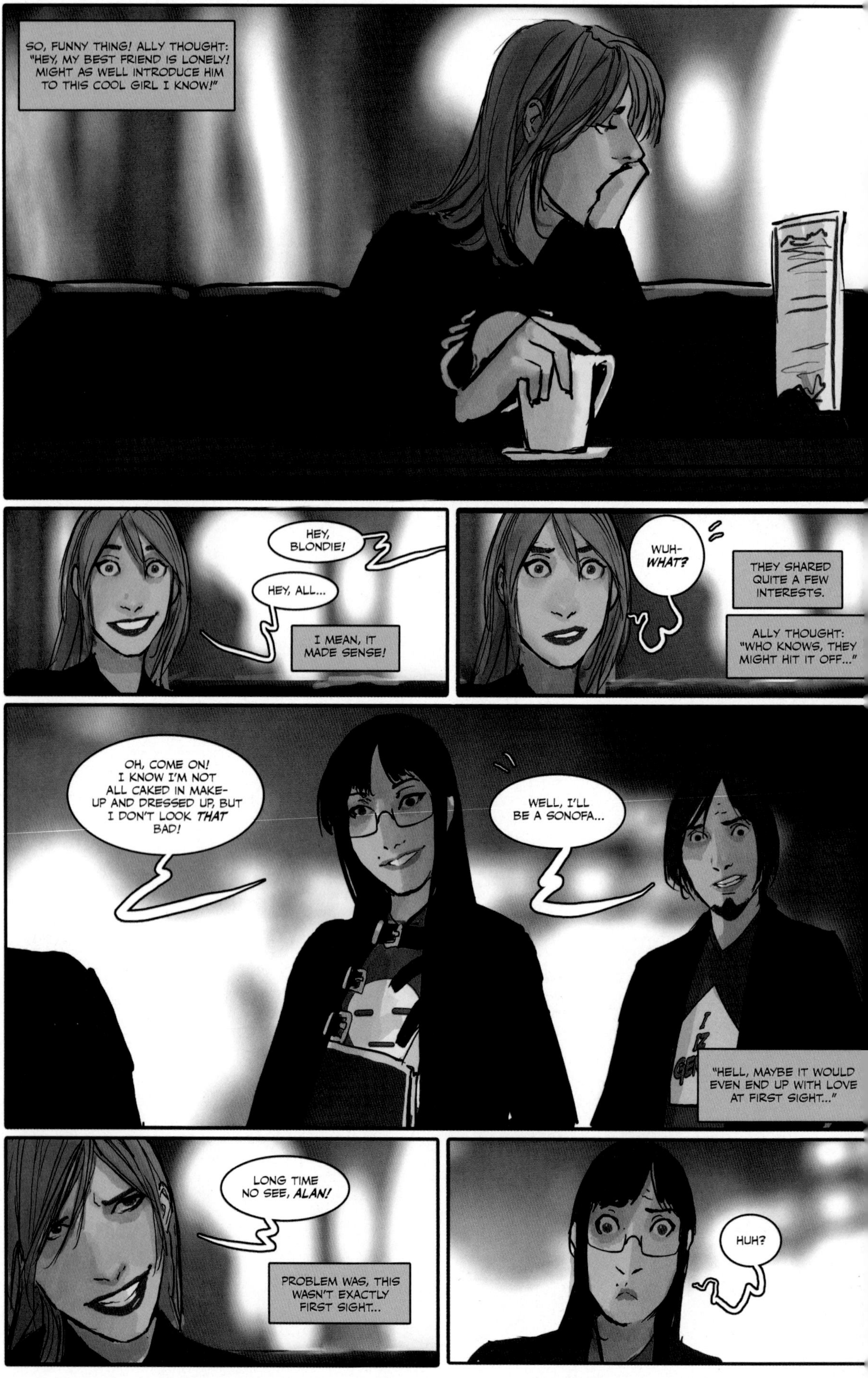

SO, FUNNY THING! ALLY THOUGHT: "HEY, MY BEST FRIEND IS LONELY! MIGHT AS WELL INTRODUCE HIM TO THIS COOL GIRL I KNOW!"
HEY, BLONDIE!
HEY, ALL...
I MEAN, IT MADE SENSE!
WUH-WHAT?
THEY SHARED QUITE A FEW INTERESTS.
ALLY THOUGHT: "WHO KNOWS, THEY MIGHT HIT IT OFF..."
OH, COME ON! I KNOW I'M NOT ALL CAKED IN MAKE-UP AND DRESSED UP, BUT I DON'T LOOK THAT BAD!
WELL, I'LL BE A SONOFA...
"HELL, MAYBE IT WOULD EVEN END UP WITH LOVE AT FIRST SIGHT..."
LONG TIME NO SEE, ALAN!
PROBLEM WAS, THIS WASN'T EXACTLY FIRST SIGHT...
HUH?

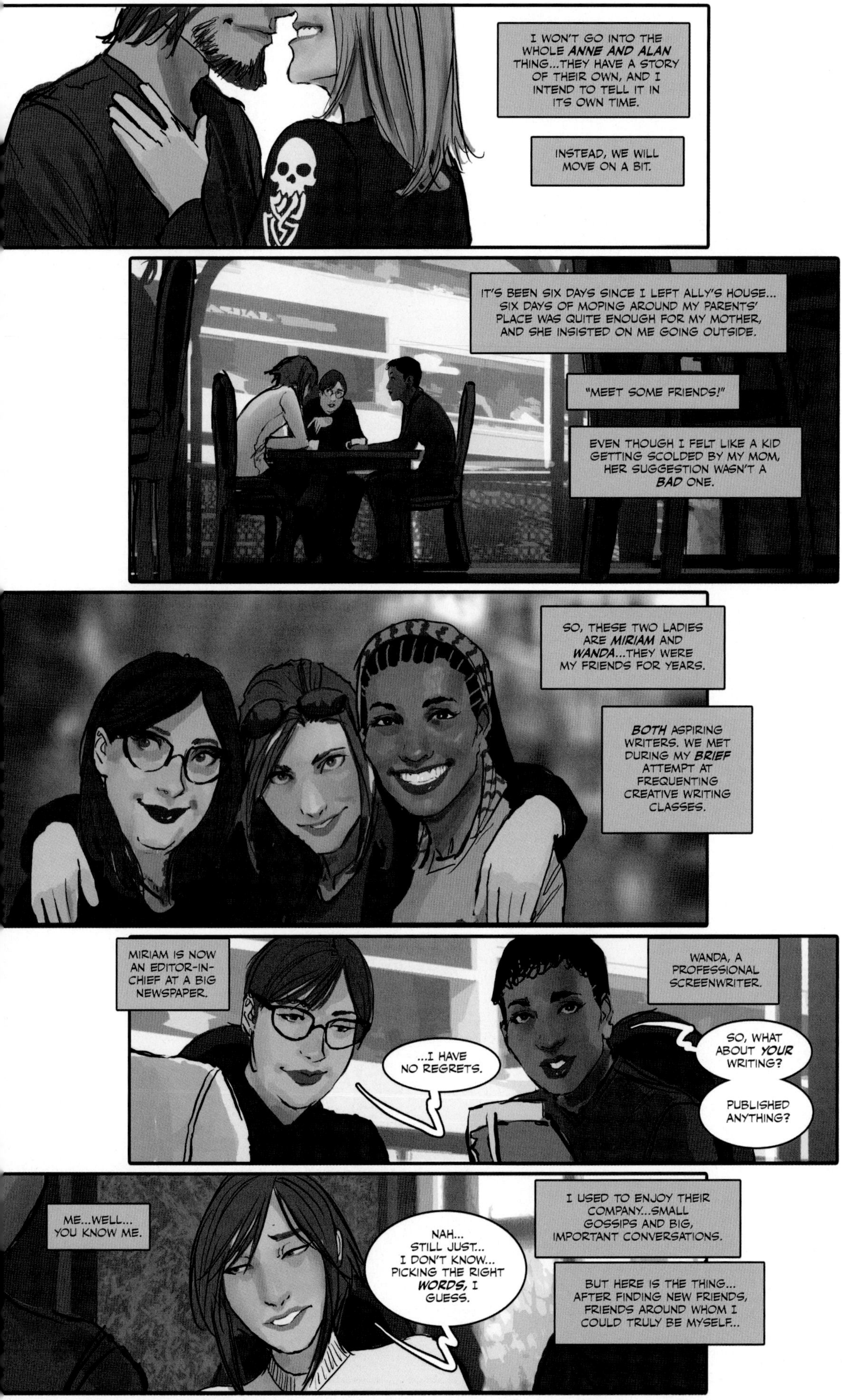
I WON'T GO INTO THE WHOLE ANNE AND ALAN THING...THEY HAVE A STORY OF THEIR OWN, AND I INTEND TO TELL IT IN ITS OWN TIME.
INSTEAD, WE WILL MOVE ON A BIT.
IT'S BEEN SIX DAYS SINCE I LEFT ALLY'S HOUSE... SIX DAYS OF MOPING AROUND MY PARENTS' PLACE WAS QUITE ENOUGH FOR MY MOTHER, AND SHE INSISTED ON ME GOING OUTSIDE.
"MEET SOME FRIENDS!"
EVEN THOUGH I FELT LIKE A KID GETTING SCOLDED BY MY MOM, HER SUGGESTION WASN'T A BAD ONE.
SO, THESE TWO LADIES ARE MIRIAM AND WANDA...THEY WERE MY FRIENDS FOR YEARS.
BOTH ASPIRING WRITERS. WE MET DURING MY BRIEF ATTEMPT AT FREQUENTING CREATIVE WRITING CLASSES.
MIRIAM IS NOW AN EDITOR-IN-CHIEF AT A BIG NEWSPAPER.
...I HAVE NO REGRETS.
WANDA, A PROFESSIONAL SCREENWRITER.
SO, WHAT ABOUT YOUR WRITING?
PUBLISHED ANYTHING?
ME...WELL... YOU KNOW ME.
NAH... STILL JUST... I DON'T KNOW... PICKING THE RIGHT WORDS, I GUESS.
I USED TO ENJOY THEIR COMPANY...SMALL GOSSIPS AND BIG, IMPORTANT CONVERSATIONS.
BUT HERE IS THE THING... AFTER FINDING NEW FRIENDS, FRIENDS AROUND WHOM I COULD TRULY BE MYSELF...

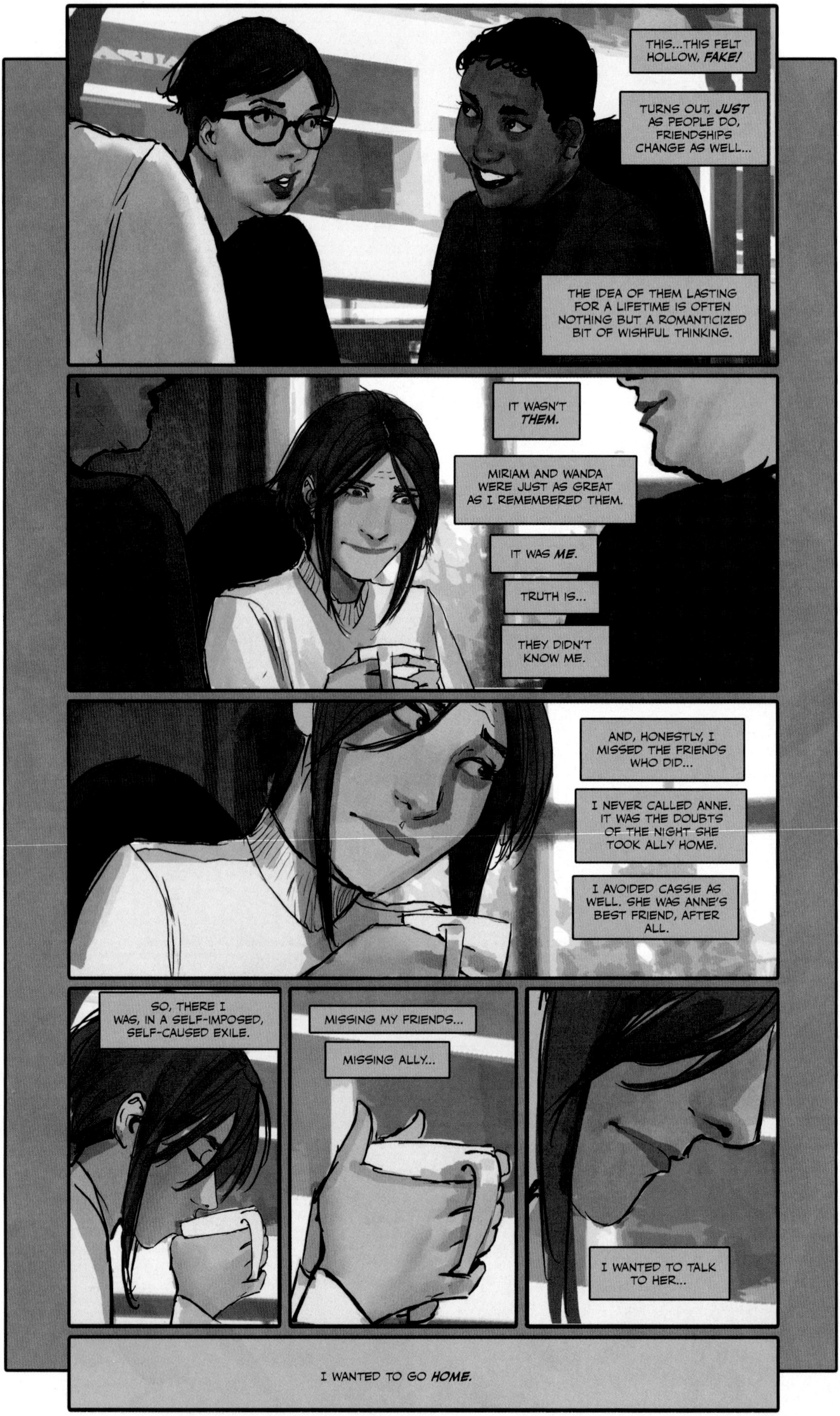
THIS...THIS FELT HOLLOW, FAKE!
TURNS OUT, JUST AS PEOPLE DO, FRIENDSHIPS CHANGE AS WELL...
THE IDEA OF THEM LASTING FOR A LIFETIME IS OFTEN NOTHING BUT A ROMANTICIZED BIT OF WISHFUL THINKING.
IT WASN'T THEM.
MIRIAM AND WANDA WERE JUST AS GREAT AS I REMEMBERED THEM.
IT WAS ME.
TRUTH IS...
THEY DIDN'T KNOW ME.
AND, HONESTLY, I MISSED THE FRIENDS WHO DID...
I NEVER CALLED ANNE. IT WAS THE DOUBTS OF THE NIGHT SHE TOOK ALLY HOME.
I AVOIDED CASSIE AS WELL. SHE WAS ANNE'S BEST FRIEND, AFTER ALL.
SO, THERE I WAS, IN A SELF-IMPOSED, SELF-CAUSED EXILE.
MISSING MY FRIENDS...
MISSING ALLY...
I WANTED TO TALK TO HER...
I WANTED TO GO HOME.

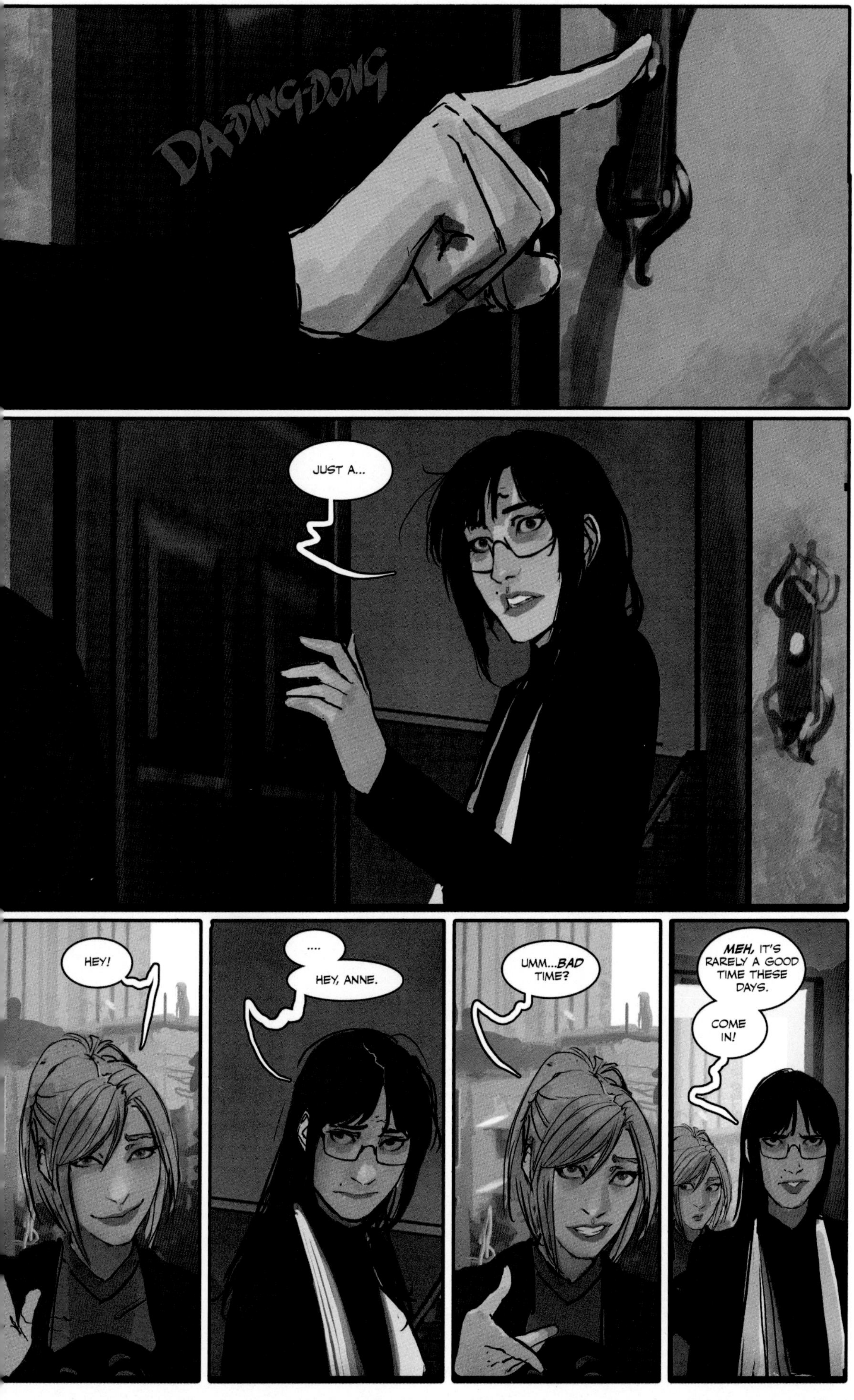
DA-DING-DONG
JUST A...
HEY!
....
HEY, ANNE.
UMM...BAD TIME?
MEH, IT'S RARELY A GOOD TIME THESE DAYS.
COME IN!

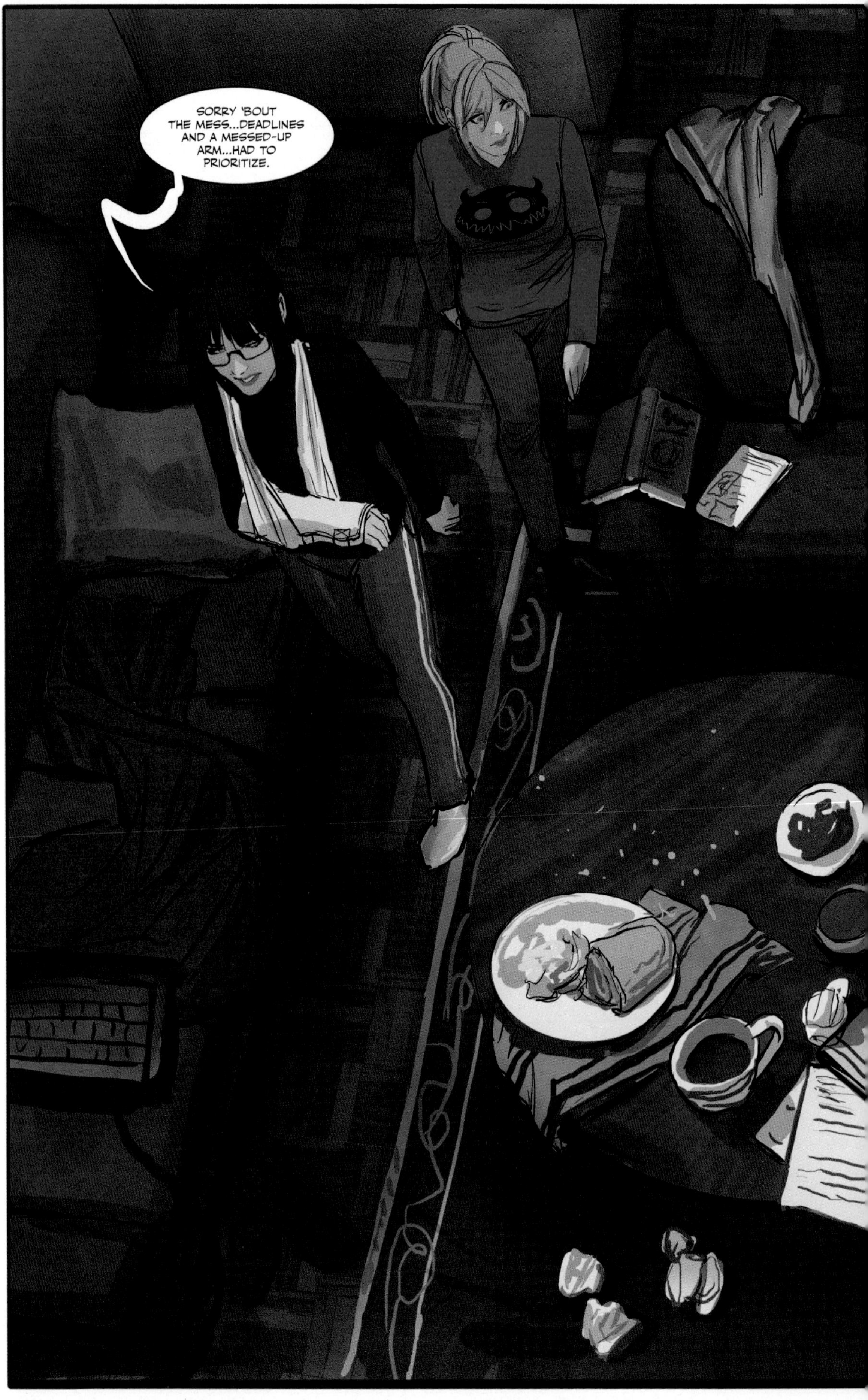
SORRY 'BOUT THE MESS...DEADLINES AND A MESSED-UP ARM...HAD TO PRIORITIZE.

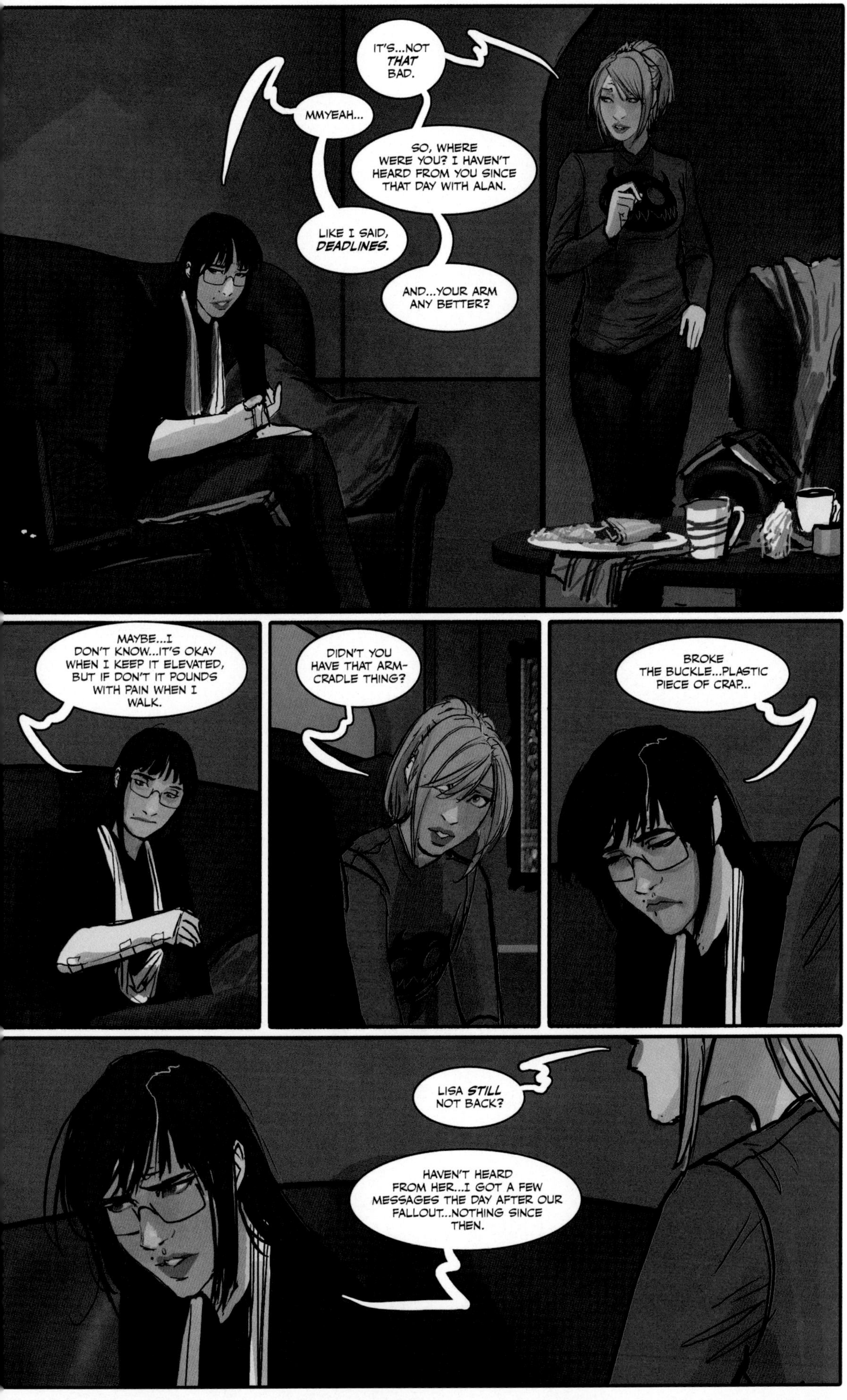
IT'S...NOT *THAT* BAD.
MMYEAH...
SO, WHERE WERE YOU? I HAVEN'T HEARD FROM YOU SINCE THAT DAY WITH ALAN.
LIKE I SAID, *DEADLINES.*
AND...YOUR ARM ANY BETTER?
MAYBE...I DON'T KNOW...IT'S OKAY WHEN I KEEP IT ELEVATED, BUT IF DON'T IT POUNDS WITH PAIN WHEN I WALK.
DIDN'T YOU HAVE THAT ARM-CRADLE THING?
BROKE THE BUCKLE...PLASTIC PIECE OF CRAP...
LISA *STILL* NOT BACK?
HAVEN'T HEARD FROM HER...I GOT A FEW MESSAGES THE DAY AFTER OUR FALLOUT...NOTHING SINCE THEN.

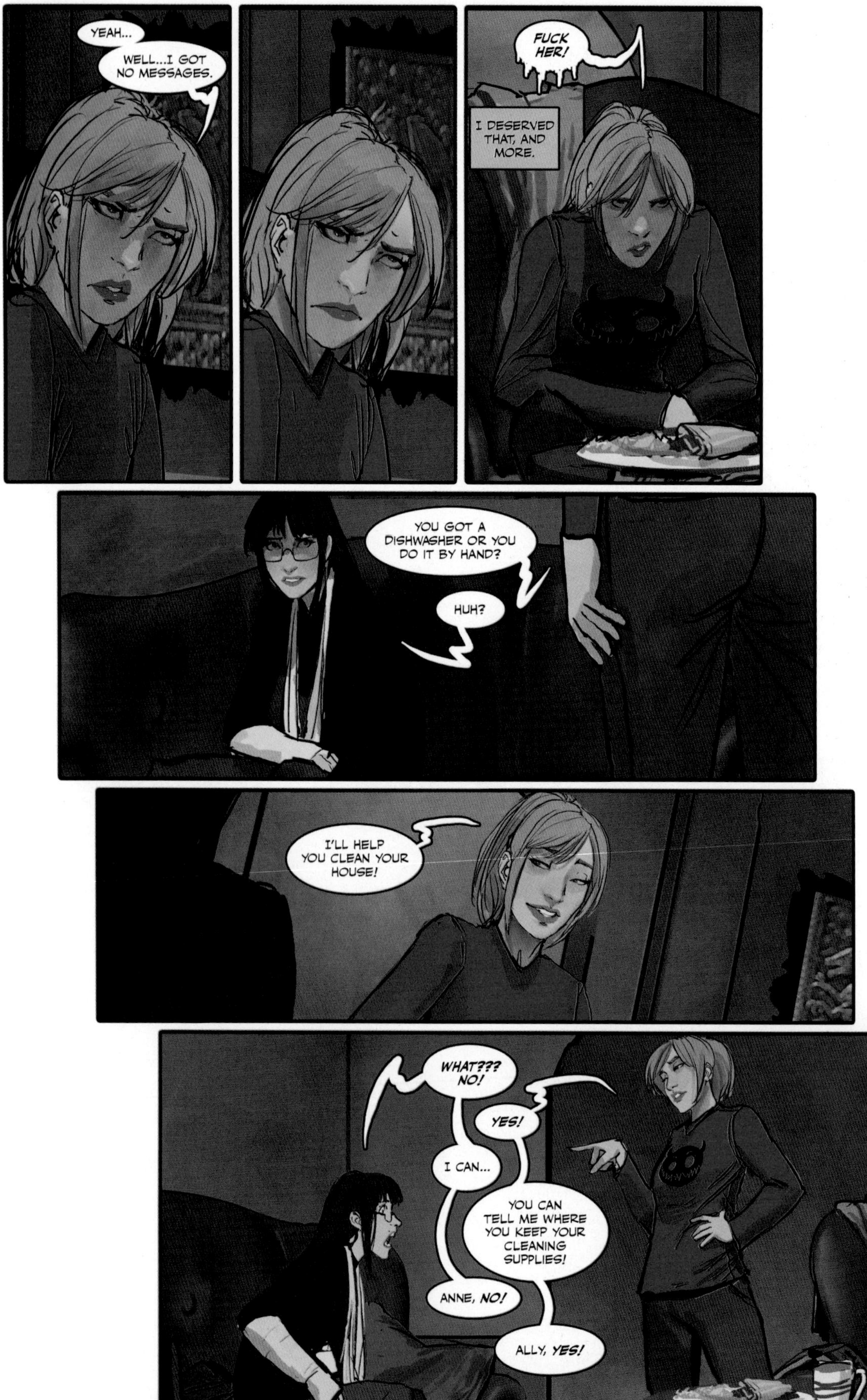
YEAH...
WELL...I GOT NO MESSAGES.
FUCK HER!
I DESERVED THAT, AND MORE.
YOU GOT A DISHWASHER OR YOU DO IT BY HAND?
HUH?
I'LL HELP YOU CLEAN YOUR HOUSE!
WHAT??? NO!
YES!
I CAN...
YOU CAN TELL ME WHERE YOU KEEP YOUR CLEANING SUPPLIES!
ANNE, NO!
ALLY, YES!

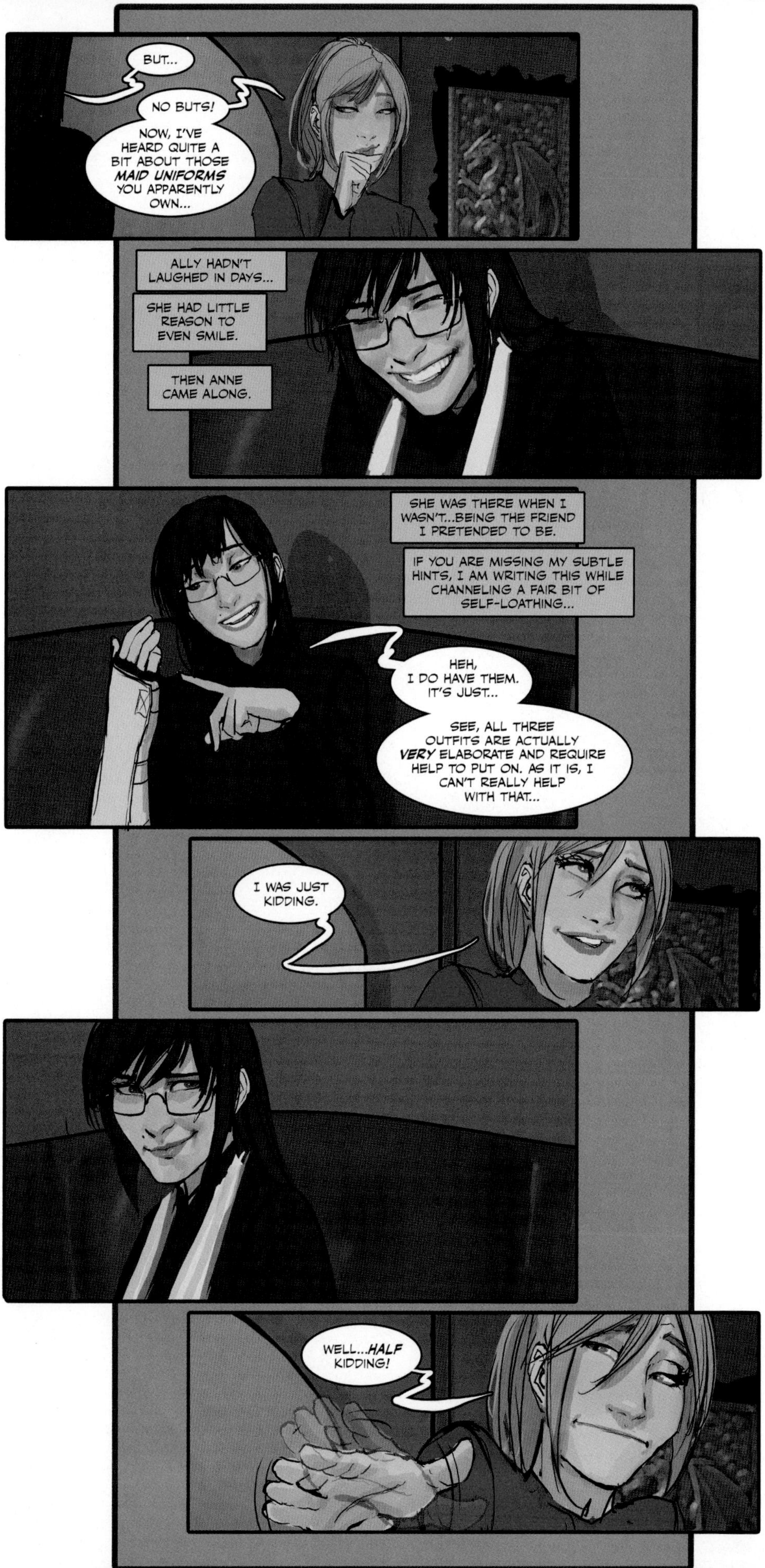
BUT...
NO BUTS!
NOW, I'VE HEARD QUITE A BIT ABOUT THOSE **MAID UNIFORMS** YOU APPARENTLY OWN...
ALLY HADN'T LAUGHED IN DAYS...
SHE HAD LITTLE REASON TO EVEN SMILE.
THEN ANNE CAME ALONG.
SHE WAS THERE WHEN I WASN'T...BEING THE FRIEND I PRETENDED TO BE.
IF YOU ARE MISSING MY SUBTLE HINTS, I AM WRITING THIS WHILE CHANNELING A FAIR BIT OF SELF-LOATHING...
HEH, I DO HAVE THEM. IT'S JUST...
SEE, ALL THREE OUTFITS ARE ACTUALLY **VERY** ELABORATE AND REQUIRE HELP TO PUT ON. AS IT IS, I CAN'T REALLY HELP WITH THAT...
I WAS JUST KIDDING.
WELL...**HALF** KIDDING!

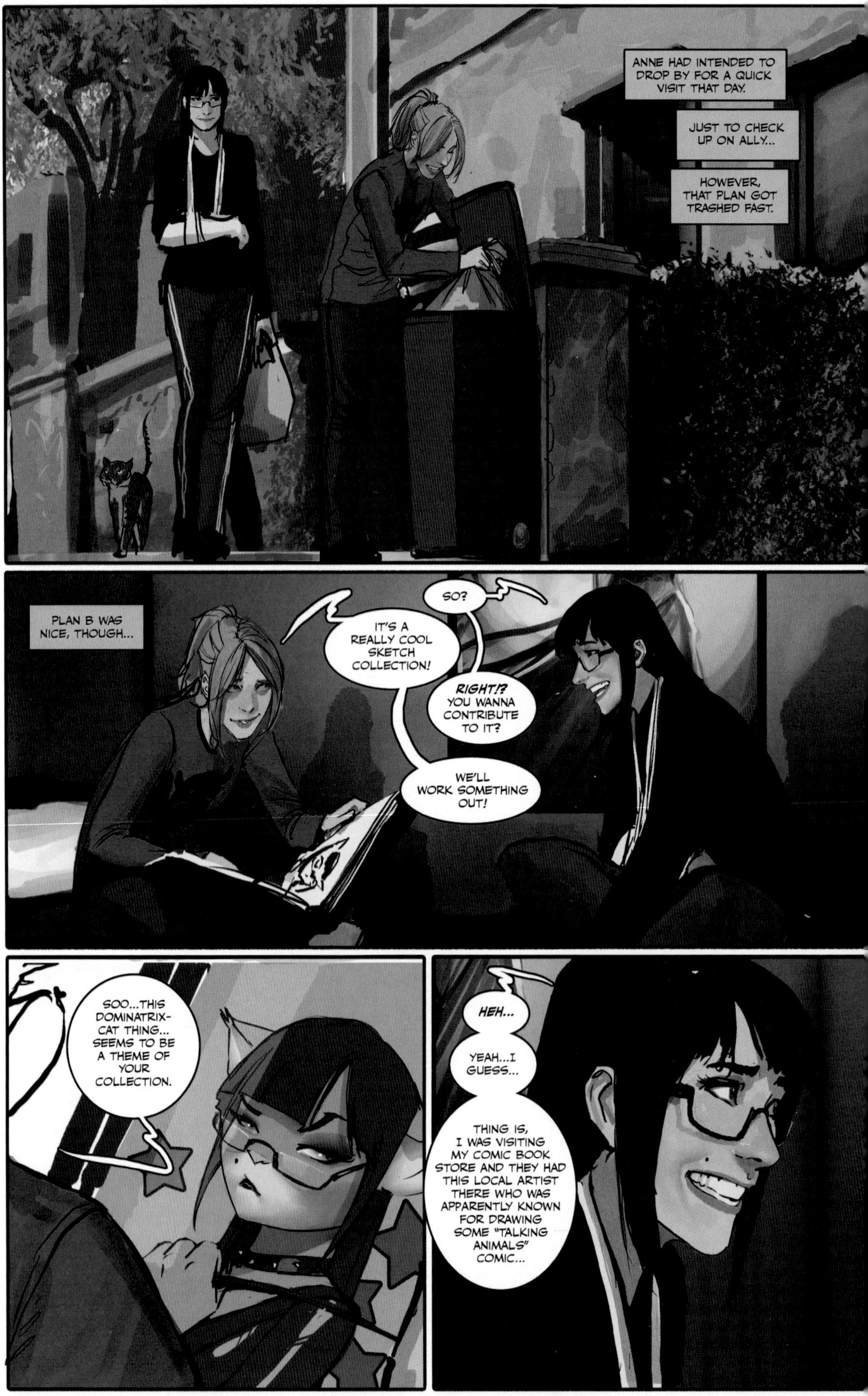
ANNE HAD INTENDED TO DROP BY FOR A QUICK VISIT THAT DAY.
JUST TO CHECK UP ON ALLY...
HOWEVER, THAT PLAN GOT TRASHED FAST.
PLAN B WAS NICE, THOUGH...
SO?
IT'S A REALLY COOL SKETCH COLLECTION!
RIGHT!? YOU WANNA CONTRIBUTE TO IT?
WE'LL WORK SOMETHING OUT!
SOO...THIS DOMINATRIX-CAT THING... SEEMS TO BE A THEME OF YOUR COLLECTION.
HEH...
YEAH...I GUESS...
THING IS, I WAS VISITING MY COMIC BOOK STORE AND THEY HAD THIS LOCAL ARTIST THERE WHO WAS APPARENTLY KNOWN FOR DRAWING SOME "TALKING ANIMALS" COMIC...

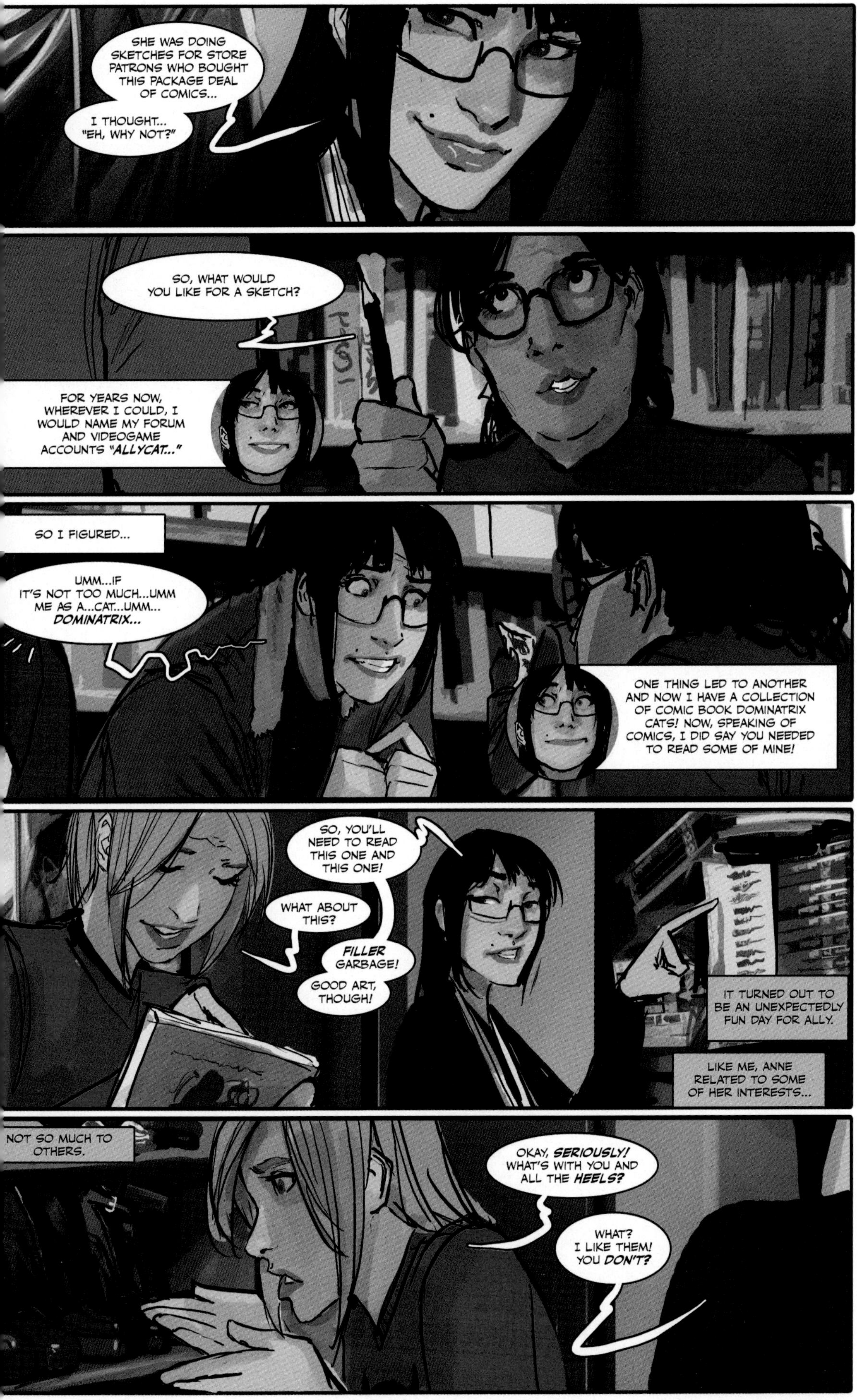

SHE WAS DOING SKETCHES FOR STORE PATRONS WHO BOUGHT THIS PACKAGE DEAL OF COMICS...
I THOUGHT... "EH, WHY NOT?"
SO, WHAT WOULD YOU LIKE FOR A SKETCH?
FOR YEARS NOW, WHEREVER I COULD, I WOULD NAME MY FORUM AND VIDEOGAME ACCOUNTS "ALLYCAT..."
SO I FIGURED...
UMM...IF IT'S NOT TOO MUCH...UMM ME AS A...CAT...UMM... DOMINATRIX...
ONE THING LED TO ANOTHER AND NOW I HAVE A COLLECTION OF COMIC BOOK DOMINATRIX CATS! NOW, SPEAKING OF COMICS, I DID SAY YOU NEEDED TO READ SOME OF MINE!
SO, YOU'LL NEED TO READ THIS ONE AND THIS ONE!
WHAT ABOUT THIS?
FILLER GARBAGE!
GOOD ART, THOUGH!
IT TURNED OUT TO BE AN UNEXPECTEDLY FUN DAY FOR ALLY.
LIKE ME, ANNE RELATED TO SOME OF HER INTERESTS...
NOT SO MUCH TO OTHERS.
OKAY, SERIOUSLY! WHAT'S WITH YOU AND ALL THE HEELS?
WHAT? I LIKE THEM! YOU DON'T?

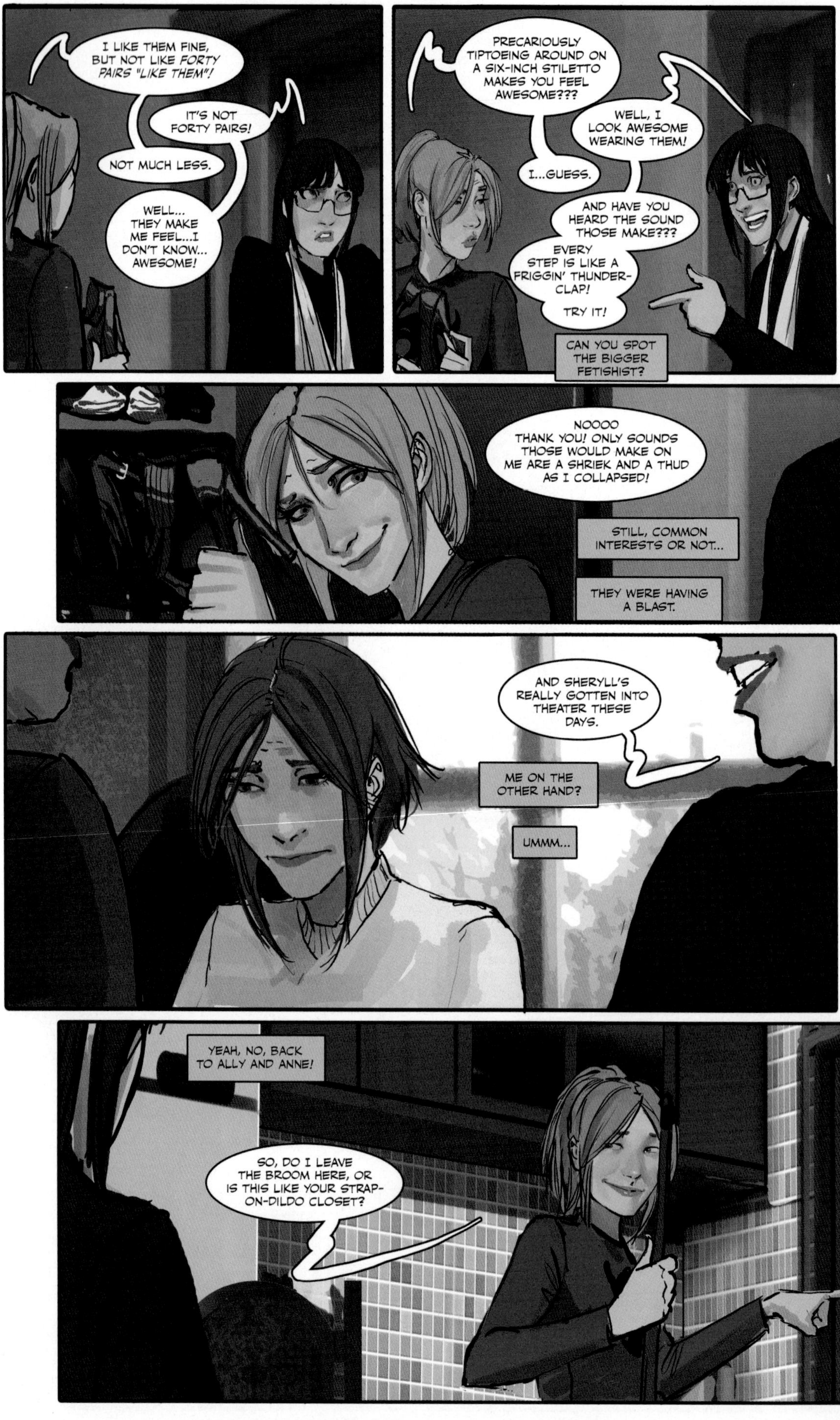
I LIKE THEM FINE, BUT NOT LIKE FORTY PAIRS "LIKE THEM"!
IT'S NOT FORTY PAIRS!
NOT MUCH LESS.
WELL... THEY MAKE ME FEEL...I DON'T KNOW... AWESOME!
PRECARIOUSLY TIPTOEING AROUND ON A SIX-INCH STILETTO MAKES YOU FEEL AWESOME???
WELL, I LOOK AWESOME WEARING THEM!
I...GUESS.
AND HAVE YOU HEARD THE SOUND THOSE MAKE???
EVERY STEP IS LIKE A FRIGGIN' THUNDER-CLAP!
TRY IT!
CAN YOU SPOT THE BIGGER FETISHIST?
NOOOO THANK YOU! ONLY SOUNDS THOSE WOULD MAKE ON ME ARE A SHRIEK AND A THUD AS I COLLAPSED!
STILL, COMMON INTERESTS OR NOT...
THEY WERE HAVING A BLAST.
AND SHERYLL'S REALLY GOTTEN INTO THEATER THESE DAYS.
ME ON THE OTHER HAND?
UMMM...
YEAH, NO, BACK TO ALLY AND ANNE!
SO, DO I LEAVE THE BROOM HERE, OR IS THIS LIKE YOUR STRAP-ON-DILDO CLOSET?

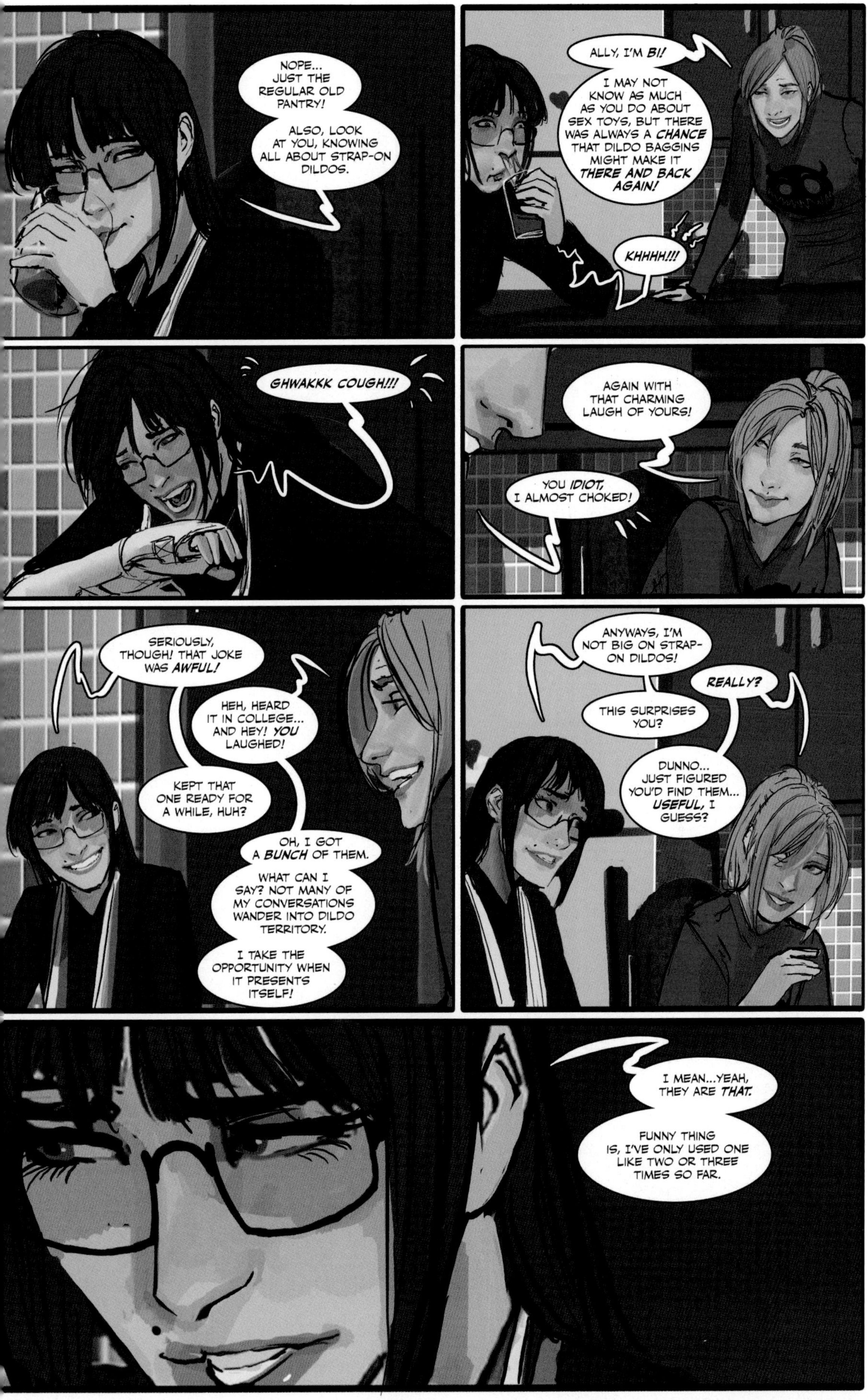
NOPE... JUST THE REGULAR OLD PANTRY!
ALSO, LOOK AT YOU, KNOWING ALL ABOUT STRAP-ON DILDOS.
ALLY, I'M BI!
I MAY NOT KNOW AS MUCH AS YOU DO ABOUT SEX TOYS, BUT THERE WAS ALWAYS A CHANCE THAT DILDO BAGGINS MIGHT MAKE IT THERE AND BACK AGAIN!
KHHHH!!!
GHWAKKK COUGH!!!
AGAIN WITH THAT CHARMING LAUGH OF YOURS!
YOU IDIOT, I ALMOST CHOKED!
SERIOUSLY, THOUGH! THAT JOKE WAS AWFUL!
HEH, HEARD IT IN COLLEGE... AND HEY! YOU LAUGHED!
KEPT THAT ONE READY FOR A WHILE, HUH?
OH, I GOT A BUNCH OF THEM.
WHAT CAN I SAY? NOT MANY OF MY CONVERSATIONS WANDER INTO DILDO TERRITORY.
I TAKE THE OPPORTUNITY WHEN IT PRESENTS ITSELF!
ANYWAYS, I'M NOT BIG ON STRAP-ON DILDOS!
REALLY?
THIS SURPRISES YOU?
DUNNO... JUST FIGURED YOU'D FIND THEM... USEFUL, I GUESS?
I MEAN...YEAH, THEY ARE THAT.
FUNNY THING IS, I'VE ONLY USED ONE LIKE TWO OR THREE TIMES SO FAR.

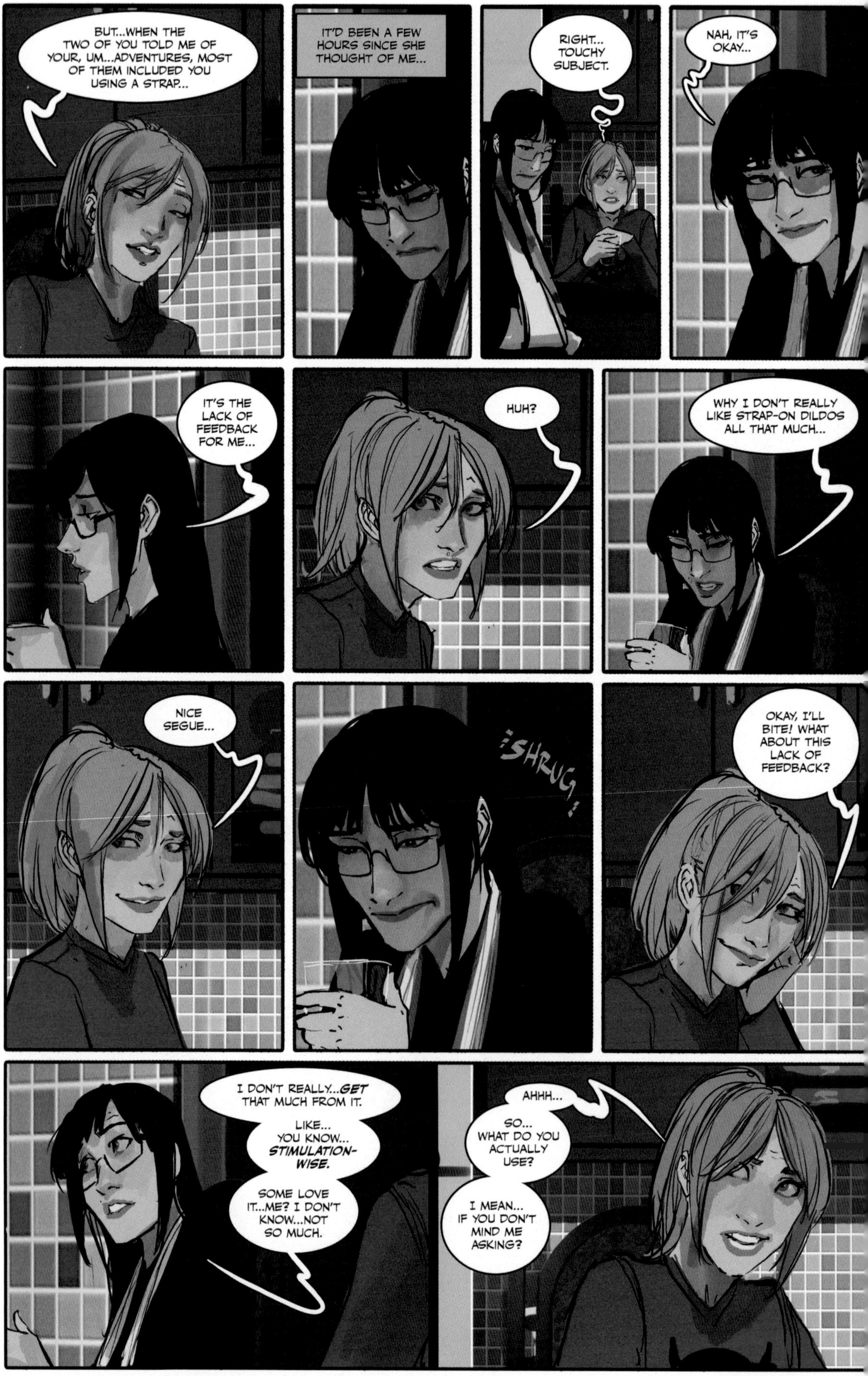
BUT...WHEN THE TWO OF YOU TOLD ME OF YOUR, UM...ADVENTURES, MOST OF THEM INCLUDED YOU USING A STRAP...
IT'D BEEN A FEW HOURS SINCE SHE THOUGHT OF ME...
RIGHT... TOUCHY SUBJECT.
NAH, IT'S OKAY...
IT'S THE LACK OF FEEDBACK FOR ME...
HUH?
WHY I DON'T REALLY LIKE STRAP-ON DILDOS ALL THAT MUCH...
NICE SEGUE...
SHRUG
OKAY, I'LL BITE! WHAT ABOUT THIS LACK OF FEEDBACK?
I DON'T REALLY...*GET* THAT MUCH FROM IT.
LIKE... YOU KNOW... ***STIMULATION-WISE.***
SOME LOVE IT...ME? I DON'T KNOW...NOT SO MUCH.
AHHH...
SO... WHAT DO YOU ACTUALLY USE?
I MEAN... IF YOU DON'T MIND ME ASKING?

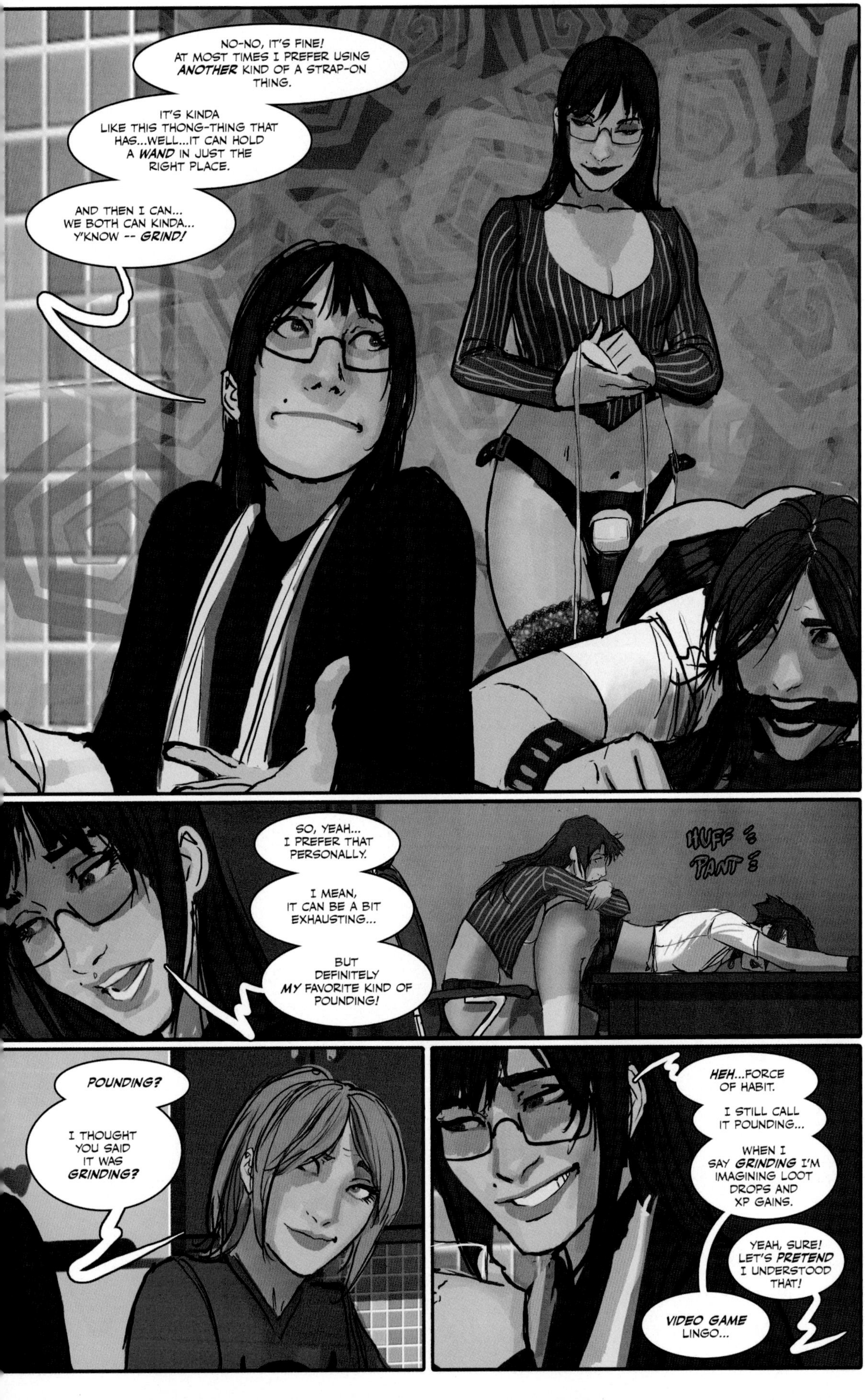
NO-NO, IT'S FINE! AT MOST TIMES I PREFER USING ANOTHER KIND OF A STRAP-ON THING.
IT'S KINDA LIKE THIS THONG-THING THAT HAS...WELL...IT CAN HOLD A WAND IN JUST THE RIGHT PLACE.
AND THEN I CAN... WE BOTH CAN KINDA... Y'KNOW -- GRIND!
SO, YEAH... I PREFER THAT PERSONALLY.
I MEAN, IT CAN BE A BIT EXHAUSTING...
BUT DEFINITELY MY FAVORITE KIND OF POUNDING!
HUFF
PANT
POUNDING?
I THOUGHT YOU SAID IT WAS GRINDING?
HEH...FORCE OF HABIT.
I STILL CALL IT POUNDING...
WHEN I SAY GRINDING I'M IMAGINING LOOT DROPS AND XP GAINS.
VIDEO GAME LINGO...
YEAH, SURE! LET'S PRETEND I UNDERSTOOD THAT!

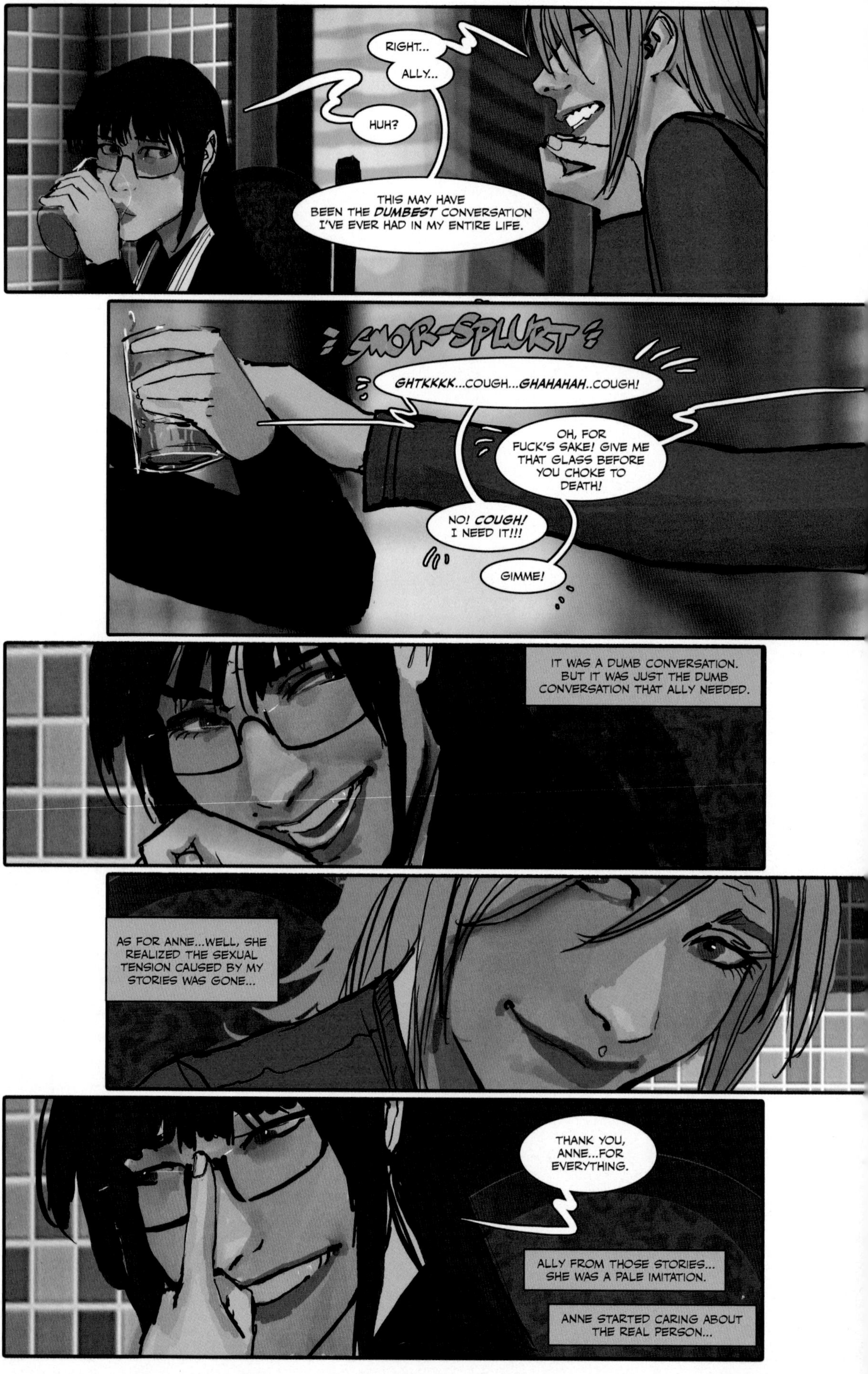
RIGHT...
ALLY...
HUH?
THIS MAY HAVE BEEN THE *DUMBEST* CONVERSATION I'VE EVER HAD IN MY ENTIRE LIFE.
SMOR-SPLURT
GHTKKKK...COUGH...*GHAHAHAH*..COUGH!
OH, FOR FUCK'S SAKE! GIVE ME THAT GLASS BEFORE YOU CHOKE TO DEATH!
NO! *COUGH!* I NEED IT!!!
GIMME!
IT WAS A DUMB CONVERSATION. BUT IT WAS JUST THE DUMB CONVERSATION THAT ALLY NEEDED.
AS FOR ANNE...WELL, SHE REALIZED THE SEXUAL TENSION CAUSED BY MY STORIES WAS GONE...
THANK YOU, ANNE...FOR EVERYTHING.
ALLY FROM THOSE STORIES... SHE WAS A PALE IMITATION.
ANNE STARTED CARING ABOUT THE REAL PERSON...

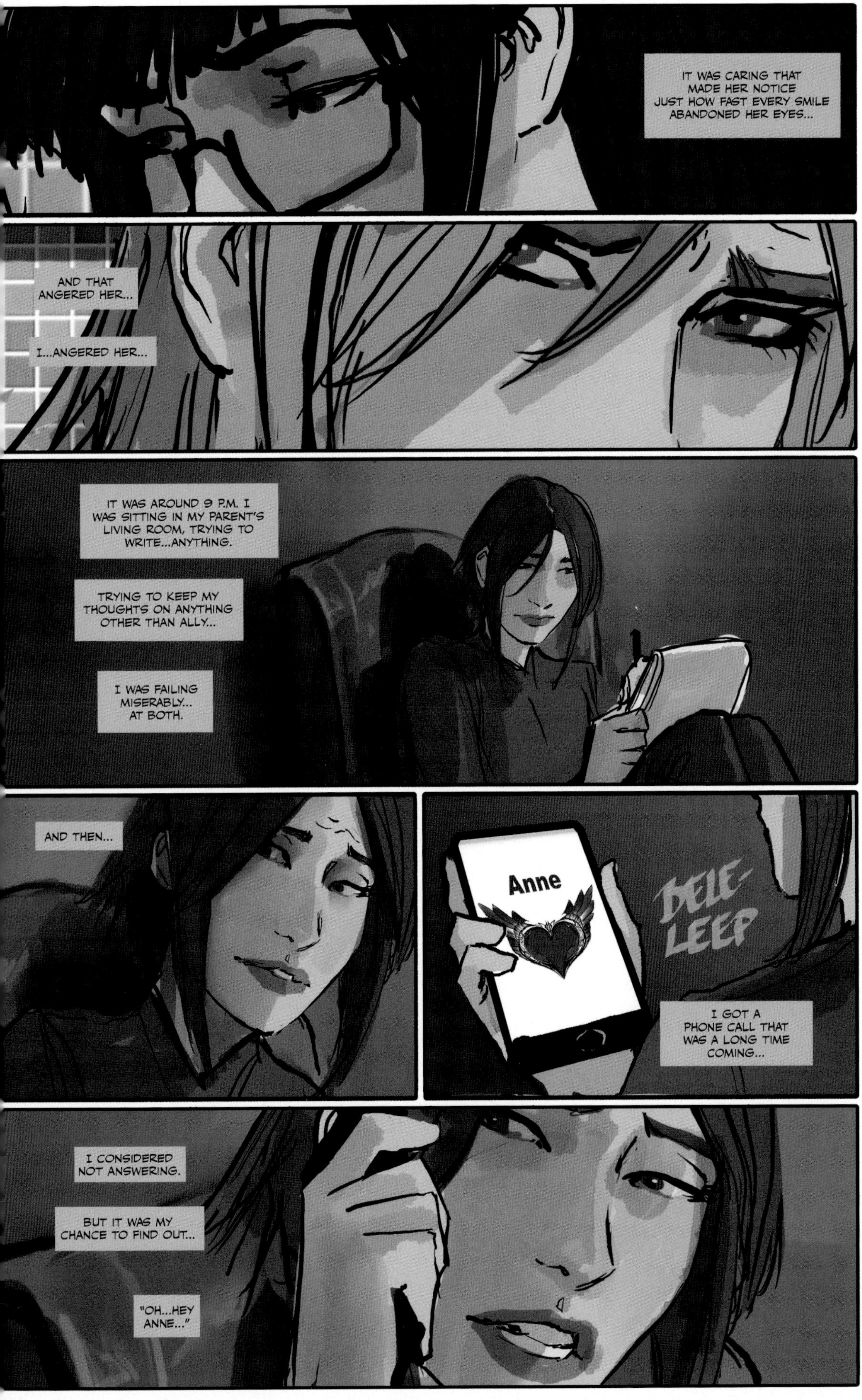
IT WAS CARING THAT MADE HER NOTICE JUST HOW FAST EVERY SMILE ABANDONED HER EYES...
AND THAT ANGERED HER...
I...ANGERED HER...
IT WAS AROUND 9 P.M. I WAS SITTING IN MY PARENT'S LIVING ROOM, TRYING TO WRITE...ANYTHING.
TRYING TO KEEP MY THOUGHTS ON ANYTHING OTHER THAN ALLY...
I WAS FAILING MISERABLY... AT BOTH.
AND THEN...
Anne
BELE-LEEP
I GOT A PHONE CALL THAT WAS A LONG TIME COMING...
I CONSIDERED NOT ANSWERING.
BUT IT WAS MY CHANCE TO FIND OUT...
"OH...HEY ANNE..."

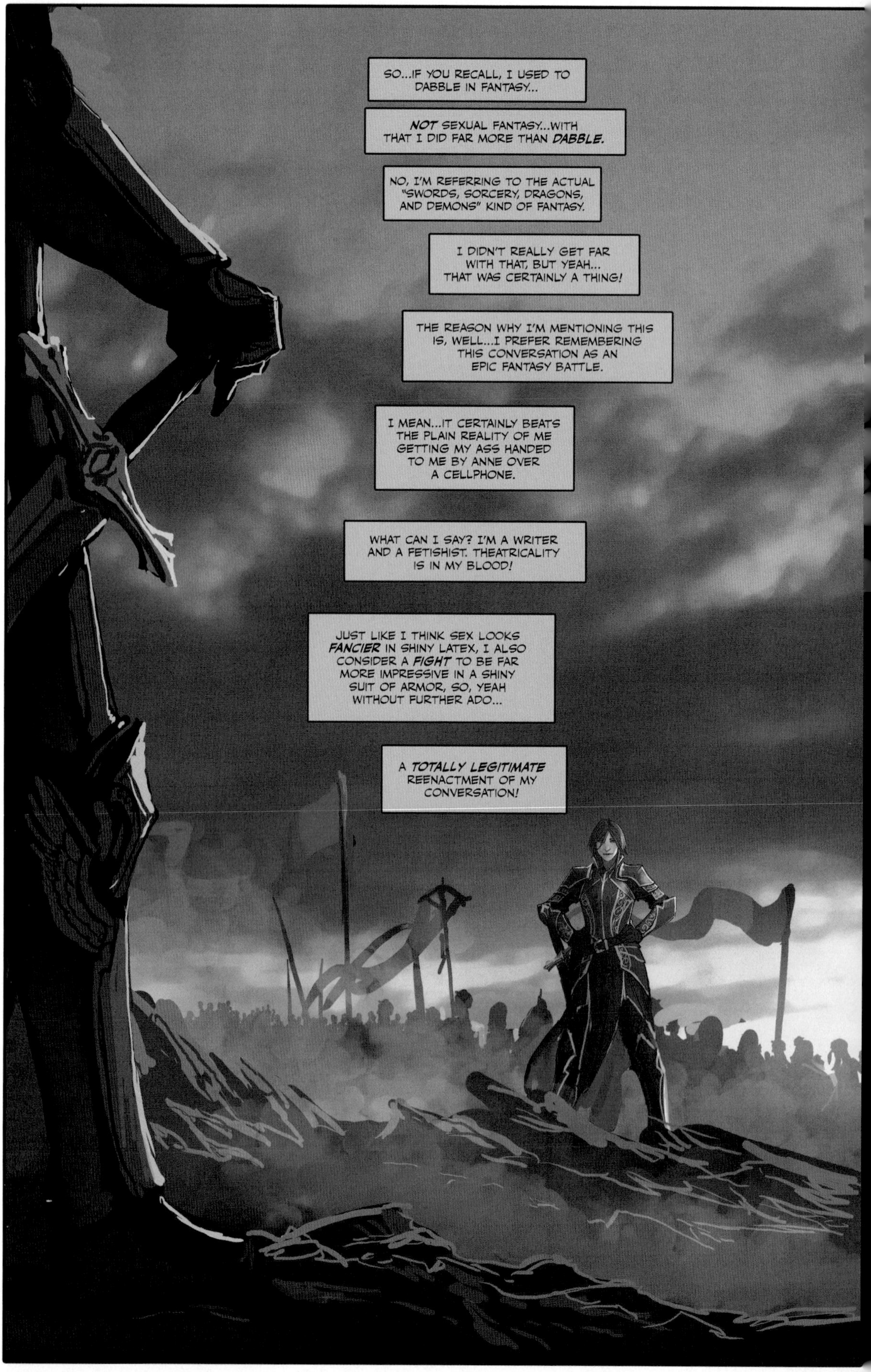

SO...IF YOU RECALL, I USED TO DABBLE IN FANTASY...
NOT SEXUAL FANTASY...WITH THAT I DID FAR MORE THAN DABBLE.
NO, I'M REFERRING TO THE ACTUAL "SWORDS, SORCERY, DRAGONS, AND DEMONS" KIND OF FANTASY.
I DIDN'T REALLY GET FAR WITH THAT, BUT YEAH... THAT WAS CERTAINLY A THING!
THE REASON WHY I'M MENTIONING THIS IS, WELL...I PREFER REMEMBERING THIS CONVERSATION AS AN EPIC FANTASY BATTLE.
I MEAN...IT CERTAINLY BEATS THE PLAIN REALITY OF ME GETTING MY ASS HANDED TO ME BY ANNE OVER A CELLPHONE.
WHAT CAN I SAY? I'M A WRITER AND A FETISHIST. THEATRICALITY IS IN MY BLOOD!
JUST LIKE I THINK SEX LOOKS FANCIER IN SHINY LATEX, I ALSO CONSIDER A FIGHT TO BE FAR MORE IMPRESSIVE IN A SHINY SUIT OF ARMOR, SO, YEAH WITHOUT FURTHER ADO...
A TOTALLY LEGITIMATE REENACTMENT OF MY CONVERSATION!

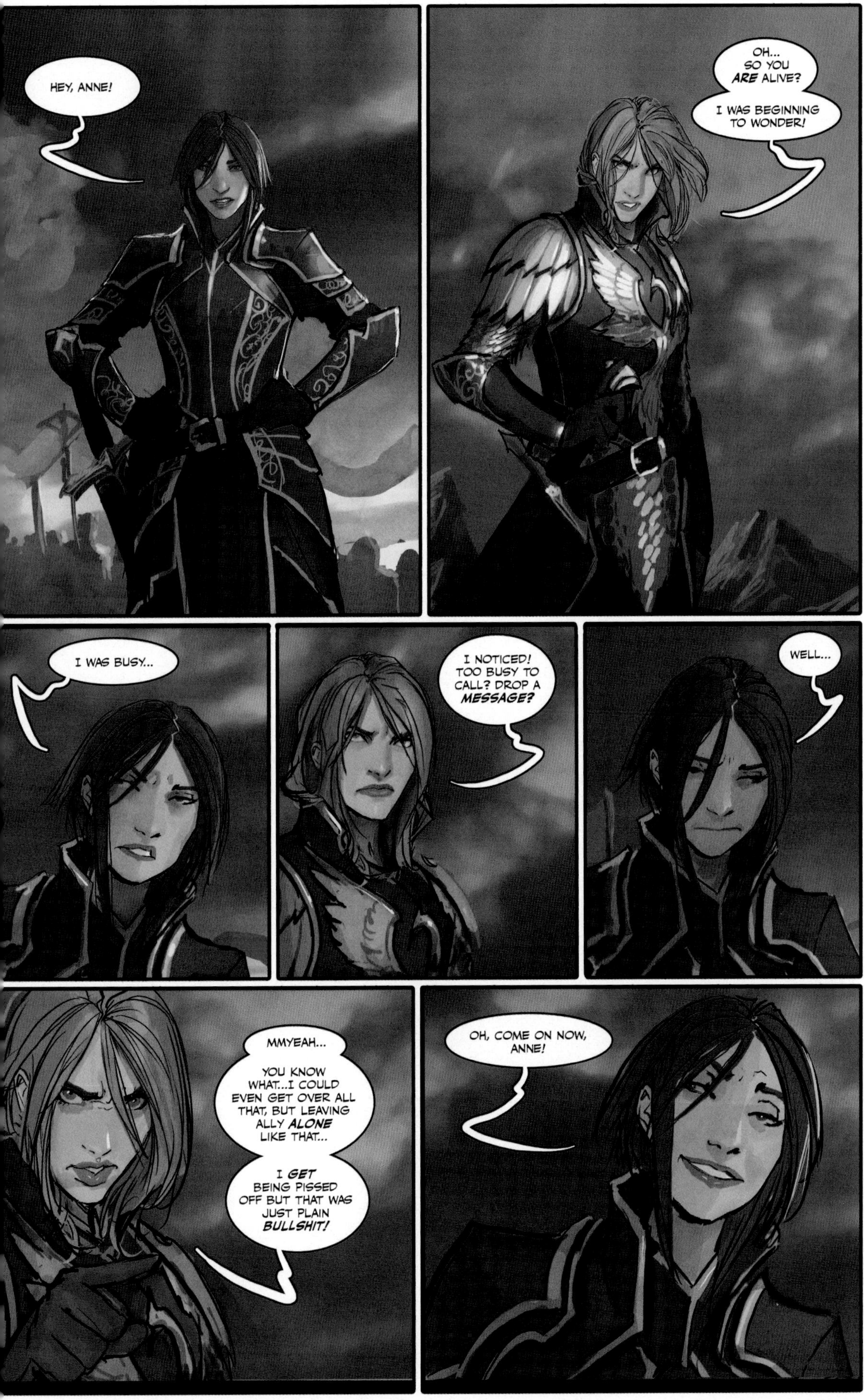
HEY, ANNE!
OH... SO YOU ARE ALIVE?
I WAS BEGINNING TO WONDER!
I WAS BUSY...
I NOTICED! TOO BUSY TO CALL? DROP A MESSAGE?
WELL...
MMYEAH...
YOU KNOW WHAT...I COULD EVEN GET OVER ALL THAT, BUT LEAVING ALLY ALONE LIKE THAT...
I GET BEING PISSED OFF BUT THAT WAS JUST PLAIN BULLSHIT!
OH, COME ON NOW, ANNE!

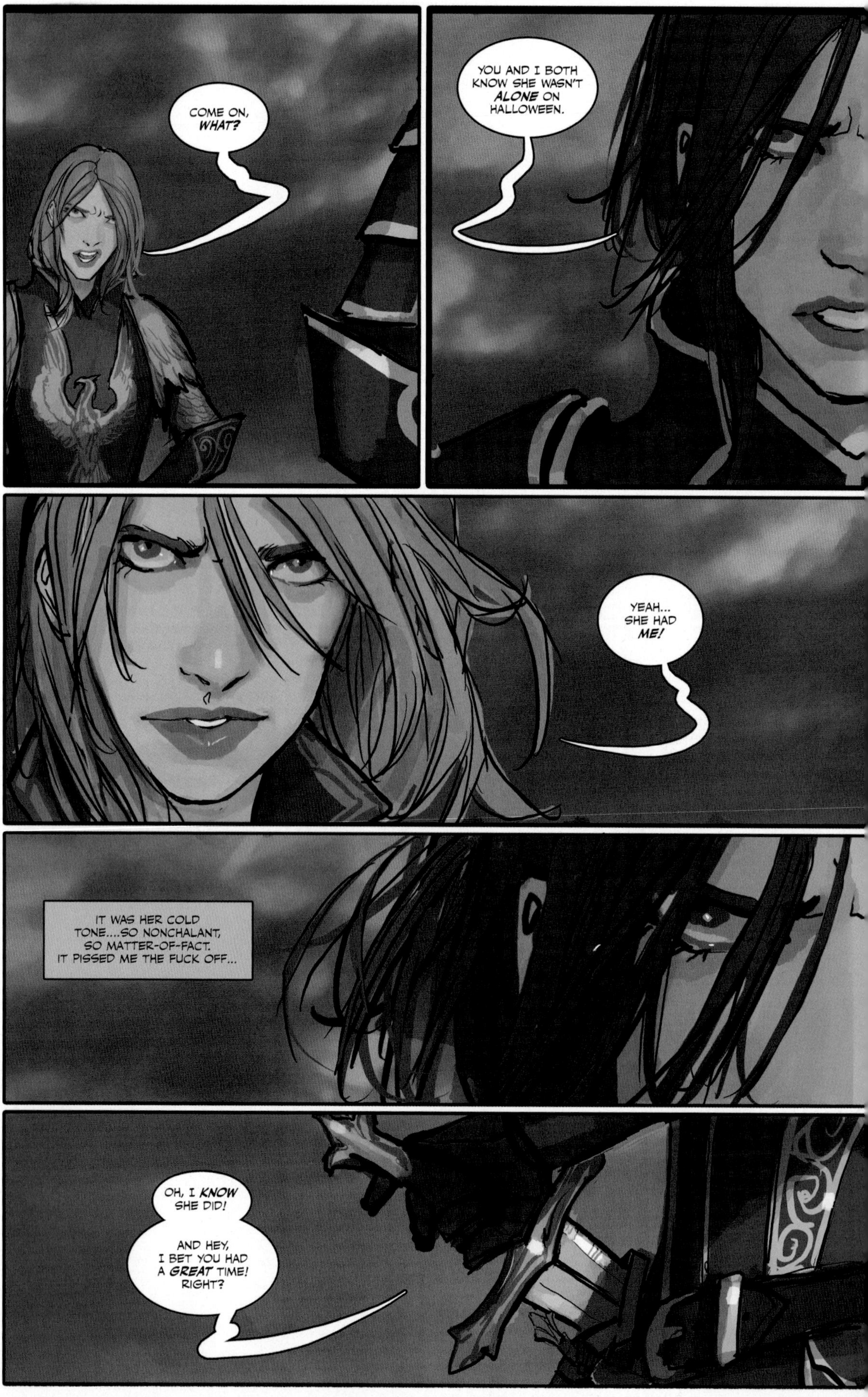
COME ON, WHAT?
YOU AND I BOTH KNOW SHE WASN'T ALONE ON HALLOWEEN.
YEAH... SHE HAD ME!
IT WAS HER COLD TONE....SO NONCHALANT, SO MATTER-OF-FACT. IT PISSED ME THE FUCK OFF...
OH, I KNOW SHE DID!
AND HEY, I BET YOU HAD A GREAT TIME! RIGHT?

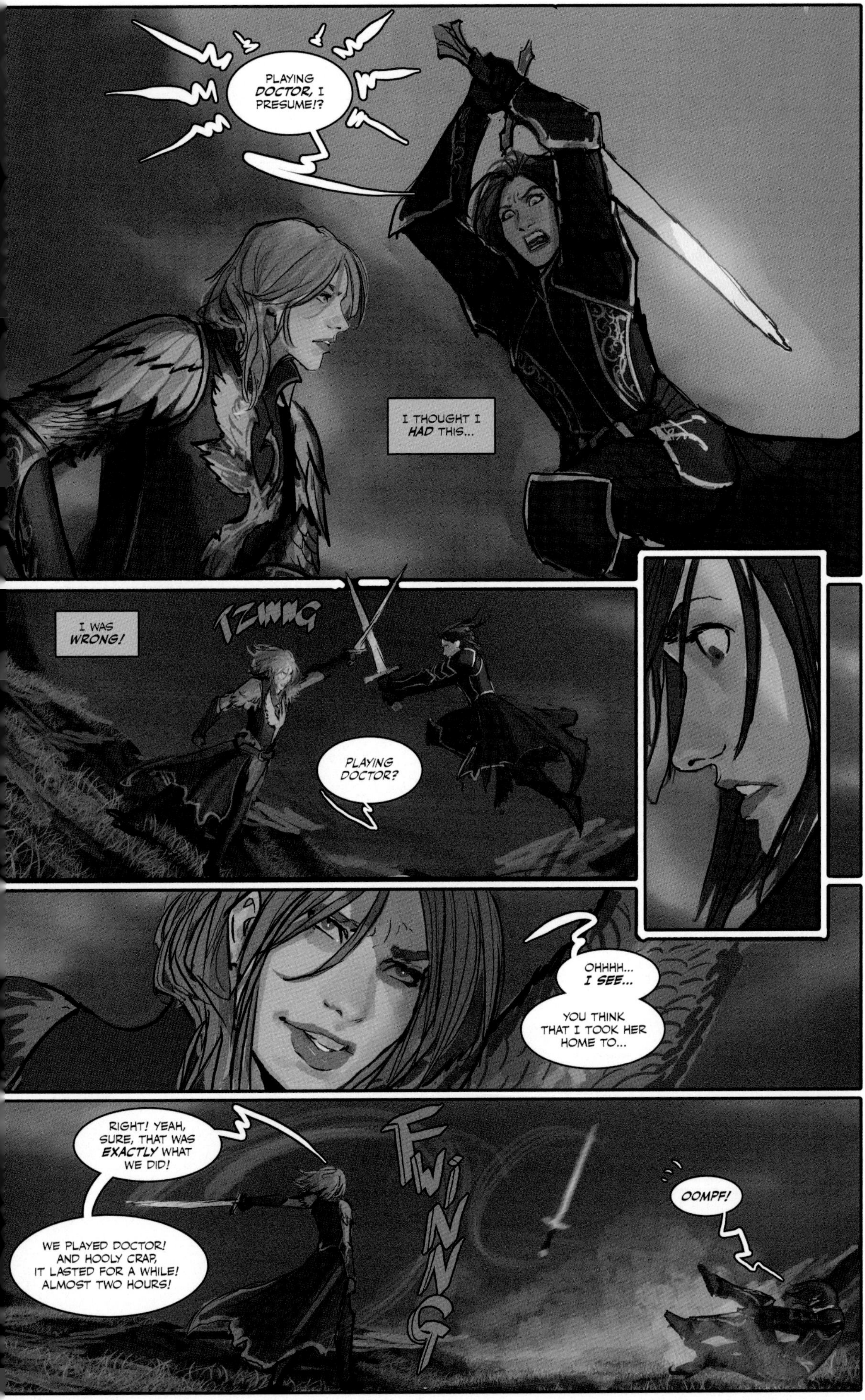
PLAYING *DOCTOR*, I PRESUME!?
I THOUGHT I *HAD* THIS...
I WAS *WRONG!*
TZING
PLAYING DOCTOR?
OHHHH... *I SEE...*
YOU THINK THAT I TOOK HER HOME TO...
RIGHT! YEAH, SURE, THAT WAS *EXACTLY* WHAT WE DID!
WE PLAYED DOCTOR! AND HOOLY CRAP, IT LASTED FOR A WHILE! ALMOST TWO HOURS!
FWINNNGT
OOMPF!

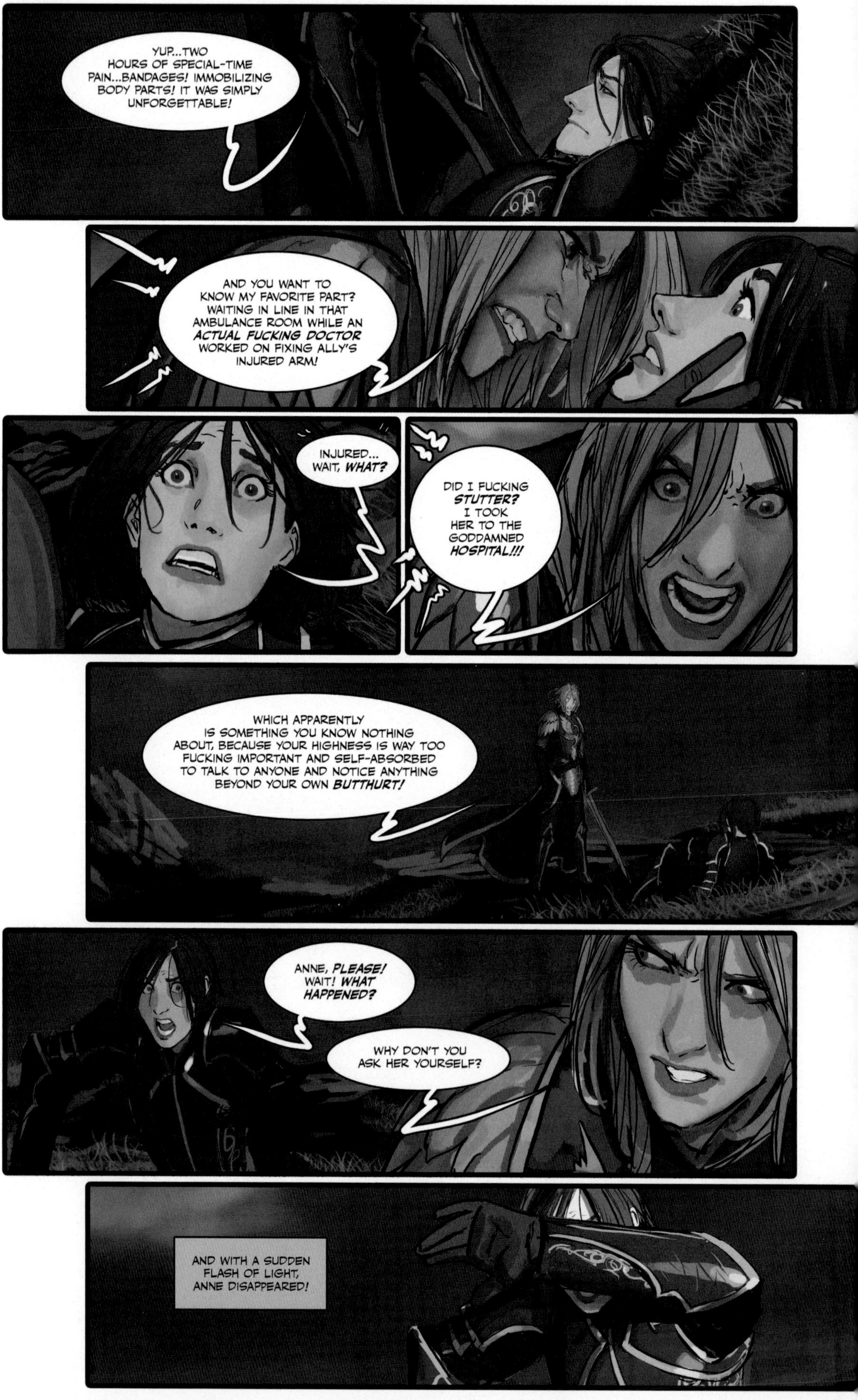
YUP...TWO HOURS OF SPECIAL-TIME PAIN...BANDAGES! IMMOBILIZING BODY PARTS! IT WAS SIMPLY UNFORGETTABLE!
AND YOU WANT TO KNOW MY FAVORITE PART? WAITING IN LINE IN THAT AMBULANCE ROOM WHILE AN *ACTUAL FUCKING DOCTOR* WORKED ON FIXING ALLY'S INJURED ARM!
INJURED... WAIT, *WHAT?*
DID I FUCKING *STUTTER?* I TOOK HER TO THE GODDAMNED *HOSPITAL!!!*
WHICH APPARENTLY IS SOMETHING YOU KNOW NOTHING ABOUT, BECAUSE YOUR HIGHNESS IS WAY TOO FUCKING IMPORTANT AND SELF-ABSORBED TO TALK TO ANYONE AND NOTICE ANYTHING BEYOND YOUR OWN *BUTTHURT!*
ANNE, *PLEASE!* WAIT! *WHAT HAPPENED?*
WHY DON'T YOU ASK HER YOURSELF?
AND WITH A SUDDEN FLASH OF LIGHT, ANNE DISAPPEARED!

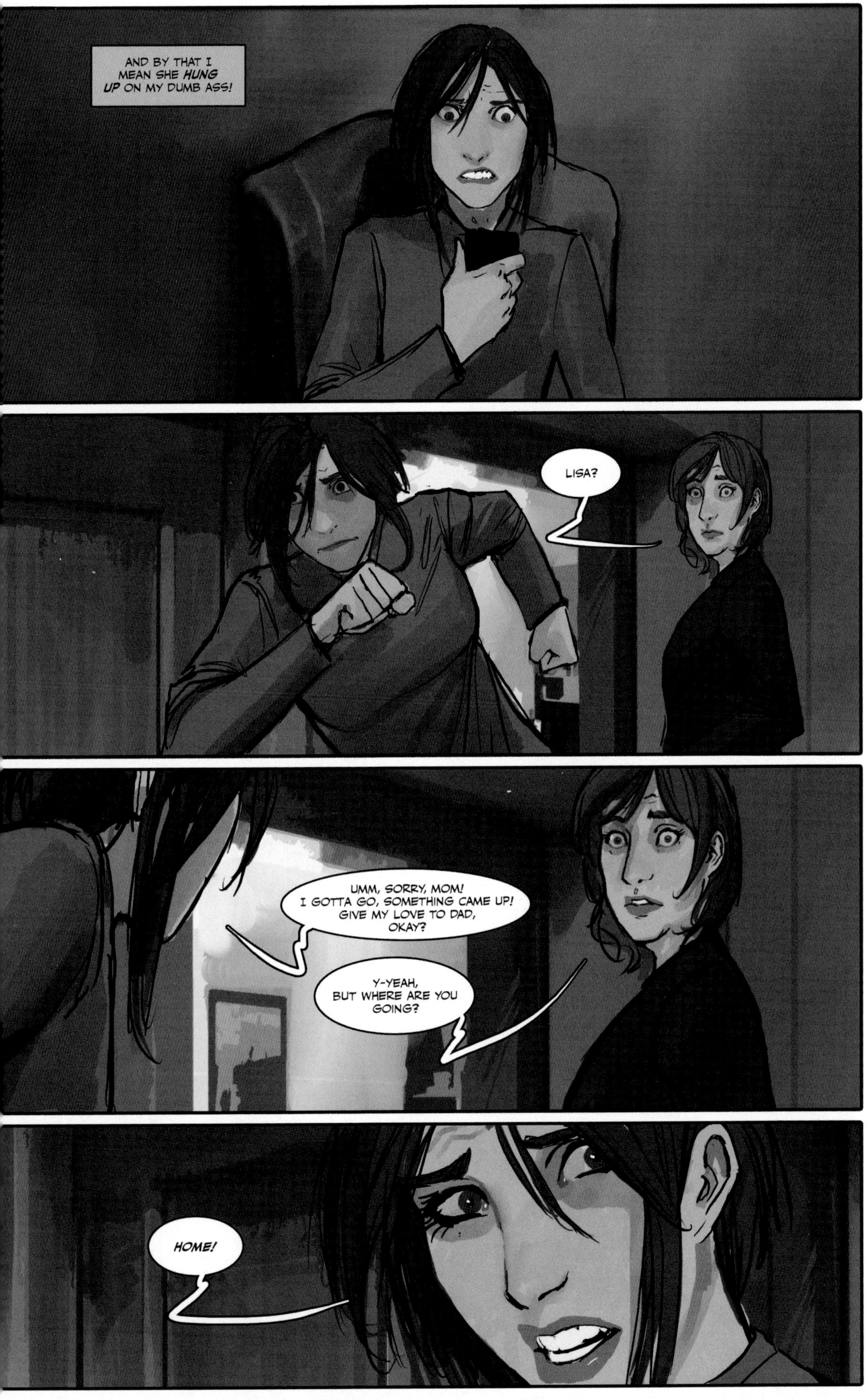
AND BY THAT I MEAN SHE HUNG UP ON MY DUMB ASS!
LISA?
UMM, SORRY, MOM! I GOTTA GO, SOMETHING CAME UP! GIVE MY LOVE TO DAD, OKAY?
Y-YEAH, BUT WHERE ARE YOU GOING?
HOME!

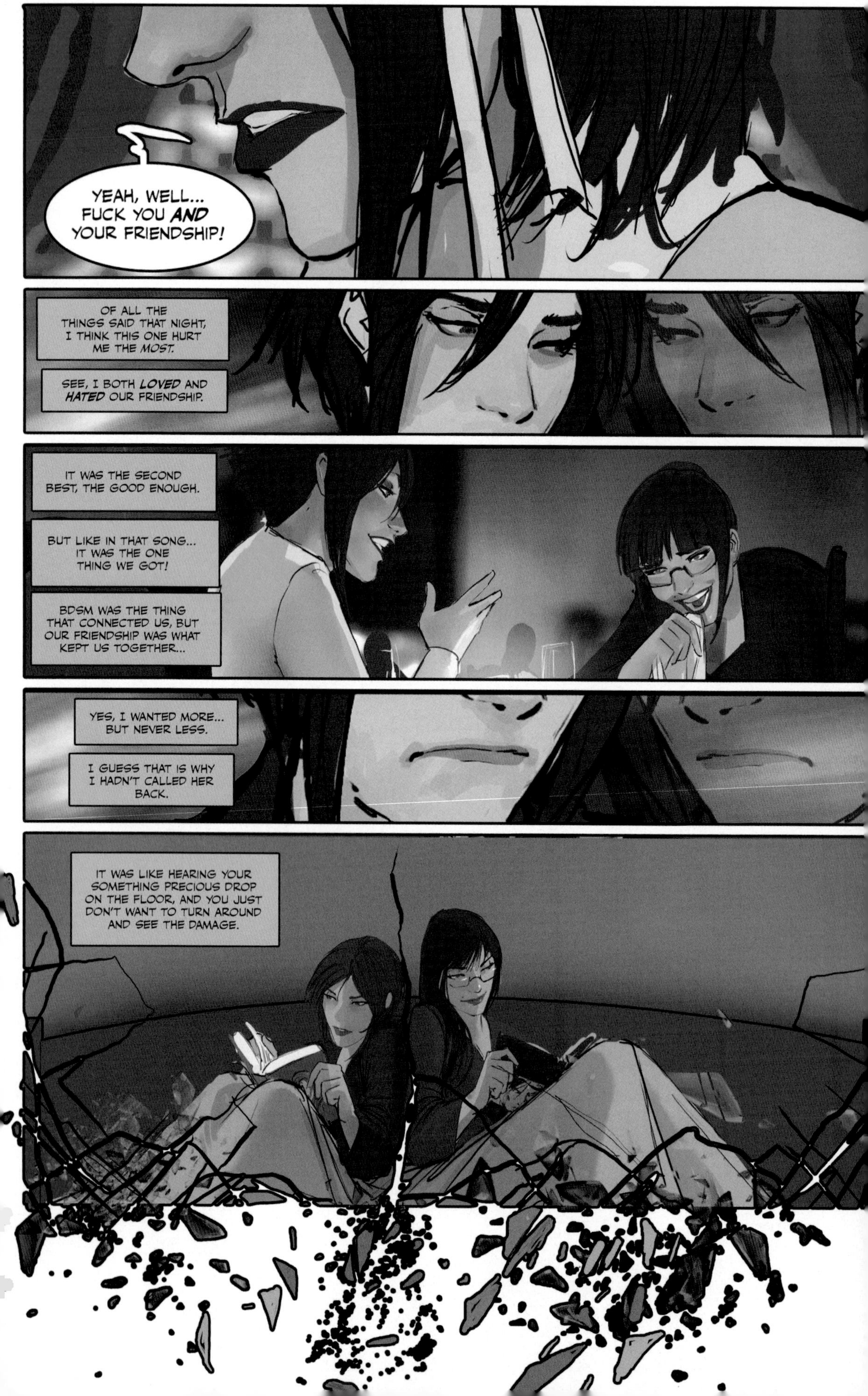
YEAH, WELL... FUCK YOU AND YOUR FRIENDSHIP!
OF ALL THE THINGS SAID THAT NIGHT, I THINK THIS ONE HURT ME THE MOST.
SEE, I BOTH LOVED AND HATED OUR FRIENDSHIP.
IT WAS THE SECOND BEST, THE GOOD ENOUGH.
BUT LIKE IN THAT SONG... IT WAS THE ONE THING WE GOT!
BDSM WAS THE THING THAT CONNECTED US, BUT OUR FRIENDSHIP WAS WHAT KEPT US TOGETHER...
YES, I WANTED MORE... BUT NEVER LESS.
I GUESS THAT IS WHY I HADN'T CALLED HER BACK.
IT WAS LIKE HEARING YOUR SOMETHING PRECIOUS DROP ON THE FLOOR, AND YOU JUST DON'T WANT TO TURN AROUND AND SEE THE DAMAGE.

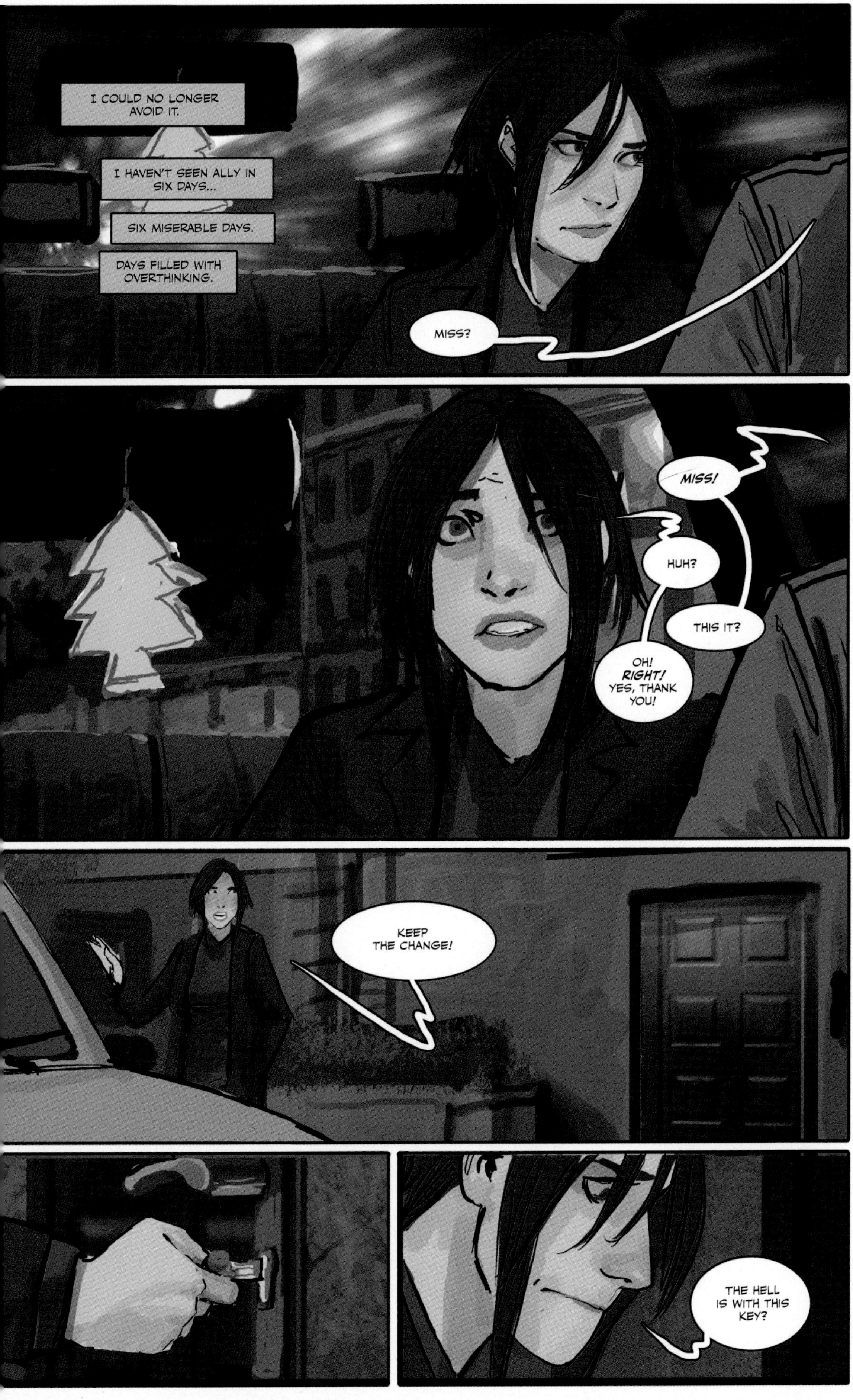
I COULD NO LONGER AVOID IT.
I HAVEN'T SEEN ALLY IN SIX DAYS...
SIX MISERABLE DAYS.
DAYS FILLED WITH OVERTHINKING.
MISS?
MISS!
HUH?
THIS IT?
OH! RIGHT! YES, THANK YOU!
KEEP THE CHANGE!
THE HELL IS WITH THIS KEY?

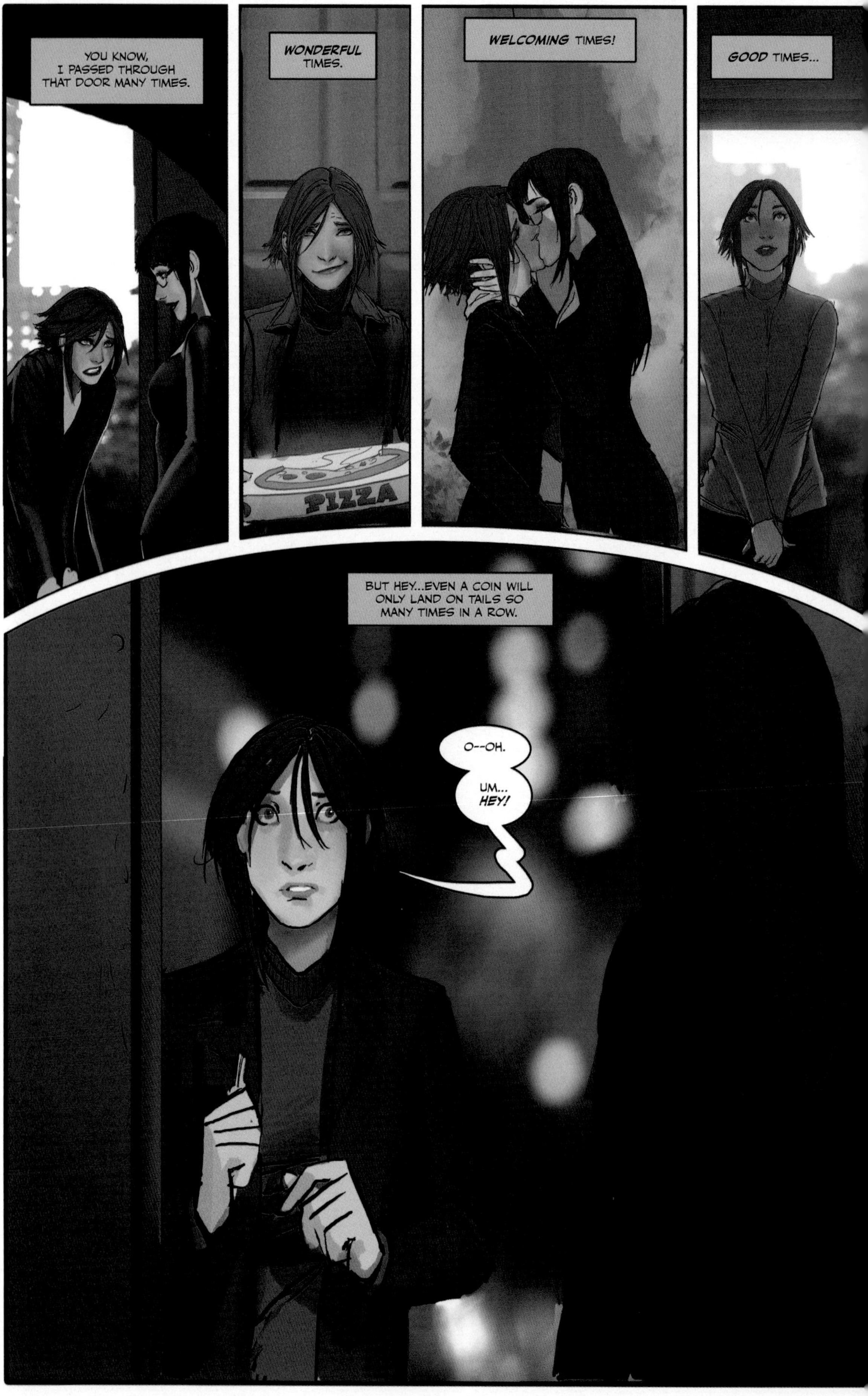
YOU KNOW, I PASSED THROUGH THAT DOOR MANY TIMES.
WONDERFUL TIMES.
PIZZA
WELCOMING TIMES!
GOOD TIMES...
BUT HEY...EVEN A COIN WILL ONLY LAND ON TAILS SO MANY TIMES IN A ROW.
O--OH.
UM... *HEY!*

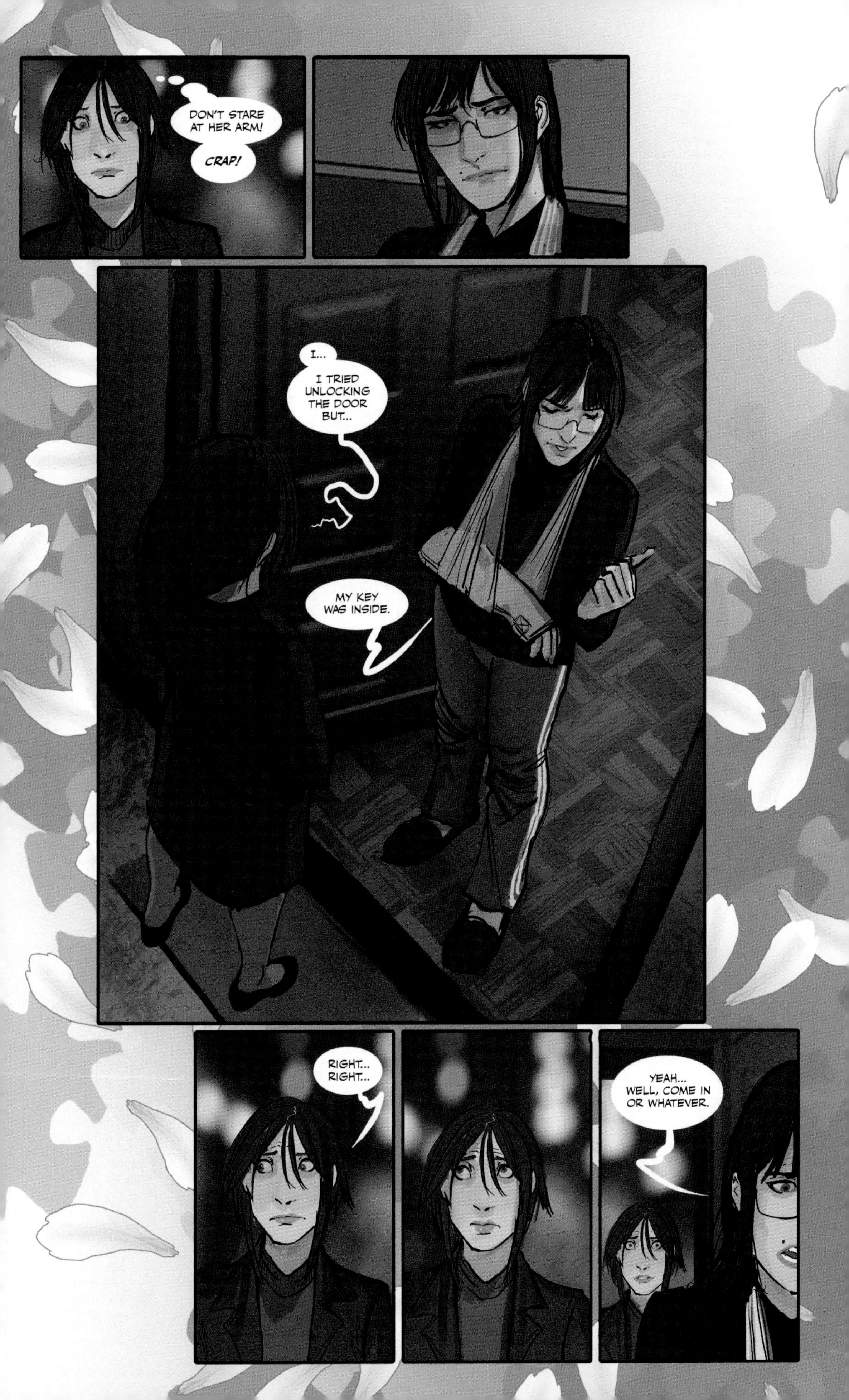
DON'T STARE AT HER ARM!
CRAP!
I...
I TRIED UNLOCKING THE DOOR BUT...
MY KEY WAS INSIDE.
RIGHT... RIGHT...
YEAH... WELL, COME IN OR WHATEVER.

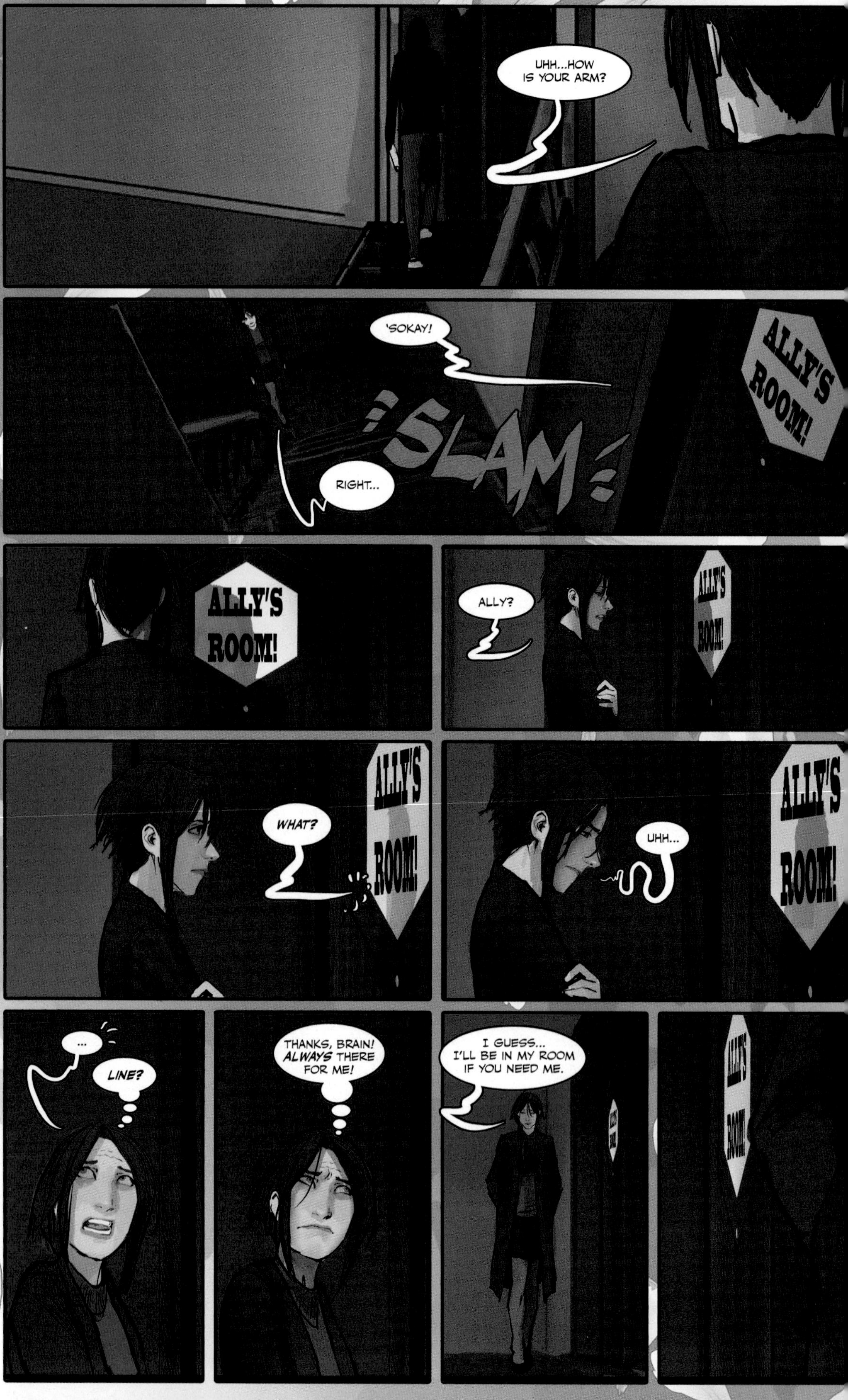
UHH...HOW IS YOUR ARM?
'SOKAY!
ALLY'S ROOM!
SLAM
RIGHT...
ALLY'S ROOM!
ALLY?
ALLY'S ROOM!
WHAT?
ALLY'S ROOM!
UHH...
ALLY'S ROOM!
...
LINE?
THANKS, BRAIN! *ALWAYS* THERE FOR ME!
I GUESS... I'LL BE IN MY ROOM IF YOU NEED ME.
ALLY'S ROOM!

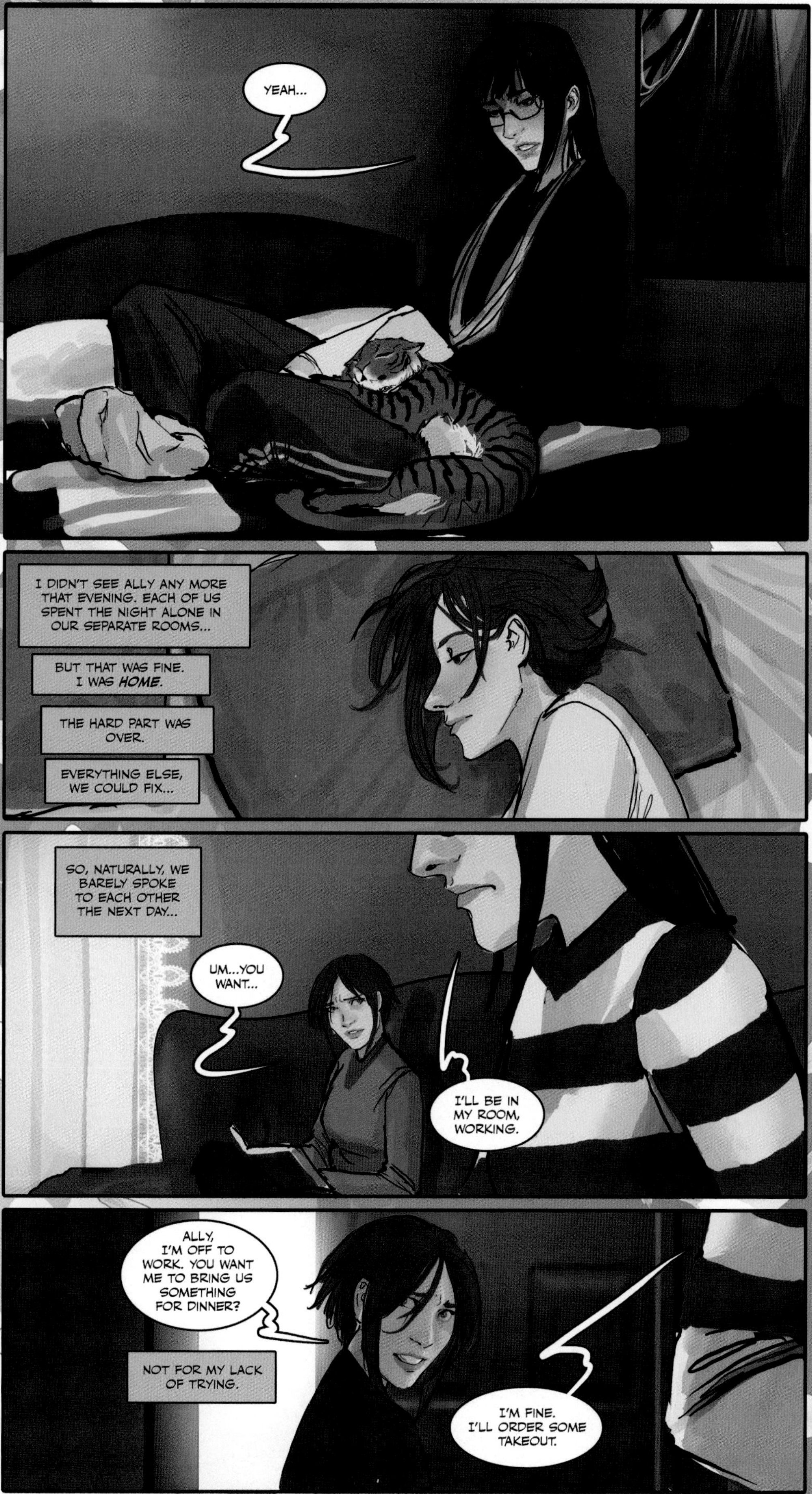
YEAH...
I DIDN'T SEE ALLY ANY MORE THAT EVENING. EACH OF US SPENT THE NIGHT ALONE IN OUR SEPARATE ROOMS...
BUT THAT WAS FINE. I WAS ***HOME***.
THE HARD PART WAS OVER.
EVERYTHING ELSE, WE COULD FIX...
SO, NATURALLY, WE BARELY SPOKE TO EACH OTHER THE NEXT DAY...
UM...YOU WANT...
I'LL BE IN MY ROOM, WORKING.
ALLY, I'M OFF TO WORK. YOU WANT ME TO BRING US SOMETHING FOR DINNER?
NOT FOR MY LACK OF TRYING.
I'M FINE. I'LL ORDER SOME TAKEOUT.

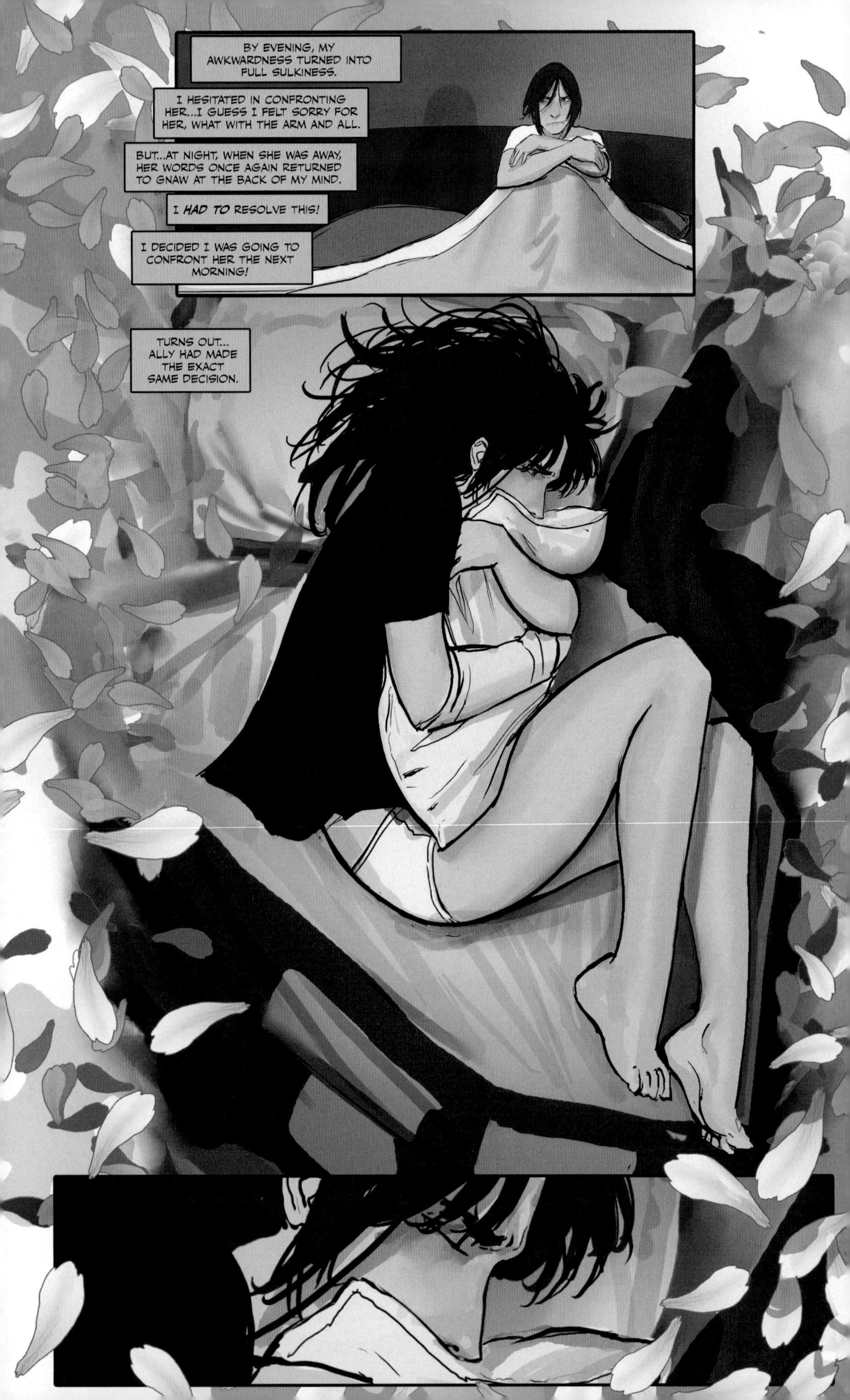
BY EVENING, MY AWKWARDNESS TURNED INTO FULL SULKINESS.
I HESITATED IN CONFRONTING HER...I GUESS I FELT SORRY FOR HER, WHAT WITH THE ARM AND ALL.
BUT...AT NIGHT, WHEN SHE WAS AWAY, HER WORDS ONCE AGAIN RETURNED TO GNAW AT THE BACK OF MY MIND.
I *HAD TO* RESOLVE THIS!
I DECIDED I WAS GOING TO CONFRONT HER THE NEXT MORNING!
TURNS OUT... ALLY HAD MADE THE EXACT SAME DECISION.

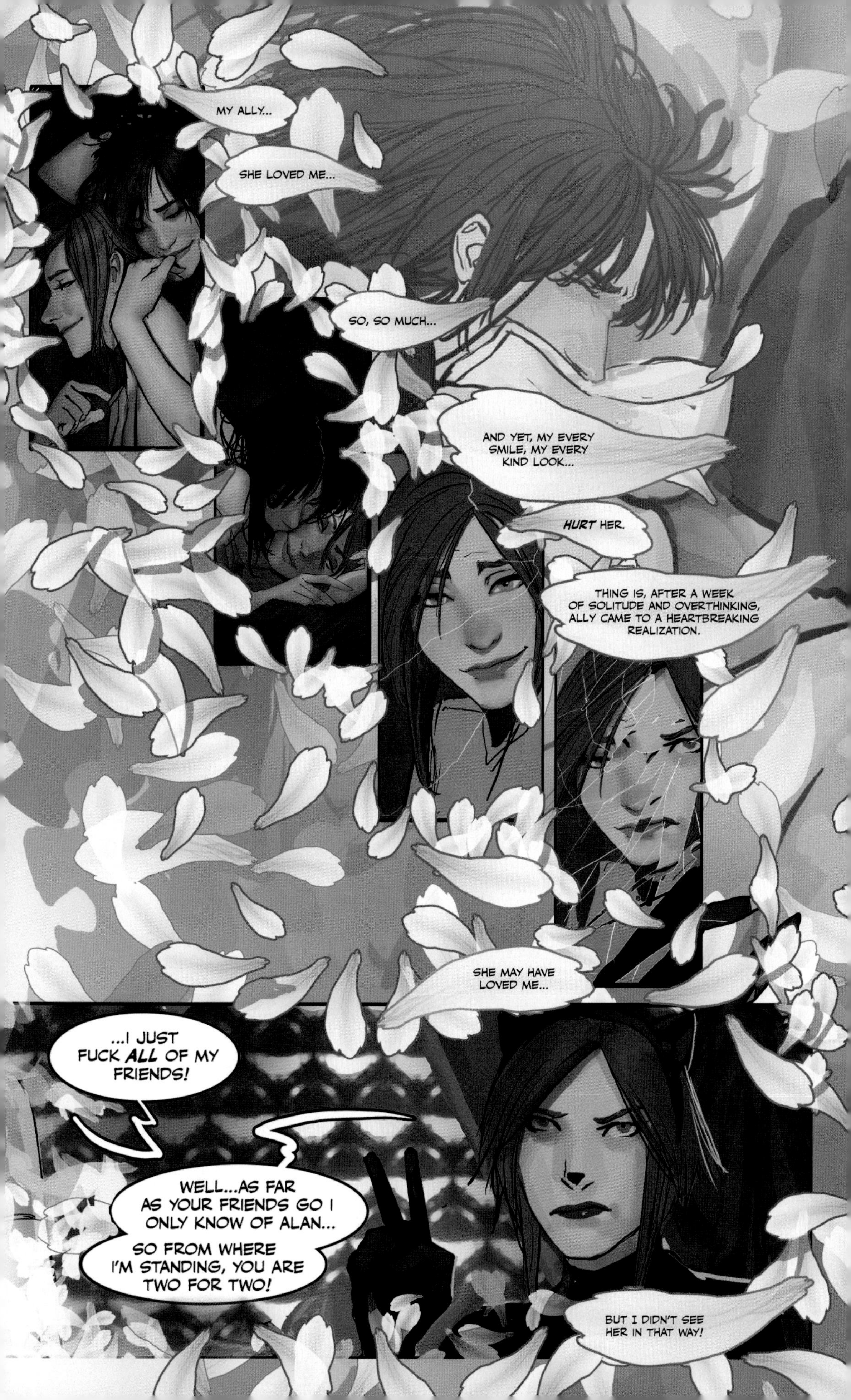
MY ALLY...
SHE LOVED ME...
SO, SO MUCH...
AND YET, MY EVERY SMILE, MY EVERY KIND LOOK...
HURT HER.
THING IS, AFTER A WEEK OF SOLITUDE AND OVERTHINKING, ALLY CAME TO A HEARTBREAKING REALIZATION.
SHE MAY HAVE LOVED ME...
BUT I DIDN'T SEE HER IN THAT WAY!
...I JUST FUCK ALL OF MY FRIENDS!
WELL...AS FAR AS YOUR FRIENDS GO I ONLY KNOW OF ALAN...
SO FROM WHERE I'M STANDING, YOU ARE TWO FOR TWO!

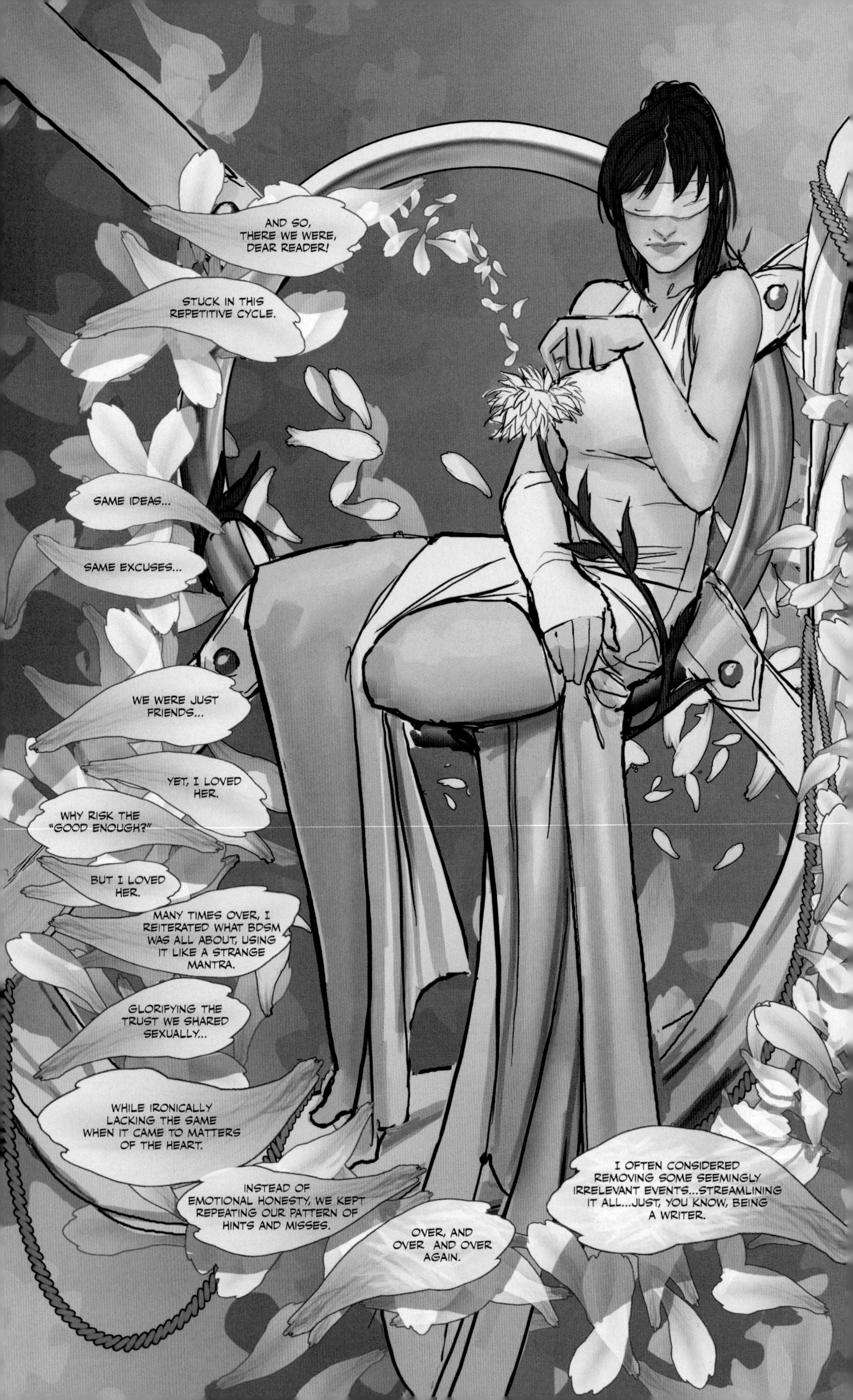
AND SO, THERE WE WERE, DEAR READER!
STUCK IN THIS REPETITIVE CYCLE.
SAME IDEAS...
SAME EXCUSES...
WE WERE JUST FRIENDS...
YET, I LOVED HER.
WHY RISK THE "GOOD ENOUGH?"
BUT I LOVED HER.
MANY TIMES OVER, I REITERATED WHAT BDSM WAS ALL ABOUT, USING IT LIKE A STRANGE MANTRA.
GLORIFYING THE TRUST WE SHARED SEXUALLY...
WHILE IRONICALLY LACKING THE SAME WHEN IT CAME TO MATTERS OF THE HEART.
INSTEAD OF EMOTIONAL HONESTY, WE KEPT REPEATING OUR PATTERN OF HINTS AND MISSES.
OVER, AND OVER AND OVER AGAIN.
I OFTEN CONSIDERED REMOVING SOME SEEMINGLY IRRELEVANT EVENTS...STREAMLINING IT ALL...JUST, YOU KNOW, BEING A WRITER.

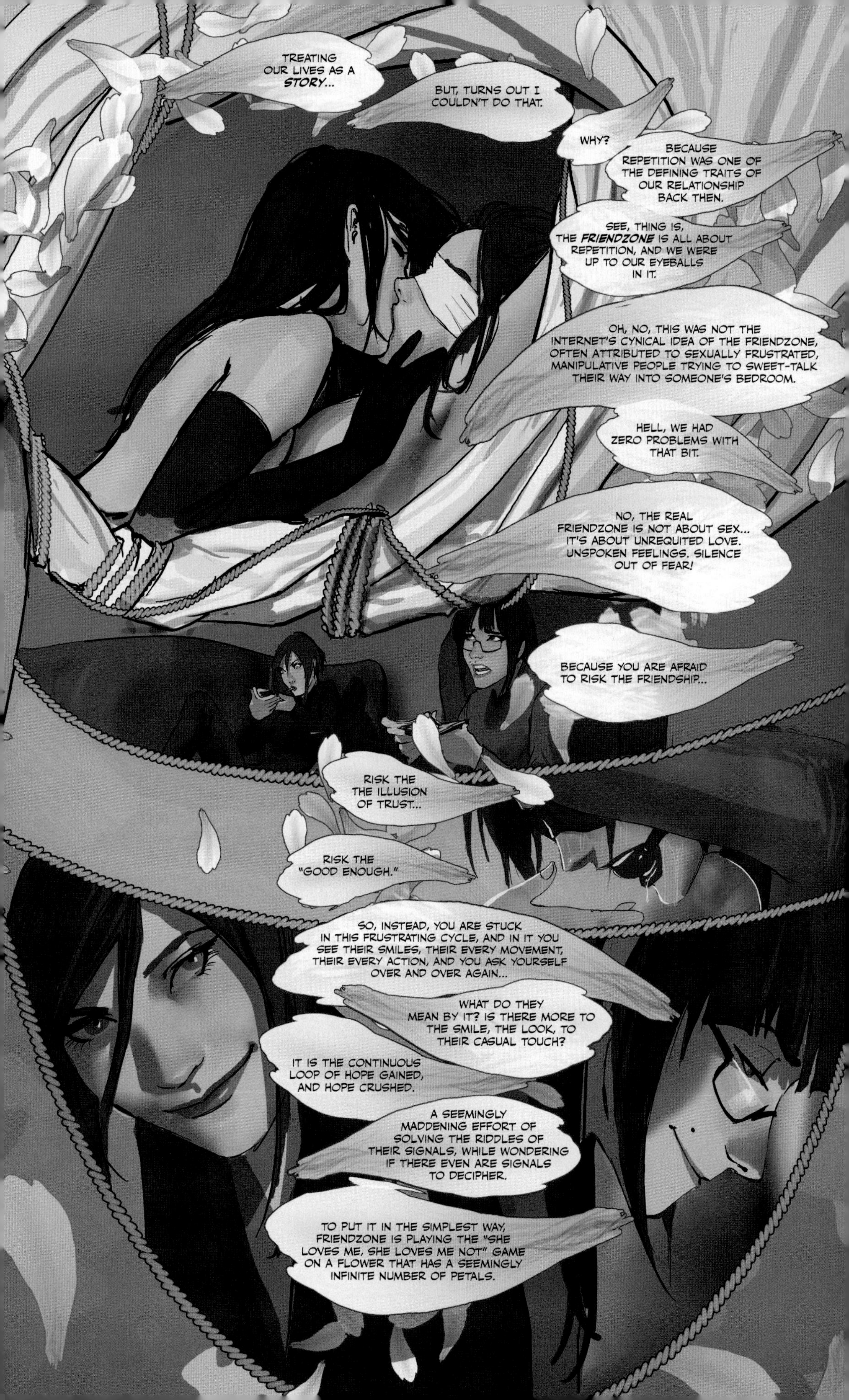
TREATING OUR LIVES AS A *STORY*...
BUT, TURNS OUT I COULDN'T DO THAT.
WHY?
BECAUSE REPETITION WAS ONE OF THE DEFINING TRAITS OF OUR RELATIONSHIP BACK THEN.
SEE, THING IS, THE ***FRIENDZONE*** IS ALL ABOUT REPETITION, AND WE WERE UP TO OUR EYEBALLS IN IT.
OH, NO, THIS WAS NOT THE INTERNET'S CYNICAL IDEA OF THE FRIENDZONE, OFTEN ATTRIBUTED TO SEXUALLY FRUSTRATED, MANIPULATIVE PEOPLE TRYING TO SWEET-TALK THEIR WAY INTO SOMEONE'S BEDROOM.
HELL, WE HAD ZERO PROBLEMS WITH THAT BIT.
NO, THE REAL FRIENDZONE IS NOT ABOUT SEX... IT'S ABOUT UNREQUITED LOVE. UNSPOKEN FEELINGS. SILENCE OUT OF FEAR!
BECAUSE YOU ARE AFRAID TO RISK THE FRIENDSHIP...
RISK THE THE ILLUSION OF TRUST...
RISK THE "GOOD ENOUGH."
SO, INSTEAD, YOU ARE STUCK IN THIS FRUSTRATING CYCLE, AND IN IT YOU SEE THEIR SMILES, THEIR EVERY MOVEMENT, THEIR EVERY ACTION, AND YOU ASK YOURSELF OVER AND OVER AGAIN...
WHAT DO THEY MEAN BY IT? IS THERE MORE TO THE SMILE, THE LOOK, TO THEIR CASUAL TOUCH?
IT IS THE CONTINUOUS LOOP OF HOPE GAINED, AND HOPE CRUSHED.
A SEEMINGLY MADDENING EFFORT OF SOLVING THE RIDDLES OF THEIR SIGNALS, WHILE WONDERING IF THERE EVEN ARE SIGNALS TO DECIPHER.
TO PUT IT IN THE SIMPLEST WAY, FRIENDZONE IS PLAYING THE "SHE LOVES ME, SHE LOVES ME NOT" GAME ON A FLOWER THAT HAS A SEEMINGLY INFINITE NUMBER OF PETALS.

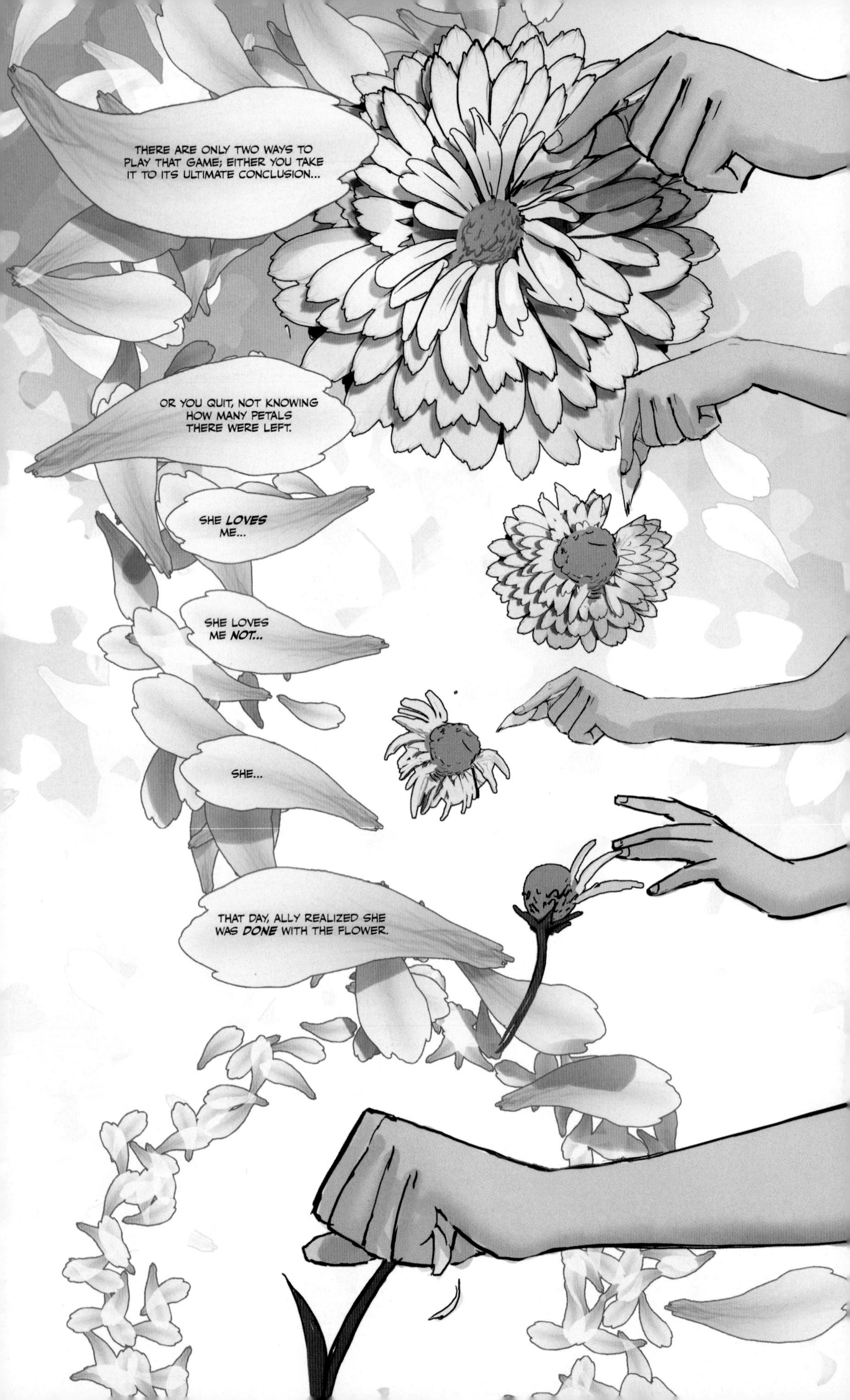

THERE ARE ONLY TWO WAYS TO PLAY THAT GAME; EITHER YOU TAKE IT TO ITS ULTIMATE CONCLUSION...
OR YOU QUIT, NOT KNOWING HOW MANY PETALS THERE WERE LEFT.
SHE *LOVES* ME...
SHE LOVES ME *NOT*...
SHE...
THAT DAY, ALLY REALIZED SHE WAS *DONE* WITH THE FLOWER.

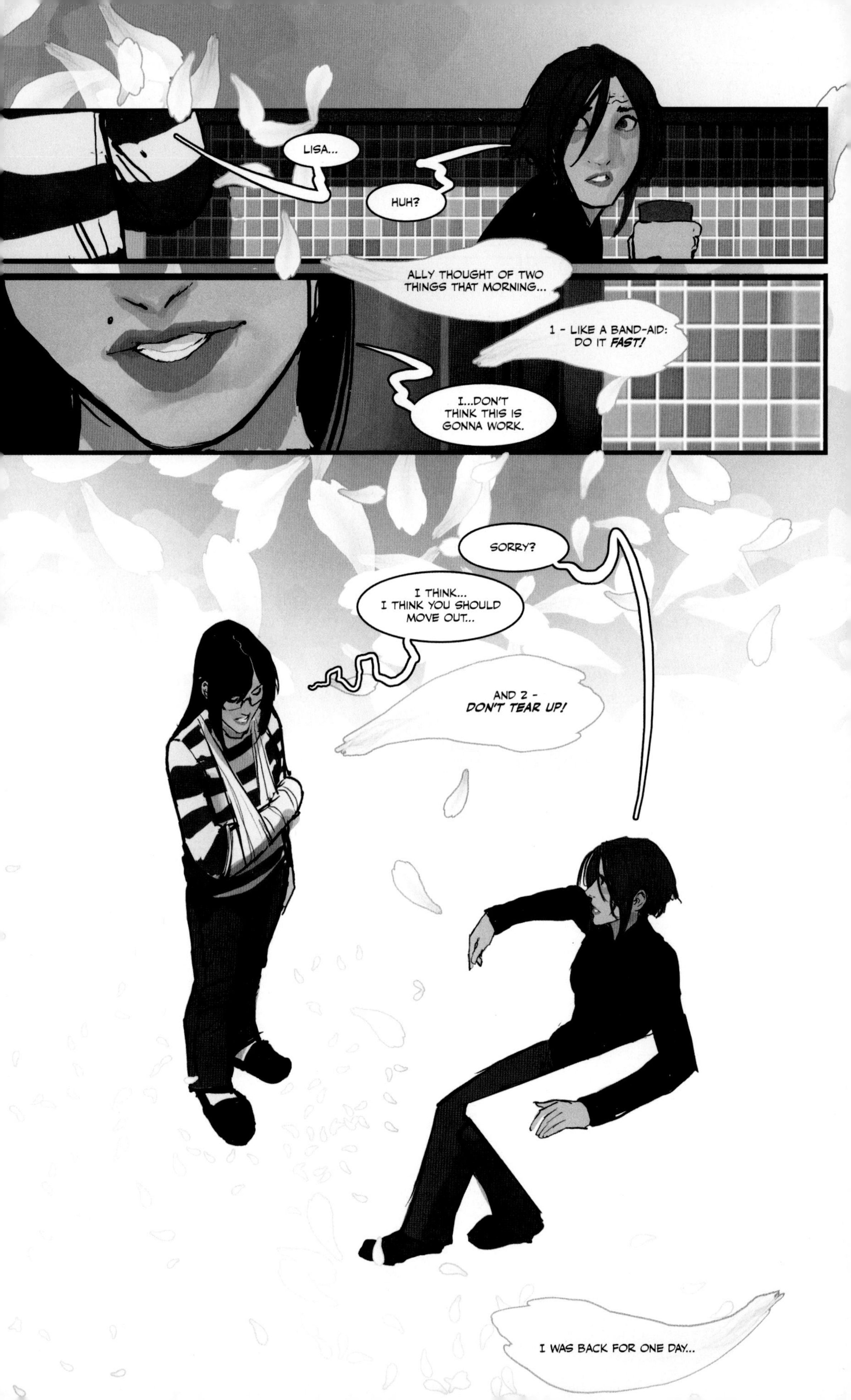
LISA...
HUH?
ALLY THOUGHT OF TWO THINGS THAT MORNING...
1 - LIKE A BAND-AID: DO IT *FAST!*
I...DON'T THINK THIS IS GONNA WORK.
SORRY?
I THINK... I THINK YOU SHOULD MOVE OUT...
AND 2 - *DON'T TEAR UP!*
I WAS BACK FOR ONE DAY...

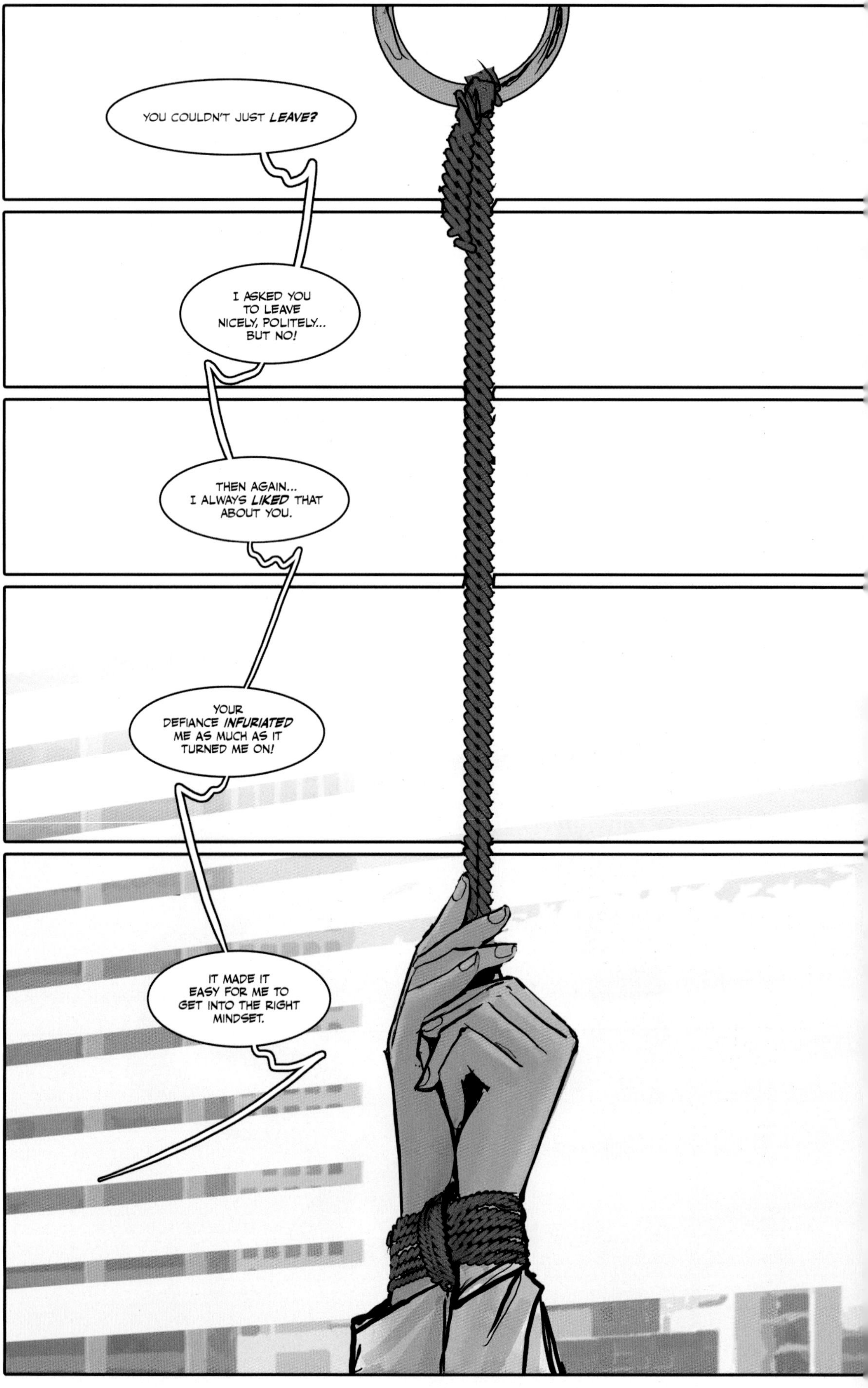

YOU COULDN'T JUST *LEAVE?*
I ASKED YOU TO LEAVE NICELY, POLITELY... BUT NO!
THEN AGAIN... I ALWAYS *LIKED* THAT ABOUT YOU.
YOUR DEFIANCE *INFURIATED* ME AS MUCH AS IT TURNED ME ON!
IT MADE IT EASY FOR ME TO GET INTO THE RIGHT MINDSET.

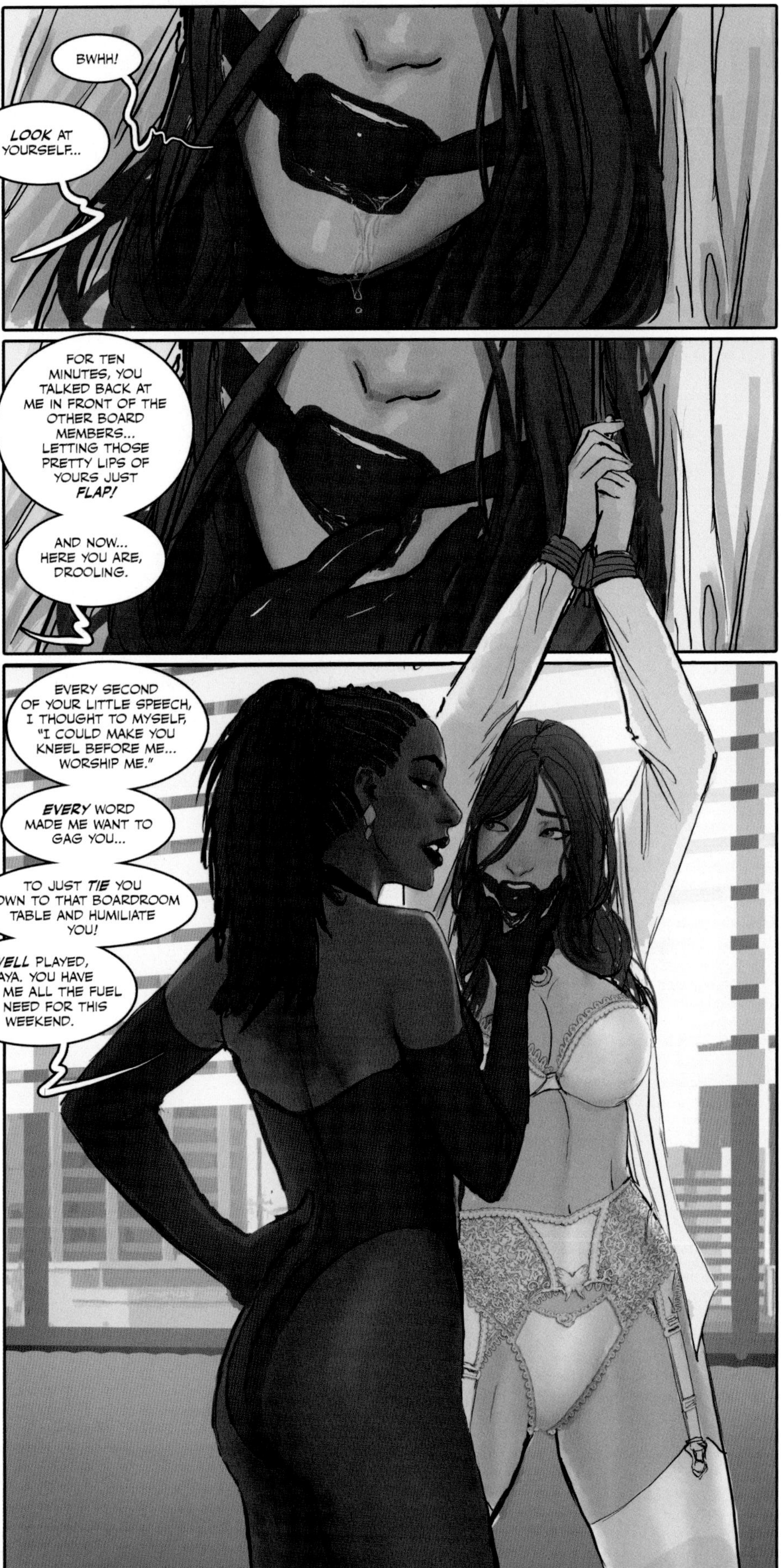
BWHH!
LOOK AT YOURSELF...
FOR TEN MINUTES, YOU TALKED BACK AT ME IN FRONT OF THE OTHER BOARD MEMBERS... LETTING THOSE PRETTY LIPS OF YOURS JUST *FLAP!*
AND NOW... HERE YOU ARE, DROOLING.
EVERY SECOND OF YOUR LITTLE SPEECH, I THOUGHT TO MYSELF, "I COULD MAKE YOU KNEEL BEFORE ME... WORSHIP ME."
EVERY WORD MADE ME WANT TO GAG YOU...
TO JUST *TIE* YOU DOWN TO THAT BOARDROOM TABLE AND HUMILIATE YOU!
WELL PLAYED, MAYA. YOU HAVE GIVEN ME ALL THE FUEL I'LL NEED FOR THIS WEEKEND.

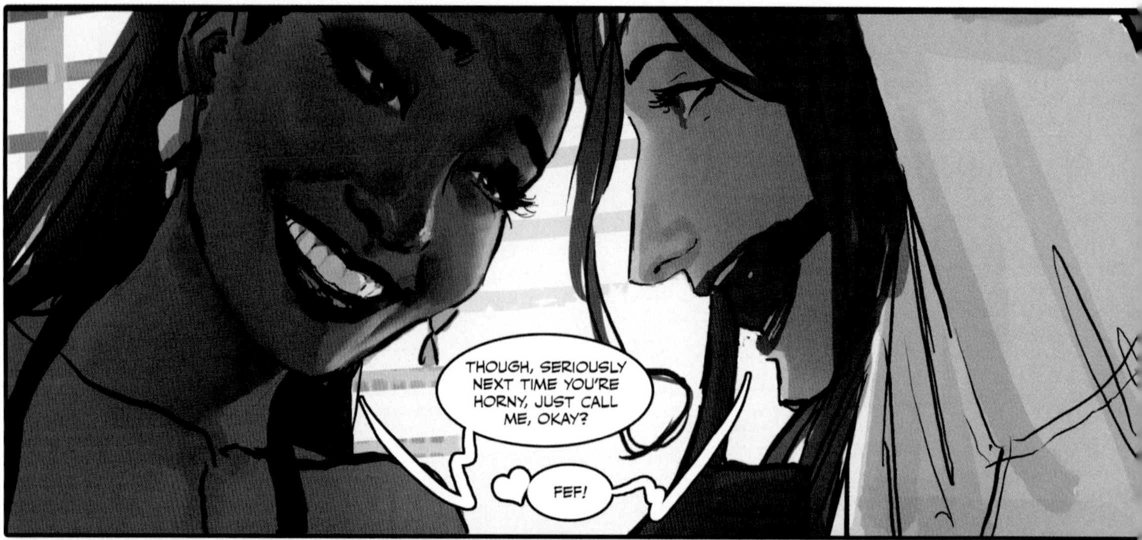
THOUGH, SERIOUSLY NEXT TIME YOU'RE HORNY, JUST CALL ME, OKAY?
FEF!

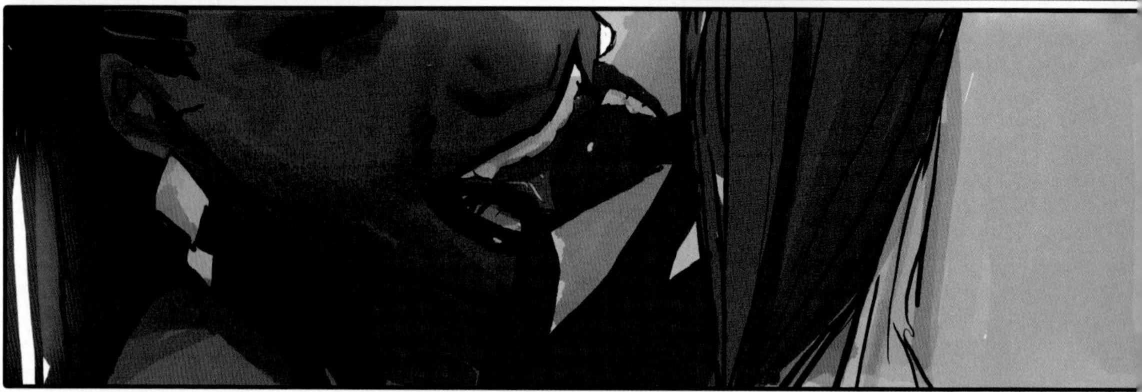

Maya closed her eyes, drinking in the feel of Jade's latex-clad hands on her skin, cool, smooth, and sliding slowly downwards. She felt that familiar pleasant twinge deep inside. She couldn't speak, she couldn't leave, she could do nothing but submit!

Grinning behind her gag, she thought... "Let's do this!"

OKAY...HERE WE GO.

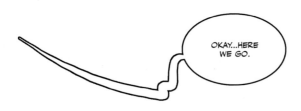

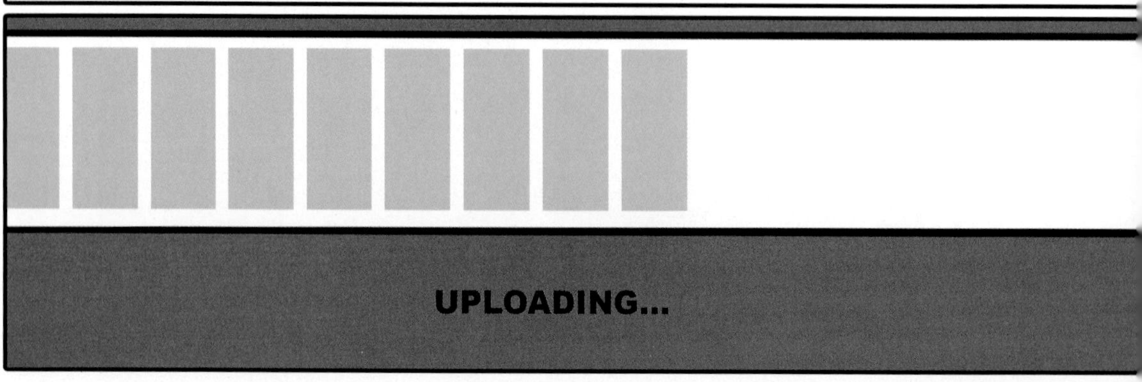
UPLOADING...

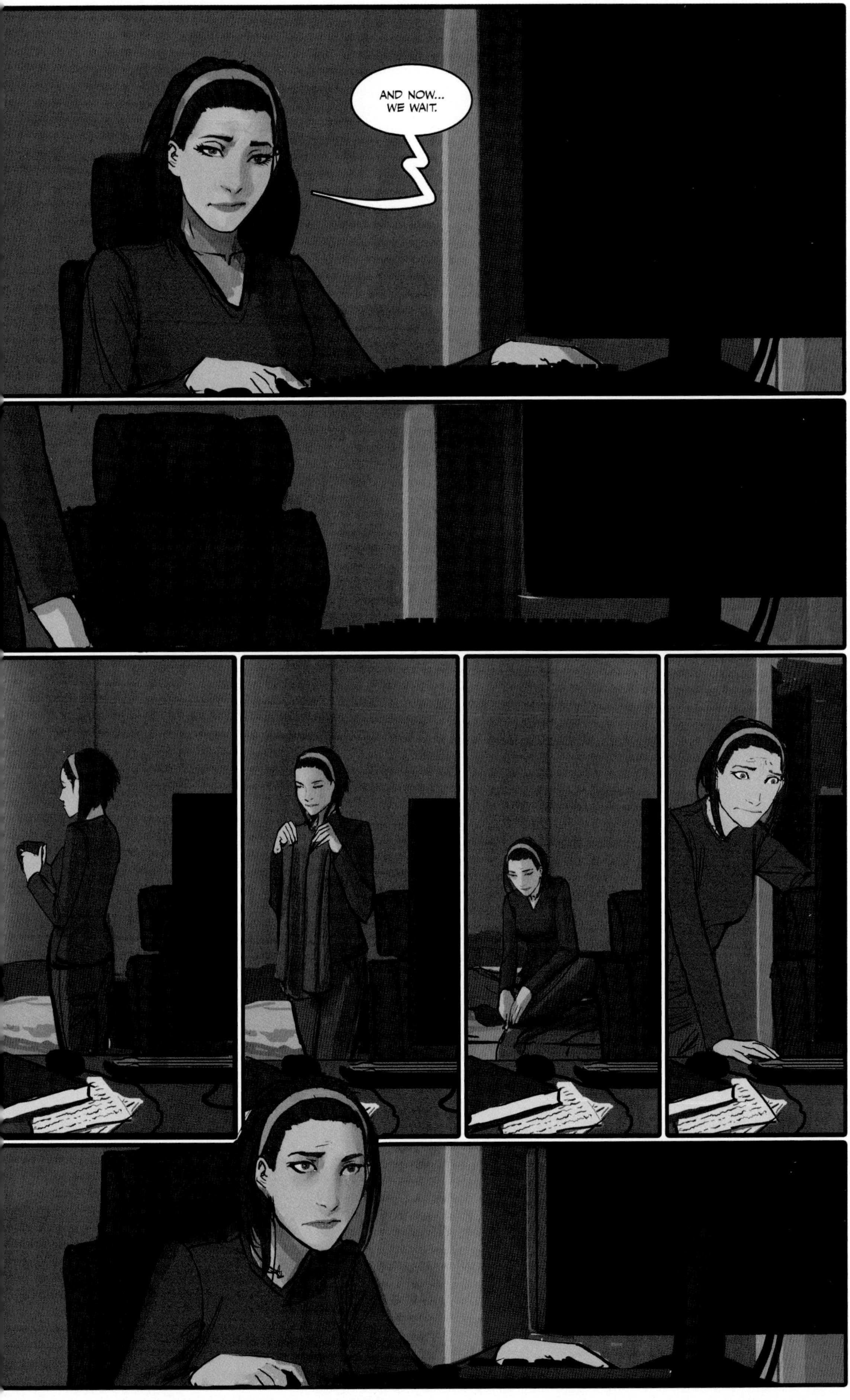
AND NOW... WE WAIT.

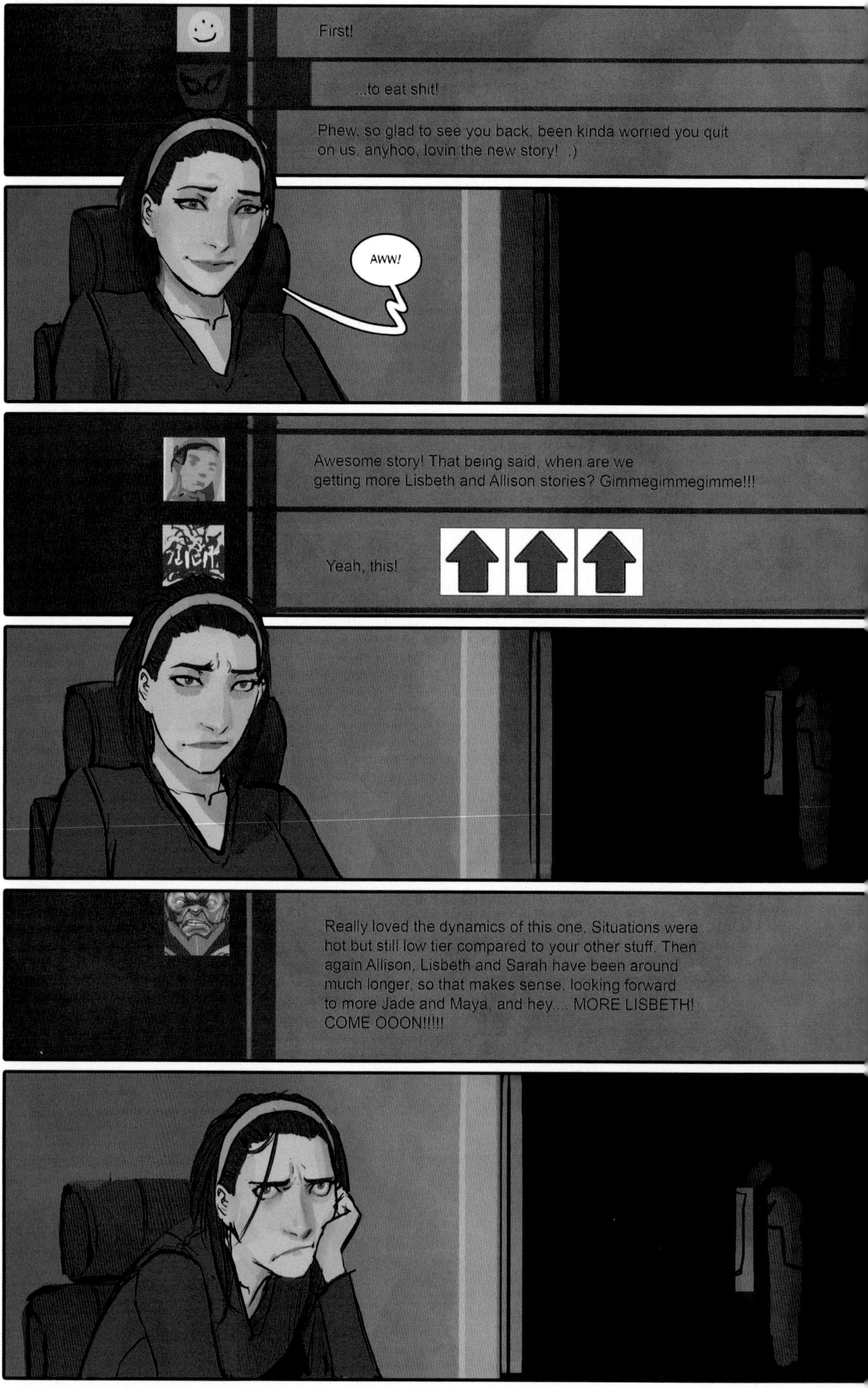
First!
...to eat shit!
Phew, so glad to see you back, been kinda worried you quit on us. anyhoo, lovin the new story! :)
AWW!
Awesome story! That being said, when are we getting more Lisbeth and Allison stories? Gimmegimmegimme!!!
Yeah, this!
Really loved the dynamics of this one. Situations were hot but still low tier compared to your other stuff. Then again Allison, Lisbeth and Sarah have been around much longer, so that makes sense. looking forward to more Jade and Maya, and hey.... MORE LISBETH! COME OOON!!!!!

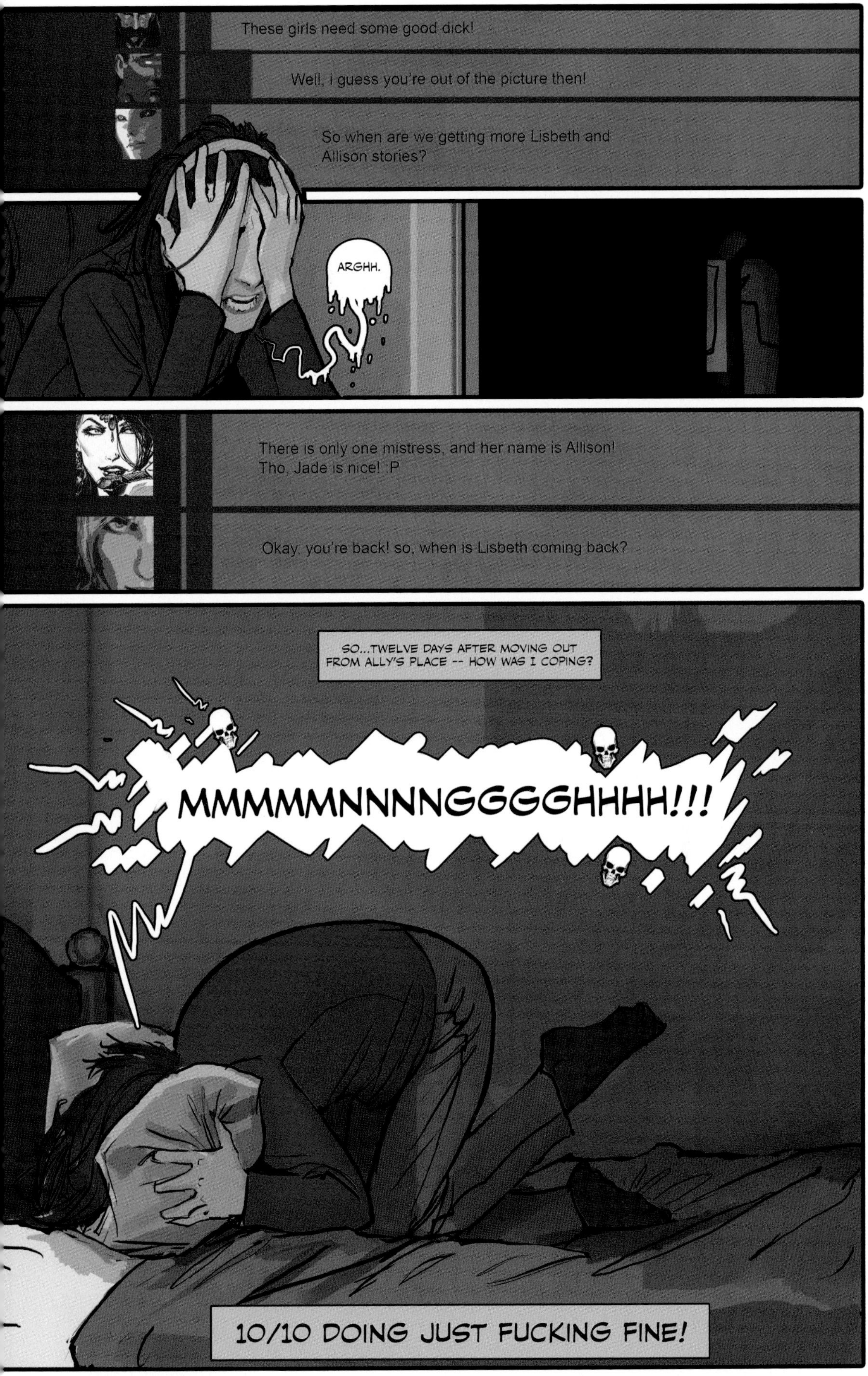
These girls need some good dick!
Well, i guess you're out of the picture then!
So when are we getting more Lisbeth and Allison stories?
ARGHH.
There is only one mistress, and her name is Allison! Tho, Jade is nice! :P
Okay, you're back! so, when is Lisbeth coming back?
SO...TWELVE DAYS AFTER MOVING OUT FROM ALLY'S PLACE -- HOW WAS I COPING?
MMMMMNNNNGGGGHHHH!!!
10/10 DOING JUST FUCKING FINE!

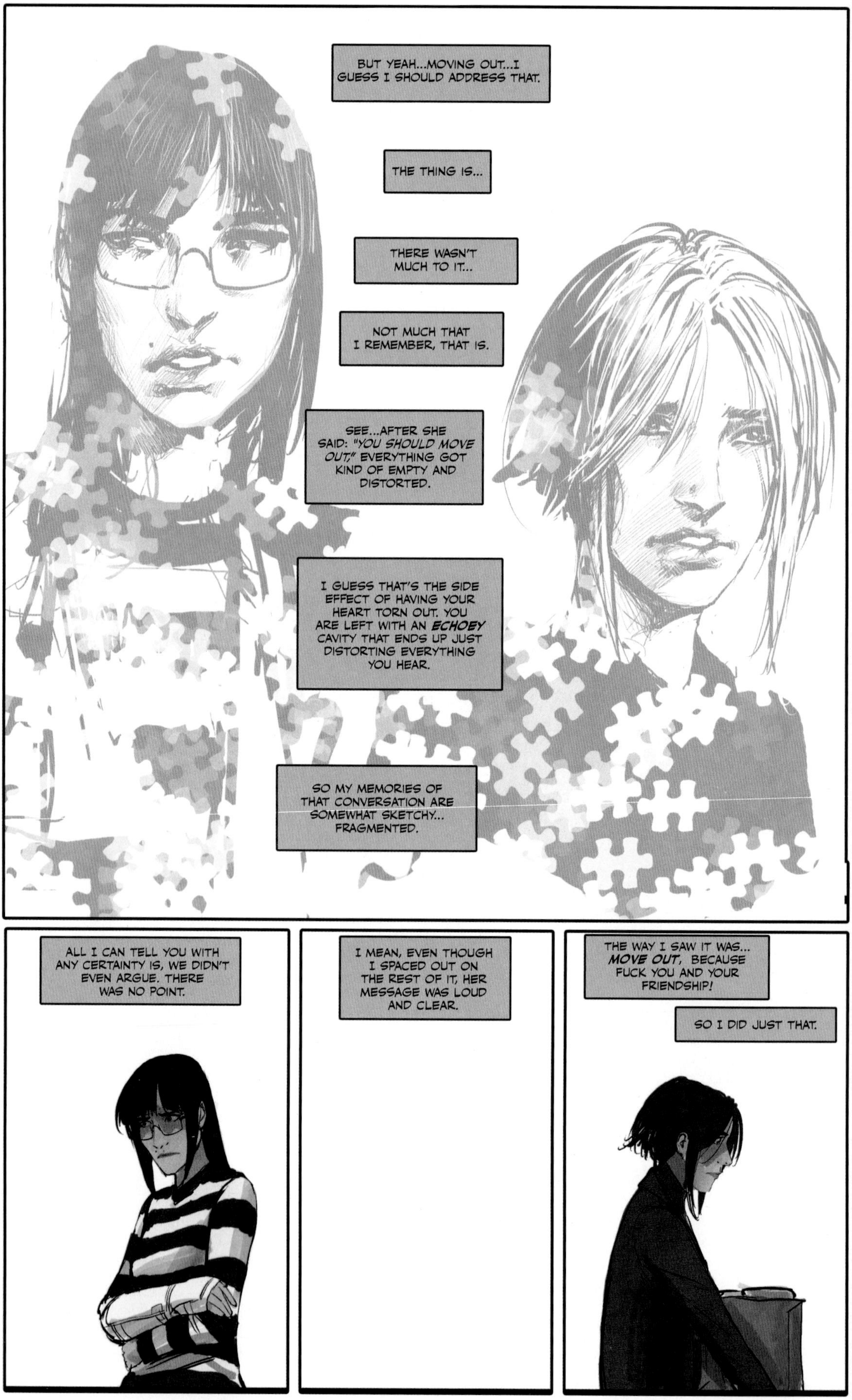
BUT YEAH...MOVING OUT...I GUESS I SHOULD ADDRESS THAT.
THE THING IS...
THERE WASN'T MUCH TO IT...
NOT MUCH THAT I REMEMBER, THAT IS.
SEE...AFTER SHE SAID: *"YOU SHOULD MOVE OUT,"* EVERYTHING GOT KIND OF EMPTY AND DISTORTED.
I GUESS THAT'S THE SIDE EFFECT OF HAVING YOUR HEART TORN OUT. YOU ARE LEFT WITH AN ***ECHOEY*** CAVITY THAT ENDS UP JUST DISTORTING EVERYTHING YOU HEAR.
SO MY MEMORIES OF THAT CONVERSATION ARE SOMEWHAT SKETCHY... FRAGMENTED.
ALL I CAN TELL YOU WITH ANY CERTAINTY IS, WE DIDN'T EVEN ARGUE. THERE WAS NO POINT.
I MEAN, EVEN THOUGH I SPACED OUT ON THE REST OF IT, HER MESSAGE WAS LOUD AND CLEAR.
THE WAY I SAW IT WAS... ***MOVE OUT,*** BECAUSE FUCK YOU AND YOUR FRIENDSHIP!
SO I DID JUST THAT.

I MOVED BACK INTO MY OLD PLACE. IT WAS AVAILABLE. I GUESS MS. DERRINGER, THE LANDLADY, DIDN'T FIND ANY TAKERS. WHAT WITH THE PRICE AND...HER CHARM.

KEEP IN MIND, I HAVE...

ZERO TOLERANCE FOR LATE RENT...I KNOW. I *LIVED* HERE.

MHMM!

HOME SWEET...

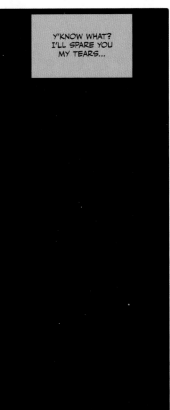

Y'KNOW WHAT? I'LL SPARE YOU MY TEARS...

I SPENT THOSE DAYS WALKING AROUND WITH A HOLLOW PAIN IN BOTH MY HEART AND STOMACH.

I GUESS HEARTACHE SOUNDS MORE ROMANTIC THAN STOMACHACHE, BUT I SWEAR THEY BOTH FELT THE SAME.

I MISSED HER. IT HURT WHEN I BROKE UP WITH DAVID, BUT WITH ALLY... OH GOD...IT WAS TEN TIMES WORSE.

SUFFICE TO SAY, MY NOVEMBER WAS OFF TO A SHITTY START.

I WAS A *ZOMBIE* AT WORK.

COFFEE?

NO, THANK YOU. UMM...YOU SEEM LIKE *YOU* COULD USE SOME.

MY ATTEMPTS AT DISTRACTING MYSELF WITH BOOKS FAILED MISERABLY.

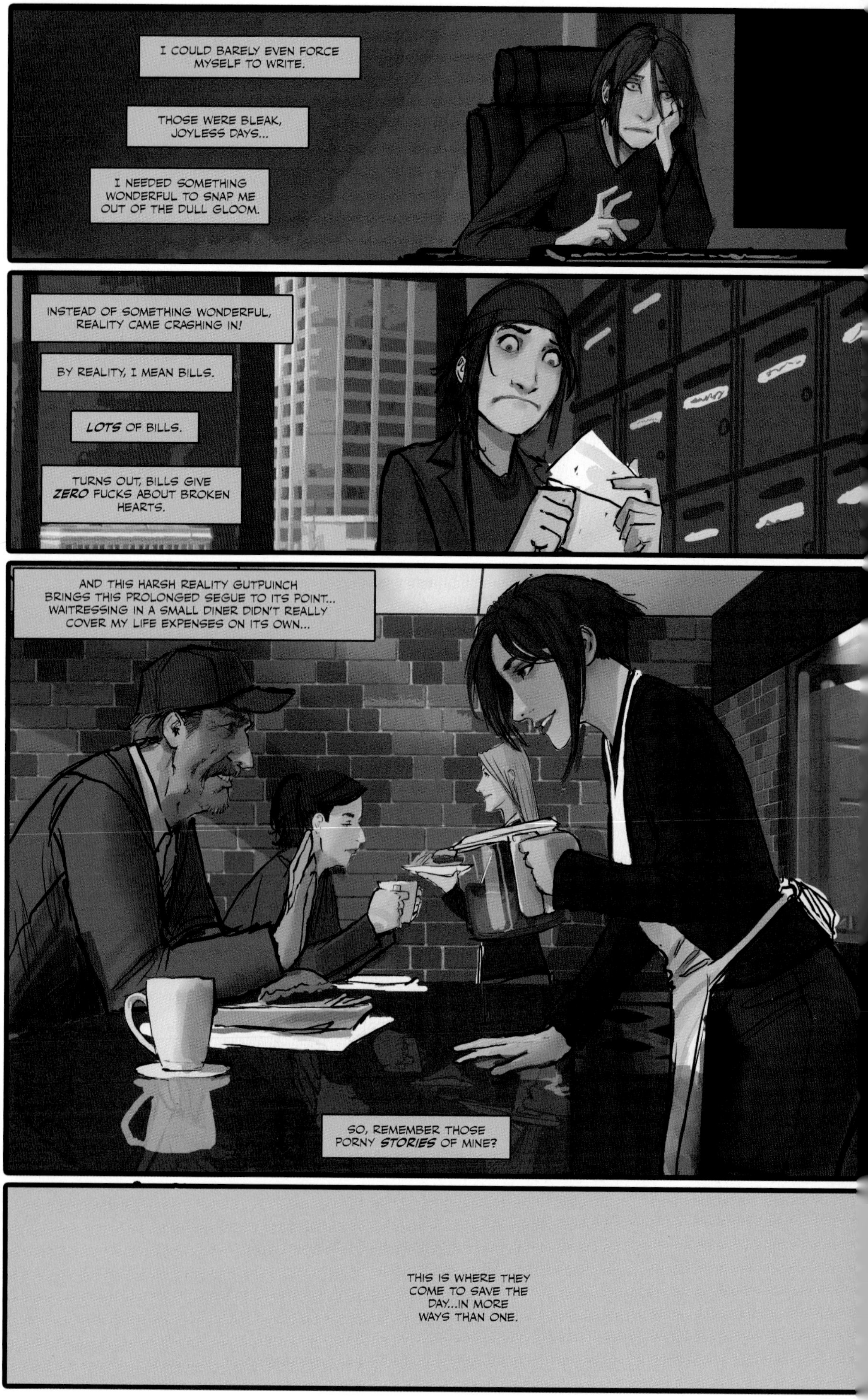
I COULD BARELY EVEN FORCE MYSELF TO WRITE.
THOSE WERE BLEAK, JOYLESS DAYS...
I NEEDED SOMETHING WONDERFUL TO SNAP ME OUT OF THE DULL GLOOM.
INSTEAD OF SOMETHING WONDERFUL, REALITY CAME CRASHING IN!
BY REALITY, I MEAN BILLS.
LOTS OF BILLS.
TURNS OUT, BILLS GIVE *ZERO* FUCKS ABOUT BROKEN HEARTS.
AND THIS HARSH REALITY GUTPUINCH BRINGS THIS PROLONGED SEGUE TO ITS POINT... WAITRESSING IN A SMALL DINER DIDN'T REALLY COVER MY LIFE EXPENSES ON ITS OWN...
SO, REMEMBER THOSE PORNY *STORIES* OF MINE?
THIS IS WHERE THEY COME TO SAVE THE DAY...IN MORE WAYS THAN ONE.

SO...HOW DO YOU BECOME AN INTERNET PORN STORY WRITER?

NO IDEA! I CAN ONLY TELL YOU HOW *I* BECAME ONE.

I WAS SEVENTEEN WHEN WE GOT OUR FIRST PC.

JUST...BEAR WITH ME, I'M *GOING* SOMEWHERE WITH THIS.

MY BROTHERS AND I NEEDED A COMPUTER...WELL, MORE SPECIFICALLY WE NEEDED INTERNET FOR SCHOOL PURPOSES.

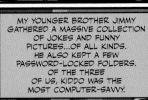

BUT, AS THAT IS OFTEN THE CASE, WE MOSTLY USED IT FOR SOCIAL NETWORKING AND JUST SEARCHING FOR RANDOM CRAP ON THE INTERNET...

PERSONALLY, I GOT BORED OF IT ALL FAST. I RETURNED TO MY BOOKS. AND ONLY USED THE COMPUTER SPORADICALLY AT BEST.

IN FACT, I PICKED UP AN ODD HABIT OF JUST LOOKING AT ALL THE SHIT MY BROTHERS STOCKPILED ON ITS ETERNALLY SHRINKING STORAGE SPACE... YOU MIGHT CALL IT INTERNET BY *PROXY.*

MY YOUNGER BROTHER JIMMY GATHERED A MASSIVE COLLECTION OF JOKES AND FUNNY PICTURES...OF ALL KINDS. HE ALSO KEPT A FEW PASSWORD-LOCKED FOLDERS. OF THE THREE OF US, KIDDO WAS THE MOST COMPUTER-SAVVY.

AND MIKE...

HEH! MIKE'S HOMEWORK FOLDER?

MIKE WAS NINETEEN, AND SINGLE BACK THEN...

ANNND HE HAD INTERNET ACCESS...

SO YEAH, *PORN...LOTSA* PORN!

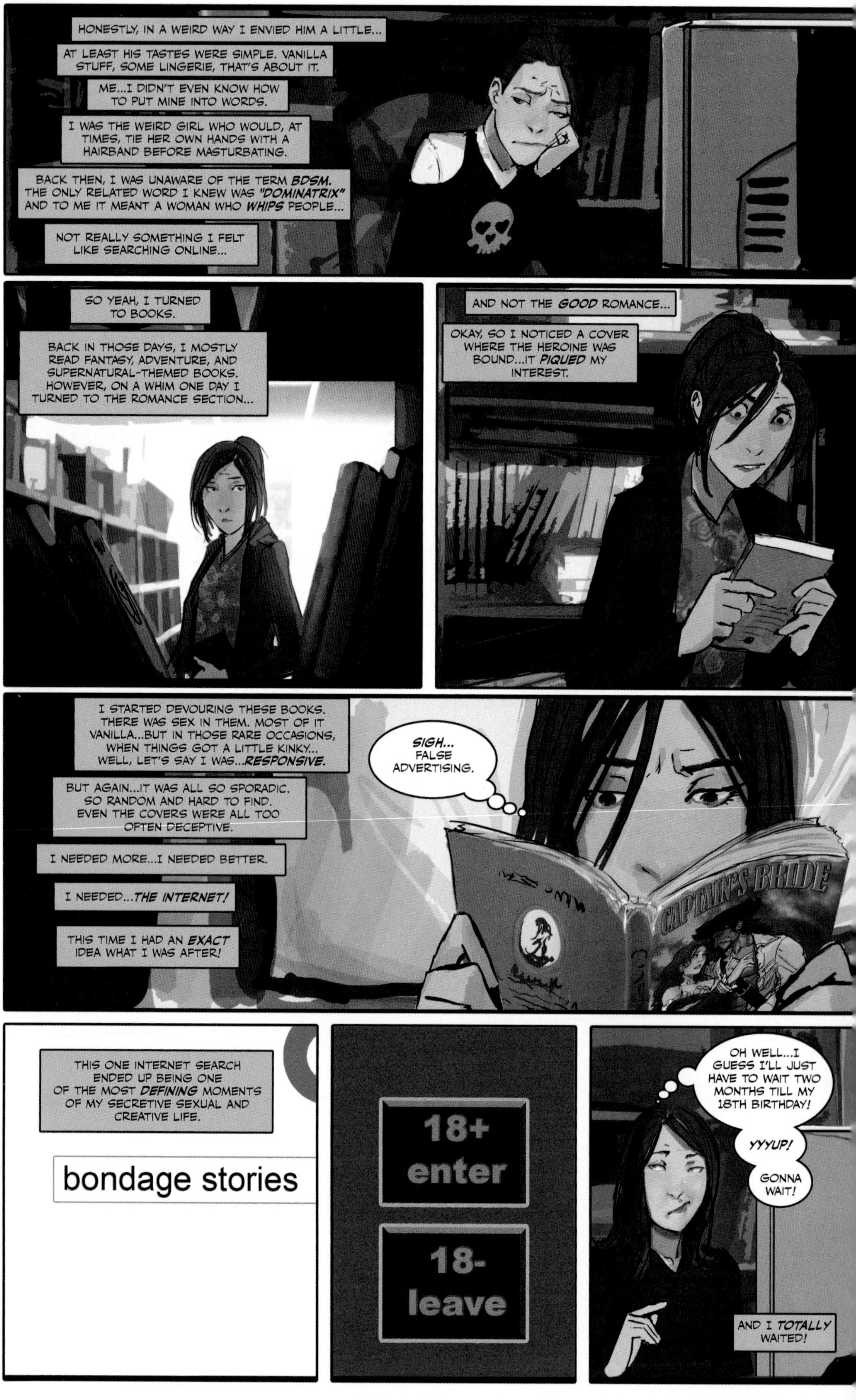
HONESTLY, IN A WEIRD WAY I ENVIED HIM A LITTLE...
AT LEAST HIS TASTES WERE SIMPLE. VANILLA STUFF, SOME LINGERIE, THAT'S ABOUT IT.
ME...I DIDN'T EVEN KNOW HOW TO PUT MINE INTO WORDS.
I WAS THE WEIRD GIRL WHO WOULD, AT TIMES, TIE HER OWN HANDS WITH A HAIRBAND BEFORE MASTURBATING.
BACK THEN, I WAS UNAWARE OF THE TERM *BDSM.* THE ONLY RELATED WORD I KNEW WAS *"DOMINATRIX"* AND TO ME IT MEANT A WOMAN WHO *WHIPS* PEOPLE...
NOT REALLY SOMETHING I FELT LIKE SEARCHING ONLINE...
SO YEAH, I TURNED TO BOOKS.
BACK IN THOSE DAYS, I MOSTLY READ FANTASY, ADVENTURE, AND SUPERNATURAL-THEMED BOOKS. HOWEVER, ON A WHIM ONE DAY I TURNED TO THE ROMANCE SECTION...
AND NOT THE *GOOD* ROMANCE...
OKAY, SO I NOTICED A COVER WHERE THE HEROINE WAS BOUND...IT *PIQUED* MY INTEREST.
I STARTED DEVOURING THESE BOOKS. THERE WAS SEX IN THEM. MOST OF IT VANILLA...BUT IN THOSE RARE OCCASIONS, WHEN THINGS GOT A LITTLE KINKY... WELL, LET'S SAY I WAS...*RESPONSIVE.*
BUT AGAIN...IT WAS ALL SO SPORADIC. SO RANDOM AND HARD TO FIND. EVEN THE COVERS WERE ALL TOO OFTEN DECEPTIVE.
I NEEDED MORE...I NEEDED BETTER.
I NEEDED...*THE INTERNET!*
THIS TIME I HAD AN *EXACT* IDEA WHAT I WAS AFTER!
SIGH... FALSE ADVERTISING.
CAPTAIN'S BRIDE
THIS ONE INTERNET SEARCH ENDED UP BEING ONE OF THE MOST *DEFINING* MOMENTS OF MY SECRETIVE SEXUAL AND CREATIVE LIFE.
bondage stories
18+ enter
18- leave
OH WELL...I GUESS I'LL JUST HAVE TO WAIT TWO MONTHS TILL MY 18TH BIRTHDAY!
YYYUP!
GONNA WAIT!
AND I *TOTALLY* WAITED!

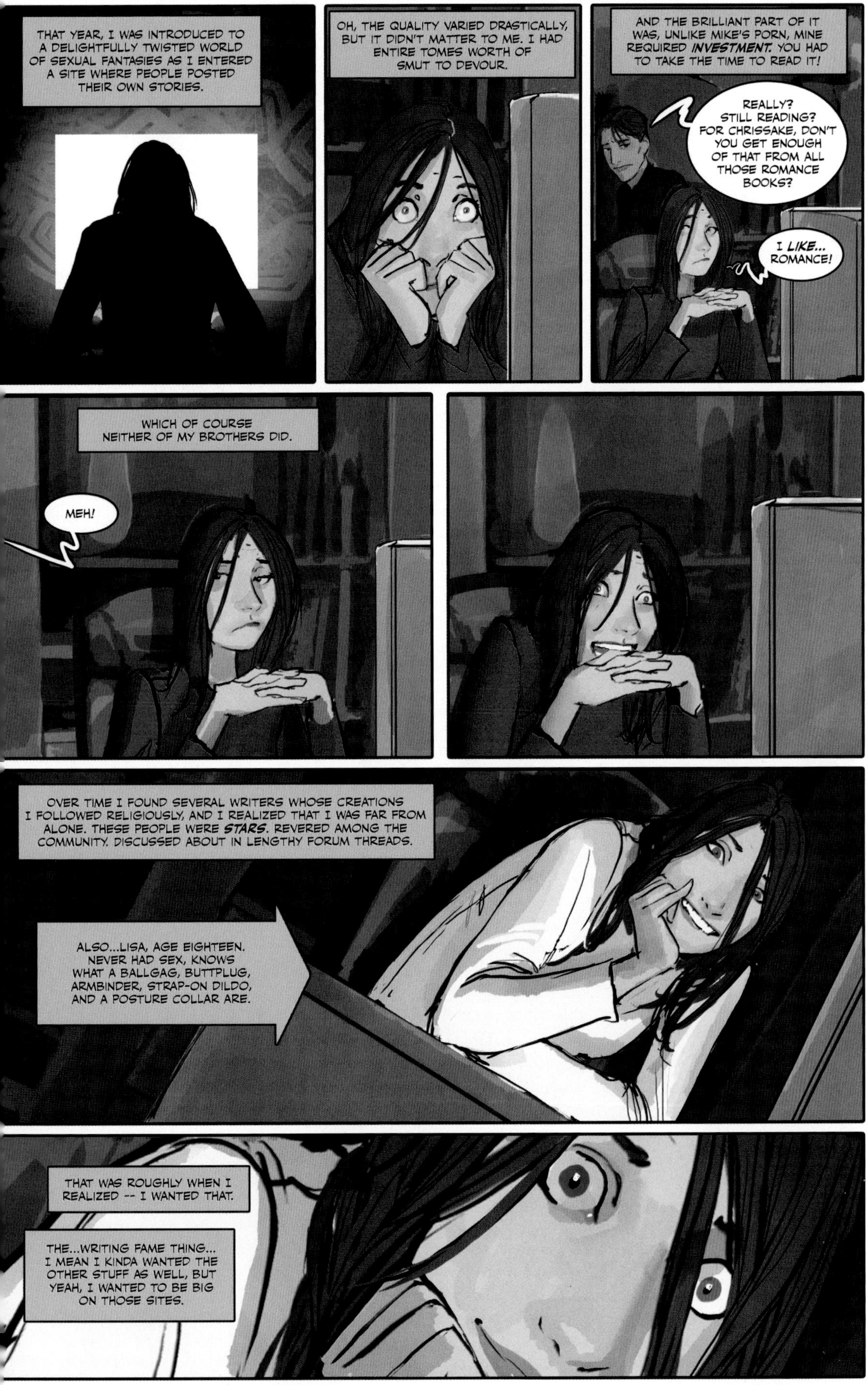
THAT YEAR, I WAS INTRODUCED TO A DELIGHTFULLY TWISTED WORLD OF SEXUAL FANTASIES AS I ENTERED A SITE WHERE PEOPLE POSTED THEIR OWN STORIES.
OH, THE QUALITY VARIED DRASTICALLY, BUT IT DIDN'T MATTER TO ME. I HAD ENTIRE TOMES WORTH OF SMUT TO DEVOUR.
AND THE BRILLIANT PART OF IT WAS, UNLIKE MIKE'S PORN, MINE REQUIRED *INVESTMENT.* YOU HAD TO TAKE THE TIME TO READ IT!
REALLY? STILL READING? FOR CHRISSAKE, DON'T YOU GET ENOUGH OF THAT FROM ALL THOSE ROMANCE BOOKS?
I *LIKE...* ROMANCE!
WHICH OF COURSE NEITHER OF MY BROTHERS DID.
MEH!
OVER TIME I FOUND SEVERAL WRITERS WHOSE CREATIONS I FOLLOWED RELIGIOUSLY, AND I REALIZED THAT I WAS FAR FROM ALONE. THESE PEOPLE WERE *STARS*. REVERED AMONG THE COMMUNITY. DISCUSSED ABOUT IN LENGTHY FORUM THREADS.
ALSO...LISA, AGE EIGHTEEN. NEVER HAD SEX, KNOWS WHAT A BALLGAG, BUTTPLUG, ARMBINDER, STRAP-ON DILDO, AND A POSTURE COLLAR ARE.
THAT WAS ROUGHLY WHEN I REALIZED -- I WANTED THAT.
THE...WRITING FAME THING... I MEAN I KINDA WANTED THE OTHER STUFF AS WELL, BUT YEAH, I WANTED TO BE BIG ON THOSE SITES.

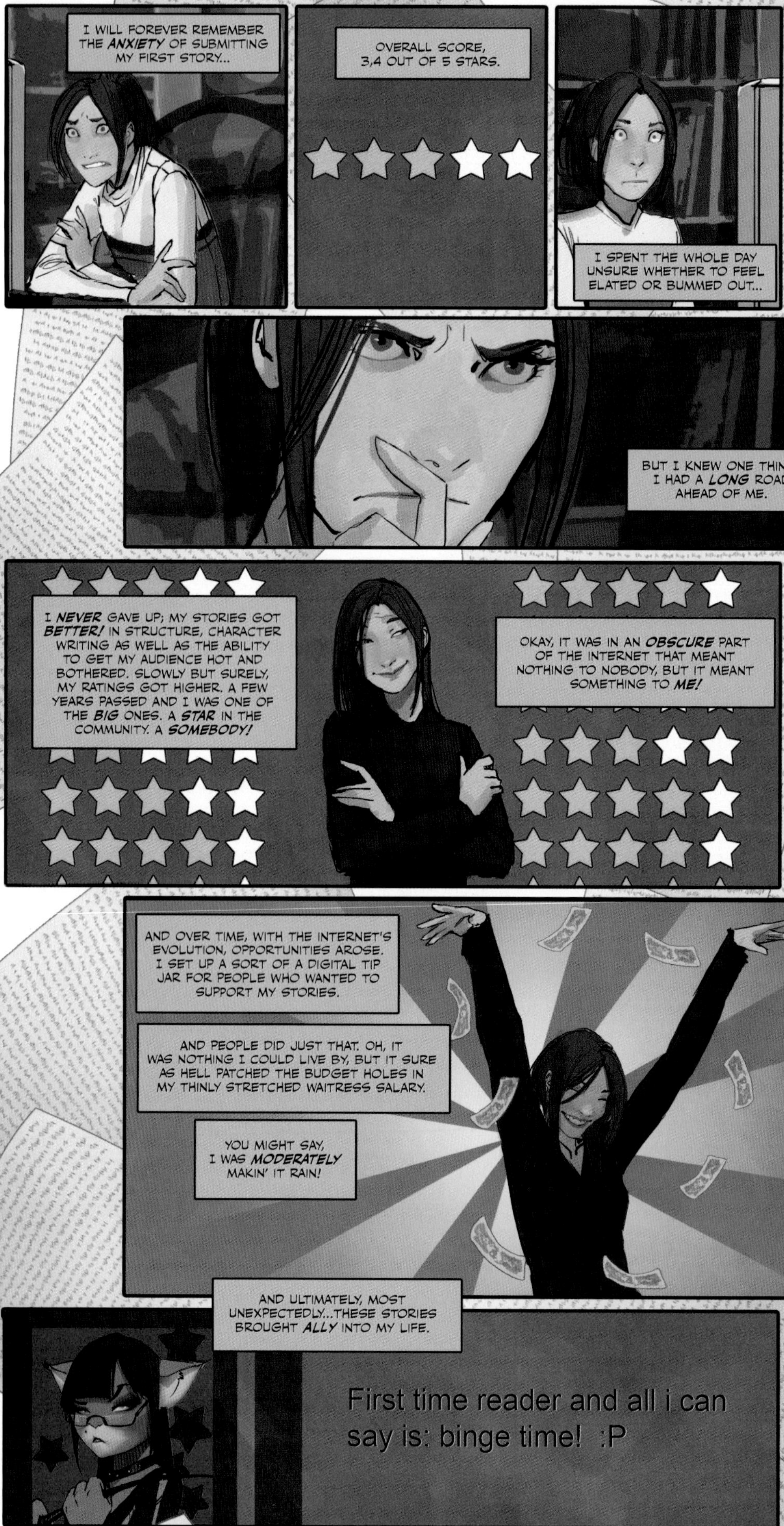

I WILL FOREVER REMEMBER THE ANXIETY OF SUBMITTING MY FIRST STORY...
OVERALL SCORE, 3,4 OUT OF 5 STARS.
I SPENT THE WHOLE DAY UNSURE WHETHER TO FEEL ELATED OR BUMMED OUT...
BUT I KNEW ONE THING. I HAD A LONG ROAD AHEAD OF ME.
I NEVER GAVE UP; MY STORIES GOT BETTER! IN STRUCTURE, CHARACTER WRITING AS WELL AS THE ABILITY TO GET MY AUDIENCE HOT AND BOTHERED. SLOWLY BUT SURELY, MY RATINGS GOT HIGHER. A FEW YEARS PASSED AND I WAS ONE OF THE BIG ONES. A STAR IN THE COMMUNITY. A SOMEBODY!
OKAY, IT WAS IN AN OBSCURE PART OF THE INTERNET THAT MEANT NOTHING TO NOBODY, BUT IT MEANT SOMETHING TO ME!
AND OVER TIME, WITH THE INTERNET'S EVOLUTION, OPPORTUNITIES AROSE. I SET UP A SORT OF A DIGITAL TIP JAR FOR PEOPLE WHO WANTED TO SUPPORT MY STORIES.
AND PEOPLE DID JUST THAT. OH, IT WAS NOTHING I COULD LIVE BY, BUT IT SURE AS HELL PATCHED THE BUDGET HOLES IN MY THINLY STRETCHED WAITRESS SALARY.
YOU MIGHT SAY, I WAS MODERATELY MAKIN' IT RAIN!
AND ULTIMATELY, MOST UNEXPECTEDLY...THESE STORIES BROUGHT ALLY INTO MY LIFE.
First time reader and all i can say is: binge time! :P

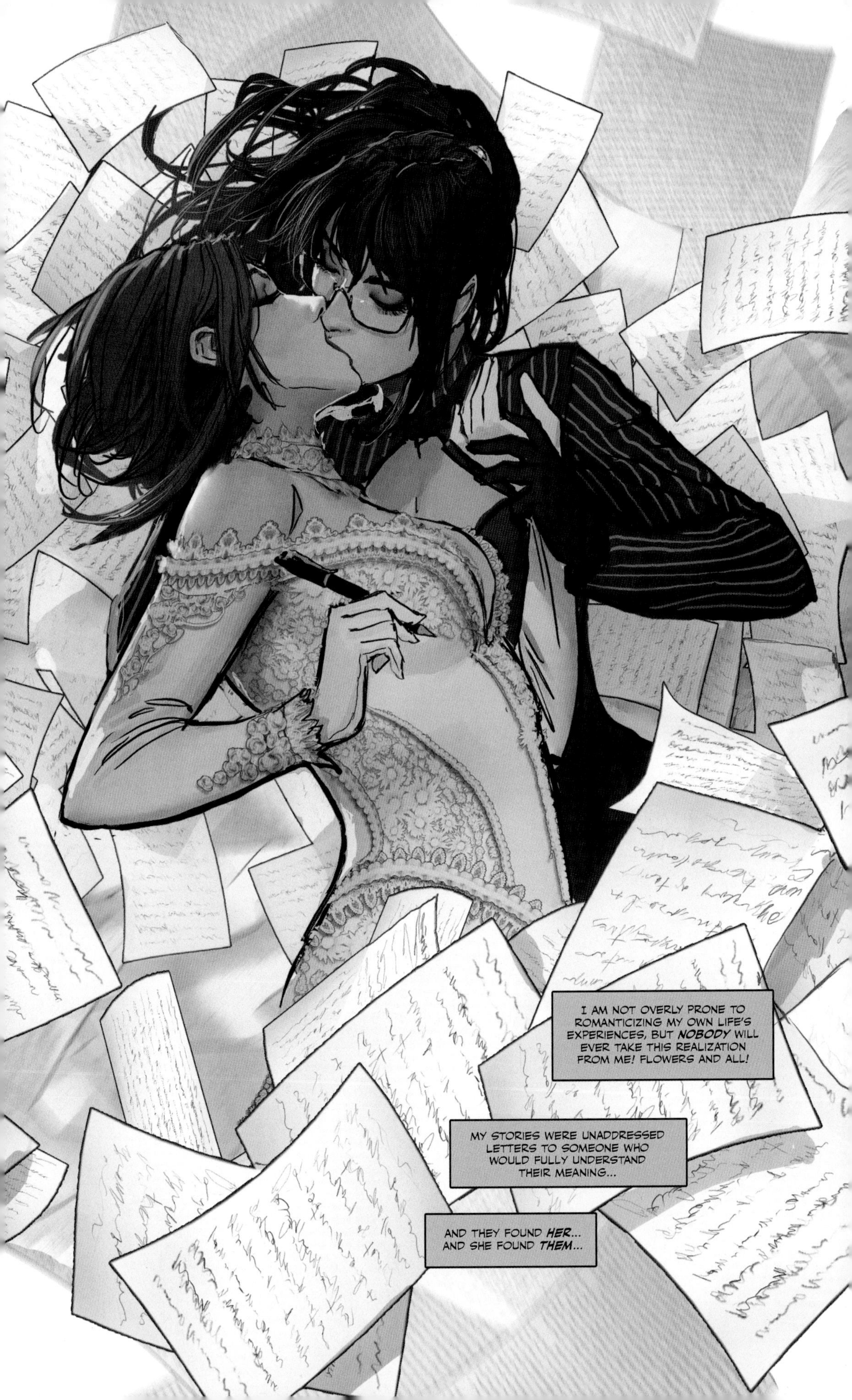
I AM NOT OVERLY PRONE TO ROMANTICIZING MY OWN LIFE'S EXPERIENCES, BUT *NOBODY* WILL EVER TAKE THIS REALIZATION FROM ME*!* FLOWERS AND ALL*!*
MY STORIES WERE UNADDRESSED LETTERS TO SOMEONE WHO WOULD FULLY UNDERSTAND THEIR MEANING...
AND THEY FOUND *HER*... AND SHE FOUND *THEM*...

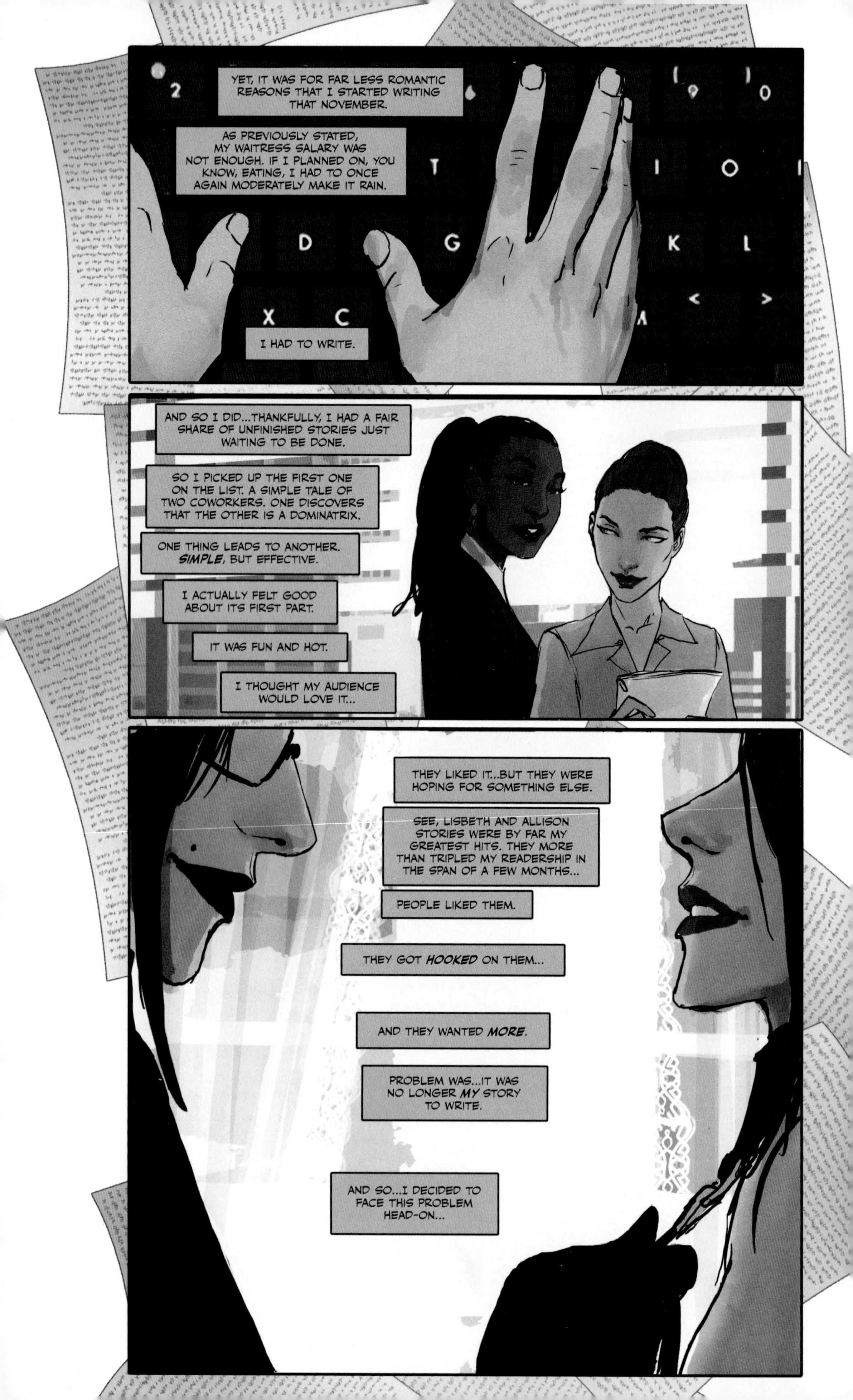
YET, IT WAS FOR FAR LESS ROMANTIC REASONS THAT I STARTED WRITING THAT NOVEMBER.
AS PREVIOUSLY STATED, MY WAITRESS SALARY WAS NOT ENOUGH. IF I PLANNED ON, YOU KNOW, EATING, I HAD TO ONCE AGAIN MODERATELY MAKE IT RAIN.
I HAD TO WRITE.
AND SO I DID...THANKFULLY, I HAD A FAIR SHARE OF UNFINISHED STORIES JUST WAITING TO BE DONE.
SO I PICKED UP THE FIRST ONE ON THE LIST. A SIMPLE TALE OF TWO COWORKERS. ONE DISCOVERS THAT THE OTHER IS A DOMINATRIX.
ONE THING LEADS TO ANOTHER. *SIMPLE*, BUT EFFECTIVE.
I ACTUALLY FELT GOOD ABOUT ITS FIRST PART.
IT WAS FUN AND HOT.
I THOUGHT MY AUDIENCE WOULD LOVE IT...
THEY LIKED IT...BUT THEY WERE HOPING FOR SOMETHING ELSE.
SEE, LISBETH AND ALLISON STORIES WERE BY FAR MY GREATEST HITS. THEY MORE THAN TRIPLED MY READERSHIP IN THE SPAN OF A FEW MONTHS...
PEOPLE LIKED THEM.
THEY GOT *HOOKED* ON THEM...
AND THEY WANTED *MORE*.
PROBLEM WAS...IT WAS NO LONGER *MY* STORY TO WRITE.
AND SO...I DECIDED TO FACE THIS PROBLEM HEAD-ON...

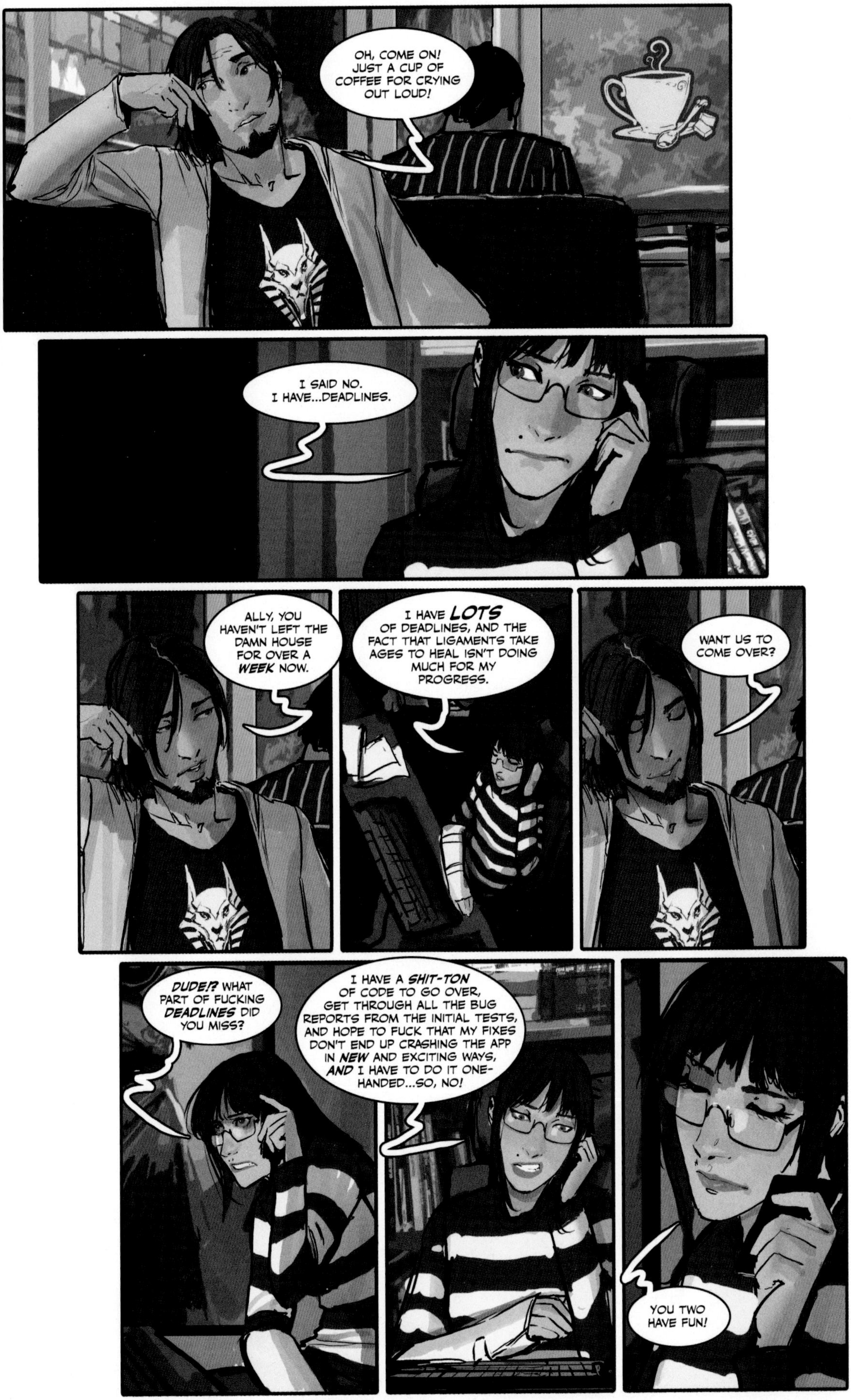
OH, COME ON! JUST A CUP OF COFFEE FOR CRYING OUT LOUD!
I SAID NO. I HAVE...DEADLINES.
ALLY, YOU HAVEN'T LEFT THE DAMN HOUSE FOR OVER A WEEK NOW.
I HAVE LOTS OF DEADLINES, AND THE FACT THAT LIGAMENTS TAKE AGES TO HEAL ISN'T DOING MUCH FOR MY PROGRESS.
WANT US TO COME OVER?
DUDE!? WHAT PART OF FUCKING DEADLINES DID YOU MISS?
I HAVE A SHIT-TON OF CODE TO GO OVER, GET THROUGH ALL THE BUG REPORTS FROM THE INITIAL TESTS, AND HOPE TO FUCK THAT MY FIXES DON'T END UP CRASHING THE APP IN NEW AND EXCITING WAYS, AND I HAVE TO DO IT ONE-HANDED...SO, NO!
YOU TWO HAVE FUN!

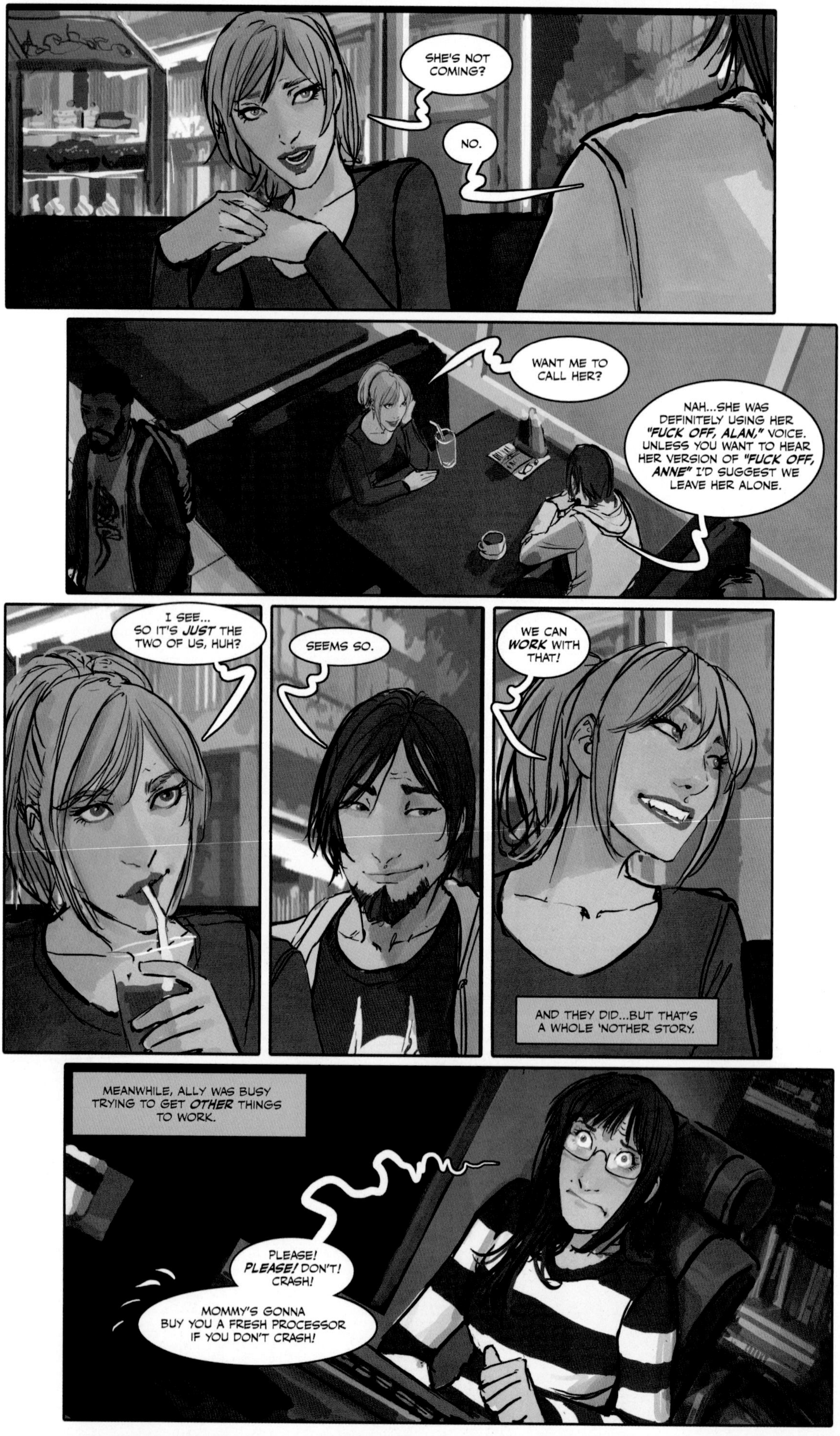

SHE'S NOT COMING?
NO.
WANT ME TO CALL HER?
NAH...SHE WAS DEFINITELY USING HER "FUCK OFF, ALAN," VOICE. UNLESS YOU WANT TO HEAR HER VERSION OF "FUCK OFF, ANNE" I'D SUGGEST WE LEAVE HER ALONE.
I SEE... SO IT'S JUST THE TWO OF US, HUH?
SEEMS SO.
WE CAN WORK WITH THAT!
AND THEY DID...BUT THAT'S A WHOLE 'NOTHER STORY.
MEANWHILE, ALLY WAS BUSY TRYING TO GET OTHER THINGS TO WORK.
PLEASE! PLEASE! DON'T! CRASH!
MOMMY'S GONNA BUY YOU A FRESH PROCESSOR IF YOU DON'T CRASH!

...
...

WELCOME TO O-WORLD!

OH, THANK THE DIGITAL GODS! ONE DOWN!

YUP...

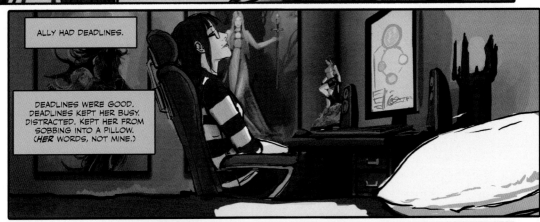

ALLY HAD DEADLINES.

DEADLINES WERE GOOD. DEADLINES KEPT HER BUSY. DISTRACTED. KEPT HER FROM SOBBING INTO A PILLOW. (*HER* WORDS, NOT MINE.)

WE'D HAD NO CONTACT FOR TWO WEEKS SINCE I MOVED OUT, AND THAT DAY, AGAINST HER BETTER JUDGEMENT... SHE VISITED MY WEBSITE.

I'LL JUST QUOTE HER:

"I DON'T KNOW WHAT I WAS LOOKING FOR...I FELT EMPTY. I GUESS. NOT HEARING FROM YOU MADE IT ALL SEEM SURREAL, LIKE YOU WERE NEVER THERE, A *DREAM*, A FIGMENT OF MY IMAGINATION.

"I WENT TO YOUR SITE THAT DAY TO...I GUESS, DOUBLECHECK.

JADE'S SECRET...ARY

"I THOUGHT...MAYBE YOU WROTE *SOMETHING*, A NEW STORY...A MESSAGE... *ANYTHING*."

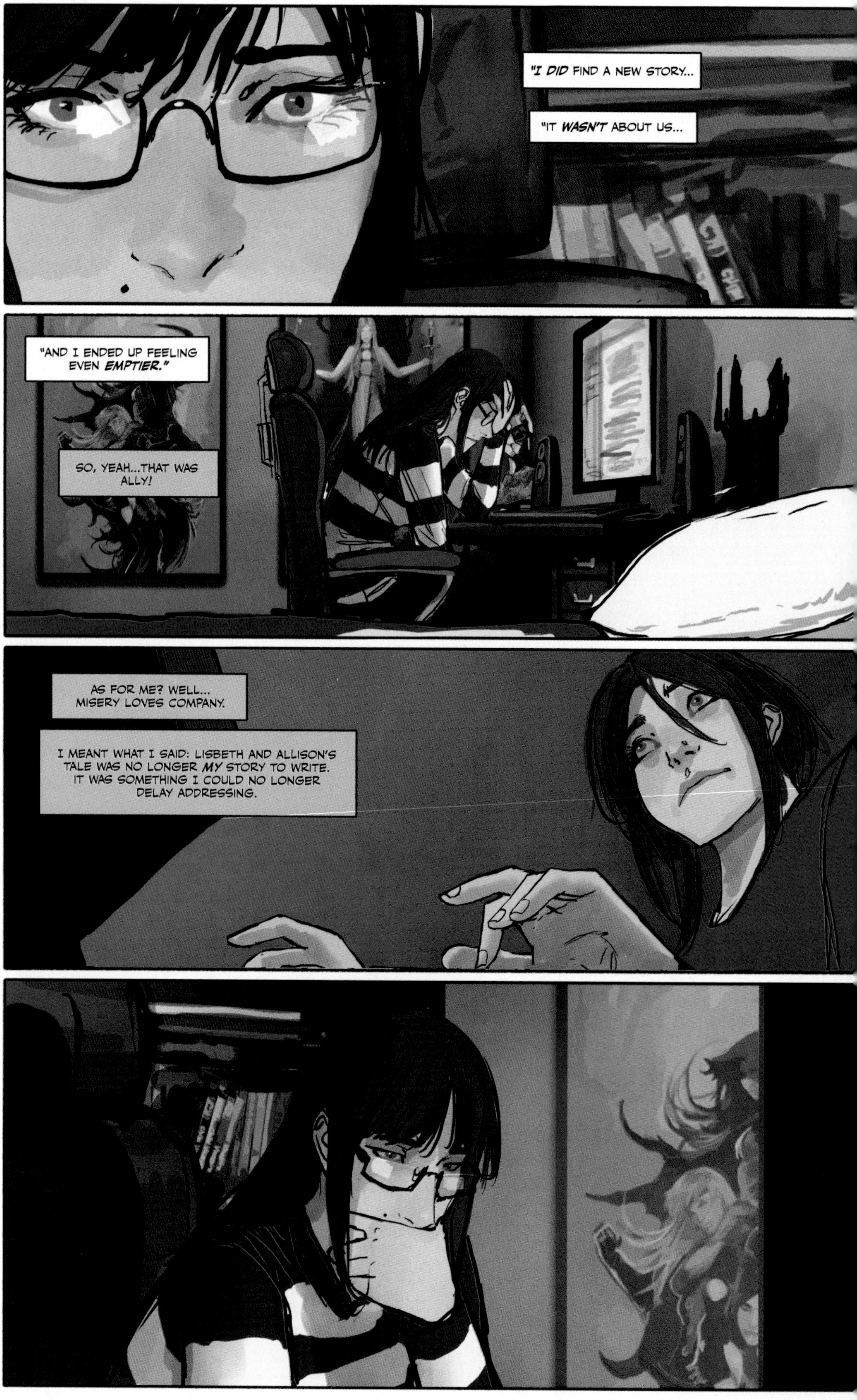

"I DID FIND A NEW STORY...
"IT WASN'T ABOUT US...
"AND I ENDED UP FEELING EVEN EMPTIER."
SO, YEAH...THAT WAS ALLY!
AS FOR ME? WELL... MISERY LOVES COMPANY.
I MEANT WHAT I SAID: LISBETH AND ALLISON'S TALE WAS NO LONGER MY STORY TO WRITE. IT WAS SOMETHING I COULD NO LONGER DELAY ADDRESSING.

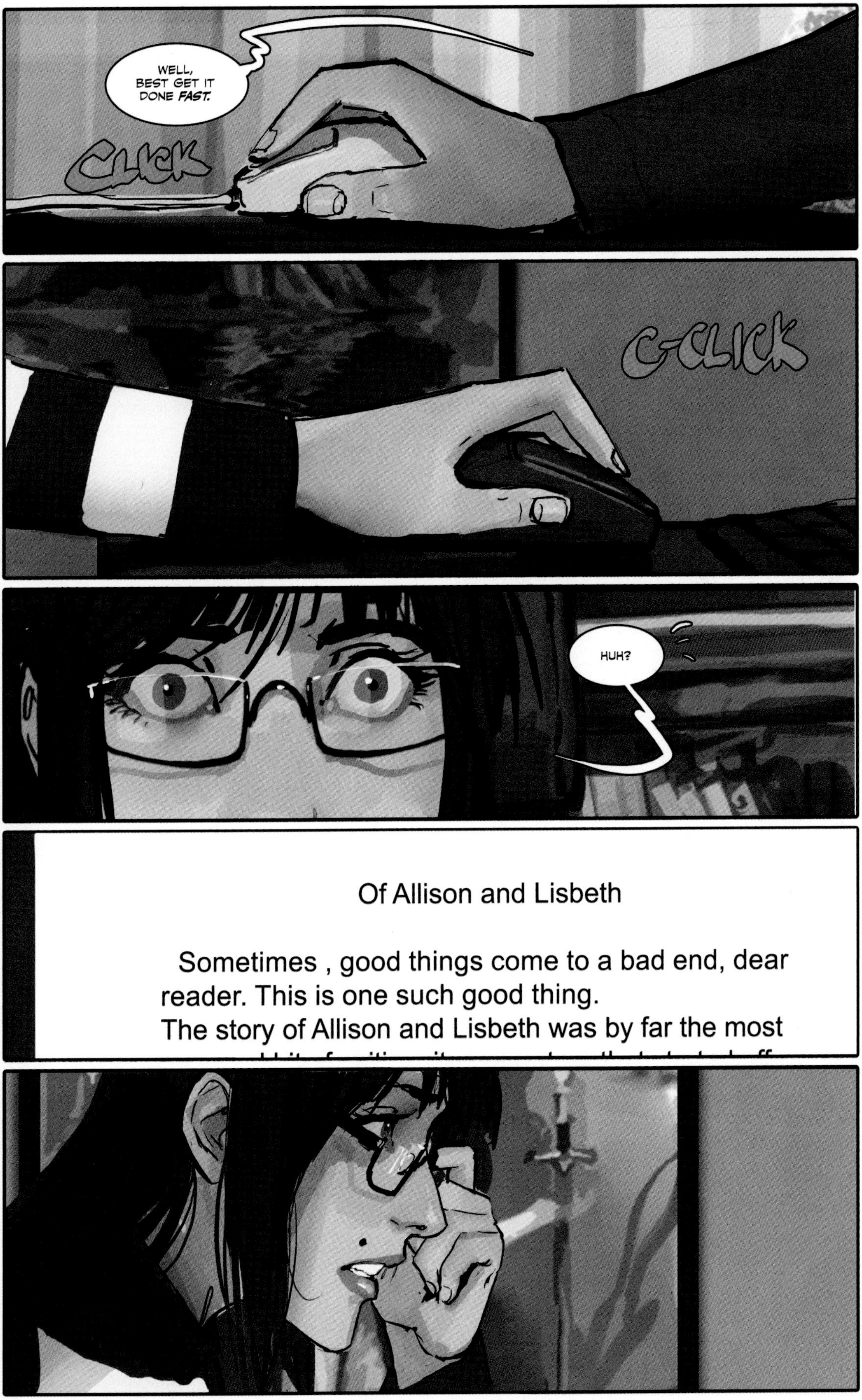
WELL, BEST GET IT DONE *FAST.*
CLICK
C-CLICK
HUH?
Of Allison and Lisbeth
Sometimes , good things come to a bad end, dear reader. This is one such good thing.
The story of Allison and Lisbeth was by far the most

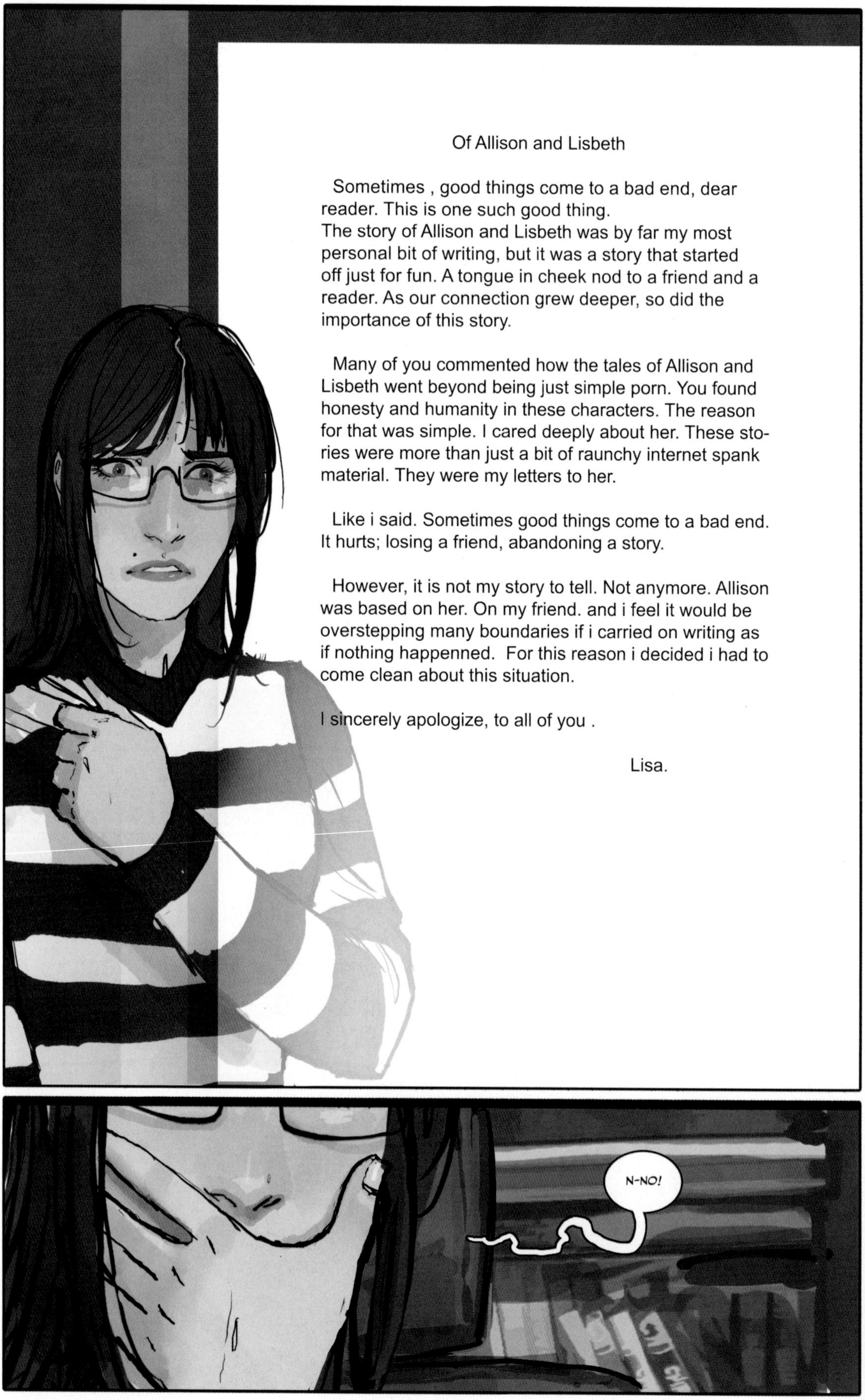

Of Allison and Lisbeth

Sometimes , good things come to a bad end, dear reader. This is one such good thing.
The story of Allison and Lisbeth was by far my most personal bit of writing, but it was a story that started off just for fun. A tongue in cheek nod to a friend and a reader. As our connection grew deeper, so did the importance of this story.

Many of you commented how the tales of Allison and Lisbeth went beyond being just simple porn. You found honesty and humanity in these characters. The reason for that was simple. I cared deeply about her. These stories were more than just a bit of raunchy internet spank material. They were my letters to her.

Like i said. Sometimes good things come to a bad end. It hurts; losing a friend, abandoning a story.

However, it is not my story to tell. Not anymore. Allison was based on her. On my friend. and i feel it would be overstepping many boundaries if i carried on writing as if nothing happenned. For this reason i decided i had to come clean about this situation.

I sincerely apologize, to all of you .

Lisa.

N-NO!

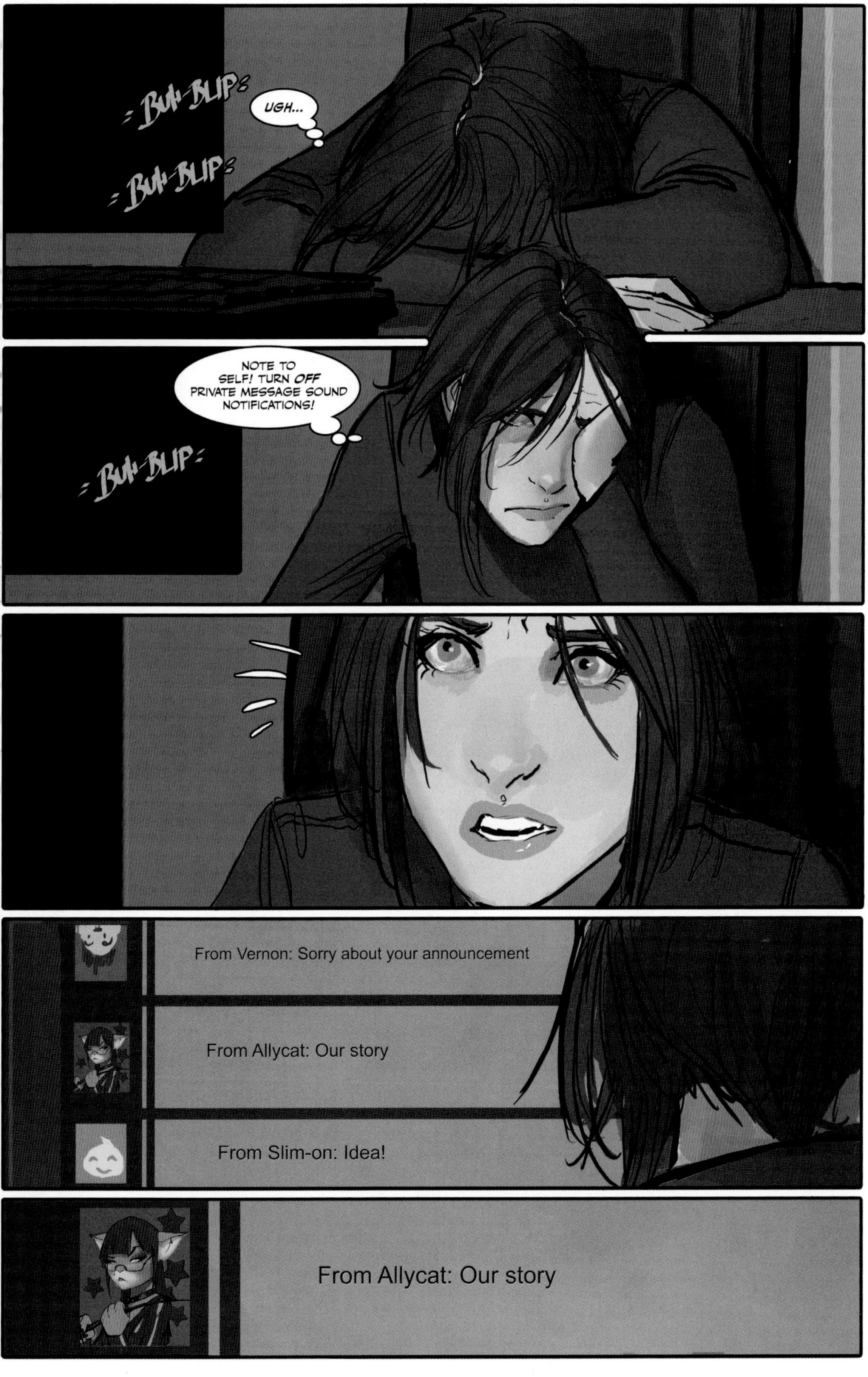
BU-BLIP
UGH...
BU-BLIP
NOTE TO SELF! TURN OFF PRIVATE MESSAGE SOUND NOTIFICATIONS!
BU-BLIP
From Vernon: Sorry about your announcement
From Allycat: Our story
From Slim-on: Idea!
From Allycat: Our story

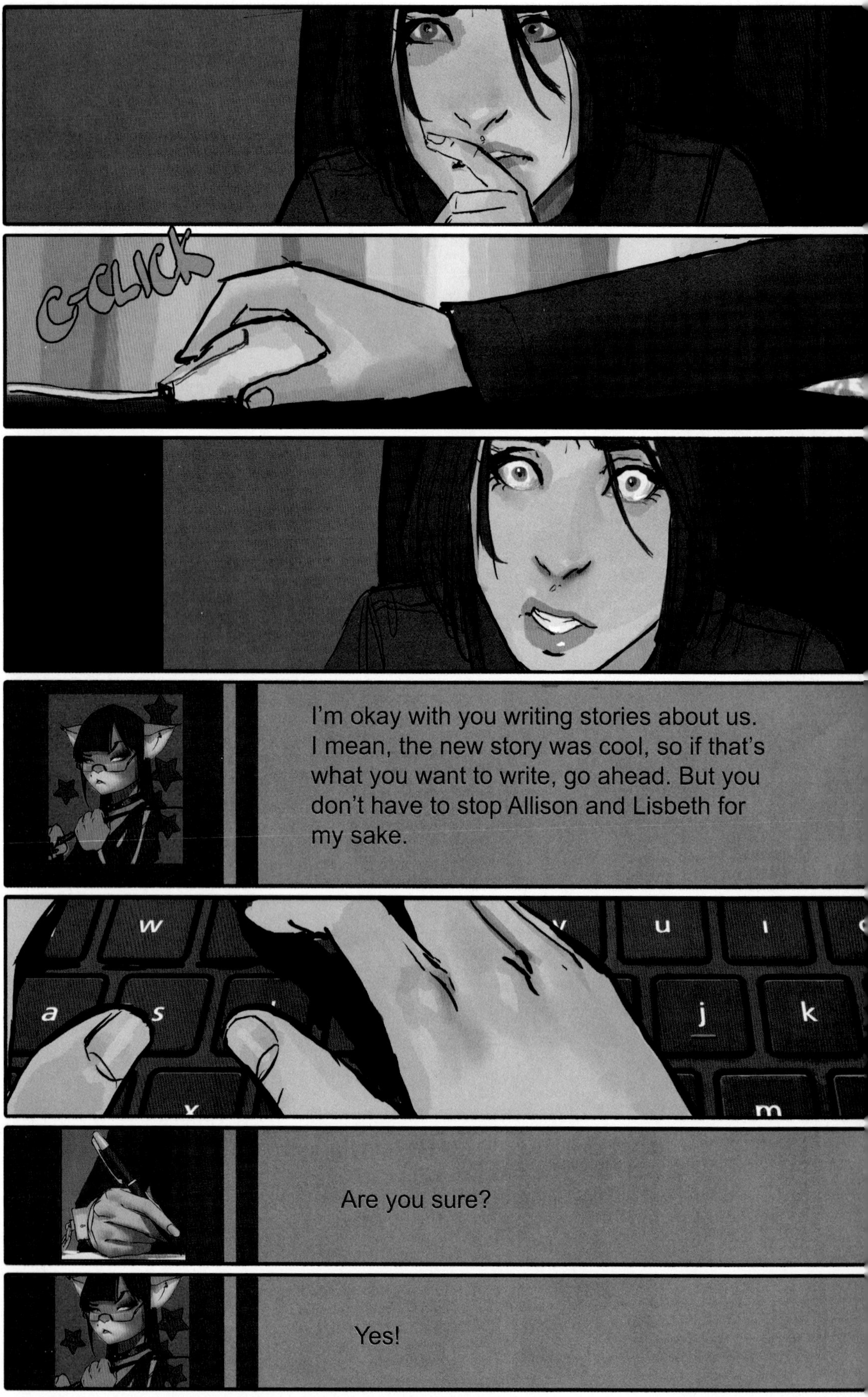
C-CLICK
I'm okay with you writing stories about us. I mean, the new story was cool, so if that's what you want to write, go ahead. But you don't have to stop Allison and Lisbeth for my sake.
Are you sure?
Yes!

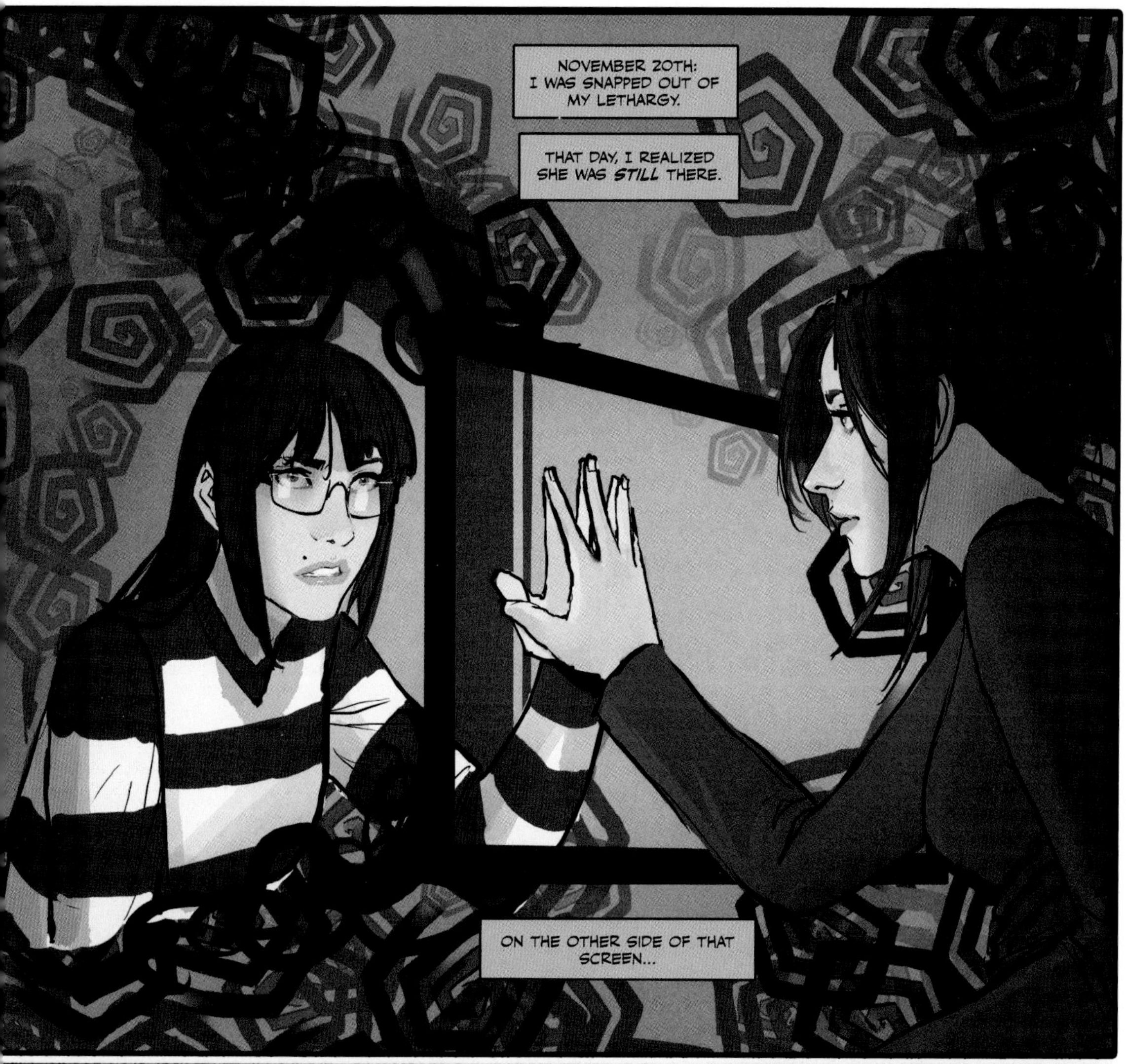
NOVEMBER 20TH: I WAS SNAPPED OUT OF MY LETHARGY.
THAT DAY, I REALIZED SHE WAS *STILL* THERE.
ON THE OTHER SIDE OF THAT SCREEN...

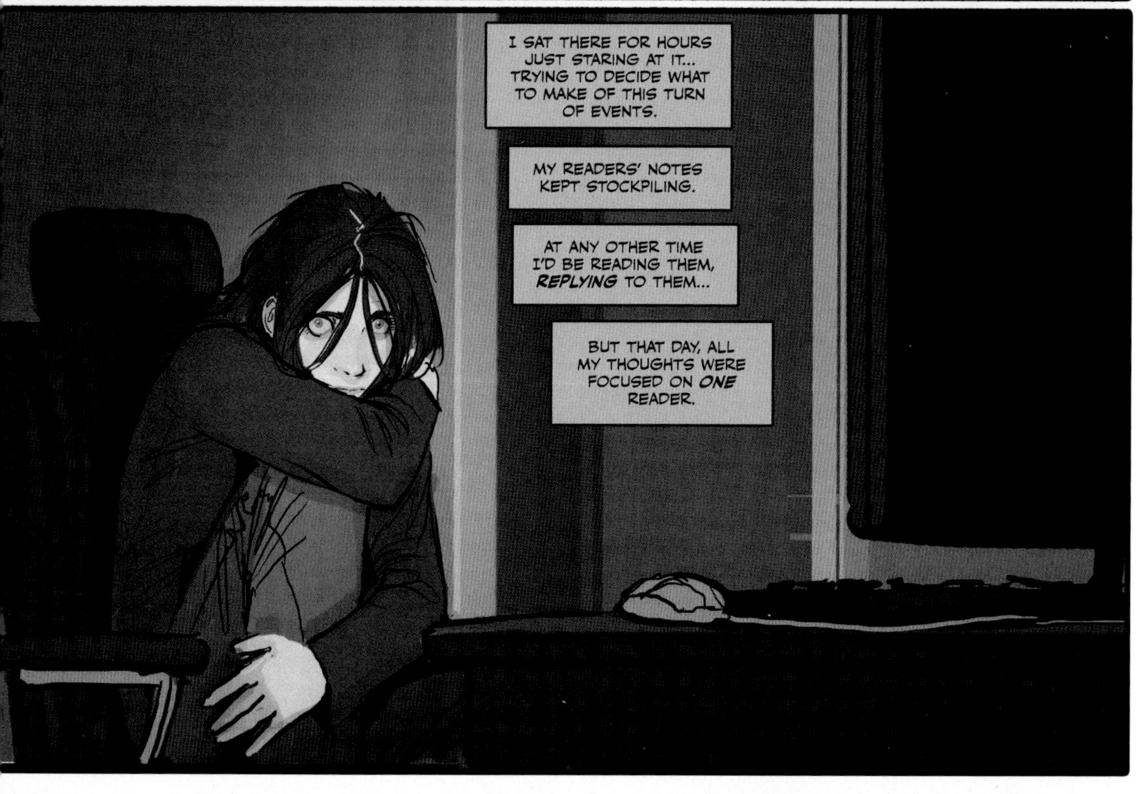
I SAT THERE FOR HOURS JUST STARING AT IT... TRYING TO DECIDE WHAT TO MAKE OF THIS TURN OF EVENTS.
MY READERS' NOTES KEPT STOCKPILING.
AT ANY OTHER TIME I'D BE READING THEM, *REPLYING* TO THEM...
BUT THAT DAY, ALL MY THOUGHTS WERE FOCUSED ON *ONE* READER.

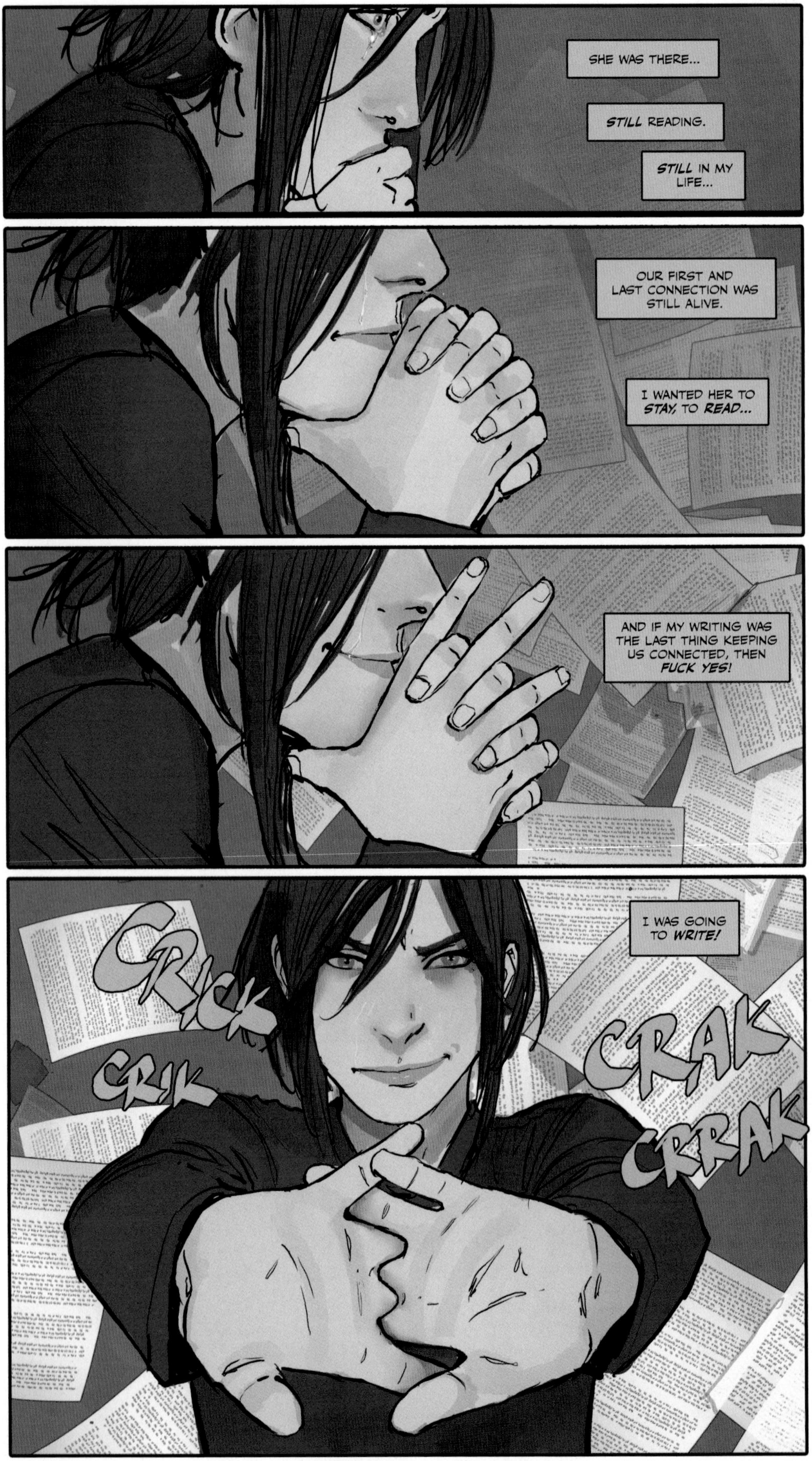
SHE WAS THERE...
STILL READING.
STILL IN MY LIFE...
OUR FIRST AND LAST CONNECTION WAS STILL ALIVE.
I WANTED HER TO STAY, TO READ...
AND IF MY WRITING WAS THE LAST THING KEEPING US CONNECTED, THEN FUCK YES!
I WAS GOING TO WRITE!
CRICK
CRIK
CRAK
CRRAK

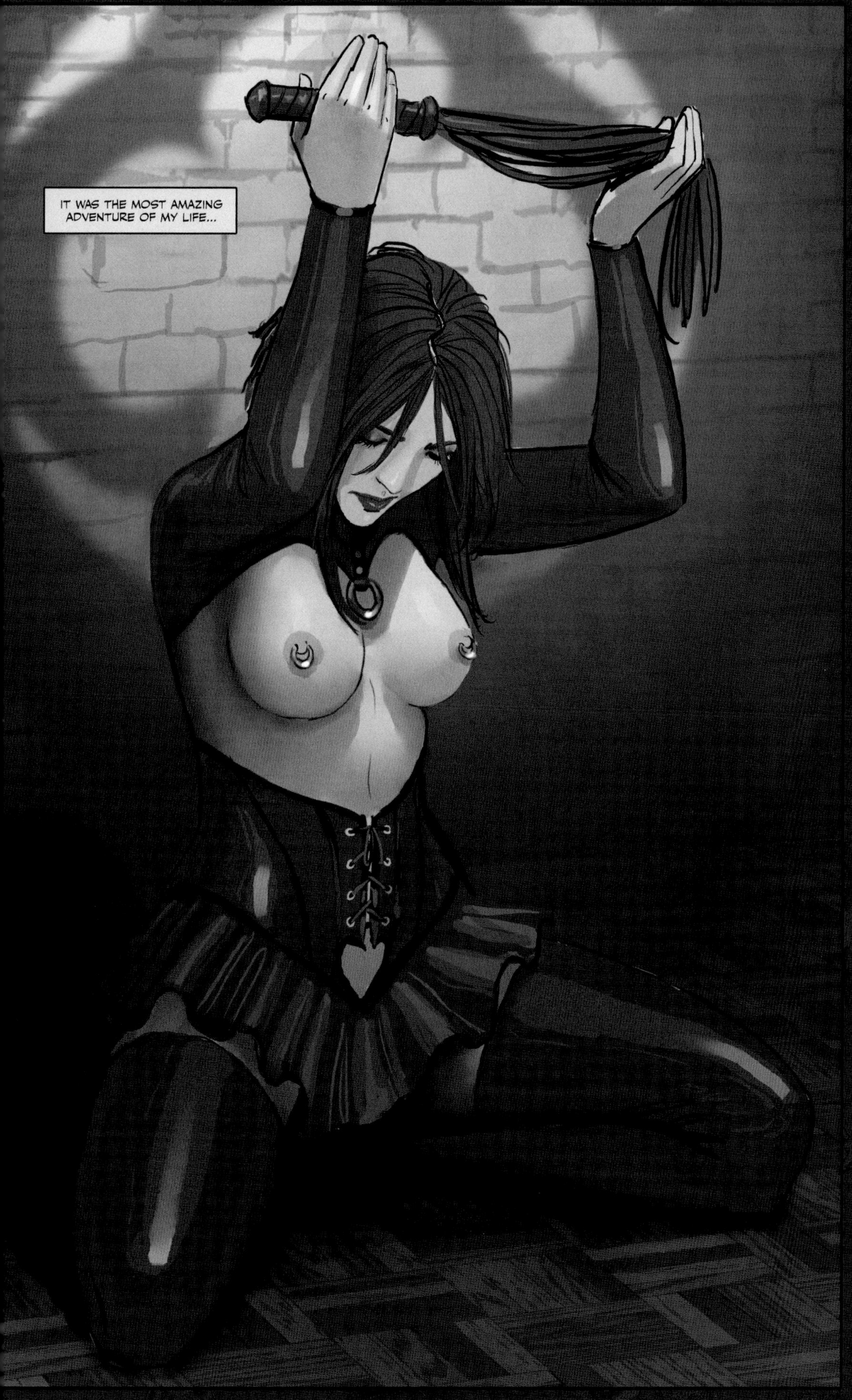
IT WAS THE MOST AMAZING
ADVENTURE OF MY LIFE...

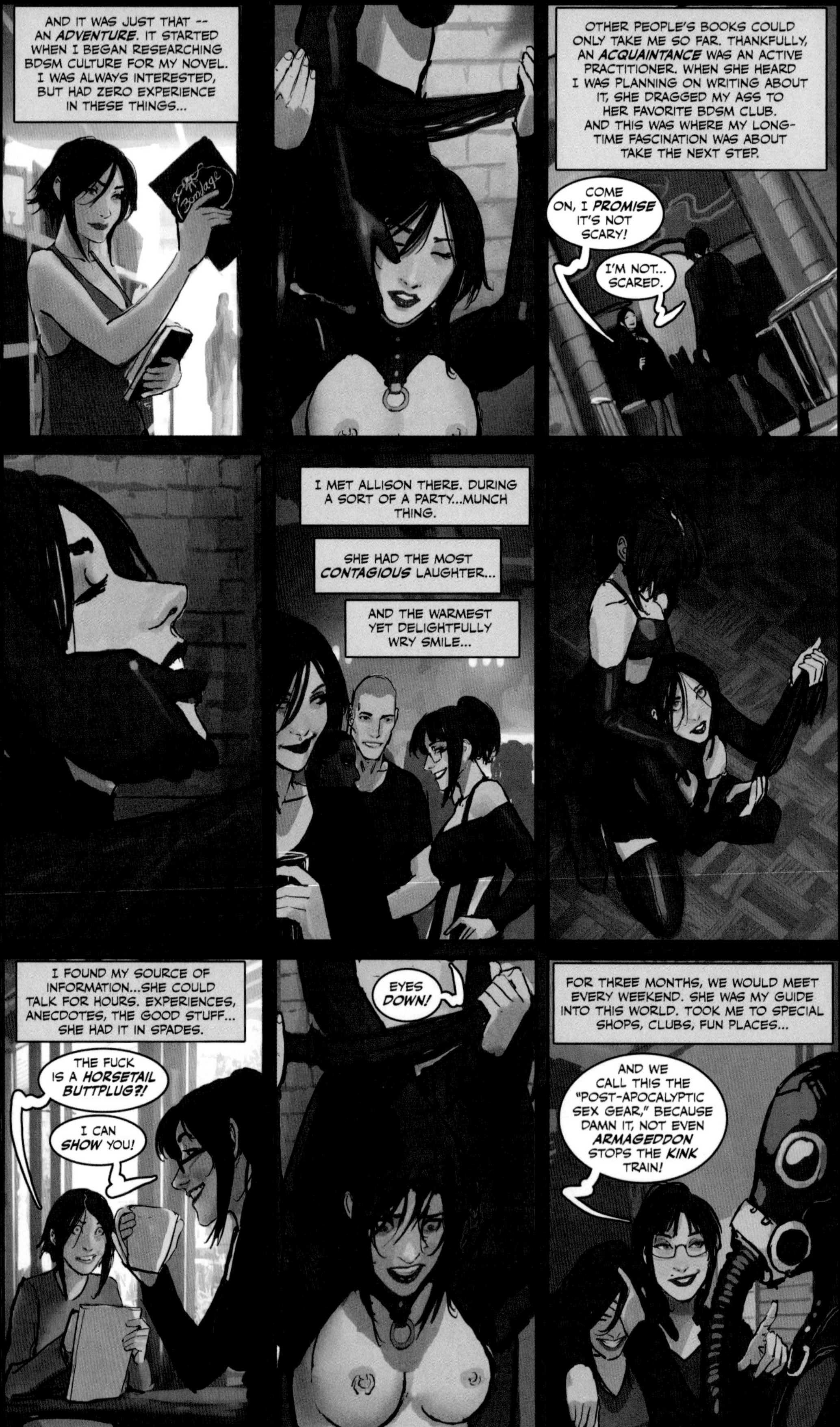
AND IT WAS JUST THAT -- AN ADVENTURE. IT STARTED WHEN I BEGAN RESEARCHING BDSM CULTURE FOR MY NOVEL. I WAS ALWAYS INTERESTED, BUT HAD ZERO EXPERIENCE IN THESE THINGS...
Bondage
OTHER PEOPLE'S BOOKS COULD ONLY TAKE ME SO FAR. THANKFULLY, AN ACQUAINTANCE WAS AN ACTIVE PRACTITIONER. WHEN SHE HEARD I WAS PLANNING ON WRITING ABOUT IT, SHE DRAGGED MY ASS TO HER FAVORITE BDSM CLUB. AND THIS WAS WHERE MY LONG-TIME FASCINATION WAS ABOUT TAKE THE NEXT STEP.
COME ON, I PROMISE IT'S NOT SCARY!
I'M NOT... SCARED.
I MET ALLISON THERE. DURING A SORT OF A PARTY...MUNCH THING.
SHE HAD THE MOST CONTAGIOUS LAUGHTER...
AND THE WARMEST YET DELIGHTFULLY WRY SMILE...
I FOUND MY SOURCE OF INFORMATION...SHE COULD TALK FOR HOURS. EXPERIENCES, ANECDOTES, THE GOOD STUFF... SHE HAD IT IN SPADES.
THE FUCK IS A HORSETAIL BUTTPLUG?!
I CAN SHOW YOU!
EYES DOWN!
FOR THREE MONTHS, WE WOULD MEET EVERY WEEKEND. SHE WAS MY GUIDE INTO THIS WORLD. TOOK ME TO SPECIAL SHOPS, CLUBS, FUN PLACES...
AND WE CALL THIS THE "POST-APOCALYPTIC SEX GEAR," BECAUSE DAMN IT, NOT EVEN ARMAGEDDON STOPS THE KINK TRAIN!

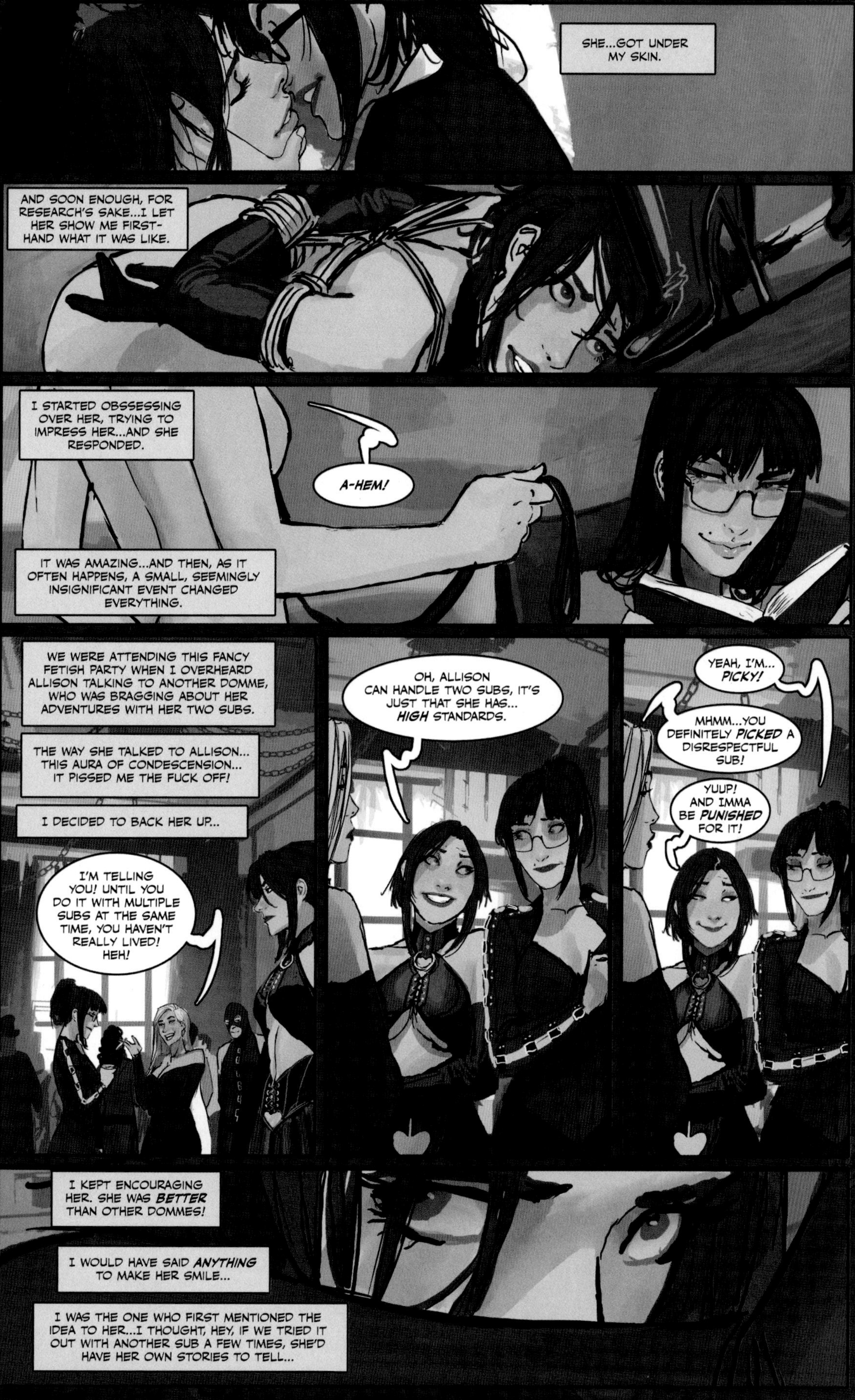
SHE...GOT UNDER MY SKIN.
AND SOON ENOUGH, FOR RESEARCH'S SAKE...I LET HER SHOW ME FIRST-HAND WHAT IT WAS LIKE.
I STARTED OBSSESSING OVER HER, TRYING TO IMPRESS HER...AND SHE RESPONDED.
A-HEM!
IT WAS AMAZING...AND THEN, AS IT OFTEN HAPPENS, A SMALL, SEEMINGLY INSIGNIFICANT EVENT CHANGED EVERYTHING.
WE WERE ATTENDING THIS FANCY FETISH PARTY WHEN I OVERHEARD ALLISON TALKING TO ANOTHER DOMME, WHO WAS BRAGGING ABOUT HER ADVENTURES WITH HER TWO SUBS.
THE WAY SHE TALKED TO ALLISON... THIS AURA OF CONDESCENSION... IT PISSED ME THE FUCK OFF!
I DECIDED TO BACK HER UP...
I'M TELLING YOU! UNTIL YOU DO IT WITH MULTIPLE SUBS AT THE SAME TIME, YOU HAVEN'T REALLY LIVED! HEH!
OH, ALLISON CAN HANDLE TWO SUBS, IT'S JUST THAT SHE HAS... HIGH STANDARDS.
YEAH, I'M... PICKY!
MHMM...YOU DEFINITELY PICKED A DISRESPECTFUL SUB!
YUUP! AND IMMA BE PUNISHED FOR IT!
I KEPT ENCOURAGING HER. SHE WAS BETTER THAN OTHER DOMMES!
I WOULD HAVE SAID ANYTHING TO MAKE HER SMILE...
I WAS THE ONE WHO FIRST MENTIONED THE IDEA TO HER...I THOUGHT, HEY, IF WE TRIED IT OUT WITH ANOTHER SUB A FEW TIMES, SHE'D HAVE HER OWN STORIES TO TELL...

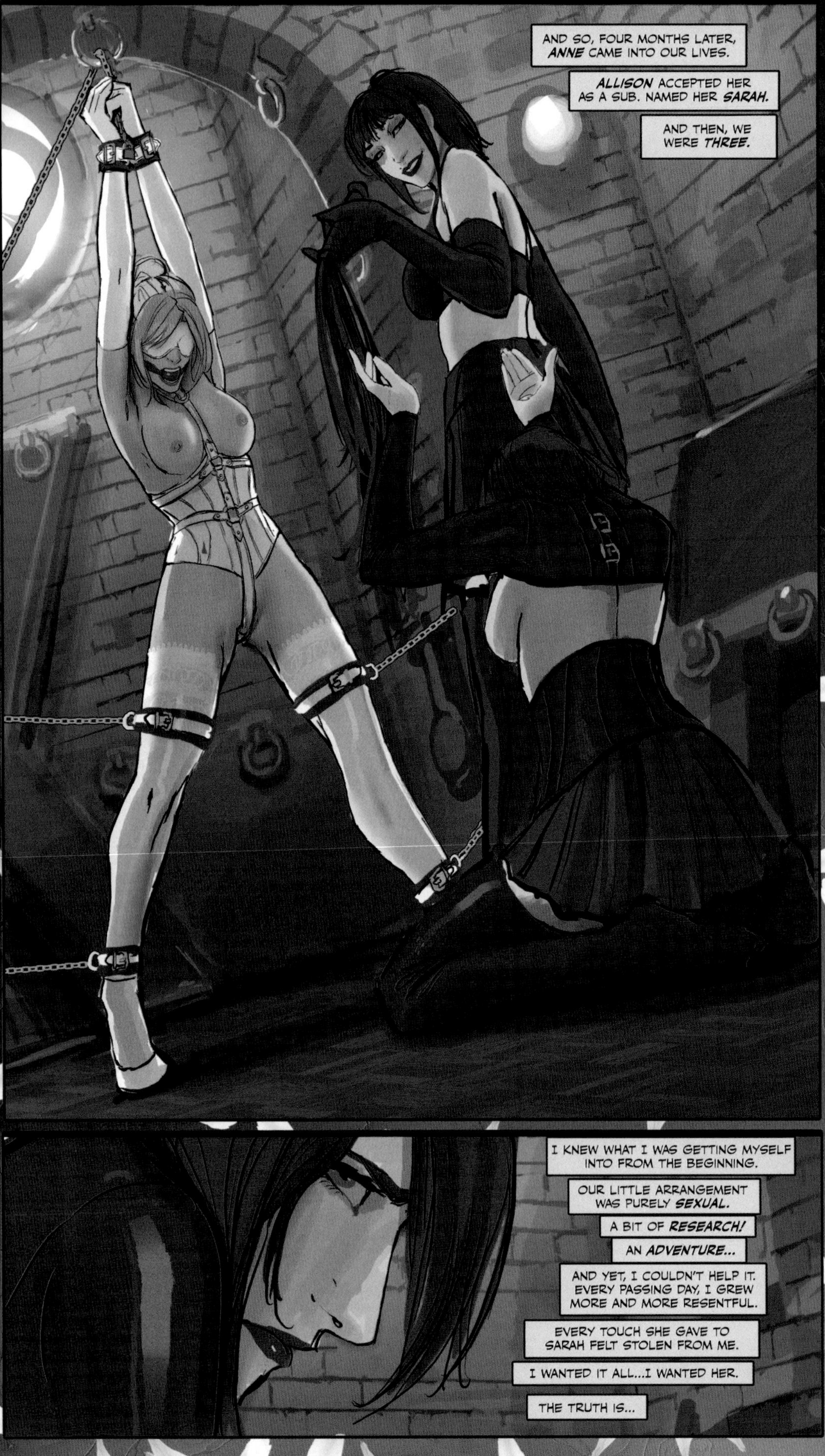
AND SO, FOUR MONTHS LATER, ANNE CAME INTO OUR LIVES.
ALLISON ACCEPTED HER AS A SUB. NAMED HER SARAH.
AND THEN, WE WERE THREE.
I KNEW WHAT I WAS GETTING MYSELF INTO FROM THE BEGINNING.
OUR LITTLE ARRANGEMENT WAS PURELY SEXUAL.
A BIT OF RESEARCH!
AN ADVENTURE...
AND YET, I COULDN'T HELP IT. EVERY PASSING DAY, I GREW MORE AND MORE RESENTFUL.
EVERY TOUCH SHE GAVE TO SARAH FELT STOLEN FROM ME.
I WANTED IT ALL...I WANTED HER.
THE TRUTH IS...

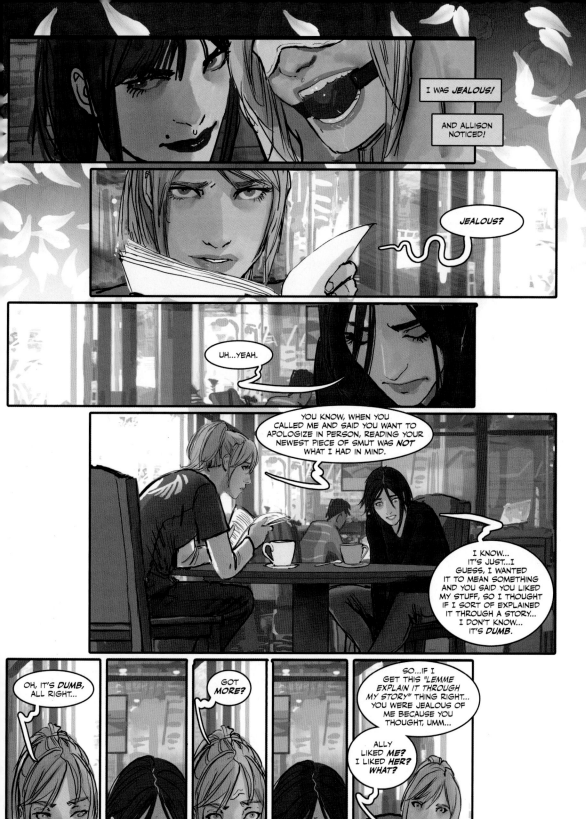

I WAS *JEALOUS!*

AND ALLISON NOTICED!

JEALOUS?

UH...YEAH.

YOU KNOW, WHEN YOU CALLED ME AND SAID YOU WANT TO APOLOGIZE IN PERSON, READING YOUR NEWEST PIECE OF SMUT WAS *NOT* WHAT I HAD IN MIND.

I KNOW... IT'S JUST...I GUESS, I WANTED IT TO MEAN SOMETHING AND YOU SAID YOU LIKED MY STUFF, SO I THOUGHT IF I SORT OF EXPLAINED IT THROUGH A STORY... I DON'T KNOW... IT'S *DUMB.*

OH, IT'S *DUMB,* ALL RIGHT...

GOT *MORE?*

SO...IF I GET THIS *"LEMME EXPLAIN IT THROUGH MY STORY"* THING RIGHT... YOU WERE JEALOUS OF ME BECAUSE YOU THOUGHT, UMM...

ALLY LIKED *ME?* I LIKED *HER?* WHAT?

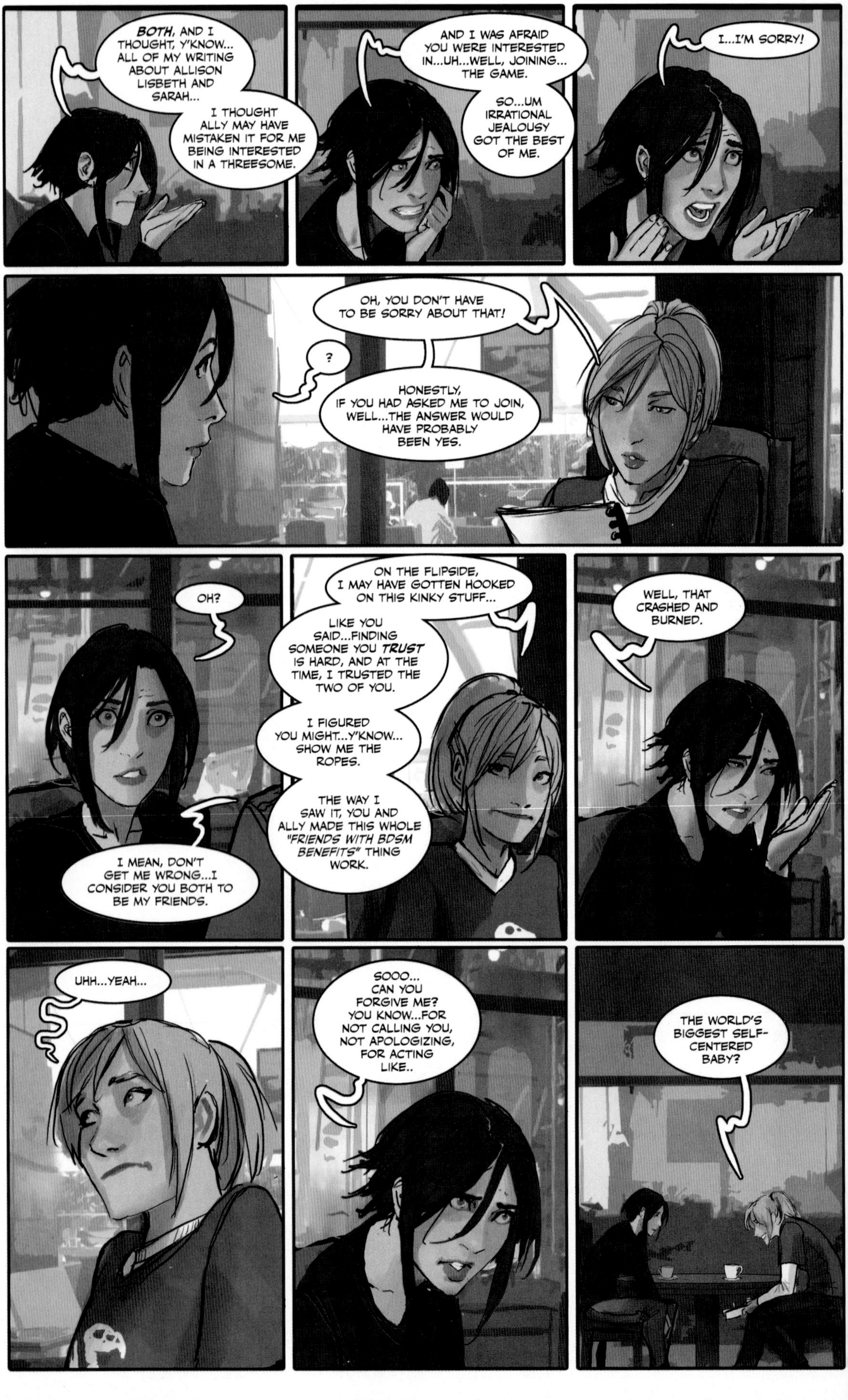
BOTH, AND I THOUGHT, Y'KNOW... ALL OF MY WRITING ABOUT ALLISON LISBETH AND SARAH...
I THOUGHT ALLY MAY HAVE MISTAKEN IT FOR ME BEING INTERESTED IN A THREESOME.
AND I WAS AFRAID YOU WERE INTERESTED IN...UH...WELL, JOINING... THE GAME.
SO...UM IRRATIONAL JEALOUSY GOT THE BEST OF ME.
I...I'M SORRY!
OH, YOU DON'T HAVE TO BE SORRY ABOUT THAT!
?
HONESTLY, IF YOU HAD ASKED ME TO JOIN, WELL...THE ANSWER WOULD HAVE PROBABLY BEEN YES.
OH?
I MEAN, DON'T GET ME WRONG...I CONSIDER YOU BOTH TO BE MY FRIENDS.
ON THE FLIPSIDE, I MAY HAVE GOTTEN HOOKED ON THIS KINKY STUFF...
LIKE YOU SAID...FINDING SOMEONE YOU TRUST IS HARD, AND AT THE TIME, I TRUSTED THE TWO OF YOU.
I FIGURED YOU MIGHT...Y'KNOW... SHOW ME THE ROPES.
THE WAY I SAW IT, YOU AND ALLY MADE THIS WHOLE "FRIENDS WITH BDSM BENEFITS" THING WORK.
WELL, THAT CRASHED AND BURNED.
UHH...YEAH...
SOOO... CAN YOU FORGIVE ME? YOU KNOW...FOR NOT CALLING YOU, NOT APOLOGIZING, FOR ACTING LIKE..
THE WORLD'S BIGGEST SELF-CENTERED BABY?

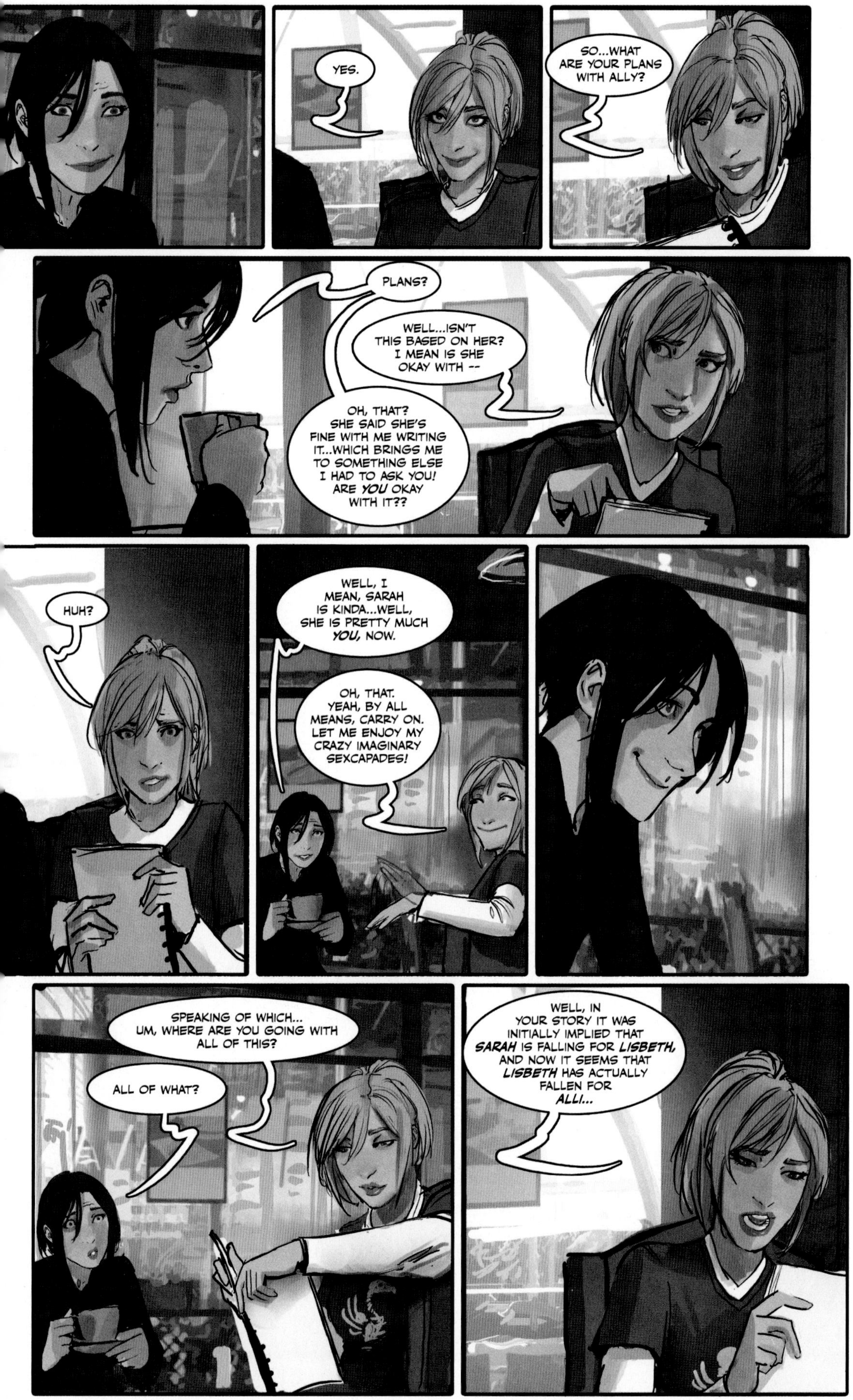
YES.
SO...WHAT ARE YOUR PLANS WITH ALLY?
PLANS?
WELL...ISN'T THIS BASED ON HER? I MEAN IS SHE OKAY WITH --
OH, THAT? SHE SAID SHE'S FINE WITH ME WRITING IT...WHICH BRINGS ME TO SOMETHING ELSE I HAD TO ASK YOU! ARE *YOU* OKAY WITH IT??
HUH?
WELL, I MEAN, SARAH IS KINDA...WELL, SHE IS PRETTY MUCH *YOU,* NOW.
OH, THAT. YEAH, BY ALL MEANS, CARRY ON. LET ME ENJOY MY CRAZY IMAGINARY SEXCAPADES!
SPEAKING OF WHICH... UM, WHERE ARE YOU GOING WITH ALL OF THIS?
ALL OF WHAT?
WELL, IN YOUR STORY IT WAS INITIALLY IMPLIED THAT *SARAH* IS FALLING FOR *LISBETH,* AND NOW IT SEEMS THAT *LISBETH* HAS ACTUALLY FALLEN FOR *ALLI...*

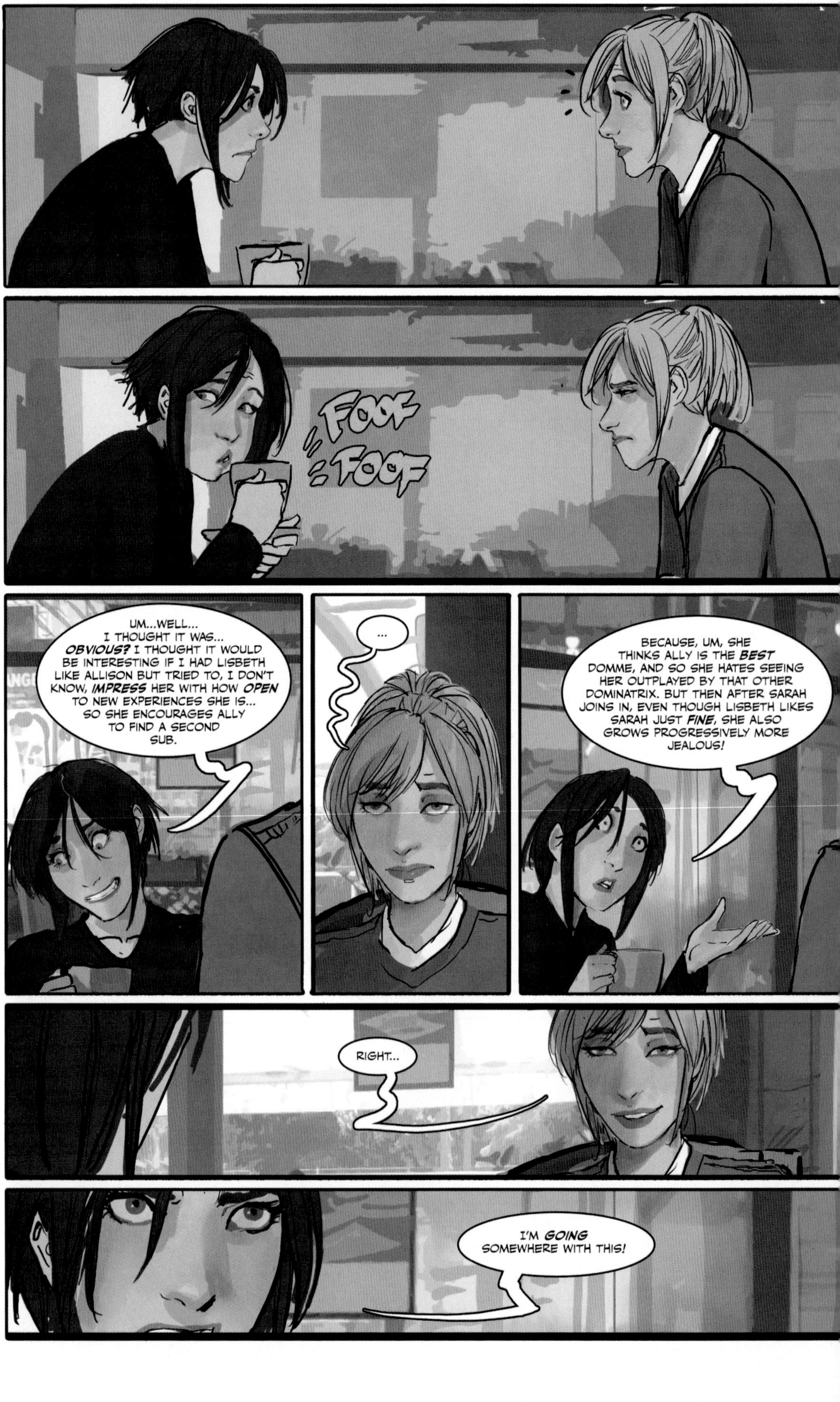
FOOF
FOOF
UM...WELL... I THOUGHT IT WAS... OBVIOUS? I THOUGHT IT WOULD BE INTERESTING IF I HAD LISBETH LIKE ALLISON BUT TRIED TO, I DON'T KNOW, IMPRESS HER WITH HOW OPEN TO NEW EXPERIENCES SHE IS... SO SHE ENCOURAGES ALLY TO FIND A SECOND SUB.
...
BECAUSE, UM, SHE THINKS ALLY IS THE BEST DOMME, AND SO SHE HATES SEEING HER OUTPLAYED BY THAT OTHER DOMINATRIX. BUT THEN AFTER SARAH JOINS IN, EVEN THOUGH LISBETH LIKES SARAH JUST FINE, SHE ALSO GROWS PROGRESSIVELY MORE JEALOUS!
RIGHT...
I'M GOING SOMEWHERE WITH THIS!

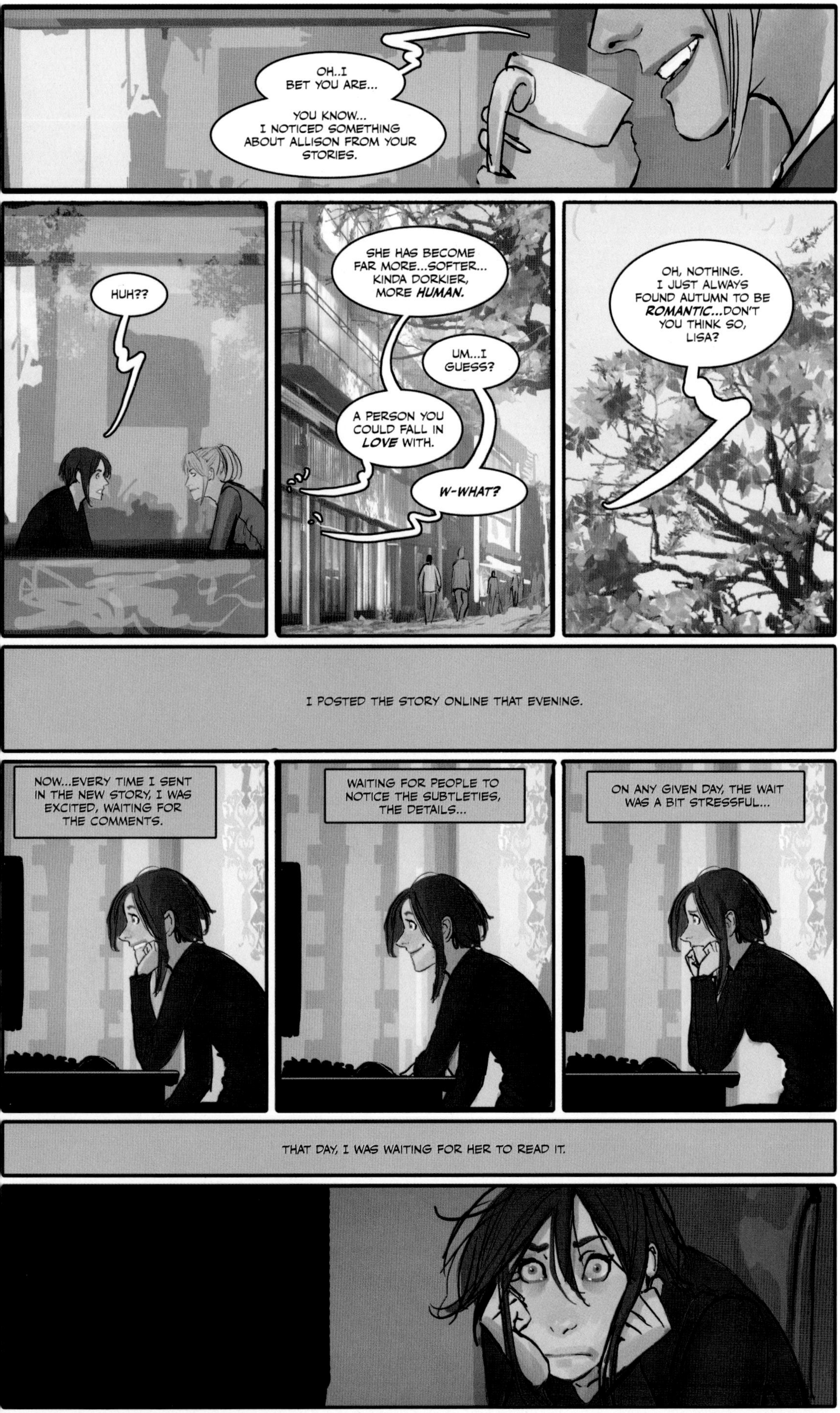
OH..I BET YOU ARE...
YOU KNOW... I NOTICED SOMETHING ABOUT ALLISON FROM YOUR STORIES.
HUH??
SHE HAS BECOME FAR MORE...SOFTER... KINDA DORKIER, MORE HUMAN.
UM...I GUESS?
A PERSON YOU COULD FALL IN LOVE WITH.
W-WHAT?
OH, NOTHING. I JUST ALWAYS FOUND AUTUMN TO BE ROMANTIC...DON'T YOU THINK SO, LISA?
I POSTED THE STORY ONLINE THAT EVENING.
NOW...EVERY TIME I SENT IN THE NEW STORY, I WAS EXCITED, WAITING FOR THE COMMENTS.
WAITING FOR PEOPLE TO NOTICE THE SUBTLETIES, THE DETAILS...
ON ANY GIVEN DAY, THE WAIT WAS A BIT STRESSFUL...
THAT DAY, I WAS WAITING FOR HER TO READ IT.

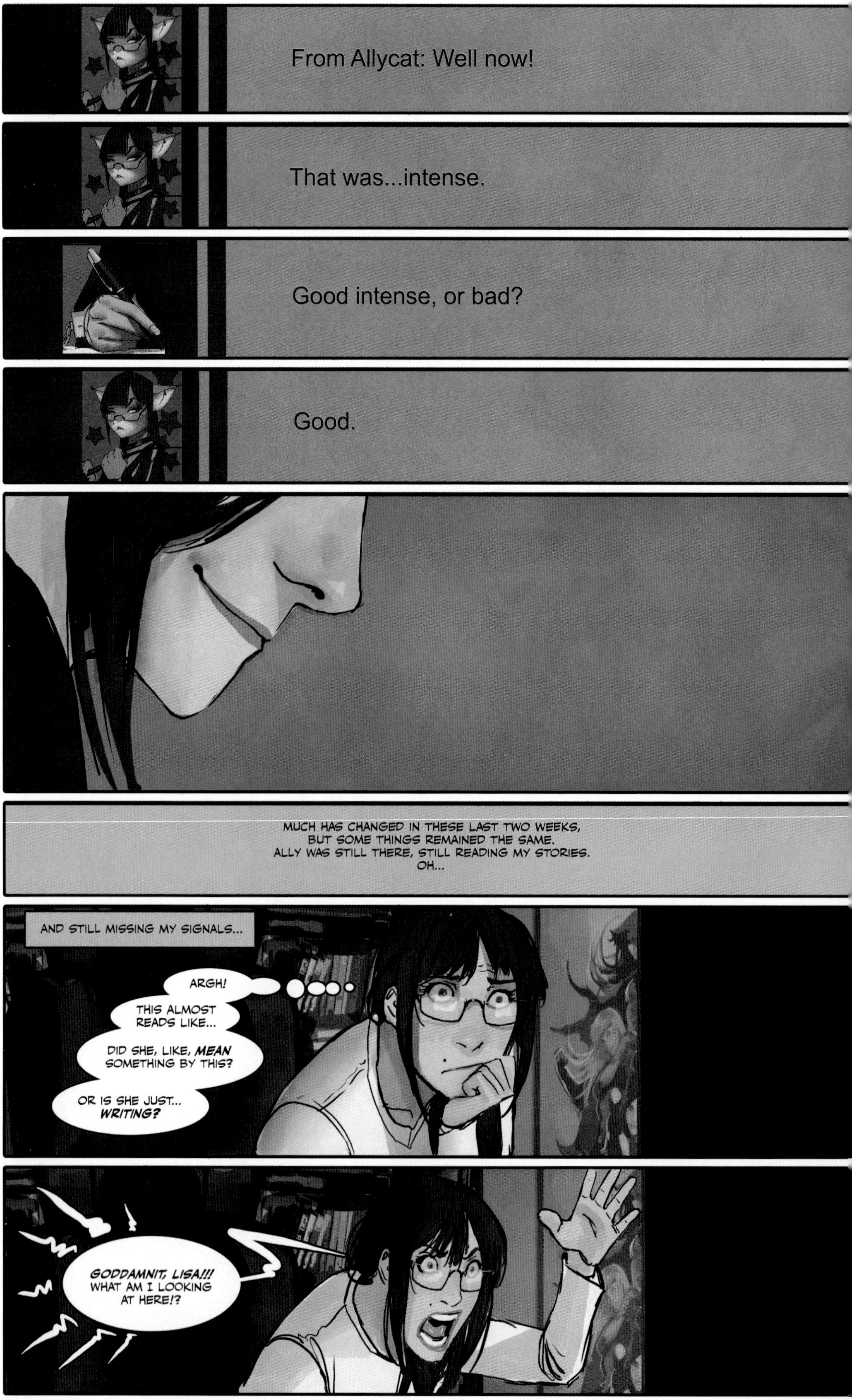
From Allycat: Well now!
That was...intense.
Good intense, or bad?
Good.
MUCH HAS CHANGED IN THESE LAST TWO WEEKS, BUT SOME THINGS REMAINED THE SAME. ALLY WAS STILL THERE, STILL READING MY STORIES. OH...
AND STILL MISSING MY SIGNALS...
ARGH!
THIS ALMOST READS LIKE...
DID SHE, LIKE, MEAN SOMETHING BY THIS?
OR IS SHE JUST... WRITING?
GODDAMNIT, LISA!!! WHAT AM I LOOKING AT HERE!?

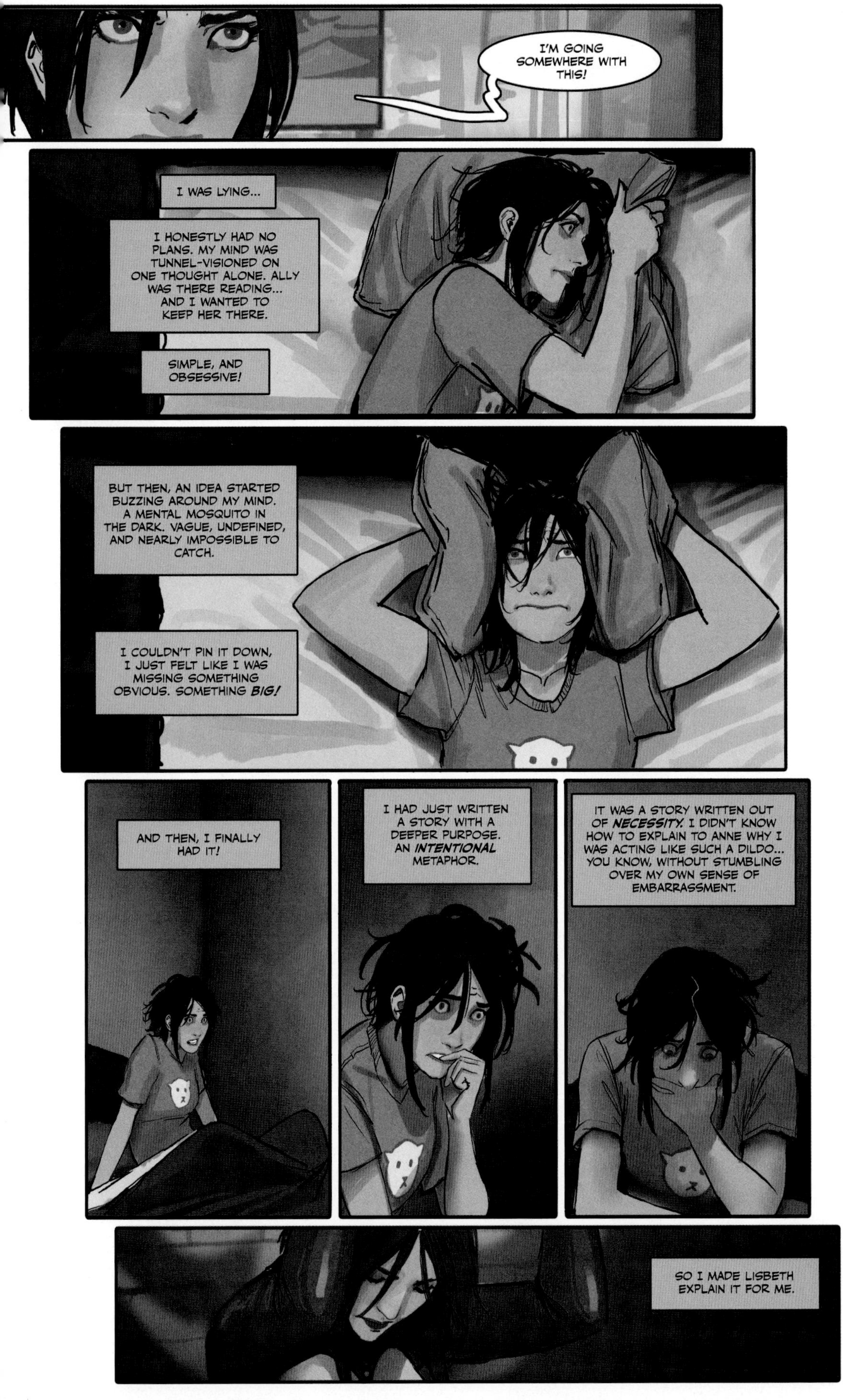
I'M GOING SOMEWHERE WITH THIS!
I WAS LYING...
I HONESTLY HAD NO PLANS. MY MIND WAS TUNNEL-VISIONED ON ONE THOUGHT ALONE. ALLY WAS THERE READING... AND I WANTED TO KEEP HER THERE.
SIMPLE, AND OBSESSIVE!
BUT THEN, AN IDEA STARTED BUZZING AROUND MY MIND. A MENTAL MOSQUITO IN THE DARK. VAGUE, UNDEFINED, AND NEARLY IMPOSSIBLE TO CATCH.
I COULDN'T PIN IT DOWN, I JUST FELT LIKE I WAS MISSING SOMETHING OBVIOUS. SOMETHING *BIG!*
AND THEN, I FINALLY HAD IT!
I HAD JUST WRITTEN A STORY WITH A DEEPER PURPOSE. AN *INTENTIONAL* METAPHOR.
IT WAS A STORY WRITTEN OUT OF *NECESSITY.* I DIDN'T KNOW HOW TO EXPLAIN TO ANNE WHY I WAS ACTING LIKE SUCH A DILDO... YOU KNOW, WITHOUT STUMBLING OVER MY OWN SENSE OF EMBARRASSMENT.
SO I MADE LISBETH EXPLAIN IT FOR ME.

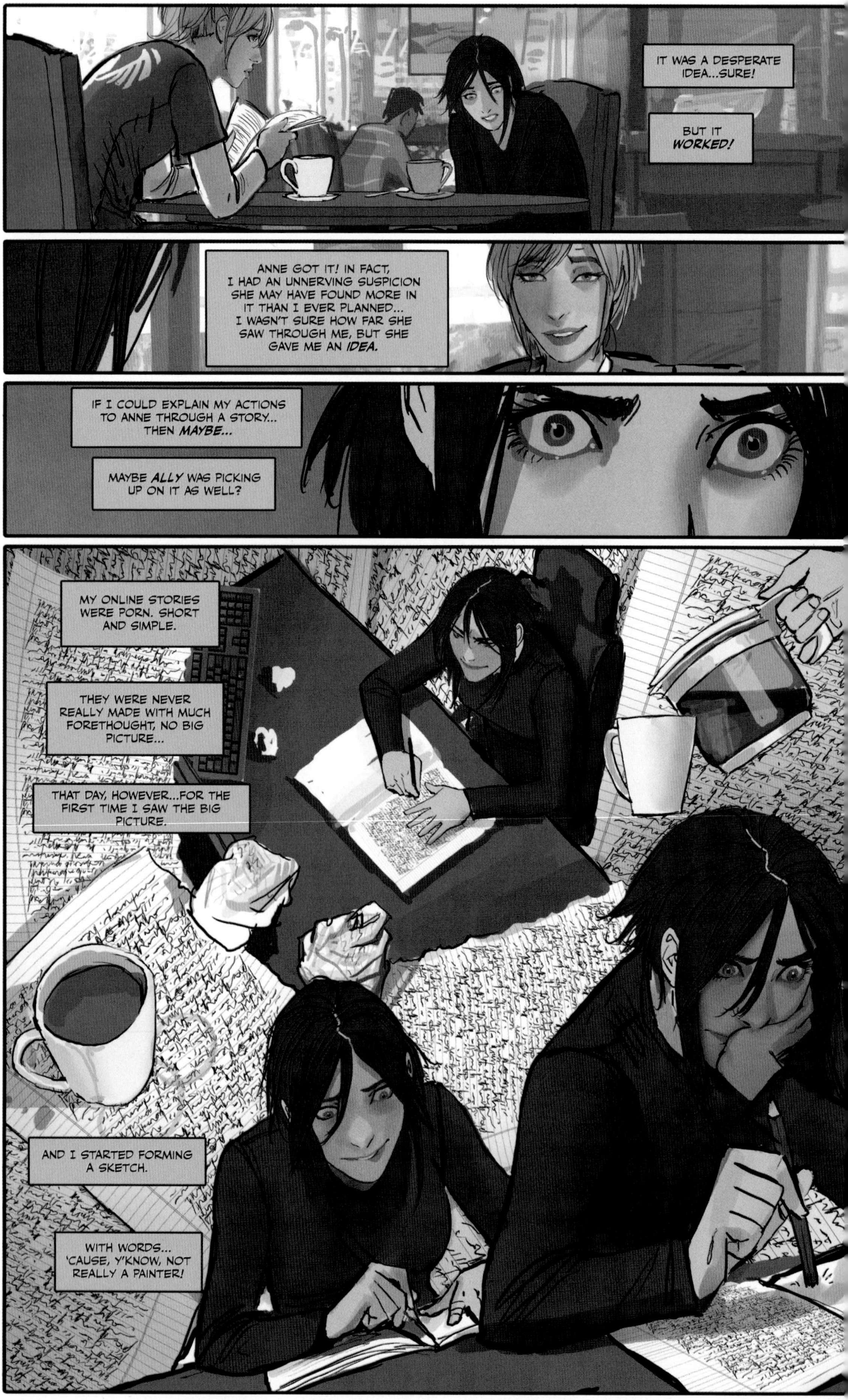
IT WAS A DESPERATE IDEA...SURE!
BUT IT WORKED!
ANNE GOT IT! IN FACT, I HAD AN UNNERVING SUSPICION SHE MAY HAVE FOUND MORE IN IT THAN I EVER PLANNED... I WASN'T SURE HOW FAR SHE SAW THROUGH ME, BUT SHE GAVE ME AN IDEA.
IF I COULD EXPLAIN MY ACTIONS TO ANNE THROUGH A STORY... THEN MAYBE...
MAYBE ALLY WAS PICKING UP ON IT AS WELL?
MY ONLINE STORIES WERE PORN. SHORT AND SIMPLE.
THEY WERE NEVER REALLY MADE WITH MUCH FORETHOUGHT, NO BIG PICTURE...
THAT DAY, HOWEVER...FOR THE FIRST TIME I SAW THE BIG PICTURE.
AND I STARTED FORMING A SKETCH.
WITH WORDS... 'CAUSE, Y'KNOW, NOT REALLY A PAINTER!

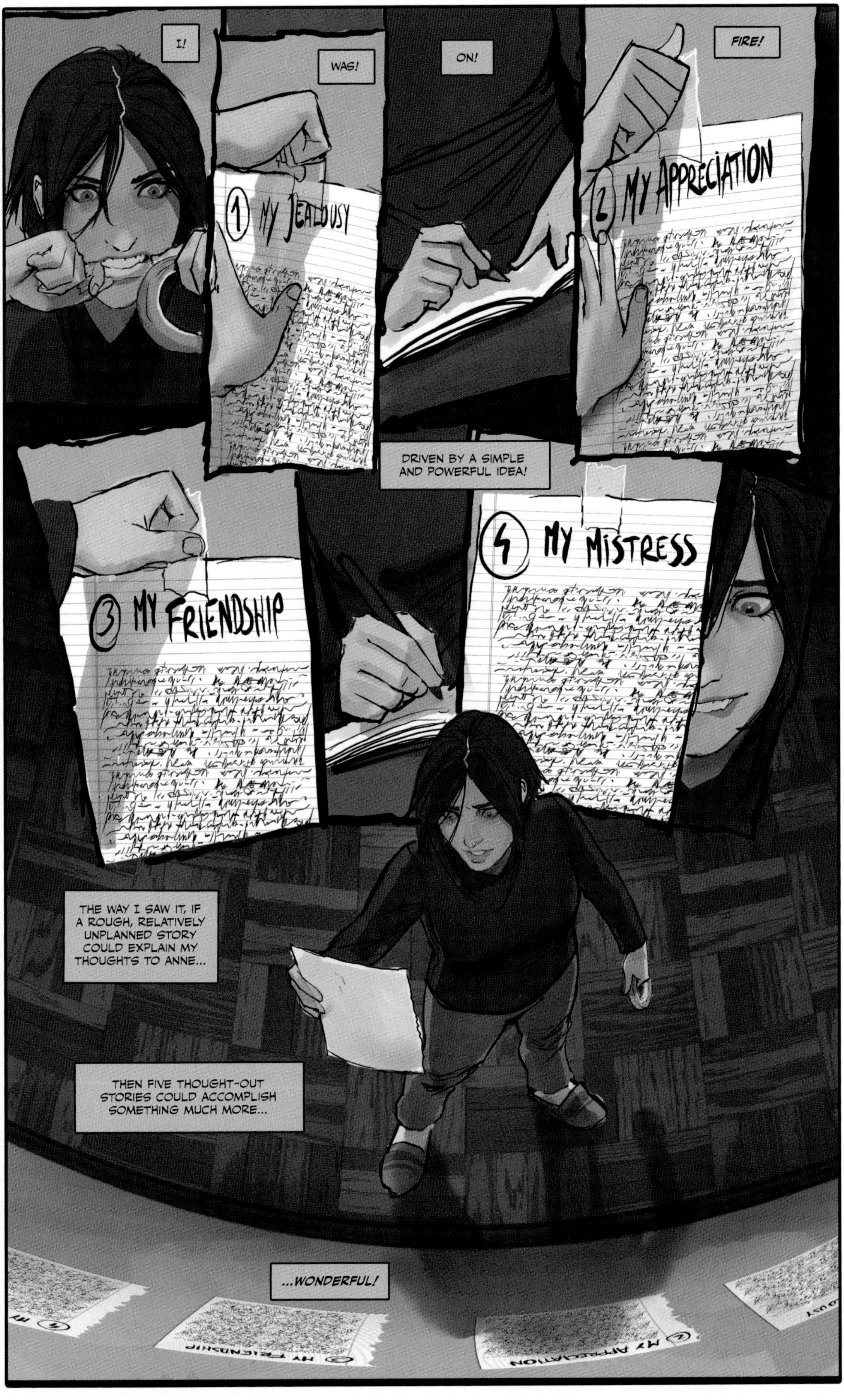
I!
WAS!
ON!
FIRE!
1 MY JEALOUSY
2 MY APPRECIATION
DRIVEN BY A SIMPLE AND POWERFUL IDEA!
3 MY FRIENDSHIP
4 MY MISTRESS
THE WAY I SAW IT, IF A ROUGH, RELATIVELY UNPLANNED STORY COULD EXPLAIN MY THOUGHTS TO ANNE...
THEN FIVE THOUGHT-OUT STORIES COULD ACCOMPLISH SOMETHING MUCH MORE...
...WONDERFUL!

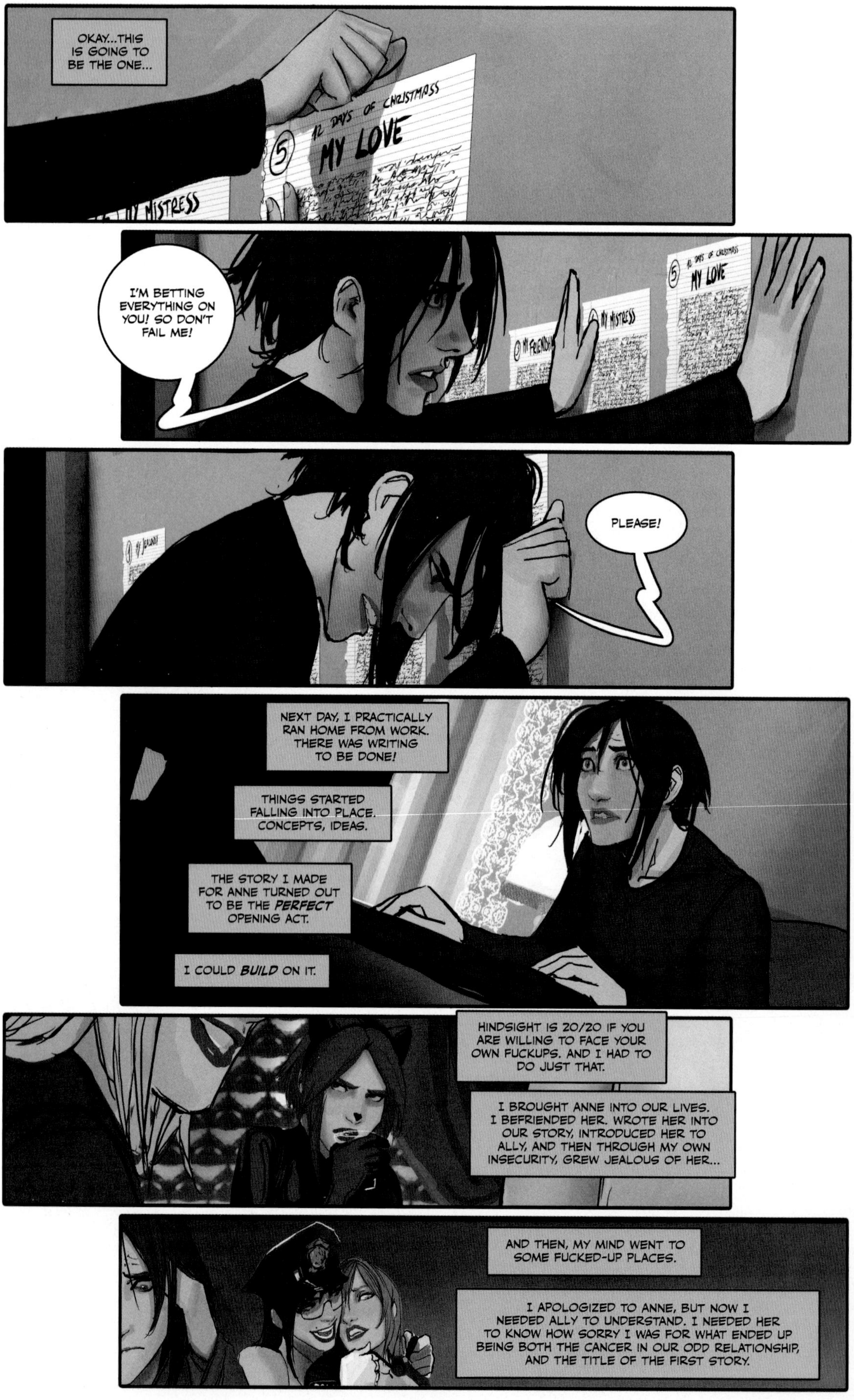
OKAY...THIS IS GOING TO BE THE ONE...
12 DAYS OF CHRISTMASS
MY LOVE
MY MISTRESS
I'M BETTING EVERYTHING ON YOU! SO DON'T FAIL ME!
PLEASE!
NEXT DAY, I PRACTICALLY RAN HOME FROM WORK. THERE WAS WRITING TO BE DONE!
THINGS STARTED FALLING INTO PLACE. CONCEPTS, IDEAS.
THE STORY I MADE FOR ANNE TURNED OUT TO BE THE *PERFECT* OPENING ACT.
I COULD *BUILD* ON IT.
HINDSIGHT IS 20/20 IF YOU ARE WILLING TO FACE YOUR OWN FUCKUPS. AND I HAD TO DO JUST THAT.
I BROUGHT ANNE INTO OUR LIVES. I BEFRIENDED HER. WROTE HER INTO OUR STORY, INTRODUCED HER TO ALLY, AND THEN THROUGH MY OWN INSECURITY, GREW JEALOUS OF HER...
AND THEN, MY MIND WENT TO SOME FUCKED-UP PLACES.
I APOLOGIZED TO ANNE, BUT NOW I NEEDED ALLY TO UNDERSTAND. I NEEDED HER TO KNOW HOW SORRY I WAS FOR WHAT ENDED UP BEING BOTH THE CANCER IN OUR ODD RELATIONSHIP, AND THE TITLE OF THE FIRST STORY.

MY JEALOUSY

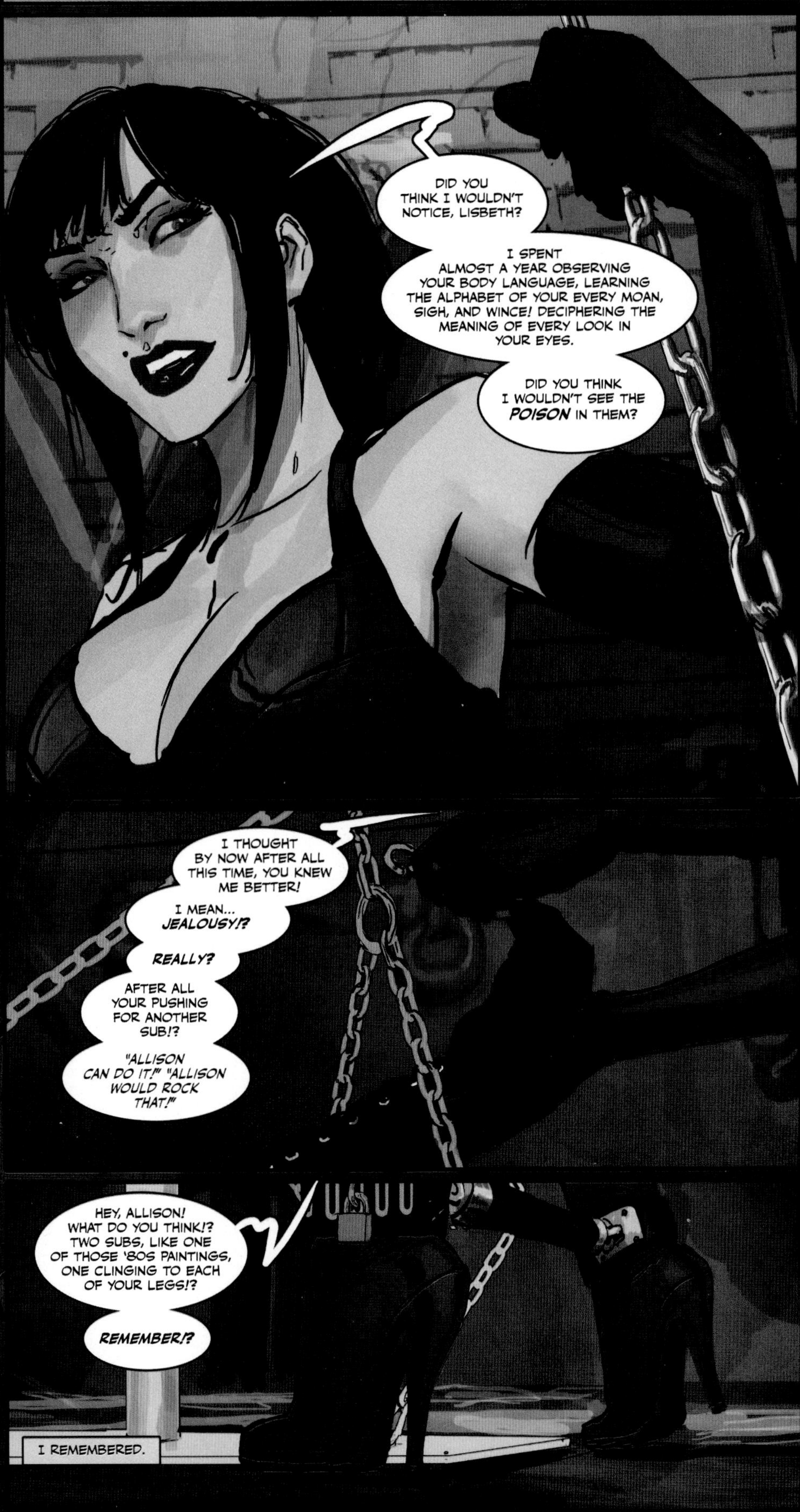
DID YOU THINK I WOULDN'T NOTICE, LISBETH?
I SPENT ALMOST A YEAR OBSERVING YOUR BODY LANGUAGE, LEARNING THE ALPHABET OF YOUR EVERY MOAN, SIGH, AND WINCE! DECIPHERING THE MEANING OF EVERY LOOK IN YOUR EYES.
DID YOU THINK I WOULDN'T SEE THE *POISON* IN THEM?
I THOUGHT BY NOW AFTER ALL THIS TIME, YOU KNEW ME BETTER!
I MEAN... *JEALOUSY!?*
REALLY?
AFTER ALL YOUR PUSHING FOR ANOTHER SUB!?
"ALLISON CAN DO IT!" "ALLISON WOULD ROCK THAT!"
HEY, ALLISON! WHAT DO YOU THINK!? TWO SUBS, LIKE ONE OF THOSE '80S PAINTINGS, ONE CLINGING TO EACH OF YOUR LEGS!?
REMEMBER!?
I REMEMBERED.

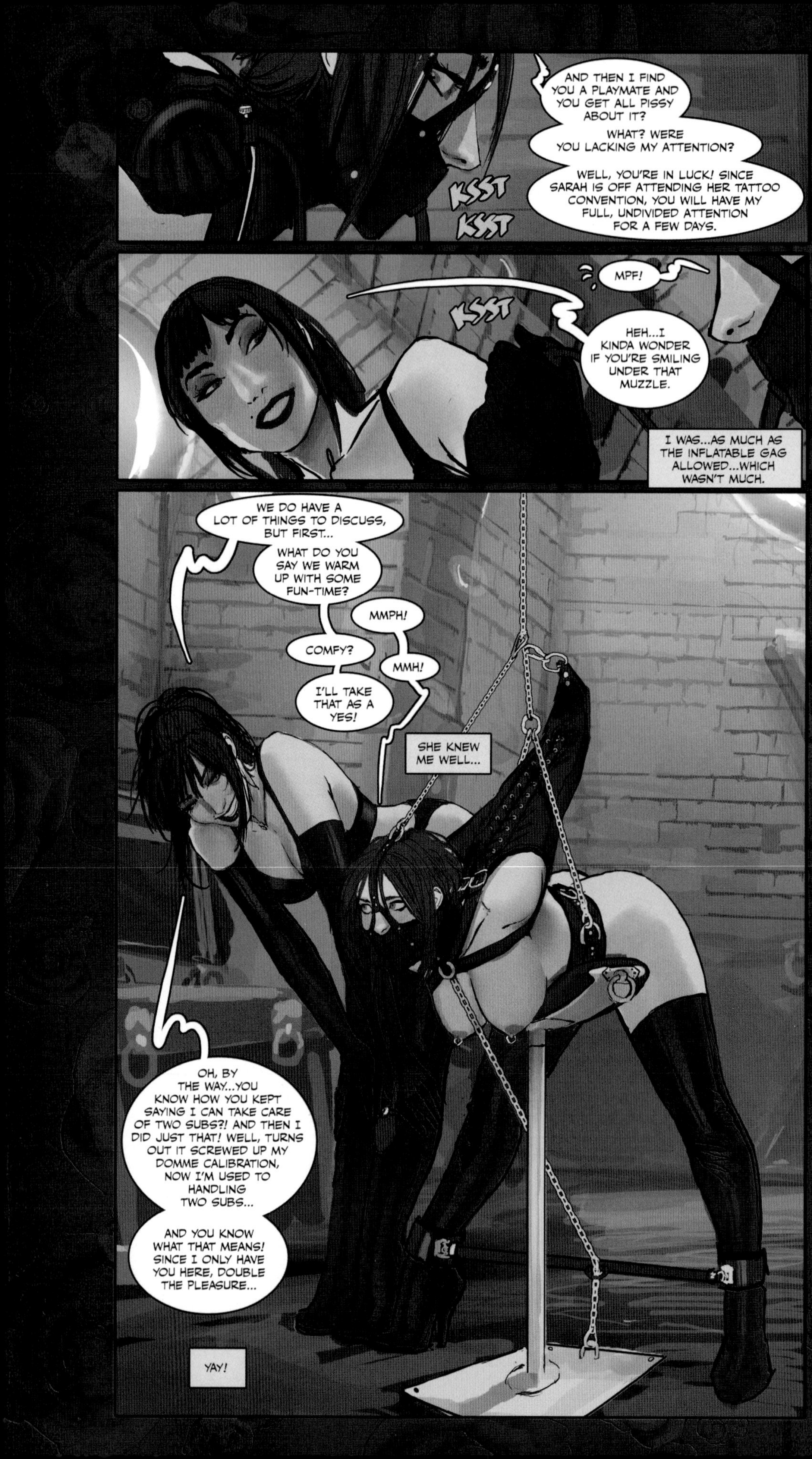
AND THEN I FIND YOU A PLAYMATE AND YOU GET ALL PISSY ABOUT IT?
WHAT? WERE YOU LACKING MY ATTENTION?
WELL, YOU'RE IN LUCK! SINCE SARAH IS OFF ATTENDING HER TATTOO CONVENTION, YOU WILL HAVE MY FULL, UNDIVIDED ATTENTION FOR A FEW DAYS.
KSST
KSST
KSST
MPF!
HEH...I KINDA WONDER IF YOU'RE SMILING UNDER THAT MUZZLE.
I WAS...AS MUCH AS THE INFLATABLE GAG ALLOWED...WHICH WASN'T MUCH.
WE DO HAVE A LOT OF THINGS TO DISCUSS, BUT FIRST...
WHAT DO YOU SAY WE WARM UP WITH SOME FUN-TIME?
MMPH!
COMFY?
MMH!
I'LL TAKE THAT AS A YES!
SHE KNEW ME WELL...
OH, BY THE WAY...YOU KNOW HOW YOU KEPT SAYING I CAN TAKE CARE OF TWO SUBS?! AND THEN I DID JUST THAT! WELL, TURNS OUT IT SCREWED UP MY DOMME CALIBRATION, NOW I'M USED TO HANDLING TWO SUBS...
AND YOU KNOW WHAT THAT MEANS! SINCE I ONLY HAVE YOU HERE, DOUBLE THE PLEASURE...
YAY!

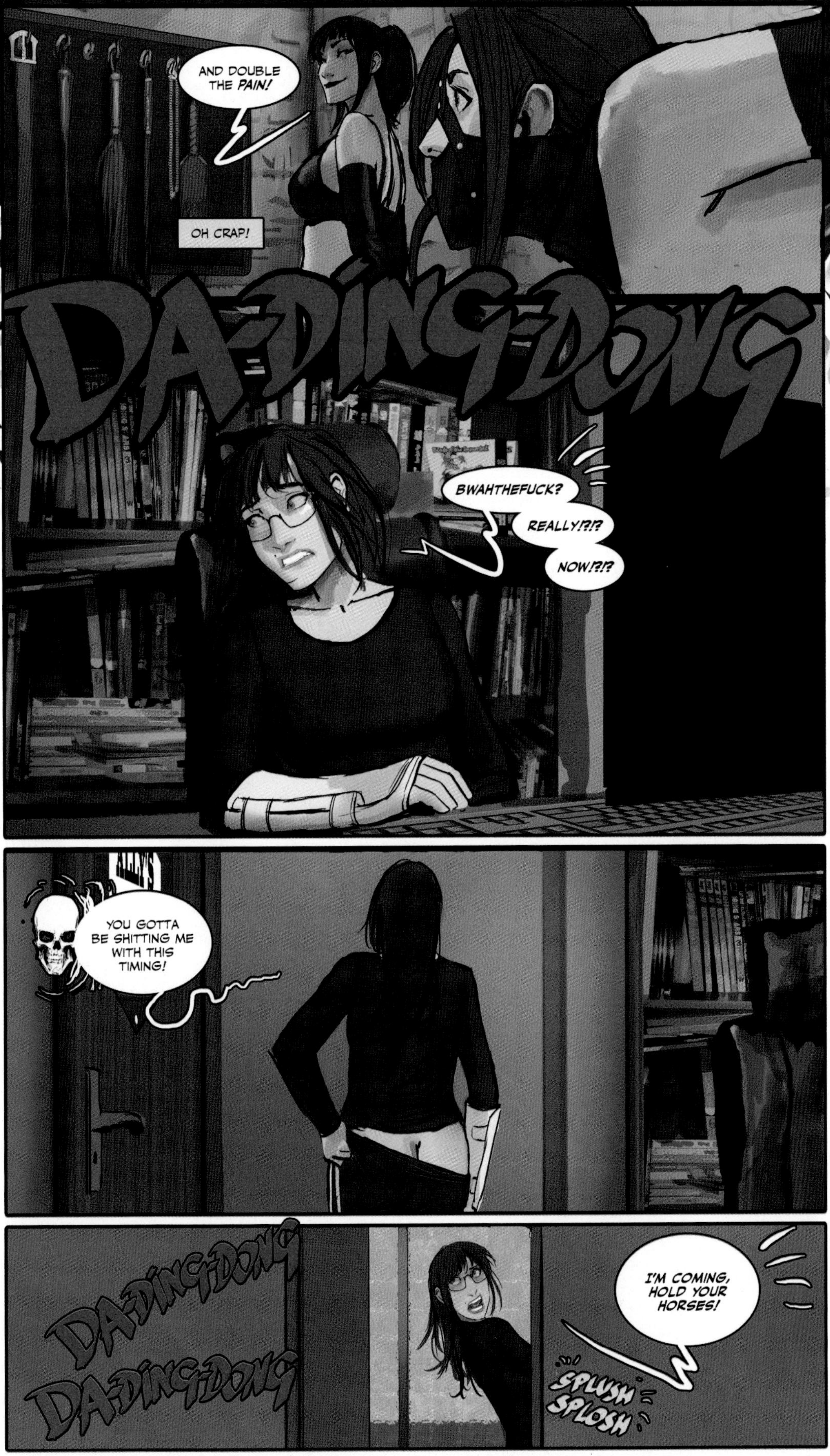

AND DOUBLE THE PAIN!
OH CRAP!
DA-DING-DONG
BWAHTHEFUCK?
REALLY!?!?
NOW!?!?
YOU GOTTA BE SHITTING ME WITH THIS TIMING!
DA-DING-DONG
DA-DING-DONG
I'M COMING, HOLD YOUR HORSES!
SPLUSH
SPLOSH

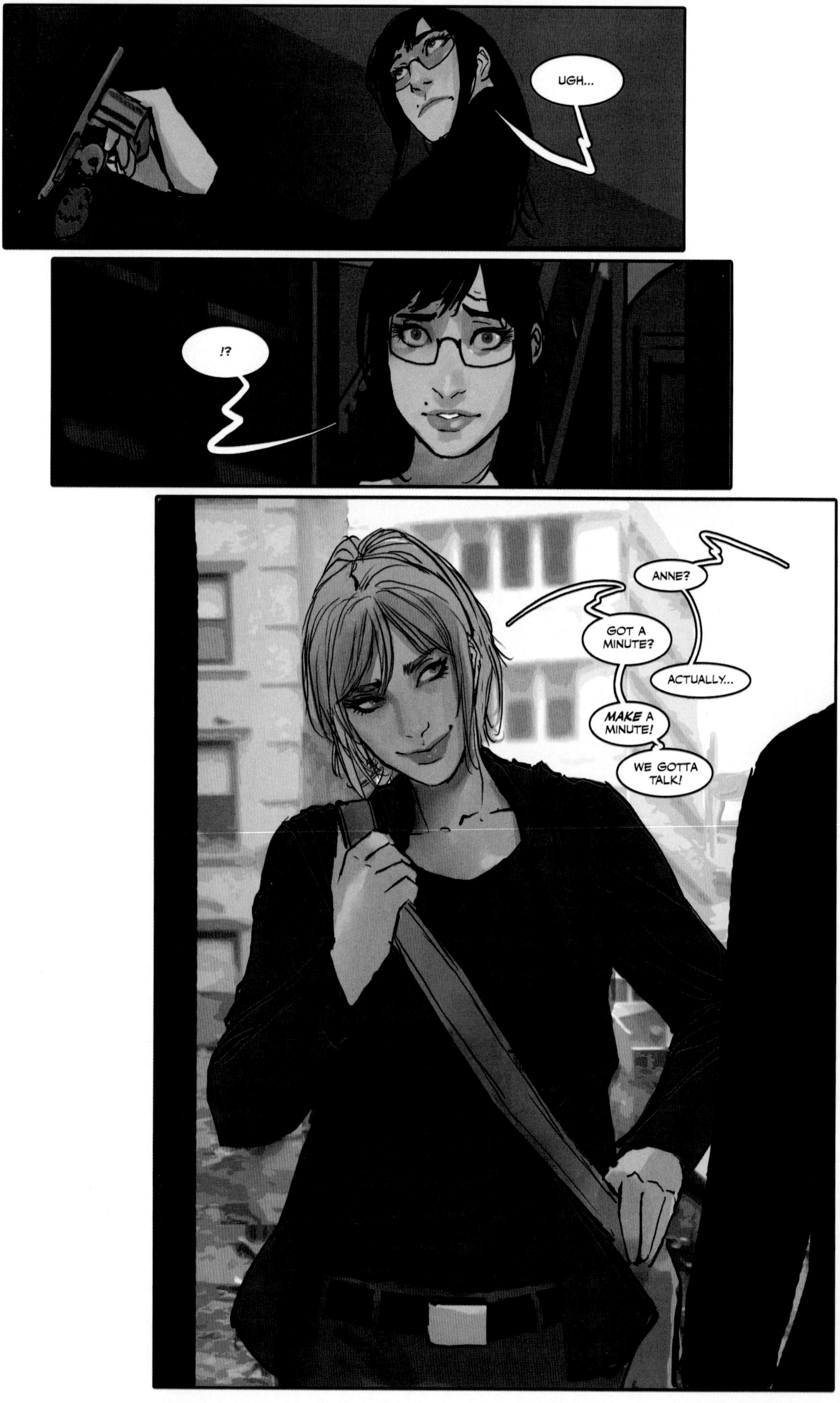
UGH...
!?
ANNE?
GOT A MINUTE?
ACTUALLY...
MAKE A MINUTE!
WE GOTTA TALK!

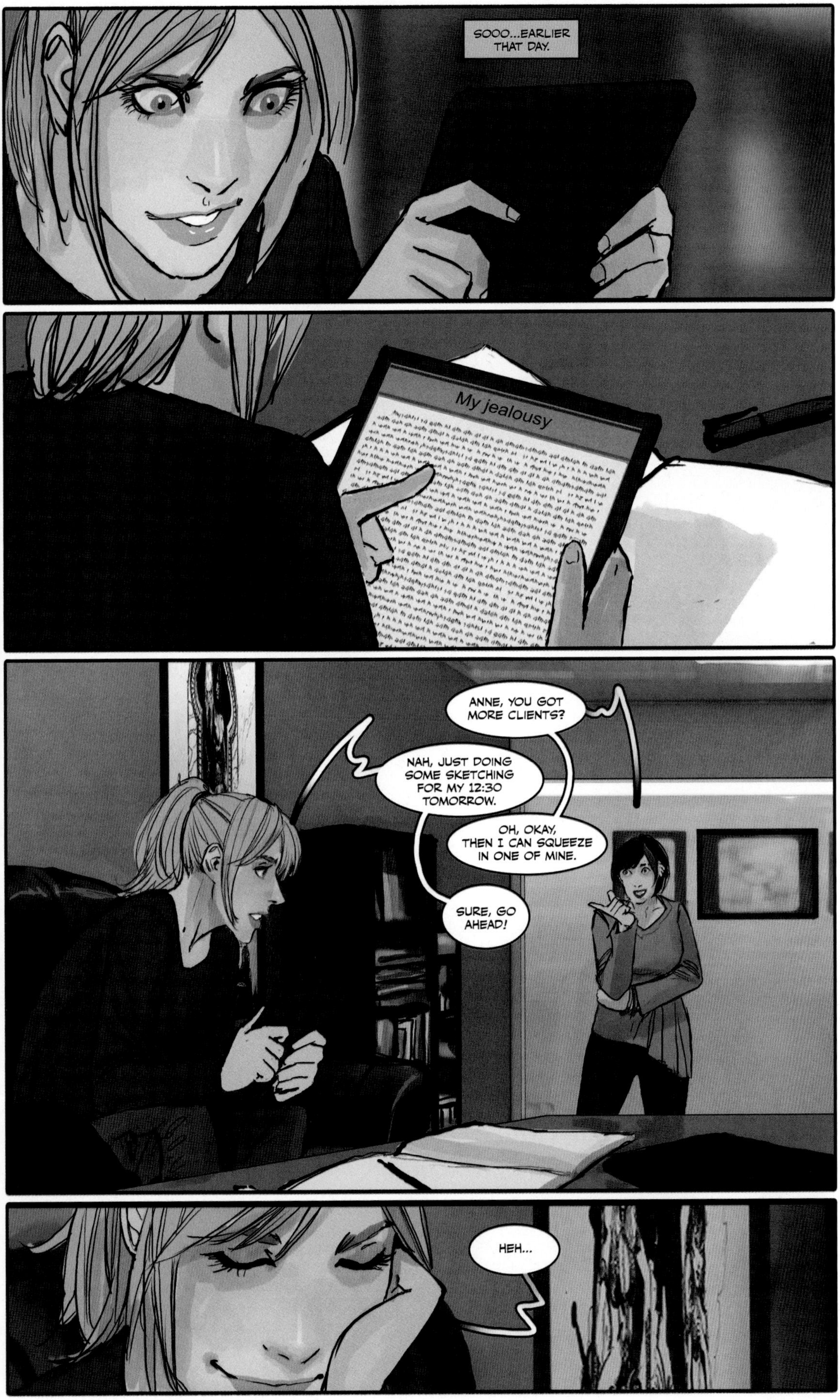
SOOO...EARLIER THAT DAY.
My jealousy
ANNE, YOU GOT MORE CLIENTS?
NAH, JUST DOING SOME SKETCHING FOR MY 12:30 TOMORROW.
OH, OKAY, THEN I CAN SQUEEZE IN ONE OF MINE.
SURE, GO AHEAD!
HEH...

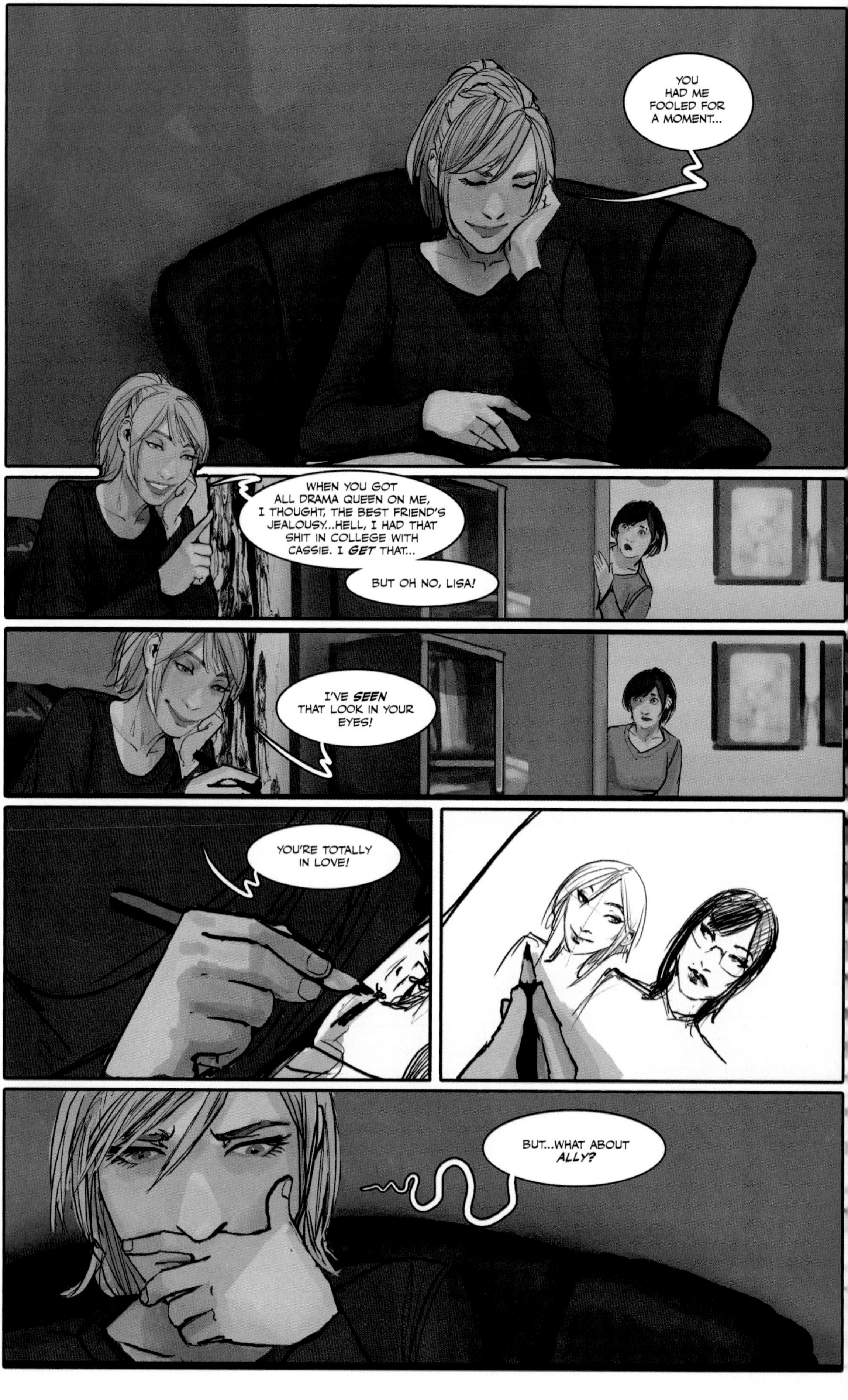
YOU HAD ME FOOLED FOR A MOMENT...
WHEN YOU GOT ALL DRAMA QUEEN ON ME, I THOUGHT, THE BEST FRIEND'S JEALOUSY...HELL, I HAD THAT SHIT IN COLLEGE WITH CASSIE. I *GET* THAT...
BUT OH NO, LISA!
I'VE *SEEN* THAT LOOK IN YOUR EYES!
YOU'RE TOTALLY IN LOVE!
BUT...WHAT ABOUT *ALLY?*

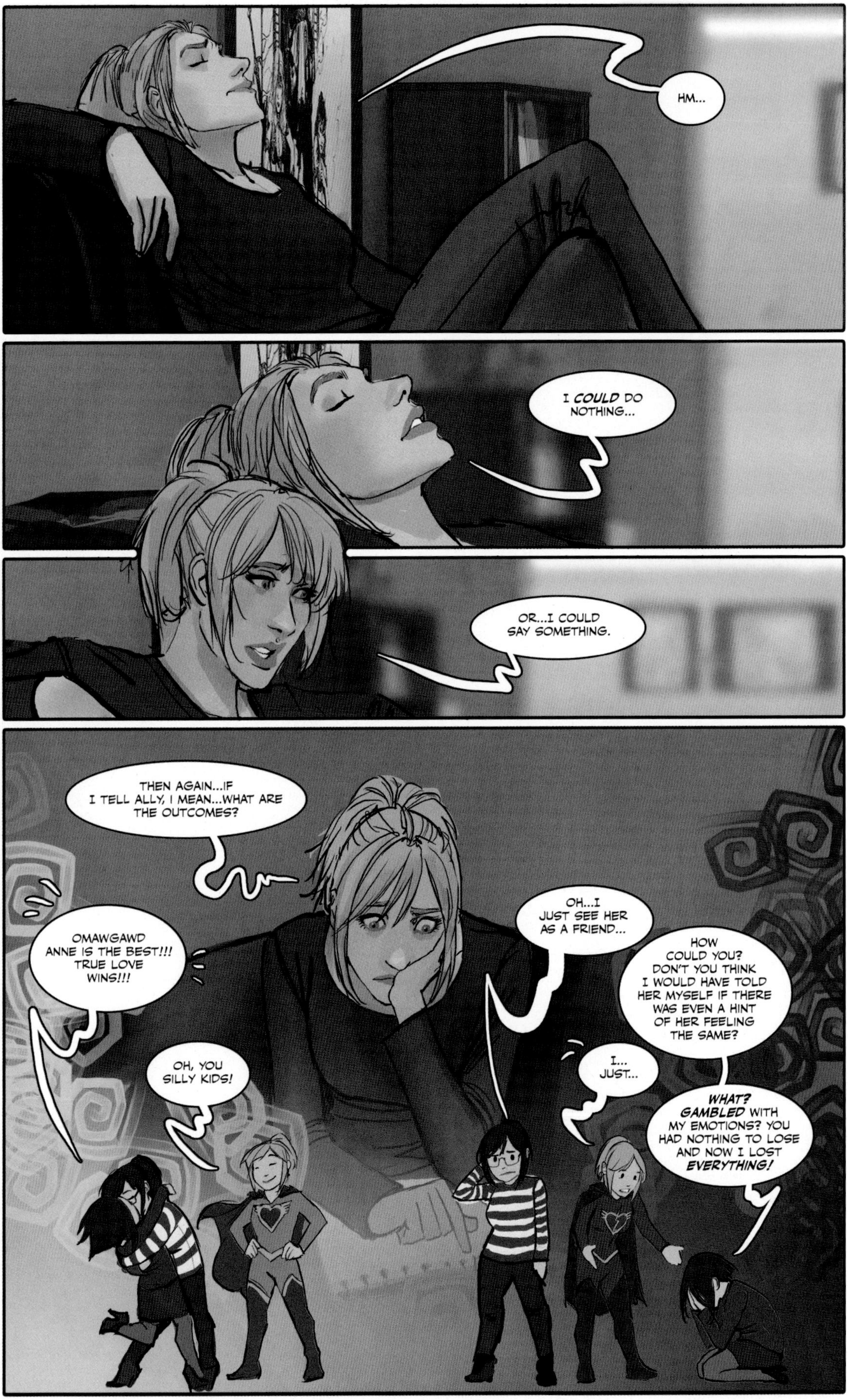
HM...
I COULD DO NOTHING...
OR...I COULD SAY SOMETHING.
THEN AGAIN...IF I TELL ALLY, I MEAN...WHAT ARE THE OUTCOMES?
OMAWGAWD ANNE IS THE BEST!!! TRUE LOVE WINS!!!
OH, YOU SILLY KIDS!
OH...I JUST SEE HER AS A FRIEND...
I... JUST...
HOW COULD YOU? DON'T YOU THINK I WOULD HAVE TOLD HER MYSELF IF THERE WAS EVEN A HINT OF HER FEELING THE SAME?
WHAT? GAMBLED WITH MY EMOTIONS? YOU HAD NOTHING TO LOSE AND NOW I LOST EVERYTHING!

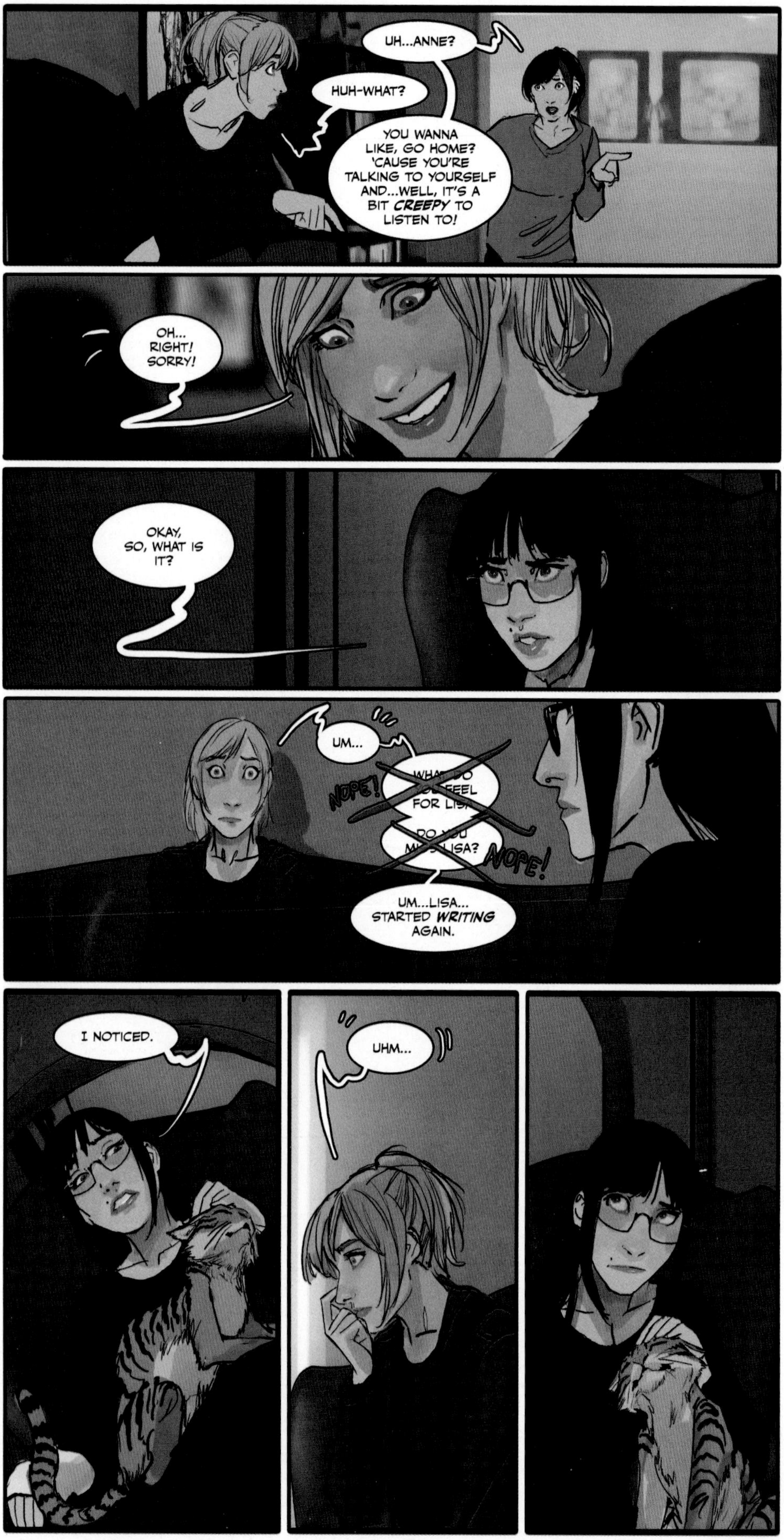
UH...ANNE?
HUH-WHAT?
YOU WANNA LIKE, GO HOME? 'CAUSE YOU'RE TALKING TO YOURSELF AND...WELL, IT'S A BIT *CREEPY* TO LISTEN TO!
OH... RIGHT! SORRY!
OKAY, SO, WHAT IS IT?
UM...
NOPE!
NOPE!
UM...LISA... STARTED *WRITING* AGAIN.
I NOTICED.
UHM...

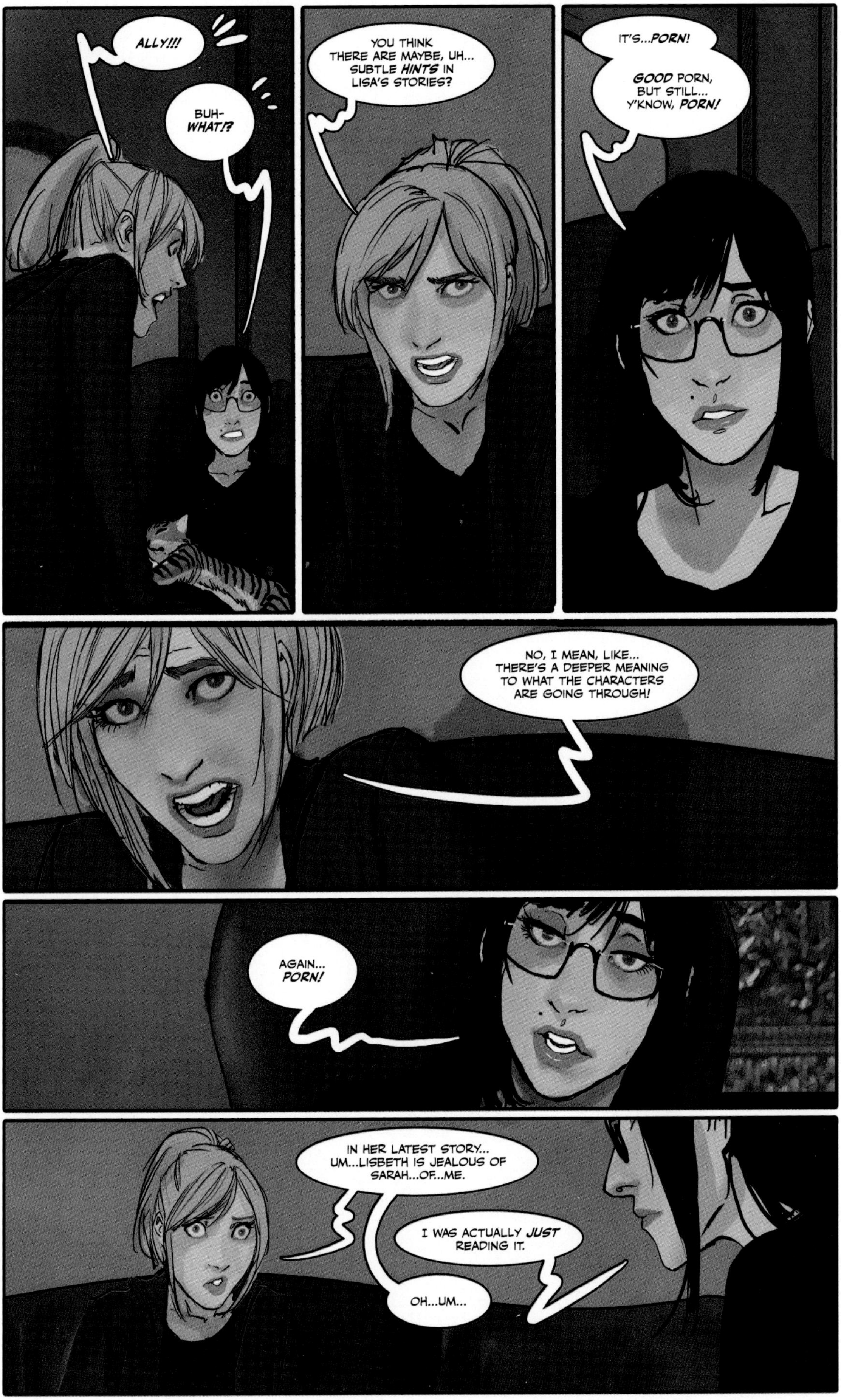
ALLY!!!
BUH-WHAT!?
YOU THINK THERE ARE MAYBE, UH... SUBTLE HINTS IN LISA'S STORIES?
IT'S...PORN!
GOOD PORN, BUT STILL... Y'KNOW, PORN!
NO, I MEAN, LIKE... THERE'S A DEEPER MEANING TO WHAT THE CHARACTERS ARE GOING THROUGH!
AGAIN... PORN!
IN HER LATEST STORY... UM...LISBETH IS JEALOUS OF SARAH...OF...ME.
I WAS ACTUALLY JUST READING IT.
OH...UM...

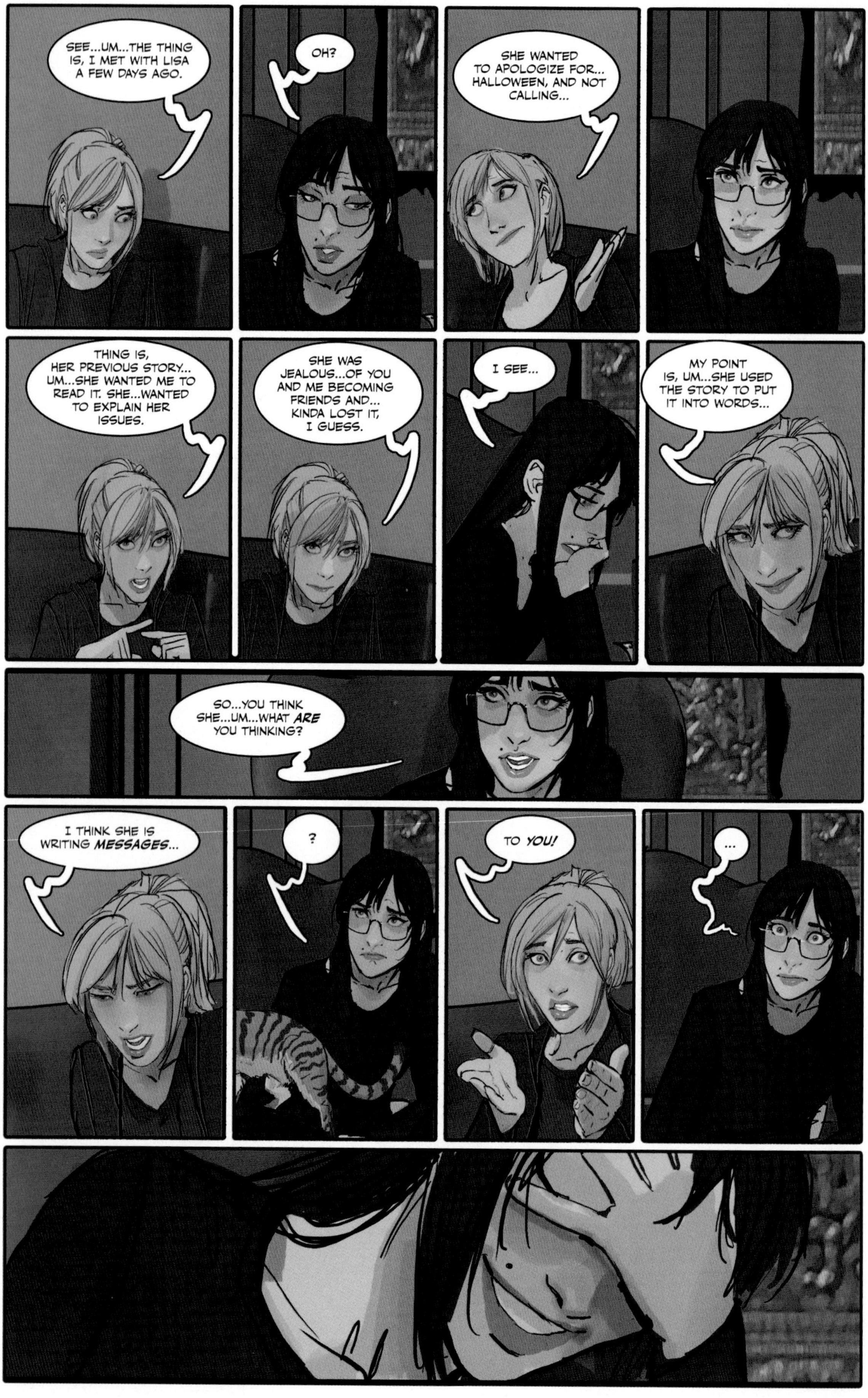
SEE...UM...THE THING IS, I MET WITH LISA A FEW DAYS AGO.
OH?
SHE WANTED TO APOLOGIZE FOR... HALLOWEEN, AND NOT CALLING...
THING IS, HER PREVIOUS STORY... UM...SHE WANTED ME TO READ IT. SHE...WANTED TO EXPLAIN HER ISSUES.
SHE WAS JEALOUS...OF YOU AND ME BECOMING FRIENDS AND... KINDA LOST IT, I GUESS.
I SEE...
MY POINT IS, UM...SHE USED THE STORY TO PUT IT INTO WORDS...
SO...YOU THINK SHE...UM...WHAT *ARE* YOU THINKING?
I THINK SHE IS WRITING ***MESSAGES***...
?
TO ***YOU!***
...

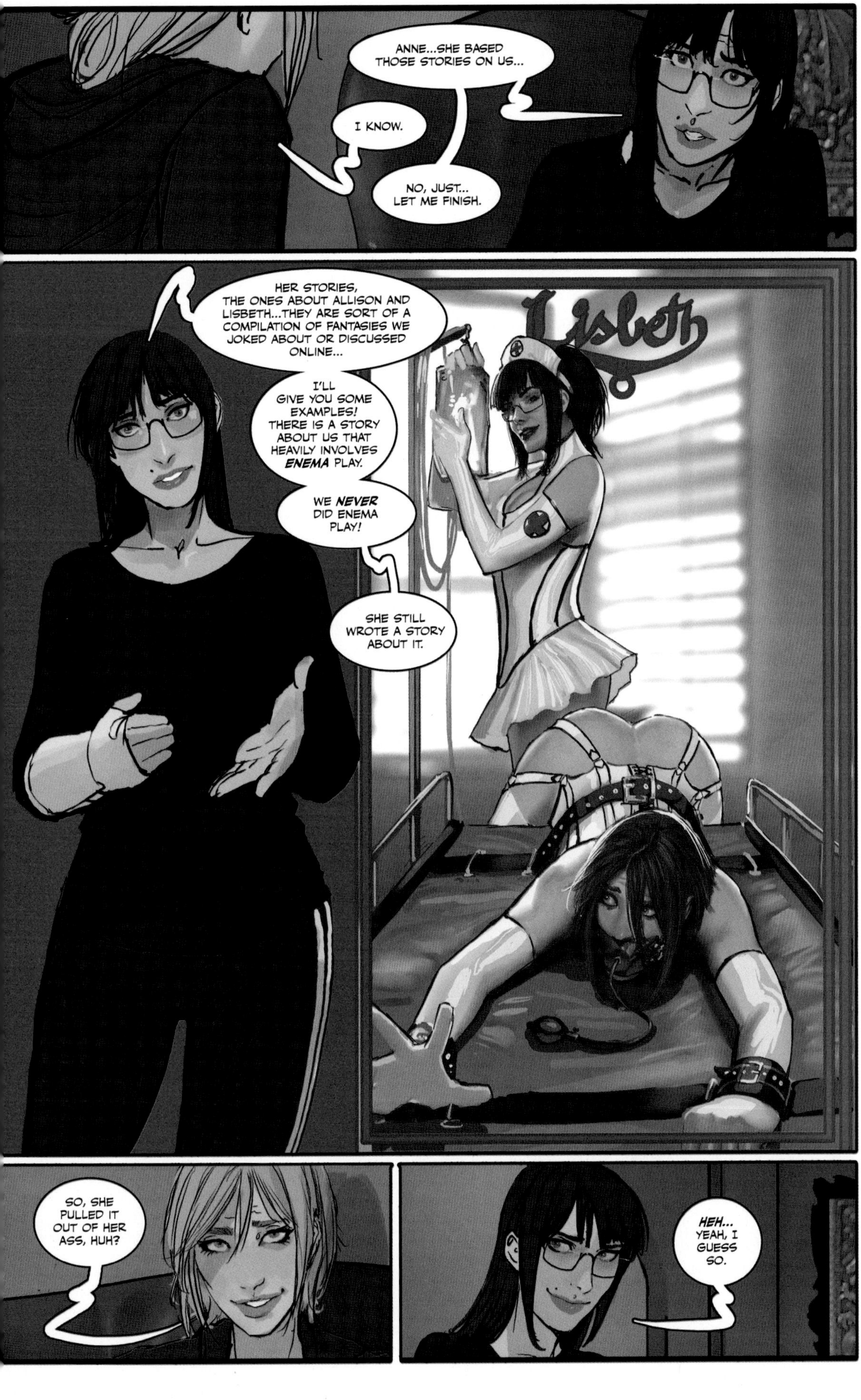
ANNE...SHE BASED THOSE STORIES ON US...
I KNOW.
NO, JUST... LET ME FINISH.
HER STORIES, THE ONES ABOUT ALLISON AND LISBETH...THEY ARE SORT OF A COMPILATION OF FANTASIES WE JOKED ABOUT OR DISCUSSED ONLINE...
Lisbeth
I'LL GIVE YOU SOME EXAMPLES! THERE IS A STORY ABOUT US THAT HEAVILY INVOLVES ENEMA PLAY.
WE NEVER DID ENEMA PLAY!
SHE STILL WROTE A STORY ABOUT IT.
SO, SHE PULLED IT OUT OF HER ASS, HUH?
HEH... YEAH, I GUESS SO.

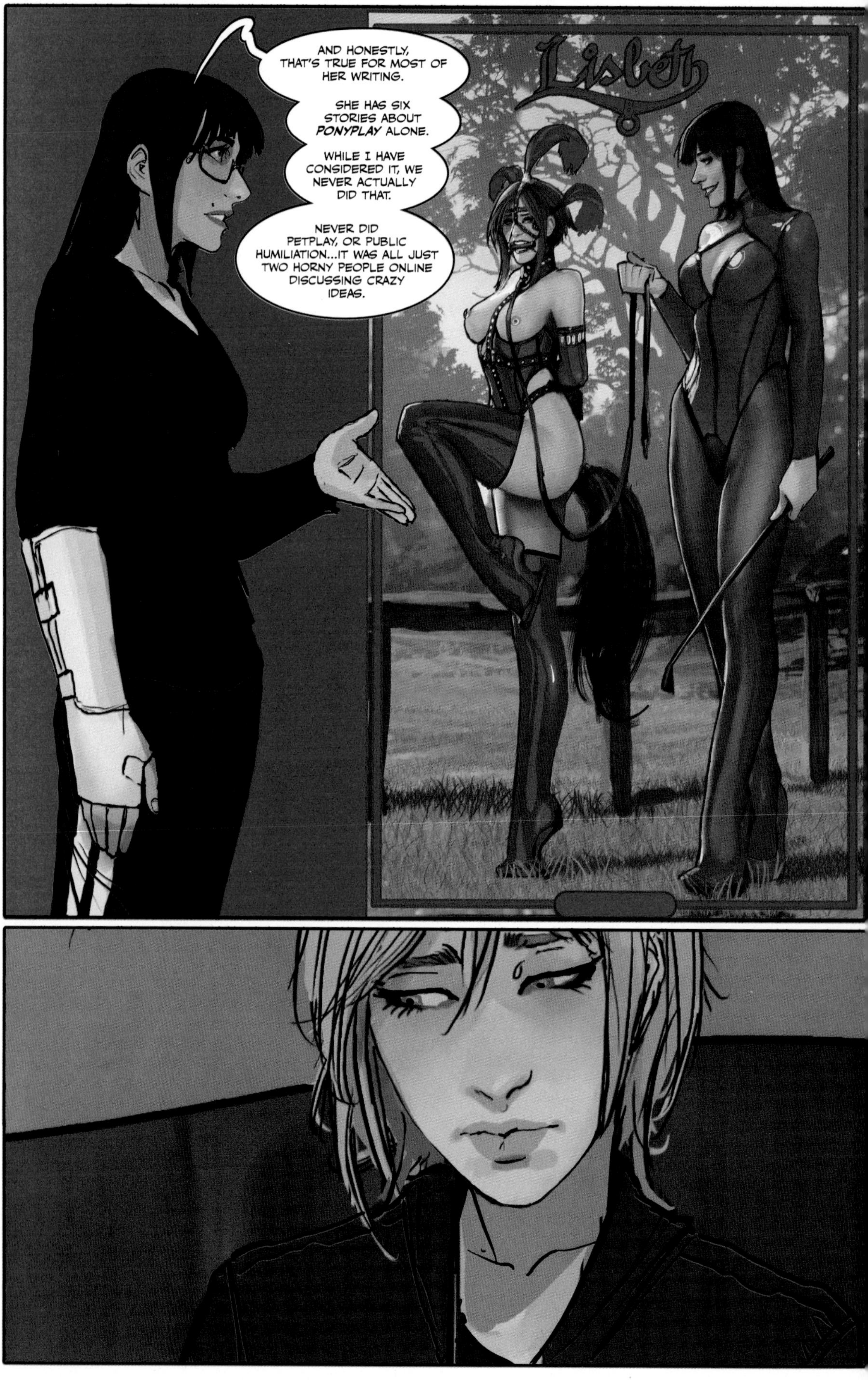
AND HONESTLY, THAT'S TRUE FOR MOST OF HER WRITING.
SHE HAS SIX STORIES ABOUT *PONYPLAY* ALONE.
WHILE I HAVE CONSIDERED IT, WE NEVER ACTUALLY DID THAT.
NEVER DID PETPLAY, OR PUBLIC HUMILIATION...IT WAS ALL JUST TWO HORNY PEOPLE ONLINE DISCUSSING CRAZY IDEAS.
Lisbeth

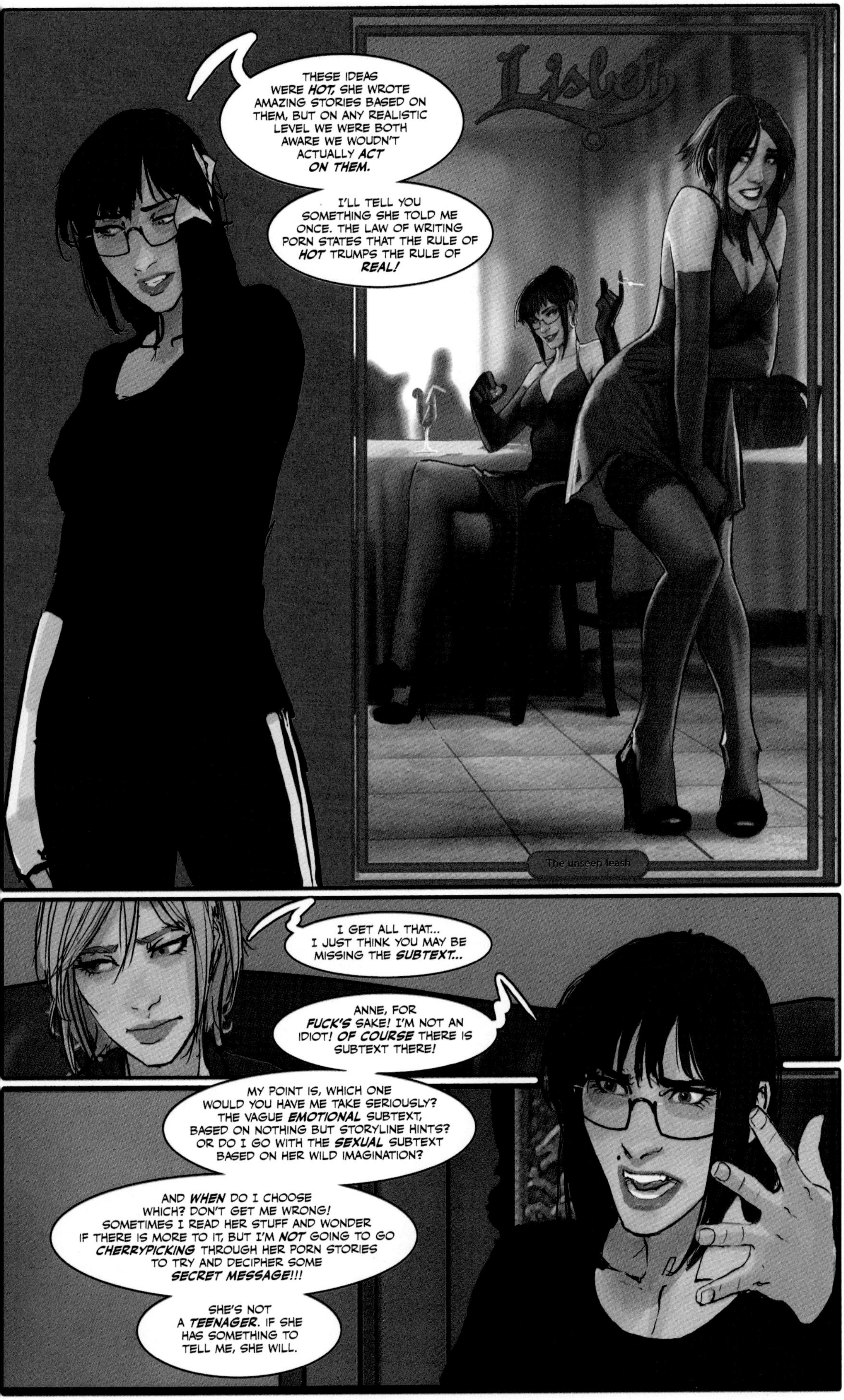

Lisbet
THESE IDEAS WERE HOT, SHE WROTE AMAZING STORIES BASED ON THEM, BUT ON ANY REALISTIC LEVEL WE WERE BOTH AWARE WE WOUDN'T ACTUALLY ACT ON THEM.
I'LL TELL YOU SOMETHING SHE TOLD ME ONCE. THE LAW OF WRITING PORN STATES THAT THE RULE OF HOT TRUMPS THE RULE OF REAL!
The unseen leash
I GET ALL THAT... I JUST THINK YOU MAY BE MISSING THE SUBTEXT...
ANNE, FOR FUCK'S SAKE! I'M NOT AN IDIOT! OF COURSE THERE IS SUBTEXT THERE!
MY POINT IS, WHICH ONE WOULD YOU HAVE ME TAKE SERIOUSLY? THE VAGUE EMOTIONAL SUBTEXT, BASED ON NOTHING BUT STORYLINE HINTS? OR DO I GO WITH THE SEXUAL SUBTEXT BASED ON HER WILD IMAGINATION?
AND WHEN DO I CHOOSE WHICH? DON'T GET ME WRONG! SOMETIMES I READ HER STUFF AND WONDER IF THERE IS MORE TO IT, BUT I'M NOT GOING TO GO CHERRYPICKING THROUGH HER PORN STORIES TO TRY AND DECIPHER SOME SECRET MESSAGE!!!
SHE'S NOT A TEENAGER. IF SHE HAS SOMETHING TO TELL ME, SHE WILL.

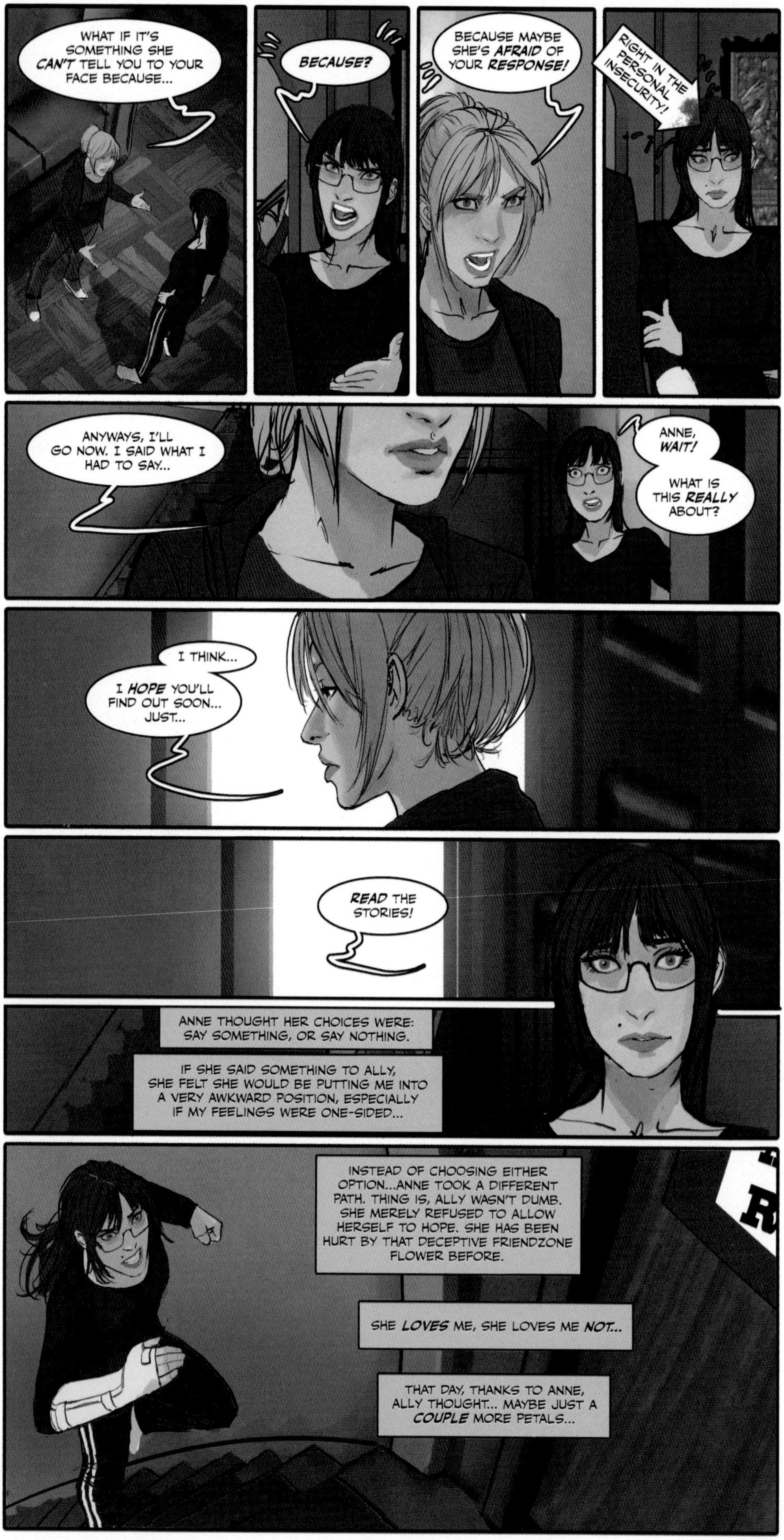
WHAT IF IT'S SOMETHING SHE CAN'T TELL YOU TO YOUR FACE BECAUSE...
BECAUSE?
BECAUSE MAYBE SHE'S AFRAID OF YOUR RESPONSE!
RIGHT IN THE PERSONAL INSECURITY!
ANYWAYS, I'LL GO NOW. I SAID WHAT I HAD TO SAY...
ANNE, WAIT!
WHAT IS THIS REALLY ABOUT?
I THINK...
I HOPE YOU'LL FIND OUT SOON... JUST...
READ THE STORIES!
ANNE THOUGHT HER CHOICES WERE: SAY SOMETHING, OR SAY NOTHING.
IF SHE SAID SOMETHING TO ALLY, SHE FELT SHE WOULD BE PUTTING ME INTO A VERY AWKWARD POSITION, ESPECIALLY IF MY FEELINGS WERE ONE-SIDED...
INSTEAD OF CHOOSING EITHER OPTION...ANNE TOOK A DIFFERENT PATH. THING IS, ALLY WASN'T DUMB. SHE MERELY REFUSED TO ALLOW HERSELF TO HOPE. SHE HAS BEEN HURT BY THAT DECEPTIVE FRIENDZONE FLOWER BEFORE.
SHE LOVES ME, SHE LOVES ME NOT...
THAT DAY, THANKS TO ANNE, ALLY THOUGHT... MAYBE JUST A COUPLE MORE PETALS...

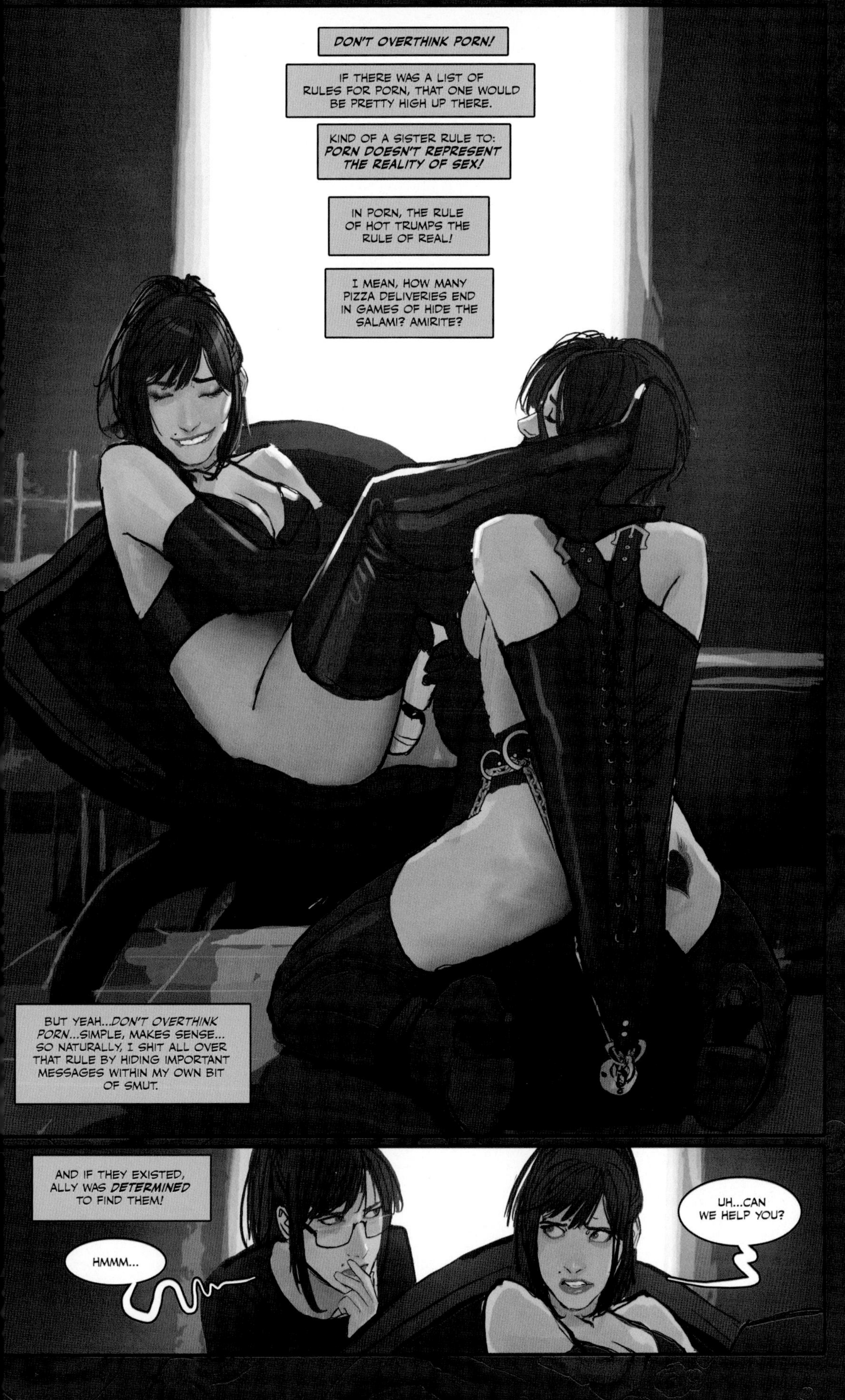
DON'T OVERTHINK PORN!
IF THERE WAS A LIST OF RULES FOR PORN, THAT ONE WOULD BE PRETTY HIGH UP THERE.
KIND OF A SISTER RULE TO: PORN DOESN'T REPRESENT THE REALITY OF SEX!
IN PORN, THE RULE OF HOT TRUMPS THE RULE OF REAL!
I MEAN, HOW MANY PIZZA DELIVERIES END IN GAMES OF HIDE THE SALAMI? AMIRITE?
BUT YEAH...DON'T OVERTHINK PORN...SIMPLE, MAKES SENSE... SO NATURALLY, I SHIT ALL OVER THAT RULE BY HIDING IMPORTANT MESSAGES WITHIN MY OWN BIT OF SMUT.
AND IF THEY EXISTED, ALLY WAS DETERMINED TO FIND THEM!
HMMM...
UH...CAN WE HELP YOU?

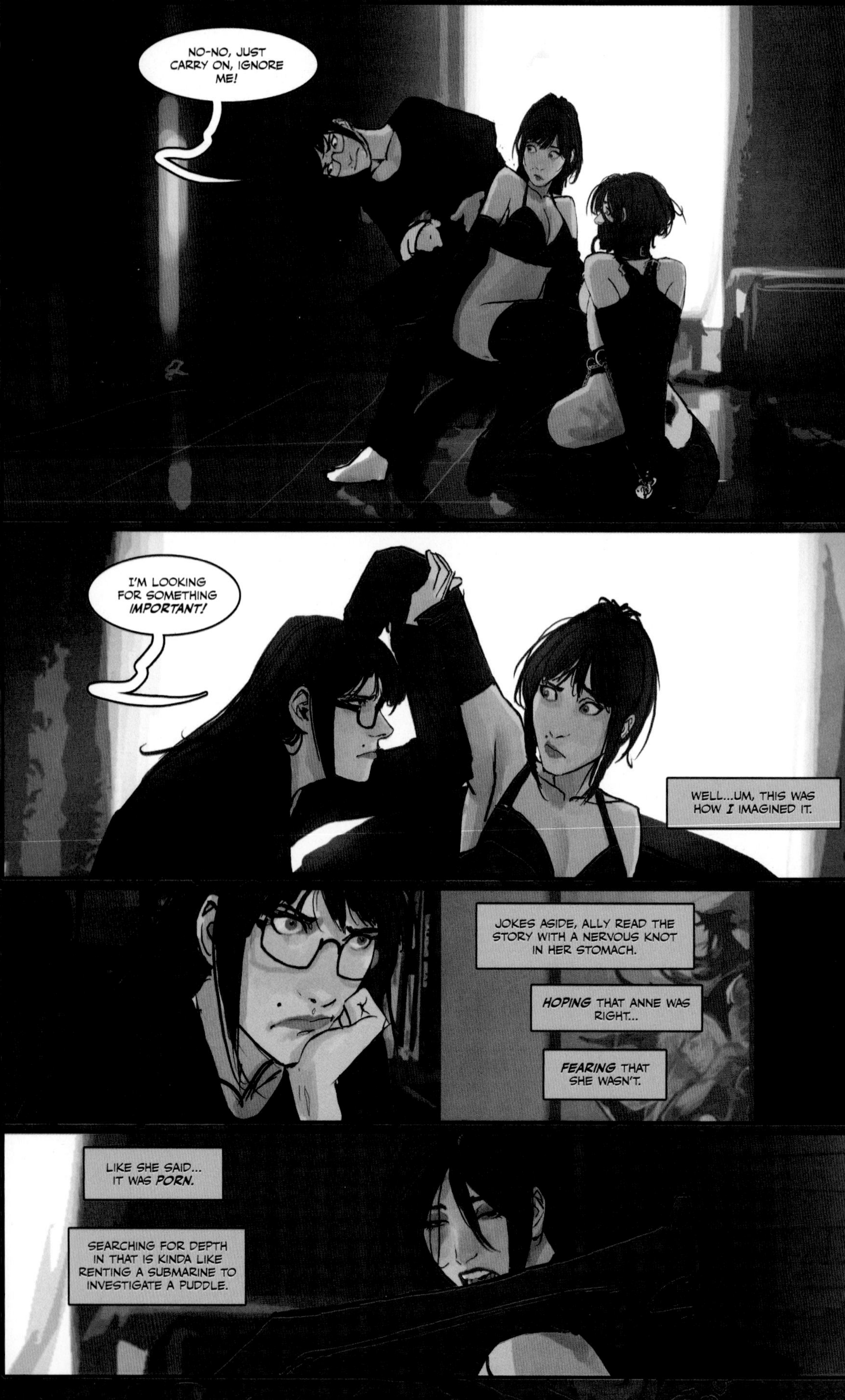
NO-NO, JUST CARRY ON, IGNORE ME!
I'M LOOKING FOR SOMETHING *IMPORTANT!*
WELL...UM, THIS WAS HOW *I* IMAGINED IT.
JOKES ASIDE, ALLY READ THE STORY WITH A NERVOUS KNOT IN HER STOMACH.
HOPING THAT ANNE WAS RIGHT...
FEARING THAT SHE WASN'T.
LIKE SHE SAID... IT WAS *PORN.*
SEARCHING FOR DEPTH IN THAT IS KINDA LIKE RENTING A SUBMARINE TO INVESTIGATE A PUDDLE.

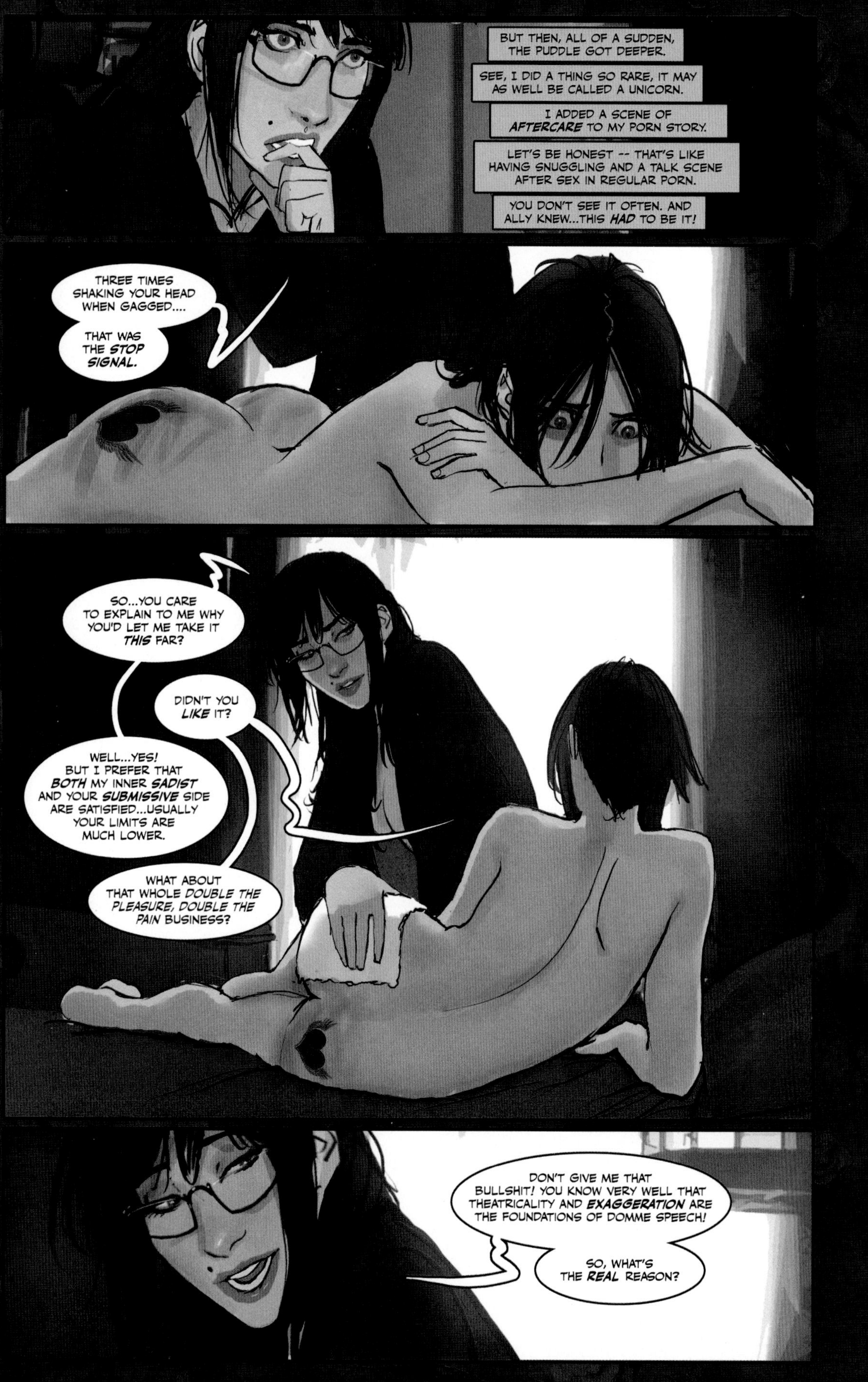
BUT THEN, ALL OF A SUDDEN, THE PUDDLE GOT DEEPER.
SEE, I DID A THING SO RARE, IT MAY AS WELL BE CALLED A UNICORN.
I ADDED A SCENE OF *AFTERCARE* TO MY PORN STORY.
LET'S BE HONEST -- THAT'S LIKE HAVING SNUGGLING AND A TALK SCENE AFTER SEX IN REGULAR PORN.
YOU DON'T SEE IT OFTEN. AND ALLY KNEW...THIS *HAD* TO BE IT!
THREE TIMES SHAKING YOUR HEAD WHEN GAGGED....
THAT WAS THE *STOP SIGNAL.*
SO...YOU CARE TO EXPLAIN TO ME WHY YOU'D LET ME TAKE IT *THIS* FAR?
DIDN'T YOU *LIKE* IT?
WELL...YES! BUT I PREFER THAT *BOTH* MY INNER *SADIST* AND YOUR *SUBMISSIVE* SIDE ARE SATISFIED...USUALLY YOUR LIMITS ARE MUCH LOWER.
WHAT ABOUT THAT WHOLE *DOUBLE THE PLEASURE, DOUBLE THE PAIN* BUSINESS?
DON'T GIVE ME THAT BULLSHIT! YOU KNOW VERY WELL THAT THEATRICALITY AND *EXAGGERATION* ARE THE FOUNDATIONS OF DOMME SPEECH!
SO, WHAT'S THE *REAL* REASON?

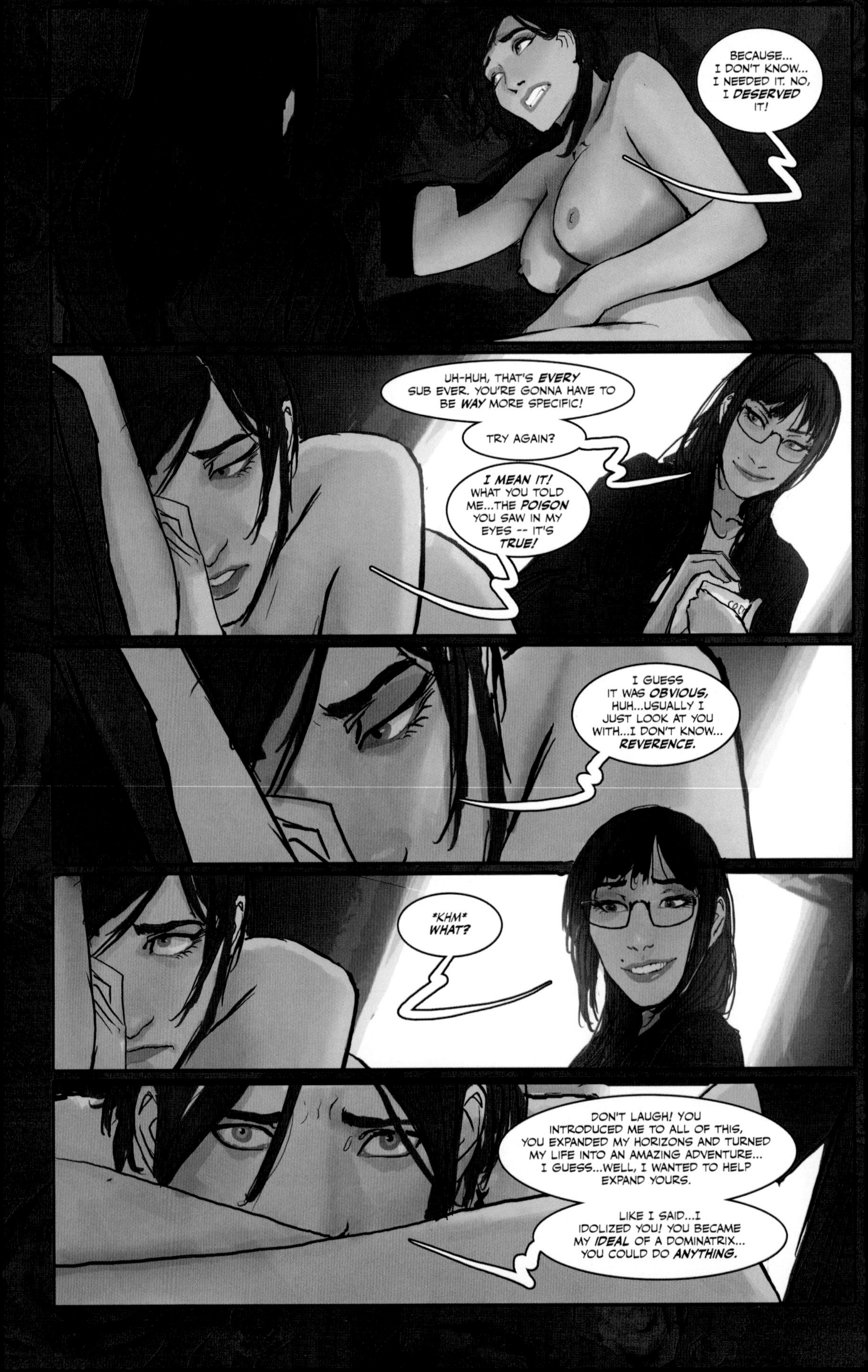
BECAUSE... I DON'T KNOW... I NEEDED IT. NO, I *DESERVED* IT!
UH-HUH, THAT'S *EVERY* SUB EVER. YOU'RE GONNA HAVE TO BE *WAY* MORE SPECIFIC!
TRY AGAIN?
I MEAN IT! WHAT YOU TOLD ME...THE *POISON* YOU SAW IN MY EYES -- IT'S *TRUE!*
I GUESS IT WAS *OBVIOUS,* HUH...USUALLY I JUST LOOK AT YOU WITH...I DON'T KNOW... *REVERENCE.*
KHM *WHAT?*
DON'T LAUGH! YOU INTRODUCED ME TO ALL OF THIS, YOU EXPANDED MY HORIZONS AND TURNED MY LIFE INTO AN AMAZING ADVENTURE... I GUESS...WELL, I WANTED TO HELP EXPAND YOURS.
LIKE I SAID...I IDOLIZED YOU! YOU BECAME MY *IDEAL* OF A DOMINATRIX... YOU COULD DO *ANYTHING.*

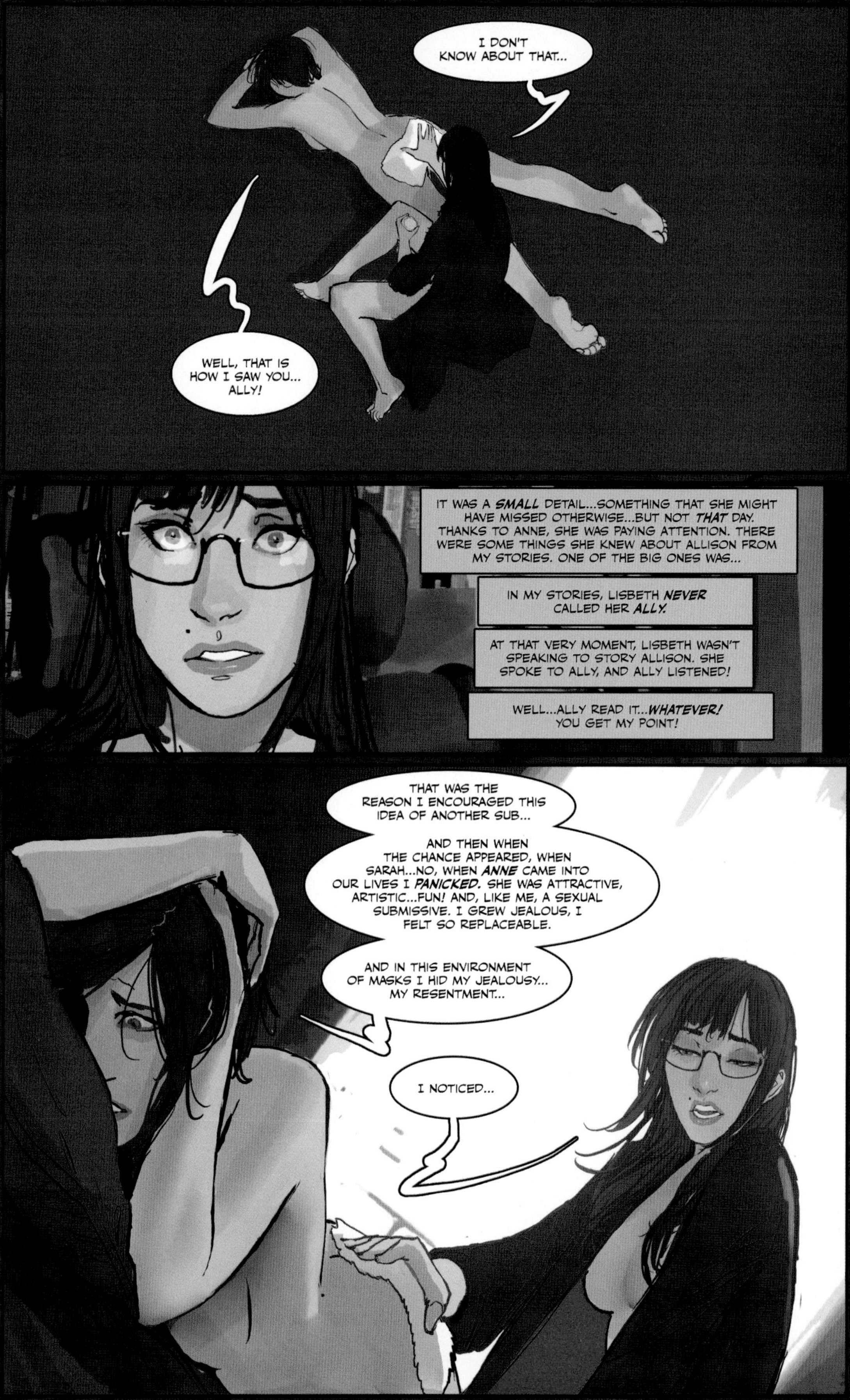

I DON'T KNOW ABOUT THAT...
WELL, THAT IS HOW I SAW YOU... ALLY!
IT WAS A SMALL DETAIL...SOMETHING THAT SHE MIGHT HAVE MISSED OTHERWISE...BUT NOT THAT DAY. THANKS TO ANNE, SHE WAS PAYING ATTENTION. THERE WERE SOME THINGS SHE KNEW ABOUT ALLISON FROM MY STORIES. ONE OF THE BIG ONES WAS...
IN MY STORIES, LISBETH NEVER CALLED HER ALLY.
AT THAT VERY MOMENT, LISBETH WASN'T SPEAKING TO STORY ALLISON. SHE SPOKE TO ALLY, AND ALLY LISTENED!
WELL...ALLY READ IT...WHATEVER! YOU GET MY POINT!
THAT WAS THE REASON I ENCOURAGED THIS IDEA OF ANOTHER SUB...
AND THEN WHEN THE CHANCE APPEARED, WHEN SARAH...NO, WHEN ANNE CAME INTO OUR LIVES I PANICKED. SHE WAS ATTRACTIVE, ARTISTIC...FUN! AND, LIKE ME, A SEXUAL SUBMISSIVE. I GREW JEALOUS, I FELT SO REPLACEABLE.
AND IN THIS ENVIRONMENT OF MASKS I HID MY JEALOUSY... MY RESENTMENT...
I NOTICED...

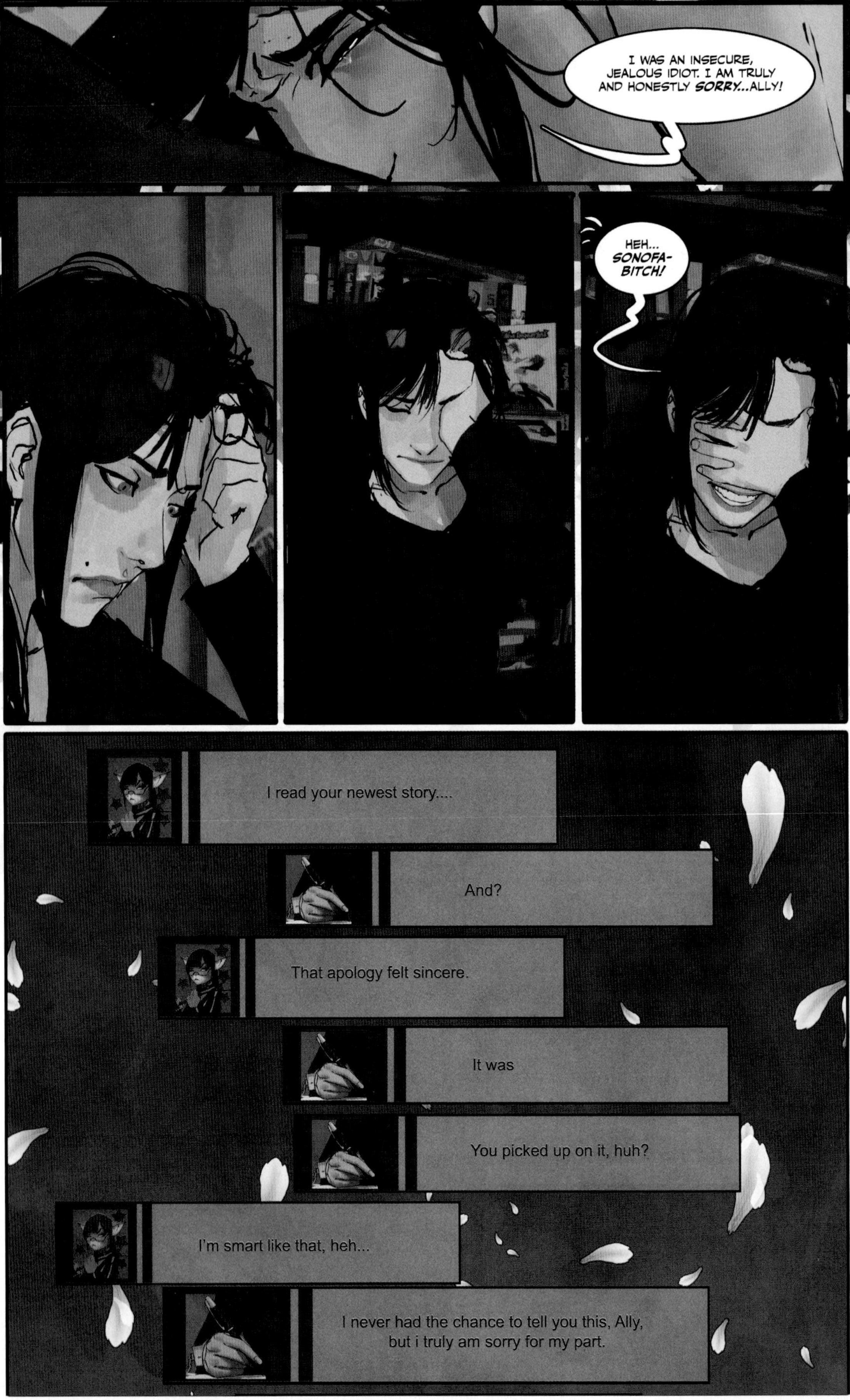
I WAS AN INSECURE, JEALOUS IDIOT. I AM TRULY AND HONESTLY *SORRY*...ALLY!
HEH... *SONOFA-BITCH!*
I read your newest story....
And?
That apology felt sincere.
It was
You picked up on it, huh?
I'm smart like that, heh...
I never had the chance to tell you this, Ally, but i truly am sorry for my part.

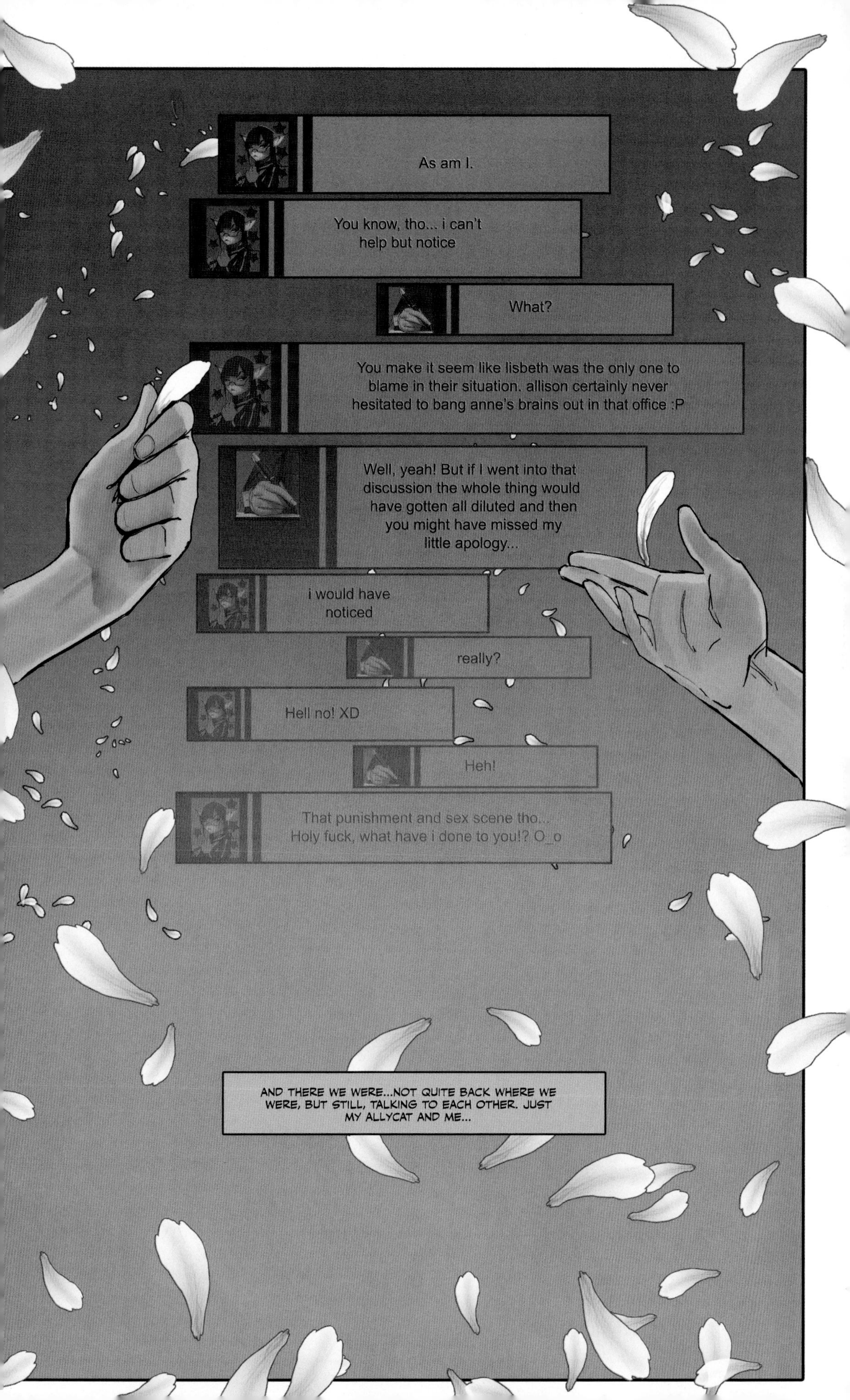
As am I.
You know, tho... i can't help but notice
What?
You make it seem like lisbeth was the only one to blame in their situation. allison certainly never hesitated to bang anne's brains out in that office :P
Well, yeah! But if I went into that discussion the whole thing would have gotten all diluted and then you might have missed my little apology...
i would have noticed
really?
Hell no! XD
Heh!
That punishment and sex scene tho... Holy fuck, what have i done to you!? O_o
AND THERE WE WERE...NOT QUITE BACK WHERE WE WERE, BUT STILL, TALKING TO EACH OTHER. JUST MY ALLYCAT AND ME...

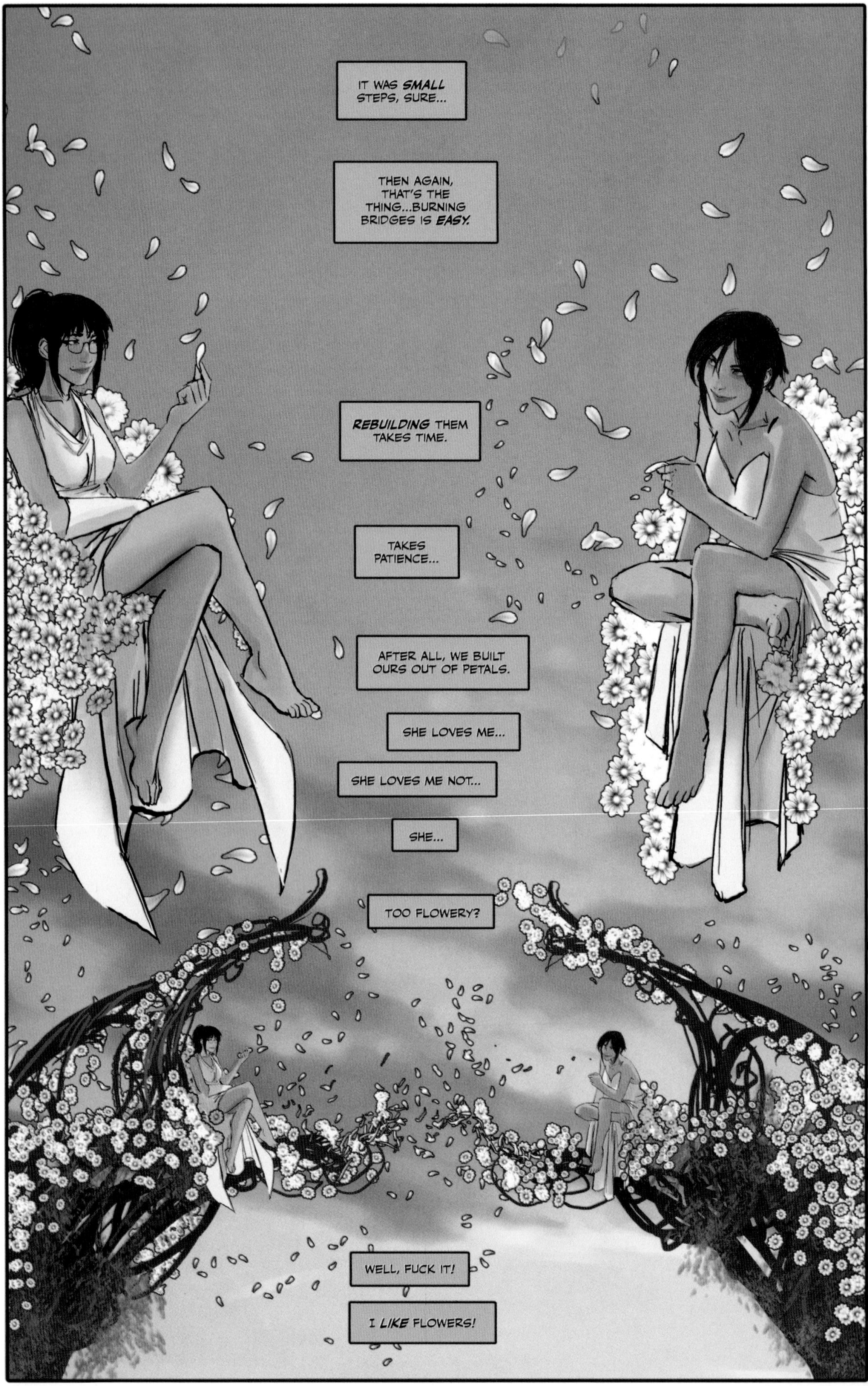
IT WAS *SMALL* STEPS, SURE...
THEN AGAIN, THAT'S THE THING...BURNING BRIDGES IS *EASY.*
REBUILDING THEM TAKES TIME.
TAKES PATIENCE...
AFTER ALL, WE BUILT OURS OUT OF PETALS.
SHE LOVES ME...
SHE LOVES ME NOT...
SHE...
TOO FLOWERY?
WELL, FUCK IT!
I *LIKE* FLOWERS!

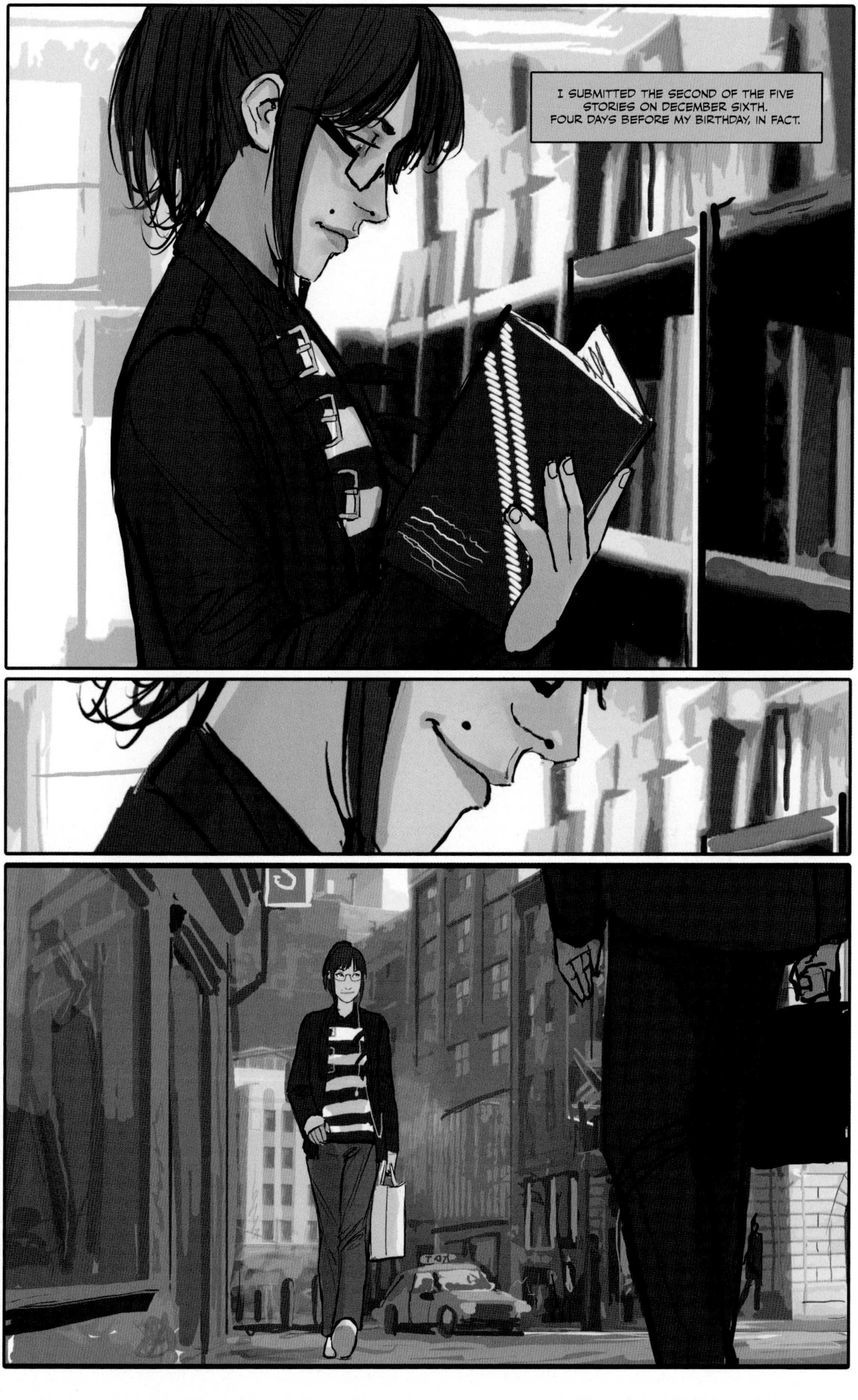
I SUBMITTED THE SECOND OF THE FIVE STORIES ON DECEMBER SIXTH. FOUR DAYS BEFORE MY BIRTHDAY, IN FACT.

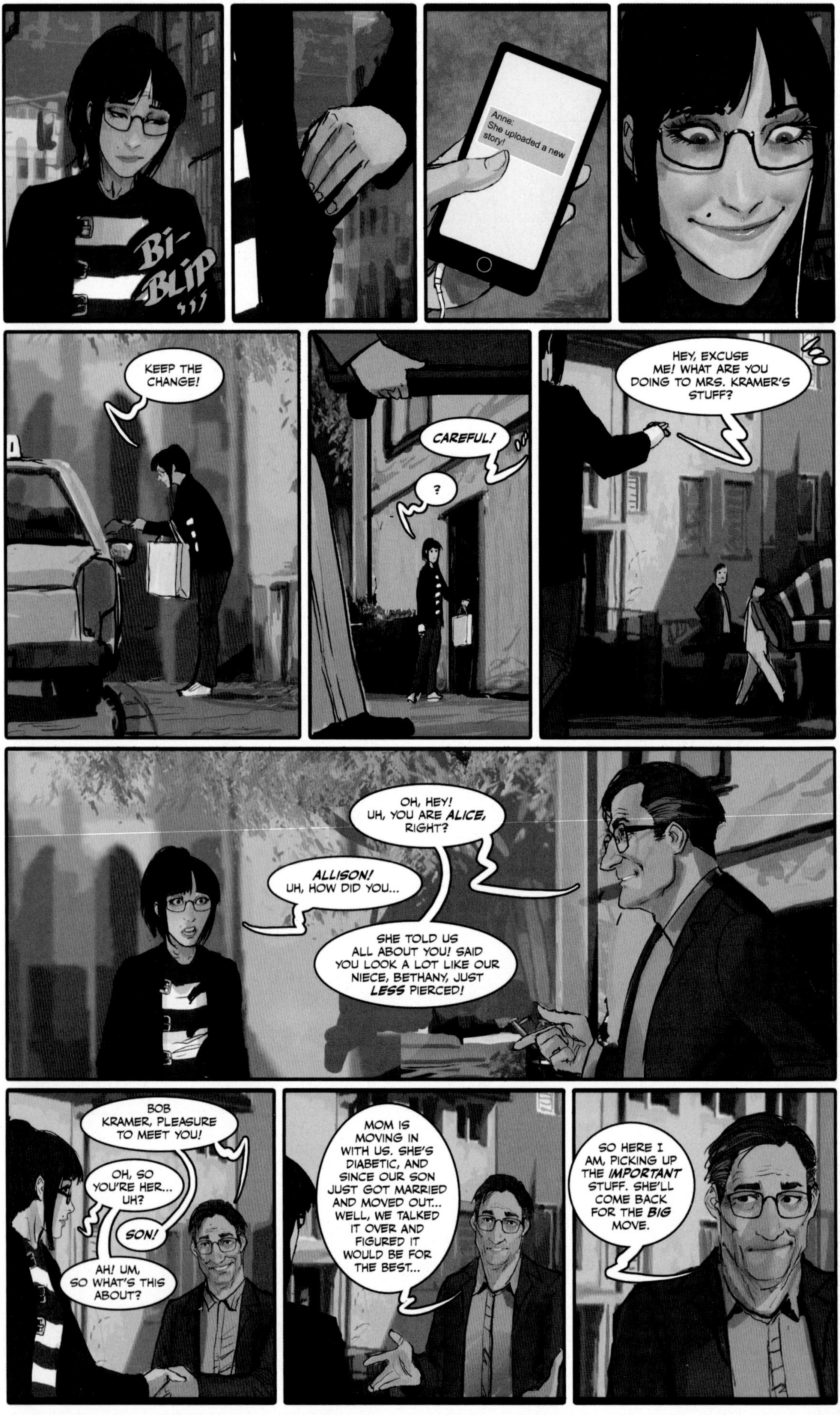
BI-BLIP
Anne: She uploaded a new story!
KEEP THE CHANGE!
CAREFUL!
?
HEY, EXCUSE ME! WHAT ARE YOU DOING TO MRS. KRAMER'S STUFF?
OH, HEY! UH, YOU ARE ALICE, RIGHT?
ALLISON! UH, HOW DID YOU...
SHE TOLD US ALL ABOUT YOU! SAID YOU LOOK A LOT LIKE OUR NIECE, BETHANY, JUST LESS PIERCED!
BOB KRAMER, PLEASURE TO MEET YOU!
OH, SO YOU'RE HER... UH?
SON!
AH! UM, SO WHAT'S THIS ABOUT?
MOM IS MOVING IN WITH US. SHE'S DIABETIC, AND SINCE OUR SON JUST GOT MARRIED AND MOVED OUT... WELL, WE TALKED IT OVER AND FIGURED IT WOULD BE FOR THE BEST...
SO HERE I AM, PICKING UP THE IMPORTANT STUFF. SHE'LL COME BACK FOR THE BIG MOVE.

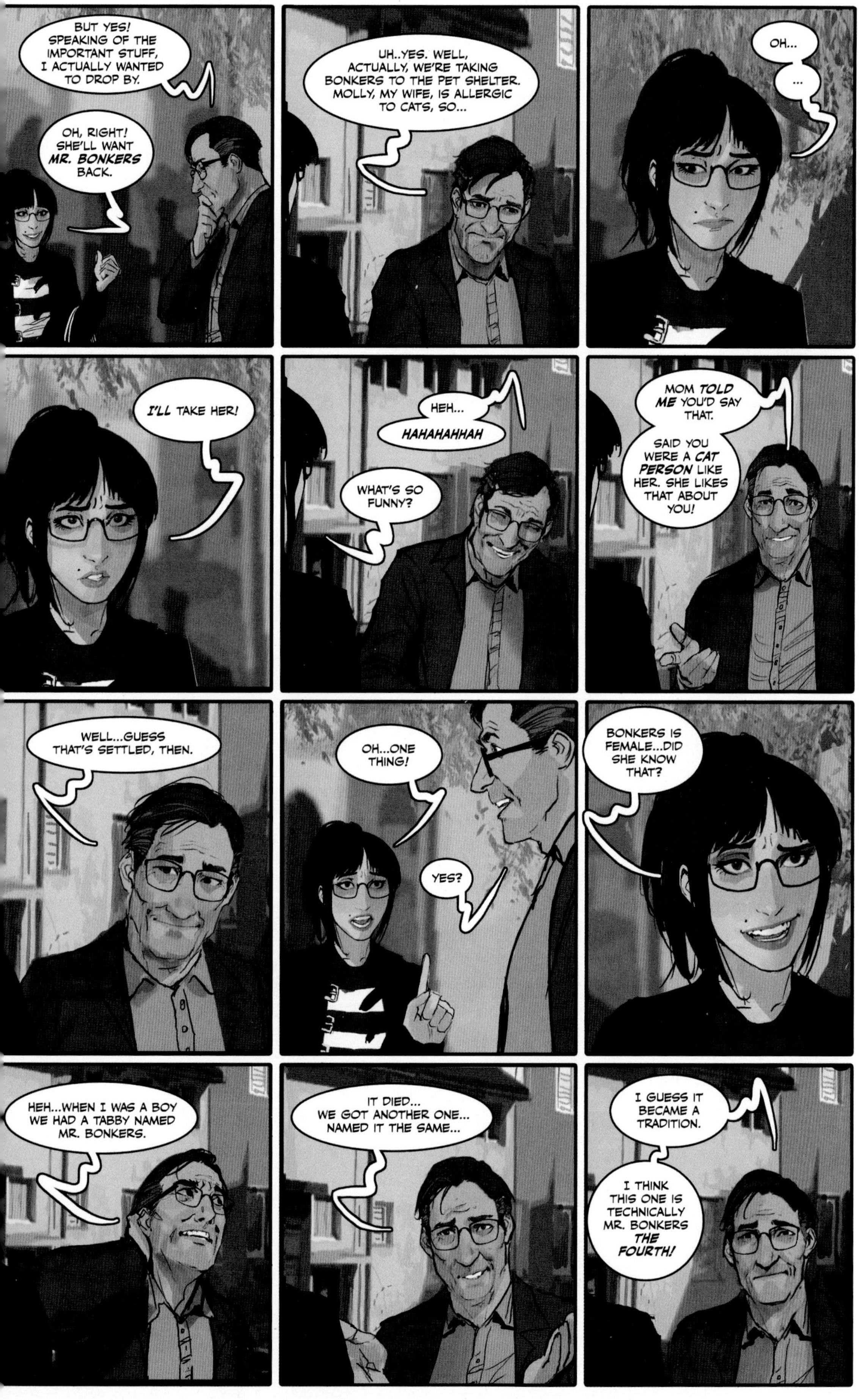
BUT YES! SPEAKING OF THE IMPORTANT STUFF, I ACTUALLY WANTED TO DROP BY.
OH, RIGHT! SHE'LL WANT MR. BONKERS BACK.
UH..YES. WELL, ACTUALLY, WE'RE TAKING BONKERS TO THE PET SHELTER. MOLLY, MY WIFE, IS ALLERGIC TO CATS, SO...
OH...
...
I'LL TAKE HER!
HEH...
HAHAHAHHAH
WHAT'S SO FUNNY?
MOM TOLD ME YOU'D SAY THAT.
SAID YOU WERE A CAT PERSON LIKE HER. SHE LIKES THAT ABOUT YOU!
WELL...GUESS THAT'S SETTLED, THEN.
OH...ONE THING!
YES?
BONKERS IS FEMALE...DID SHE KNOW THAT?
HEH...WHEN I WAS A BOY WE HAD A TABBY NAMED MR. BONKERS.
IT DIED... WE GOT ANOTHER ONE... NAMED IT THE SAME...
I GUESS IT BECAME A TRADITION.
I THINK THIS ONE IS TECHNICALLY MR. BONKERS THE FOURTH!

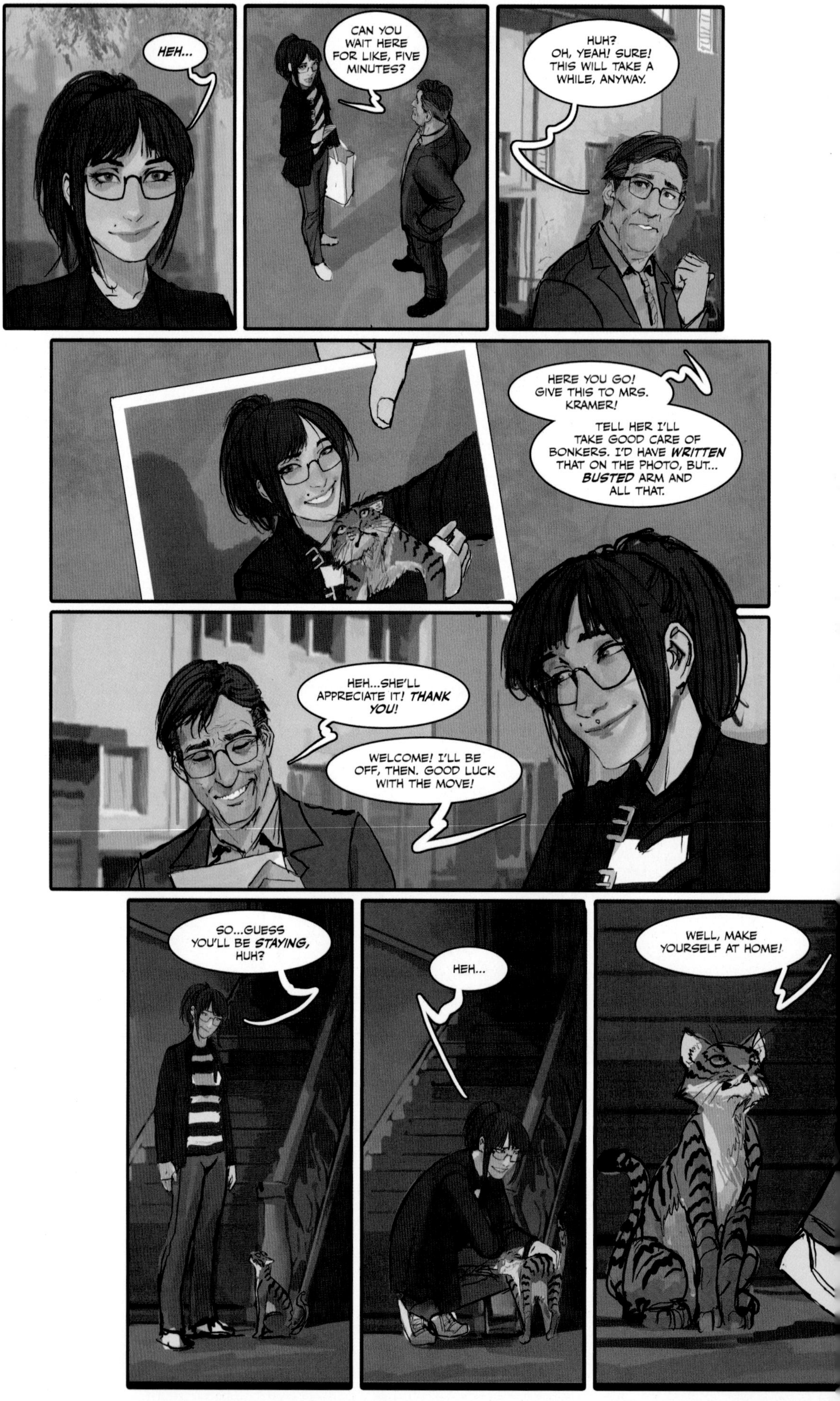
HEH...
CAN YOU WAIT HERE FOR LIKE, FIVE MINUTES?
HUH? OH, YEAH! SURE! THIS WILL TAKE A WHILE, ANYWAY.
HERE YOU GO! GIVE THIS TO MRS. KRAMER!
TELL HER I'LL TAKE GOOD CARE OF BONKERS. I'D HAVE WRITTEN THAT ON THE PHOTO, BUT... BUSTED ARM AND ALL THAT.
HEH...SHE'LL APPRECIATE IT! THANK YOU!
WELCOME! I'LL BE OFF, THEN. GOOD LUCK WITH THE MOVE!
SO...GUESS YOU'LL BE STAYING, HUH?
HEH...
WELL, MAKE YOURSELF AT HOME!

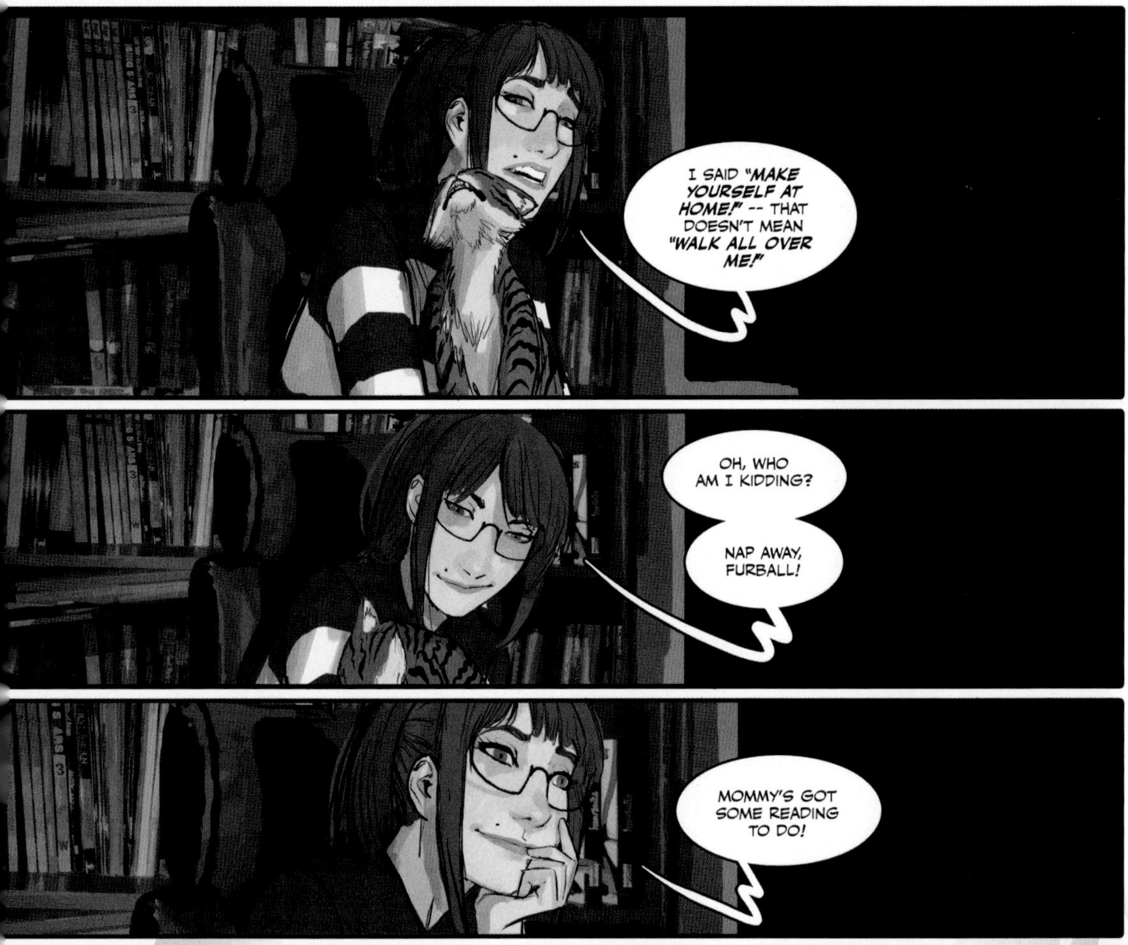

I SAID "MAKE YOURSELF AT HOME!" -- THAT DOESN'T MEAN "WALK ALL OVER ME!"
OH, WHO AM I KIDDING?
NAP AWAY, FURBALL!
MOMMY'S GOT SOME READING TO DO!

MY APPRECIATION

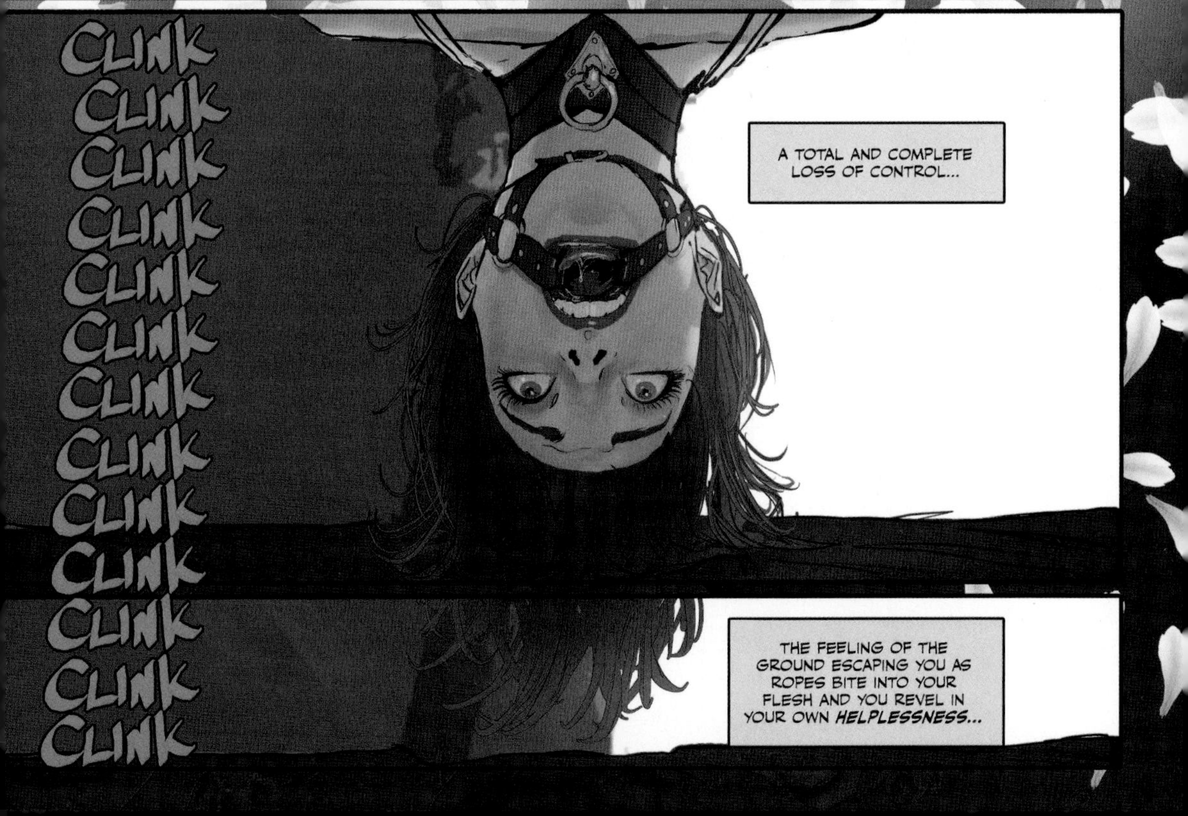

CLINK
CLINK
CLINK
CLINK
CLINK
CLINK
CLINK
CLINK
CLINK
CLINK
CLINK
CLINK
CLINK
A TOTAL AND COMPLETE LOSS OF CONTROL...
THE FEELING OF THE GROUND ESCAPING YOU AS ROPES BITE INTO YOUR FLESH AND YOU REVEL IN YOUR OWN HELPLESSNESS...

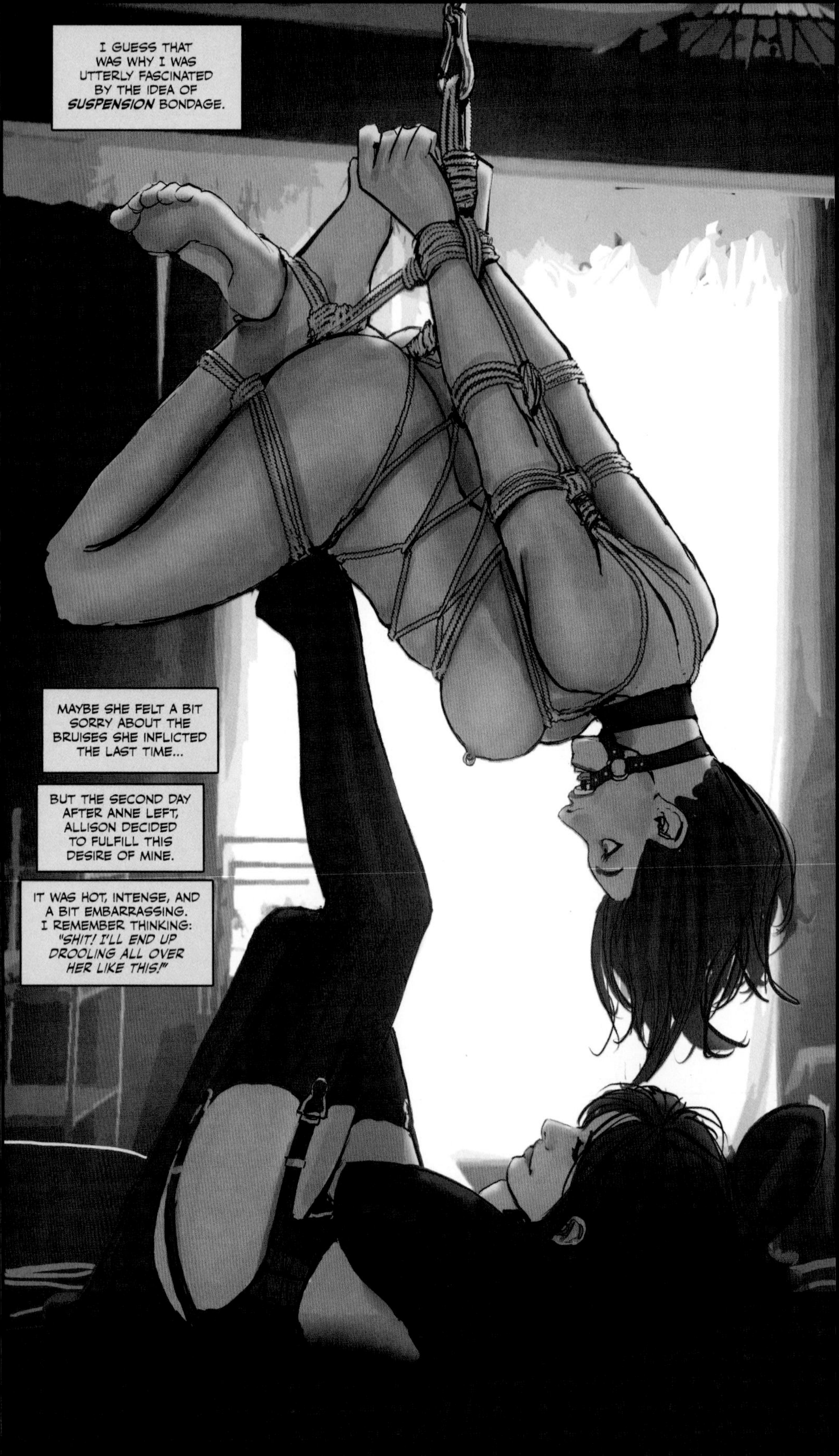
I GUESS THAT WAS WHY I WAS UTTERLY FASCINATED BY THE IDEA OF *SUSPENSION* BONDAGE.
MAYBE SHE FELT A BIT SORRY ABOUT THE BRUISES SHE INFLICTED THE LAST TIME...
BUT THE SECOND DAY AFTER ANNE LEFT, ALLISON DECIDED TO FULFILL THIS DESIRE OF MINE.
IT WAS HOT, INTENSE, AND A BIT EMBARRASSING. I REMEMBER THINKING: *"SHIT! I'LL END UP DROOLING ALL OVER HER LIKE THIS!"*

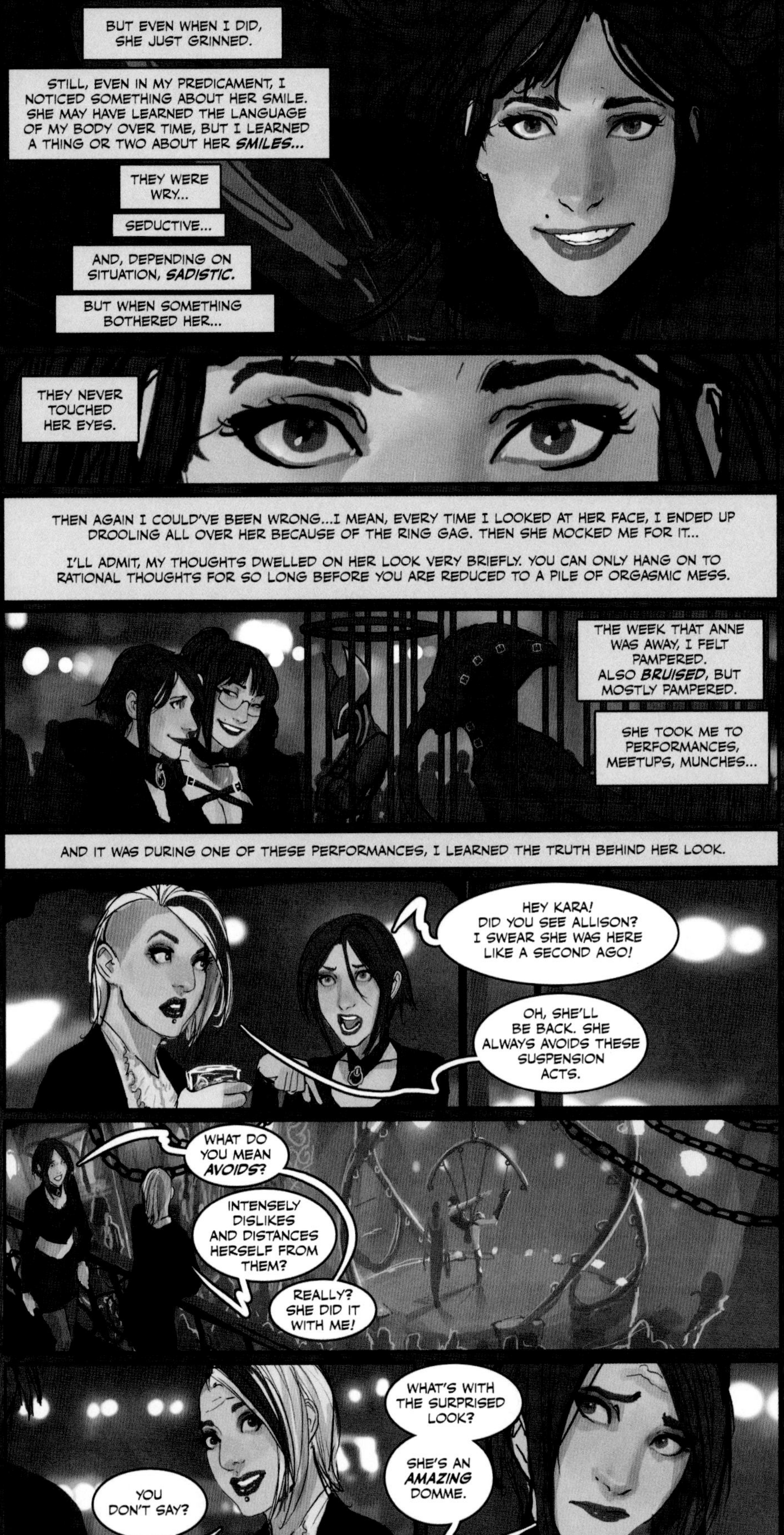

BUT EVEN WHEN I DID, SHE JUST GRINNED.
STILL, EVEN IN MY PREDICAMENT, I NOTICED SOMETHING ABOUT HER SMILE. SHE MAY HAVE LEARNED THE LANGUAGE OF MY BODY OVER TIME, BUT I LEARNED A THING OR TWO ABOUT HER *SMILES...*
THEY WERE WRY...
SEDUCTIVE...
AND, DEPENDING ON SITUATION, *SADISTIC.*
BUT WHEN SOMETHING BOTHERED HER...
THEY NEVER TOUCHED HER EYES.
THEN AGAIN I COULD'VE BEEN WRONG...I MEAN, EVERY TIME I LOOKED AT HER FACE, I ENDED UP DROOLING ALL OVER HER BECAUSE OF THE RING GAG. THEN SHE MOCKED ME FOR IT...
I'LL ADMIT, MY THOUGHTS DWELLED ON HER LOOK VERY BRIEFLY. YOU CAN ONLY HANG ON TO RATIONAL THOUGHTS FOR SO LONG BEFORE YOU ARE REDUCED TO A PILE OF ORGASMIC MESS.
THE WEEK THAT ANNE WAS AWAY, I FELT PAMPERED. ALSO *BRUISED*, BUT MOSTLY PAMPERED.
SHE TOOK ME TO PERFORMANCES, MEETUPS, MUNCHES...
AND IT WAS DURING ONE OF THESE PERFORMANCES, I LEARNED THE TRUTH BEHIND HER LOOK.
HEY KARA! DID YOU SEE ALLISON? I SWEAR SHE WAS HERE LIKE A SECOND AGO!
OH, SHE'LL BE BACK. SHE ALWAYS AVOIDS THESE SUSPENSION ACTS.
WHAT DO YOU MEAN *AVOIDS?*
INTENSELY DISLIKES AND DISTANCES HERSELF FROM THEM?
REALLY? SHE DID IT WITH ME!
WHAT'S WITH THE SURPRISED LOOK?
SHE'S AN *AMAZING* DOMME.
YOU DON'T SAY?

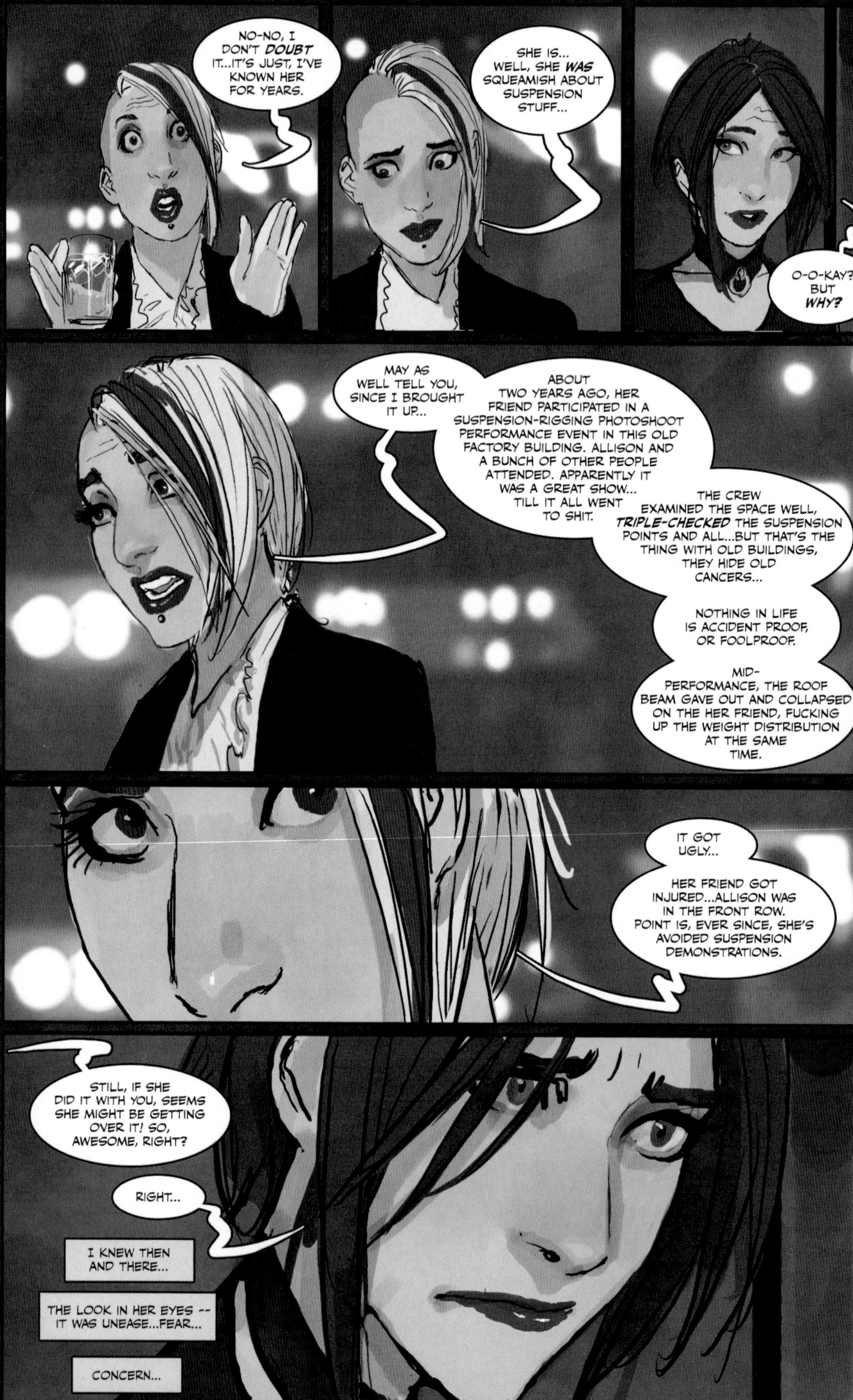
NO-NO, I DON'T *DOUBT* IT...IT'S JUST, I'VE KNOWN HER FOR YEARS.
SHE IS... WELL, SHE *WAS* SQUEAMISH ABOUT SUSPENSION STUFF...
O-O-KAY? BUT *WHY?*
MAY AS WELL TELL YOU, SINCE I BROUGHT IT UP...
ABOUT TWO YEARS AGO, HER FRIEND PARTICIPATED IN A SUSPENSION-RIGGING PHOTOSHOOT PERFORMANCE EVENT IN THIS OLD FACTORY BUILDING. ALLISON AND A BUNCH OF OTHER PEOPLE ATTENDED. APPARENTLY IT WAS A GREAT SHOW... TILL IT ALL WENT TO SHIT.
THE CREW EXAMINED THE SPACE WELL, *TRIPLE-CHECKED* THE SUSPENSION POINTS AND ALL...BUT THAT'S THE THING WITH OLD BUILDINGS, THEY HIDE OLD CANCERS...
NOTHING IN LIFE IS ACCIDENT PROOF, OR FOOLPROOF.
MID-PERFORMANCE, THE ROOF BEAM GAVE OUT AND COLLAPSED ON THE HER FRIEND, FUCKING UP THE WEIGHT DISTRIBUTION AT THE SAME TIME.
IT GOT UGLY...
HER FRIEND GOT INJURED...ALLISON WAS IN THE FRONT ROW. POINT IS, EVER SINCE, SHE'S AVOIDED SUSPENSION DEMONSTRATIONS.
STILL, IF SHE DID IT WITH YOU, SEEMS SHE MIGHT BE GETTING OVER IT! SO, AWESOME, RIGHT?
RIGHT...
I KNEW THEN AND THERE...
THE LOOK IN HER EYES -- IT WAS UNEASE...FEAR...
CONCERN...

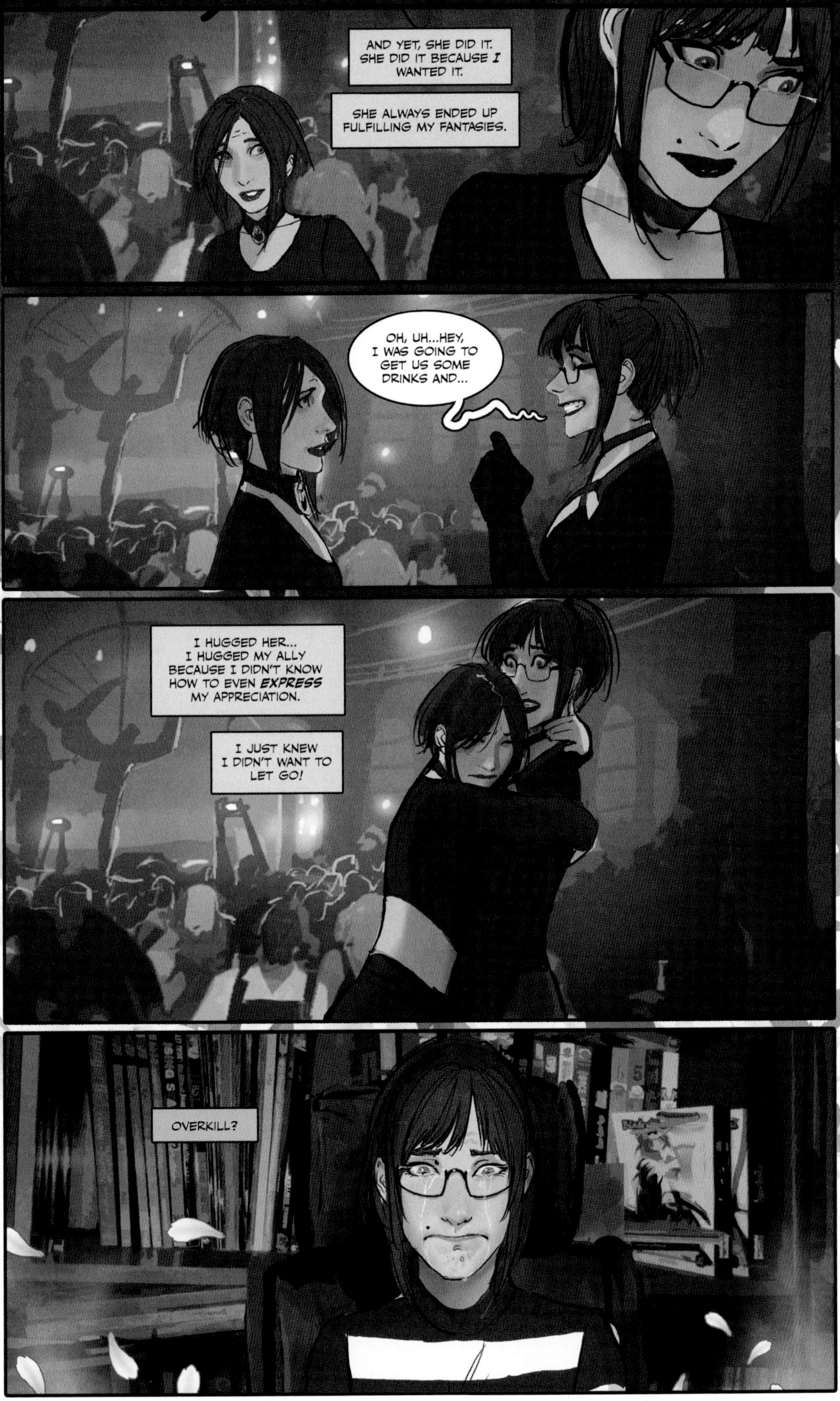
AND YET, SHE DID IT. SHE DID IT BECAUSE *I* WANTED IT.
SHE ALWAYS ENDED UP FULFILLING MY FANTASIES.
OH, UH...HEY, I WAS GOING TO GET US SOME DRINKS AND...
I HUGGED HER... I HUGGED MY ALLY BECAUSE I DIDN'T KNOW HOW TO EVEN ***EXPRESS*** MY APPRECIATION.
I JUST KNEW I DIDN'T WANT TO LET GO!
OVERKILL?

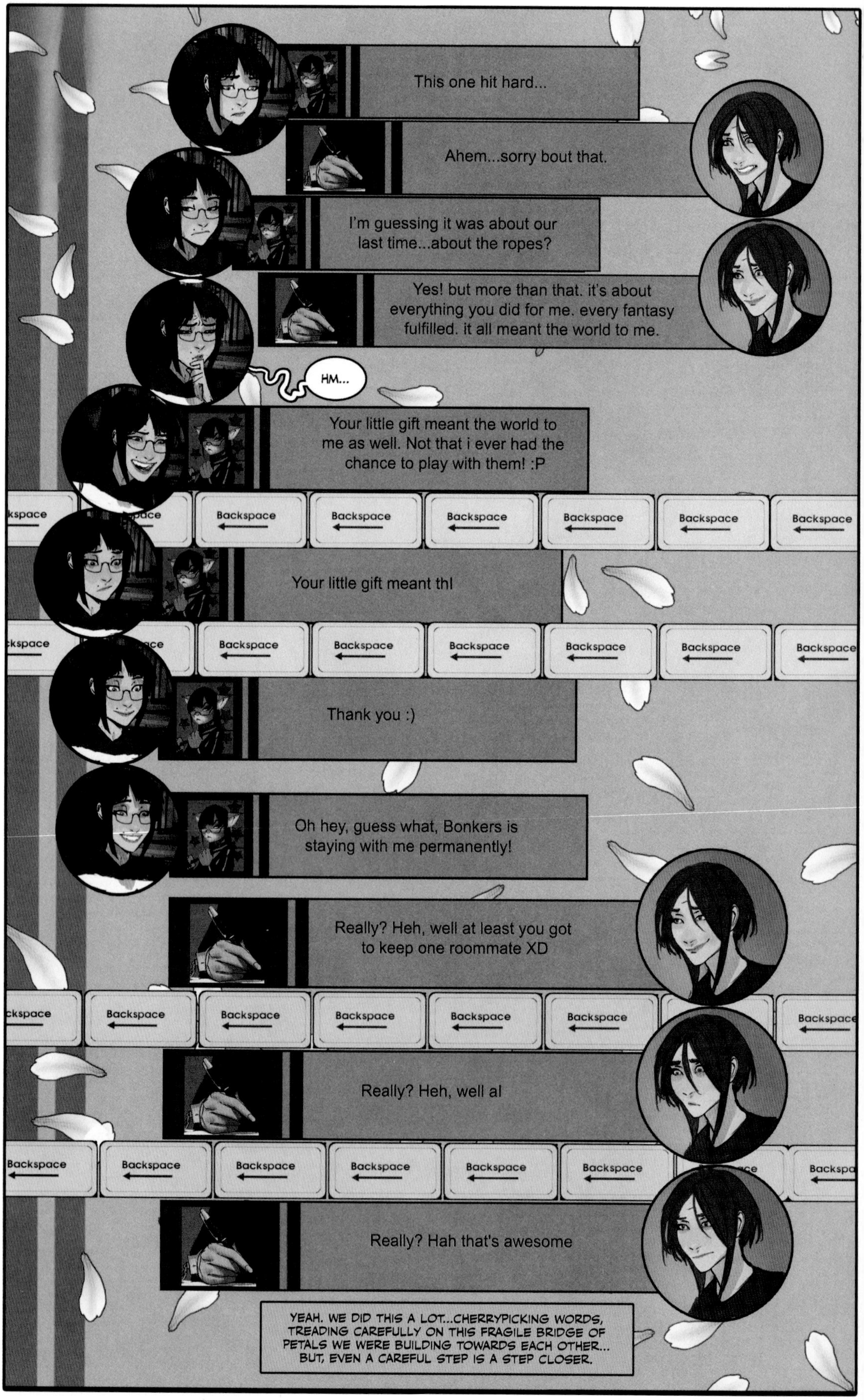

This one hit hard...
Ahem...sorry bout that.
I'm guessing it was about our last time...about the ropes?
Yes! but more than that. it's about everything you did for me. every fantasy fulfilled. it all meant the world to me.
HM...
Your little gift meant the world to me as well. Not that i ever had the chance to play with them! :P
Backspace
Your little gift meant thl
Backspace
Thank you :)
Oh hey, guess what, Bonkers is staying with me permanently!
Really? Heh, well at least you got to keep one roommate XD
Backspace
Really? Heh, well al
Backspace
Really? Hah that's awesome
YEAH. WE DID THIS A LOT...CHERRYPICKING WORDS, TREADING CAREFULLY ON THIS FRAGILE BRIDGE OF PETALS WE WERE BUILDING TOWARDS EACH OTHER... BUT, EVEN A CAREFUL STEP IS A STEP CLOSER.

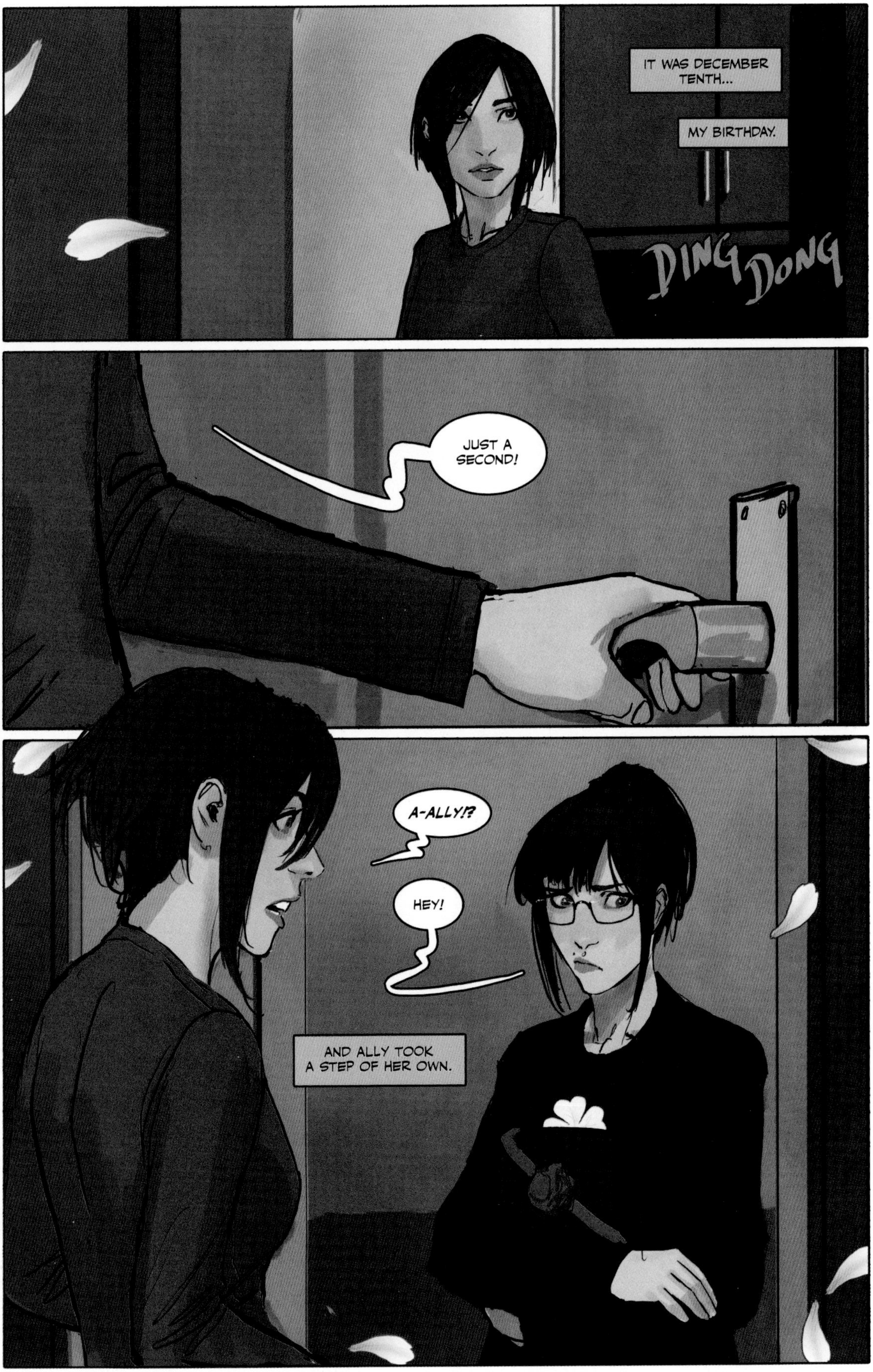

IT WAS DECEMBER TENTH...
MY BIRTHDAY.
DING DONG
JUST A SECOND!
A-ALLY!?
HEY!
AND ALLY TOOK A STEP OF HER OWN.

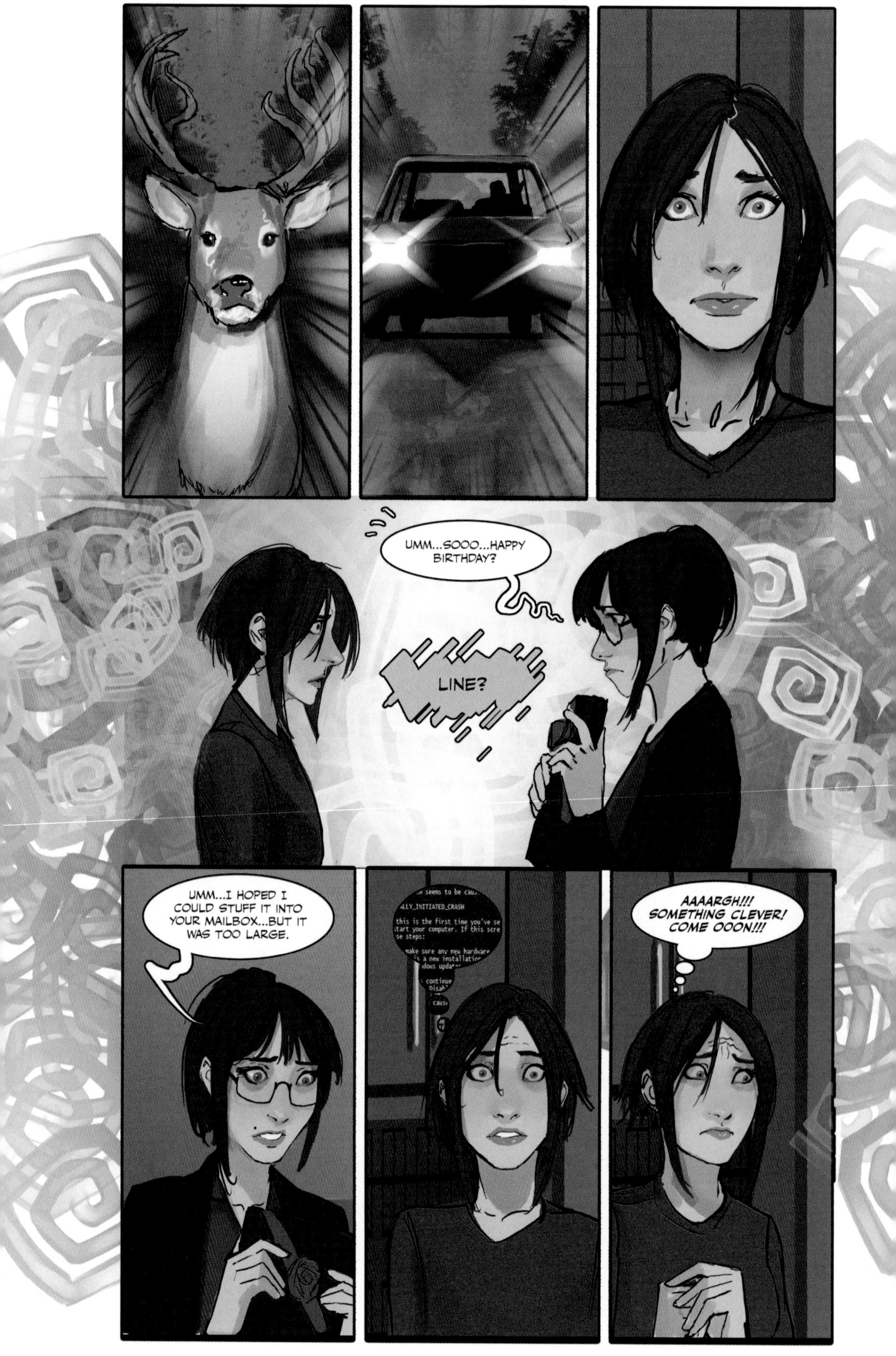
UMM...SOOO...HAPPY BIRTHDAY?
LINE?
UMM...I HOPED I COULD STUFF IT INTO YOUR MAILBOX...BUT IT WAS TOO LARGE.
AAAARGH!!! SOMETHING CLEVER! COME OOON!!!

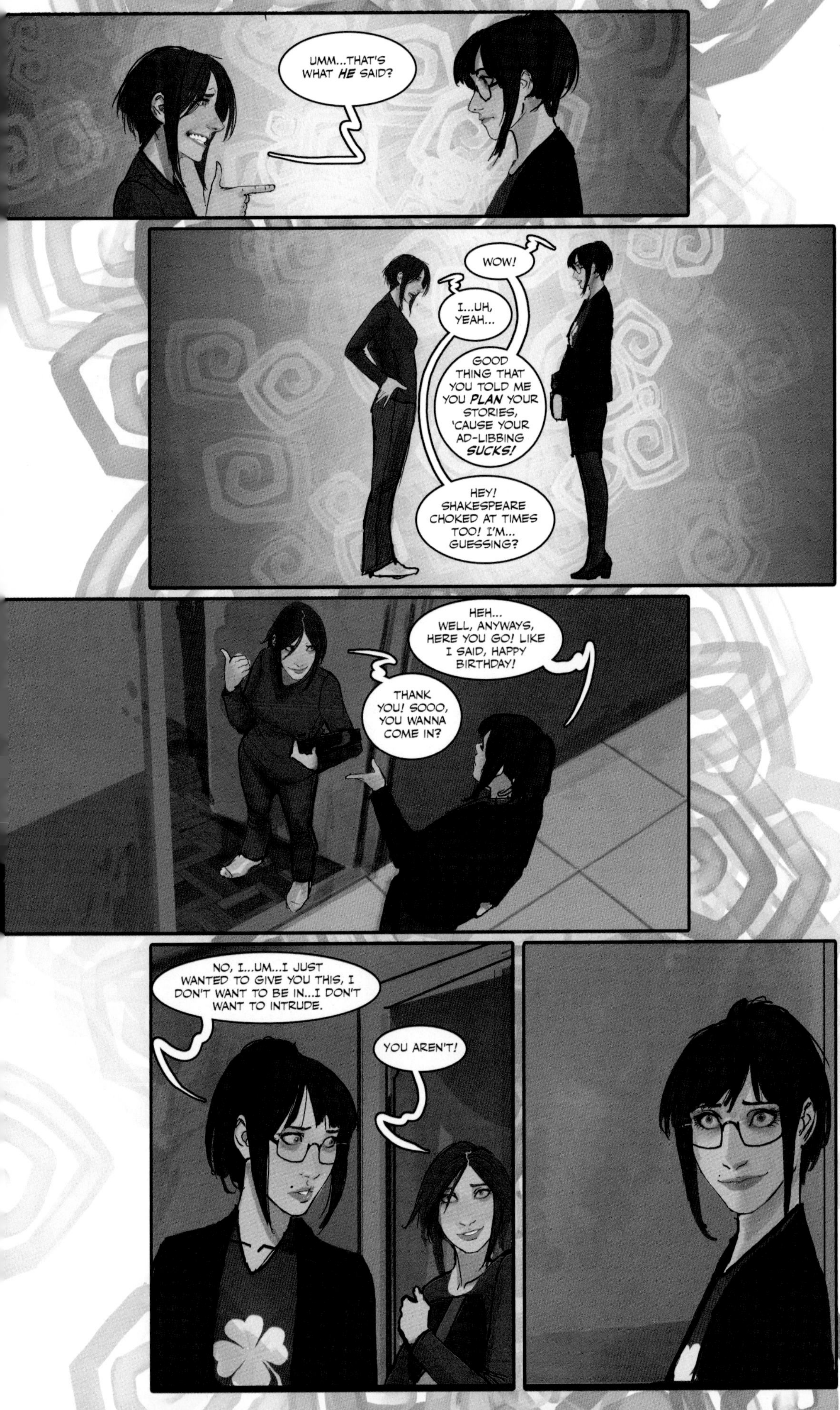
UMM...THAT'S WHAT HE SAID?
WOW!
I...UH, YEAH...
GOOD THING THAT YOU TOLD ME YOU PLAN YOUR STORIES, 'CAUSE YOUR AD-LIBBING SUCKS!
HEY! SHAKESPEARE CHOKED AT TIMES TOO! I'M... GUESSING?
HEH... WELL, ANYWAYS, HERE YOU GO! LIKE I SAID, HAPPY BIRTHDAY!
THANK YOU! SOOO, YOU WANNA COME IN?
NO, I...UM...I JUST WANTED TO GIVE YOU THIS, I DON'T WANT TO BE IN...I DON'T WANT TO INTRUDE.
YOU AREN'T!

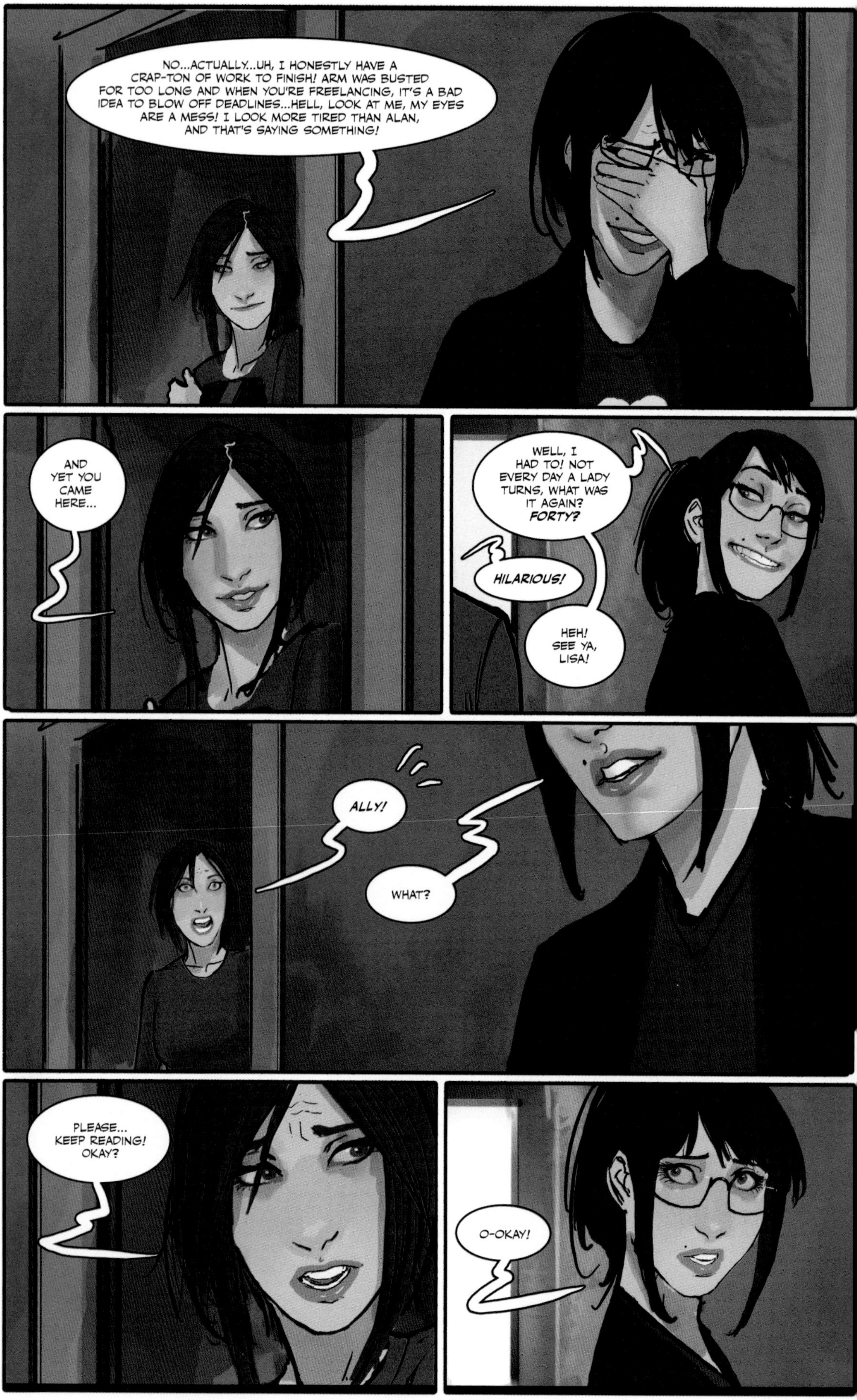
NO...ACTUALLY...UH, I HONESTLY HAVE A CRAP-TON OF WORK TO FINISH! ARM WAS BUSTED FOR TOO LONG AND WHEN YOU'RE FREELANCING, IT'S A BAD IDEA TO BLOW OFF DEADLINES...HELL, LOOK AT ME, MY EYES ARE A MESS! I LOOK MORE TIRED THAN ALAN, AND THAT'S SAYING SOMETHING!
AND YET YOU CAME HERE...
WELL, I HAD TO! NOT EVERY DAY A LADY TURNS, WHAT WAS IT AGAIN? FORTY?
HILARIOUS!
HEH! SEE YA, LISA!
ALLY!
WHAT?
PLEASE... KEEP READING! OKAY?
O-OKAY!

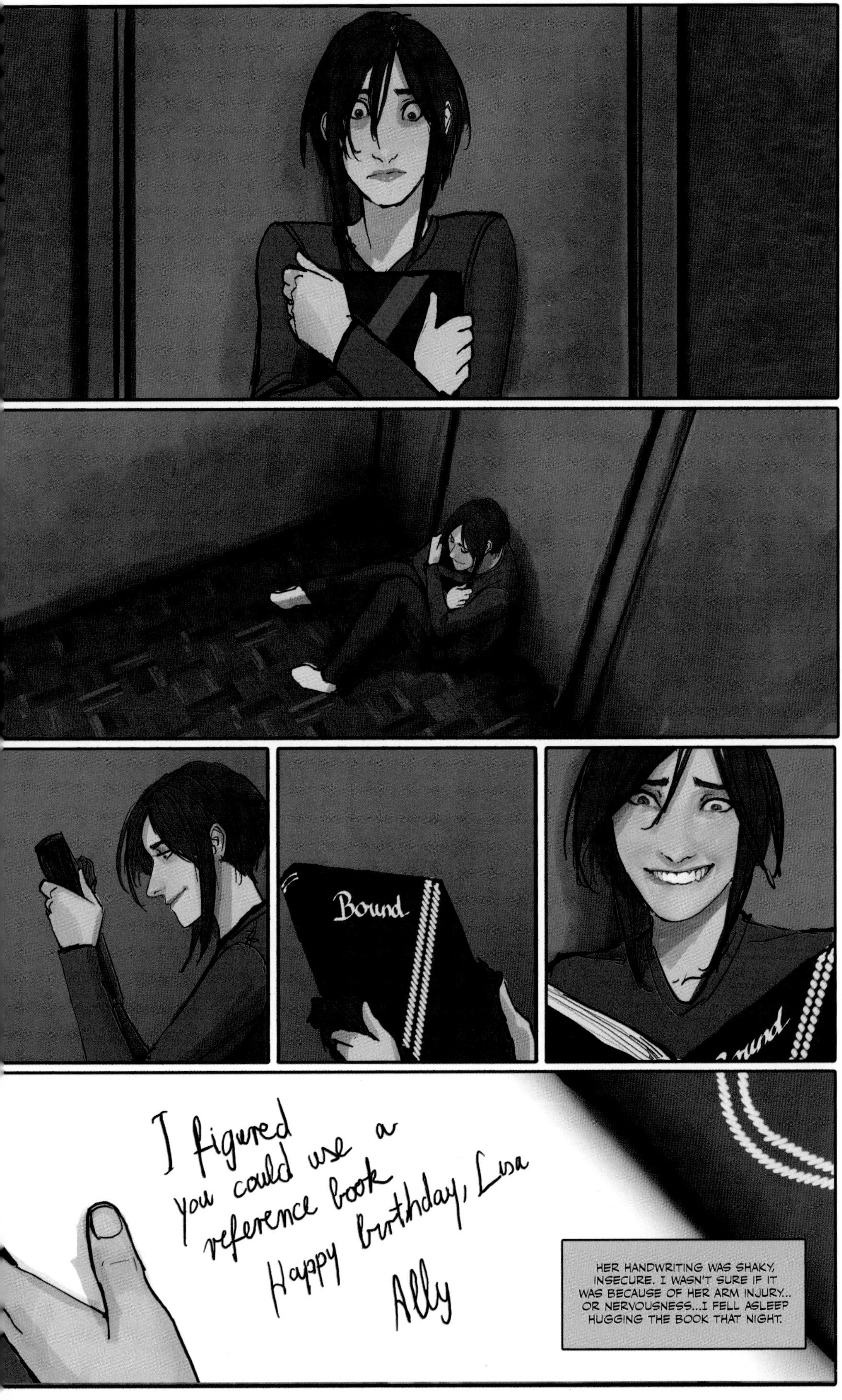
Bound
I figured you could use a reference book
Happy birthday, Lisa
Ally
HER HANDWRITING WAS SHAKY, INSECURE. I WASN'T SURE IF IT WAS BECAUSE OF HER ARM INJURY... OR NERVOUSNESS...I FELL ASLEEP HUGGING THE BOOK THAT NIGHT.

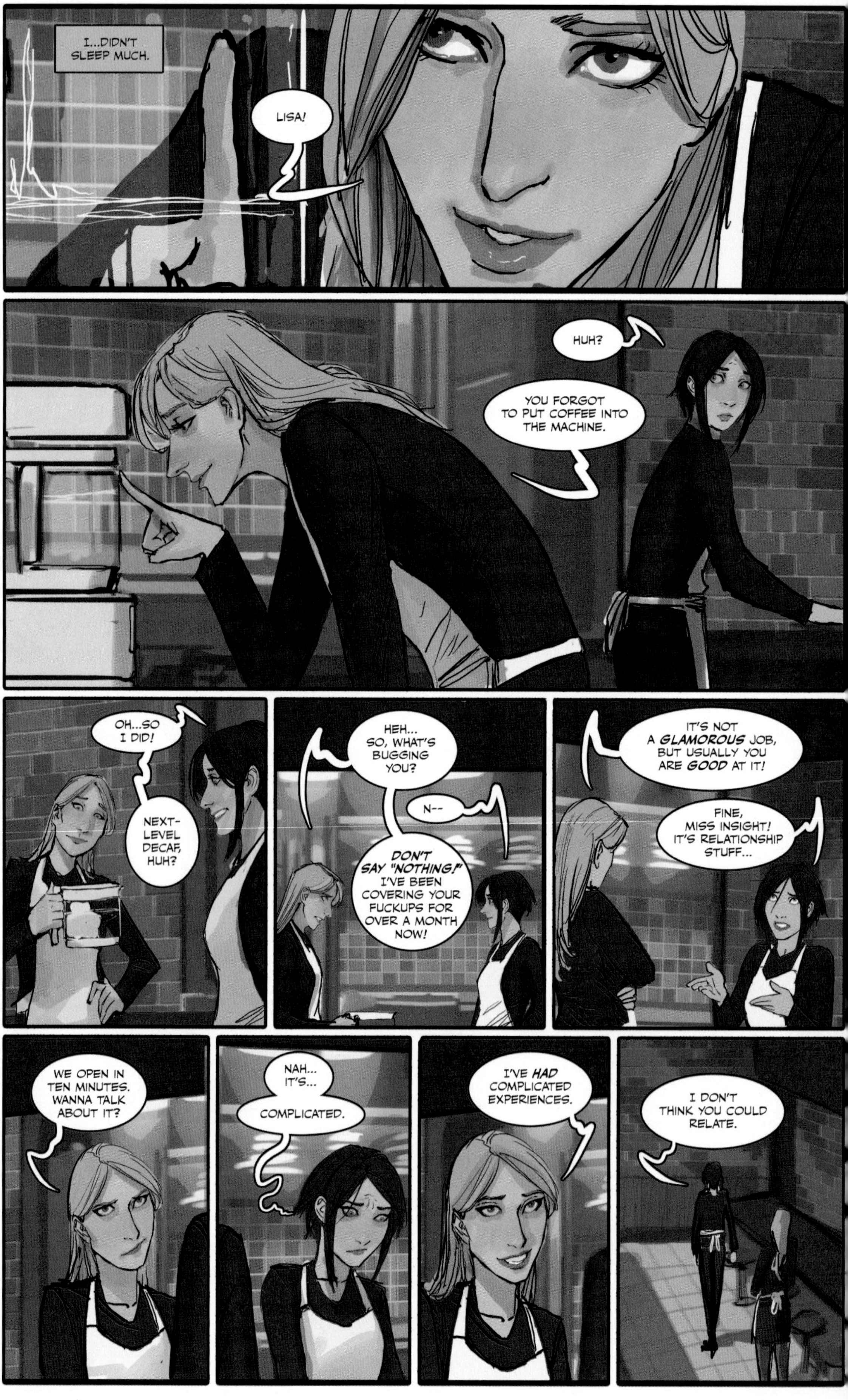
I...DIDN'T SLEEP MUCH.
LISA!
HUH?
YOU FORGOT TO PUT COFFEE INTO THE MACHINE.
OH...SO I DID!
NEXT-LEVEL DECAF, HUH?
HEH... SO, WHAT'S BUGGING YOU?
N--
DON'T SAY "NOTHING!" I'VE BEEN COVERING YOUR FUCKUPS FOR OVER A MONTH NOW!
IT'S NOT A GLAMOROUS JOB, BUT USUALLY YOU ARE GOOD AT IT!
FINE, MISS INSIGHT! IT'S RELATIONSHIP STUFF...
WE OPEN IN TEN MINUTES. WANNA TALK ABOUT IT?
NAH... IT'S...
COMPLICATED.
I'VE HAD COMPLICATED EXPERIENCES.
I DON'T THINK YOU COULD RELATE.

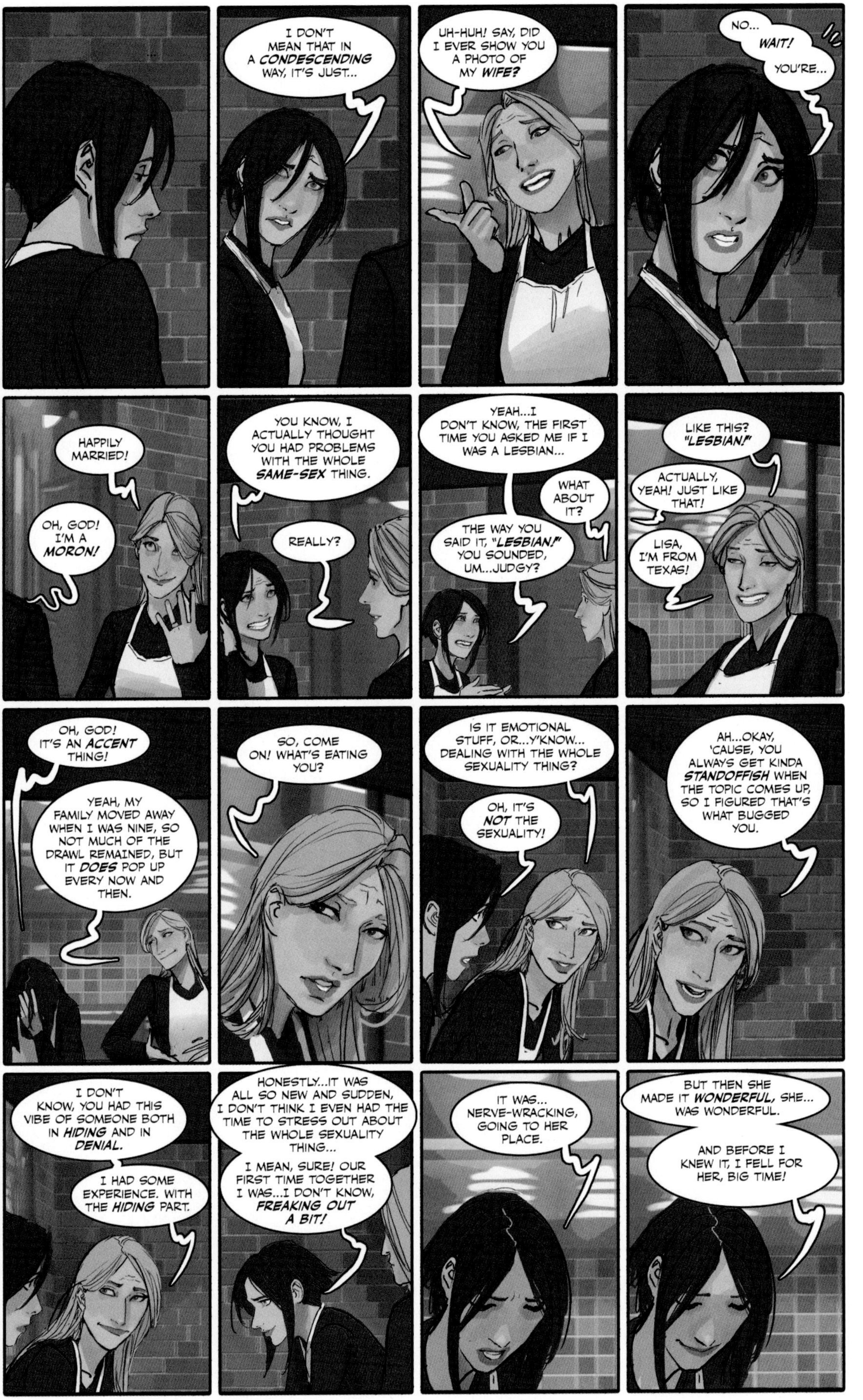
I DON'T MEAN THAT IN A CONDESCENDING WAY, IT'S JUST...
UH-HUH! SAY, DID I EVER SHOW YOU A PHOTO OF MY WIFE?
NO...
WAIT!
YOU'RE...
HAPPILY MARRIED!
OH, GOD! I'M A MORON!
YOU KNOW, I ACTUALLY THOUGHT YOU HAD PROBLEMS WITH THE WHOLE SAME-SEX THING.
REALLY?
YEAH...I DON'T KNOW, THE FIRST TIME YOU ASKED ME IF I WAS A LESBIAN...
WHAT ABOUT IT?
THE WAY YOU SAID IT, "LESBIAN!" YOU SOUNDED, UM...JUDGY?
LIKE THIS? "LESBIAN!"
ACTUALLY, YEAH! JUST LIKE THAT!
LISA, I'M FROM TEXAS!
OH, GOD! IT'S AN ACCENT THING!
YEAH, MY FAMILY MOVED AWAY WHEN I WAS NINE, SO NOT MUCH OF THE DRAWL REMAINED, BUT IT DOES POP UP EVERY NOW AND THEN.
SO, COME ON! WHAT'S EATING YOU?
IS IT EMOTIONAL STUFF, OR...Y'KNOW... DEALING WITH THE WHOLE SEXUALITY THING?
OH, IT'S NOT THE SEXUALITY!
AH...OKAY, 'CAUSE, YOU ALWAYS GET KINDA STANDOFFISH WHEN THE TOPIC COMES UP, SO I FIGURED THAT'S WHAT BUGGED YOU.
I DON'T KNOW, YOU HAD THIS VIBE OF SOMEONE BOTH IN HIDING AND IN DENIAL.
I HAD SOME EXPERIENCE. WITH THE HIDING PART.
HONESTLY...IT WAS ALL SO NEW AND SUDDEN, I DON'T THINK I EVEN HAD THE TIME TO STRESS OUT ABOUT THE WHOLE SEXUALITY THING...
I MEAN, SURE! OUR FIRST TIME TOGETHER I WAS...I DON'T KNOW, FREAKING OUT A BIT!
IT WAS... NERVE-WRACKING, GOING TO HER PLACE.
BUT THEN SHE MADE IT WONDERFUL, SHE... WAS WONDERFUL.
AND BEFORE I KNEW IT, I FELL FOR HER, BIG TIME!

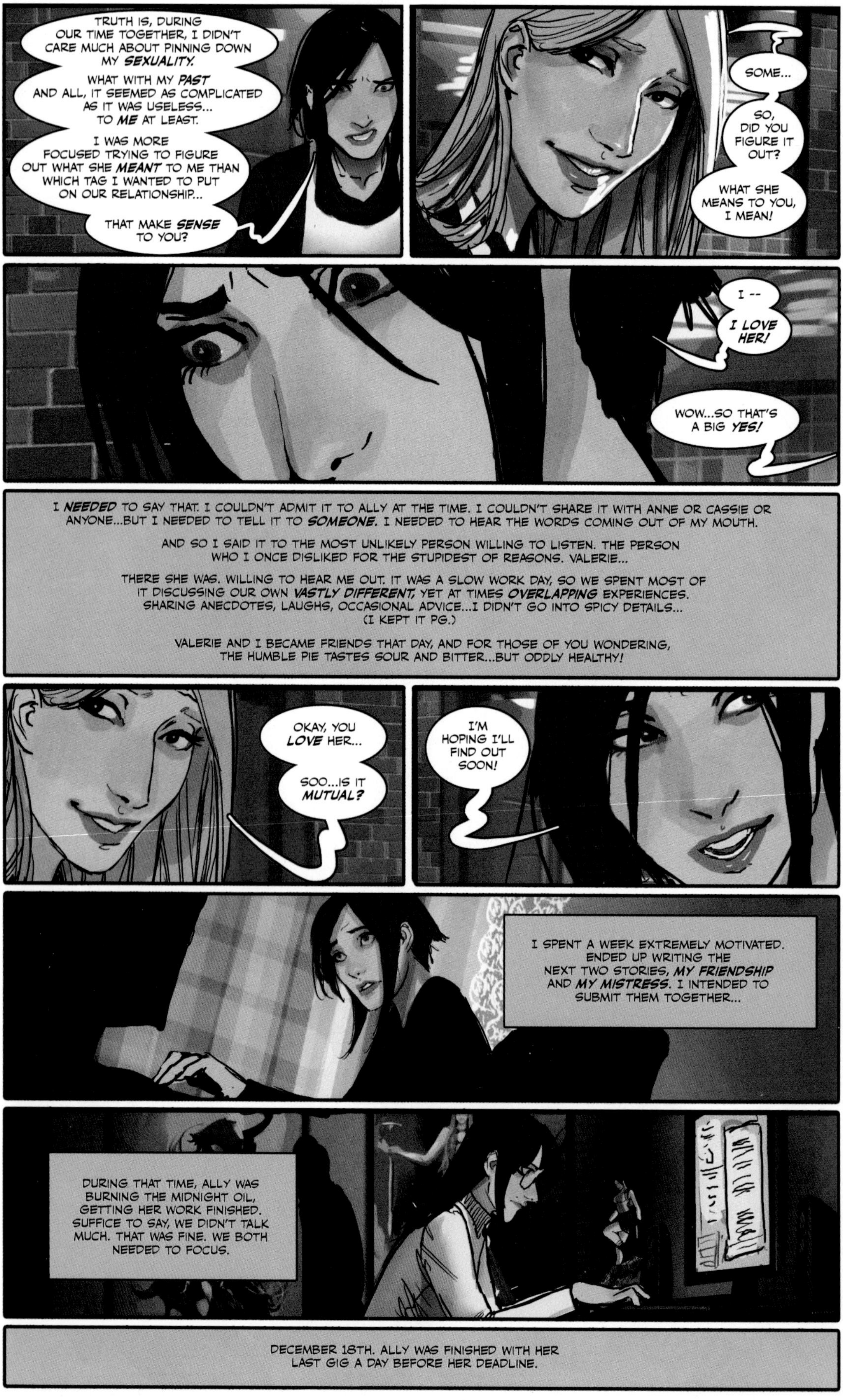
TRUTH IS, DURING OUR TIME TOGETHER, I DIDN'T CARE MUCH ABOUT PINNING DOWN MY SEXUALITY.
WHAT WITH MY PAST AND ALL, IT SEEMED AS COMPLICATED AS IT WAS USELESS... TO ME AT LEAST.
I WAS MORE FOCUSED TRYING TO FIGURE OUT WHAT SHE MEANT TO ME THAN WHICH TAG I WANTED TO PUT ON OUR RELATIONSHIP...
THAT MAKE SENSE TO YOU?
SOME...
SO, DID YOU FIGURE IT OUT?
WHAT SHE MEANS TO YOU, I MEAN!
I --
I LOVE HER!
WOW...SO THAT'S A BIG YES!
I NEEDED TO SAY THAT. I COULDN'T ADMIT IT TO ALLY AT THE TIME. I COULDN'T SHARE IT WITH ANNE OR CASSIE OR ANYONE...BUT I NEEDED TO TELL IT TO SOMEONE. I NEEDED TO HEAR THE WORDS COMING OUT OF MY MOUTH.
AND SO I SAID IT TO THE MOST UNLIKELY PERSON WILLING TO LISTEN. THE PERSON WHO I ONCE DISLIKED FOR THE STUPIDEST OF REASONS. VALERIE...
THERE SHE WAS. WILLING TO HEAR ME OUT. IT WAS A SLOW WORK DAY, SO WE SPENT MOST OF IT DISCUSSING OUR OWN VASTLY DIFFERENT, YET AT TIMES OVERLAPPING EXPERIENCES. SHARING ANECDOTES, LAUGHS, OCCASIONAL ADVICE...I DIDN'T GO INTO SPICY DETAILS... (I KEPT IT PG.)
VALERIE AND I BECAME FRIENDS THAT DAY, AND FOR THOSE OF YOU WONDERING, THE HUMBLE PIE TASTES SOUR AND BITTER...BUT ODDLY HEALTHY!
OKAY, YOU LOVE HER...
SOO...IS IT MUTUAL?
I'M HOPING I'LL FIND OUT SOON!
I SPENT A WEEK EXTREMELY MOTIVATED. ENDED UP WRITING THE NEXT TWO STORIES, MY FRIENDSHIP AND MY MISTRESS. I INTENDED TO SUBMIT THEM TOGETHER...
DURING THAT TIME, ALLY WAS BURNING THE MIDNIGHT OIL, GETTING HER WORK FINISHED. SUFFICE TO SAY, WE DIDN'T TALK MUCH. THAT WAS FINE. WE BOTH NEEDED TO FOCUS.
DECEMBER 18TH. ALLY WAS FINISHED WITH HER LAST GIG A DAY BEFORE HER DEADLINE.

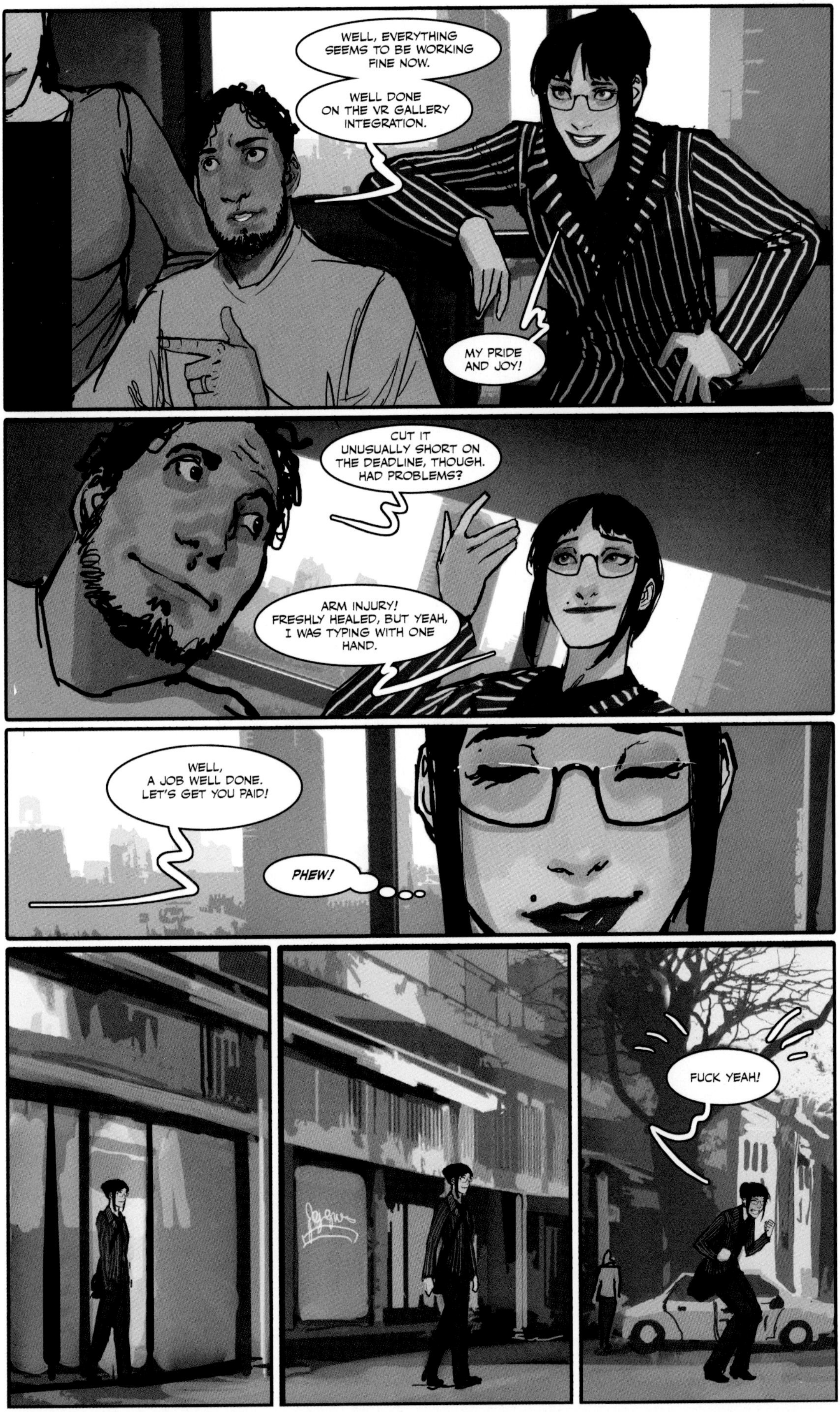
WELL, EVERYTHING SEEMS TO BE WORKING FINE NOW.
WELL DONE ON THE VR GALLERY INTEGRATION.
MY PRIDE AND JOY!
CUT IT UNUSUALLY SHORT ON THE DEADLINE, THOUGH. HAD PROBLEMS?
ARM INJURY! FRESHLY HEALED, BUT YEAH, I WAS TYPING WITH ONE HAND.
WELL, A JOB WELL DONE. LET'S GET YOU PAID!
PHEW!
FUCK YEAH!

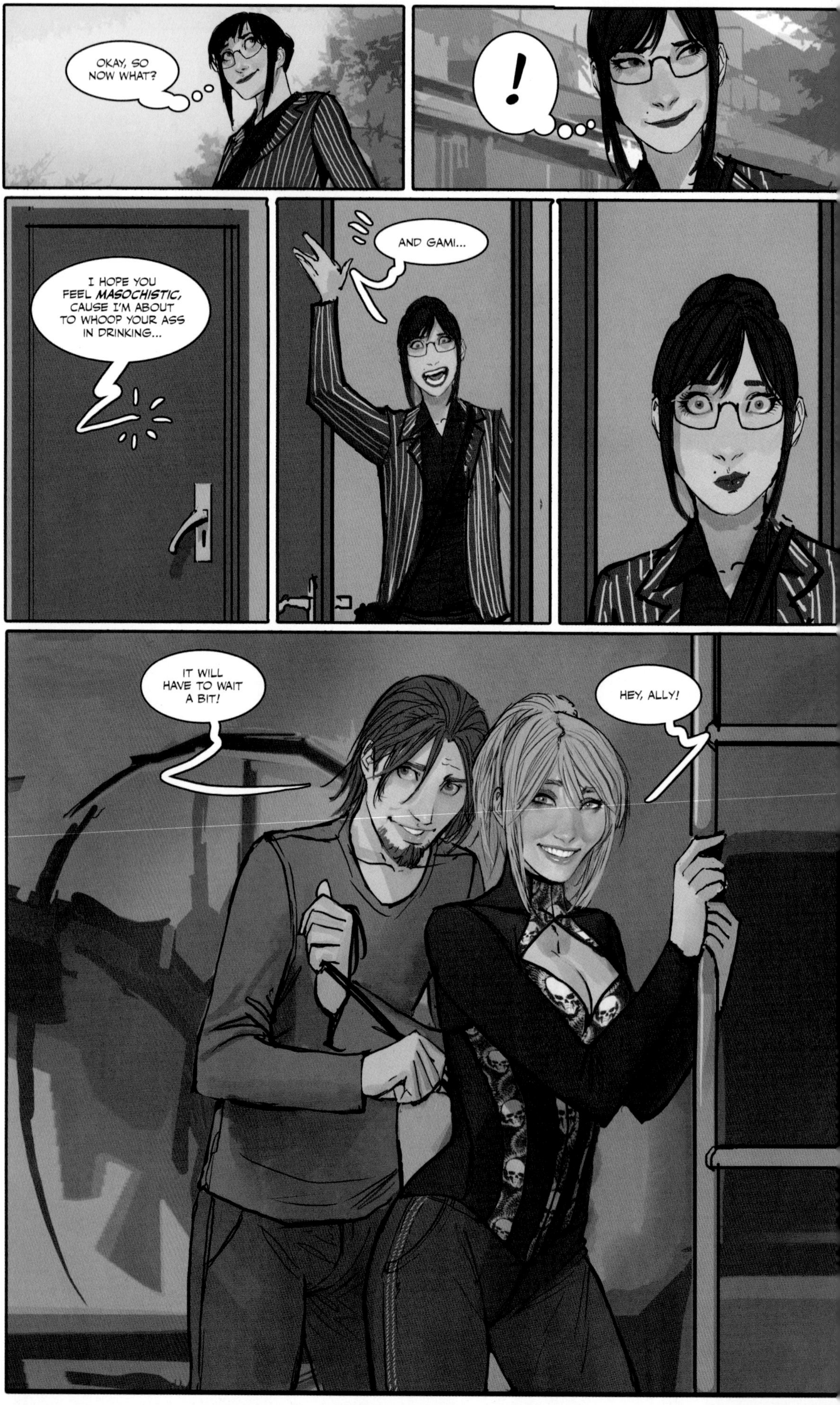
OKAY, SO NOW WHAT?
!
I HOPE YOU FEEL MASOCHISTIC, CAUSE I'M ABOUT TO WHOOP YOUR ASS IN DRINKING...
AND GAMI...
IT WILL HAVE TO WAIT A BIT!
HEY, ALLY!

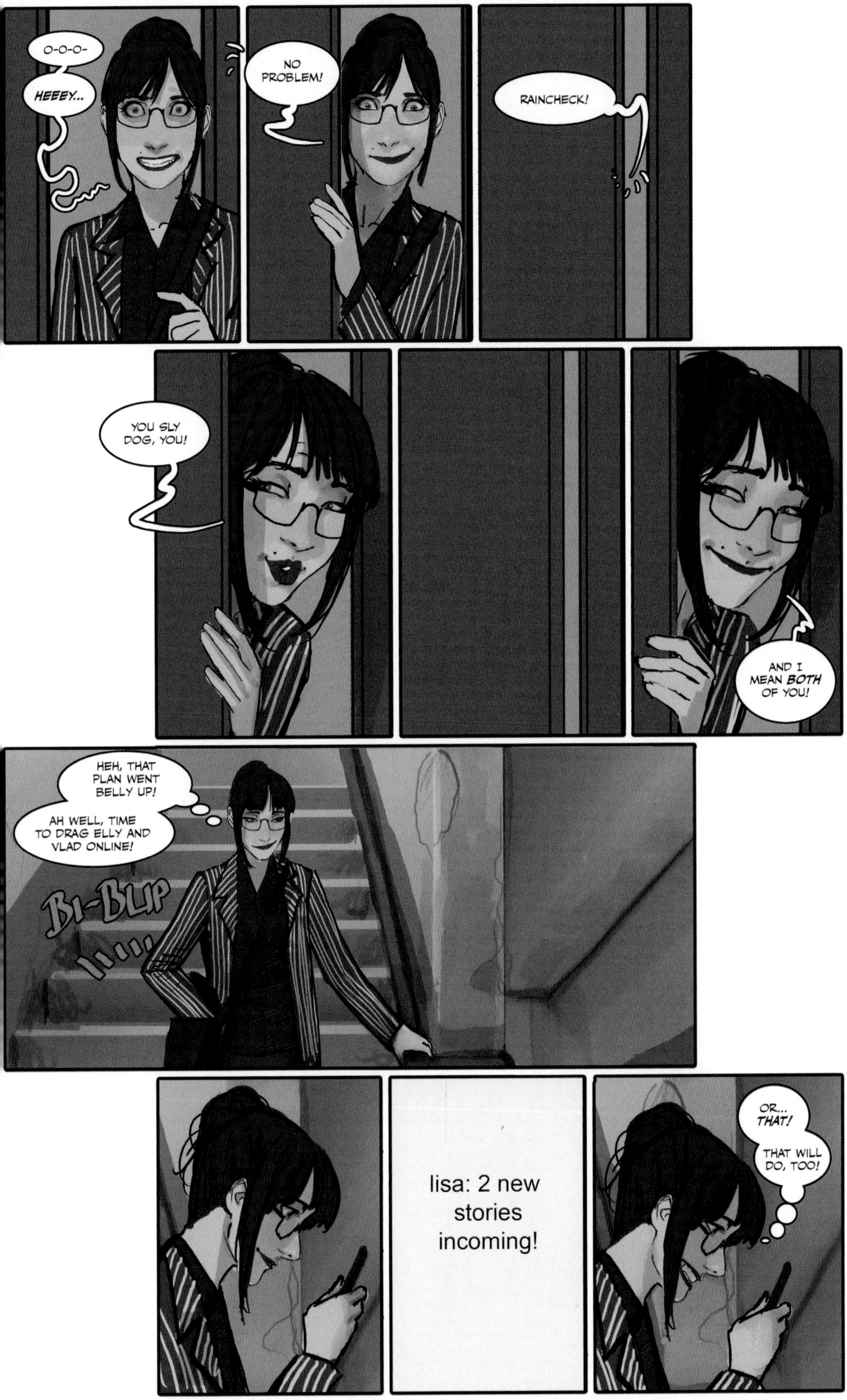

O-O-O-
HEEEY...
NO PROBLEM!
RAINCHECK!
YOU SLY DOG, YOU!
AND I MEAN BOTH OF YOU!
HEH, THAT PLAN WENT BELLY UP!
AH WELL, TIME TO DRAG ELLY AND VLAD ONLINE!
BI-BLIP
lisa: 2 new stories incoming!
OR... THAT!
THAT WILL DO, TOO!

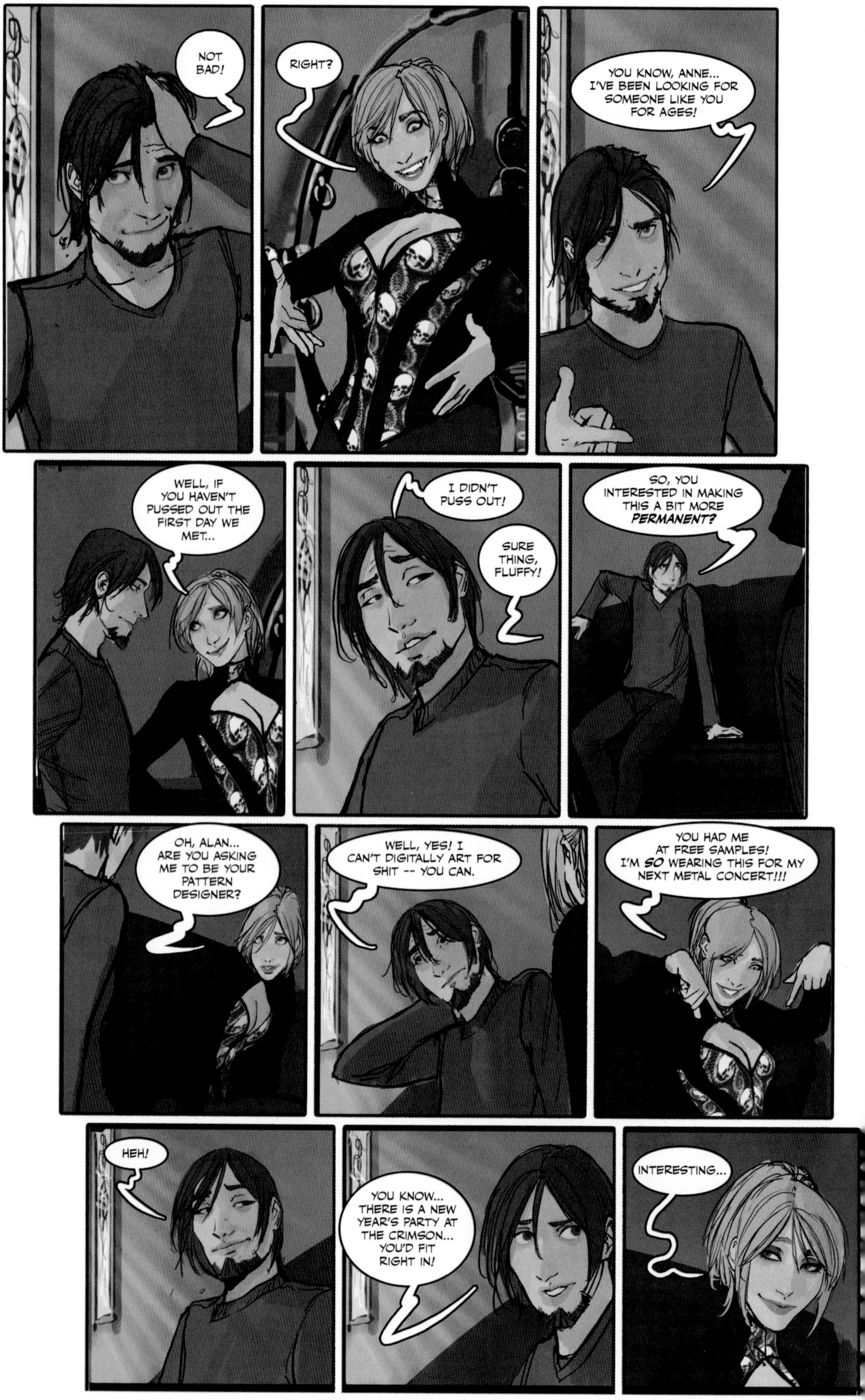
NOT BAD!
RIGHT?
YOU KNOW, ANNE... I'VE BEEN LOOKING FOR SOMEONE LIKE YOU FOR AGES!
WELL, IF YOU HAVEN'T PUSSED OUT THE FIRST DAY WE MET...
I DIDN'T PUSS OUT!
SURE THING, FLUFFY!
SO, YOU INTERESTED IN MAKING THIS A BIT MORE PERMANENT?
OH, ALAN... ARE YOU ASKING ME TO BE YOUR PATTERN DESIGNER?
WELL, YES! I CAN'T DIGITALLY ART FOR SHIT -- YOU CAN.
YOU HAD ME AT FREE SAMPLES! I'M SO WEARING THIS FOR MY NEXT METAL CONCERT!!!
HEH!
YOU KNOW... THERE IS A NEW YEAR'S PARTY AT THE CRIMSON... YOU'D FIT RIGHT IN!
INTERESTING...

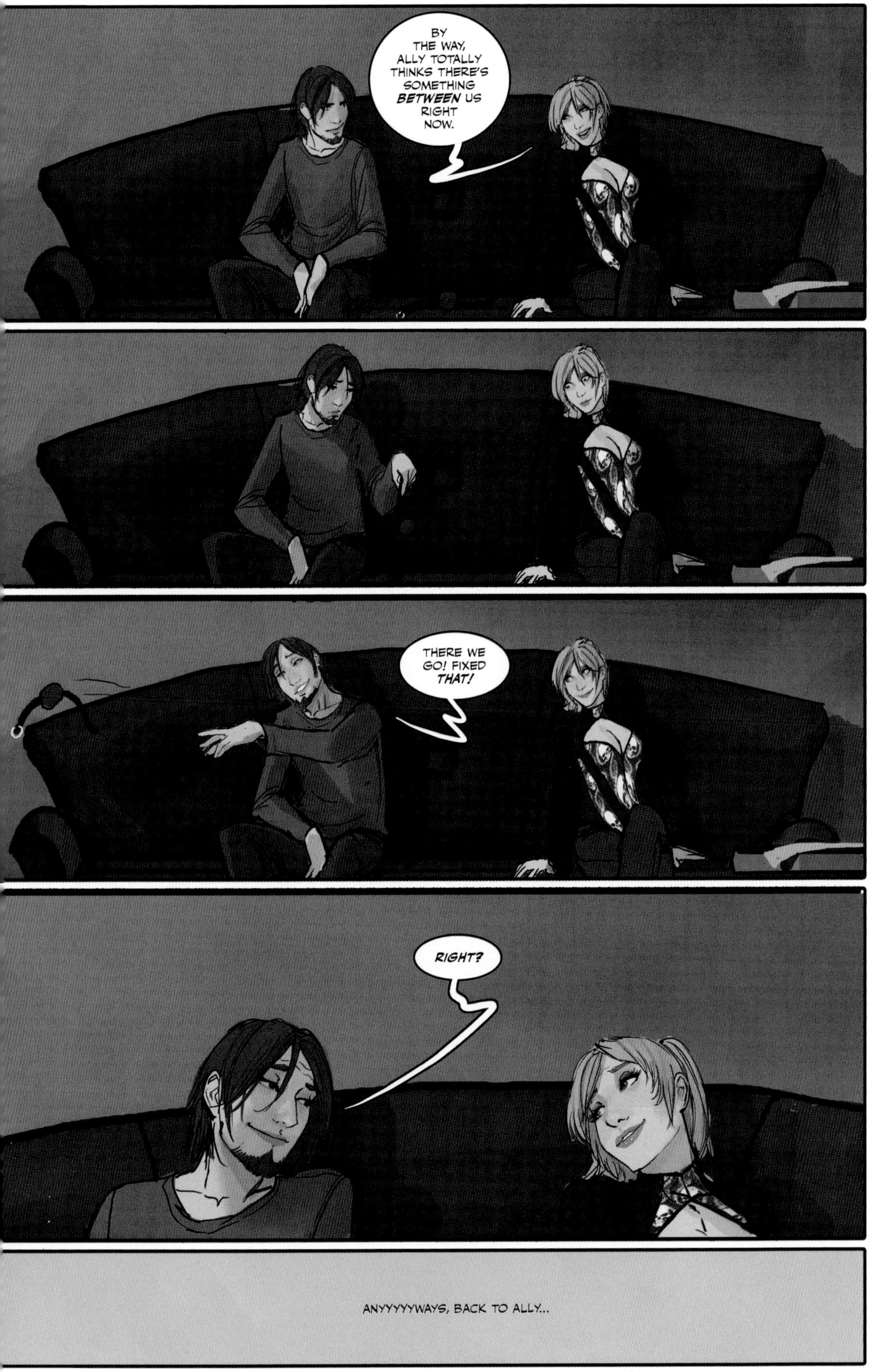
BY THE WAY, ALLY TOTALLY THINKS THERE'S SOMETHING *BETWEEN* US RIGHT NOW.
THERE WE GO! FIXED *THAT!*
RIGHT?
ANYYYYYWAYS, BACK TO ALLY...

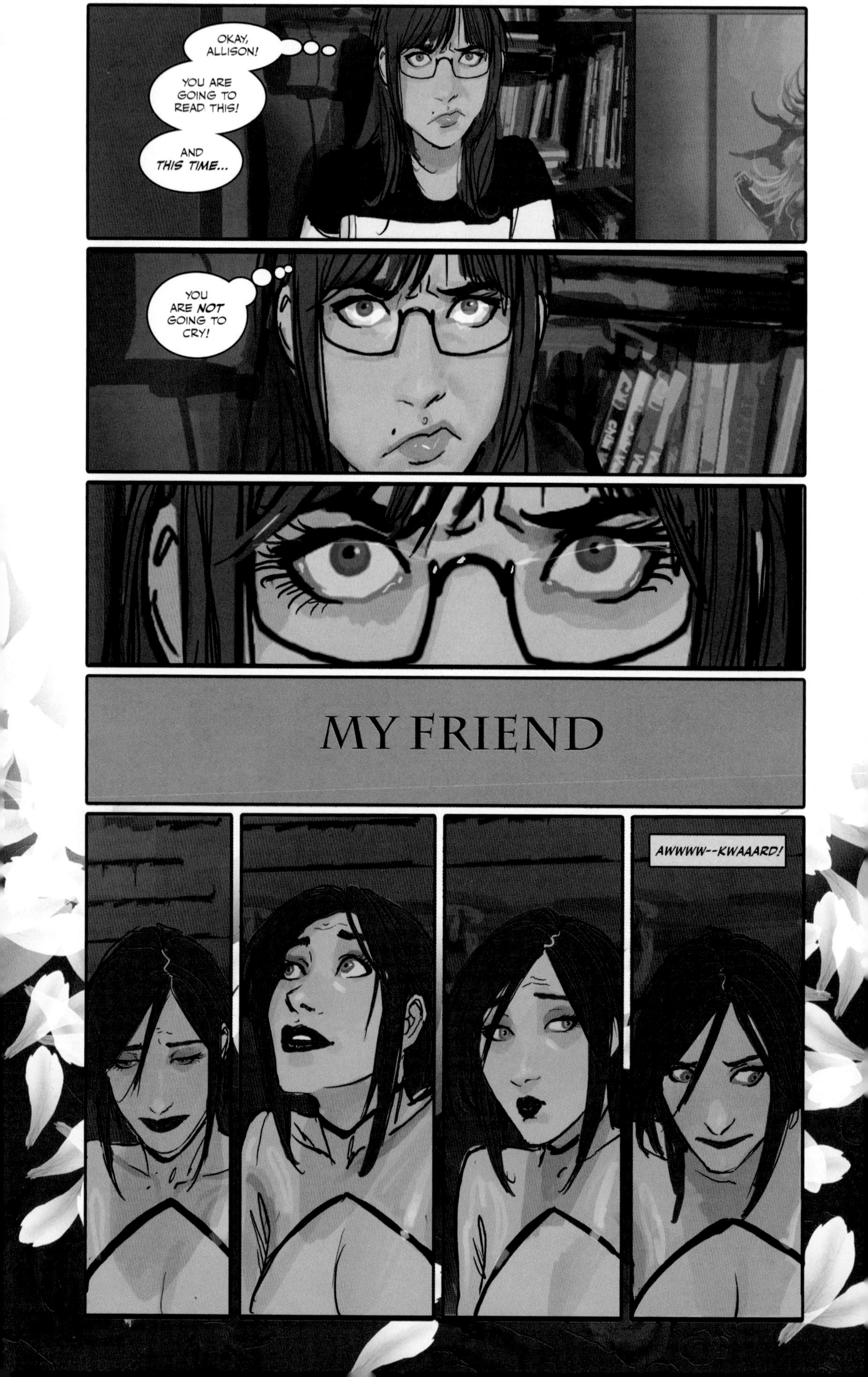
OKAY, ALLISON!
YOU ARE GOING TO READ THIS!
AND *THIS TIME...*
YOU ARE *NOT* GOING TO CRY!
MY FRIEND
AWWWW--KWAAARD!

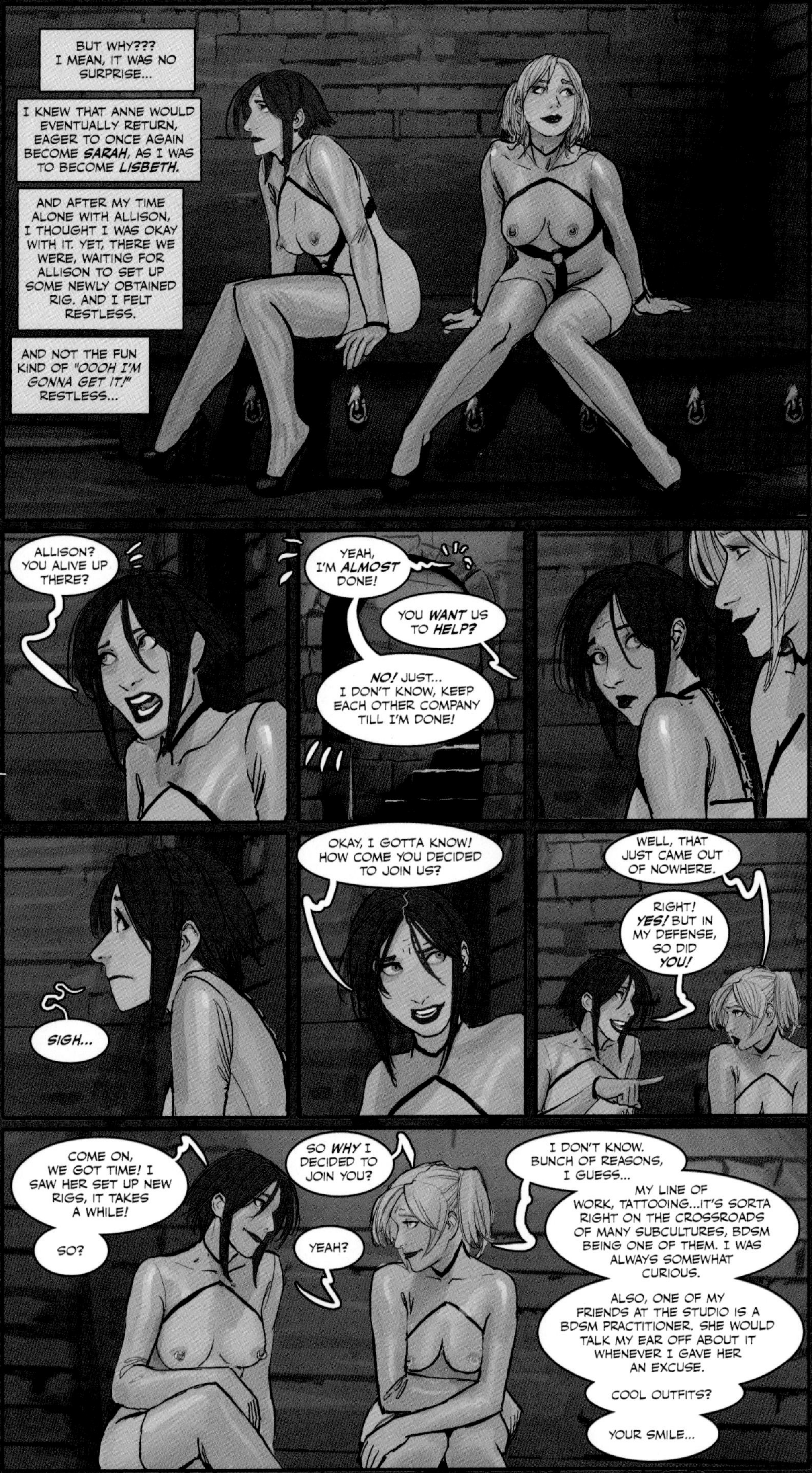
BUT WHY??? I MEAN, IT WAS NO SURPRISE...
I KNEW THAT ANNE WOULD EVENTUALLY RETURN, EAGER TO ONCE AGAIN BECOME SARAH, AS I WAS TO BECOME LISBETH.
AND AFTER MY TIME ALONE WITH ALLISON, I THOUGHT I WAS OKAY WITH IT. YET, THERE WE WERE, WAITING FOR ALLISON TO SET UP SOME NEWLY OBTAINED RIG. AND I FELT RESTLESS.
AND NOT THE FUN KIND OF "OOOH I'M GONNA GET IT!" RESTLESS...
ALLISON? YOU ALIVE UP THERE?
YEAH, I'M ALMOST DONE!
YOU WANT US TO HELP?
NO! JUST... I DON'T KNOW, KEEP EACH OTHER COMPANY TILL I'M DONE!
SIGH...
OKAY, I GOTTA KNOW! HOW COME YOU DECIDED TO JOIN US?
WELL, THAT JUST CAME OUT OF NOWHERE.
RIGHT! YES! BUT IN MY DEFENSE, SO DID YOU!
COME ON, WE GOT TIME! I SAW HER SET UP NEW RIGS, IT TAKES A WHILE!
SO WHY I DECIDED TO JOIN YOU?
SO?
YEAH?
I DON'T KNOW. BUNCH OF REASONS, I GUESS...
MY LINE OF WORK, TATTOOING...IT'S SORTA RIGHT ON THE CROSSROADS OF MANY SUBCULTURES, BDSM BEING ONE OF THEM. I WAS ALWAYS SOMEWHAT CURIOUS.
ALSO, ONE OF MY FRIENDS AT THE STUDIO IS A BDSM PRACTITIONER. SHE WOULD TALK MY EAR OFF ABOUT IT WHENEVER I GAVE HER AN EXCUSE.
COOL OUTFITS?
YOUR SMILE...

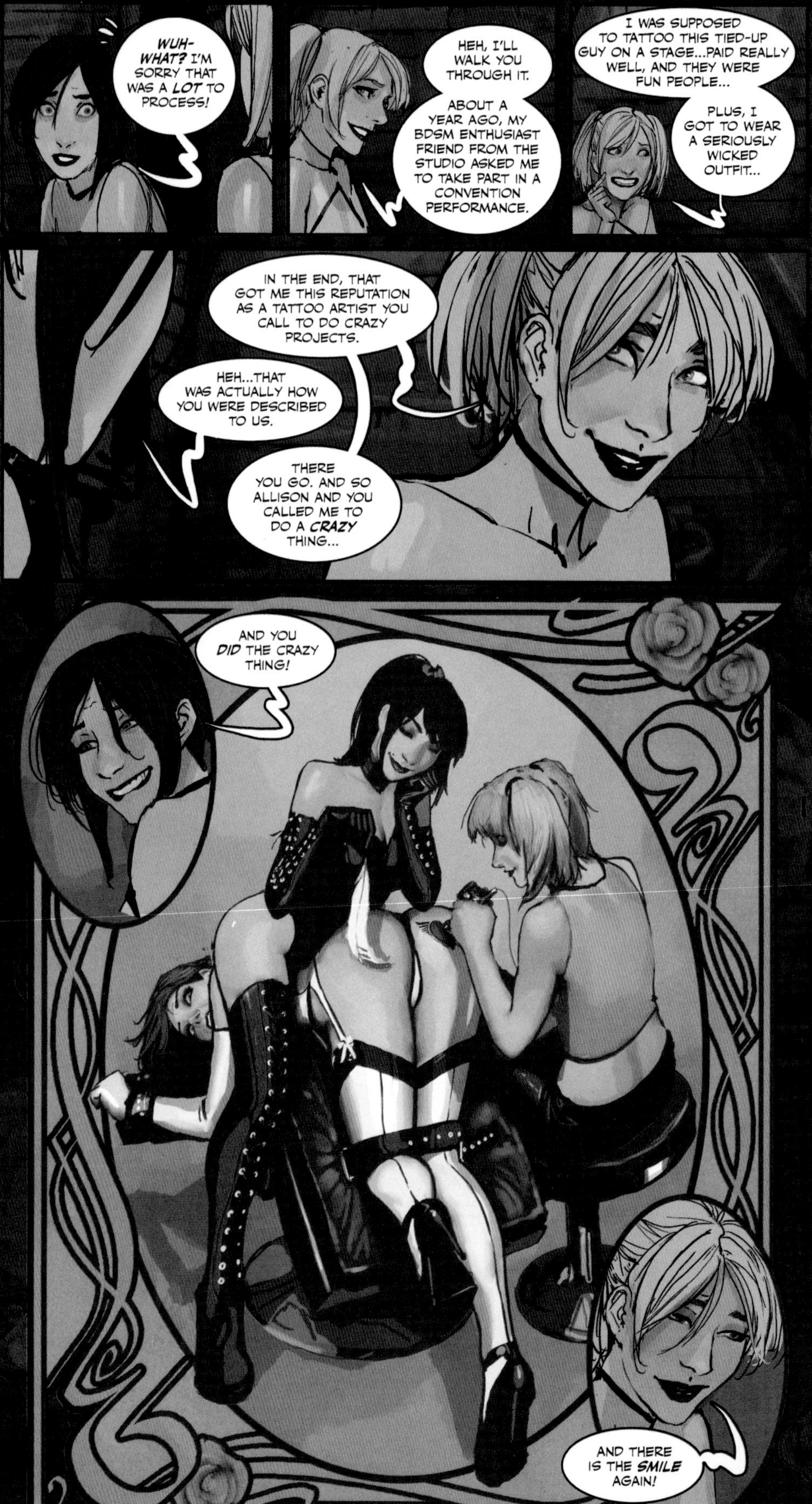
WUH-WHAT? I'M SORRY THAT WAS A LOT TO PROCESS!
HEH, I'LL WALK YOU THROUGH IT.
ABOUT A YEAR AGO, MY BDSM ENTHUSIAST FRIEND FROM THE STUDIO ASKED ME TO TAKE PART IN A CONVENTION PERFORMANCE.
I WAS SUPPOSED TO TATTOO THIS TIED-UP GUY ON A STAGE...PAID REALLY WELL, AND THEY WERE FUN PEOPLE...
PLUS, I GOT TO WEAR A SERIOUSLY WICKED OUTFIT...
IN THE END, THAT GOT ME THIS REPUTATION AS A TATTOO ARTIST YOU CALL TO DO CRAZY PROJECTS.
HEH...THAT WAS ACTUALLY HOW YOU WERE DESCRIBED TO US.
THERE YOU GO. AND SO ALLISON AND YOU CALLED ME TO DO A CRAZY THING...
AND YOU DID THE CRAZY THING!
AND THERE IS THE SMILE AGAIN!

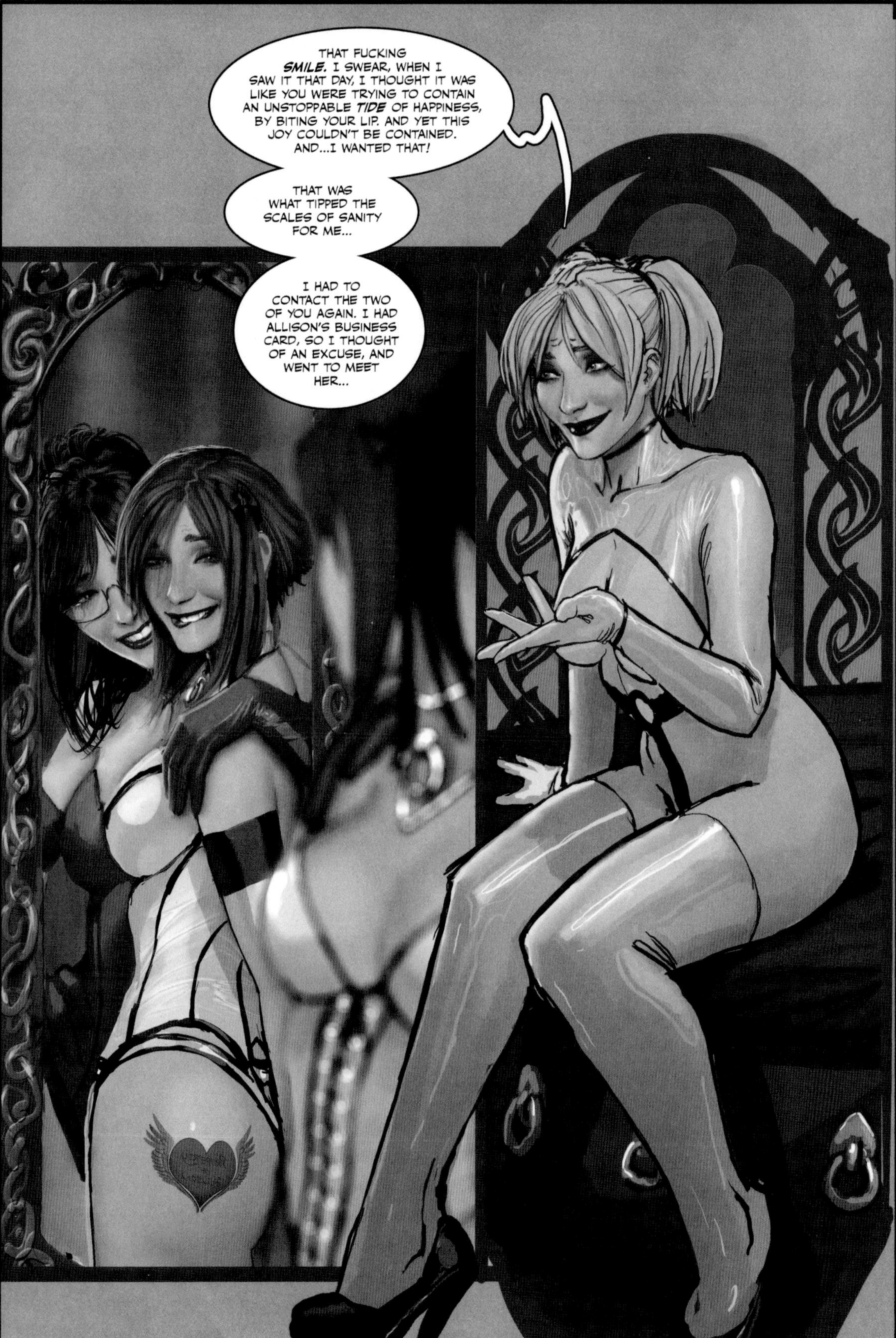
THAT FUCKING **SMILE.** I SWEAR, WHEN I SAW IT THAT DAY, I THOUGHT IT WAS LIKE YOU WERE TRYING TO CONTAIN AN UNSTOPPABLE ***TIDE*** OF HAPPINESS, BY BITING YOUR LIP. AND YET THIS JOY COULDN'T BE CONTAINED. AND...I WANTED THAT!
THAT WAS WHAT TIPPED THE SCALES OF SANITY FOR ME...
I HAD TO CONTACT THE TWO OF YOU AGAIN. I HAD ALLISON'S BUSINESS CARD, SO I THOUGHT OF AN EXCUSE, AND WENT TO MEET HER...

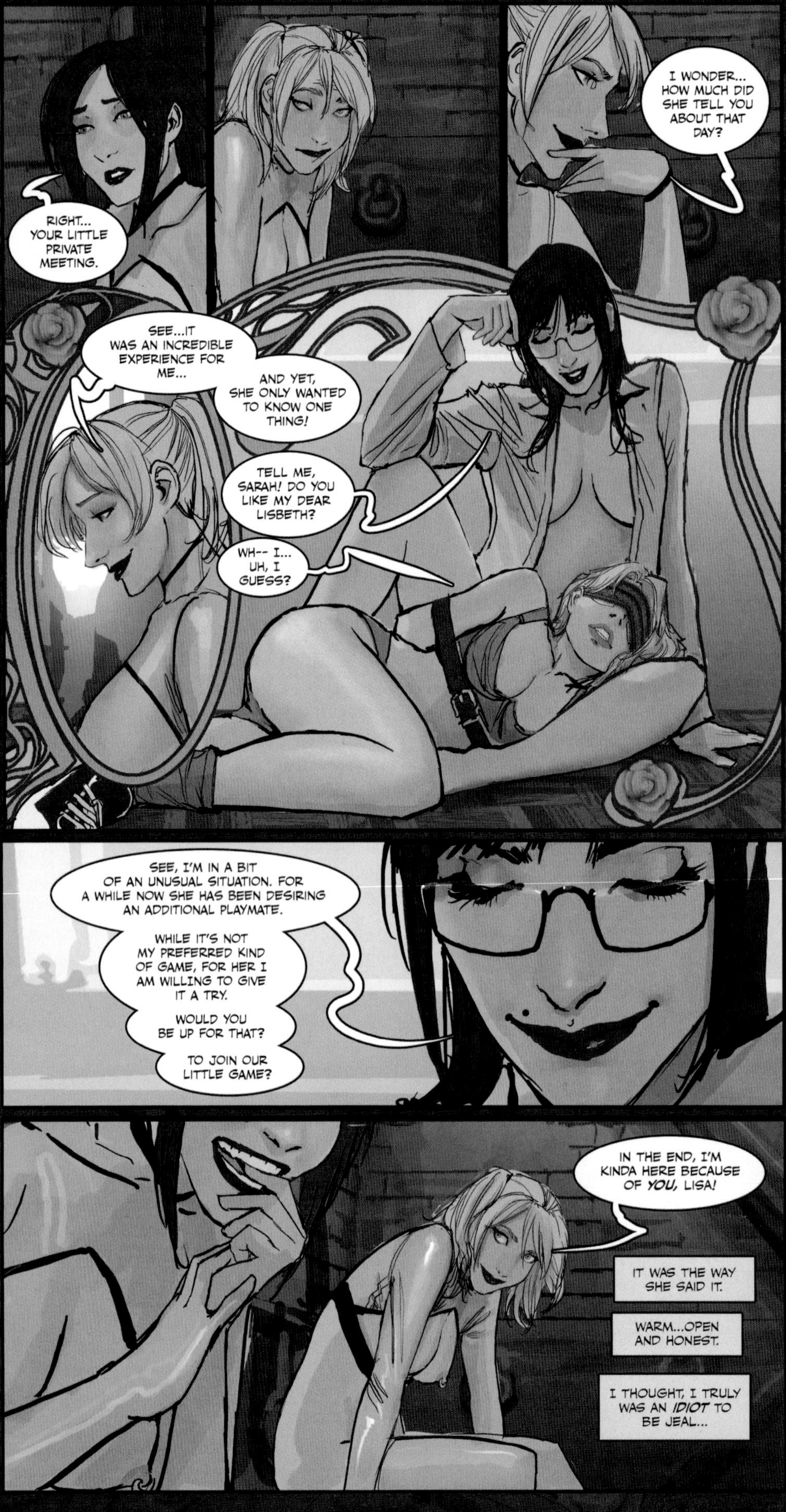
RIGHT... YOUR LITTLE PRIVATE MEETING.
I WONDER... HOW MUCH DID SHE TELL YOU ABOUT THAT DAY?
SEE...IT WAS AN INCREDIBLE EXPERIENCE FOR ME...
AND YET, SHE ONLY WANTED TO KNOW ONE THING!
TELL ME, SARAH! DO YOU LIKE MY DEAR LISBETH?
WH-- I... UH, I GUESS?
SEE, I'M IN A BIT OF AN UNUSUAL SITUATION. FOR A WHILE NOW SHE HAS BEEN DESIRING AN ADDITIONAL PLAYMATE.
WHILE IT'S NOT MY PREFERRED KIND OF GAME, FOR HER I AM WILLING TO GIVE IT A TRY.
WOULD YOU BE UP FOR THAT?
TO JOIN OUR LITTLE GAME?
IN THE END, I'M KINDA HERE BECAUSE OF *YOU,* LISA!
IT WAS THE WAY SHE SAID IT.
WARM...OPEN AND HONEST.
I THOUGHT, I TRULY WAS AN *IDIOT* TO BE JEAL...

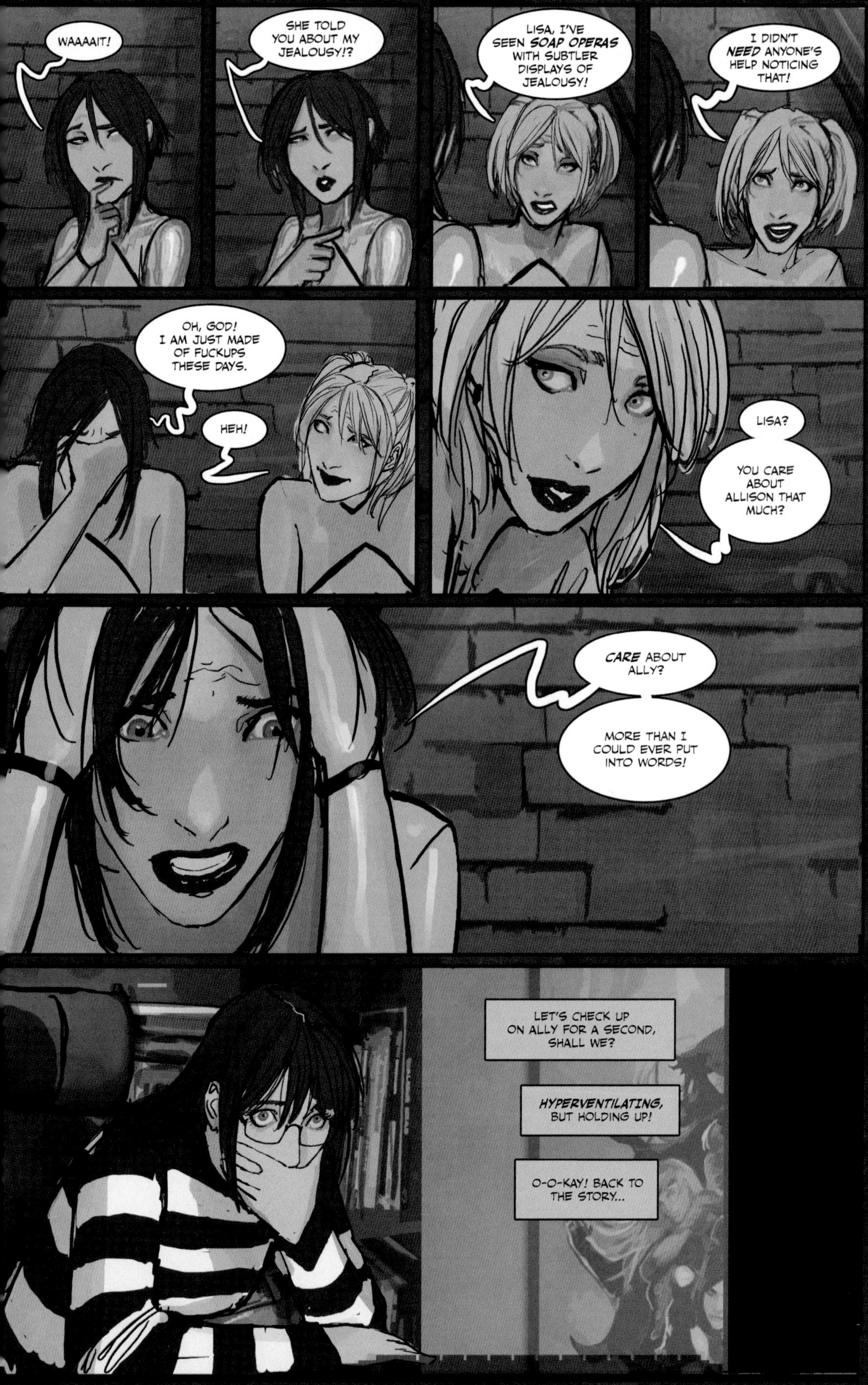
WAAAAIT!
SHE TOLD YOU ABOUT MY JEALOUSY!?
LISA, I'VE SEEN SOAP OPERAS WITH SUBTLER DISPLAYS OF JEALOUSY!
I DIDN'T NEED ANYONE'S HELP NOTICING THAT!
OH, GOD! I AM JUST MADE OF FUCKUPS THESE DAYS.
HEH!
LISA?
YOU CARE ABOUT ALLISON THAT MUCH?
CARE ABOUT ALLY?
MORE THAN I COULD EVER PUT INTO WORDS!
LET'S CHECK UP ON ALLY FOR A SECOND, SHALL WE?
HYPERVENTILATING, BUT HOLDING UP!
O-O-KAY! BACK TO THE STORY...

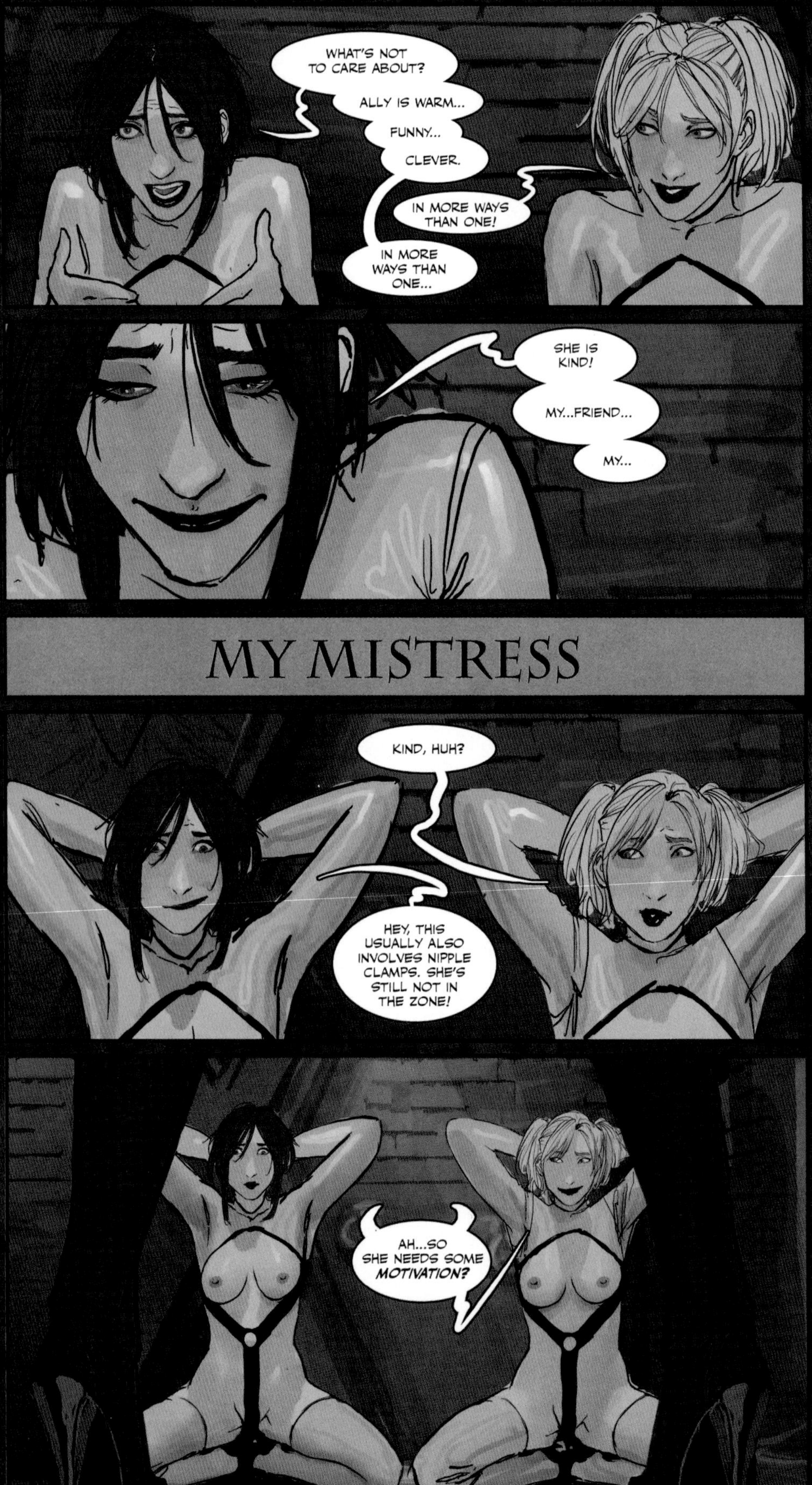

WHAT'S NOT TO CARE ABOUT?
ALLY IS WARM...
FUNNY...
CLEVER.
IN MORE WAYS THAN ONE!
IN MORE WAYS THAN ONE...
SHE IS KIND!
MY...FRIEND...
MY...
MY MISTRESS
KIND, HUH?
HEY, THIS USUALLY ALSO INVOLVES NIPPLE CLAMPS. SHE'S STILL NOT IN THE ZONE!
AH...SO SHE NEEDS SOME *MOTIVATION?*

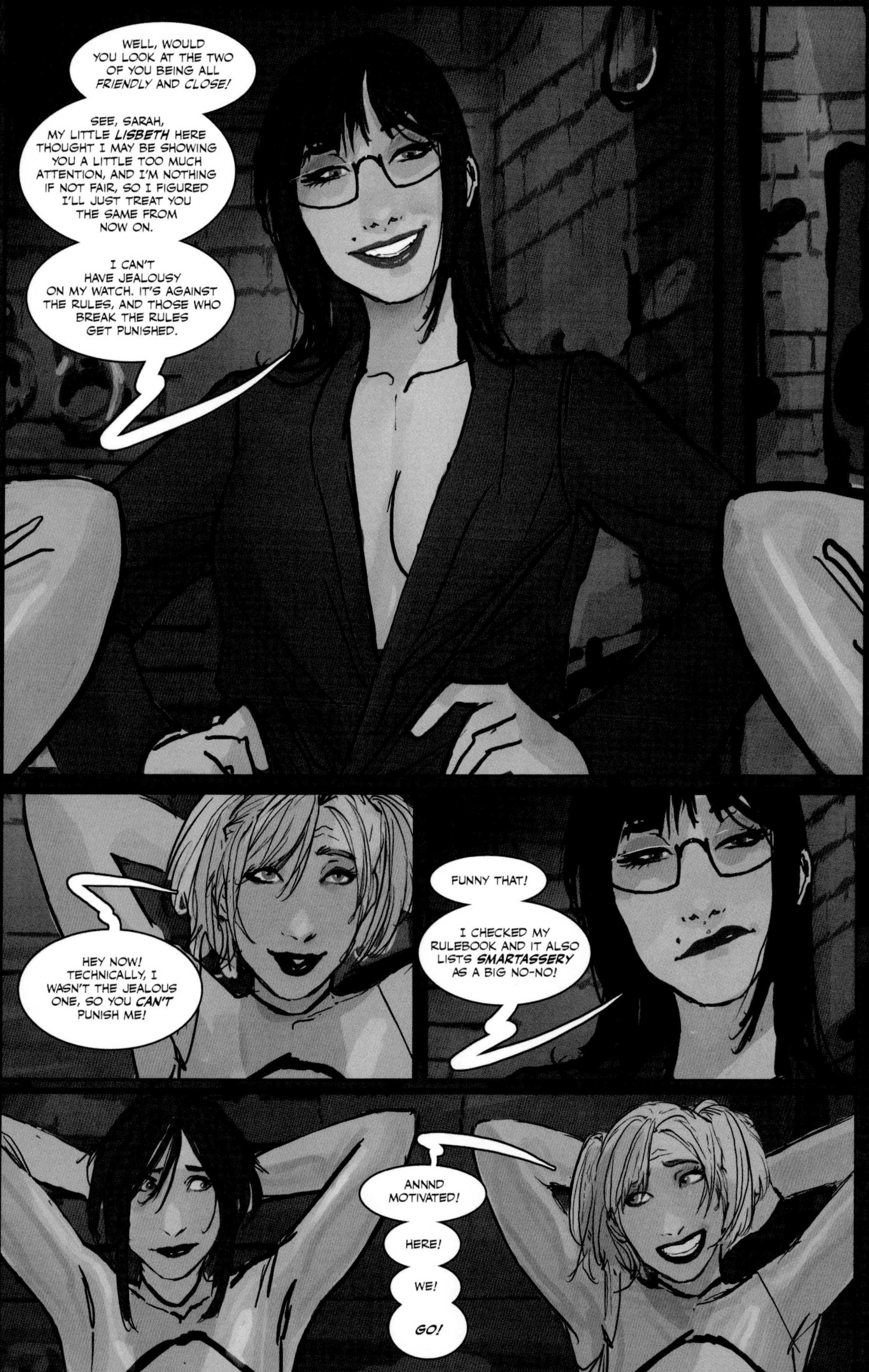
WELL, WOULD YOU LOOK AT THE TWO OF YOU BEING ALL *FRIENDLY* AND *CLOSE!*
SEE, SARAH, MY LITTLE ***LISBETH*** HERE THOUGHT I MAY BE SHOWING YOU A LITTLE TOO MUCH ATTENTION, AND I'M NOTHING IF NOT FAIR, SO I FIGURED I'LL JUST TREAT YOU THE SAME FROM NOW ON.
I CAN'T HAVE JEALOUSY ON MY WATCH. IT'S AGAINST THE RULES, AND THOSE WHO BREAK THE RULES GET PUNISHED.
HEY NOW! TECHNICALLY, I WASN'T THE JEALOUS ONE, SO YOU ***CAN'T*** PUNISH ME!
FUNNY THAT!
I CHECKED MY RULEBOOK AND IT ALSO LISTS ***SMARTASSERY*** AS A BIG NO-NO!
ANNND MOTIVATED!
HERE!
WE!
GO!

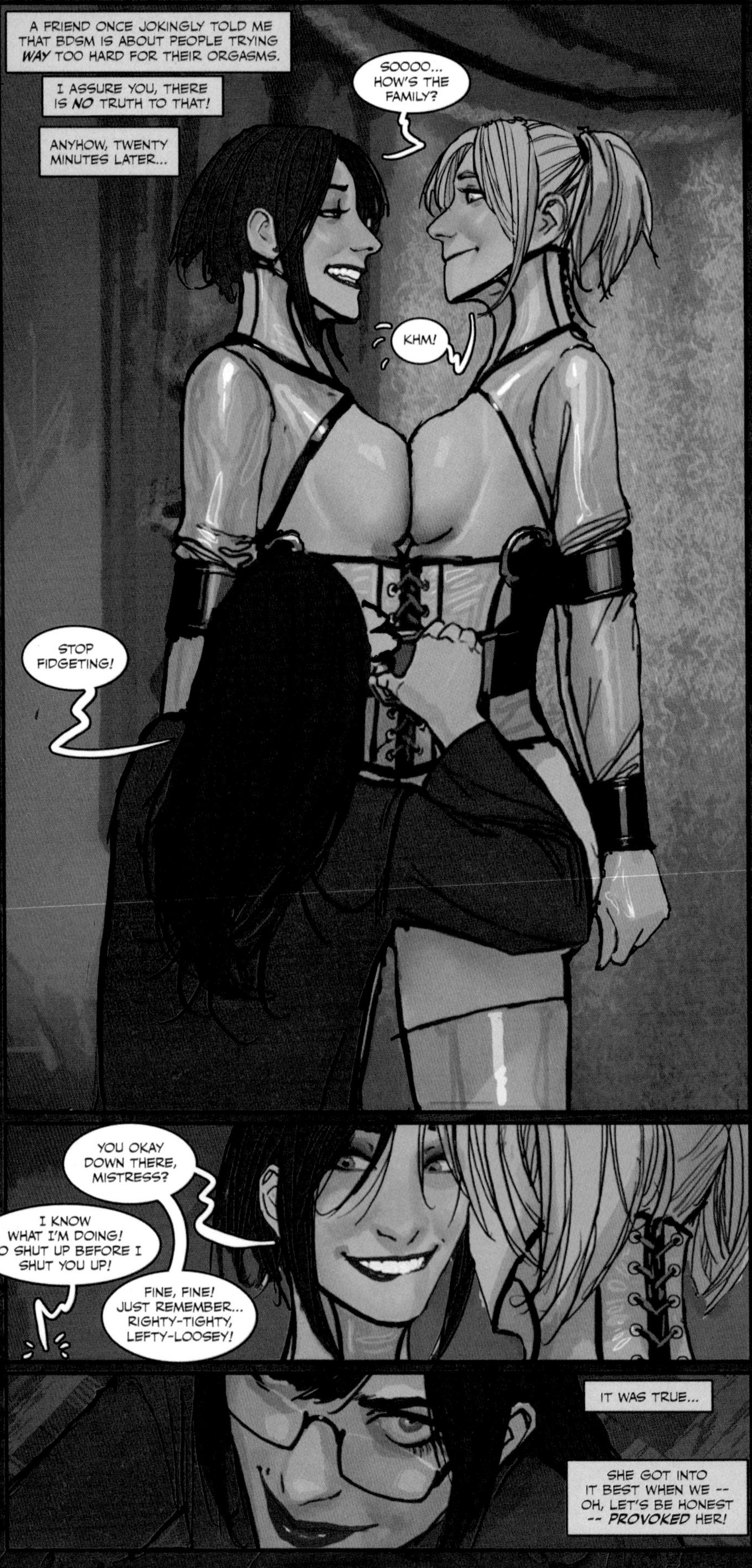

A FRIEND ONCE JOKINGLY TOLD ME THAT BDSM IS ABOUT PEOPLE TRYING *WAY* TOO HARD FOR THEIR ORGASMS.
I ASSURE YOU, THERE IS *NO* TRUTH TO THAT!
ANYHOW, TWENTY MINUTES LATER...
SOOOO... HOW'S THE FAMILY?
KHM!
STOP FIDGETING!
YOU OKAY DOWN THERE, MISTRESS?
I KNOW WHAT I'M DOING! SO SHUT UP BEFORE I SHUT YOU UP!
FINE, FINE! JUST REMEMBER... RIGHTY-TIGHTY, LEFTY-LOOSEY!
IT WAS TRUE...
SHE GOT INTO IT BEST WHEN WE -- OH, LET'S BE HONEST -- *PROVOKED* HER!

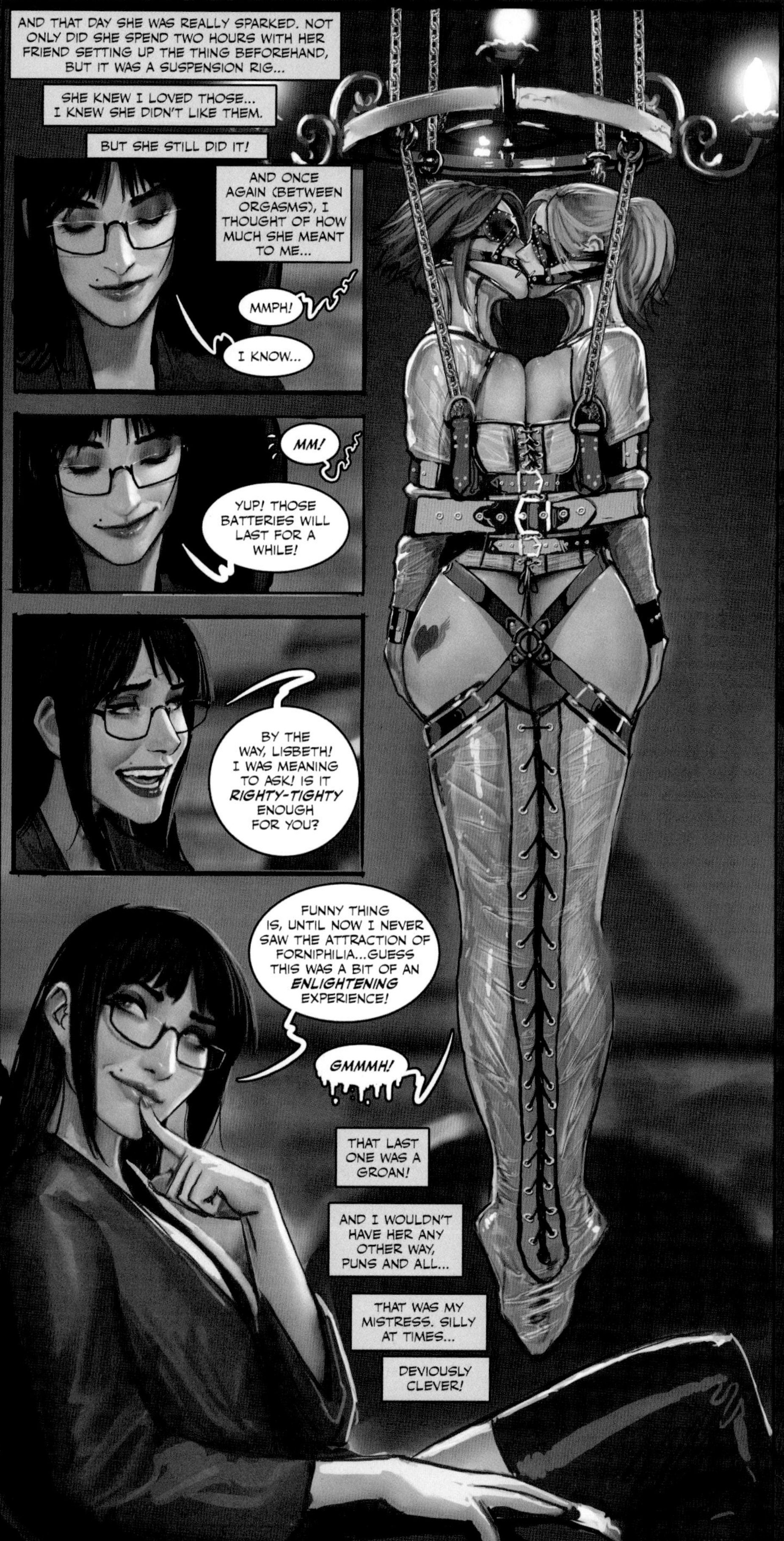
AND THAT DAY SHE WAS REALLY SPARKED. NOT ONLY DID SHE SPEND TWO HOURS WITH HER FRIEND SETTING UP THE THING BEFOREHAND, BUT IT WAS A SUSPENSION RIG...
SHE KNEW I LOVED THOSE... I KNEW SHE DIDN'T LIKE THEM.
BUT SHE STILL DID IT!
AND ONCE AGAIN (BETWEEN ORGASMS), I THOUGHT OF HOW MUCH SHE MEANT TO ME...
MMPH!
I KNOW...
MM!
YUP! THOSE BATTERIES WILL LAST FOR A WHILE!
BY THE WAY, LISBETH! I WAS MEANING TO ASK! IS IT RIGHTY-TIGHTY ENOUGH FOR YOU?
FUNNY THING IS, UNTIL NOW I NEVER SAW THE ATTRACTION OF FORNIPHILIA...GUESS THIS WAS A BIT OF AN ENLIGHTENING EXPERIENCE!
GMMMH!
THAT LAST ONE WAS A GROAN!
AND I WOULDN'T HAVE HER ANY OTHER WAY, PUNS AND ALL...
THAT WAS MY MISTRESS. SILLY AT TIMES...
DEVIOUSLY CLEVER!

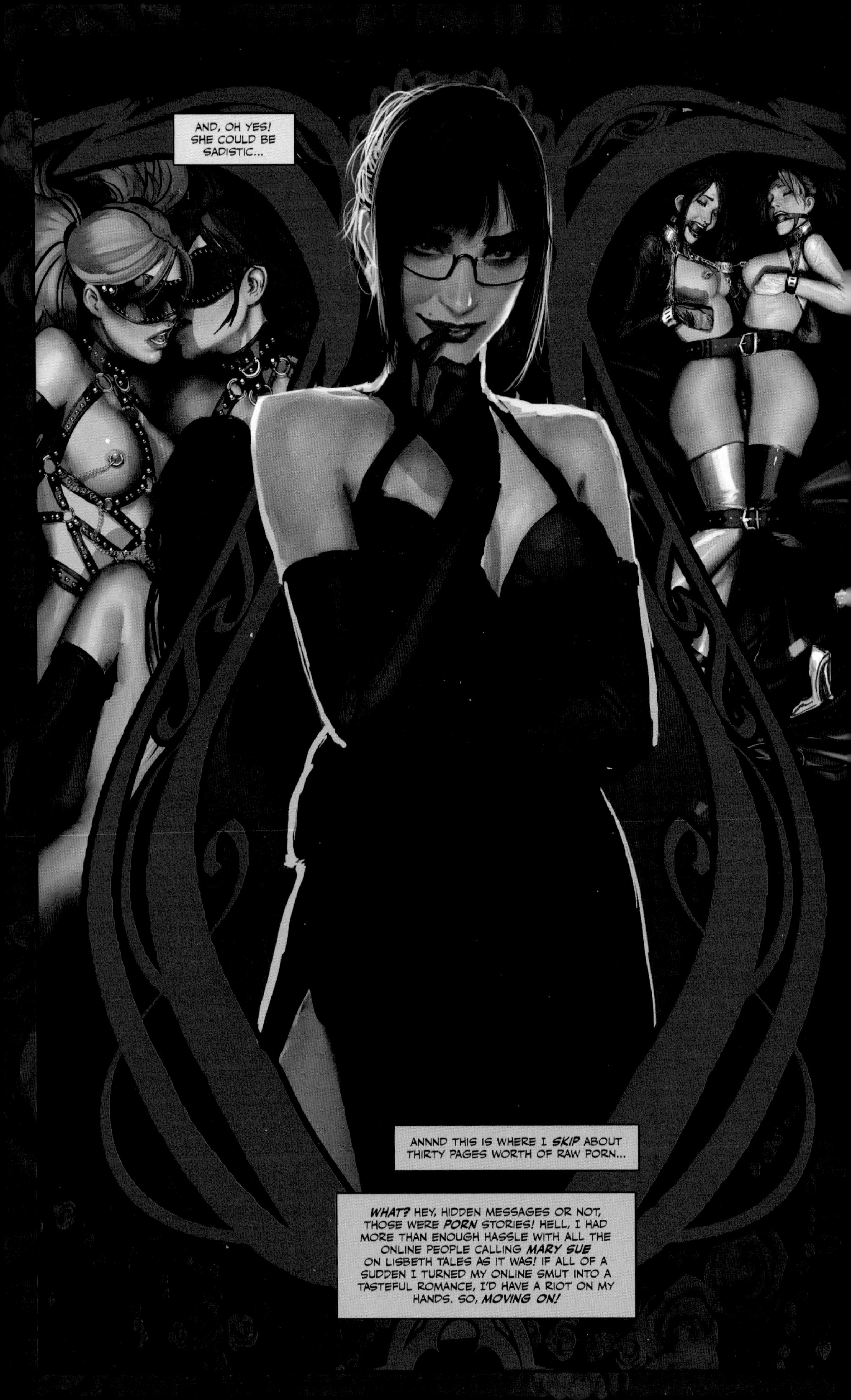
AND, OH YES! SHE COULD BE SADISTIC...
ANNND THIS IS WHERE I *SKIP* ABOUT THIRTY PAGES WORTH OF RAW PORN...
WHAT? HEY, HIDDEN MESSAGES OR NOT, THOSE WERE *PORN* STORIES! HELL, I HAD MORE THAN ENOUGH HASSLE WITH ALL THE ONLINE PEOPLE CALLING *MARY SUE* ON LISBETH TALES AS IT WAS! IF ALL OF A SUDDEN I TURNED MY ONLINE SMUT INTO A TASTEFUL ROMANCE, I'D HAVE A RIOT ON MY HANDS. SO, *MOVING ON!*

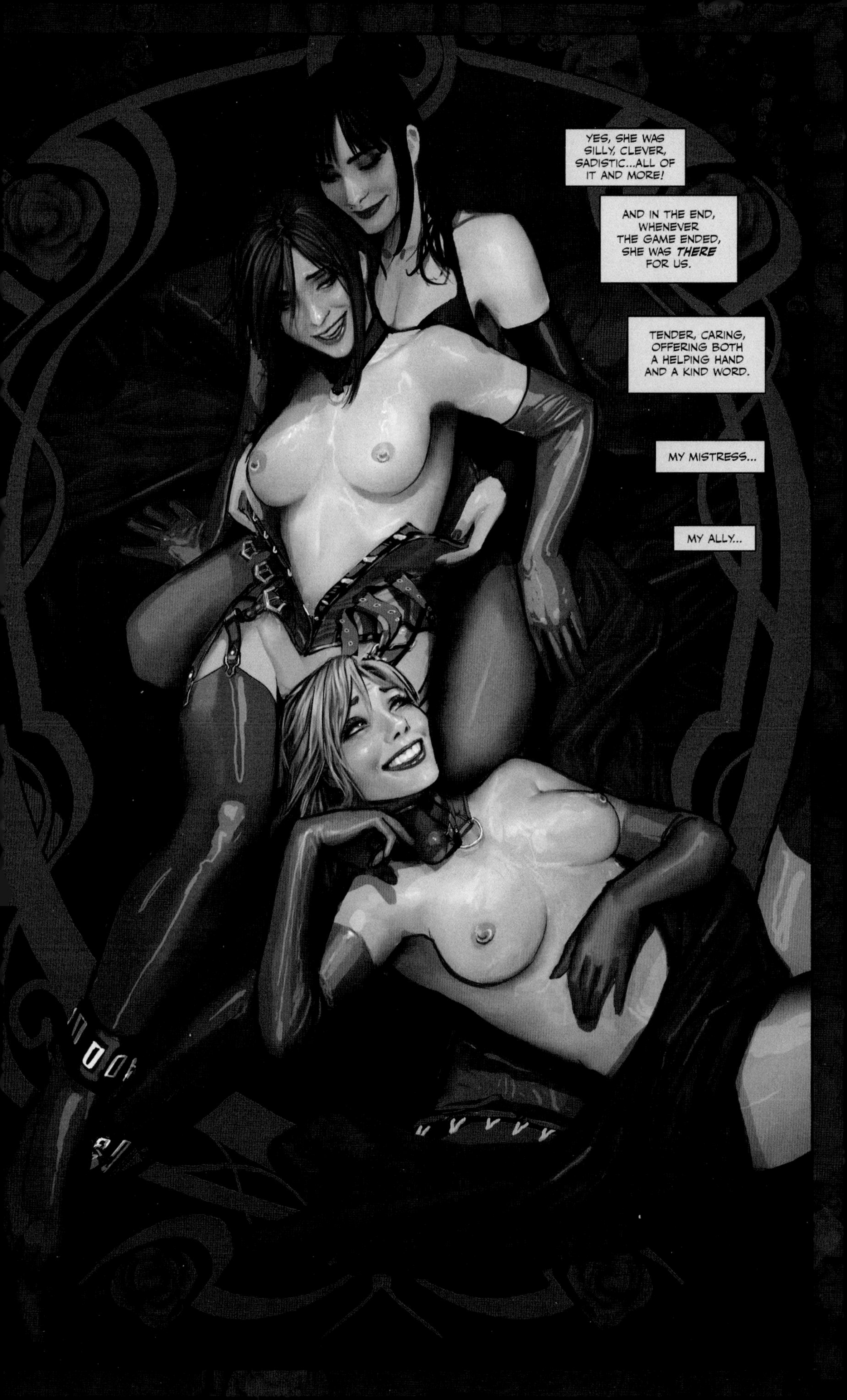
YES, SHE WAS SILLY, CLEVER, SADISTIC...ALL OF IT AND MORE!
AND IN THE END, WHENEVER THE GAME ENDED, SHE WAS *THERE* FOR US.
TENDER, CARING, OFFERING BOTH A HELPING HAND AND A KIND WORD.
MY MISTRESS...
MY ALLY...

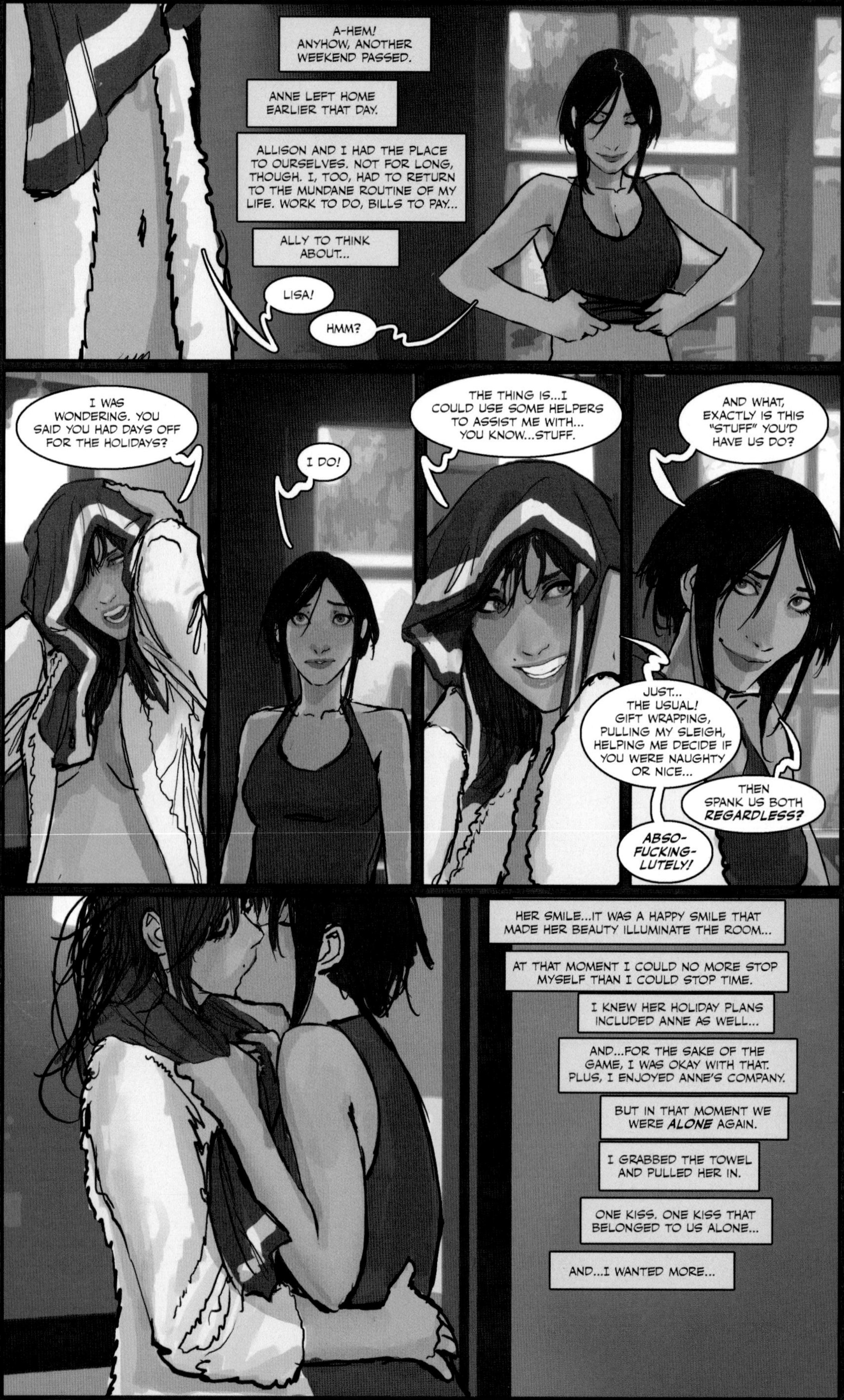

A-HEM! ANYHOW, ANOTHER WEEKEND PASSED.
ANNE LEFT HOME EARLIER THAT DAY.
ALLISON AND I HAD THE PLACE TO OURSELVES. NOT FOR LONG, THOUGH. I, TOO, HAD TO RETURN TO THE MUNDANE ROUTINE OF MY LIFE. WORK TO DO, BILLS TO PAY...
ALLY TO THINK ABOUT...
LISA!
HMM?
I WAS WONDERING. YOU SAID YOU HAD DAYS OFF FOR THE HOLIDAYS?
I DO!
THE THING IS...I COULD USE SOME HELPERS TO ASSIST ME WITH... YOU KNOW...STUFF.
AND WHAT, EXACTLY IS THIS "STUFF" YOU'D HAVE US DO?
JUST... THE USUAL! GIFT WRAPPING, PULLING MY SLEIGH, HELPING ME DECIDE IF YOU WERE NAUGHTY OR NICE...
THEN SPANK US BOTH *REGARDLESS?*
ABSO-FUCKING-LUTELY!
HER SMILE...IT WAS A HAPPY SMILE THAT MADE HER BEAUTY ILLUMINATE THE ROOM...
AT THAT MOMENT I COULD NO MORE STOP MYSELF THAN I COULD STOP TIME.
I KNEW HER HOLIDAY PLANS INCLUDED ANNE AS WELL...
AND...FOR THE SAKE OF THE GAME, I WAS OKAY WITH THAT. PLUS, I ENJOYED ANNE'S COMPANY.
BUT IN THAT MOMENT WE WERE *ALONE* AGAIN.
I GRABBED THE TOWEL AND PULLED HER IN.
ONE KISS. ONE KISS THAT BELONGED TO US ALONE...
AND...I WANTED MORE...

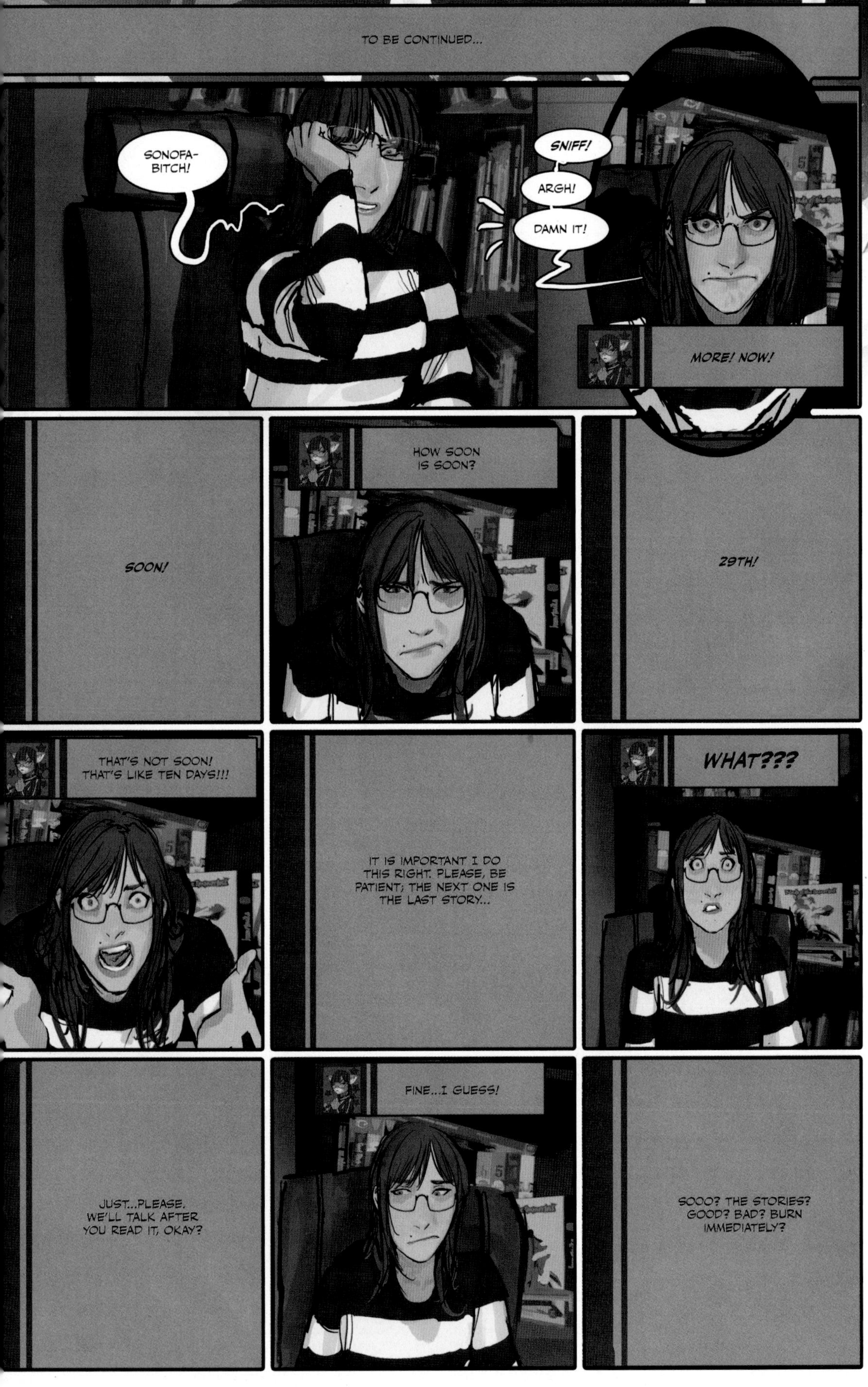
TO BE CONTINUED...
SONOFA-BITCH!
SNIFF!
ARGH!
DAMN IT!
MORE! NOW!
SOON!
HOW SOON IS SOON?
29TH!
THAT'S NOT SOON! THAT'S LIKE TEN DAYS!!!
IT IS IMPORTANT I DO THIS RIGHT. PLEASE, BE PATIENT; THE NEXT ONE IS THE LAST STORY...
WHAT???
JUST...PLEASE. WE'LL TALK AFTER YOU READ IT, OKAY?
FINE...I GUESS!
SOOO? THE STORIES? GOOD? BAD? BURN IMMEDIATELY?

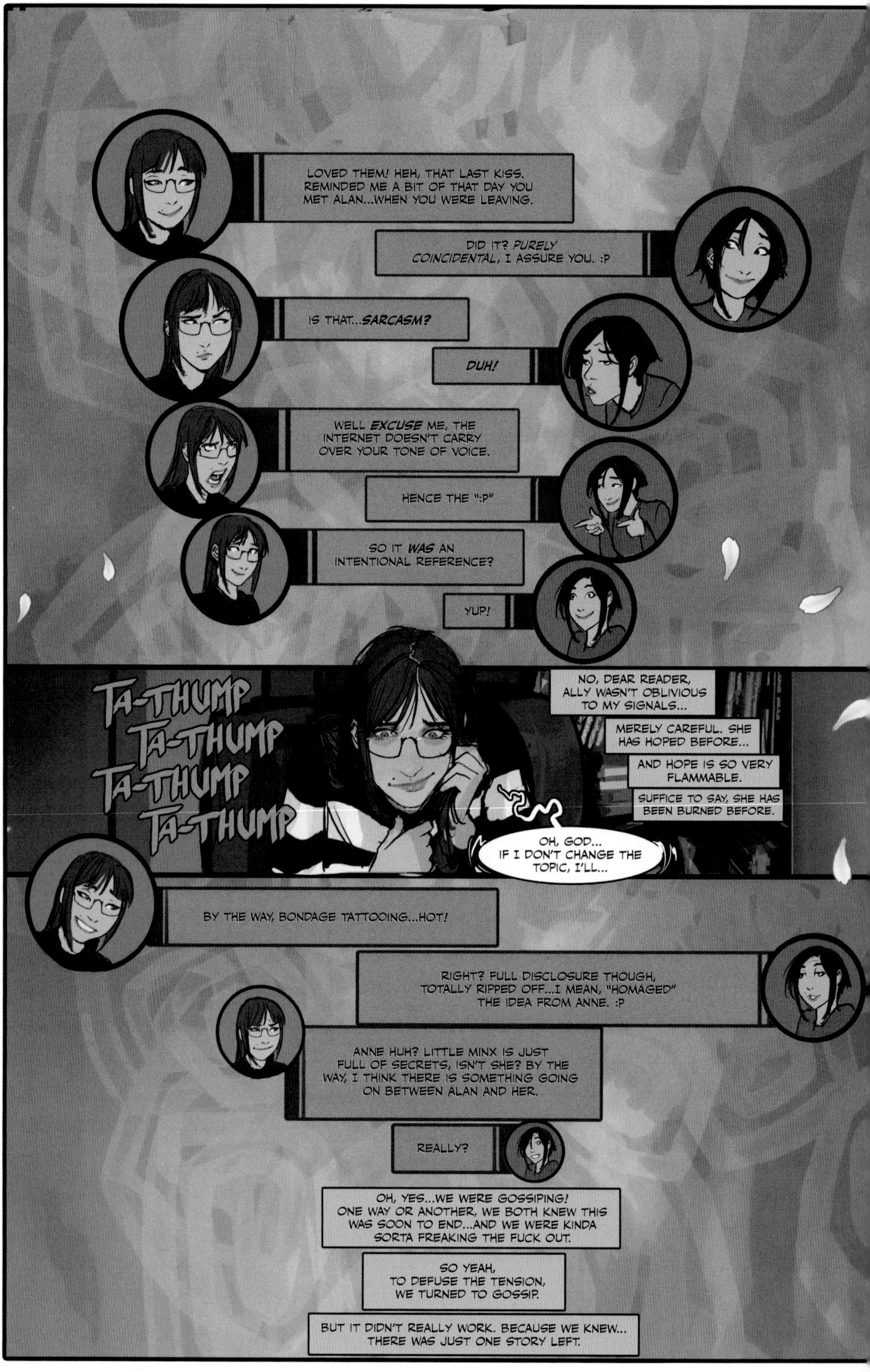

LOVED THEM! HEH, THAT LAST KISS. REMINDED ME A BIT OF THAT DAY YOU MET ALAN...WHEN YOU WERE LEAVING.
DID IT? PURELY COINCIDENTAL, I ASSURE YOU. :P
IS THAT...SARCASM?
DUH!
WELL EXCUSE ME, THE INTERNET DOESN'T CARRY OVER YOUR TONE OF VOICE.
HENCE THE ":P"
SO IT WAS AN INTENTIONAL REFERENCE?
YUP!
TA-THUMP TA-THUMP TA-THUMP TA-THUMP
NO, DEAR READER, ALLY WASN'T OBLIVIOUS TO MY SIGNALS...
MERELY CAREFUL. SHE HAS HOPED BEFORE...
AND HOPE IS SO VERY FLAMMABLE.
SUFFICE TO SAY, SHE HAS BEEN BURNED BEFORE.
OH, GOD... IF I DON'T CHANGE THE TOPIC, I'LL...
BY THE WAY, BONDAGE TATTOOING...HOT!
RIGHT? FULL DISCLOSURE THOUGH, TOTALLY RIPPED OFF...I MEAN, "HOMAGED" THE IDEA FROM ANNE. :P
ANNE HUH? LITTLE MINX IS JUST FULL OF SECRETS, ISN'T SHE? BY THE WAY, I THINK THERE IS SOMETHING GOING ON BETWEEN ALAN AND HER.
REALLY?
OH, YES...WE WERE GOSSIPING! ONE WAY OR ANOTHER, WE BOTH KNEW THIS WAS SOON TO END...AND WE WERE KINDA SORTA FREAKING THE FUCK OUT.
SO YEAH, TO DEFUSE THE TENSION, WE TURNED TO GOSSIP.
BUT IT DIDN'T REALLY WORK. BECAUSE WE KNEW... THERE WAS JUST ONE STORY LEFT.

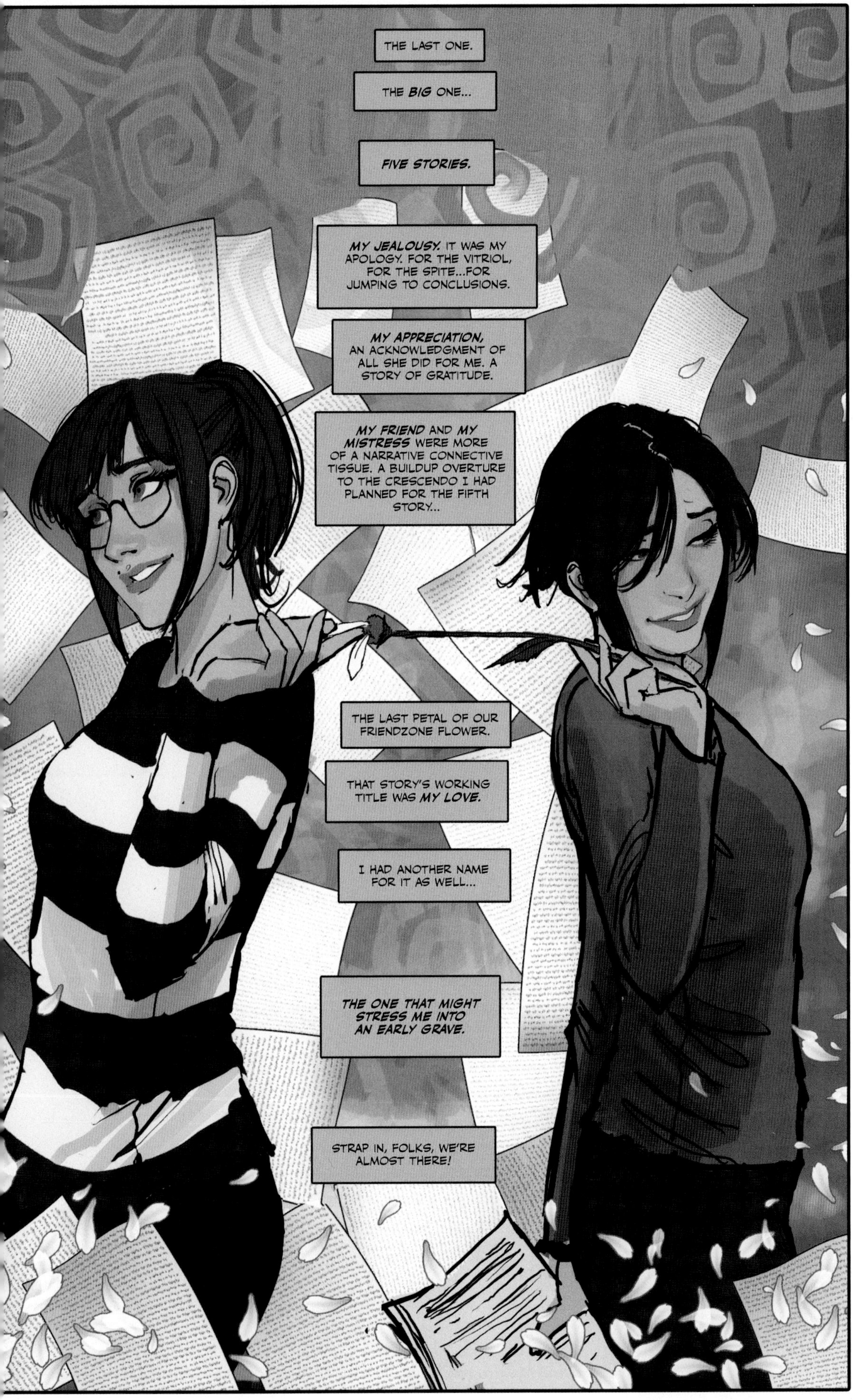
THE LAST ONE.
THE BIG ONE...
FIVE STORIES.
MY JEALOUSY. IT WAS MY APOLOGY. FOR THE VITRIOL, FOR THE SPITE...FOR JUMPING TO CONCLUSIONS.
MY APPRECIATION, AN ACKNOWLEDGMENT OF ALL SHE DID FOR ME. A STORY OF GRATITUDE.
MY FRIEND AND MY MISTRESS WERE MORE OF A NARRATIVE CONNECTIVE TISSUE. A BUILDUP OVERTURE TO THE CRESCENDO I HAD PLANNED FOR THE FIFTH STORY...
THE LAST PETAL OF OUR FRIENDZONE FLOWER.
THAT STORY'S WORKING TITLE WAS MY LOVE.
I HAD ANOTHER NAME FOR IT AS WELL...
THE ONE THAT MIGHT STRESS ME INTO AN EARLY GRAVE.
STRAP IN, FOLKS, WE'RE ALMOST THERE!

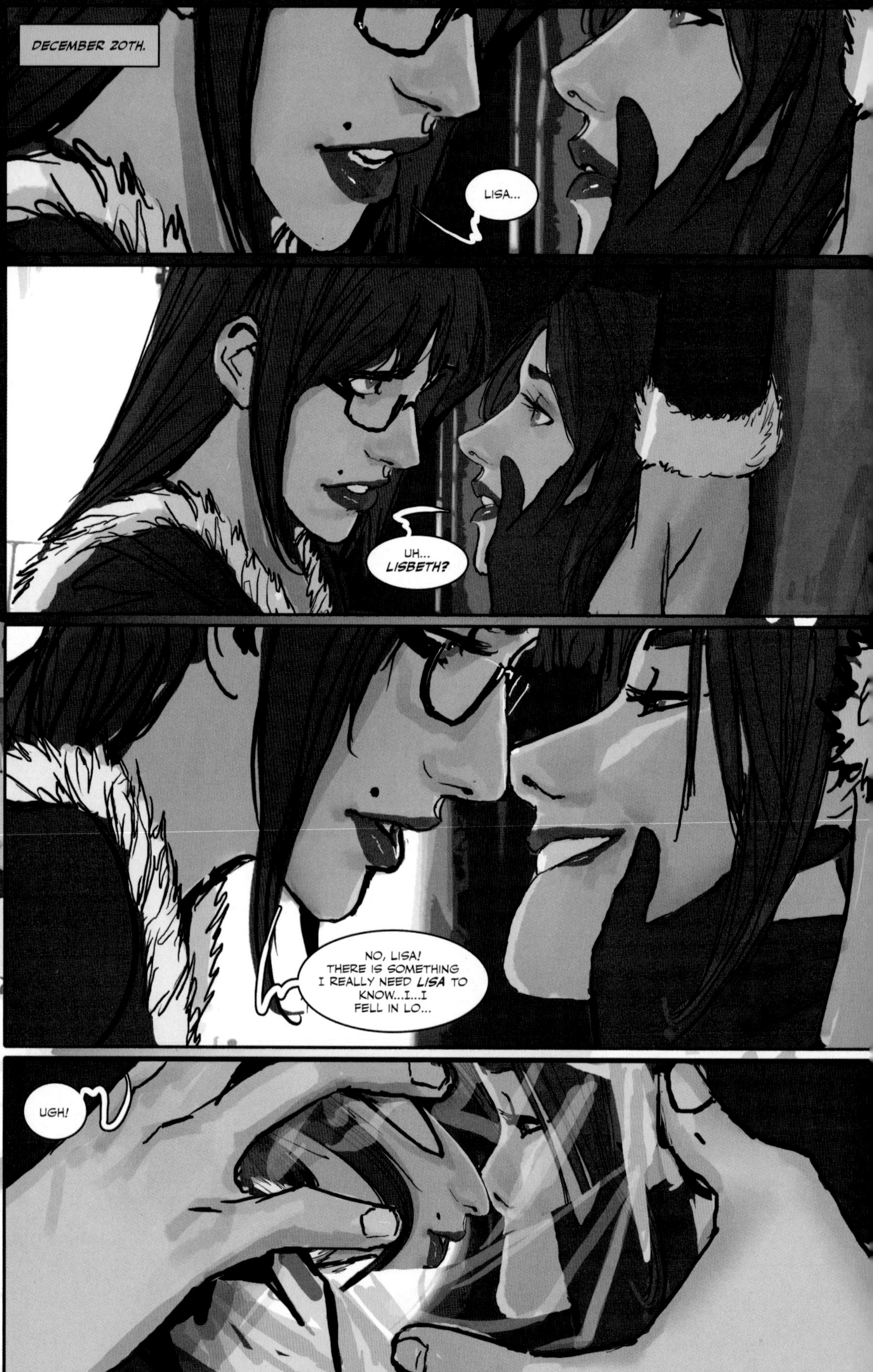
DECEMBER 20TH.
LISA...
UH... LISBETH?
NO, LISA! THERE IS SOMETHING I REALLY NEED LISA TO KNOW...I...I FELL IN LO...
UGH!

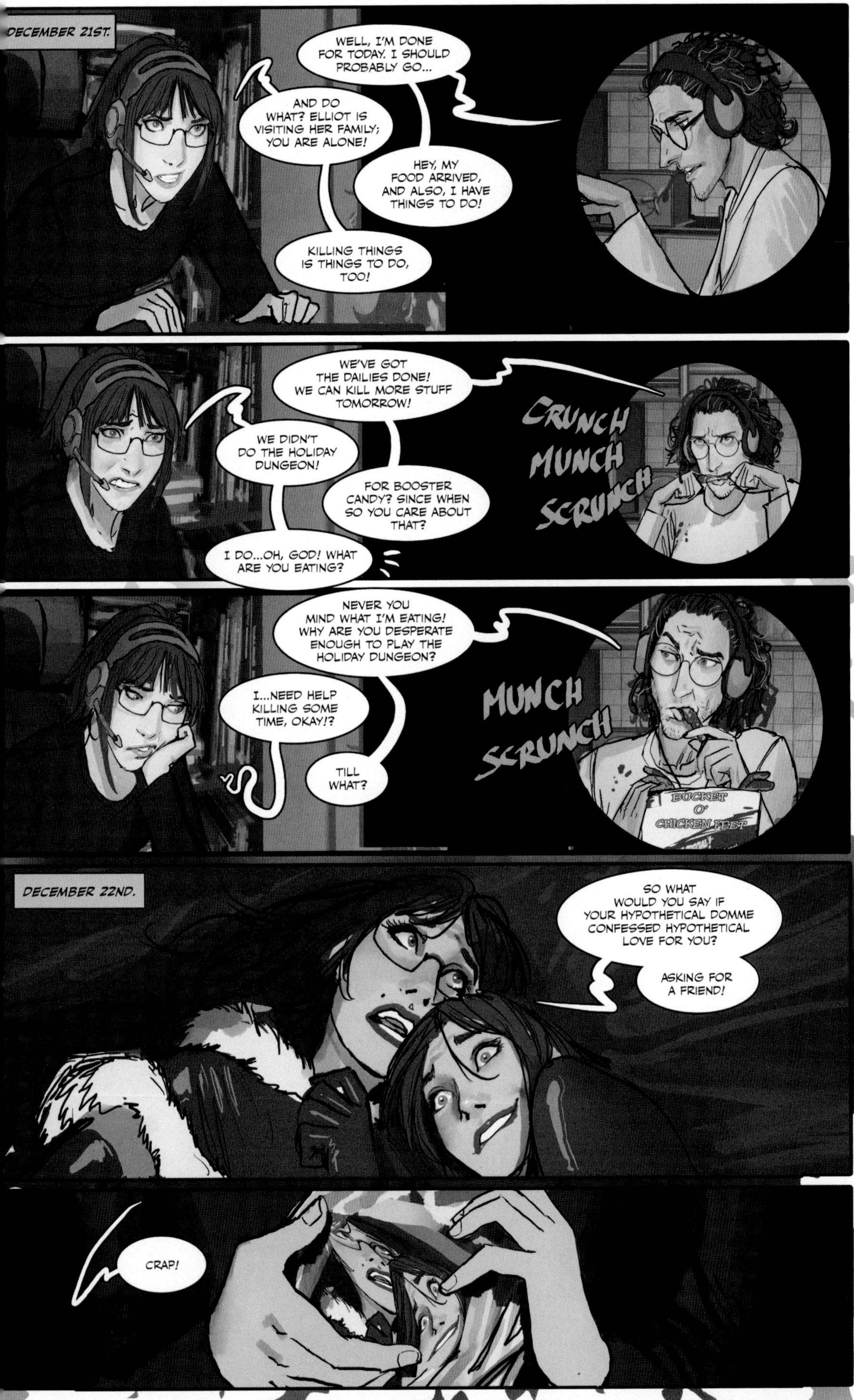
DECEMBER 21ST.
WELL, I'M DONE FOR TODAY. I SHOULD PROBABLY GO...
AND DO WHAT? ELLIOT IS VISITING HER FAMILY; YOU ARE ALONE!
HEY, MY FOOD ARRIVED, AND ALSO, I HAVE THINGS TO DO!
KILLING THINGS IS THINGS TO DO, TOO!
WE'VE GOT THE DAILIES DONE! WE CAN KILL MORE STUFF TOMORROW!
CRUNCH MUNCH SCRUNCH
WE DIDN'T DO THE HOLIDAY DUNGEON!
FOR BOOSTER CANDY? SINCE WHEN SO YOU CARE ABOUT THAT?
I DO...OH, GOD! WHAT ARE YOU EATING?
NEVER YOU MIND WHAT I'M EATING! WHY ARE YOU DESPERATE ENOUGH TO PLAY THE HOLIDAY DUNGEON?
MUNCH SCRUNCH
I...NEED HELP KILLING SOME TIME, OKAY!?
TILL WHAT?
BUCKET O' CHICKEN FEET
DECEMBER 22ND.
SO WHAT WOULD YOU SAY IF YOUR HYPOTHETICAL DOMME CONFESSED HYPOTHETICAL LOVE FOR YOU?
ASKING FOR A FRIEND!
CRAP!

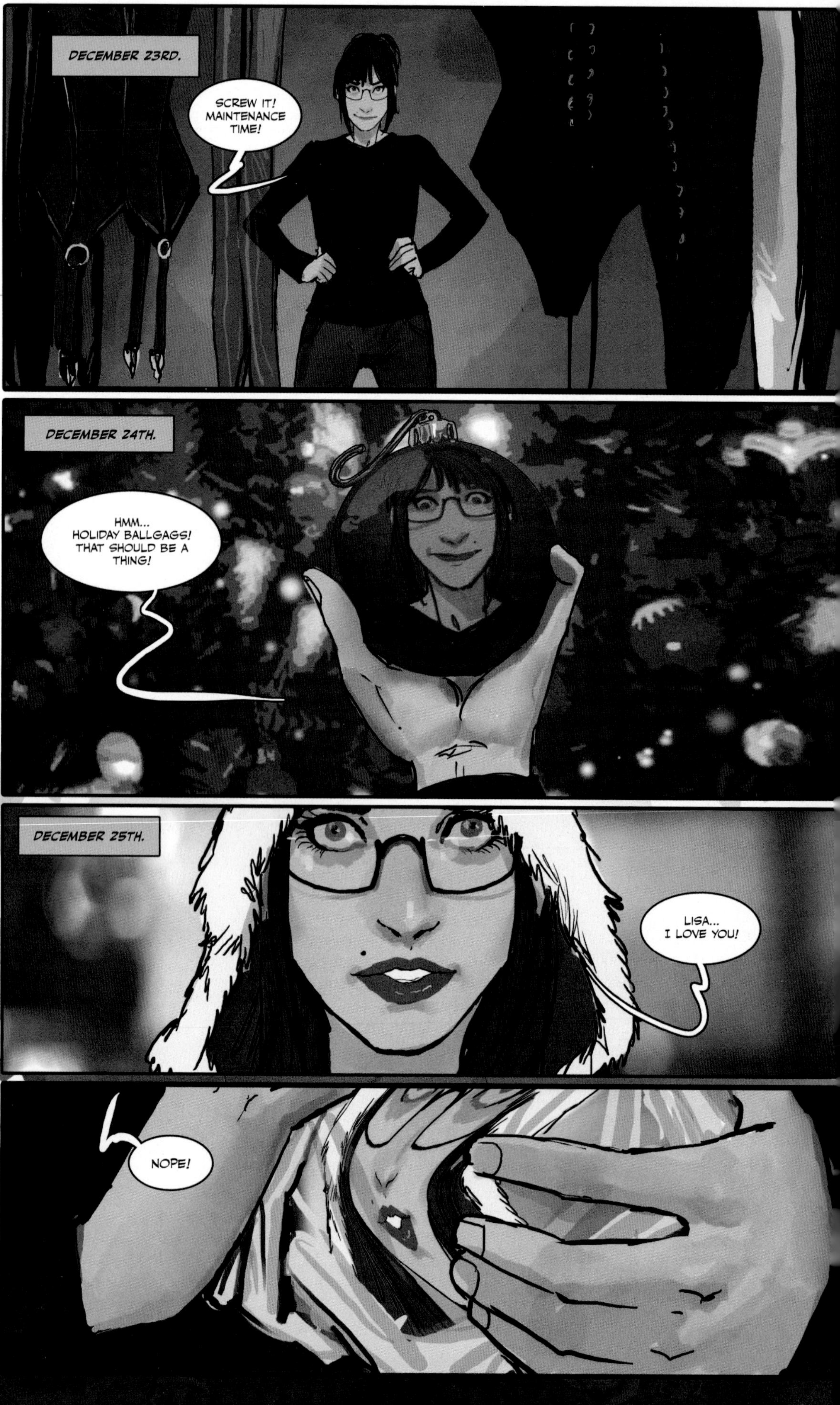
DECEMBER 23RD.
SCREW IT! MAINTENANCE TIME!
DECEMBER 24TH.
HMM... HOLIDAY BALLGAGS! THAT SHOULD BE A THING!
DECEMBER 25TH.
LISA... I LOVE YOU!
NOPE!

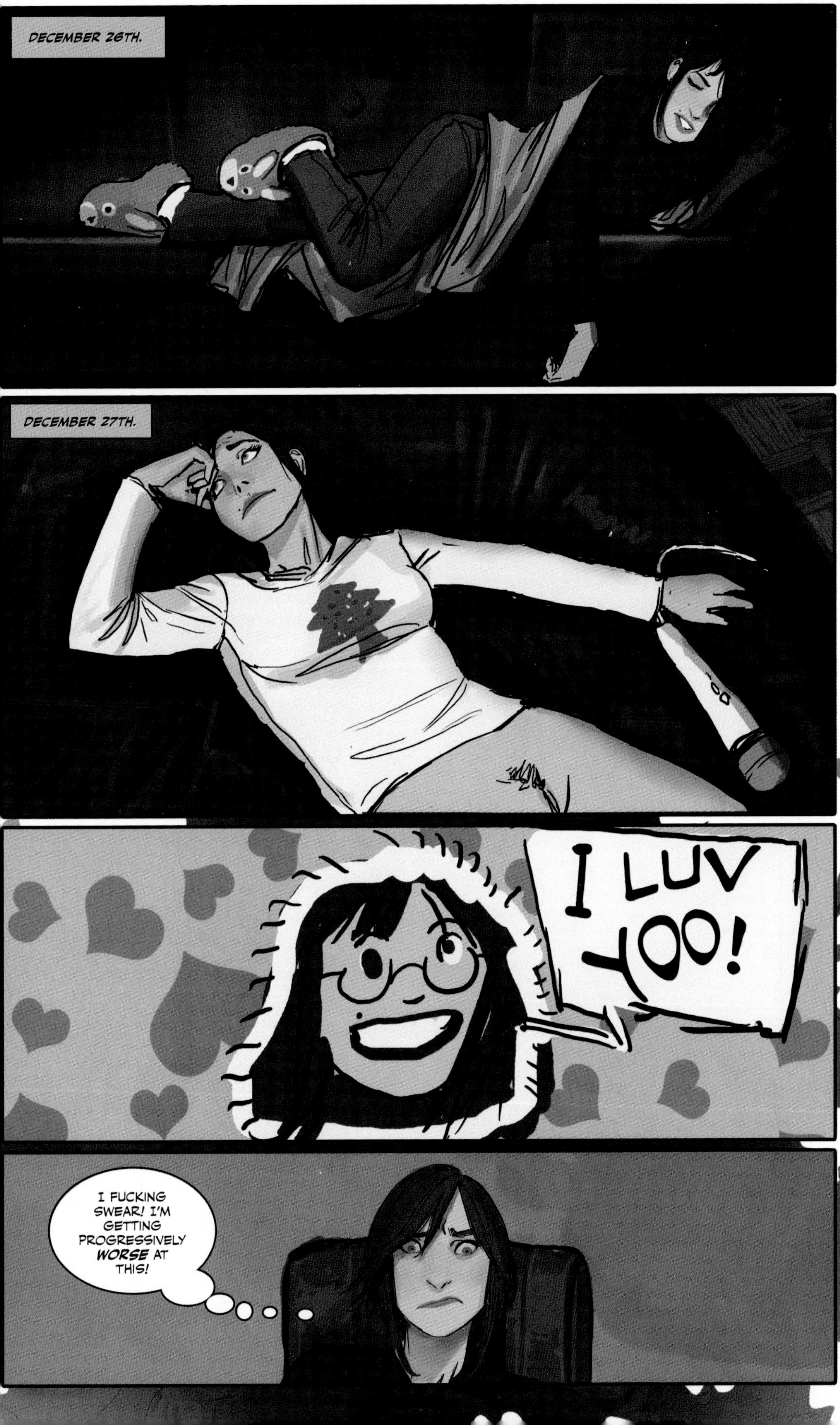
DECEMBER 26TH.
DECEMBER 27TH.
I LUV YOO!
I FUCKING SWEAR! I'M GETTING PROGRESSIVELY WORSE AT THIS!

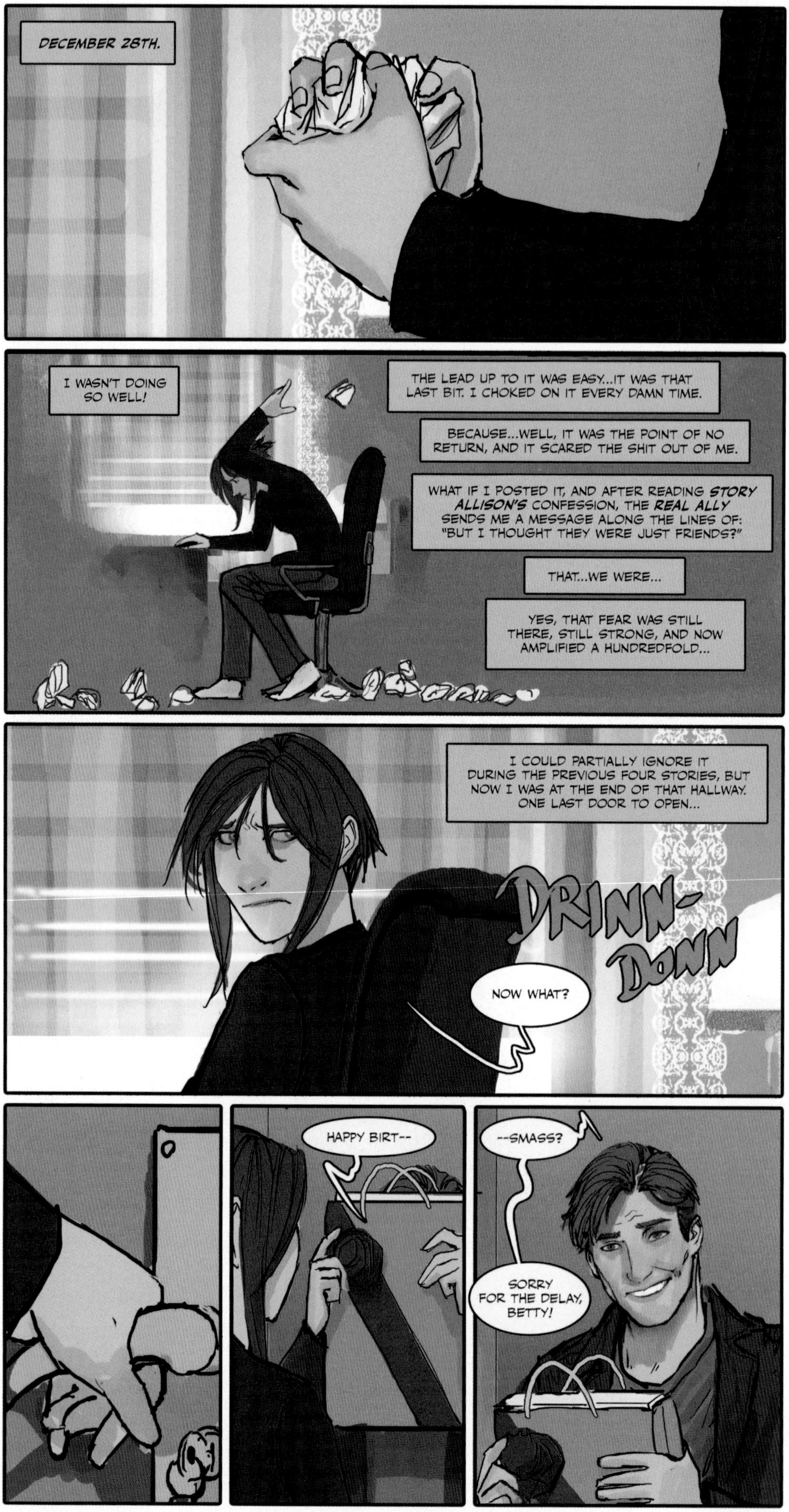

DECEMBER 28TH.
I WASN'T DOING SO WELL!
THE LEAD UP TO IT WAS EASY...IT WAS THAT LAST BIT. I CHOKED ON IT EVERY DAMN TIME.
BECAUSE...WELL, IT WAS THE POINT OF NO RETURN, AND IT SCARED THE SHIT OUT OF ME.
WHAT IF I POSTED IT, AND AFTER READING STORY ALLISON'S CONFESSION, THE REAL ALLY SENDS ME A MESSAGE ALONG THE LINES OF: "BUT I THOUGHT THEY WERE JUST FRIENDS?"
THAT...WE WERE...
YES, THAT FEAR WAS STILL THERE, STILL STRONG, AND NOW AMPLIFIED A HUNDREDFOLD...
I COULD PARTIALLY IGNORE IT DURING THE PREVIOUS FOUR STORIES, BUT NOW I WAS AT THE END OF THAT HALLWAY. ONE LAST DOOR TO OPEN...
DRINN-DONN
NOW WHAT?
HAPPY BIRT--
--SMASS?
SORRY FOR THE DELAY, BETTY!

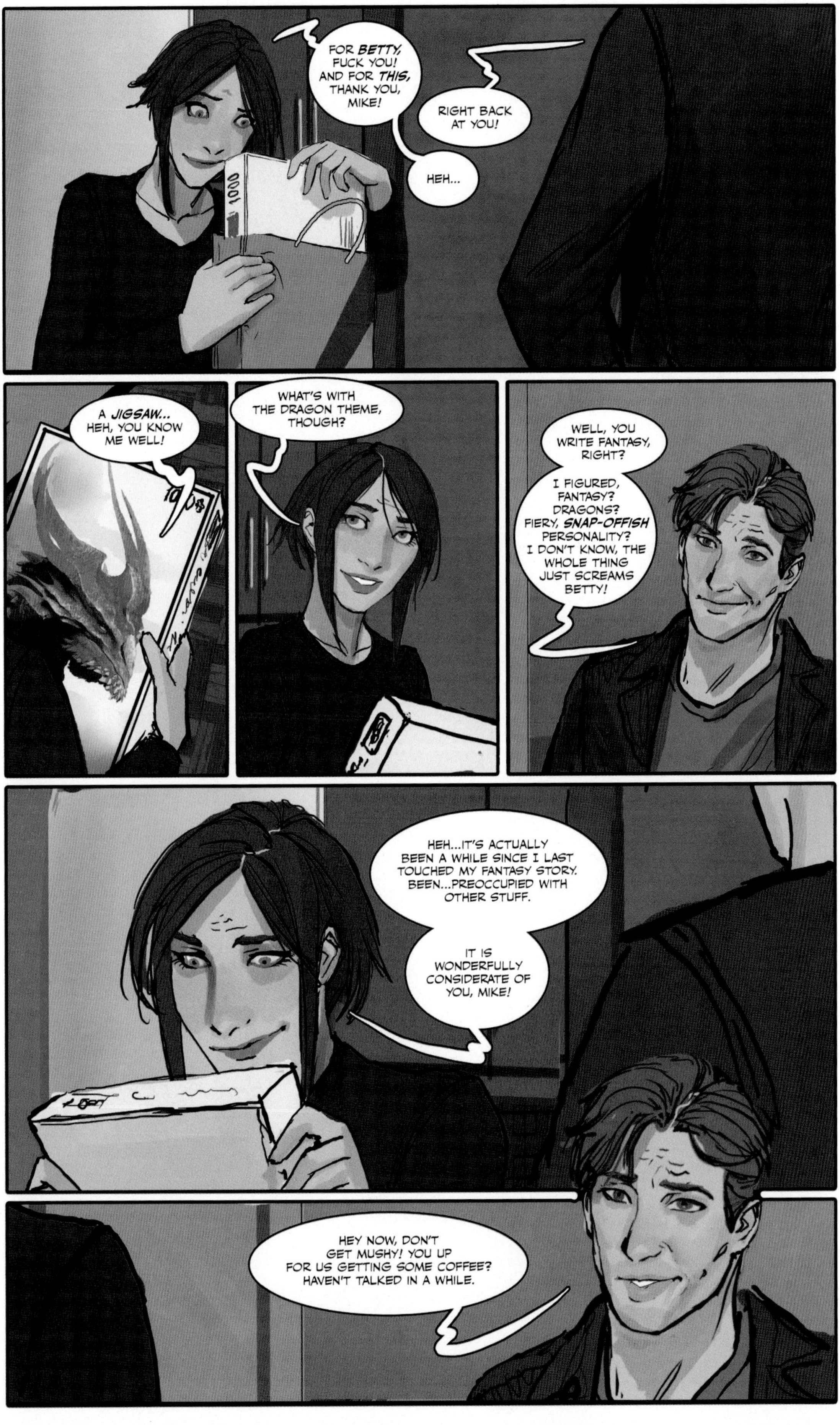

FOR BETTY, FUCK YOU! AND FOR THIS, THANK YOU, MIKE!
RIGHT BACK AT YOU!
HEH...
A JIGSAW... HEH, YOU KNOW ME WELL!
WHAT'S WITH THE DRAGON THEME, THOUGH?
WELL, YOU WRITE FANTASY, RIGHT?
I FIGURED, FANTASY? DRAGONS? FIERY, SNAP-OFFISH PERSONALITY? I DON'T KNOW, THE WHOLE THING JUST SCREAMS BETTY!
HEH...IT'S ACTUALLY BEEN A WHILE SINCE I LAST TOUCHED MY FANTASY STORY. BEEN...PREOCCUPIED WITH OTHER STUFF.
IT IS WONDERFULLY CONSIDERATE OF YOU, MIKE!
HEY NOW, DON'T GET MUSHY! YOU UP FOR US GETTING SOME COFFEE? HAVEN'T TALKED IN A WHILE.

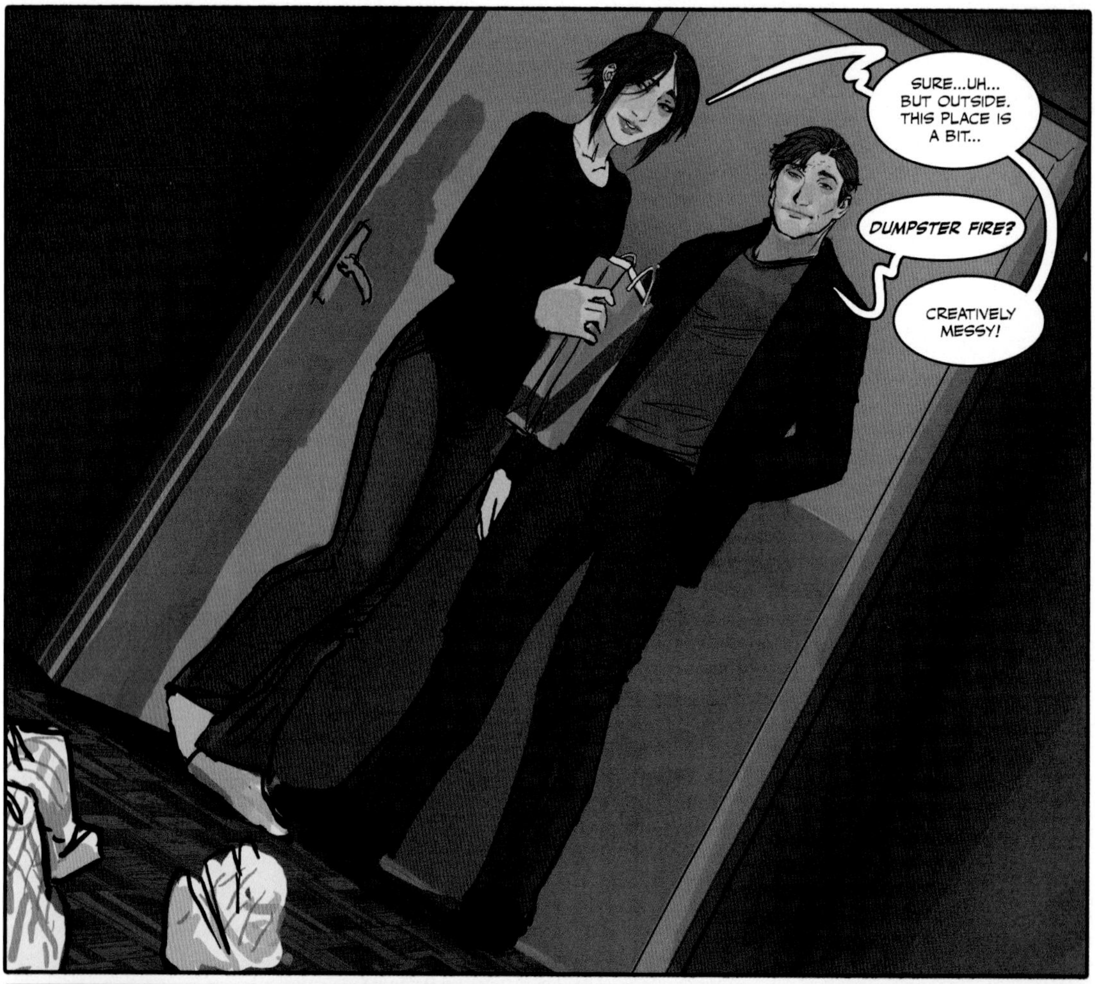
SURE...UH... BUT OUTSIDE. THIS PLACE IS A BIT...
DUMPSTER FIRE?
CREATIVELY MESSY!

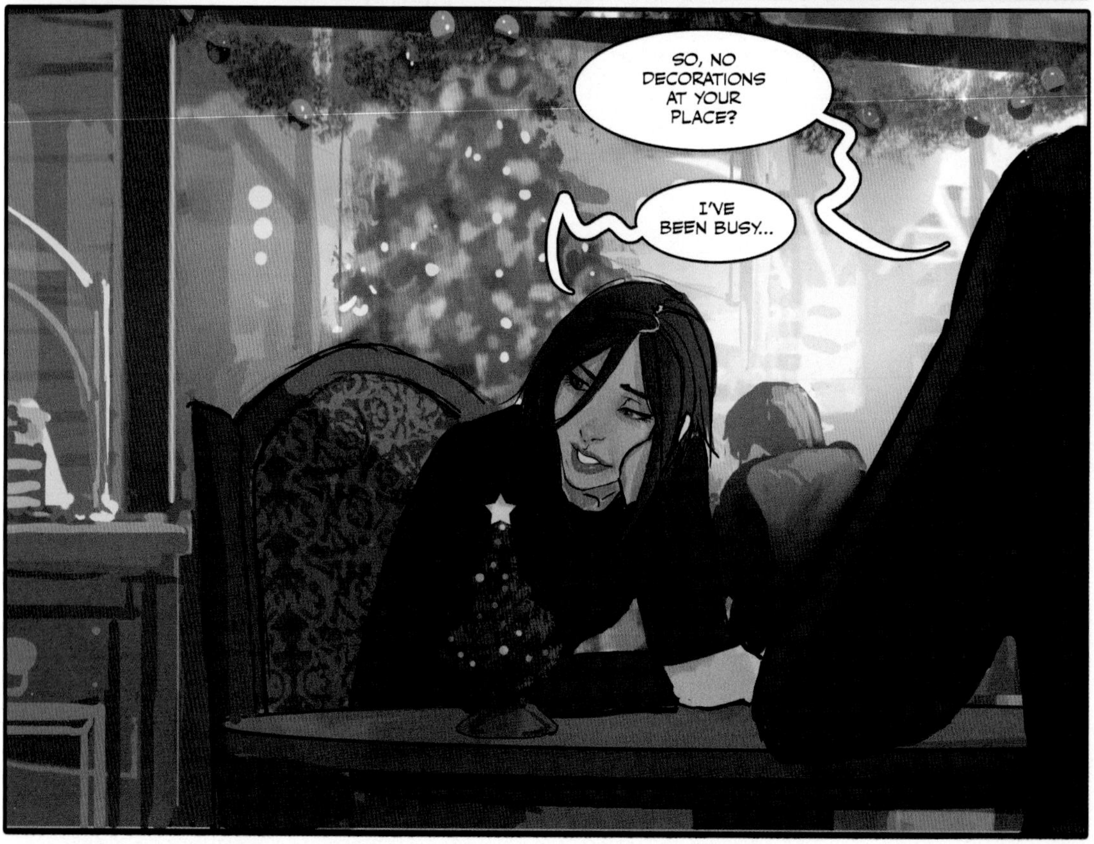
SO, NO DECORATIONS AT YOUR PLACE?
I'VE BEEN BUSY...

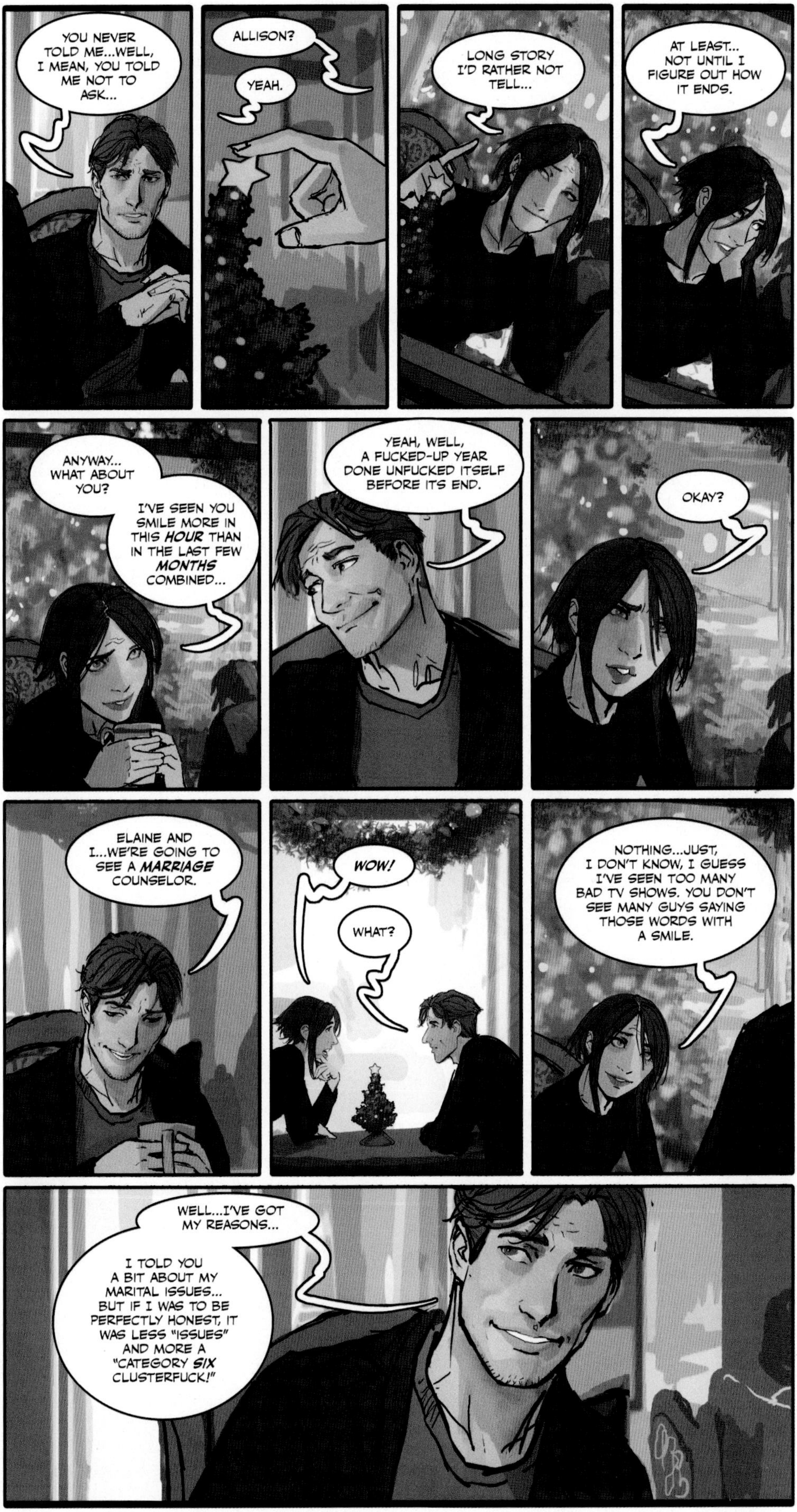
YOU NEVER TOLD ME...WELL, I MEAN, YOU TOLD ME NOT TO ASK...
ALLISON?
YEAH.
LONG STORY I'D RATHER NOT TELL...
AT LEAST... NOT UNTIL I FIGURE OUT HOW IT ENDS.
ANYWAY... WHAT ABOUT YOU?
I'VE SEEN YOU SMILE MORE IN THIS *HOUR* THAN IN THE LAST FEW *MONTHS* COMBINED...
YEAH, WELL, A FUCKED-UP YEAR DONE UNFUCKED ITSELF BEFORE ITS END.
OKAY?
ELAINE AND I...WE'RE GOING TO SEE A *MARRIAGE* COUNSELOR.
WOW!
WHAT?
NOTHING...JUST, I DON'T KNOW, I GUESS I'VE SEEN TOO MANY BAD TV SHOWS. YOU DON'T SEE MANY GUYS SAYING THOSE WORDS WITH A SMILE.
WELL...I'VE GOT MY REASONS...
I TOLD YOU A BIT ABOUT MY MARITAL ISSUES... BUT IF I WAS TO BE PERFECTLY HONEST, IT WAS LESS "ISSUES" AND MORE A "CATEGORY *SIX* CLUSTERFUCK!"

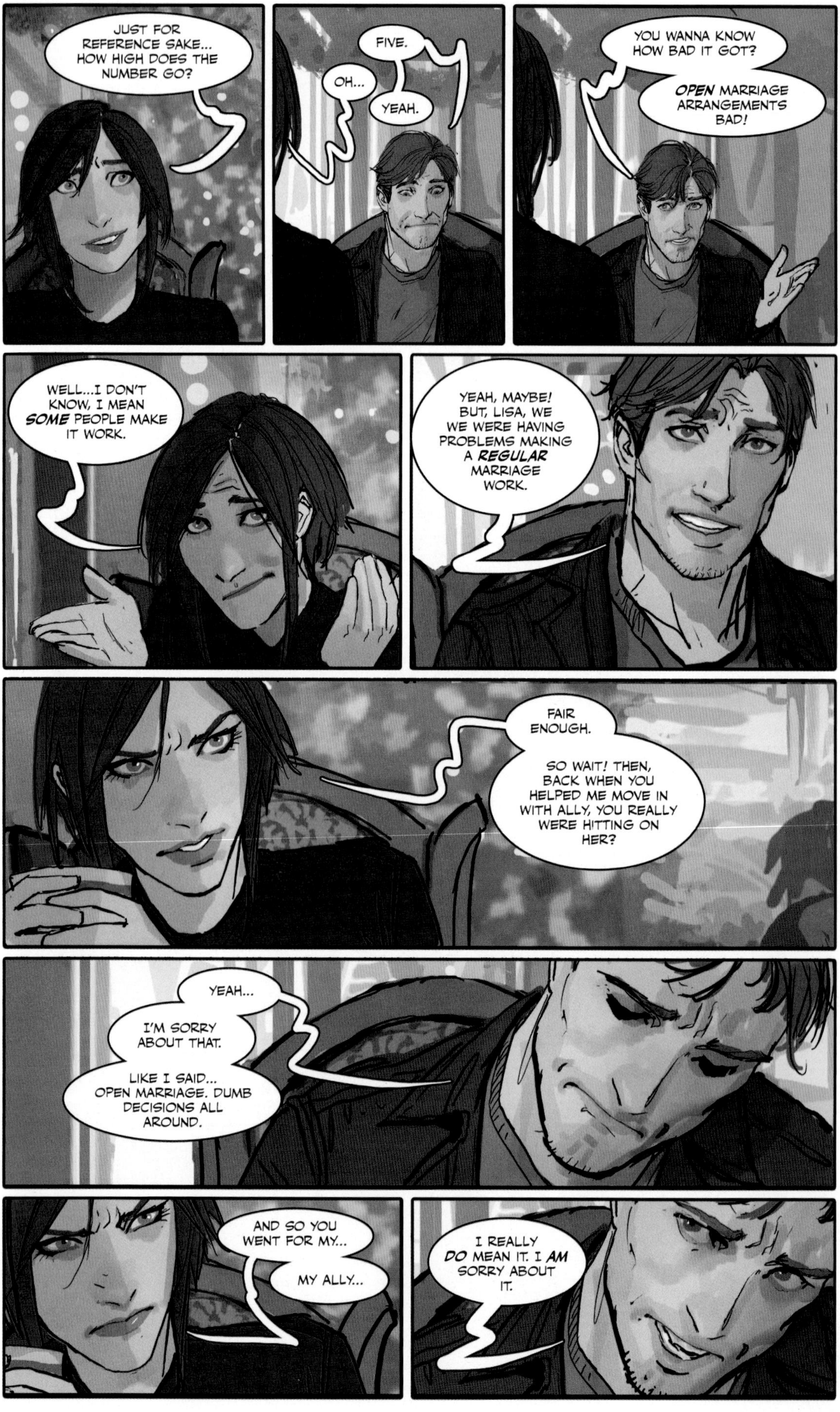

JUST FOR REFERENCE SAKE... HOW HIGH DOES THE NUMBER GO?
FIVE.
OH...
YEAH.
YOU WANNA KNOW HOW BAD IT GOT?
OPEN MARRIAGE ARRANGEMENTS BAD!
WELL...I DON'T KNOW, I MEAN SOME PEOPLE MAKE IT WORK.
YEAH, MAYBE! BUT, LISA, WE WE WERE HAVING PROBLEMS MAKING A REGULAR MARRIAGE WORK.
FAIR ENOUGH.
SO WAIT! THEN, BACK WHEN YOU HELPED ME MOVE IN WITH ALLY, YOU REALLY WERE HITTING ON HER?
YEAH...
I'M SORRY ABOUT THAT.
LIKE I SAID... OPEN MARRIAGE. DUMB DECISIONS ALL AROUND.
AND SO YOU WENT FOR MY...
MY ALLY...
I REALLY DO MEAN IT. I AM SORRY ABOUT IT.

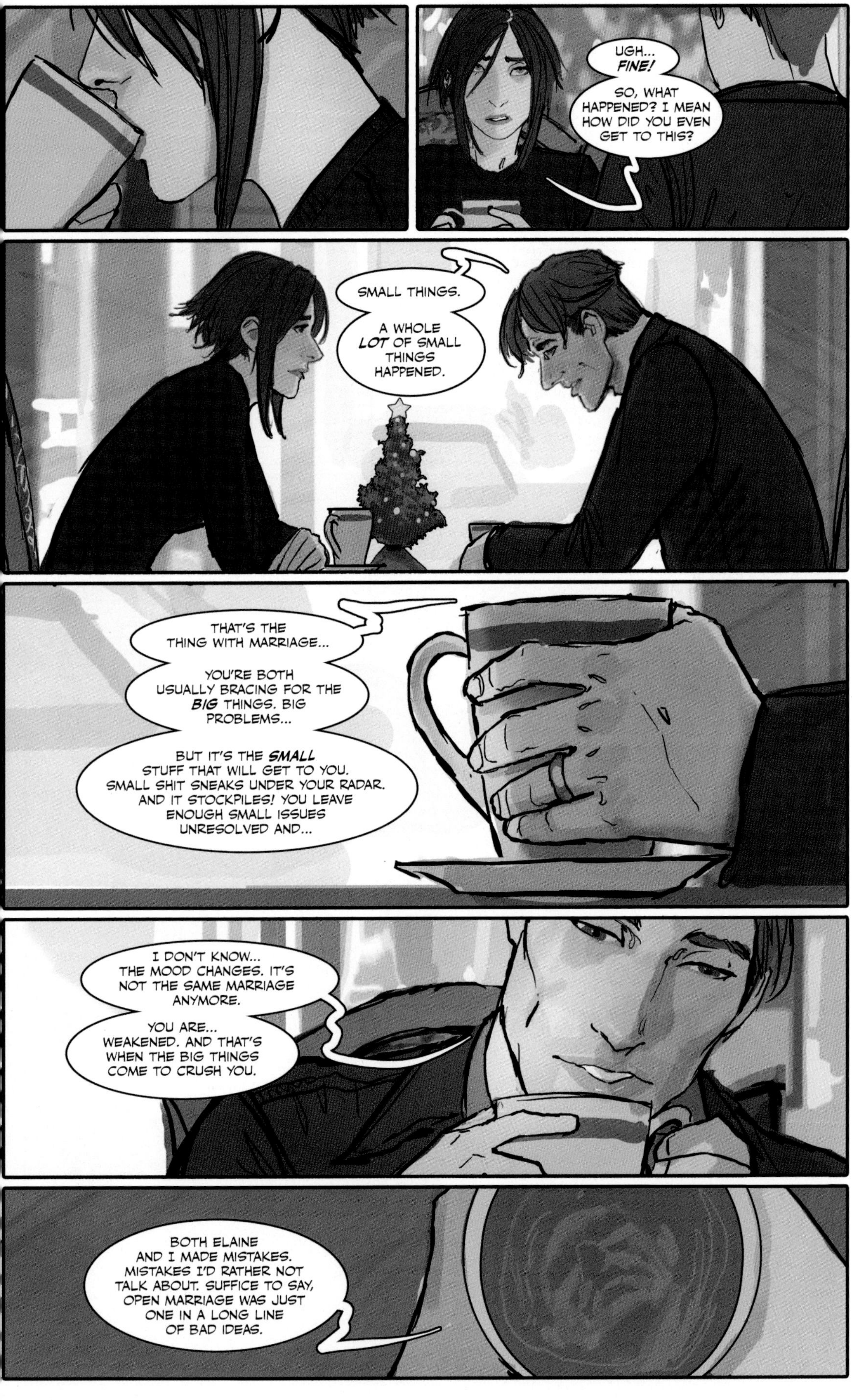
UGH... FINE!
SO, WHAT HAPPENED? I MEAN HOW DID YOU EVEN GET TO THIS?
SMALL THINGS.
A WHOLE LOT OF SMALL THINGS HAPPENED.
THAT'S THE THING WITH MARRIAGE...
YOU'RE BOTH USUALLY BRACING FOR THE BIG THINGS. BIG PROBLEMS...
BUT IT'S THE SMALL STUFF THAT WILL GET TO YOU. SMALL SHIT SNEAKS UNDER YOUR RADAR. AND IT STOCKPILES! YOU LEAVE ENOUGH SMALL ISSUES UNRESOLVED AND...
I DON'T KNOW... THE MOOD CHANGES. IT'S NOT THE SAME MARRIAGE ANYMORE.
YOU ARE... WEAKENED. AND THAT'S WHEN THE BIG THINGS COME TO CRUSH YOU.
BOTH ELAINE AND I MADE MISTAKES. MISTAKES I'D RATHER NOT TALK ABOUT. SUFFICE TO SAY, OPEN MARRIAGE WAS JUST ONE IN A LONG LINE OF BAD IDEAS.

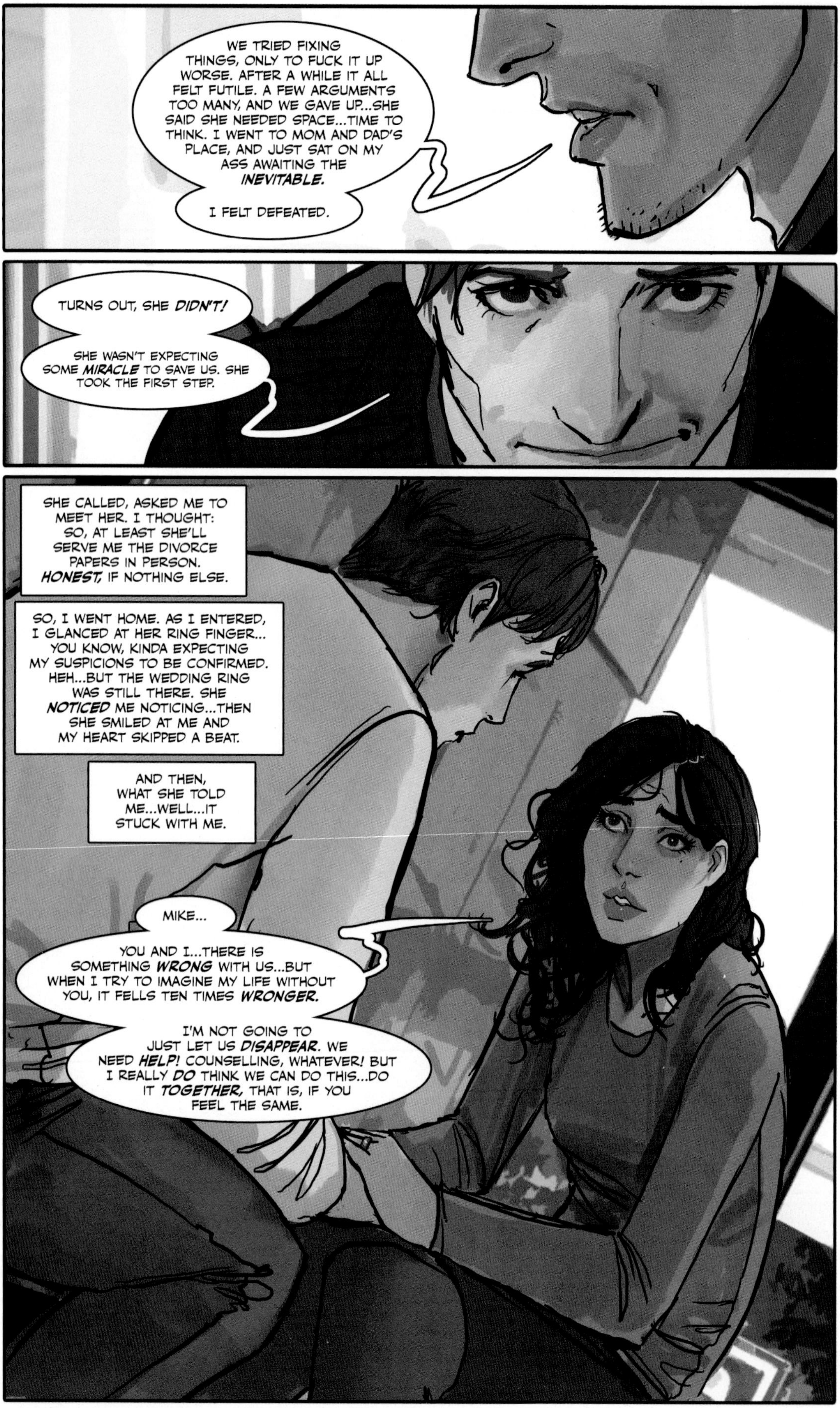
WE TRIED FIXING THINGS, ONLY TO FUCK IT UP WORSE. AFTER A WHILE IT ALL FELT FUTILE. A FEW ARGUMENTS TOO MANY, AND WE GAVE UP...SHE SAID SHE NEEDED SPACE...TIME TO THINK. I WENT TO MOM AND DAD'S PLACE, AND JUST SAT ON MY ASS AWAITING THE *INEVITABLE.*
I FELT DEFEATED.
TURNS OUT, SHE *DIDN'T!*
SHE WASN'T EXPECTING SOME *MIRACLE* TO SAVE US. SHE TOOK THE FIRST STEP.
SHE CALLED, ASKED ME TO MEET HER. I THOUGHT: SO, AT LEAST SHE'LL SERVE ME THE DIVORCE PAPERS IN PERSON. *HONEST,* IF NOTHING ELSE.
SO, I WENT HOME. AS I ENTERED, I GLANCED AT HER RING FINGER... YOU KNOW, KINDA EXPECTING MY SUSPICIONS TO BE CONFIRMED. HEH...BUT THE WEDDING RING WAS STILL THERE. SHE *NOTICED* ME NOTICING...THEN SHE SMILED AT ME AND MY HEART SKIPPED A BEAT.
AND THEN, WHAT SHE TOLD ME...WELL...IT STUCK WITH ME.
MIKE...
YOU AND I...THERE IS SOMETHING *WRONG* WITH US...BUT WHEN I TRY TO IMAGINE MY LIFE WITHOUT YOU, IT FELLS TEN TIMES *WRONGER.*
I'M NOT GOING TO JUST LET US *DISAPPEAR.* WE NEED *HELP!* COUNSELLING, WHATEVER! BUT I REALLY *DO* THINK WE CAN DO THIS...DO IT *TOGETHER,* THAT IS, IF YOU FEEL THE SAME.

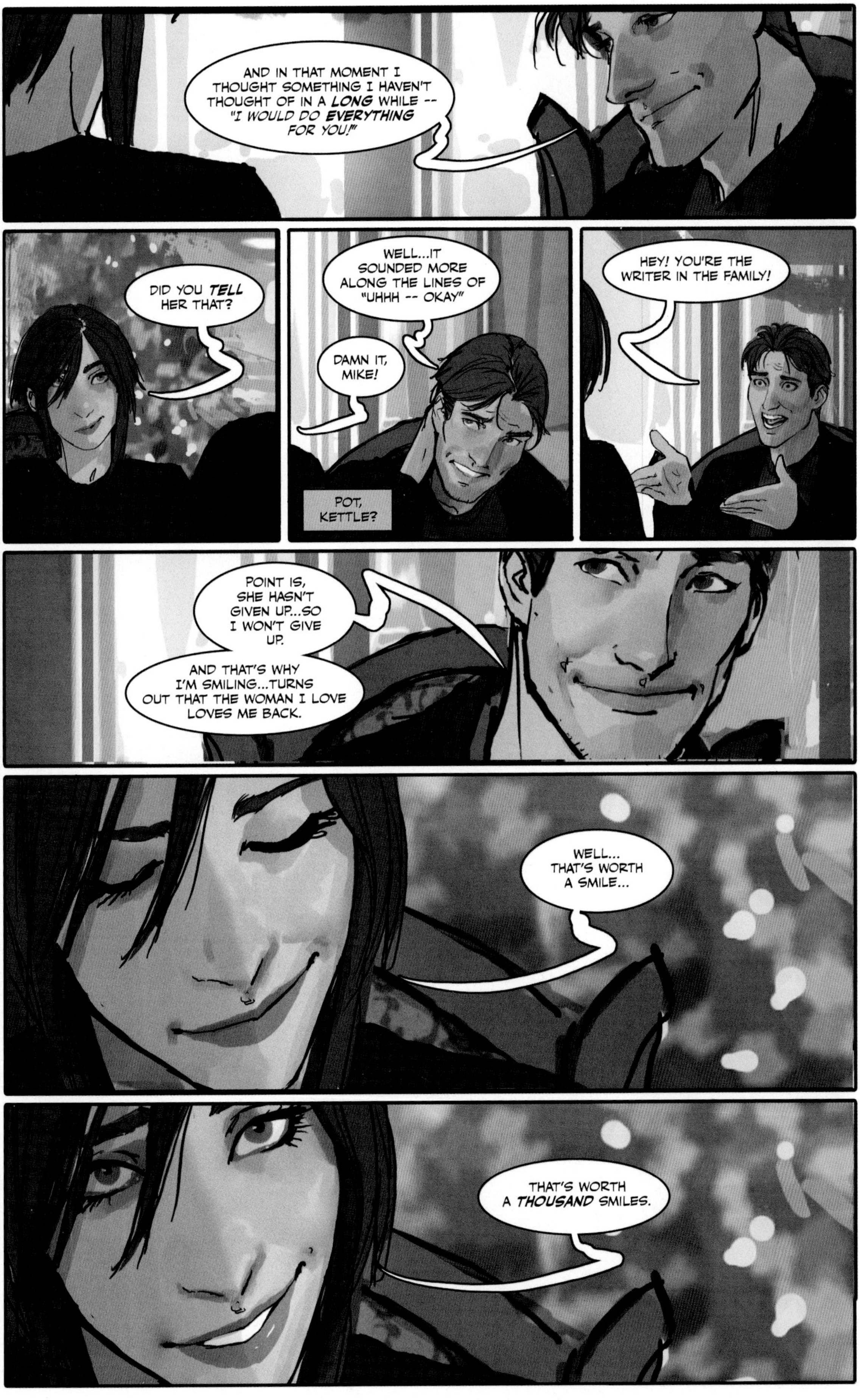
AND IN THAT MOMENT I THOUGHT SOMETHING I HAVEN'T THOUGHT OF IN A *LONG* WHILE -- "I WOULD DO ***EVERYTHING*** FOR YOU!"
DID YOU ***TELL*** HER THAT?
WELL...IT SOUNDED MORE ALONG THE LINES OF "UHHH -- OKAY"
DAMN IT, MIKE!
POT, KETTLE?
HEY! YOU'RE THE WRITER IN THE FAMILY!
POINT IS, SHE HASN'T GIVEN UP...SO I WON'T GIVE UP.
AND THAT'S WHY I'M SMILING...TURNS OUT THAT THE WOMAN I LOVE LOVES ME BACK.
WELL... THAT'S WORTH A SMILE...
THAT'S WORTH A ***THOUSAND*** SMILES.

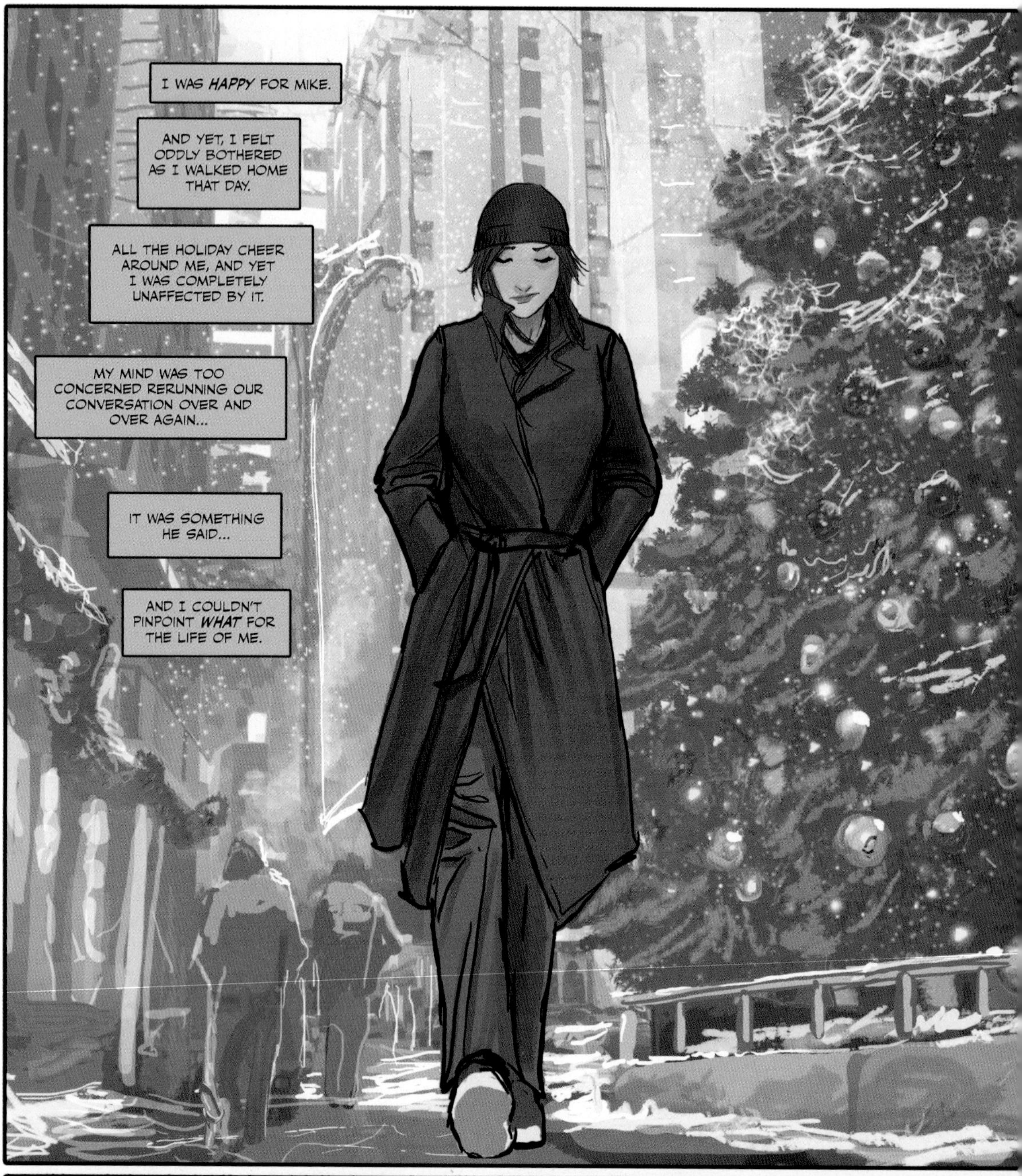
I WAS *HAPPY* FOR MIKE.
AND YET, I FELT ODDLY BOTHERED AS I WALKED HOME THAT DAY.
ALL THE HOLIDAY CHEER AROUND ME, AND YET I WAS COMPLETELY UNAFFECTED BY IT.
MY MIND WAS TOO CONCERNED RERUNNING OUR CONVERSATION OVER AND OVER AGAIN...
IT WAS SOMETHING HE SAID...
AND I COULDN'T PINPOINT *WHAT* FOR THE LIFE OF ME.

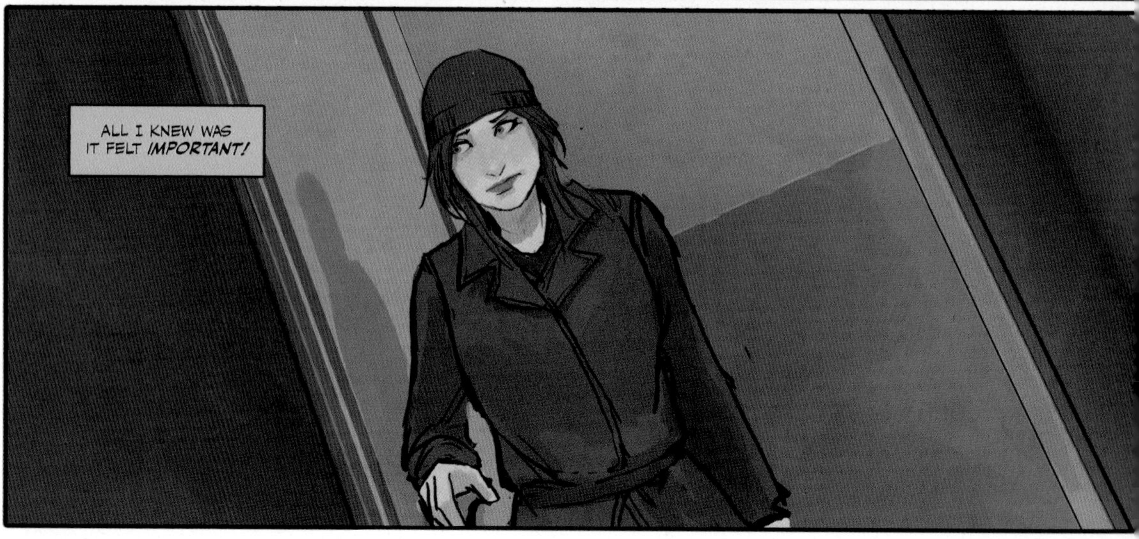
ALL I KNEW WAS IT FELT *IMPORTANT!*

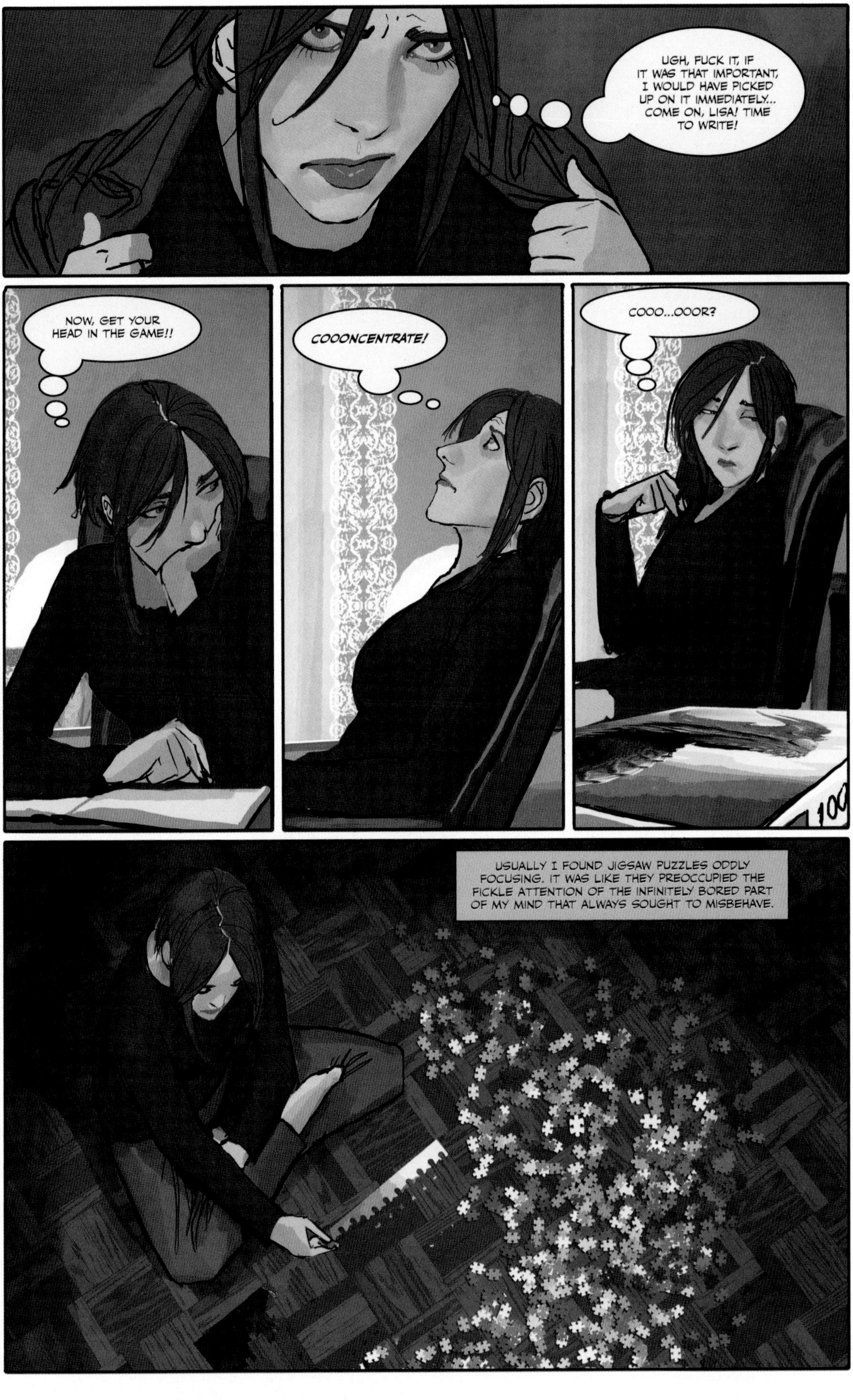
UGH, FUCK IT, IF IT WAS THAT IMPORTANT, I WOULD HAVE PICKED UP ON IT IMMEDIATELY... COME ON, LISA! TIME TO WRITE!
NOW, GET YOUR HEAD IN THE GAME!!
COOONCENTRATE!
COOO...OOOR?
USUALLY I FOUND JIGSAW PUZZLES ODDLY FOCUSING. IT WAS LIKE THEY PREOCCUPIED THE FICKLE ATTENTION OF THE INFINITELY BORED PART OF MY MIND THAT ALWAYS SOUGHT TO MISBEHAVE.

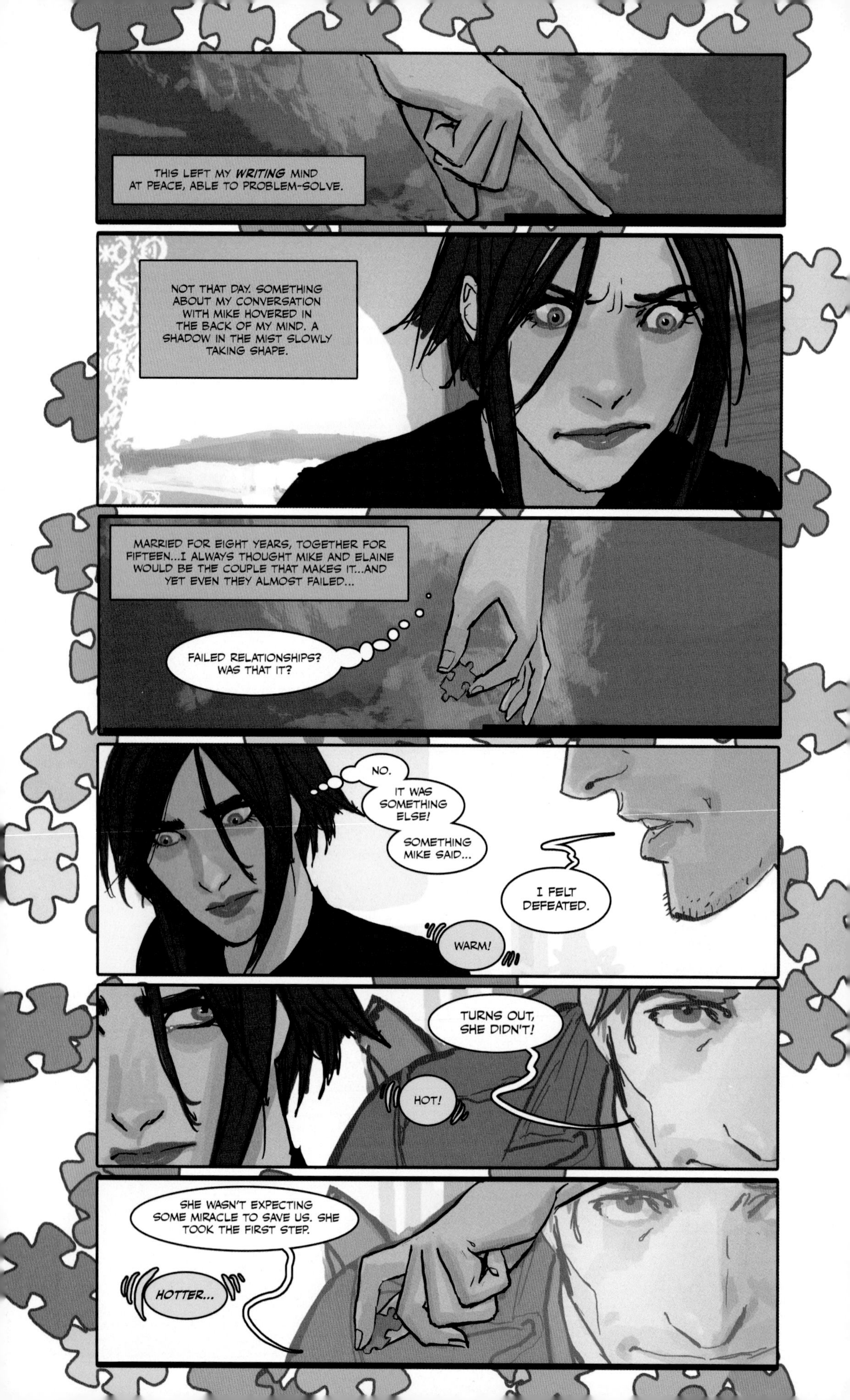
THIS LEFT MY *WRITING* MIND AT PEACE, ABLE TO PROBLEM-SOLVE.
NOT THAT DAY. SOMETHING ABOUT MY CONVERSATION WITH MIKE HOVERED IN THE BACK OF MY MIND. A SHADOW IN THE MIST SLOWLY TAKING SHAPE.
MARRIED FOR EIGHT YEARS, TOGETHER FOR FIFTEEN...I ALWAYS THOUGHT MIKE AND ELAINE WOULD BE THE COUPLE THAT MAKES IT...AND YET EVEN THEY ALMOST FAILED...
FAILED RELATIONSHIPS? WAS THAT IT?
NO.
IT WAS SOMETHING ELSE!
SOMETHING MIKE SAID...
I FELT DEFEATED.
WARM!
TURNS OUT, SHE DIDN'T!
HOT!
SHE WASN'T EXPECTING SOME MIRACLE TO SAVE US. SHE TOOK THE FIRST STEP.
HOTTER...

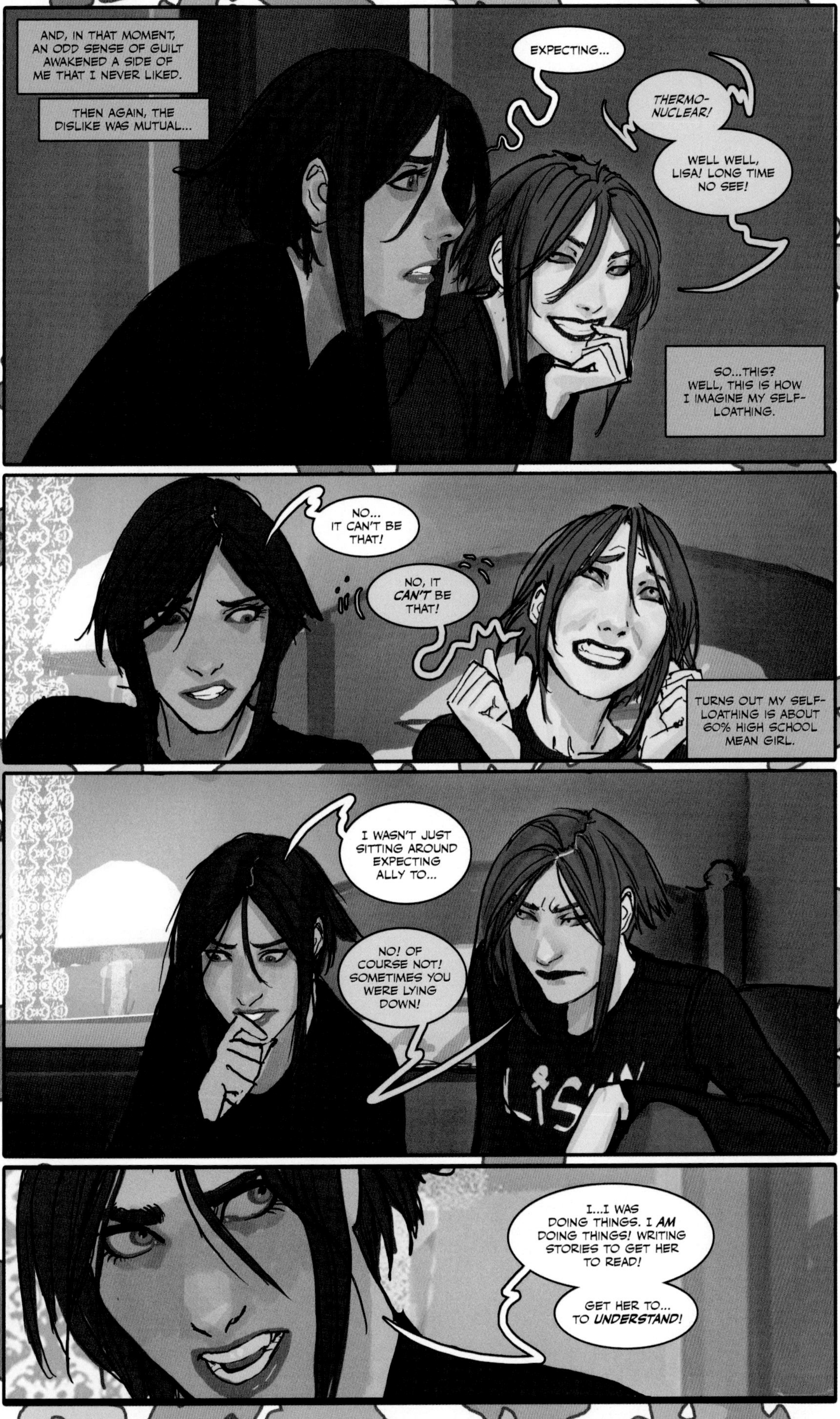
AND, IN THAT MOMENT, AN ODD SENSE OF GUILT AWAKENED A SIDE OF ME THAT I NEVER LIKED.
THEN AGAIN, THE DISLIKE WAS MUTUAL...
EXPECTING...
THERMO-NUCLEAR!
WELL WELL, LISA! LONG TIME NO SEE!
SO...THIS? WELL, THIS IS HOW I IMAGINE MY SELF-LOATHING.
NO... IT CAN'T BE THAT!
NO, IT CAN'T BE THAT!
TURNS OUT MY SELF-LOATHING IS ABOUT 60% HIGH SCHOOL MEAN GIRL.
I WASN'T JUST SITTING AROUND EXPECTING ALLY TO...
NO! OF COURSE NOT! SOMETIMES YOU WERE LYING DOWN!
I...I WAS DOING THINGS. I AM DOING THINGS! WRITING STORIES TO GET HER TO READ!
GET HER TO... TO UNDERSTAND!

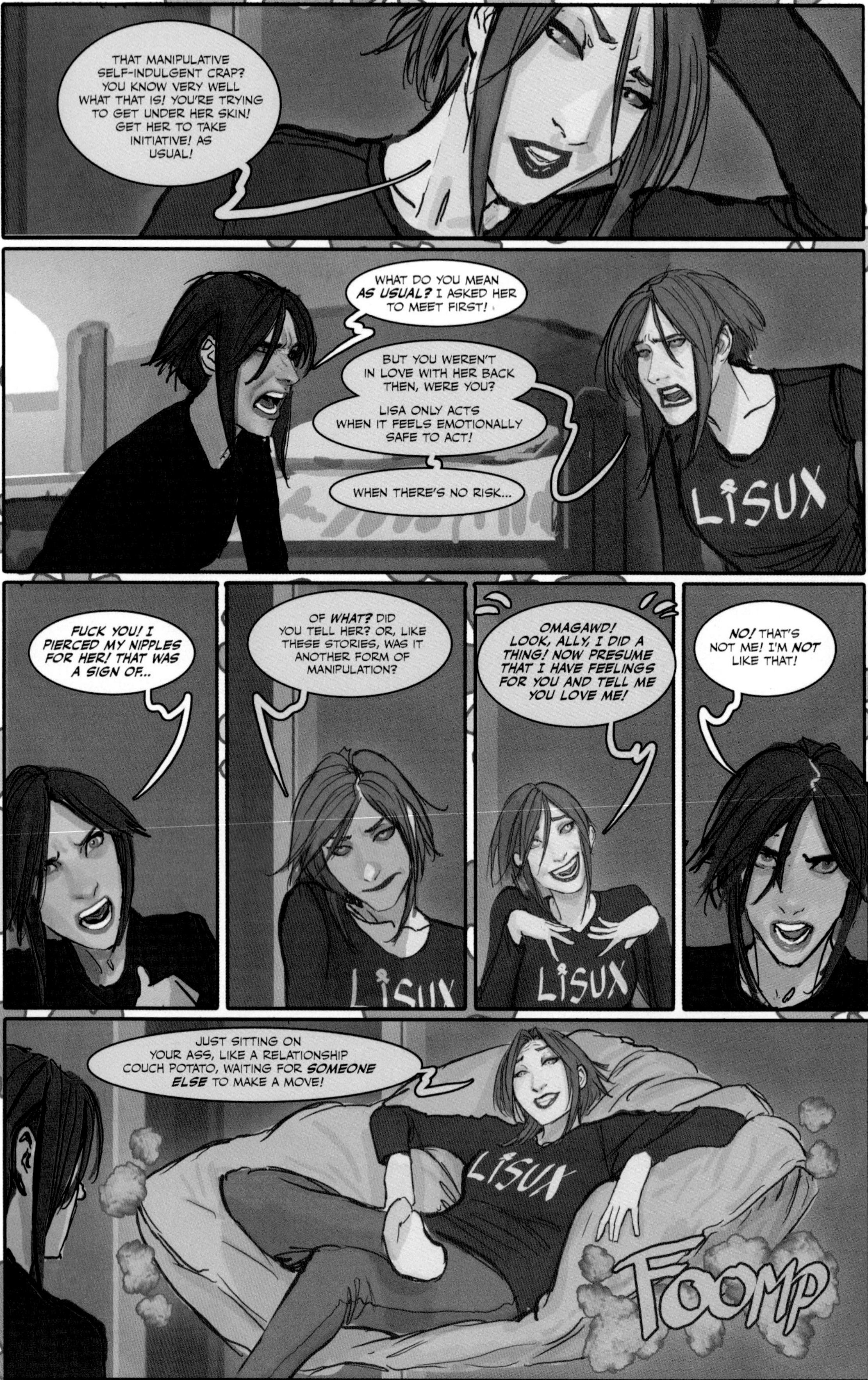
THAT MANIPULATIVE SELF-INDULGENT CRAP? YOU KNOW VERY WELL WHAT THAT IS! YOU'RE TRYING TO GET UNDER HER SKIN! GET HER TO TAKE INITIATIVE! AS USUAL!
WHAT DO YOU MEAN AS USUAL? I ASKED HER TO MEET FIRST!
BUT YOU WEREN'T IN LOVE WITH HER BACK THEN, WERE YOU?
LISA ONLY ACTS WHEN IT FEELS EMOTIONALLY SAFE TO ACT!
WHEN THERE'S NO RISK...
LISUX
FUCK YOU! I PIERCED MY NIPPLES FOR HER! THAT WAS A SIGN OF...
OF WHAT? DID YOU TELL HER? OR, LIKE THESE STORIES, WAS IT ANOTHER FORM OF MANIPULATION?
OMAGAWD! LOOK, ALLY, I DID A THING! NOW PRESUME THAT I HAVE FEELINGS FOR YOU AND TELL ME YOU LOVE ME!
NO! THAT'S NOT ME! I'M NOT LIKE THAT!
JUST SITTING ON YOUR ASS, LIKE A RELATIONSHIP COUCH POTATO, WAITING FOR SOMEONE ELSE TO MAKE A MOVE!
FOOMP

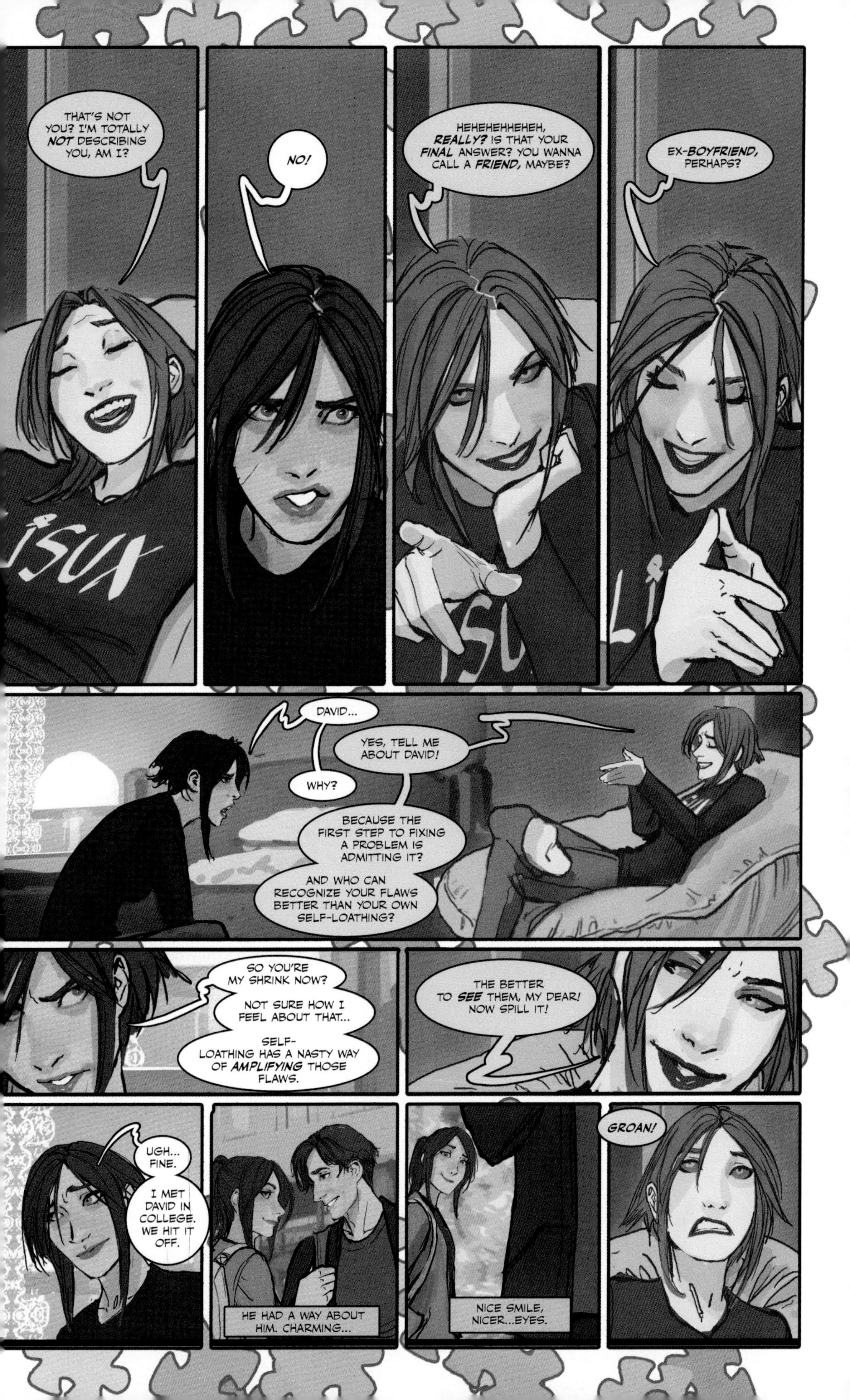

THAT'S NOT YOU? I'M TOTALLY *NOT* DESCRIBING YOU, AM I?
NO!
HEHEHEHHEHEH, *REALLY?* IS THAT YOUR *FINAL* ANSWER? YOU WANNA CALL A *FRIEND,* MAYBE?
EX-*BOYFRIEND,* PERHAPS?
DAVID...
YES, TELL ME ABOUT DAVID!
WHY?
BECAUSE THE FIRST STEP TO FIXING A PROBLEM IS ADMITTING IT?
AND WHO CAN RECOGNIZE YOUR FLAWS BETTER THAN YOUR OWN SELF-LOATHING?
SO YOU'RE MY SHRINK NOW?
NOT SURE HOW I FEEL ABOUT THAT...
SELF-LOATHING HAS A NASTY WAY OF *AMPLIFYING* THOSE FLAWS.
THE BETTER TO *SEE* THEM, MY DEAR! NOW SPILL IT!
UGH... FINE.
I MET DAVID IN COLLEGE. WE HIT IT OFF.
HE HAD A WAY ABOUT HIM. CHARMING...
NICE SMILE, NICER...EYES.
GROAN!

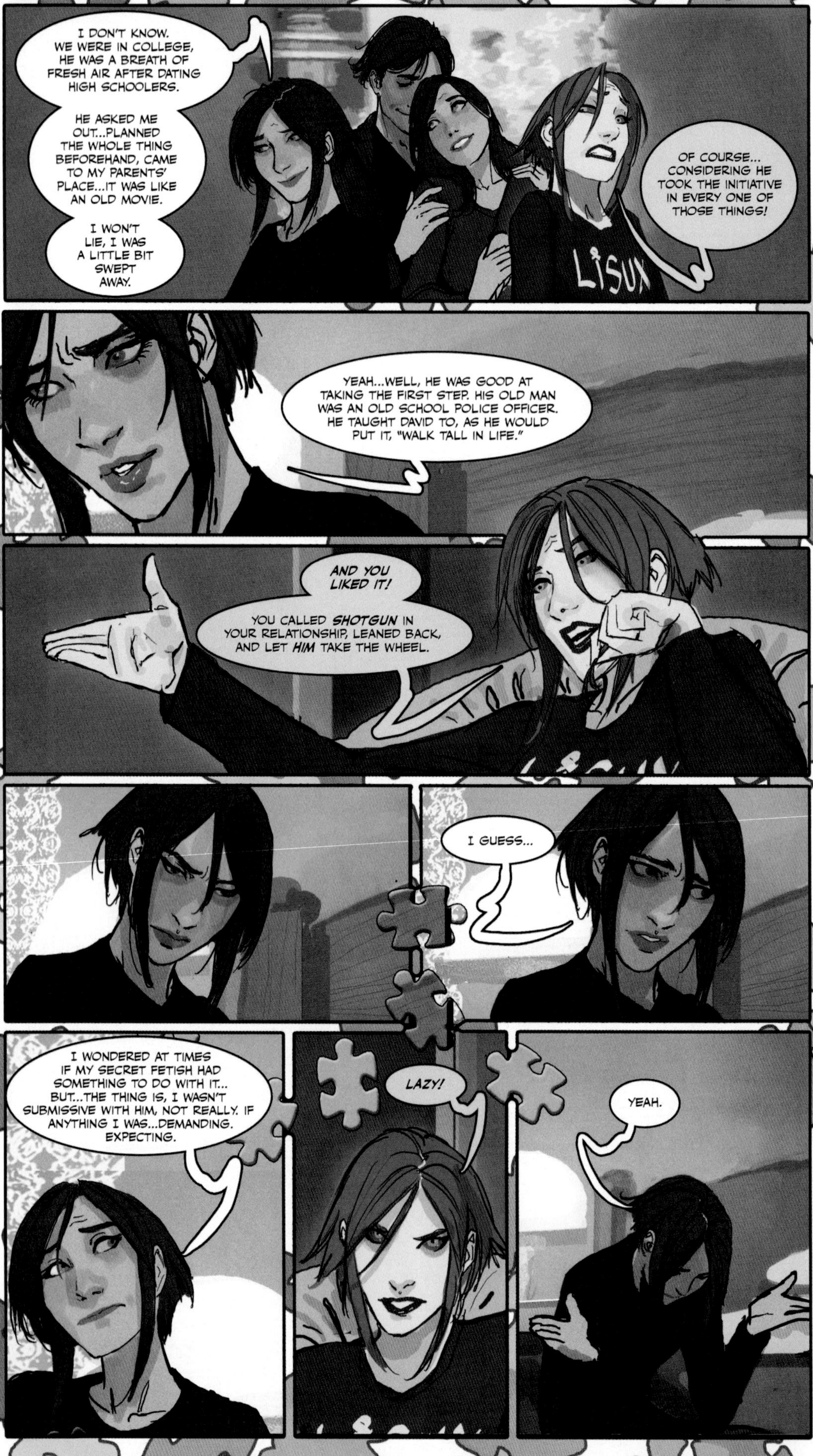
I DON'T KNOW. WE WERE IN COLLEGE, HE WAS A BREATH OF FRESH AIR AFTER DATING HIGH SCHOOLERS.
HE ASKED ME OUT...PLANNED THE WHOLE THING BEFOREHAND, CAME TO MY PARENTS' PLACE...IT WAS LIKE AN OLD MOVIE.
I WON'T LIE, I WAS A LITTLE BIT SWEPT AWAY.
OF COURSE... CONSIDERING HE TOOK THE INITIATIVE IN EVERY ONE OF THOSE THINGS!
LISUX
YEAH...WELL, HE WAS GOOD AT TAKING THE FIRST STEP. HIS OLD MAN WAS AN OLD SCHOOL POLICE OFFICER. HE TAUGHT DAVID TO, AS HE WOULD PUT IT, "WALK TALL IN LIFE."
AND YOU LIKED IT!
YOU CALLED SHOTGUN IN YOUR RELATIONSHIP, LEANED BACK, AND LET HIM TAKE THE WHEEL.
I GUESS...
I WONDERED AT TIMES IF MY SECRET FETISH HAD SOMETHING TO DO WITH IT... BUT...THE THING IS, I WASN'T SUBMISSIVE WITH HIM, NOT REALLY. IF ANYTHING I WAS...DEMANDING. EXPECTING.
LAZY!
YEAH.

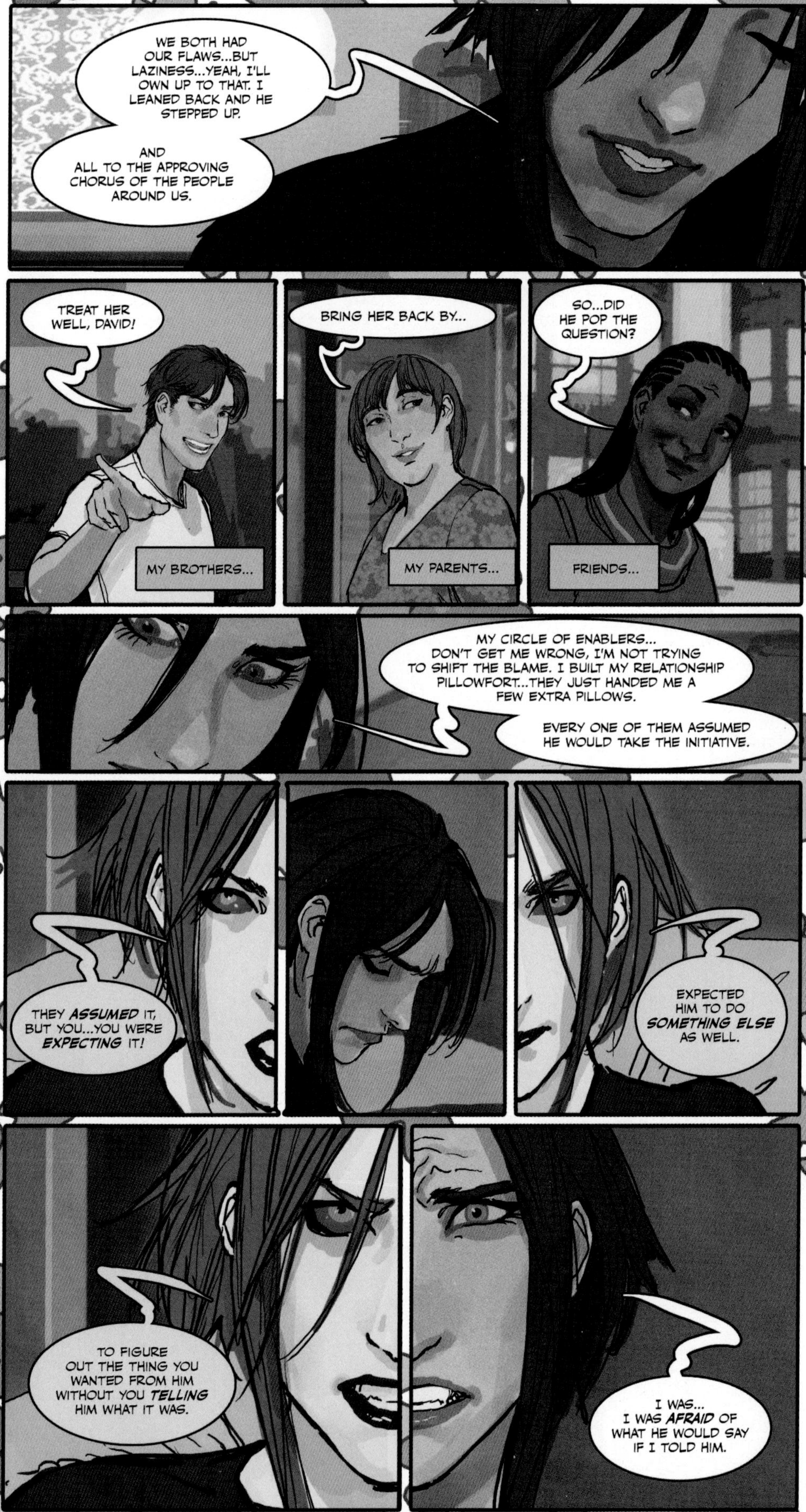
WE BOTH HAD OUR FLAWS...BUT LAZINESS...YEAH, I'LL OWN UP TO THAT. I LEANED BACK AND HE STEPPED UP.
AND ALL TO THE APPROVING CHORUS OF THE PEOPLE AROUND US.
TREAT HER WELL, DAVID!
MY BROTHERS...
BRING HER BACK BY...
MY PARENTS...
SO...DID HE POP THE QUESTION?
FRIENDS...
MY CIRCLE OF ENABLERS... DON'T GET ME WRONG, I'M NOT TRYING TO SHIFT THE BLAME. I BUILT MY RELATIONSHIP PILLOWFORT...THEY JUST HANDED ME A FEW EXTRA PILLOWS.
EVERY ONE OF THEM ASSUMED HE WOULD TAKE THE INITIATIVE.
THEY *ASSUMED* IT, BUT YOU...YOU WERE *EXPECTING* IT!
EXPECTED HIM TO DO *SOMETHING ELSE* AS WELL.
TO FIGURE OUT THE THING YOU WANTED FROM HIM WITHOUT YOU *TELLING* HIM WHAT IT WAS.
I WAS... I WAS *AFRAID* OF WHAT HE WOULD SAY IF I TOLD HIM.

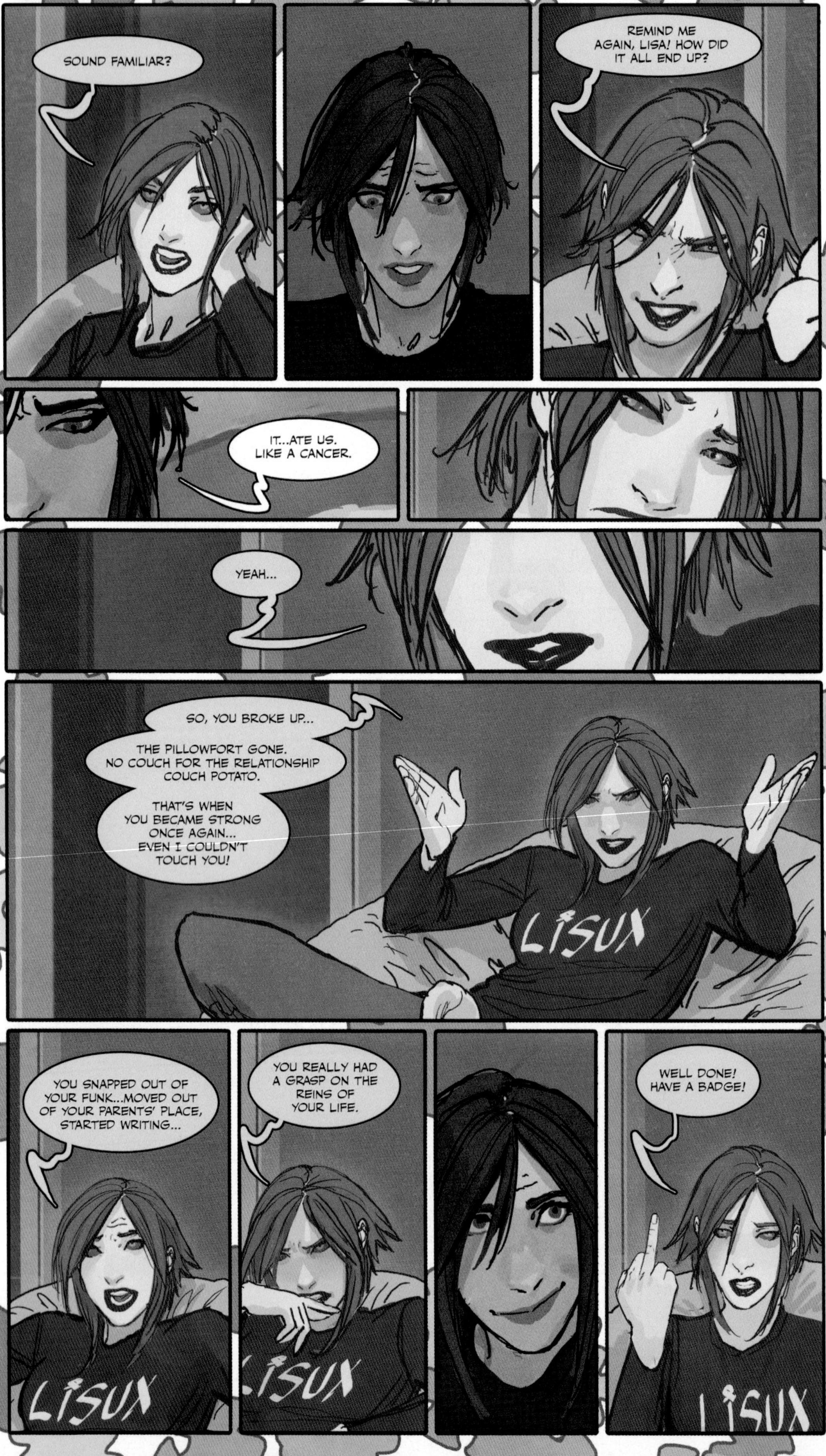
SOUND FAMILIAR?
REMIND ME AGAIN, LISA! HOW DID IT ALL END UP?
IT...ATE US. LIKE A CANCER.
YEAH...
SO, YOU BROKE UP...
THE PILLOWFORT GONE. NO COUCH FOR THE RELATIONSHIP COUCH POTATO.
THAT'S WHEN YOU BECAME STRONG ONCE AGAIN... EVEN I COULDN'T TOUCH YOU!
LISUX
YOU SNAPPED OUT OF YOUR FUNK...MOVED OUT OF YOUR PARENTS' PLACE, STARTED WRITING...
YOU REALLY HAD A GRASP ON THE REINS OF YOUR LIFE.
WELL DONE! HAVE A BADGE!

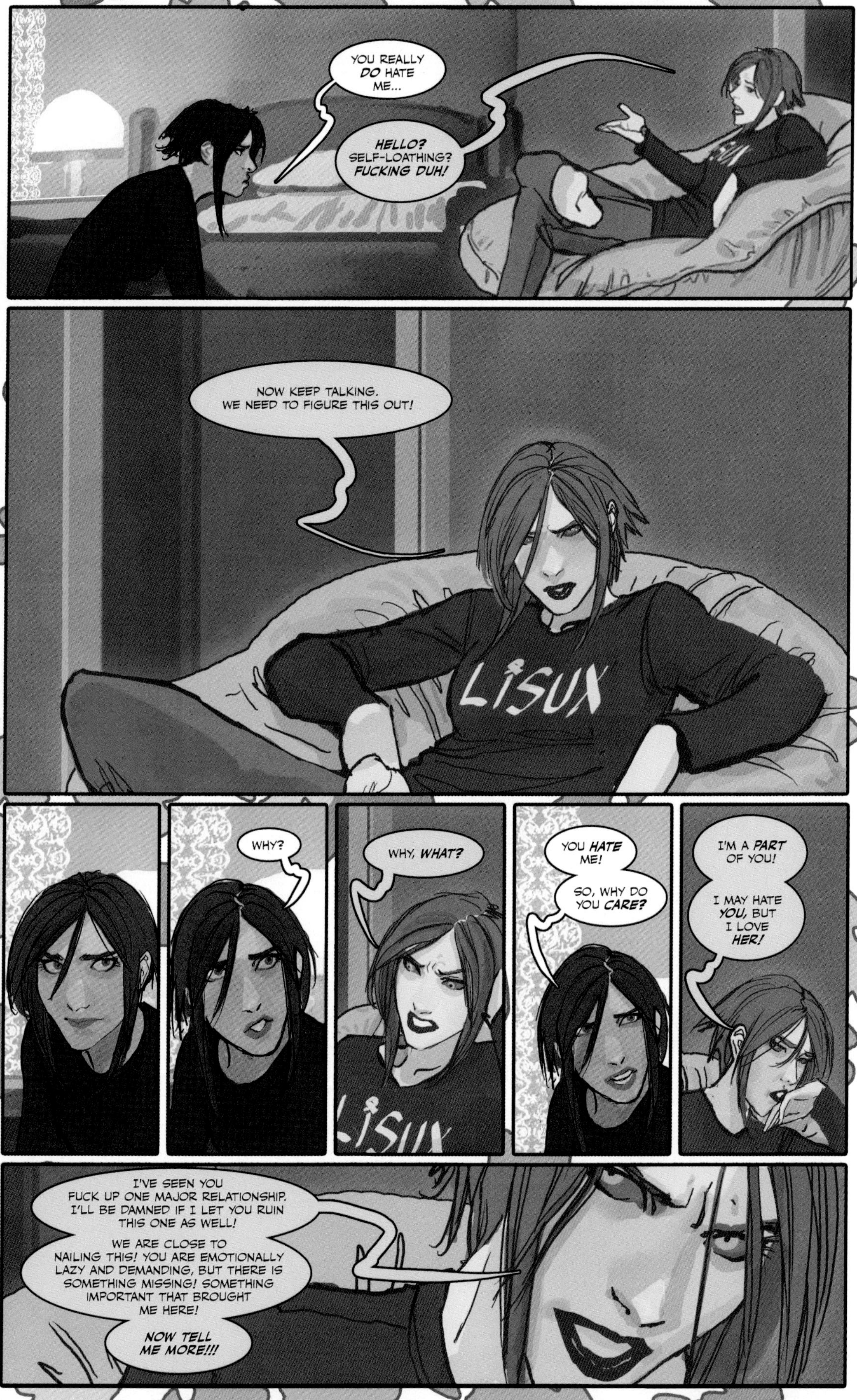
YOU REALLY DO HATE ME...
HELLO? SELF-LOATHING? FUCKING DUH!
NOW KEEP TALKING. WE NEED TO FIGURE THIS OUT!
LISUX
WHY?
WHY, WHAT?
LISUX
YOU HATE ME!
SO, WHY DO YOU CARE?
I'M A PART OF YOU!
I MAY HATE YOU, BUT I LOVE HER!
I'VE SEEN YOU FUCK UP ONE MAJOR RELATIONSHIP. I'LL BE DAMNED IF I LET YOU RUIN THIS ONE AS WELL!
WE ARE CLOSE TO NAILING THIS! YOU ARE EMOTIONALLY LAZY AND DEMANDING, BUT THERE IS SOMETHING MISSING! SOMETHING IMPORTANT THAT BROUGHT ME HERE!
NOW TELL ME MORE!!!

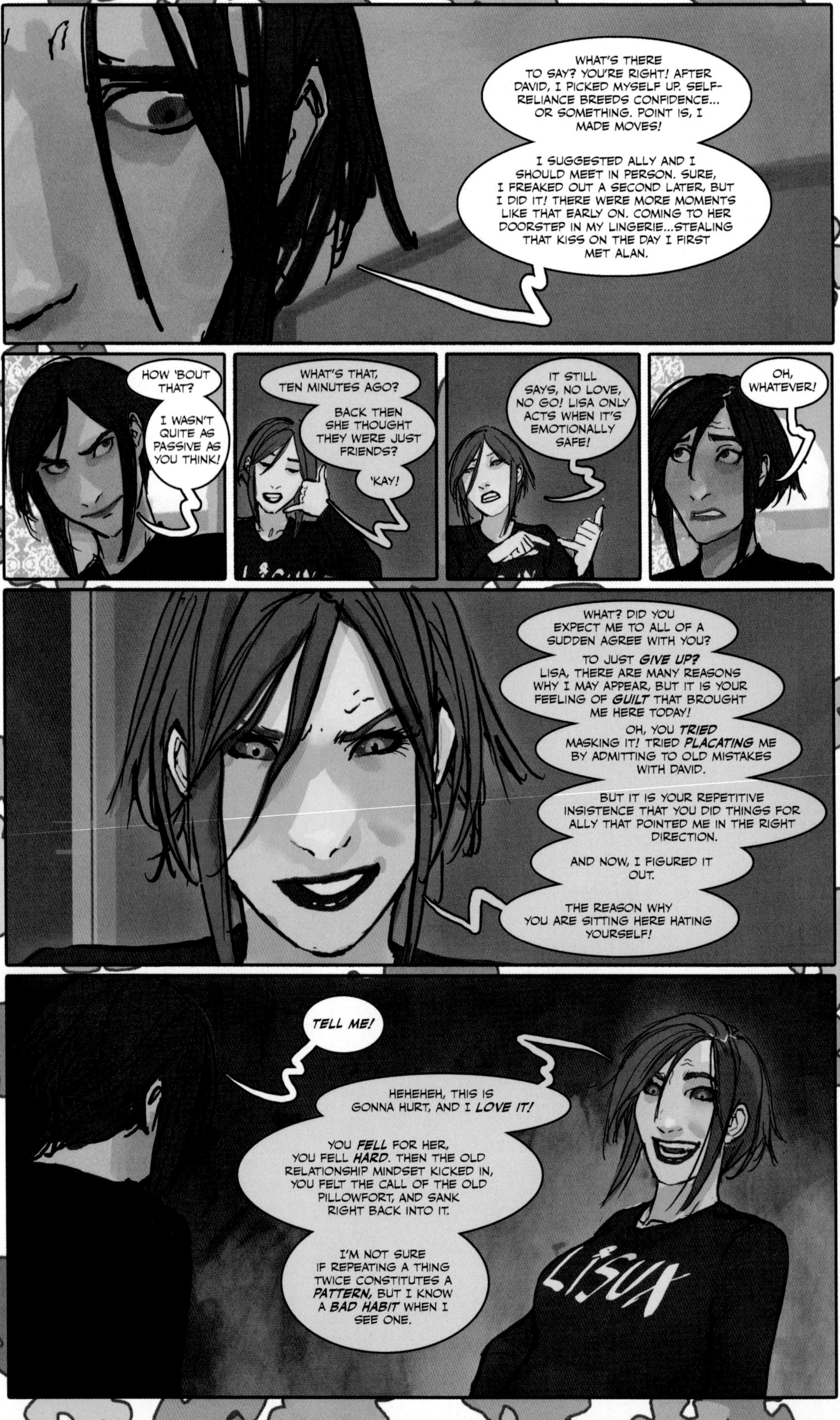
WHAT'S THERE TO SAY? YOU'RE RIGHT! AFTER DAVID, I PICKED MYSELF UP. SELF-RELIANCE BREEDS CONFIDENCE... OR SOMETHING. POINT IS, I MADE MOVES!
I SUGGESTED ALLY AND I SHOULD MEET IN PERSON. SURE, I FREAKED OUT A SECOND LATER, BUT I DID IT! THERE WERE MORE MOMENTS LIKE THAT EARLY ON. COMING TO HER DOORSTEP IN MY LINGERIE...STEALING THAT KISS ON THE DAY I FIRST MET ALAN.
HOW 'BOUT THAT?
I WASN'T QUITE AS PASSIVE AS YOU THINK!
WHAT'S THAT, TEN MINUTES AGO?
BACK THEN SHE THOUGHT THEY WERE JUST FRIENDS?
'KAY!
IT STILL SAYS, NO LOVE, NO GO! LISA ONLY ACTS WHEN IT'S EMOTIONALLY SAFE!
OH, WHATEVER!
WHAT? DID YOU EXPECT ME TO ALL OF A SUDDEN AGREE WITH YOU?
TO JUST GIVE UP? LISA, THERE ARE MANY REASONS WHY I MAY APPEAR, BUT IT IS YOUR FEELING OF GUILT THAT BROUGHT ME HERE TODAY!
OH, YOU TRIED MASKING IT! TRIED PLACATING ME BY ADMITTING TO OLD MISTAKES WITH DAVID.
BUT IT IS YOUR REPETITIVE INSISTENCE THAT YOU DID THINGS FOR ALLY THAT POINTED ME IN THE RIGHT DIRECTION.
AND NOW, I FIGURED IT OUT.
THE REASON WHY YOU ARE SITTING HERE HATING YOURSELF!
TELL ME!
HEHEHEH, THIS IS GONNA HURT, AND I LOVE IT!
YOU FELL FOR HER, YOU FELL HARD. THEN THE OLD RELATIONSHIP MINDSET KICKED IN, YOU FELT THE CALL OF THE OLD PILLOWFORT, AND SANK RIGHT BACK INTO IT.
I'M NOT SURE IF REPEATING A THING TWICE CONSTITUTES A PATTERN, BUT I KNOW A BAD HABIT WHEN I SEE ONE.
LISA

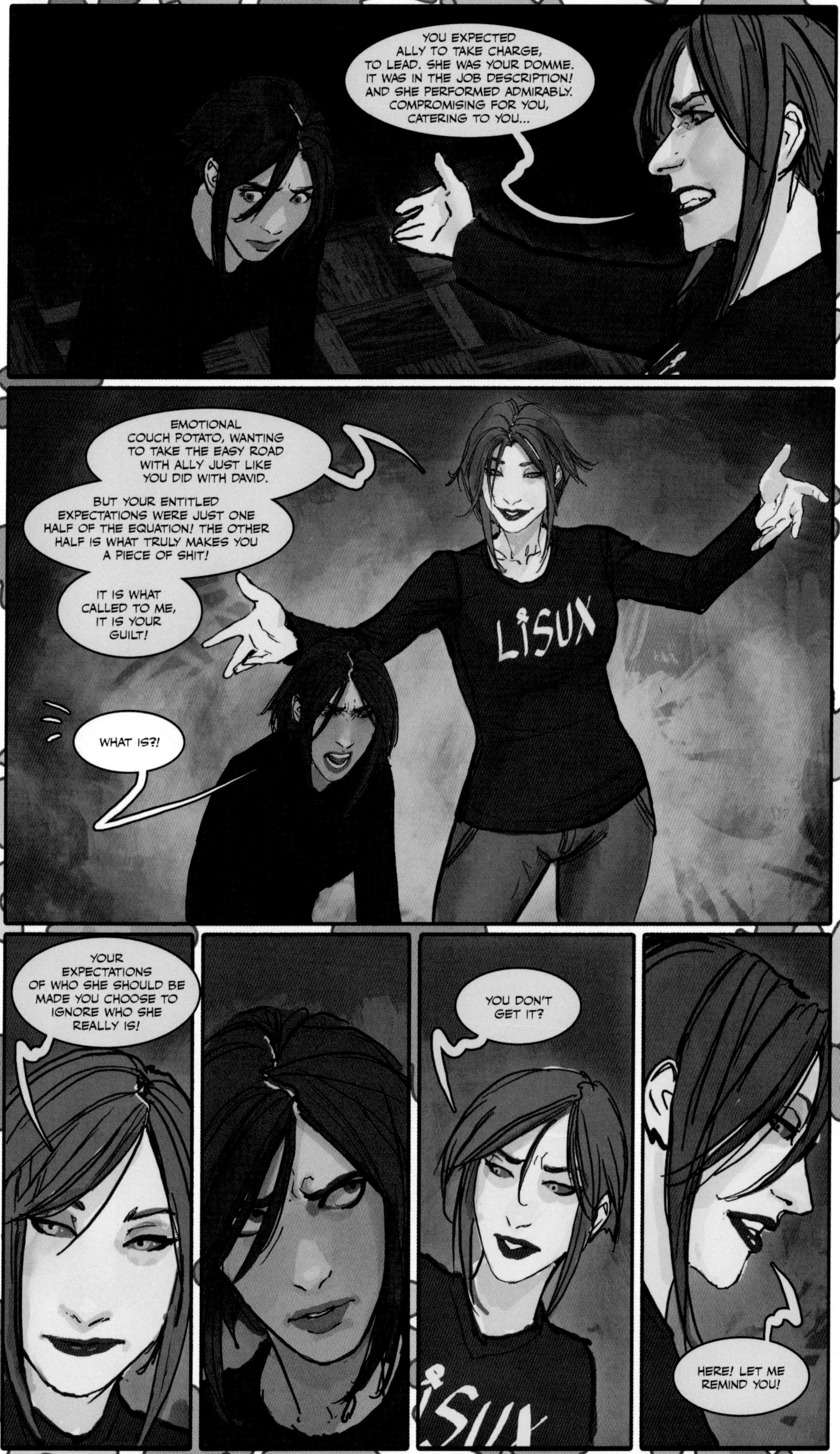
YOU EXPECTED ALLY TO TAKE CHARGE, TO LEAD. SHE WAS YOUR DOMME. IT WAS IN THE JOB DESCRIPTION! AND SHE PERFORMED ADMIRABLY. COMPROMISING FOR YOU, CATERING TO YOU...
EMOTIONAL COUCH POTATO, WANTING TO TAKE THE EASY ROAD WITH ALLY JUST LIKE YOU DID WITH DAVID.
BUT YOUR ENTITLED EXPECTATIONS WERE JUST ONE HALF OF THE EQUATION! THE OTHER HALF IS WHAT TRULY MAKES YOU A PIECE OF SHIT!
IT IS WHAT CALLED TO ME, IT IS YOUR GUILT!
LISUX
WHAT IS?!
YOUR EXPECTATIONS OF WHO SHE SHOULD BE MADE YOU CHOOSE TO IGNORE WHO SHE REALLY IS!
YOU DON'T GET IT?
HERE! LET ME REMIND YOU!

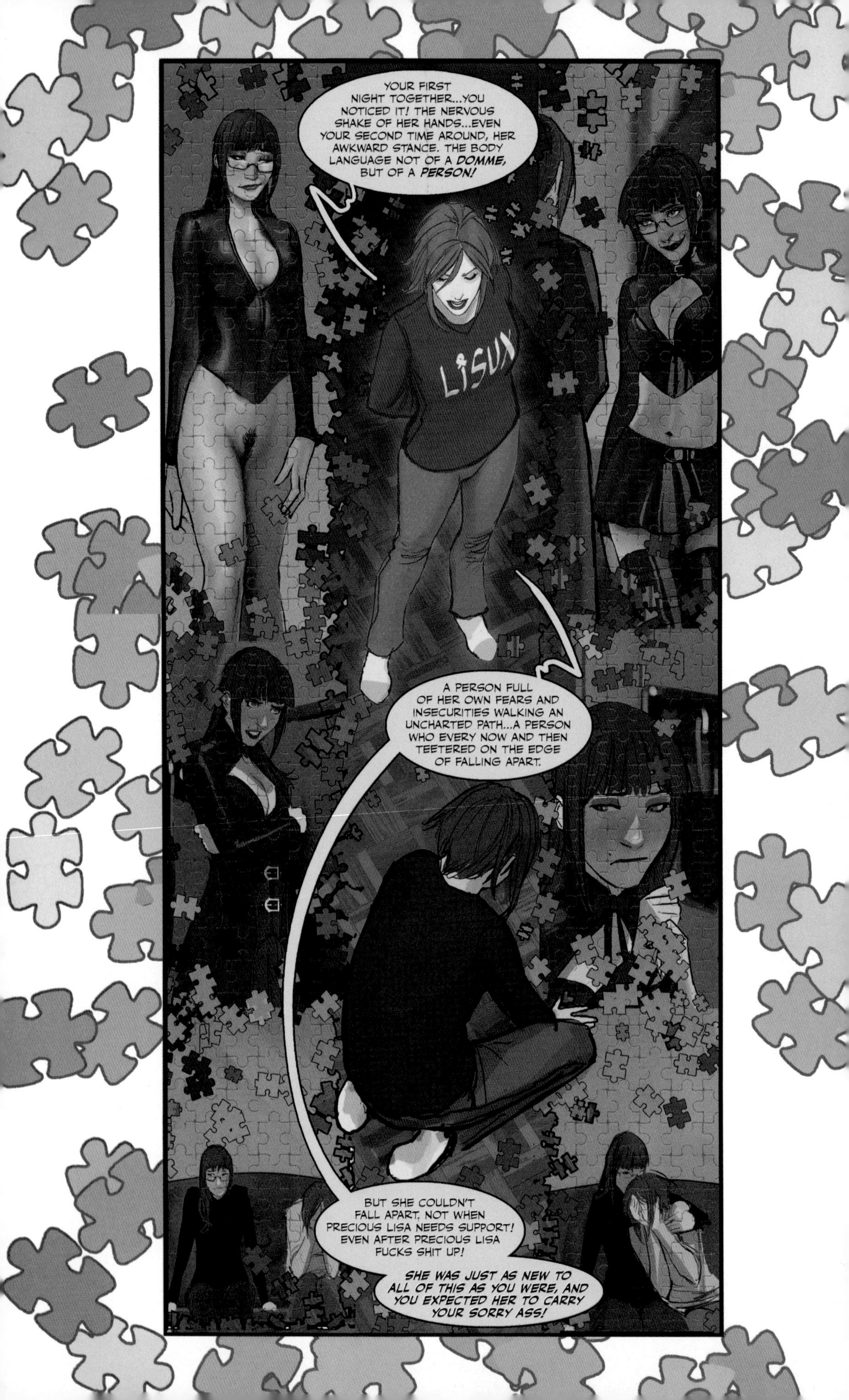
YOUR FIRST NIGHT TOGETHER...YOU NOTICED IT! THE NERVOUS SHAKE OF HER HANDS...EVEN YOUR SECOND TIME AROUND, HER AWKWARD STANCE. THE BODY LANGUAGE NOT OF A *DOMME,* BUT OF A *PERSON!*
LISUX
A PERSON FULL OF HER OWN FEARS AND INSECURITIES WALKING AN UNCHARTED PATH...A PERSON WHO EVERY NOW AND THEN TEETERED ON THE EDGE OF FALLING APART.
BUT SHE COULDN'T FALL APART, NOT WHEN PRECIOUS LISA NEEDS SUPPORT! EVEN AFTER PRECIOUS LISA FUCKS SHIT UP!
SHE WAS JUST AS NEW TO ALL OF THIS AS YOU WERE, AND YOU EXPECTED HER TO CARRY YOUR SORRY ASS!

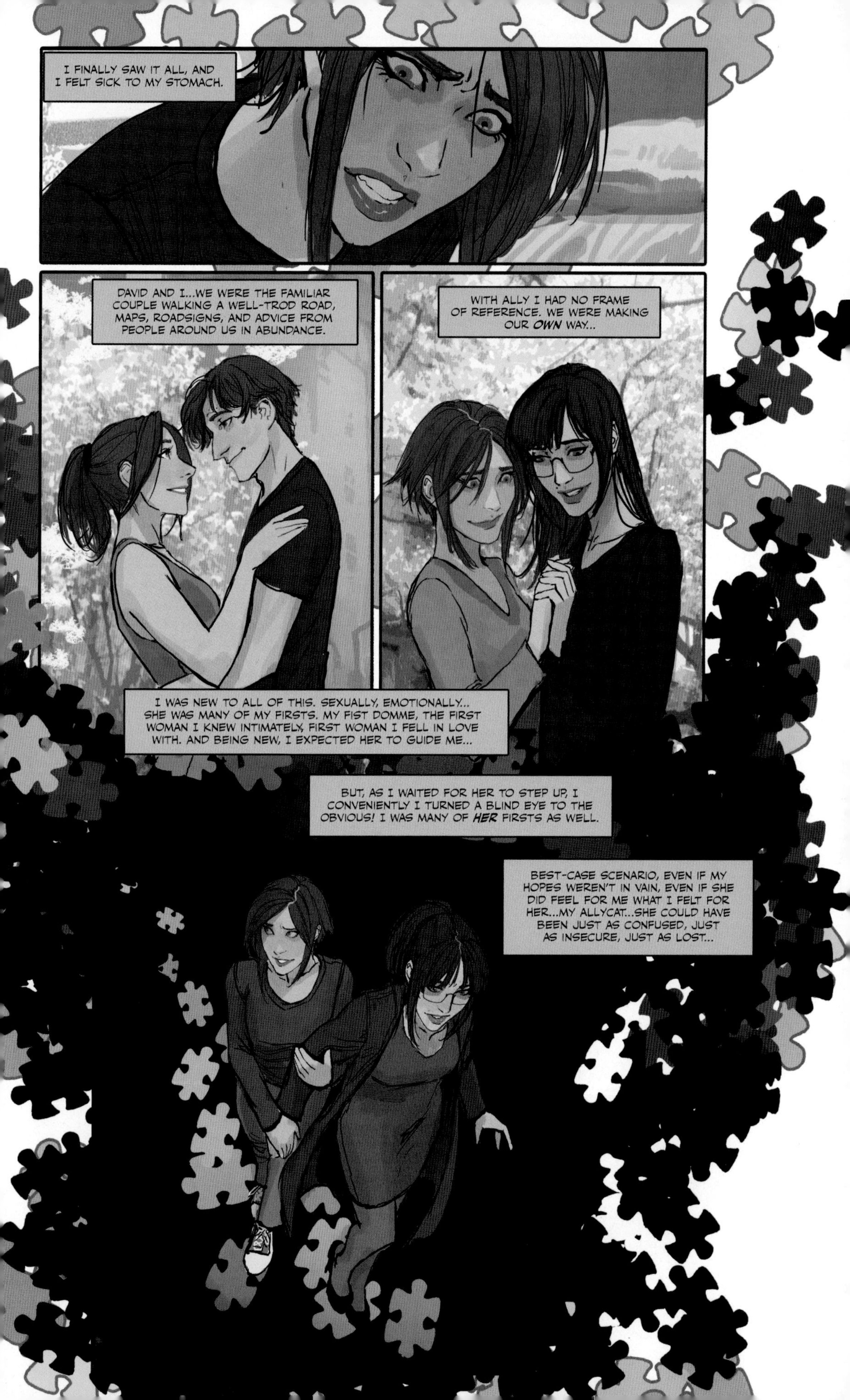
I FINALLY SAW IT ALL, AND I FELT SICK TO MY STOMACH.
DAVID AND I...WE WERE THE FAMILIAR COUPLE WALKING A WELL-TROD ROAD, MAPS, ROADSIGNS, AND ADVICE FROM PEOPLE AROUND US IN ABUNDANCE.
WITH ALLY I HAD NO FRAME OF REFERENCE. WE WERE MAKING OUR *OWN* WAY...
I WAS NEW TO ALL OF THIS. SEXUALLY, EMOTIONALLY... SHE WAS MANY OF MY FIRSTS. MY FIST DOMME, THE FIRST WOMAN I KNEW INTIMATELY, FIRST WOMAN I FELL IN LOVE WITH. AND BEING NEW, I EXPECTED HER TO GUIDE ME...
BUT, AS I WAITED FOR HER TO STEP UP, I CONVENIENTLY I TURNED A BLIND EYE TO THE OBVIOUS! I WAS MANY OF ***HER*** FIRSTS AS WELL.
BEST-CASE SCENARIO, EVEN IF MY HOPES WEREN'T IN VAIN, EVEN IF SHE DID FEEL FOR ME WHAT I FELT FOR HER...MY ALLYCAT...SHE COULD HAVE BEEN JUST AS CONFUSED, JUST AS INSECURE, JUST AS LOST...

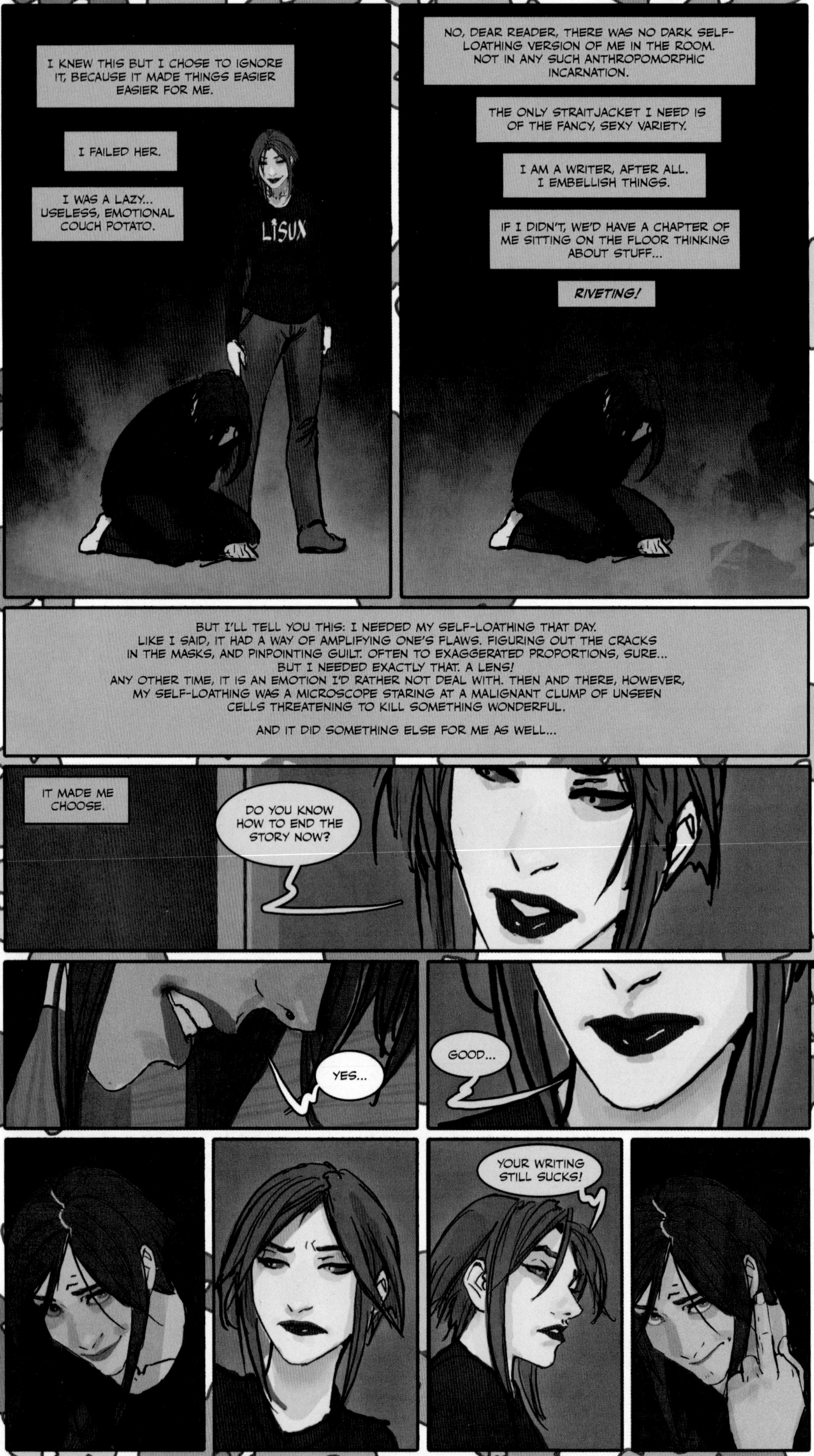
I KNEW THIS BUT I CHOSE TO IGNORE IT, BECAUSE IT MADE THINGS EASIER EASIER FOR ME.
I FAILED HER.
I WAS A LAZY... USELESS, EMOTIONAL COUCH POTATO.
LISUX
NO, DEAR READER, THERE WAS NO DARK SELF-LOATHING VERSION OF ME IN THE ROOM. NOT IN ANY SUCH ANTHROPOMORPHIC INCARNATION.
THE ONLY STRAITJACKET I NEED IS OF THE FANCY, SEXY VARIETY.
I AM A WRITER, AFTER ALL. I EMBELLISH THINGS.
IF I DIDN'T, WE'D HAVE A CHAPTER OF ME SITTING ON THE FLOOR THINKING ABOUT STUFF...
RIVETING!
BUT I'LL TELL YOU THIS: I NEEDED MY SELF-LOATHING THAT DAY. LIKE I SAID, IT HAD A WAY OF AMPLIFYING ONE'S FLAWS. FIGURING OUT THE CRACKS IN THE MASKS, AND PINPOINTING GUILT. OFTEN TO EXAGGERATED PROPORTIONS, SURE... BUT I NEEDED EXACTLY THAT. A LENS! ANY OTHER TIME, IT IS AN EMOTION I'D RATHER NOT DEAL WITH. THEN AND THERE, HOWEVER, MY SELF-LOATHING WAS A MICROSCOPE STARING AT A MALIGNANT CLUMP OF UNSEEN CELLS THREATENING TO KILL SOMETHING WONDERFUL.
AND IT DID SOMETHING ELSE FOR ME AS WELL...
IT MADE ME CHOOSE.
DO YOU KNOW HOW TO END THE STORY NOW?
YES...
GOOD...
YOUR WRITING STILL SUCKS!

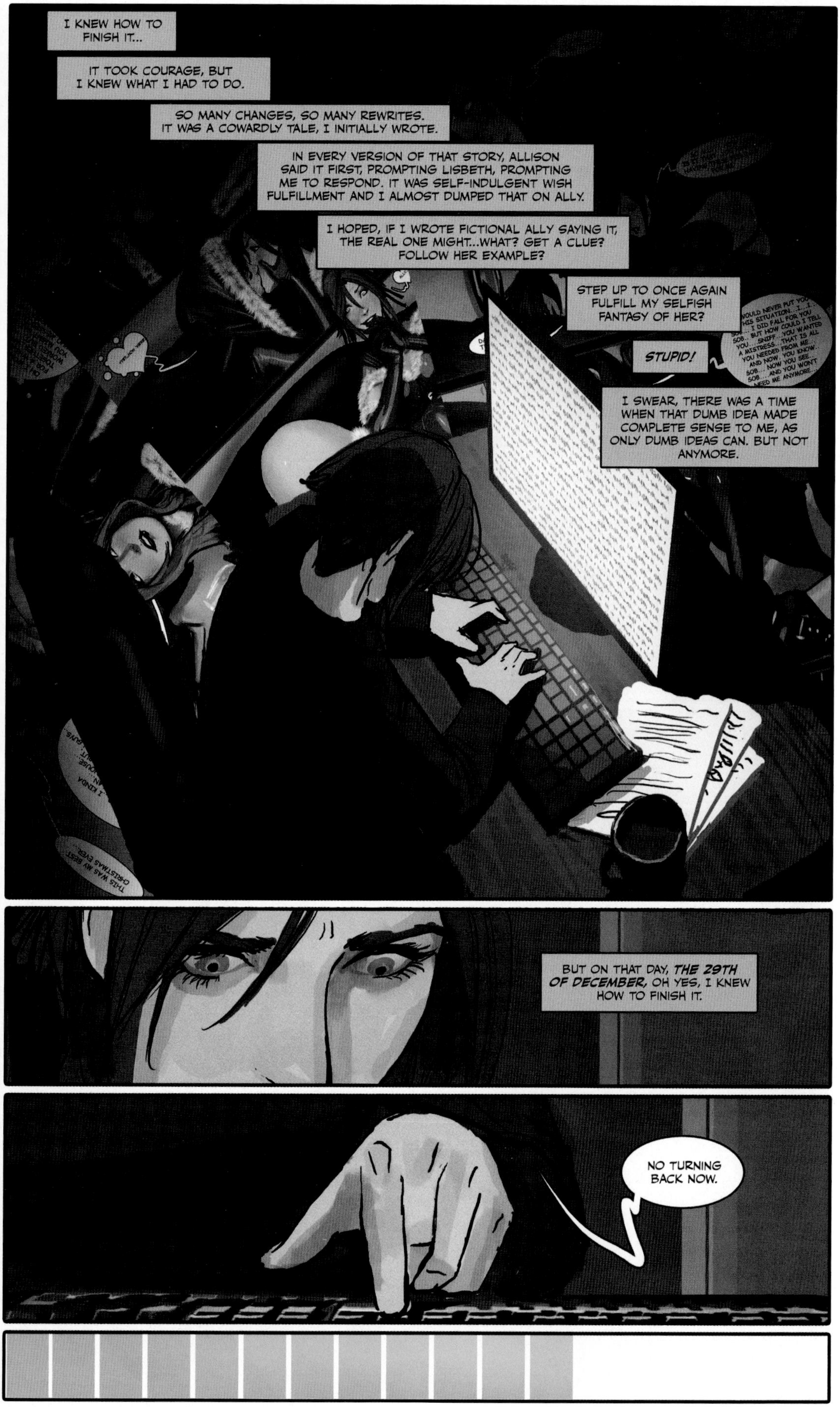
I KNEW HOW TO FINISH IT...
IT TOOK COURAGE, BUT I KNEW WHAT I HAD TO DO.
SO MANY CHANGES, SO MANY REWRITES. IT WAS A COWARDLY TALE, I INITIALLY WROTE.
IN EVERY VERSION OF THAT STORY, ALLISON SAID IT FIRST, PROMPTING LISBETH, PROMPTING ME TO RESPOND. IT WAS SELF-INDULGENT WISH FULFILLMENT AND I ALMOST DUMPED THAT ON ALLY.
I HOPED, IF I WROTE FICTIONAL ALLY SAYING IT, THE REAL ONE MIGHT...WHAT? GET A CLUE? FOLLOW HER EXAMPLE?
STEP UP TO ONCE AGAIN FULFILL MY SELFISH FANTASY OF HER?
STUPID!
I SWEAR, THERE WAS A TIME WHEN THAT DUMB IDEA MADE COMPLETE SENSE TO ME, AS ONLY DUMB IDEAS CAN. BUT NOT ANYMORE.
BUT ON THAT DAY, THE 29TH OF DECEMBER, OH YES, I KNEW HOW TO FINISH IT.
NO TURNING BACK NOW.

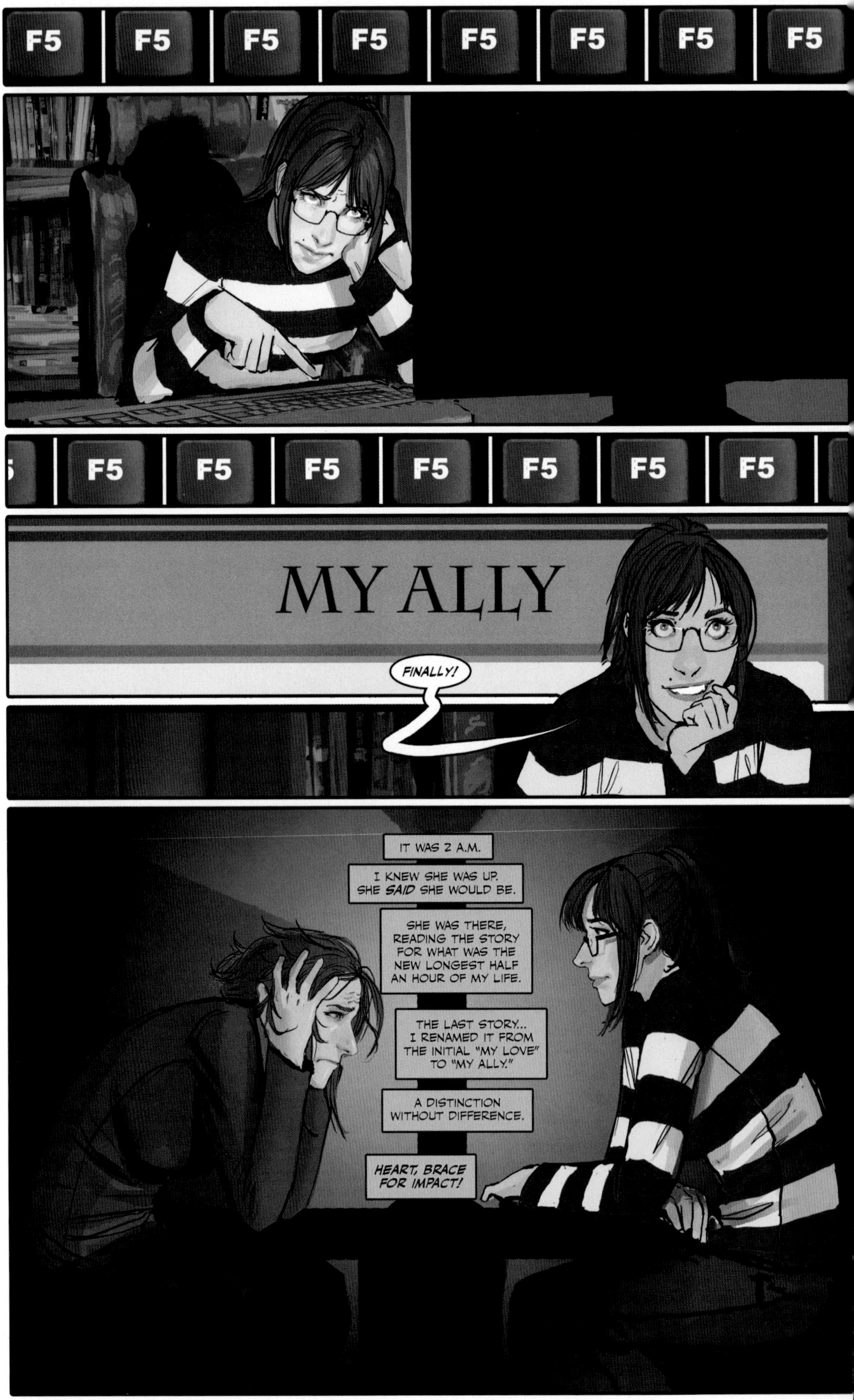
F5 F5 F5 F5 F5 F5 F5 F5
F5 F5 F5 F5 F5 F5 F5
MY ALLY
FINALLY!
IT WAS 2 A.M.
I KNEW SHE WAS UP. SHE SAID SHE WOULD BE.
SHE WAS THERE, READING THE STORY FOR WHAT WAS THE NEW LONGEST HALF AN HOUR OF MY LIFE.
THE LAST STORY... I RENAMED IT FROM THE INITIAL "MY LOVE" TO "MY ALLY."
A DISTINCTION WITHOUT DIFFERENCE.
HEART, BRACE FOR IMPACT!

MY ALLY

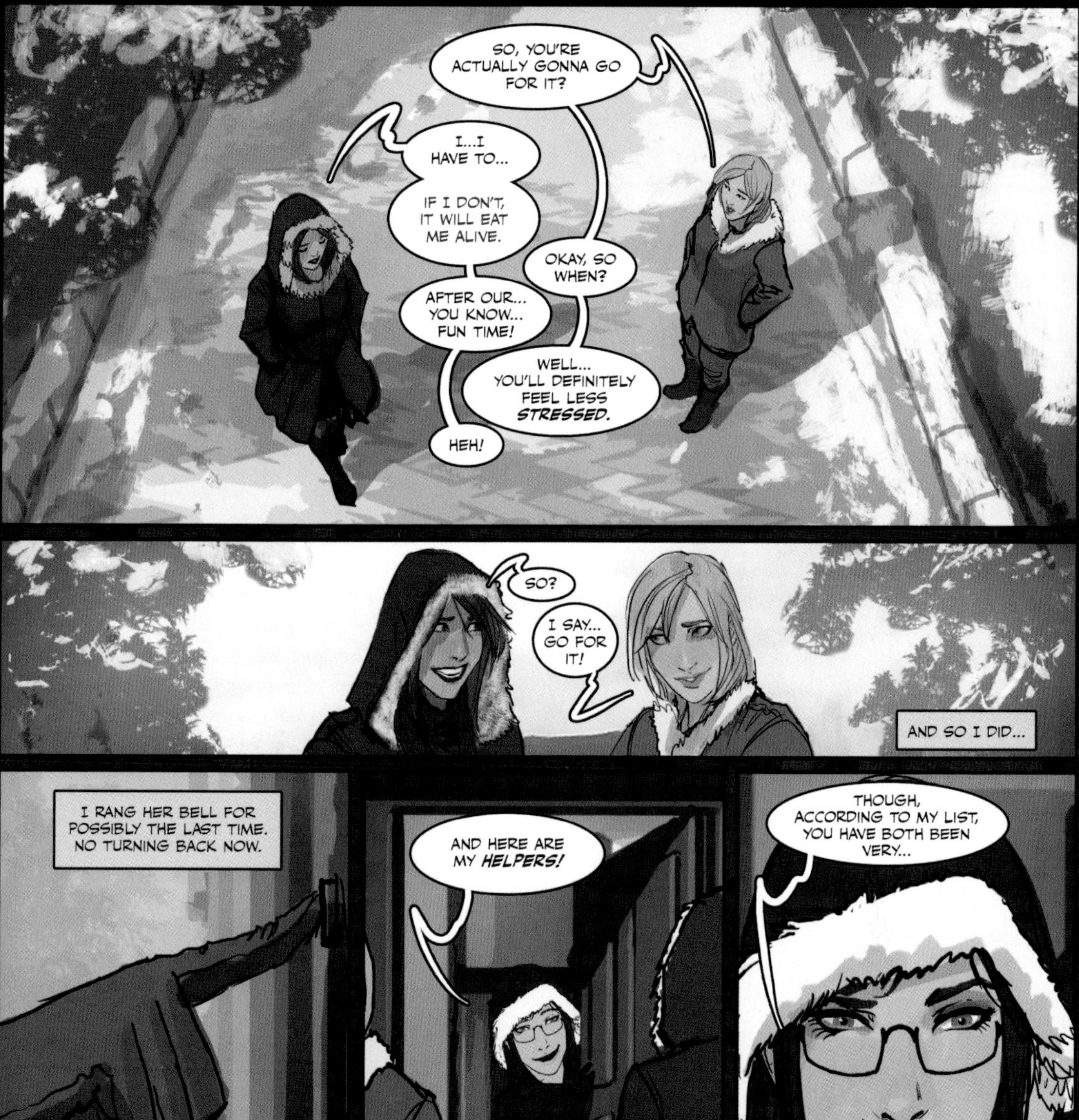
SO, YOU'RE ACTUALLY GONNA GO FOR IT?
I...I HAVE TO...
IF I DON'T, IT WILL EAT ME ALIVE.
OKAY, SO WHEN?
AFTER OUR... YOU KNOW... FUN TIME!
WELL... YOU'LL DEFINITELY FEEL LESS *STRESSED.*
HEH!
SO?
I SAY... GO FOR IT!
AND SO I DID...
I RANG HER BELL FOR POSSIBLY THE LAST TIME. NO TURNING BACK NOW.
AND HERE ARE MY *HELPERS!*
THOUGH, ACCORDING TO MY LIST, YOU HAVE BOTH BEEN VERY...

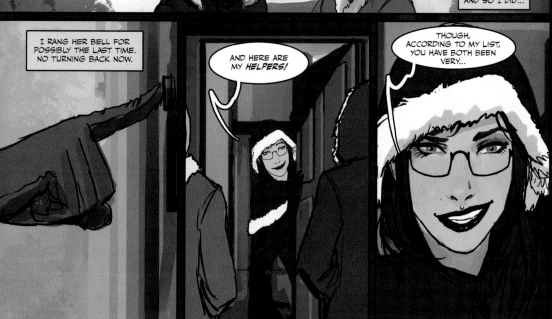

HEY, IT'S PORN, OKAY? I TEND TO INDULGE IN SOME LOWBROW CHEESINESS, THIS SEEMED OBVIOUS SO I WENT FOR IT!

AND I WENT FOR MORE THAN JUST THAT. THIS ENDED UP BEING ONE OF MY MOST POPULAR STORIES... WHY? WELL...

I GUESS, IT WAS JUST ***BRIMMING*** WITH HOLIDAY SPIRIT.

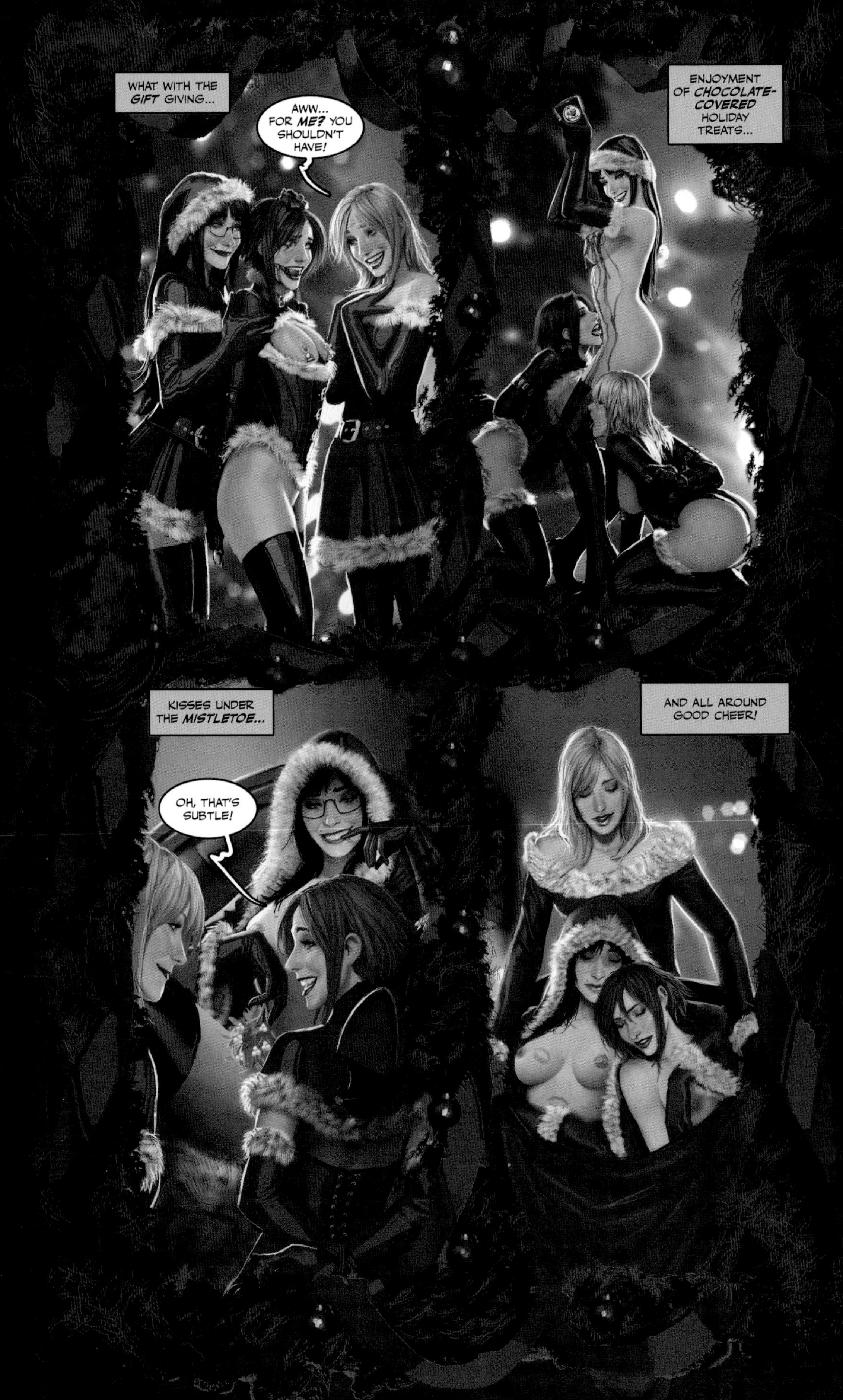
WHAT WITH THE GIFT GIVING...
AWW... FOR ME? YOU SHOULDN'T HAVE!
ENJOYMENT OF CHOCOLATE-COVERED HOLIDAY TREATS...
KISSES UNDER THE MISTLETOE...
OH, THAT'S SUBTLE!
AND ALL AROUND GOOD CHEER!

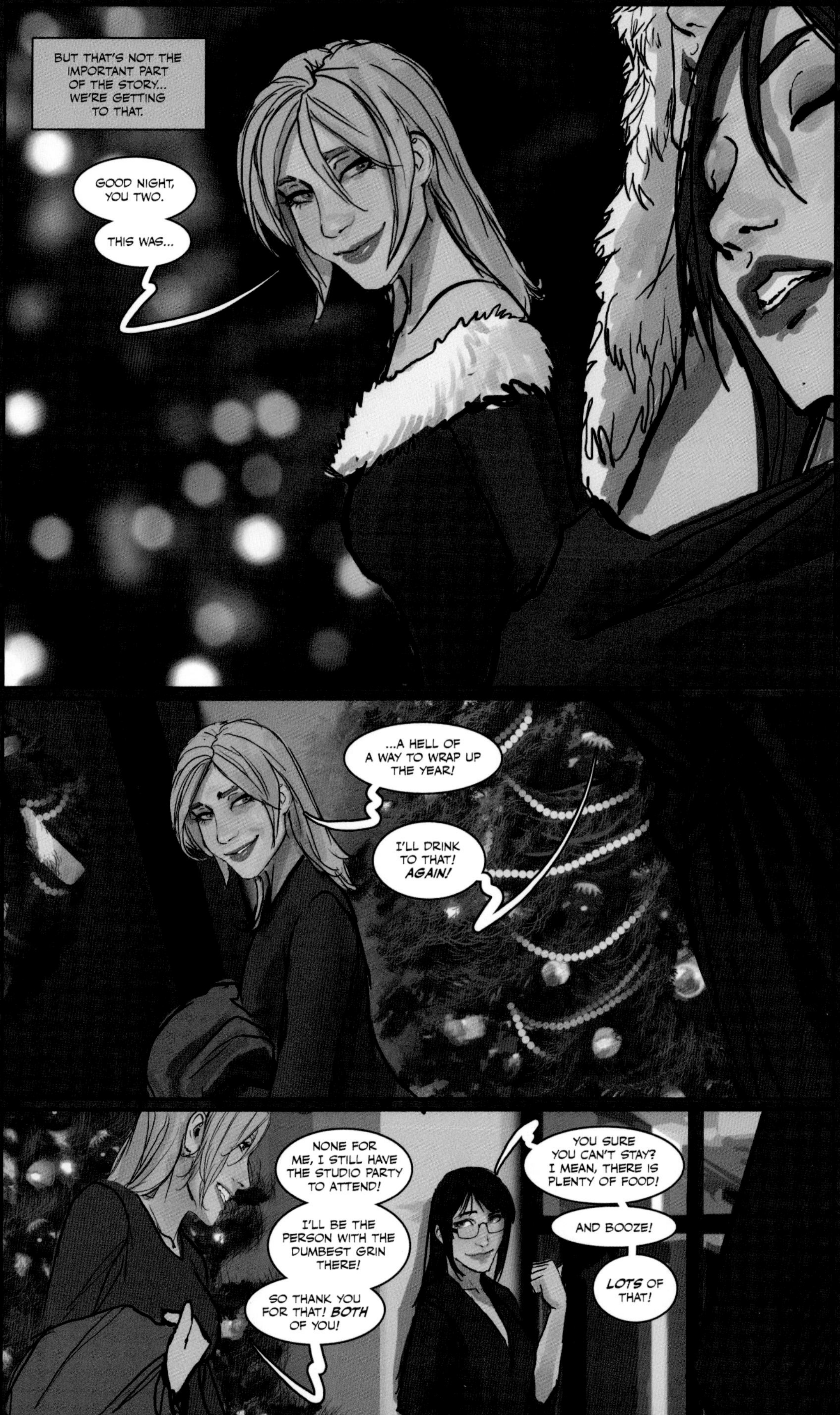
BUT THAT'S NOT THE IMPORTANT PART OF THE STORY... WE'RE GETTING TO THAT.
GOOD NIGHT, YOU TWO.
THIS WAS...
...A HELL OF A WAY TO WRAP UP THE YEAR!
I'LL DRINK TO THAT! AGAIN!
NONE FOR ME, I STILL HAVE THE STUDIO PARTY TO ATTEND!
I'LL BE THE PERSON WITH THE DUMBEST GRIN THERE!
SO THANK YOU FOR THAT! BOTH OF YOU!
YOU SURE YOU CAN'T STAY? I MEAN, THERE IS PLENTY OF FOOD!
AND BOOZE!
LOTS OF THAT!

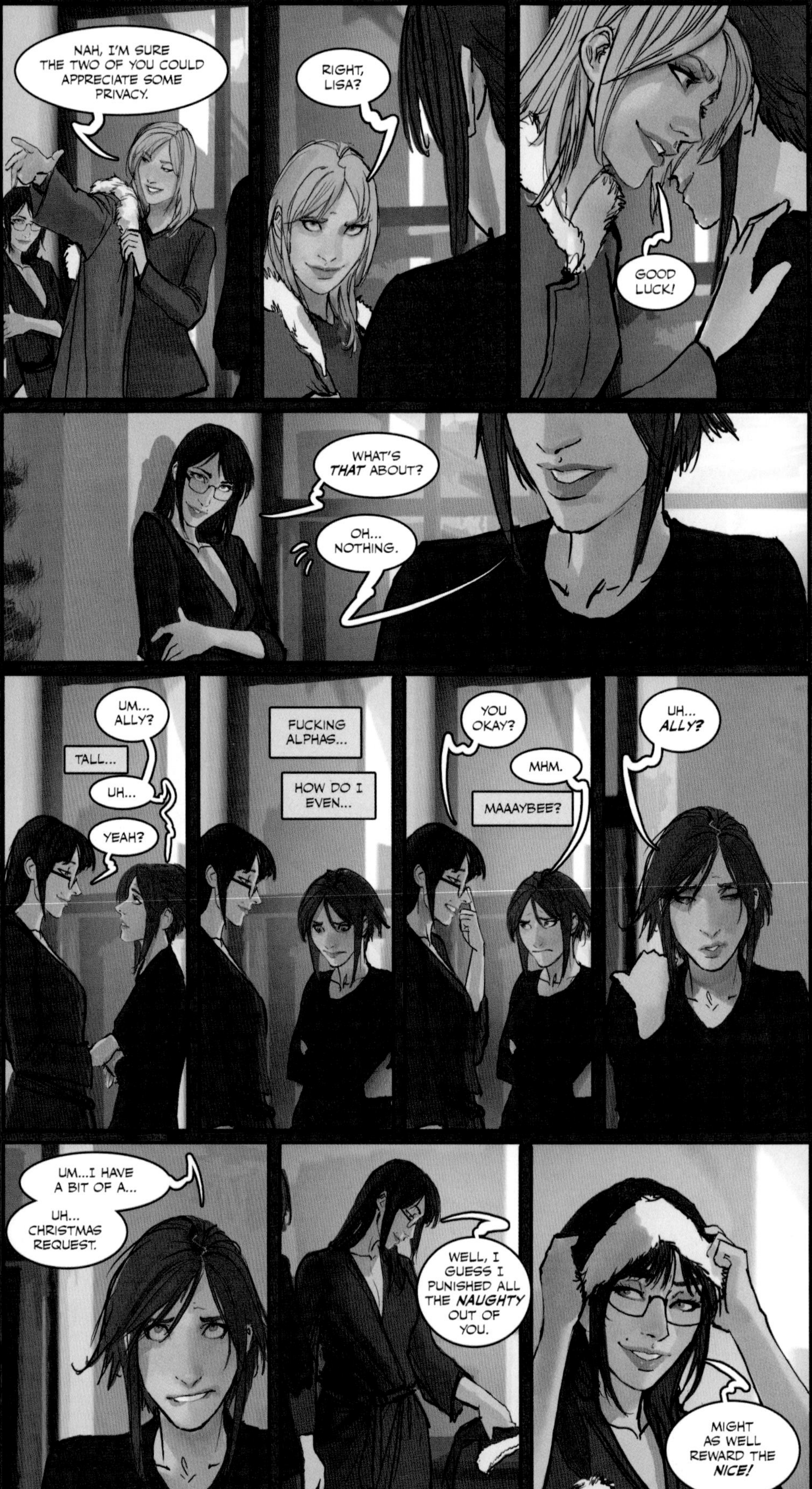
NAH, I'M SURE THE TWO OF YOU COULD APPRECIATE SOME PRIVACY.
RIGHT, LISA?
GOOD LUCK!
WHAT'S *THAT* ABOUT?
OH... NOTHING.
UM... ALLY?
TALL...
UH...
YEAH?
FUCKING ALPHAS...
HOW DO I EVEN...
YOU OKAY?
MHM.
MAAAYBEE?
UH... *ALLY?*
UM...I HAVE A BIT OF A...
UH... CHRISTMAS REQUEST.
WELL, I GUESS I PUNISHED ALL THE *NAUGHTY* OUT OF YOU.
MIGHT AS WELL REWARD THE *NICE!*

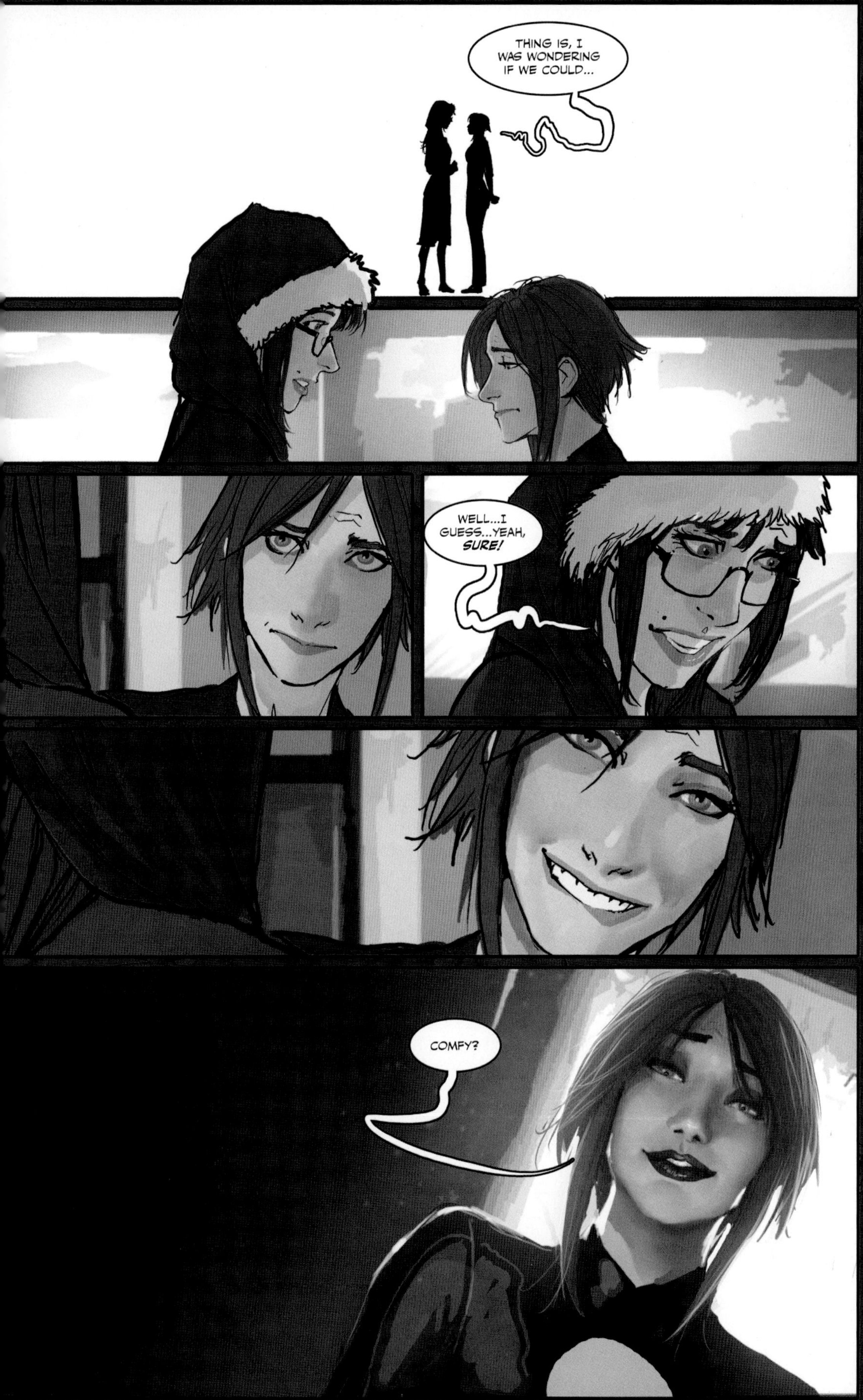
THING IS, I WAS WONDERING IF WE COULD...
WELL...I GUESS...YEAH, SURE!
COMFY?

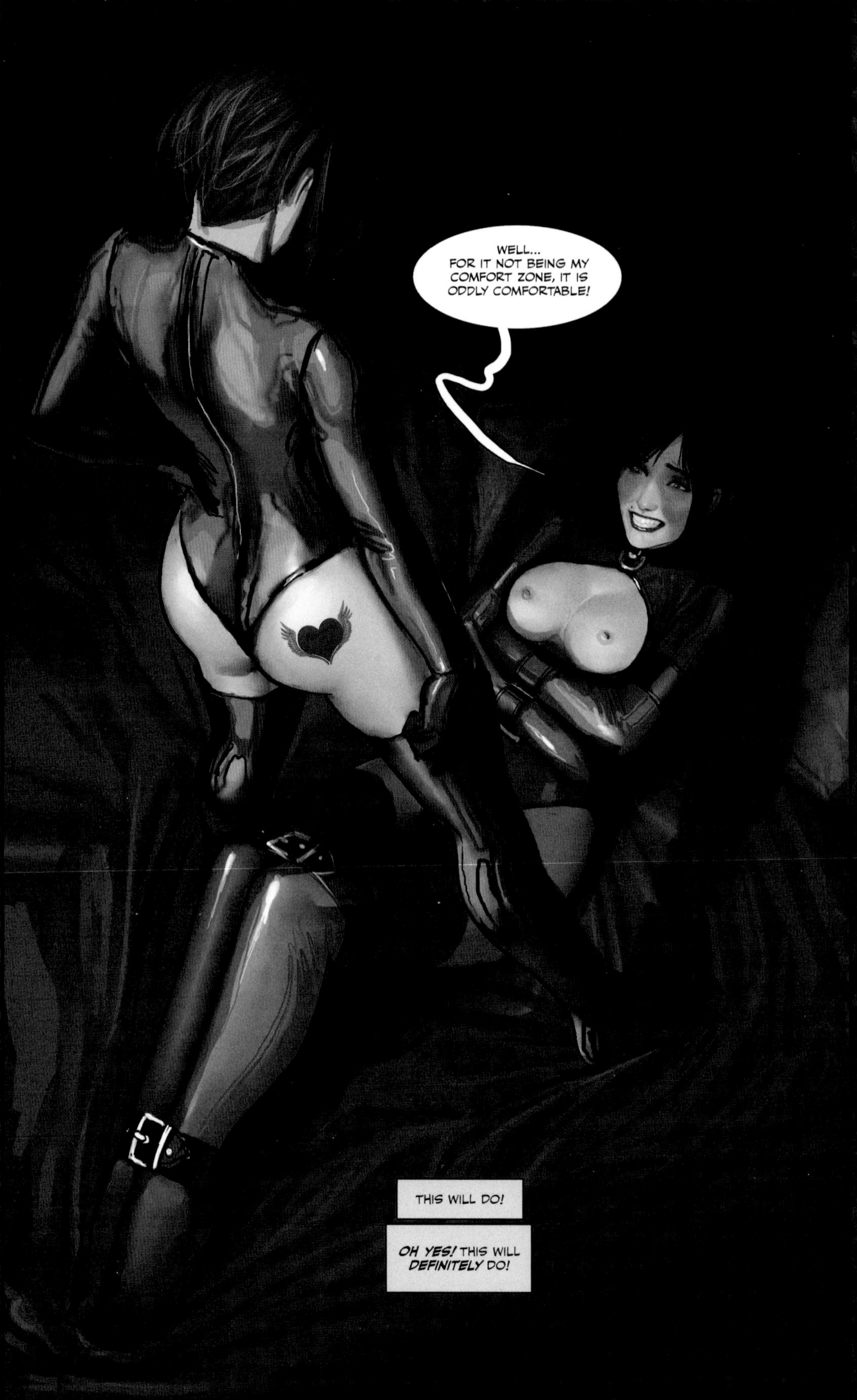
WELL...
FOR IT NOT BEING MY COMFORT ZONE, IT IS ODDLY COMFORTABLE!
THIS WILL DO!
OH YES! THIS WILL DEFINITELY DO!

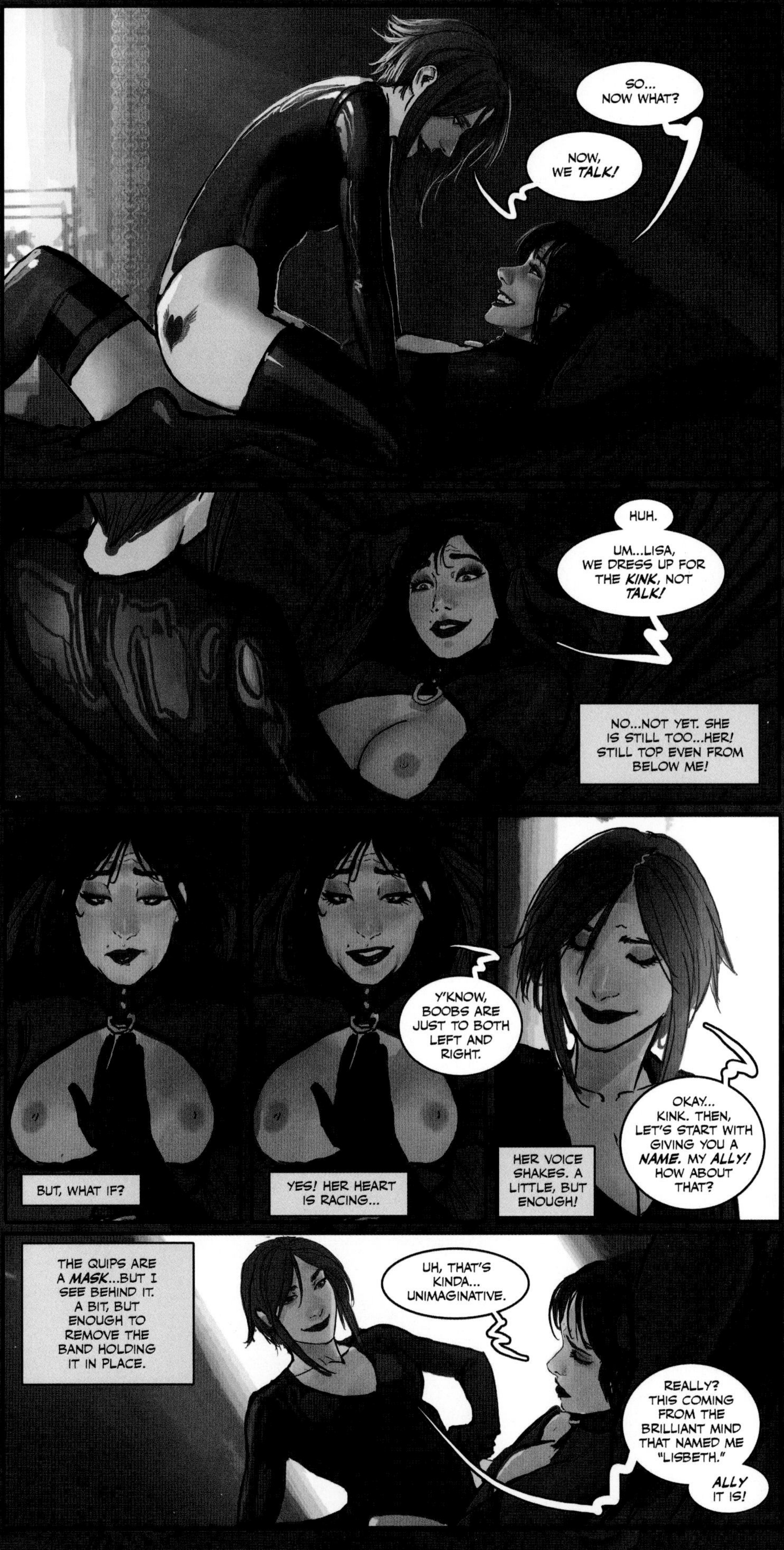
SO... NOW WHAT?
NOW, WE *TALK!*
HUH.
UM...LISA, WE DRESS UP FOR THE *KINK*, NOT *TALK!*
NO...NOT YET. SHE IS STILL TOO...HER! STILL TOP EVEN FROM BELOW ME!
BUT, WHAT IF?
YES! HER HEART IS RACING...
Y'KNOW, BOOBS ARE JUST TO BOTH LEFT AND RIGHT.
HER VOICE SHAKES. A LITTLE, BUT ENOUGH!
OKAY... KINK. THEN, LET'S START WITH GIVING YOU A *NAME.* MY *ALLY!* HOW ABOUT THAT?
THE QUIPS ARE A *MASK*...BUT I SEE BEHIND IT. A BIT, BUT ENOUGH TO REMOVE THE BAND HOLDING IT IN PLACE.
UH, THAT'S KINDA... UNIMAGINATIVE.
REALLY? THIS COMING FROM THE BRILLIANT MIND THAT NAMED ME "LISBETH."
ALLY IT IS!

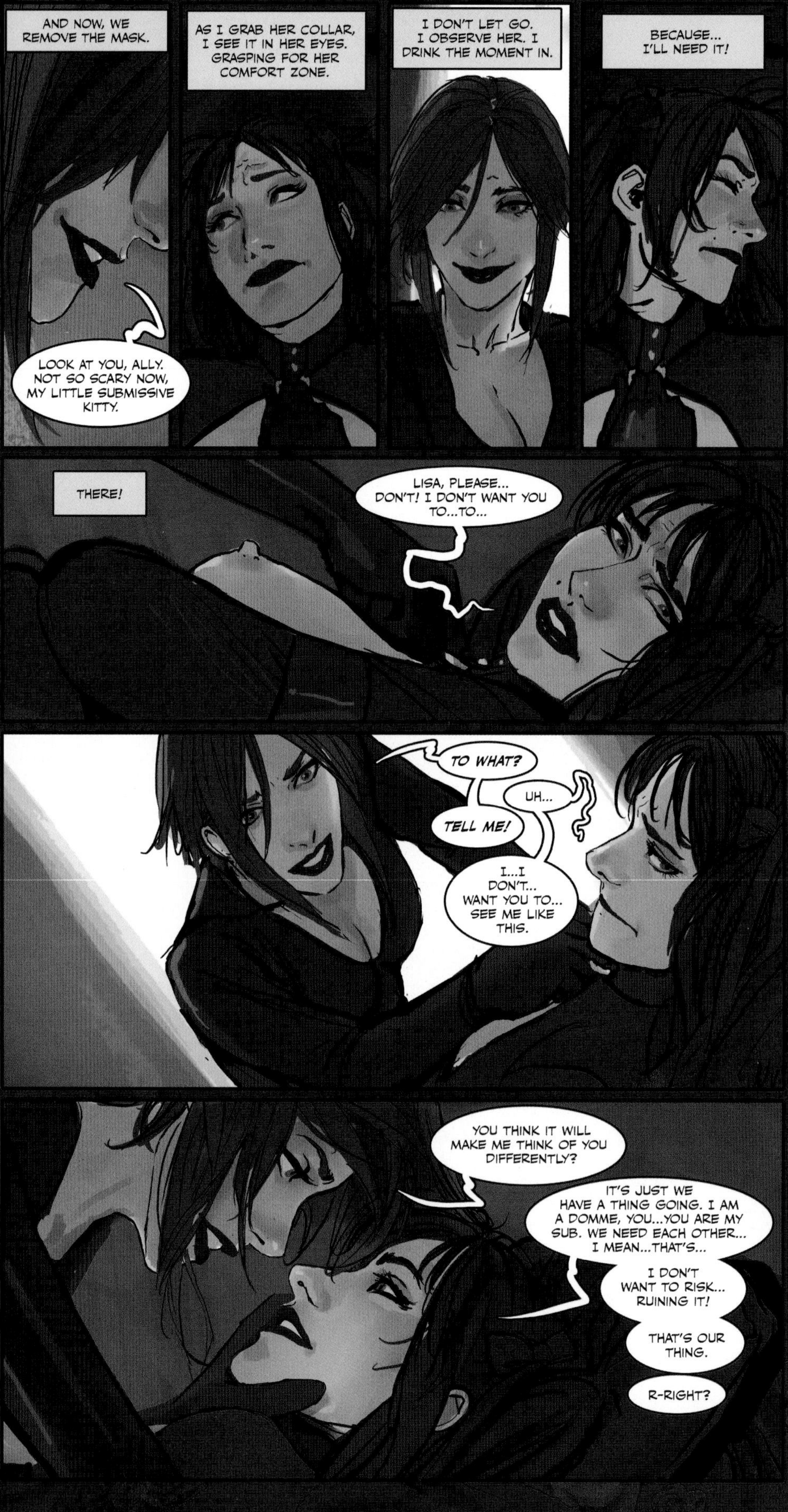

AND NOW, WE REMOVE THE MASK.
LOOK AT YOU, ALLY. NOT SO SCARY NOW, MY LITTLE SUBMISSIVE KITTY.
AS I GRAB HER COLLAR, I SEE IT IN HER EYES. GRASPING FOR HER COMFORT ZONE.
I DON'T LET GO. I OBSERVE HER. I DRINK THE MOMENT IN.
BECAUSE... I'LL NEED IT!
THERE!
LISA, PLEASE... DON'T! I DON'T WANT YOU TO...TO...
TO WHAT?
TELL ME!
UH...
I...I DON'T... WANT YOU TO... SEE ME LIKE THIS.
YOU THINK IT WILL MAKE ME THINK OF YOU DIFFERENTLY?
IT'S JUST WE HAVE A THING GOING. I AM A DOMME, YOU...YOU ARE MY SUB. WE NEED EACH OTHER... I MEAN...THAT'S...
I DON'T WANT TO RISK... RUINING IT!
THAT'S OUR THING.
R-RIGHT?

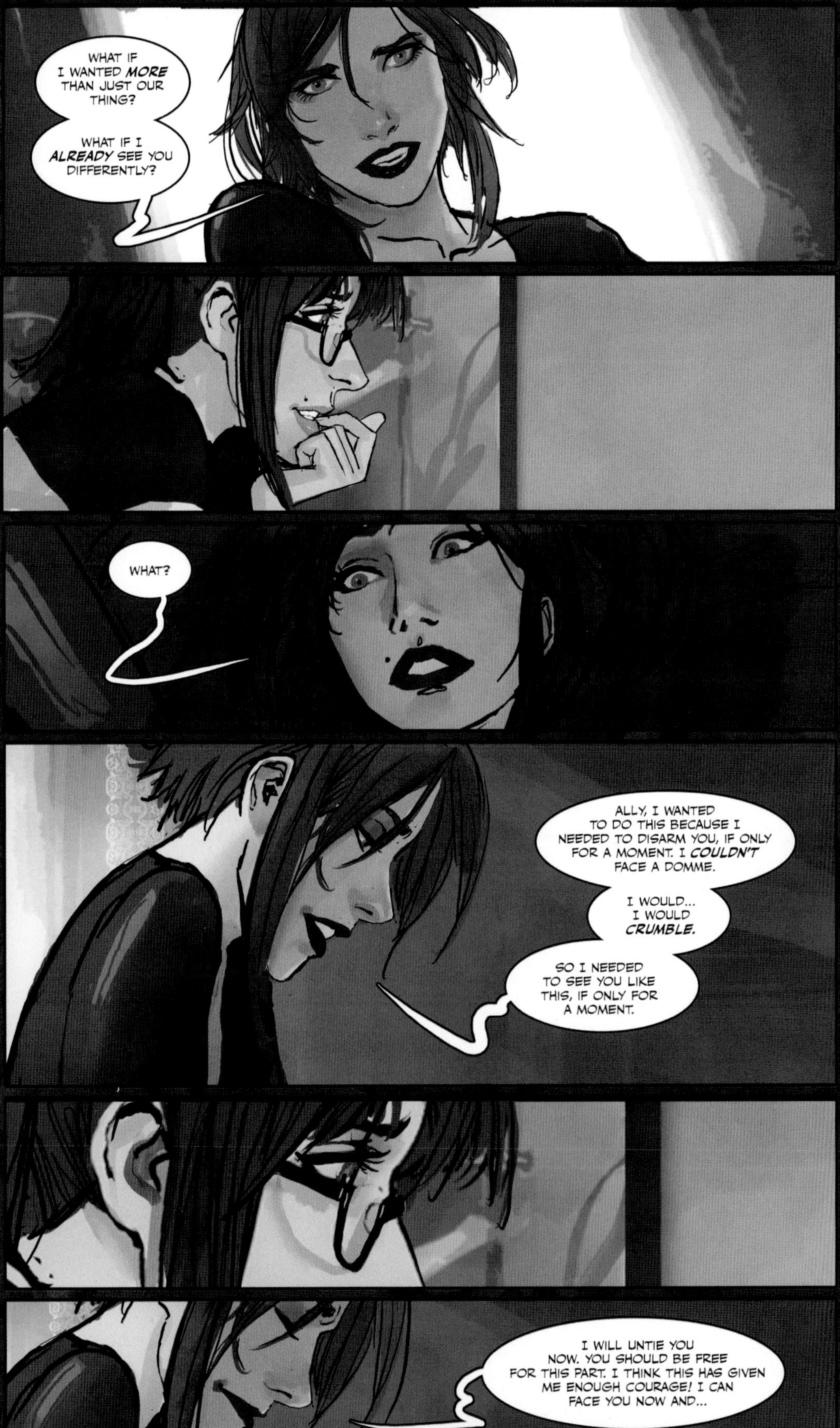
WHAT IF I WANTED MORE THAN JUST OUR THING?
WHAT IF I ALREADY SEE YOU DIFFERENTLY?
WHAT?
ALLY, I WANTED TO DO THIS BECAUSE I NEEDED TO DISARM YOU, IF ONLY FOR A MOMENT. I COULDN'T FACE A DOMME.
I WOULD... I WOULD CRUMBLE.
SO I NEEDED TO SEE YOU LIKE THIS, IF ONLY FOR A MOMENT.
I WILL UNTIE YOU NOW. YOU SHOULD BE FREE FOR THIS PART. I THINK THIS HAS GIVEN ME ENOUGH COURAGE! I CAN FACE YOU NOW AND...

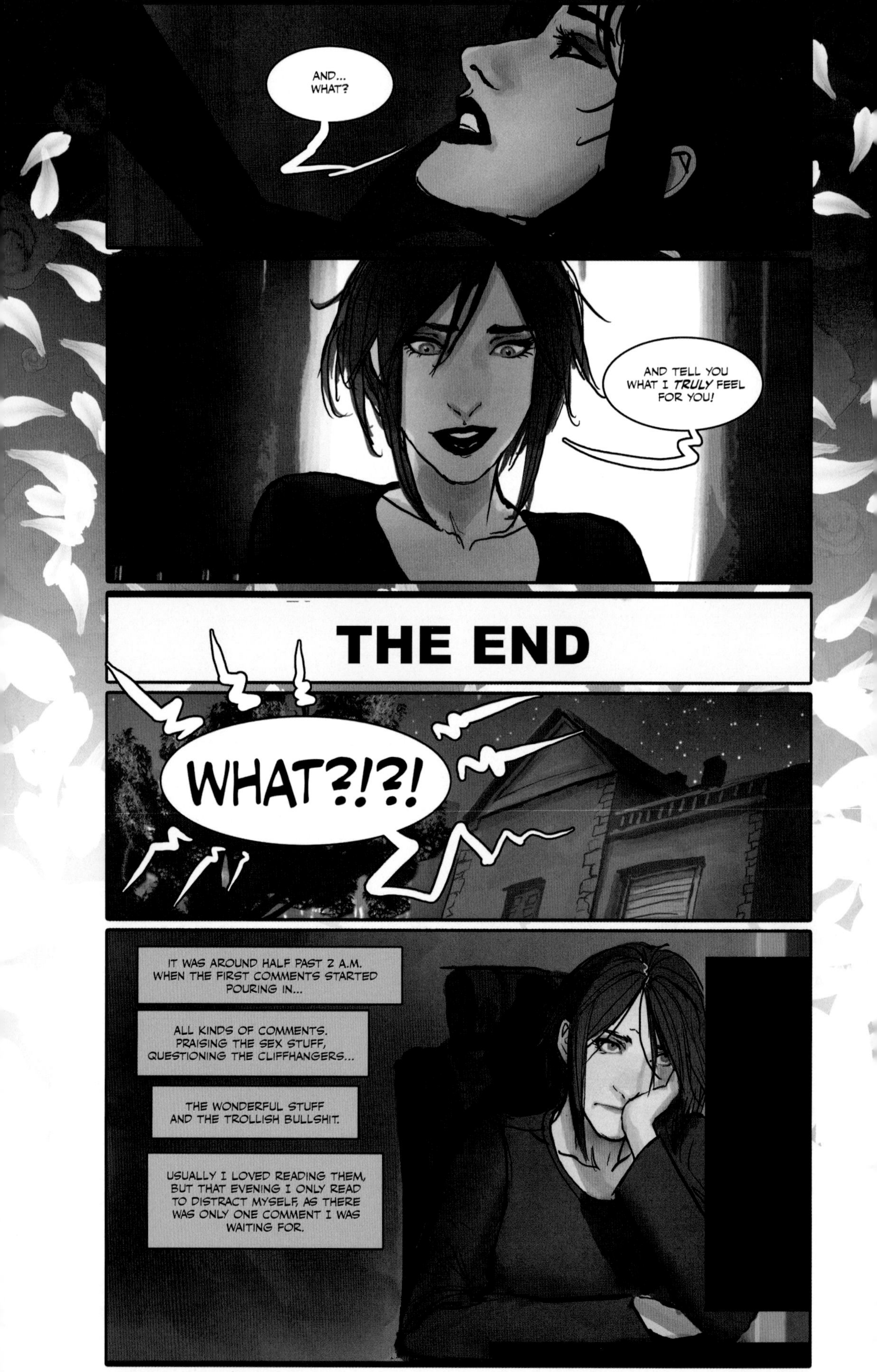
AND... WHAT?
AND TELL YOU WHAT I TRULY FEEL FOR YOU!
THE END
WHAT?!?!
IT WAS AROUND HALF PAST 2 A.M. WHEN THE FIRST COMMENTS STARTED POURING IN...
ALL KINDS OF COMMENTS. PRAISING THE SEX STUFF, QUESTIONING THE CLIFFHANGERS...
THE WONDERFUL STUFF AND THE TROLLISH BULLSHIT.
USUALLY I LOVED READING THEM, BUT THAT EVENING I ONLY READ TO DISTRACT MYSELF, AS THERE WAS ONLY ONE COMMENT I WAS WAITING FOR.

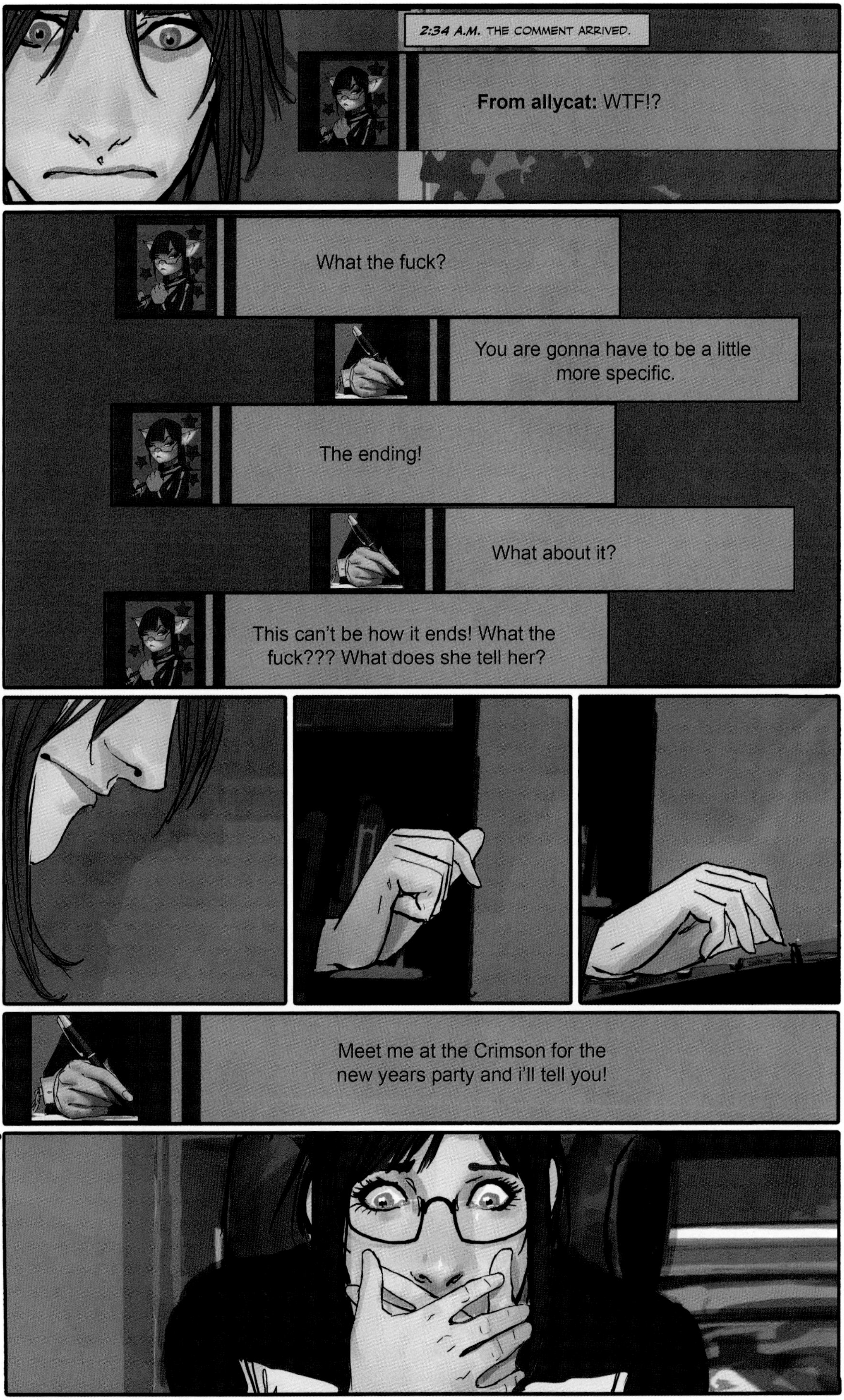

2:34 A.M. THE COMMENT ARRIVED.
From allycat: WTF!?
What the fuck?
You are gonna have to be a little more specific.
The ending!
What about it?
This can't be how it ends! What the fuck??? What does she tell her?
Meet me at the Crimson for the new years party and i'll tell you!

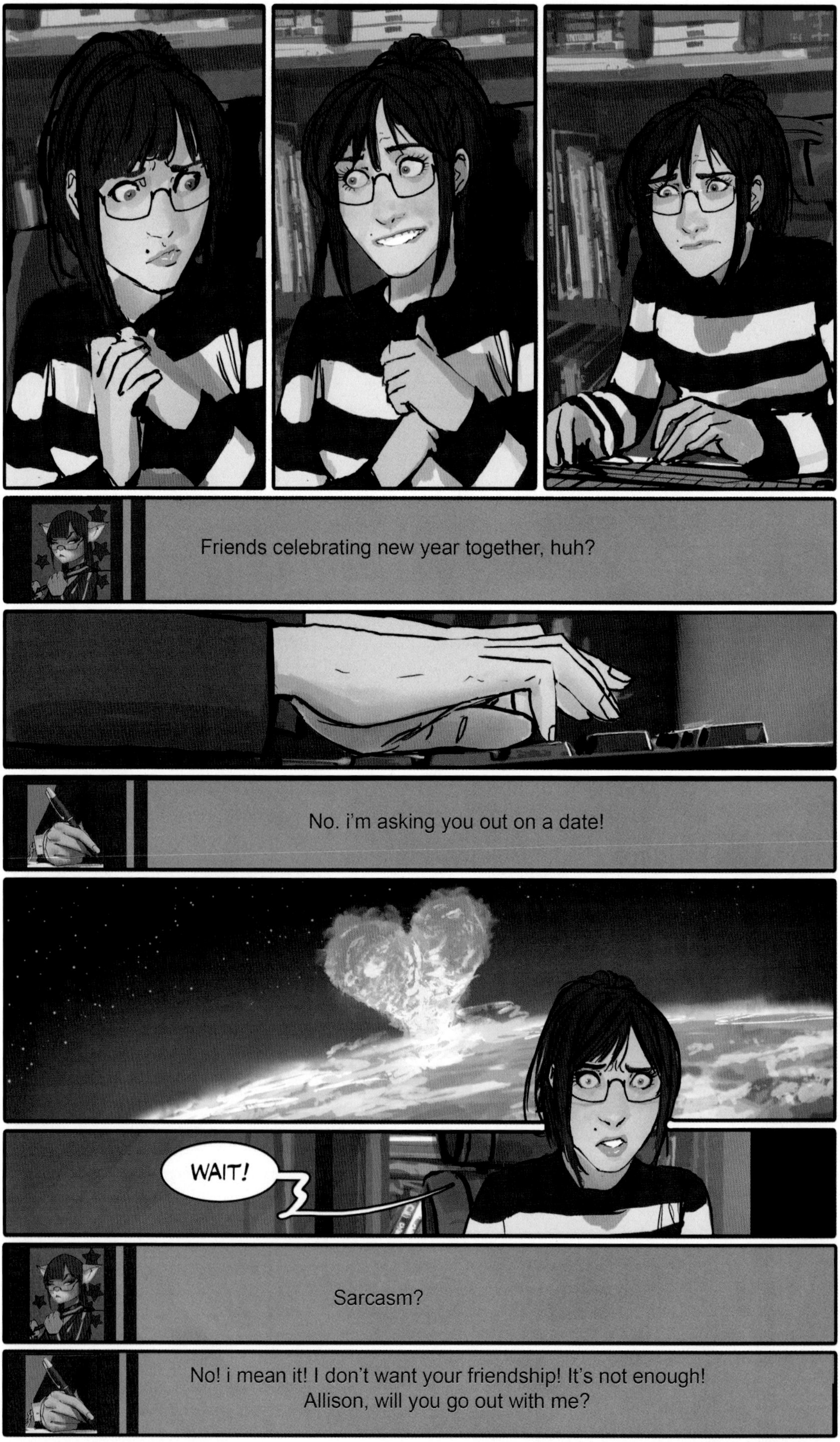
Friends celebrating new year together, huh?
No. i'm asking you out on a date!
WAIT!
Sarcasm?
No! i mean it! I don't want your friendship! It's not enough!
Allison, will you go out with me?

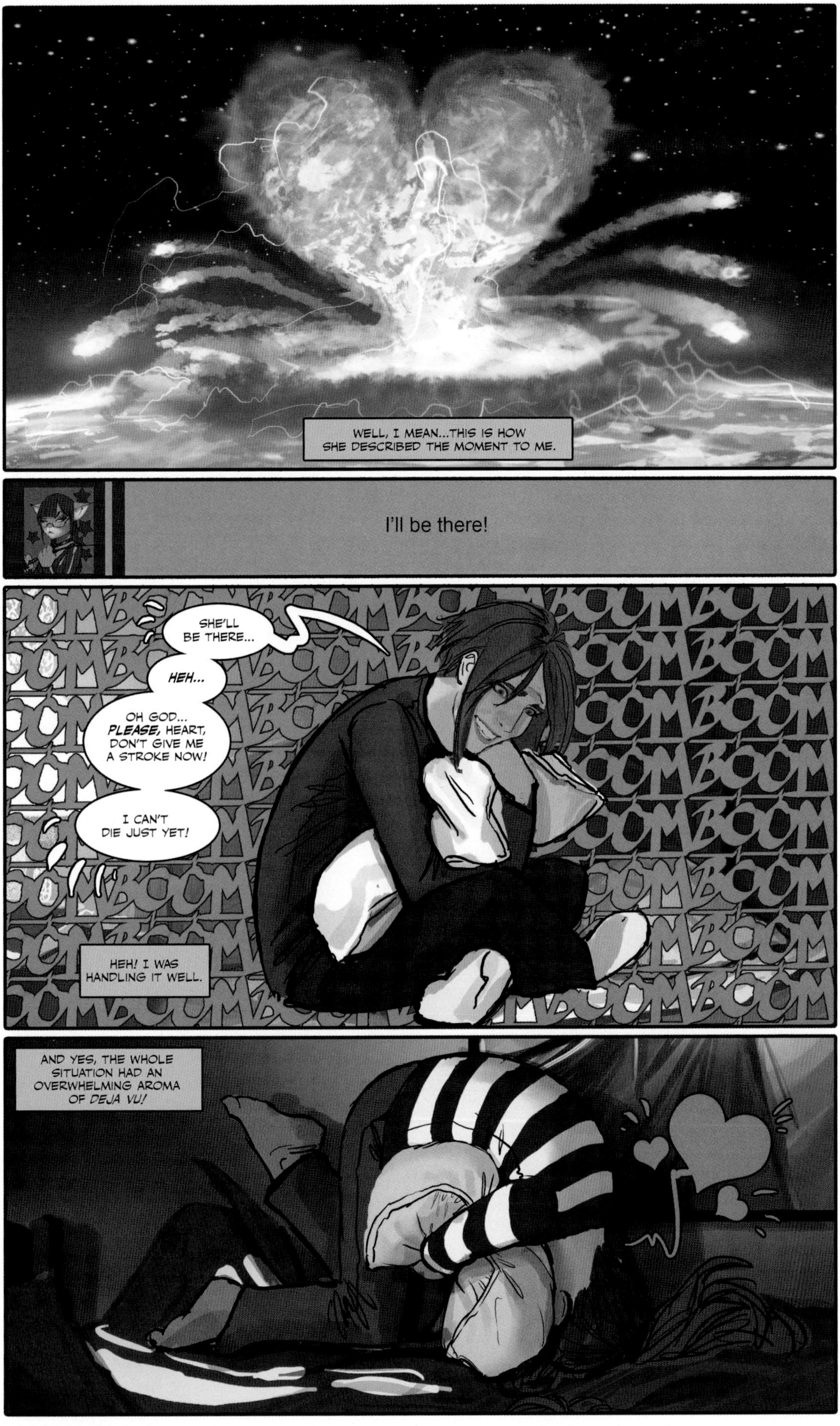

WELL, I MEAN...THIS IS HOW SHE DESCRIBED THE MOMENT TO ME.
I'll be there!
SHE'LL BE THERE...
HEH...
OH GOD... PLEASE, HEART, DON'T GIVE ME A STROKE NOW!
I CAN'T DIE JUST YET!
HEH! I WAS HANDLING IT WELL.
BOOM BOOM BOOM
AND YES, THE WHOLE SITUATION HAD AN OVERWHELMING AROMA OF DEJA VU!

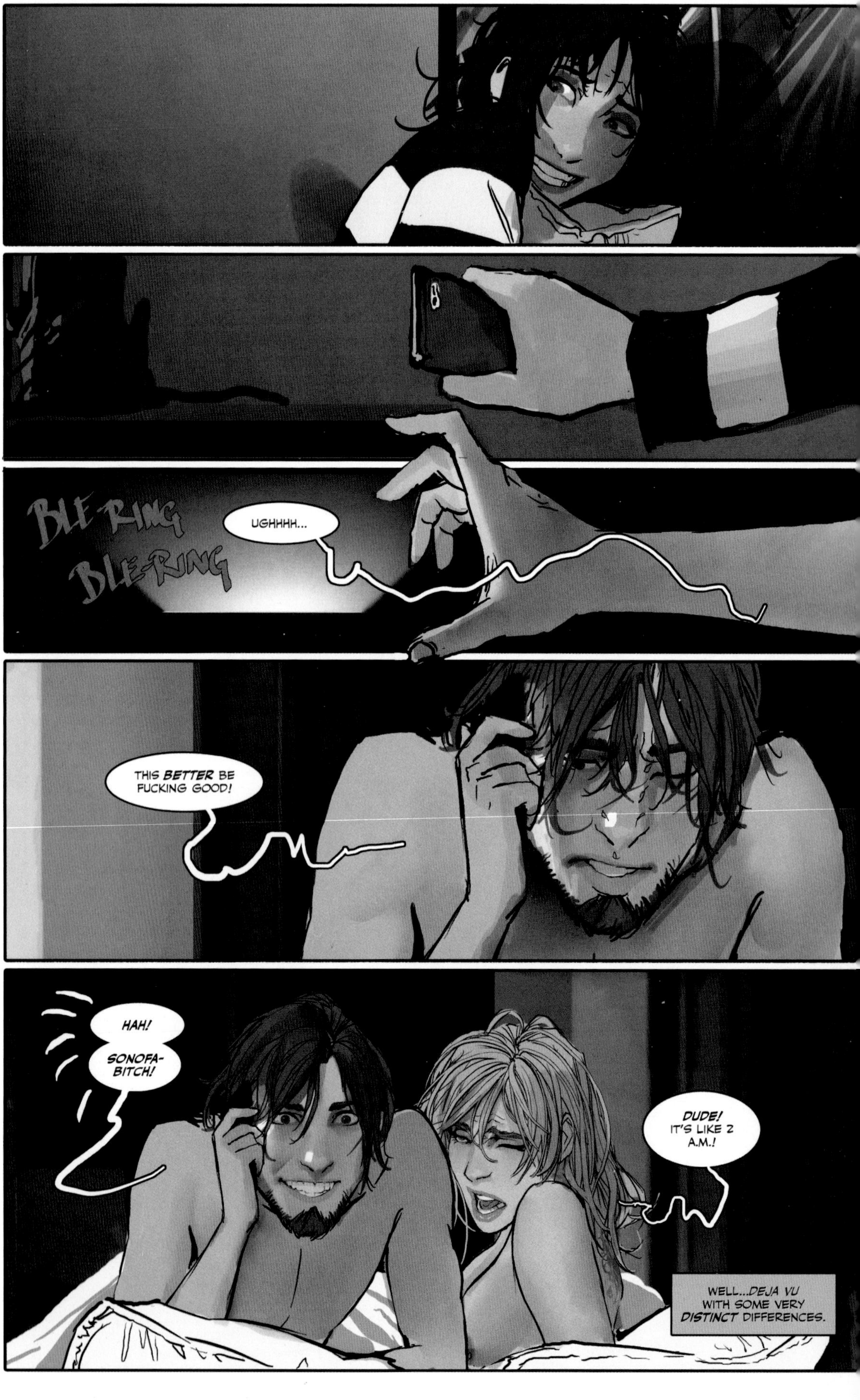
BLE-RING
BLE-RING
UGHHHH...
THIS BETTER BE FUCKING GOOD!
HAH!
SONOFA-BITCH!
DUDE! IT'S LIKE 2 A.M.!
WELL...DEJA VU WITH SOME VERY DISTINCT DIFFERENCES.

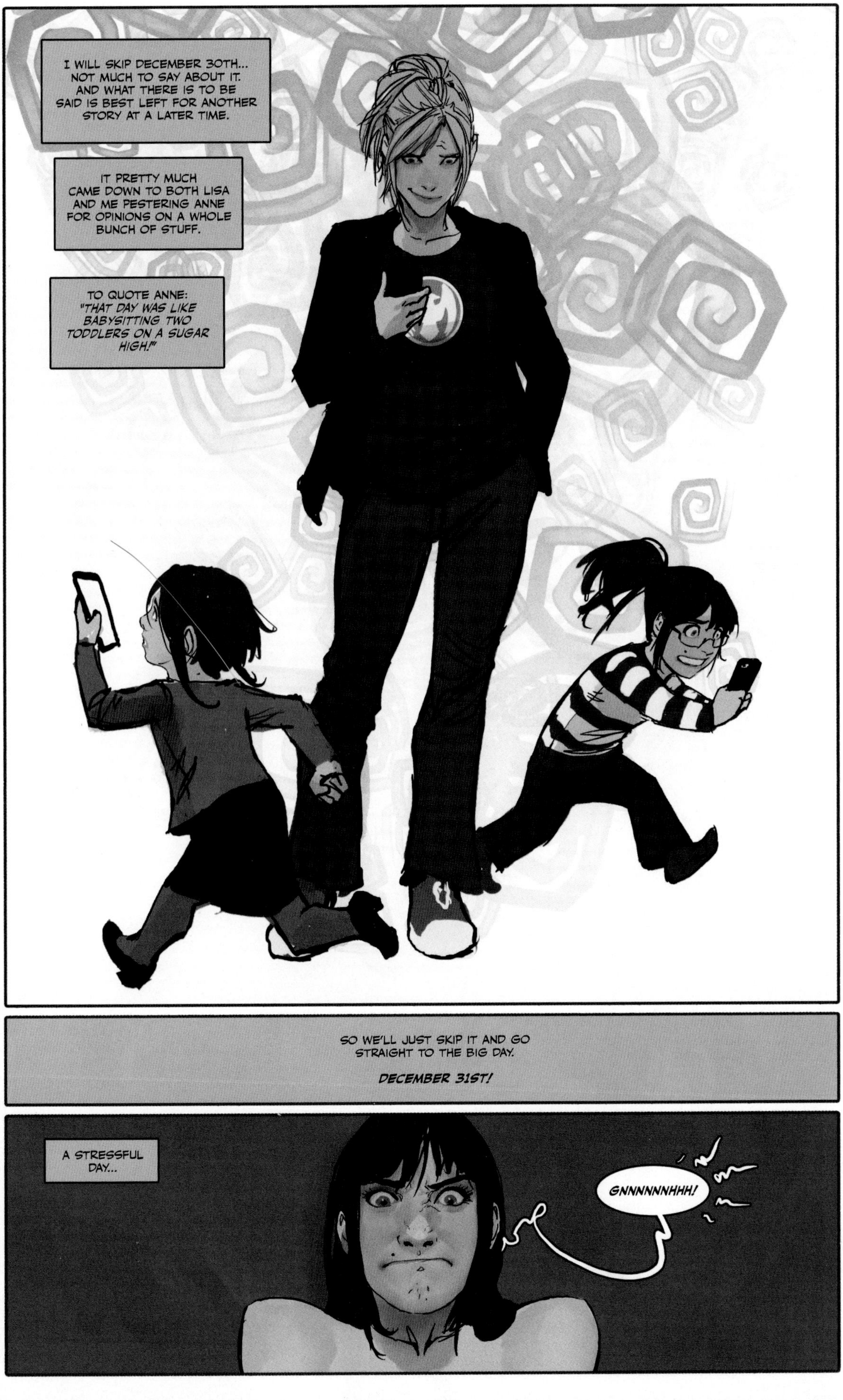
I WILL SKIP DECEMBER 30TH... NOT MUCH TO SAY ABOUT IT. AND WHAT THERE IS TO BE SAID IS BEST LEFT FOR ANOTHER STORY AT A LATER TIME.
IT PRETTY MUCH CAME DOWN TO BOTH LISA AND ME PESTERING ANNE FOR OPINIONS ON A WHOLE BUNCH OF STUFF.
TO QUOTE ANNE: "THAT DAY WAS LIKE BABYSITTING TWO TODDLERS ON A SUGAR HIGH!"
SO WE'LL JUST SKIP IT AND GO STRAIGHT TO THE BIG DAY.
DECEMBER 31ST!
A STRESSFUL DAY...
GNNNNNNHHH!

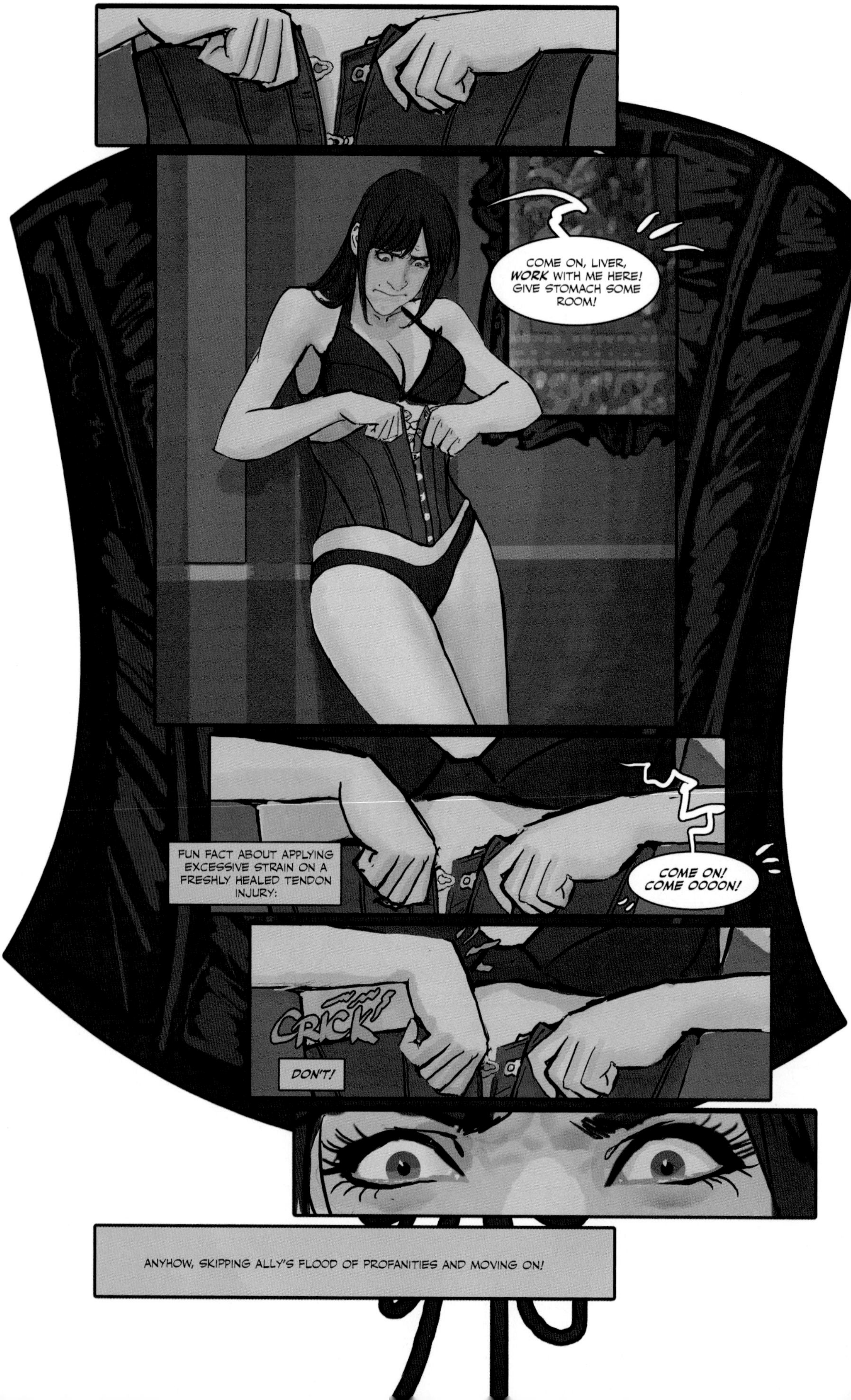

COME ON, LIVER, **WORK** WITH ME HERE! GIVE STOMACH SOME ROOM!
FUN FACT ABOUT APPLYING EXCESSIVE STRAIN ON A FRESHLY HEALED TENDON INJURY:
COME ON! COME OOOON!
CRICK
DON'T!
ANYHOW, SKIPPING ALLY'S FLOOD OF PROFANITIES AND MOVING ON!

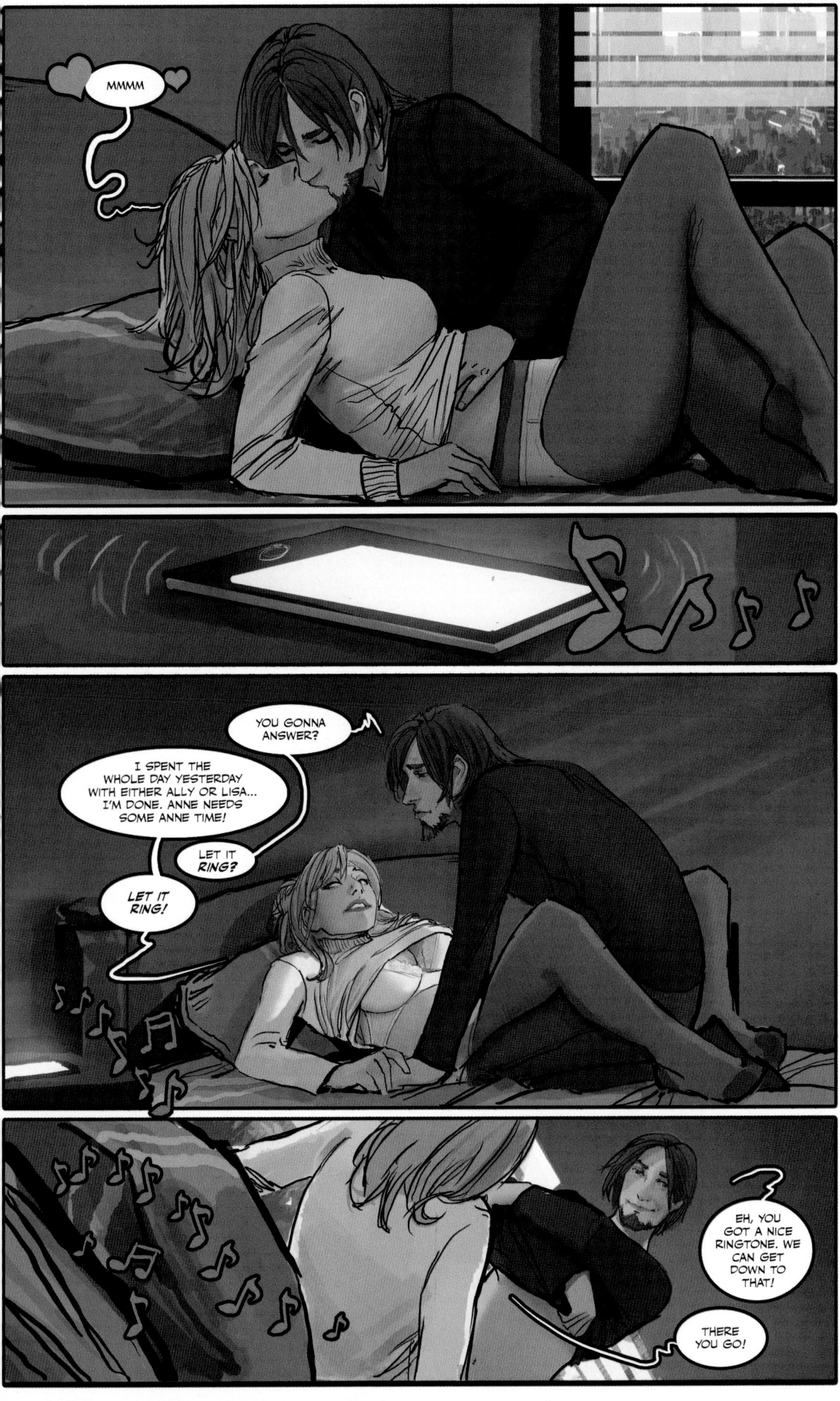
MMMM
YOU GONNA ANSWER?
I SPENT THE WHOLE DAY YESTERDAY WITH EITHER ALLY OR LISA... I'M DONE. ANNE NEEDS SOME ANNE TIME!
LET IT RING?
LET IT RING!
EH, YOU GOT A NICE RINGTONE. WE CAN GET DOWN TO THAT!
THERE YOU GO!

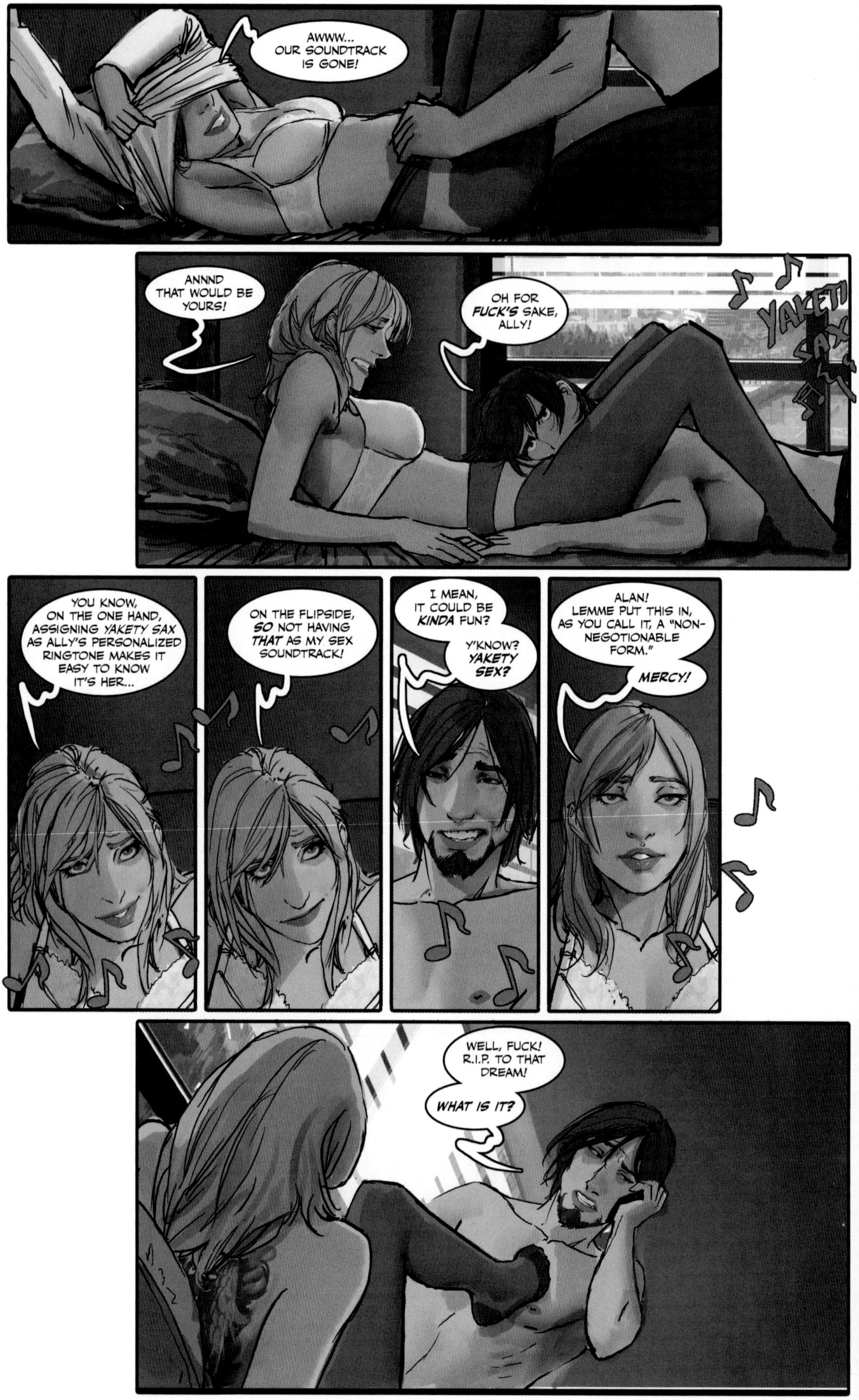
AWWW... OUR SOUNDTRACK IS GONE!
ANNND THAT WOULD BE YOURS!
OH FOR FUCK'S SAKE, ALLY!
YAKETY SAX
YOU KNOW, ON THE ONE HAND, ASSIGNING YAKETY SAX AS ALLY'S PERSONALIZED RINGTONE MAKES IT EASY TO KNOW IT'S HER...
ON THE FLIPSIDE, SO NOT HAVING THAT AS MY SEX SOUNDTRACK!
I MEAN, IT COULD BE KINDA FUN?
Y'KNOW? YAKETY SEX?
ALAN! LEMME PUT THIS IN, AS YOU CALL IT, A "NON-NEGOTIONABLE FORM."
MERCY!
WELL, FUCK! R.I.P. TO THAT DREAM!
WHAT IS IT?

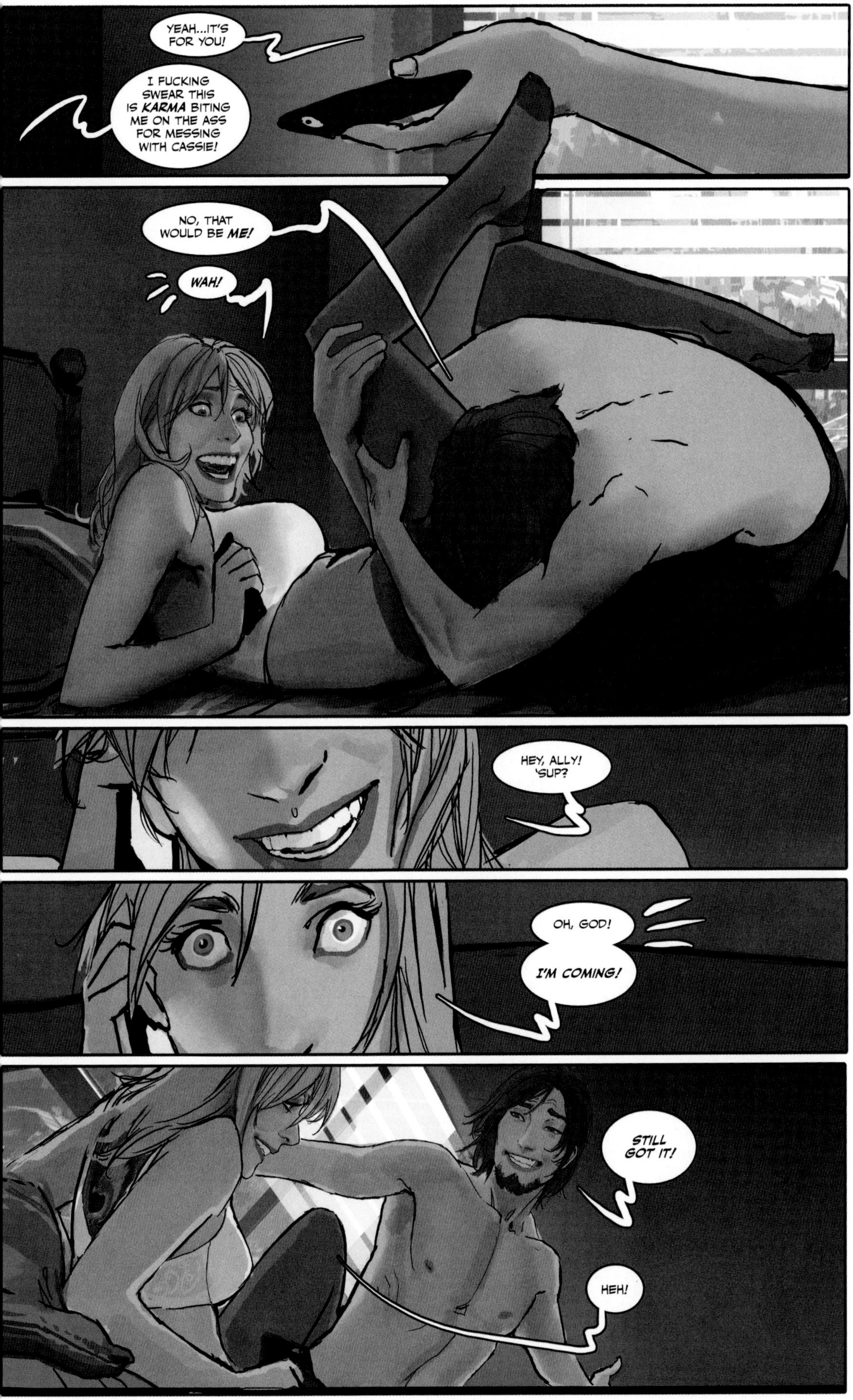
YEAH...IT'S FOR YOU!
I FUCKING SWEAR THIS IS KARMA BITING ME ON THE ASS FOR MESSING WITH CASSIE!
NO, THAT WOULD BE ME!
WAH!
HEY, ALLY! 'SUP?
OH, GOD!
I'M COMING!
STILL GOT IT!
HEH!

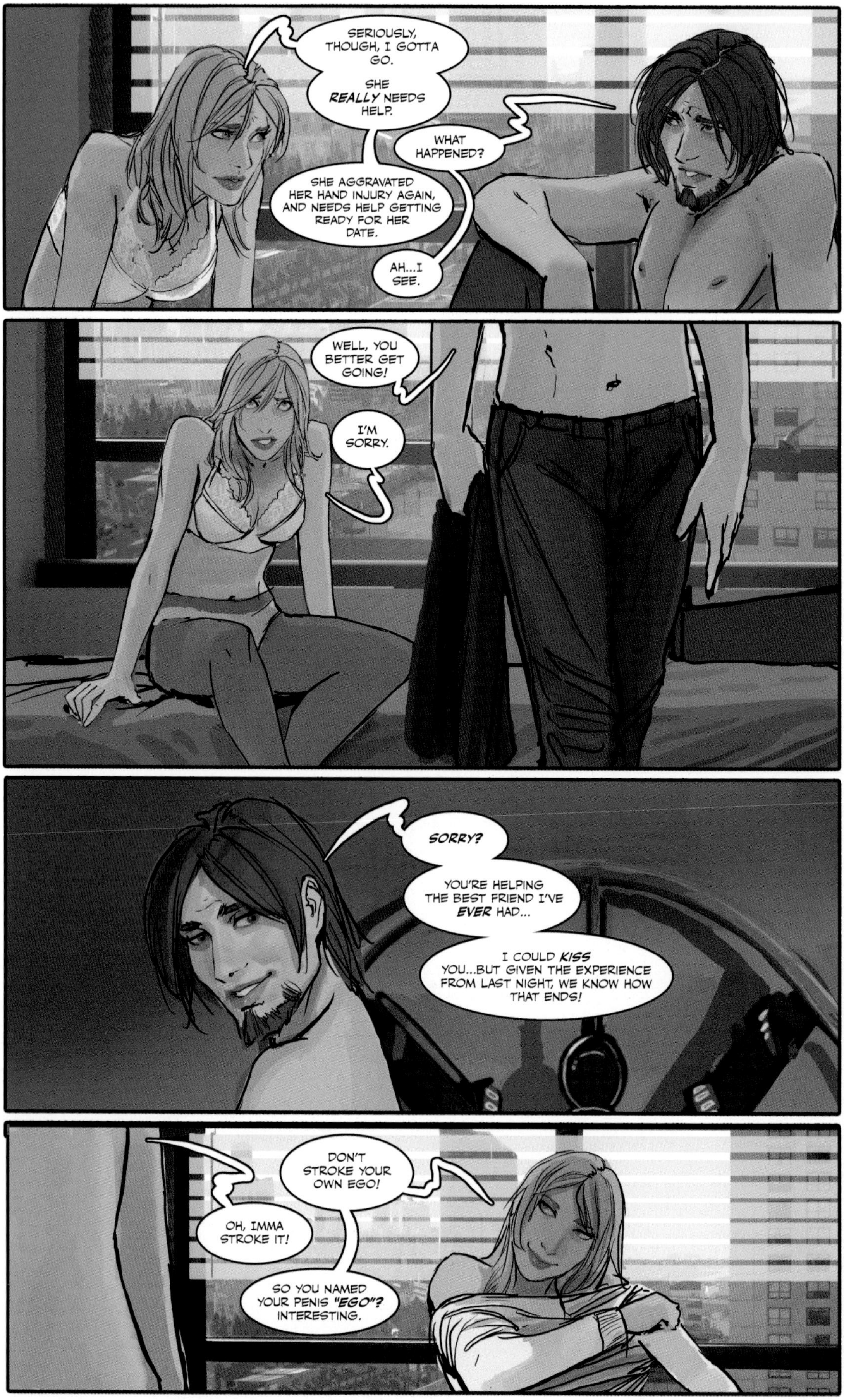
SERIOUSLY, THOUGH, I GOTTA GO.
SHE *REALLY* NEEDS HELP.
WHAT HAPPENED?
SHE AGGRAVATED HER HAND INJURY AGAIN, AND NEEDS HELP GETTING READY FOR HER DATE.
AH...I SEE.
WELL, YOU BETTER GET GOING!
I'M SORRY.
SORRY?
YOU'RE HELPING THE BEST FRIEND I'VE *EVER* HAD...
I COULD *KISS* YOU...BUT GIVEN THE EXPERIENCE FROM LAST NIGHT, WE KNOW HOW THAT ENDS!
DON'T STROKE YOUR OWN EGO!
OH, IMMA STROKE IT!
SO YOU NAMED YOUR PENIS *"EGO"?* INTERESTING.

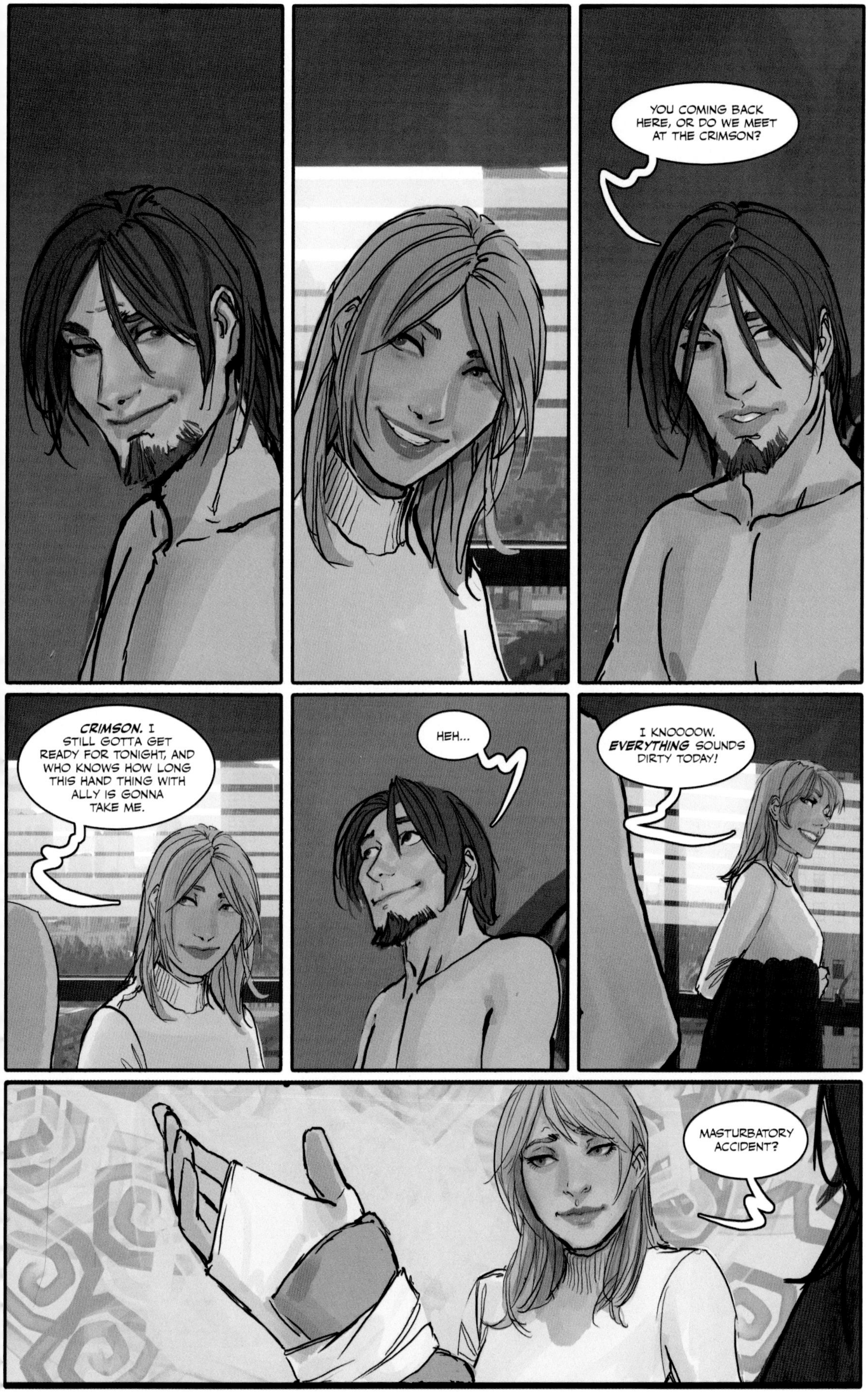
YOU COMING BACK HERE, OR DO WE MEET AT THE CRIMSON?
CRIMSON. I STILL GOTTA GET READY FOR TONIGHT, AND WHO KNOWS HOW LONG THIS HAND THING WITH ALLY IS GONNA TAKE ME.
HEH...
I KNOOOOW. EVERYTHING SOUNDS DIRTY TODAY!
MASTURBATORY ACCIDENT?

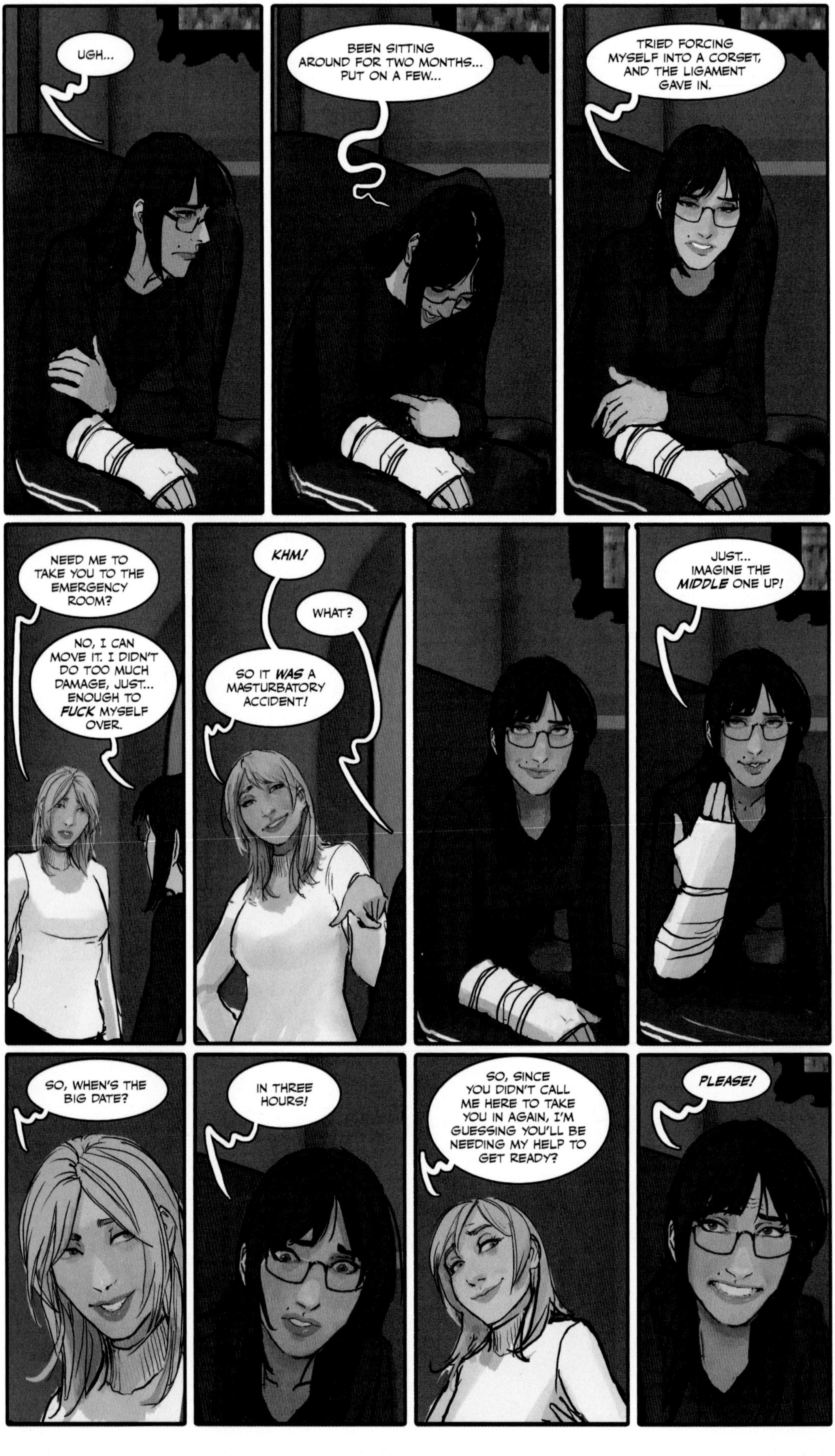
UGH...
BEEN SITTING AROUND FOR TWO MONTHS... PUT ON A FEW...
TRIED FORCING MYSELF INTO A CORSET, AND THE LIGAMENT GAVE IN.
NEED ME TO TAKE YOU TO THE EMERGENCY ROOM?
NO, I CAN MOVE IT. I DIDN'T DO TOO MUCH DAMAGE, JUST... ENOUGH TO FUCK MYSELF OVER.
KHM!
WHAT?
SO IT WAS A MASTURBATORY ACCIDENT!
JUST... IMAGINE THE MIDDLE ONE UP!
SO, WHEN'S THE BIG DATE?
IN THREE HOURS!
SO, SINCE YOU DIDN'T CALL ME HERE TO TAKE YOU IN AGAIN, I'M GUESSING YOU'LL BE NEEDING MY HELP TO GET READY?
PLEASE!

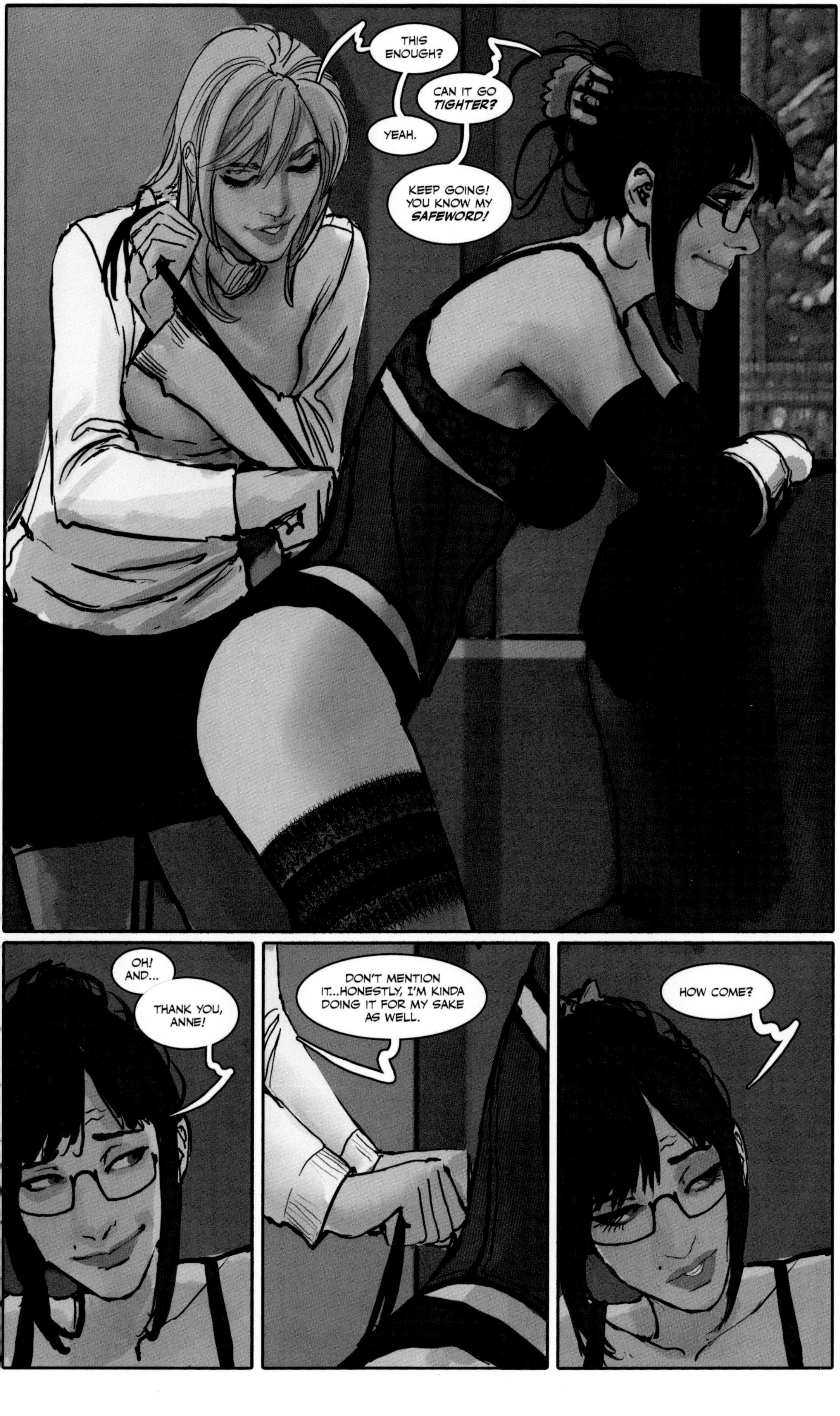
THIS ENOUGH?
YEAH.
CAN IT GO TIGHTER?
KEEP GOING! YOU KNOW MY SAFEWORD!
OH! AND...
THANK YOU, ANNE!
DON'T MENTION IT...HONESTLY, I'M KINDA DOING IT FOR MY SAKE AS WELL.
HOW COME?

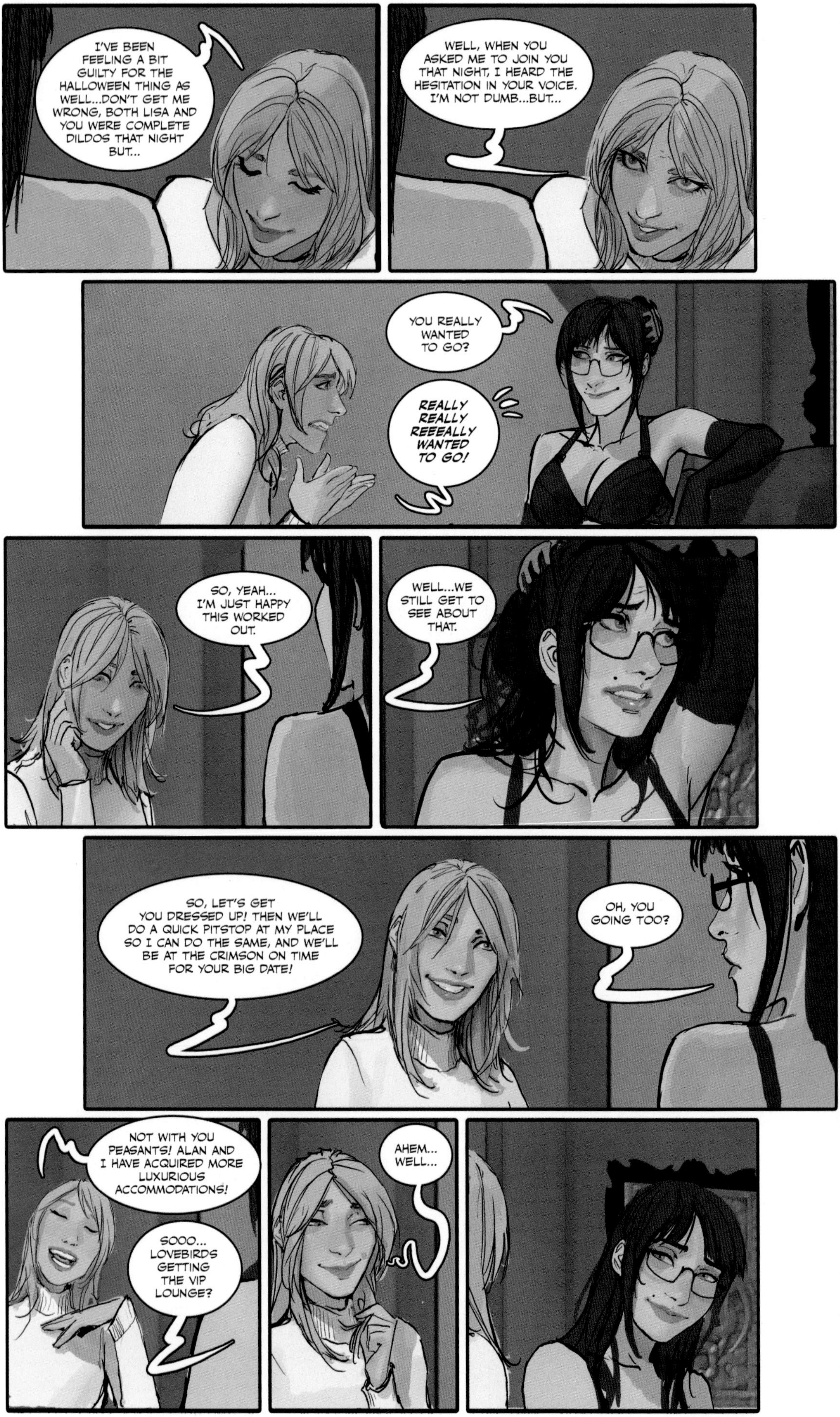

I'VE BEEN FEELING A BIT GUILTY FOR THE HALLOWEEN THING AS WELL...DON'T GET ME WRONG, BOTH LISA AND YOU WERE COMPLETE DILDOS THAT NIGHT BUT...
WELL, WHEN YOU ASKED ME TO JOIN YOU THAT NIGHT, I HEARD THE HESITATION IN YOUR VOICE. I'M NOT DUMB...BUT...
YOU REALLY WANTED TO GO?
REALLY REALLY REEEALLY WANTED TO GO!
SO, YEAH... I'M JUST HAPPY THIS WORKED OUT.
WELL...WE STILL GET TO SEE ABOUT THAT.
SO, LET'S GET YOU DRESSED UP! THEN WE'LL DO A QUICK PITSTOP AT MY PLACE SO I CAN DO THE SAME, AND WE'LL BE AT THE CRIMSON ON TIME FOR YOUR BIG DATE!
OH, YOU GOING TOO?
NOT WITH YOU PEASANTS! ALAN AND I HAVE ACQUIRED MORE LUXURIOUS ACCOMMODATIONS!
SOOO... LOVEBIRDS GETTING THE VIP LOUNGE?
AHEM... WELL...

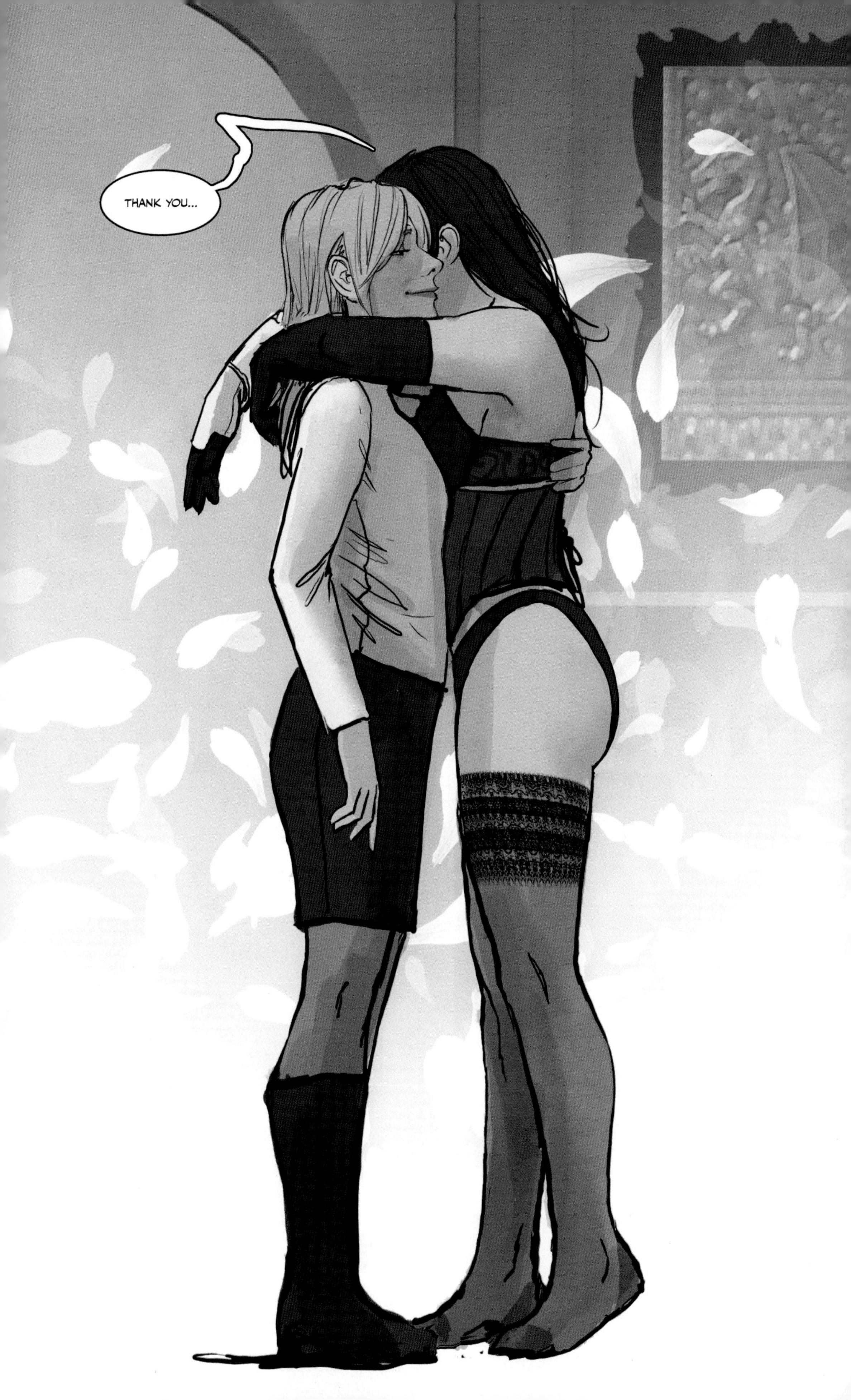
THANK YOU...

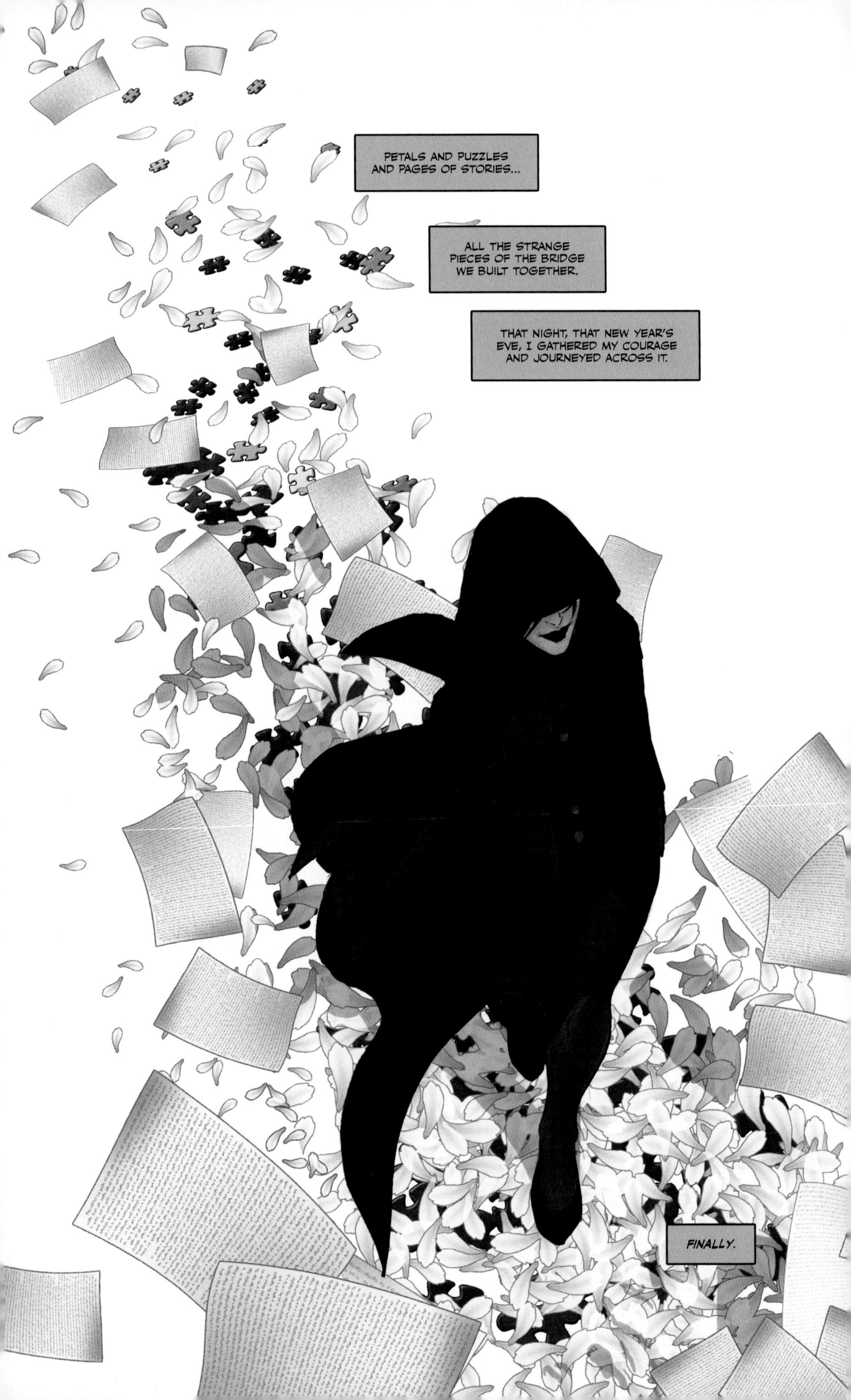
PETALS AND PUZZLES AND PAGES OF STORIES...
ALL THE STRANGE PIECES OF THE BRIDGE WE BUILT TOGETHER.
THAT NIGHT, THAT NEW YEAR'S EVE, I GATHERED MY COURAGE AND JOURNEYED ACROSS IT.
FINALLY.

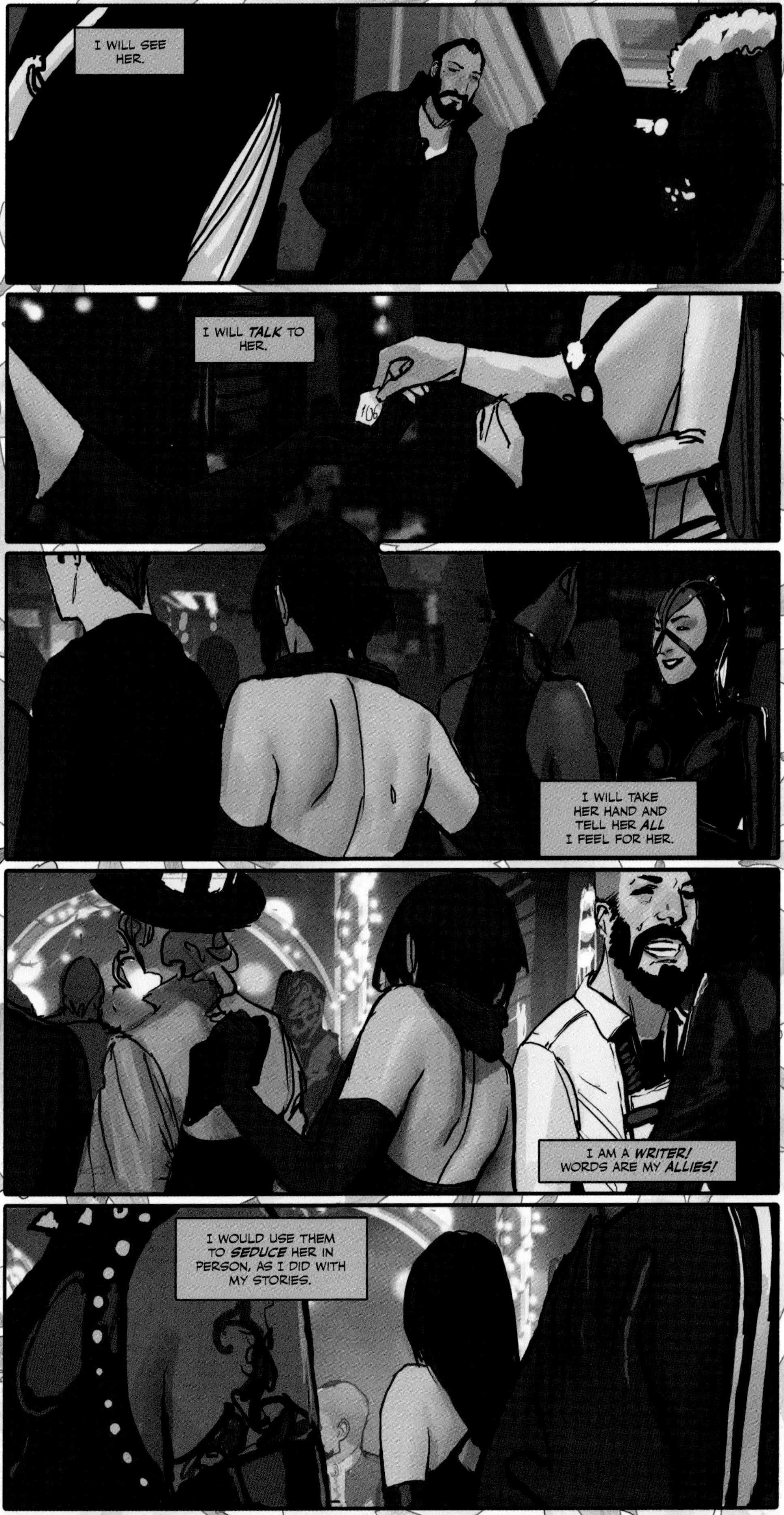
I WILL SEE HER.
I WILL *TALK* TO HER.
106
I WILL TAKE HER HAND AND TELL HER *ALL* I FEEL FOR HER.
I AM A *WRITER!* WORDS ARE MY *ALLIES!*
I WOULD USE THEM TO *SEDUCE* HER IN PERSON, AS I DID WITH MY STORIES.

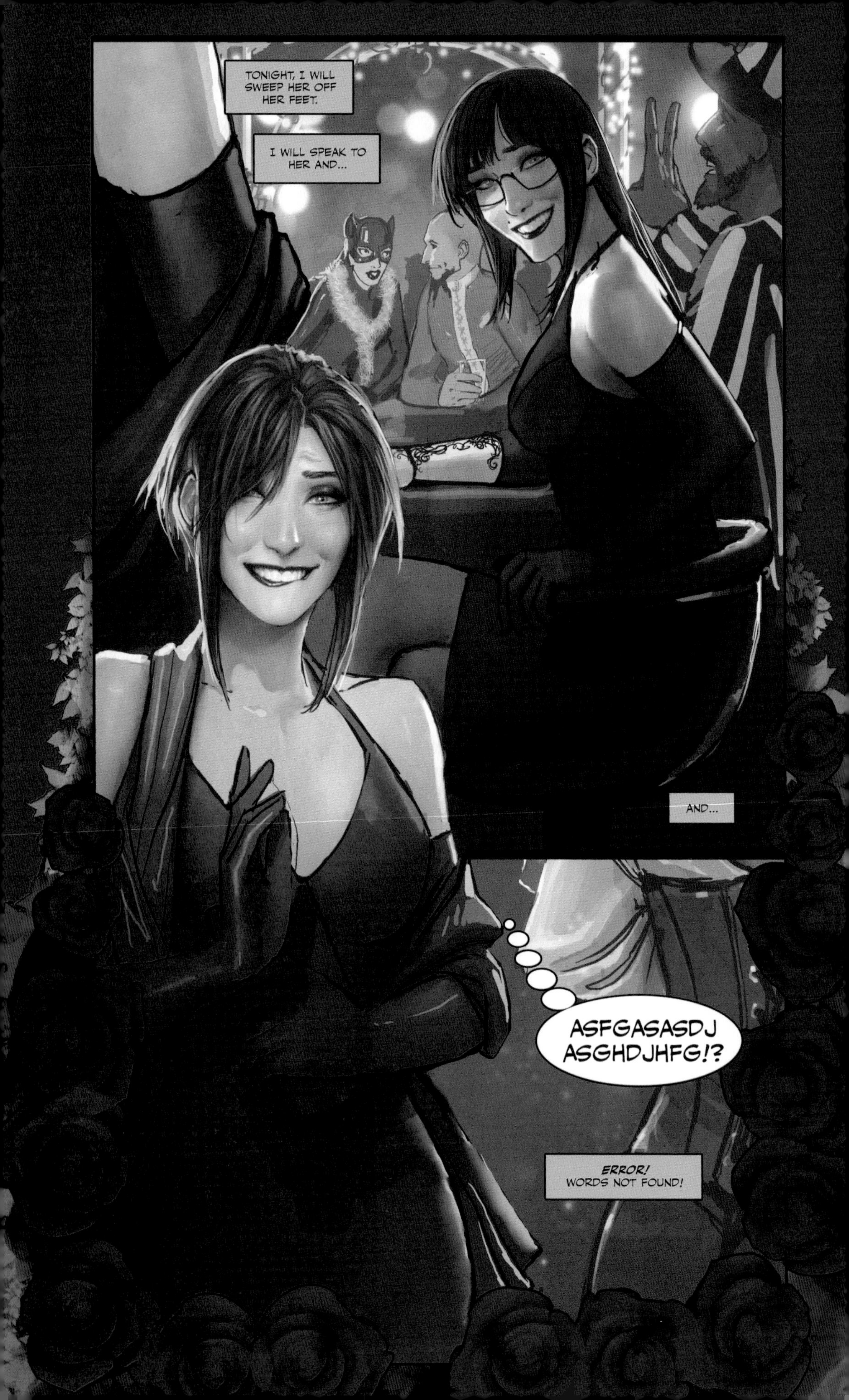
TONIGHT, I WILL SWEEP HER OFF HER FEET.
I WILL SPEAK TO HER AND...
AND...
ASFGASASDJ ASGHDJHFG!?
ERROR! WORDS NOT FOUND!

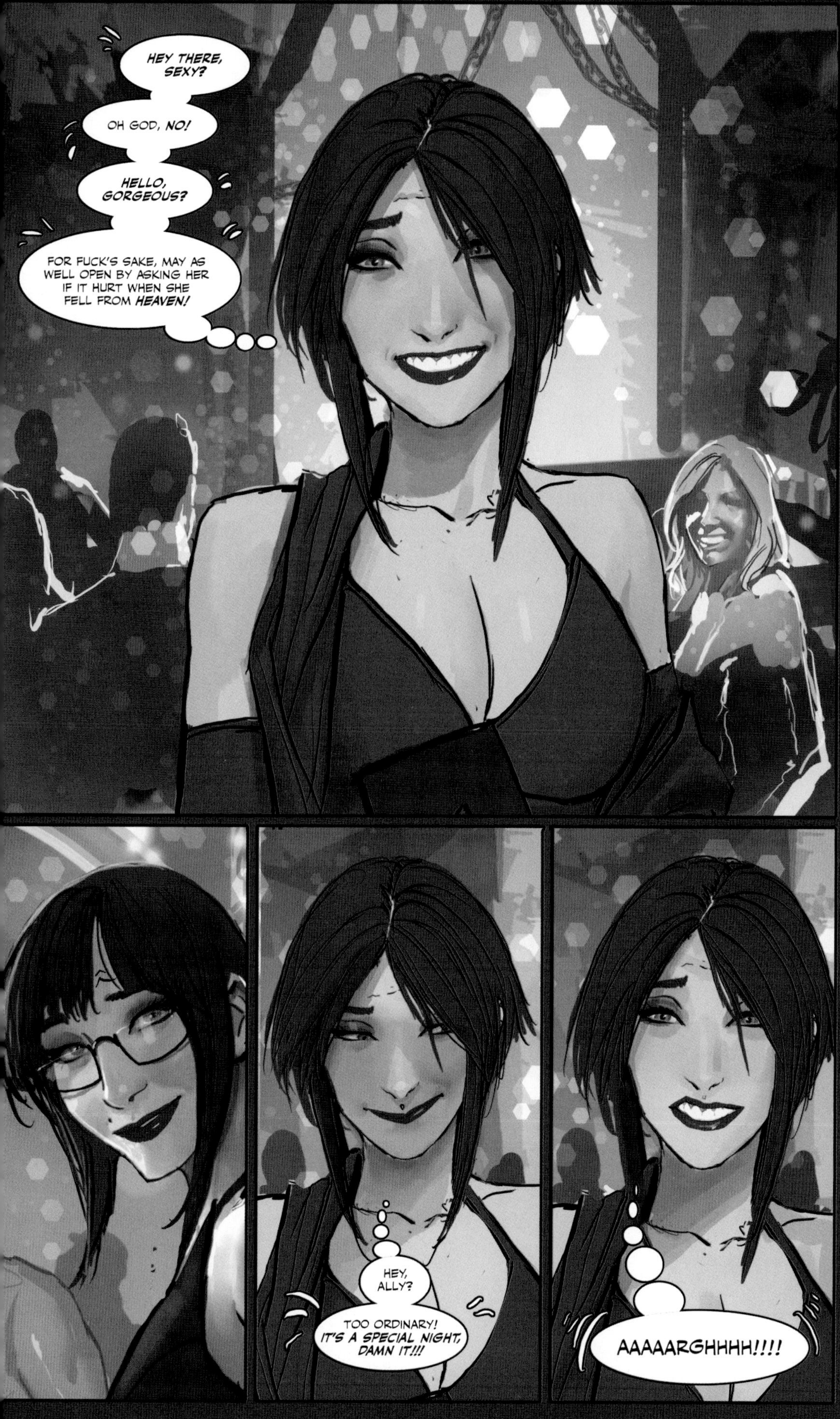
HEY THERE, SEXY?
OH GOD, NO!
HELLO, GORGEOUS?
FOR FUCK'S SAKE, MAY AS WELL OPEN BY ASKING HER IF IT HURT WHEN SHE FELL FROM HEAVEN!
HEY, ALLY?
TOO ORDINARY! IT'S A SPECIAL NIGHT, DAMN IT!!!
AAAAARGHHHH!!!!

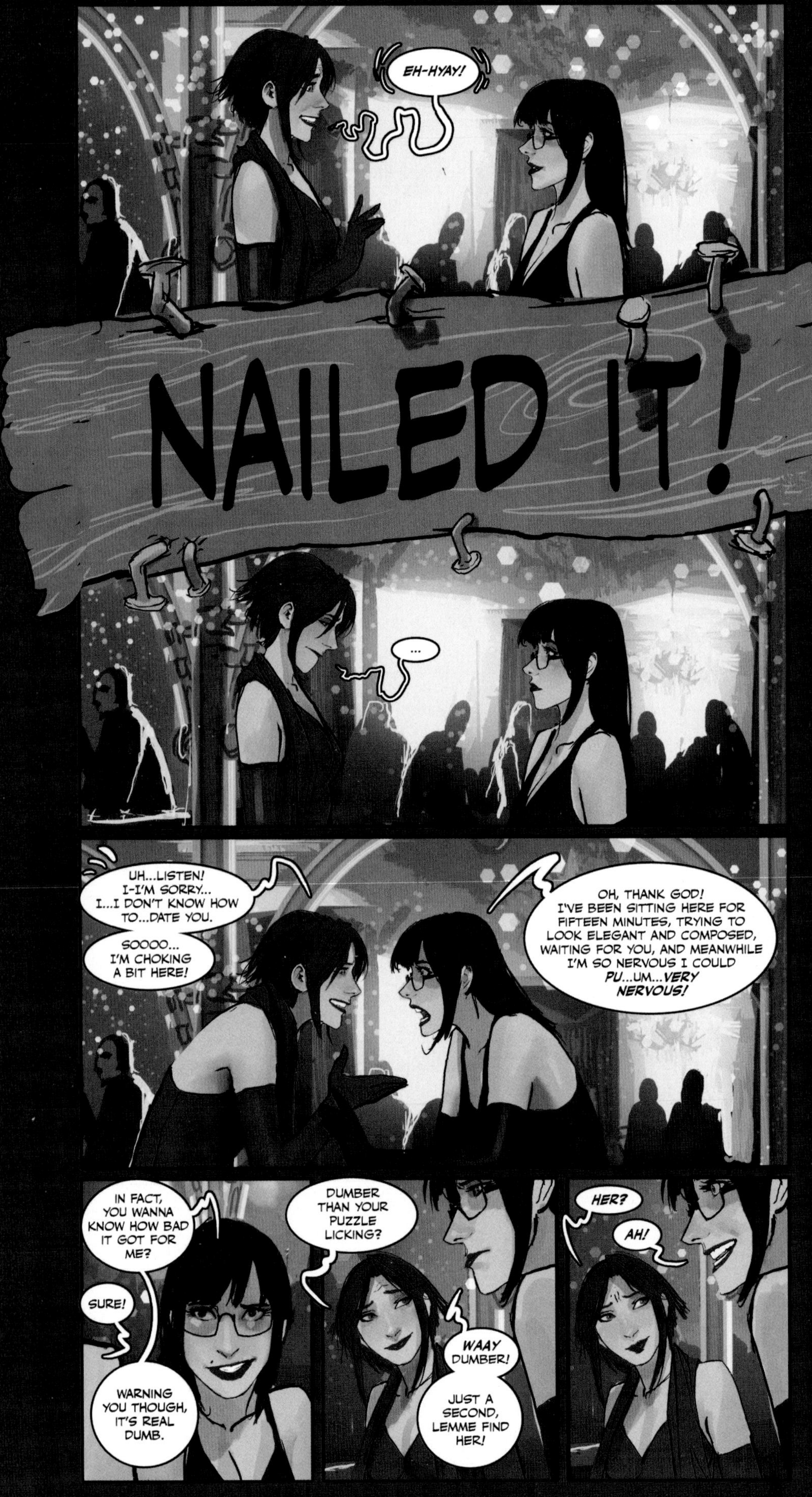
EH-HYAY!
NAILED IT!
...
UH...LISTEN! I-I'M SORRY... I...I DON'T KNOW HOW TO...DATE YOU.
SOOOO... I'M CHOKING A BIT HERE!
OH, THANK GOD! I'VE BEEN SITTING HERE FOR FIFTEEN MINUTES, TRYING TO LOOK ELEGANT AND COMPOSED, WAITING FOR YOU, AND MEANWHILE I'M SO NERVOUS I COULD PU...UM...VERY NERVOUS!
IN FACT, YOU WANNA KNOW HOW BAD IT GOT FOR ME?
SURE!
WARNING YOU THOUGH, IT'S REAL DUMB.
DUMBER THAN YOUR PUZZLE LICKING?
WAAY DUMBER!
JUST A SECOND, LEMME FIND HER!
HER?
AH!

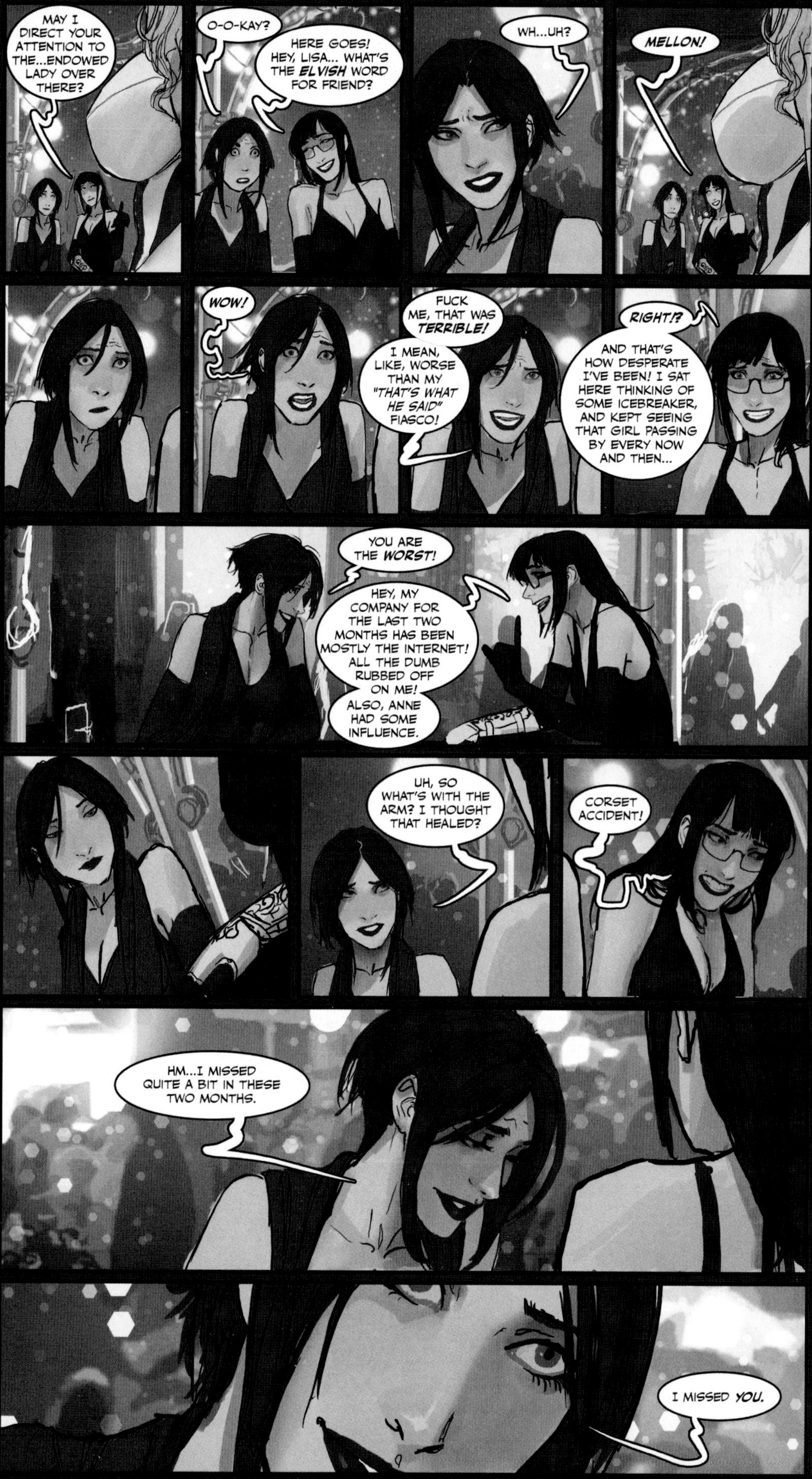

MAY I DIRECT YOUR ATTENTION TO THE...ENDOWED LADY OVER THERE?
O-O-KAY?
HERE GOES! HEY, LISA... WHAT'S THE *ELVISH* WORD FOR FRIEND?
WH...UH?
MELLON!
WOW!
FUCK ME, THAT WAS *TERRIBLE!*
I MEAN, LIKE, WORSE THAN MY *"THAT'S WHAT HE SAID"* FIASCO!
RIGHT!?
AND THAT'S HOW DESPERATE I'VE BEEN! I SAT HERE THINKING OF SOME ICEBREAKER, AND KEPT SEEING THAT GIRL PASSING BY EVERY NOW AND THEN...
YOU ARE THE *WORST!*
HEY, MY COMPANY FOR THE LAST TWO MONTHS HAS BEEN MOSTLY THE INTERNET! ALL THE DUMB RUBBED OFF ON ME!
ALSO, ANNE HAD SOME INFLUENCE.
UH, SO WHAT'S WITH THE ARM? I THOUGHT THAT HEALED?
CORSET ACCIDENT!
HM...I MISSED QUITE A BIT IN THESE TWO MONTHS.
I MISSED *YOU.*

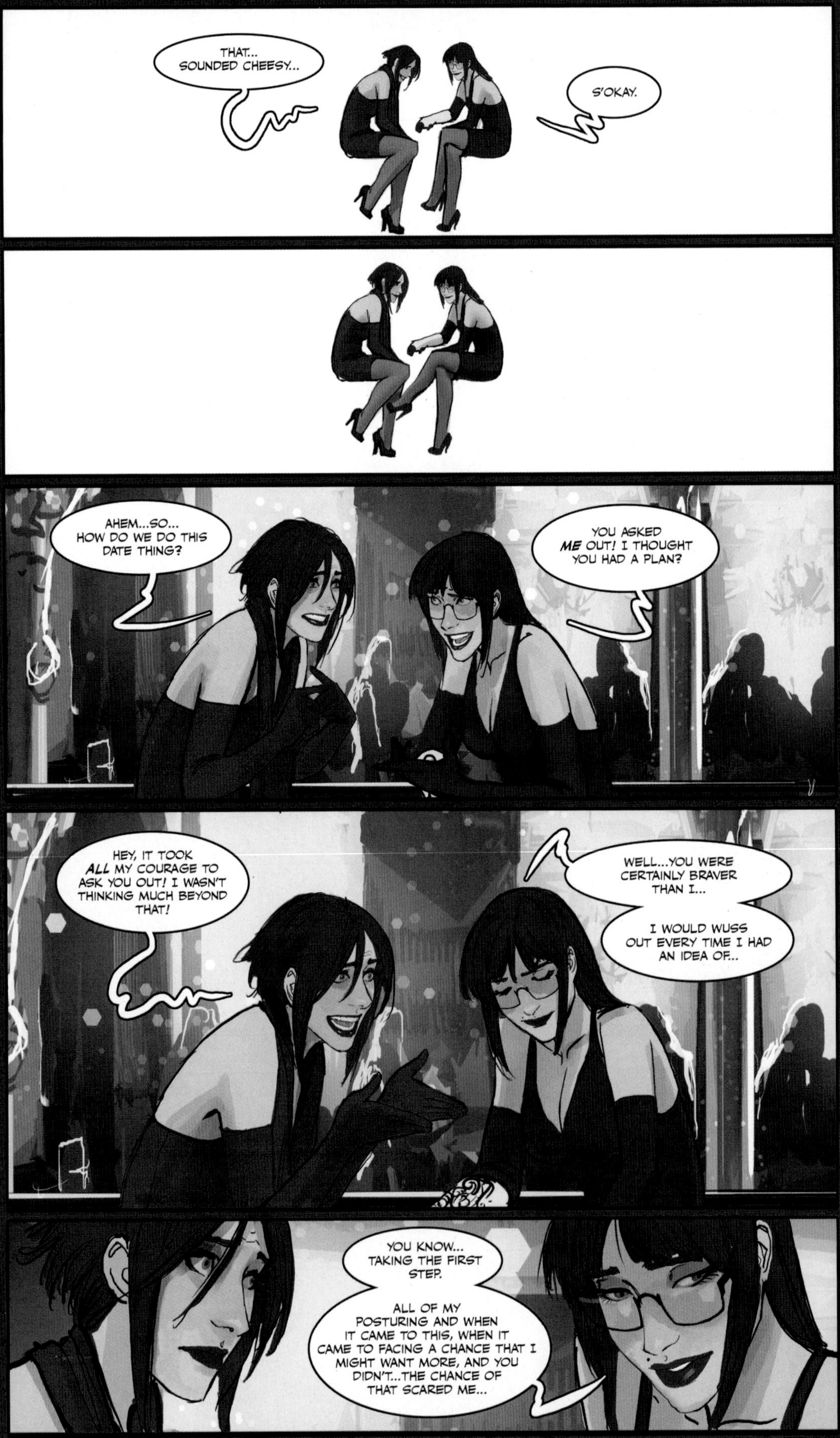
THAT... SOUNDED CHEESY...
S'OKAY.
AHEM...SO... HOW DO WE DO THIS DATE THING?
YOU ASKED **ME** OUT! I THOUGHT YOU HAD A PLAN?
HEY, IT TOOK **ALL** MY COURAGE TO ASK YOU OUT! I WASN'T THINKING MUCH BEYOND THAT!
WELL...YOU WERE CERTAINLY BRAVER THAN I...
I WOULD WUSS OUT EVERY TIME I HAD AN IDEA OF...
YOU KNOW... TAKING THE FIRST STEP.
ALL OF MY POSTURING AND WHEN IT CAME TO THIS, WHEN IT CAME TO FACING A CHANCE THAT I MIGHT WANT MORE, AND YOU DIDN'T...THE CHANCE OF THAT SCARED ME...

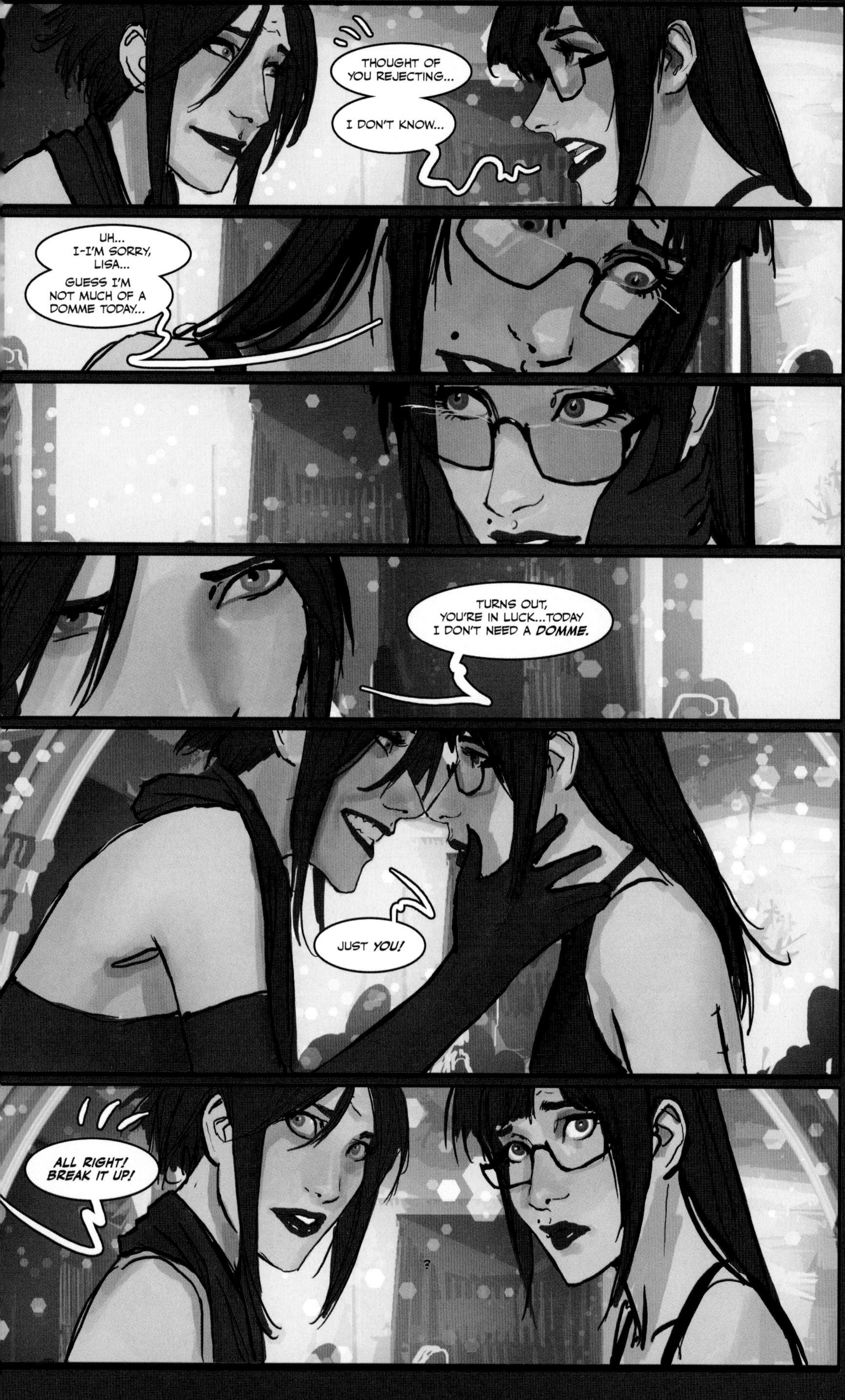
THOUGHT OF YOU REJECTING...
I DON'T KNOW...
UH... I-I'M SORRY, LISA...
GUESS I'M NOT MUCH OF A DOMME TODAY...
TURNS OUT, YOU'RE IN LUCK...TODAY I DON'T NEED A *DOMME.*
JUST *YOU!*
ALL RIGHT! BREAK IT UP!
?

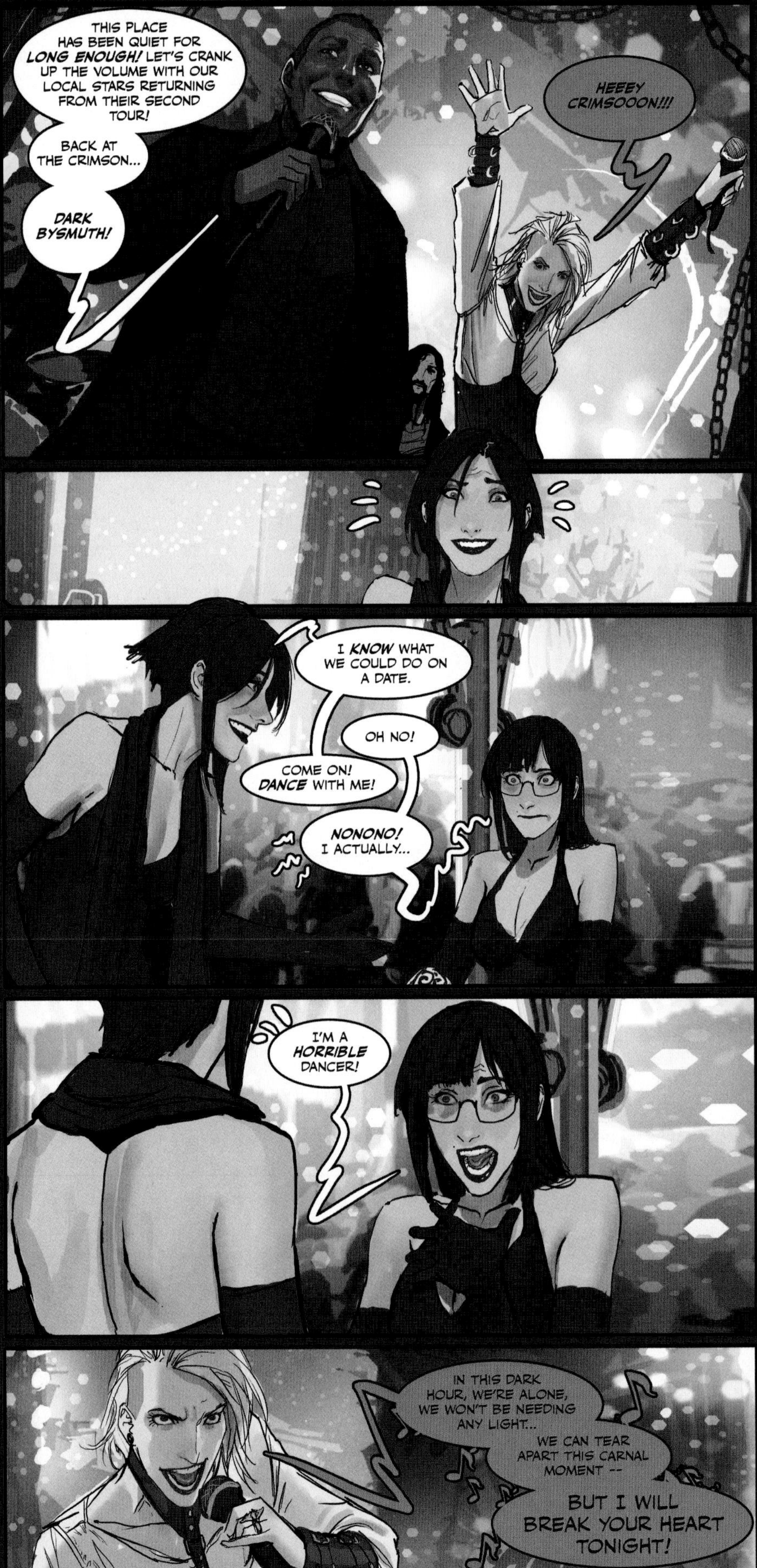
THIS PLACE HAS BEEN QUIET FOR LONG ENOUGH! LET'S CRANK UP THE VOLUME WITH OUR LOCAL STARS RETURNING FROM THEIR SECOND TOUR!
BACK AT THE CRIMSON...
DARK BYSMUTH!
HEEEY CRIMSOOON!!!
I KNOW WHAT WE COULD DO ON A DATE.
OH NO!
COME ON! DANCE WITH ME!
NONONO! I ACTUALLY...
I'M A HORRIBLE DANCER!
IN THIS DARK HOUR, WE'RE ALONE, WE WON'T BE NEEDING ANY LIGHT...
WE CAN TEAR APART THIS CARNAL MOMENT --
BUT I WILL BREAK YOUR HEART TONIGHT!

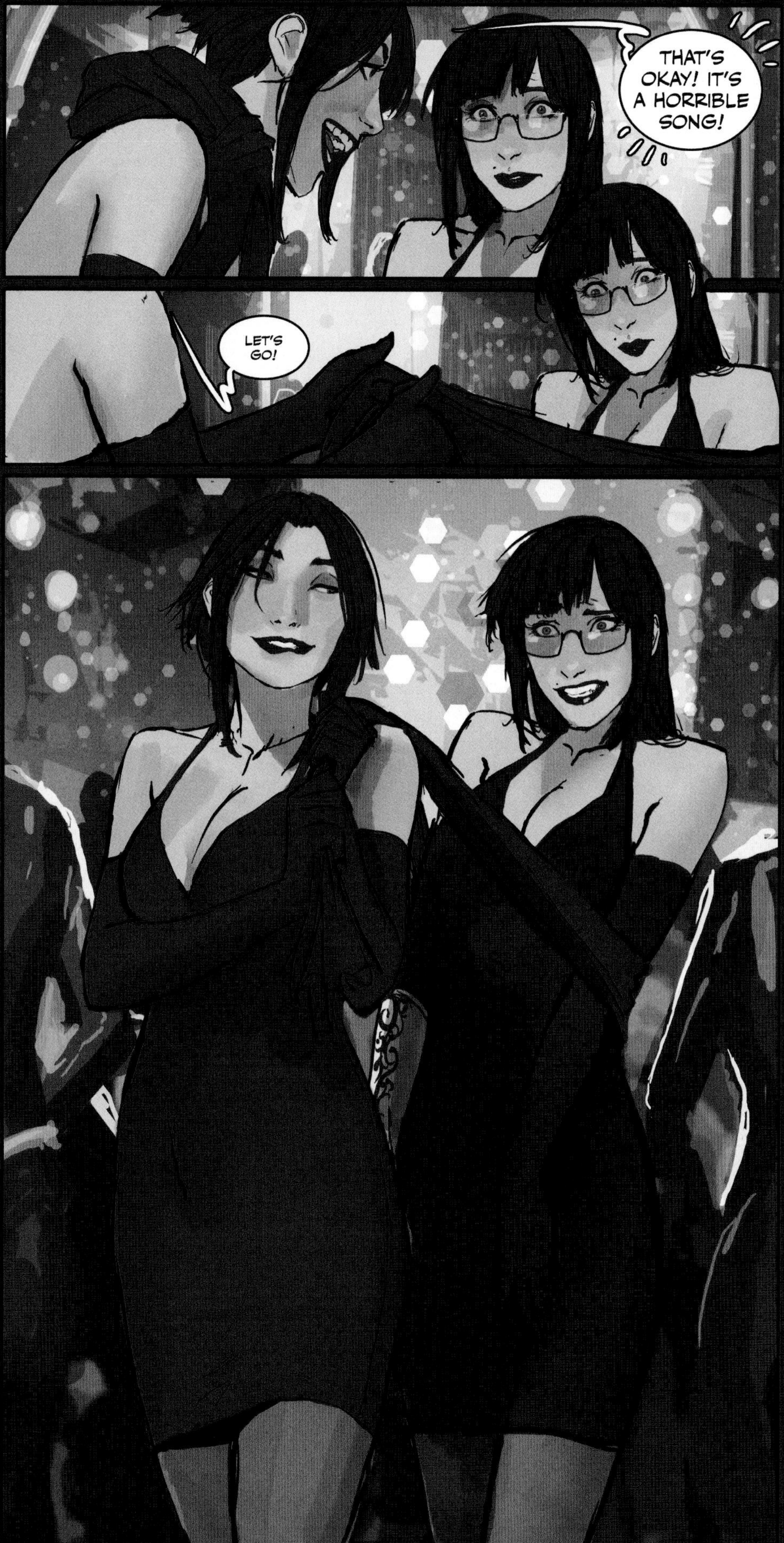
THAT'S OKAY! IT'S A HORRIBLE SONG!
LET'S GO!

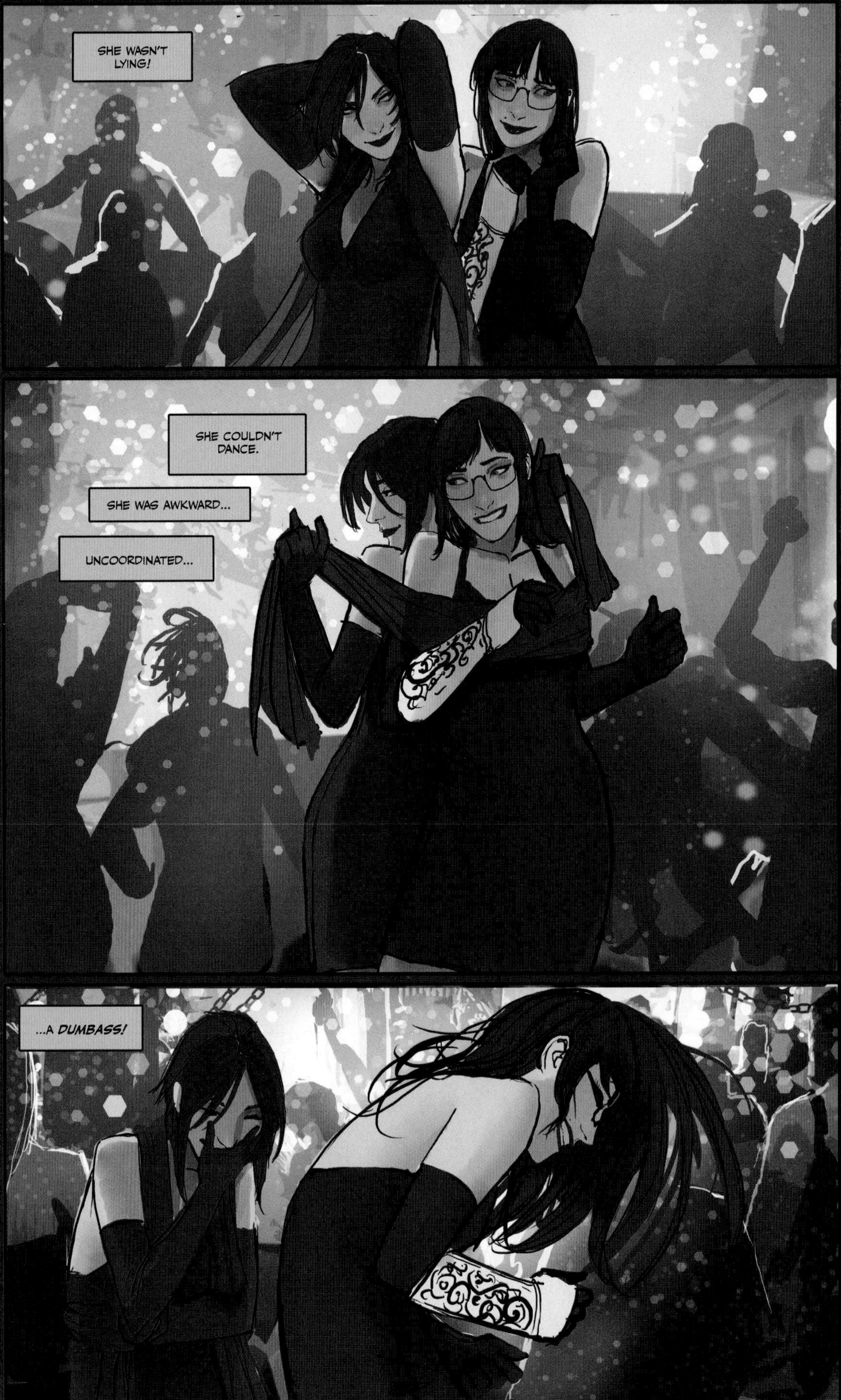
SHE WASN'T LYING!
SHE COULDN'T DANCE.
SHE WAS AWKWARD...
UNCOORDINATED...
...A *DUMBASS!*

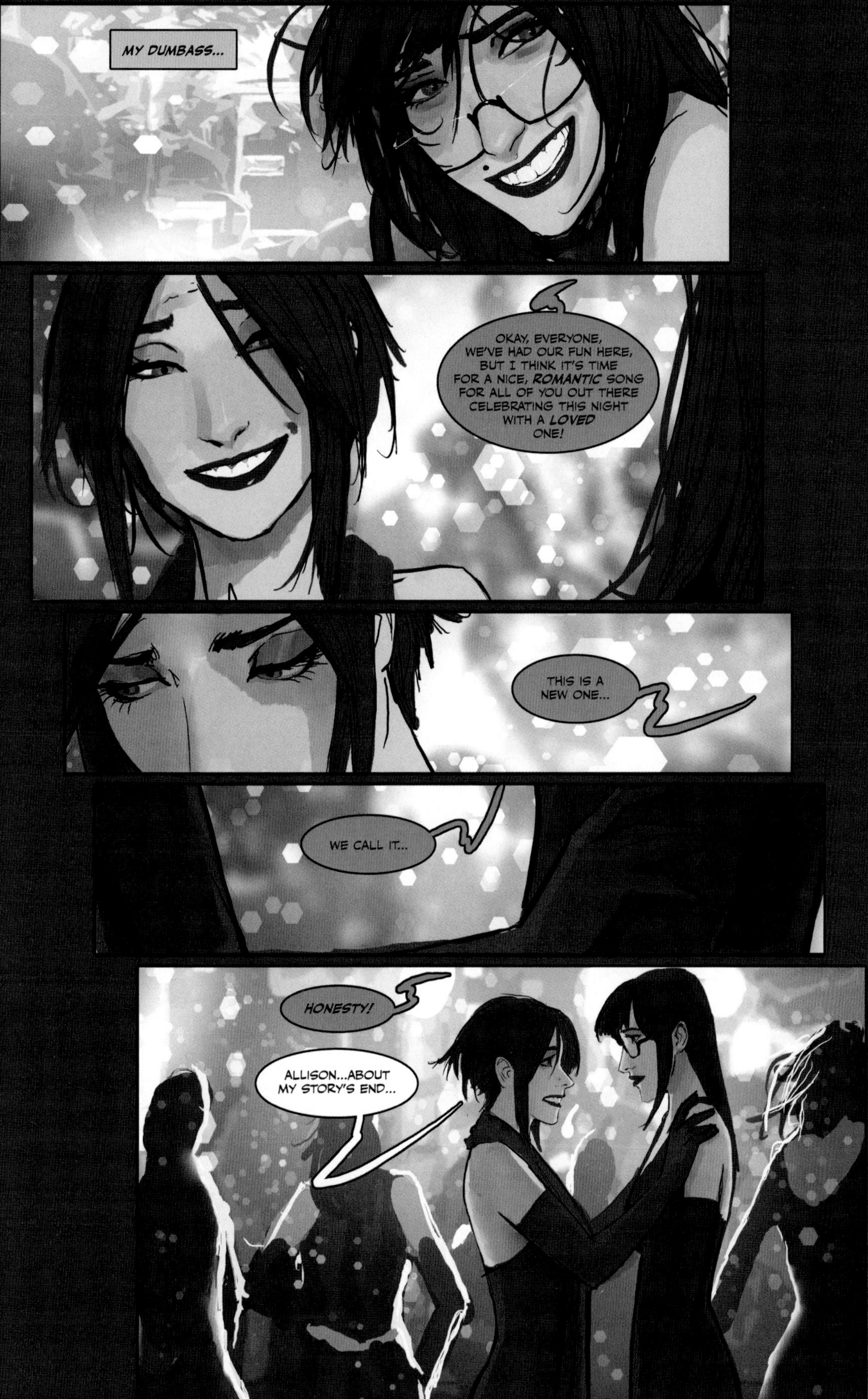
MY DUMBASS...
OKAY, EVERYONE, WE'VE HAD OUR FUN HERE, BUT I THINK IT'S TIME FOR A NICE, ROMANTIC SONG FOR ALL OF YOU OUT THERE CELEBRATING THIS NIGHT WITH A LOVED ONE!
THIS IS A NEW ONE...
WE CALL IT...
HONESTY!
ALLISON...ABOUT MY STORY'S END...

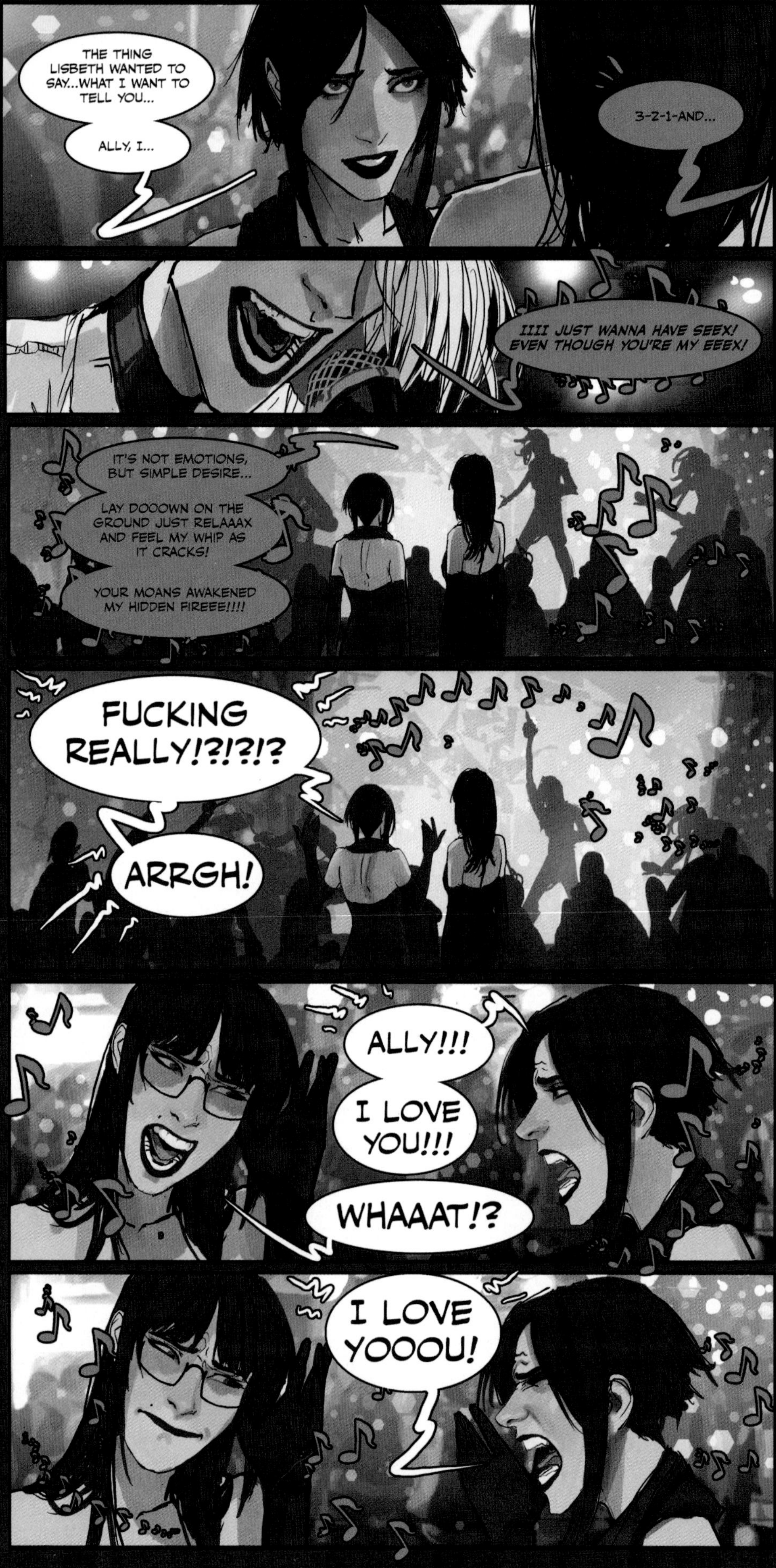
THE THING LISBETH WANTED TO SAY...WHAT I WANT TO TELL YOU...
ALLY, I...
3-2-1-AND...
IIII JUST WANNA HAVE SEEX! EVEN THOUGH YOU'RE MY EEEX!
IT'S NOT EMOTIONS, BUT SIMPLE DESIRE...
LAY DOOOWN ON THE GROUND JUST RELAAAX AND FEEL MY WHIP AS IT CRACKS!
YOUR MOANS AWAKENED MY HIDDEN FIREEE!!!!
FUCKING REALLY!?!?!?
ARRGH!
ALLY!!!
I LOVE YOU!!!
WHAAAT!?
I LOVE YOOOU!

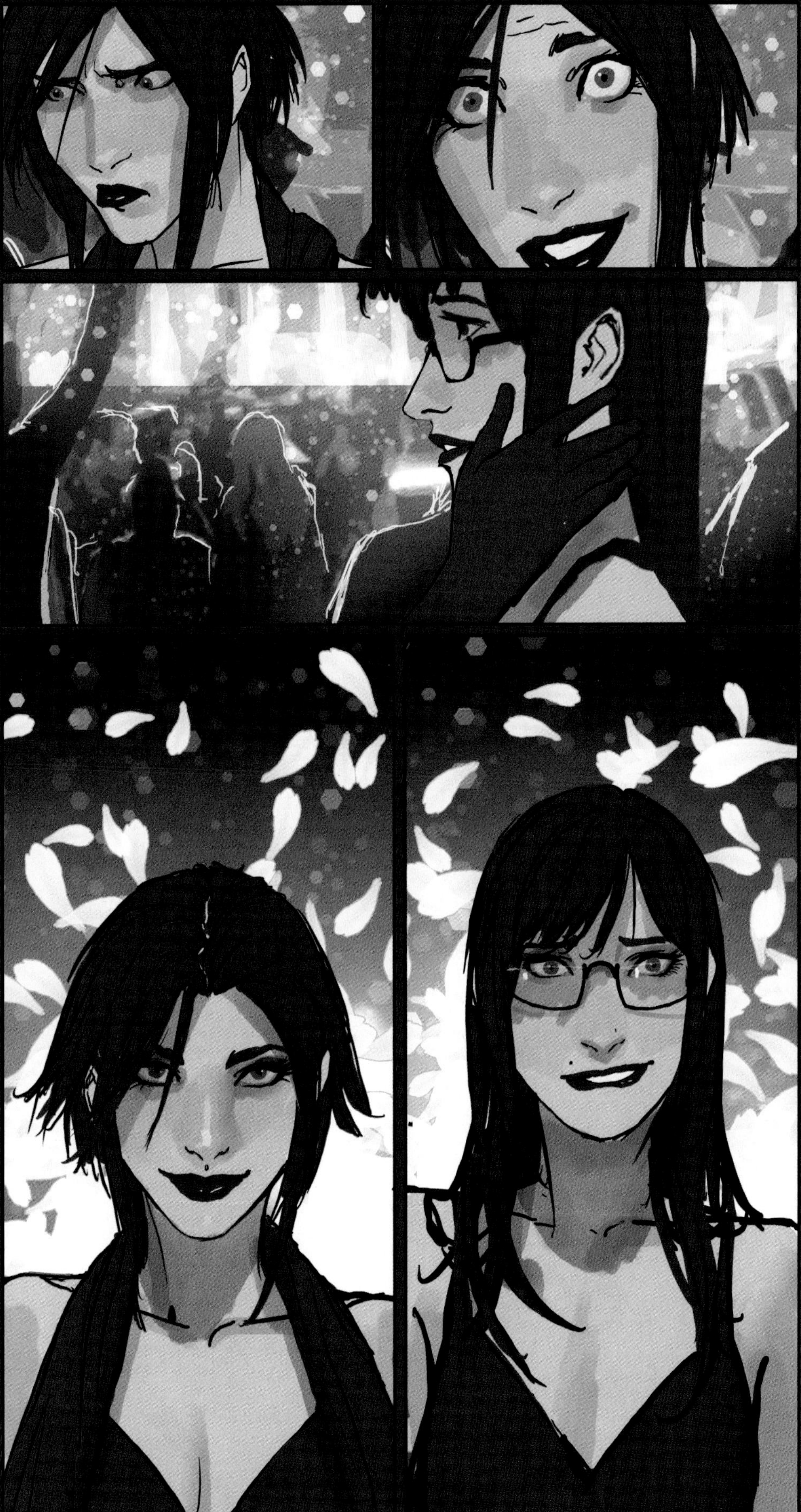

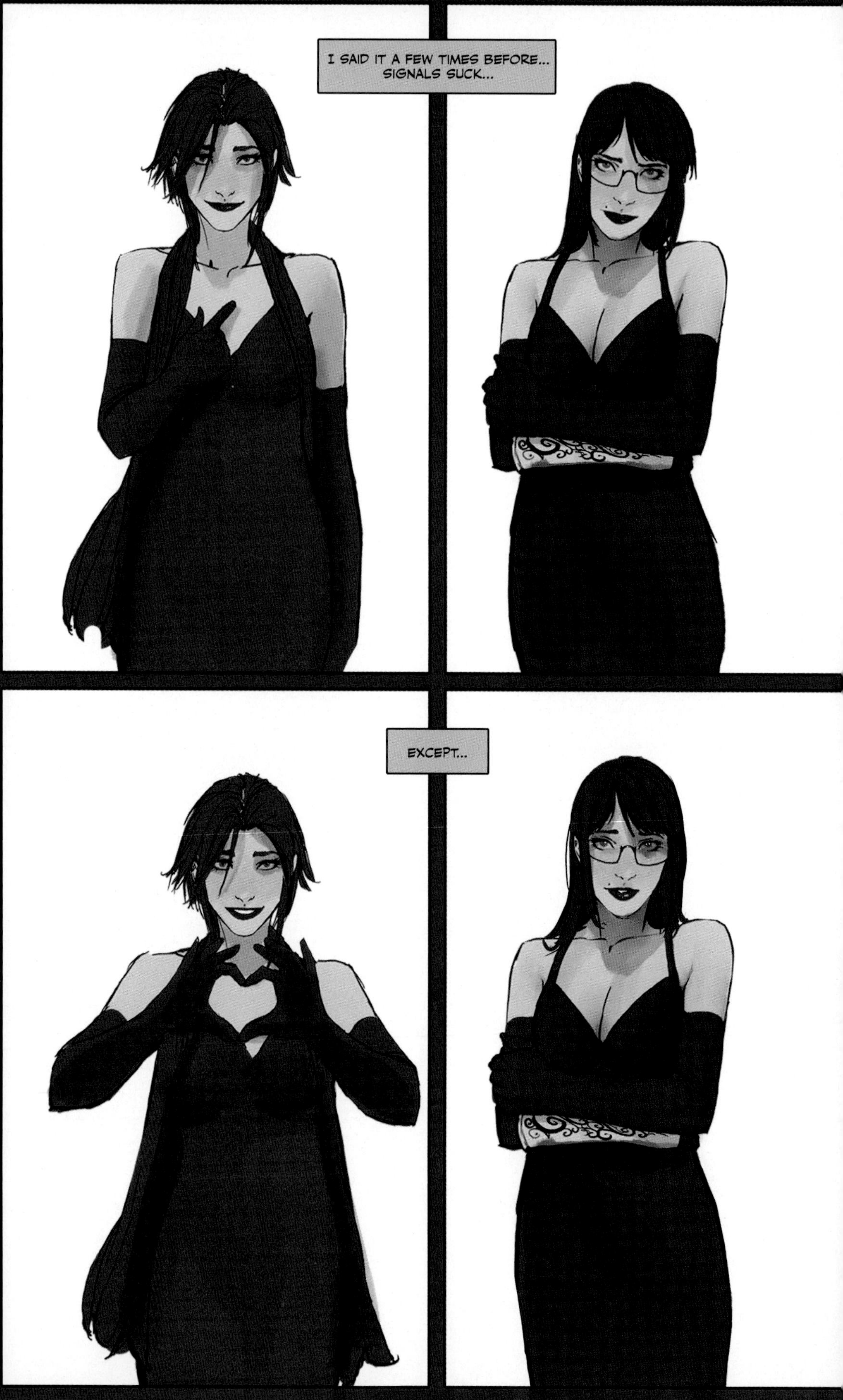
I SAID IT A FEW TIMES BEFORE...
SIGNALS SUCK...
EXCEPT...

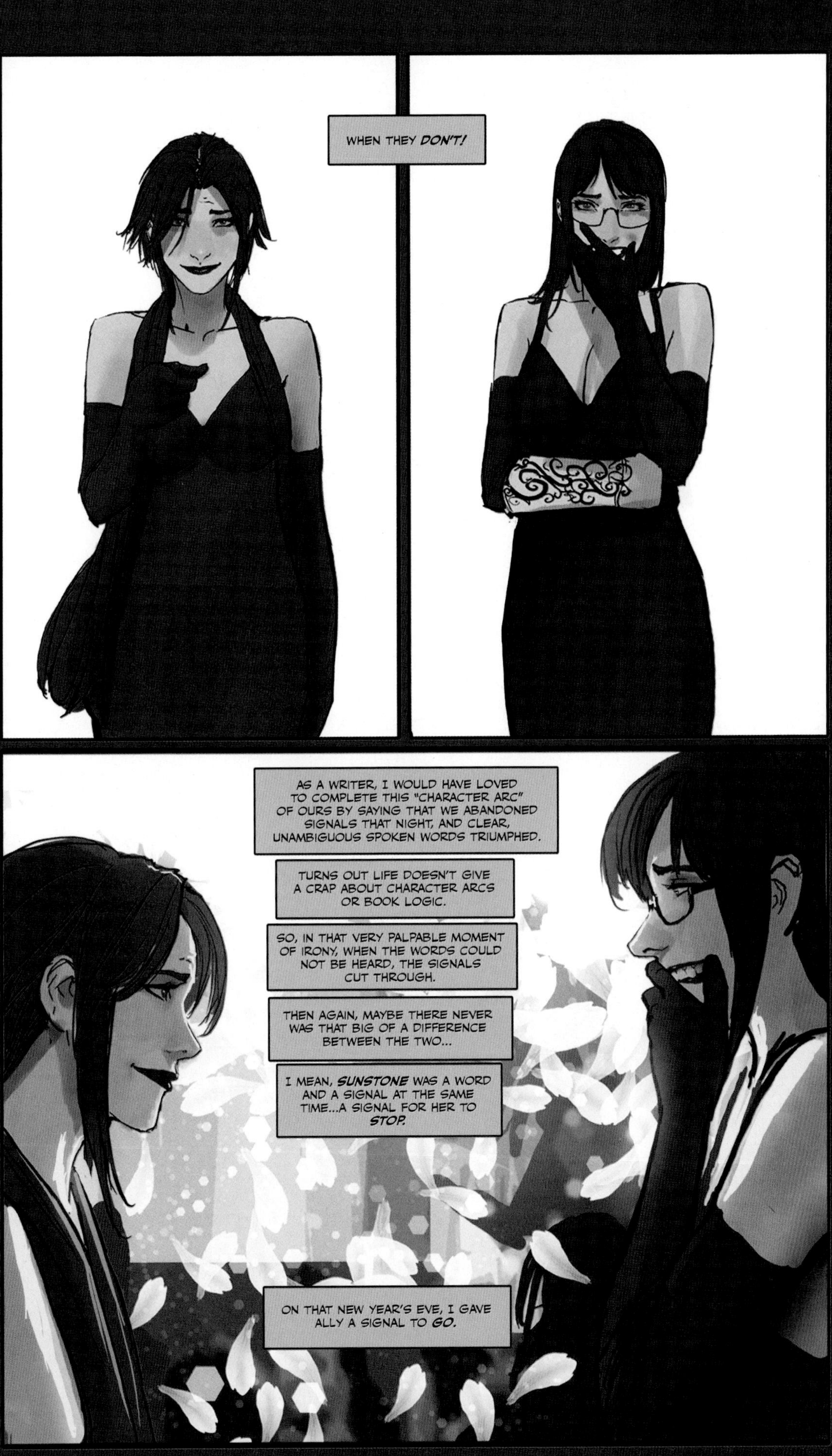
WHEN THEY *DON'T!*
AS A WRITER, I WOULD HAVE LOVED TO COMPLETE THIS "CHARACTER ARC" OF OURS BY SAYING THAT WE ABANDONED SIGNALS THAT NIGHT, AND CLEAR, UNAMBIGUOUS SPOKEN WORDS TRIUMPHED.
TURNS OUT LIFE DOESN'T GIVE A CRAP ABOUT CHARACTER ARCS OR BOOK LOGIC.
SO, IN THAT VERY PALPABLE MOMENT OF IRONY, WHEN THE WORDS COULD NOT BE HEARD, THE SIGNALS CUT THROUGH.
THEN AGAIN, MAYBE THERE NEVER WAS THAT BIG OF A DIFFERENCE BETWEEN THE TWO...
I MEAN, ***SUNSTONE*** WAS A WORD AND A SIGNAL AT THE SAME TIME...A SIGNAL FOR HER TO ***STOP.***
ON THAT NEW YEAR'S EVE, I GAVE ALLY A SIGNAL TO ***GO.***

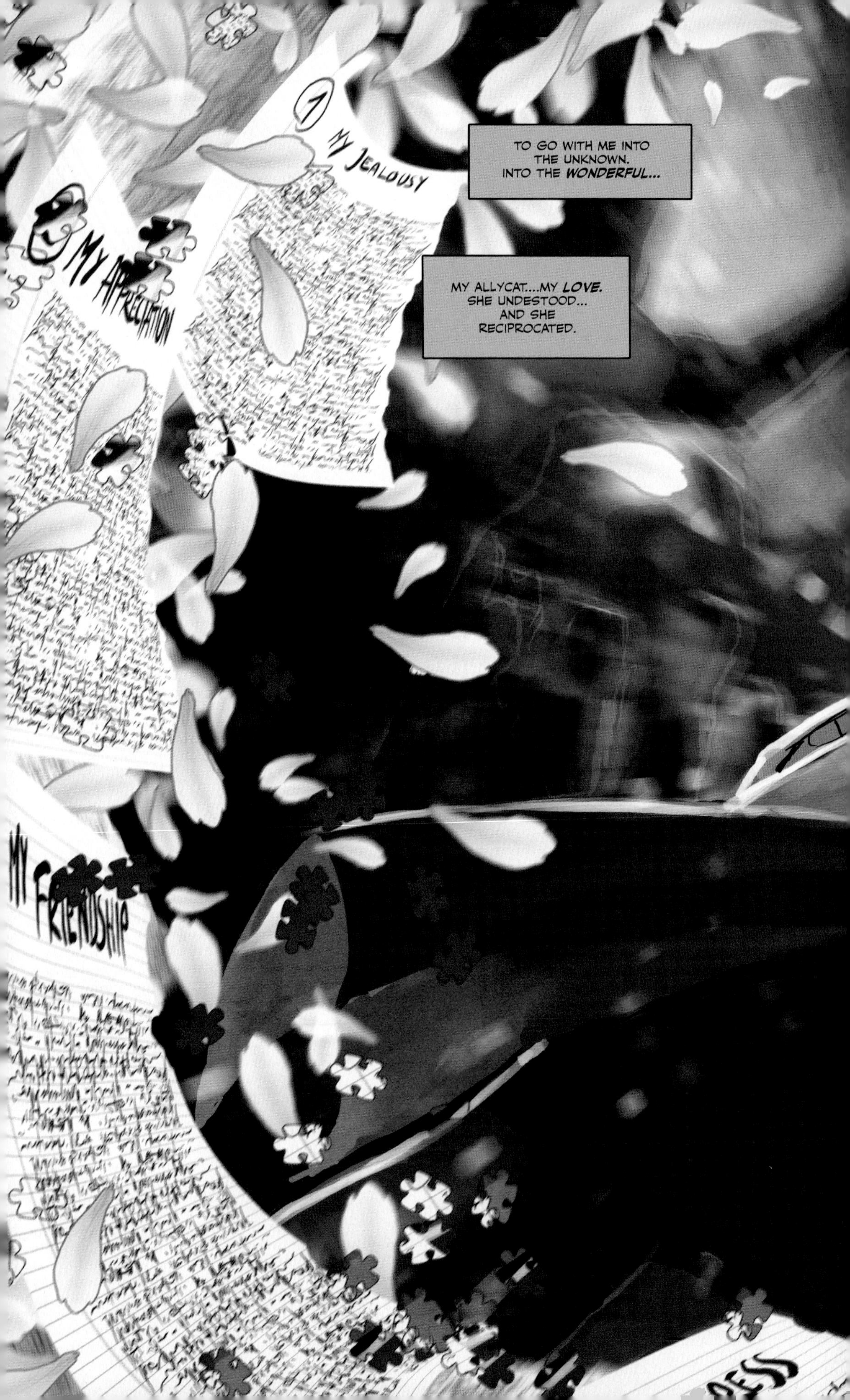
TO GO WITH ME INTO
THE UNKNOWN.
INTO THE ***WONDERFUL...***
MY ALLYCAT....MY ***LOVE.***
SHE UNDESTOOD...
AND SHE
RECIPROCATED.
MY JEALOUSY
MY APPRECIATION
MY FRIENDSHIP

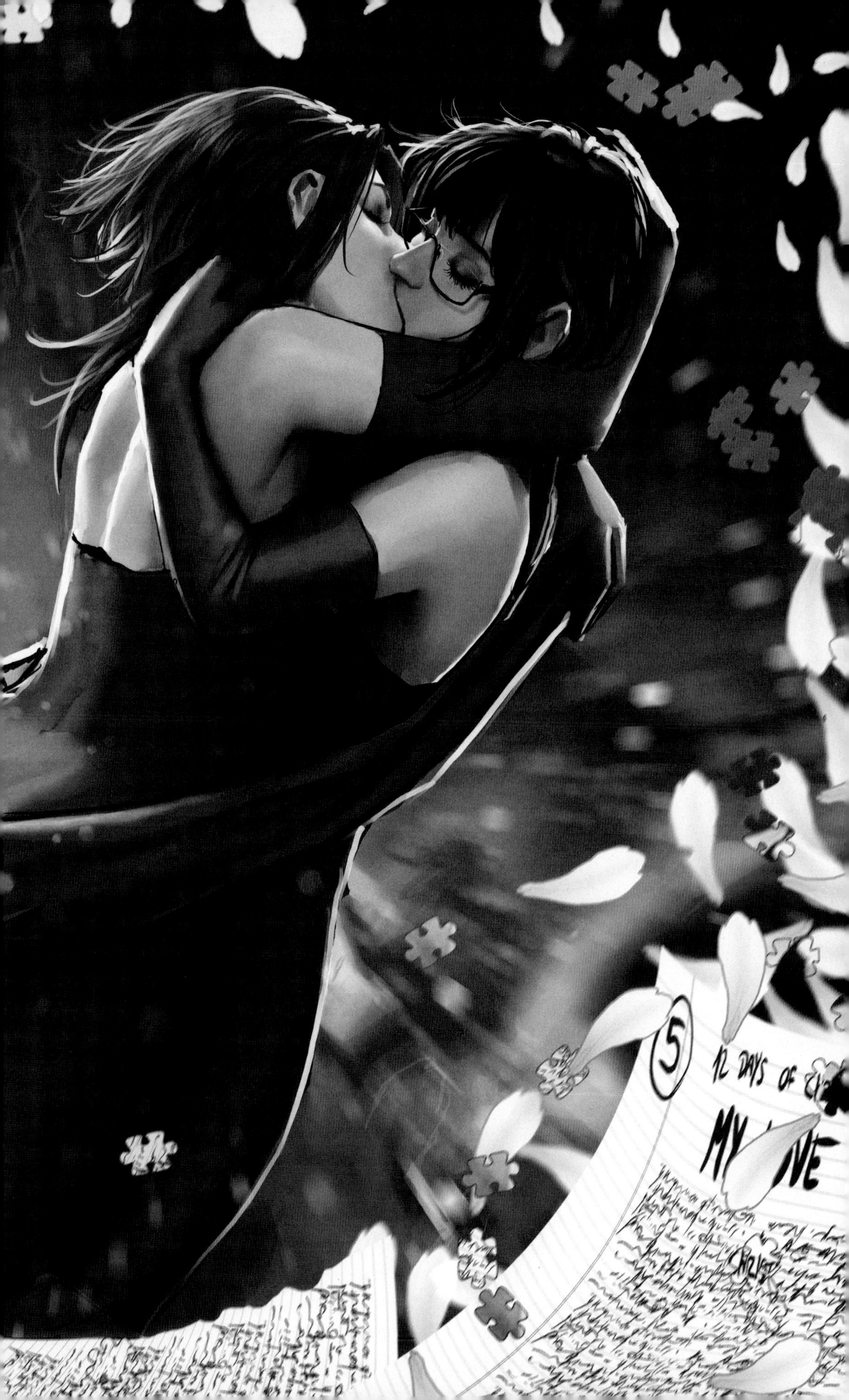
5
12 DAYS OF
MY

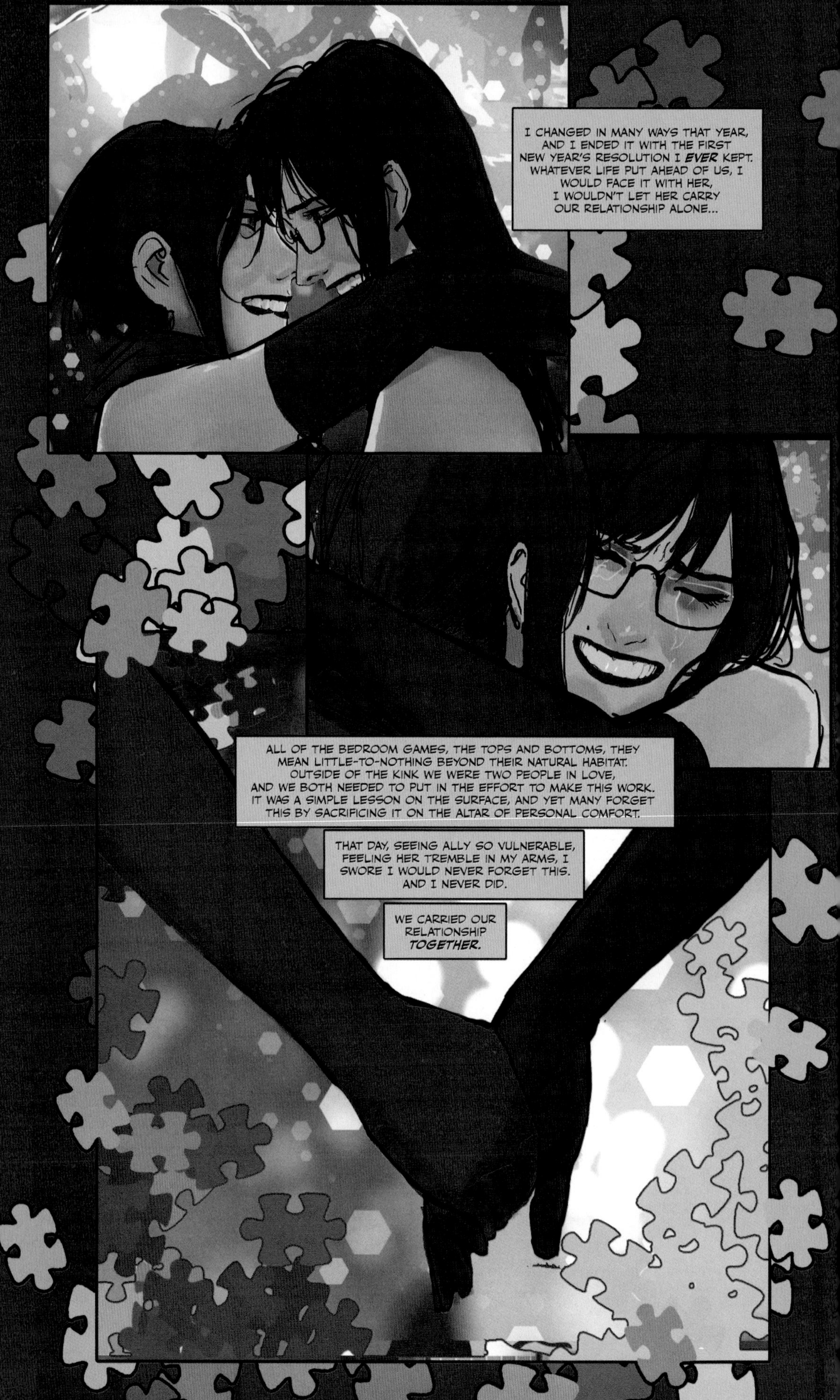

I CHANGED IN MANY WAYS THAT YEAR, AND I ENDED IT WITH THE FIRST NEW YEAR'S RESOLUTION I ***EVER*** KEPT. WHATEVER LIFE PUT AHEAD OF US, I WOULD FACE IT WITH HER, I WOULDN'T LET HER CARRY OUR RELATIONSHIP ALONE...
ALL OF THE BEDROOM GAMES, THE TOPS AND BOTTOMS, THEY MEAN LITTLE-TO-NOTHING BEYOND THEIR NATURAL HABITAT. OUTSIDE OF THE KINK WE WERE TWO PEOPLE IN LOVE, AND WE BOTH NEEDED TO PUT IN THE EFFORT TO MAKE THIS WORK. IT WAS A SIMPLE LESSON ON THE SURFACE, AND YET MANY FORGET THIS BY SACRIFICING IT ON THE ALTAR OF PERSONAL COMFORT.
THAT DAY, SEEING ALLY SO VULNERABLE, FEELING HER TREMBLE IN MY ARMS, I SWORE I WOULD NEVER FORGET THIS. AND I NEVER DID.
WE CARRIED OUR RELATIONSHIP ***TOGETHER.***

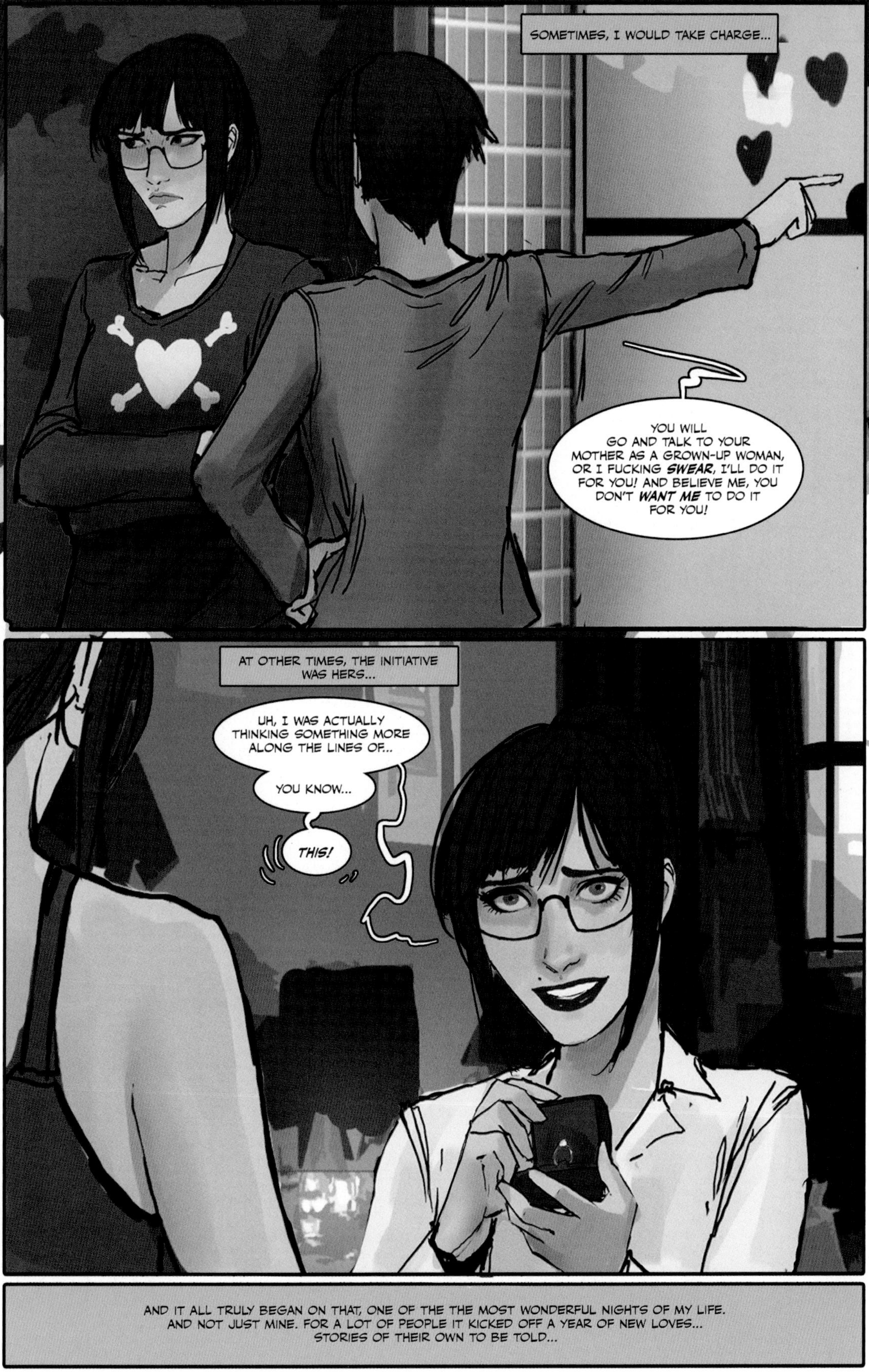
SOMETIMES, I WOULD TAKE CHARGE...
YOU WILL GO AND TALK TO YOUR MOTHER AS A GROWN-UP WOMAN, OR I FUCKING *SWEAR*, I'LL DO IT FOR YOU! AND BELIEVE ME, YOU DON'T *WANT ME* TO DO IT FOR YOU!
AT OTHER TIMES, THE INITIATIVE WAS HERS...
UH, I WAS ACTUALLY THINKING SOMETHING MORE ALONG THE LINES OF...
YOU KNOW...
THIS!
AND IT ALL TRULY BEGAN ON THAT, ONE OF THE THE MOST WONDERFUL NIGHTS OF MY LIFE. AND NOT JUST MINE. FOR A LOT OF PEOPLE IT KICKED OFF A YEAR OF NEW LOVES... STORIES OF THEIR OWN TO BE TOLD...

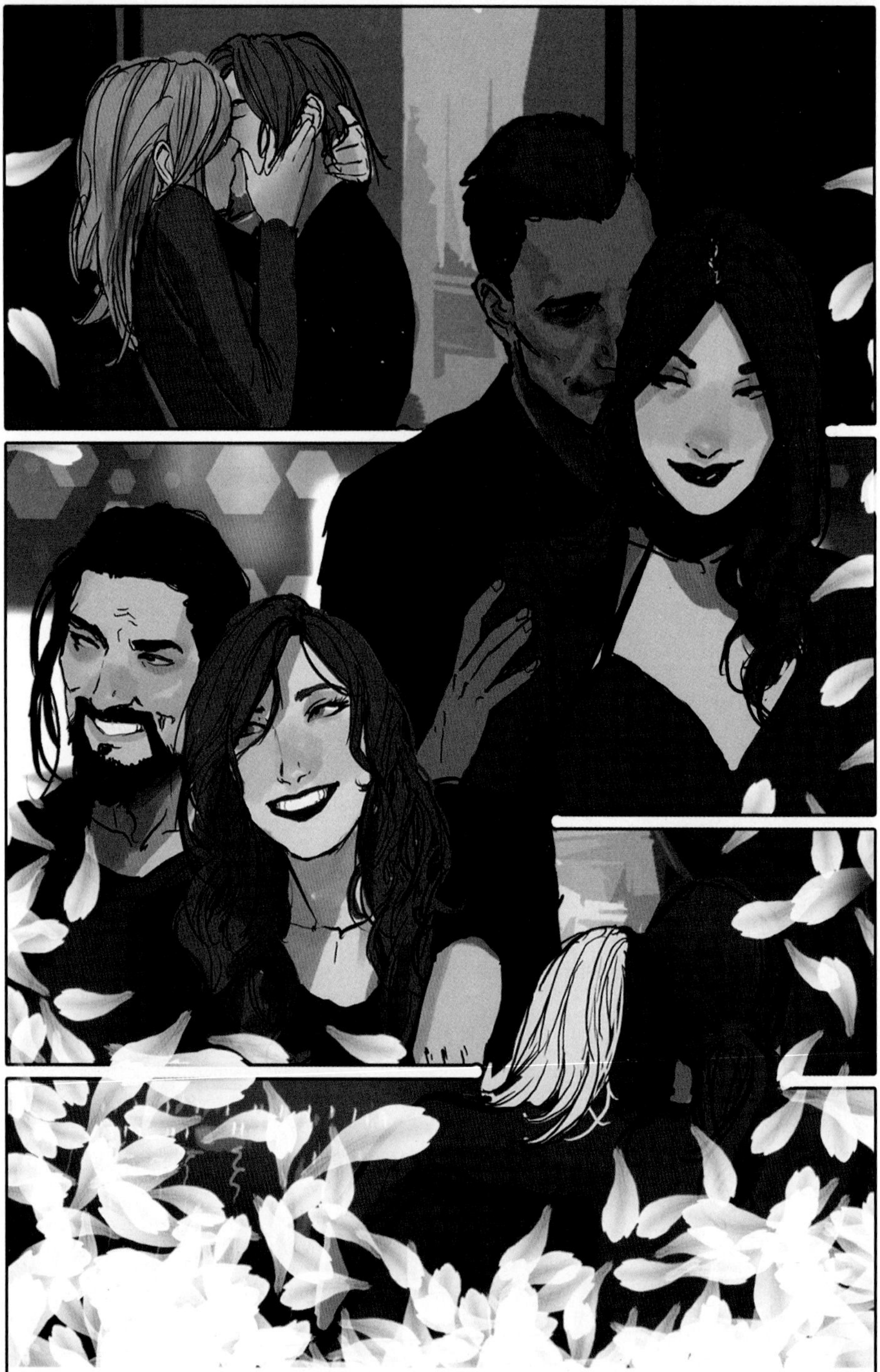

Oh, yes!
We'll get to all of those later...

As for Ally and me, we went home.
No dommes, no subs,
not that night.

That night we made love for the first time.

And I swear, it was only
partially because Ally's arm
was too busted to tie me up.

THE END

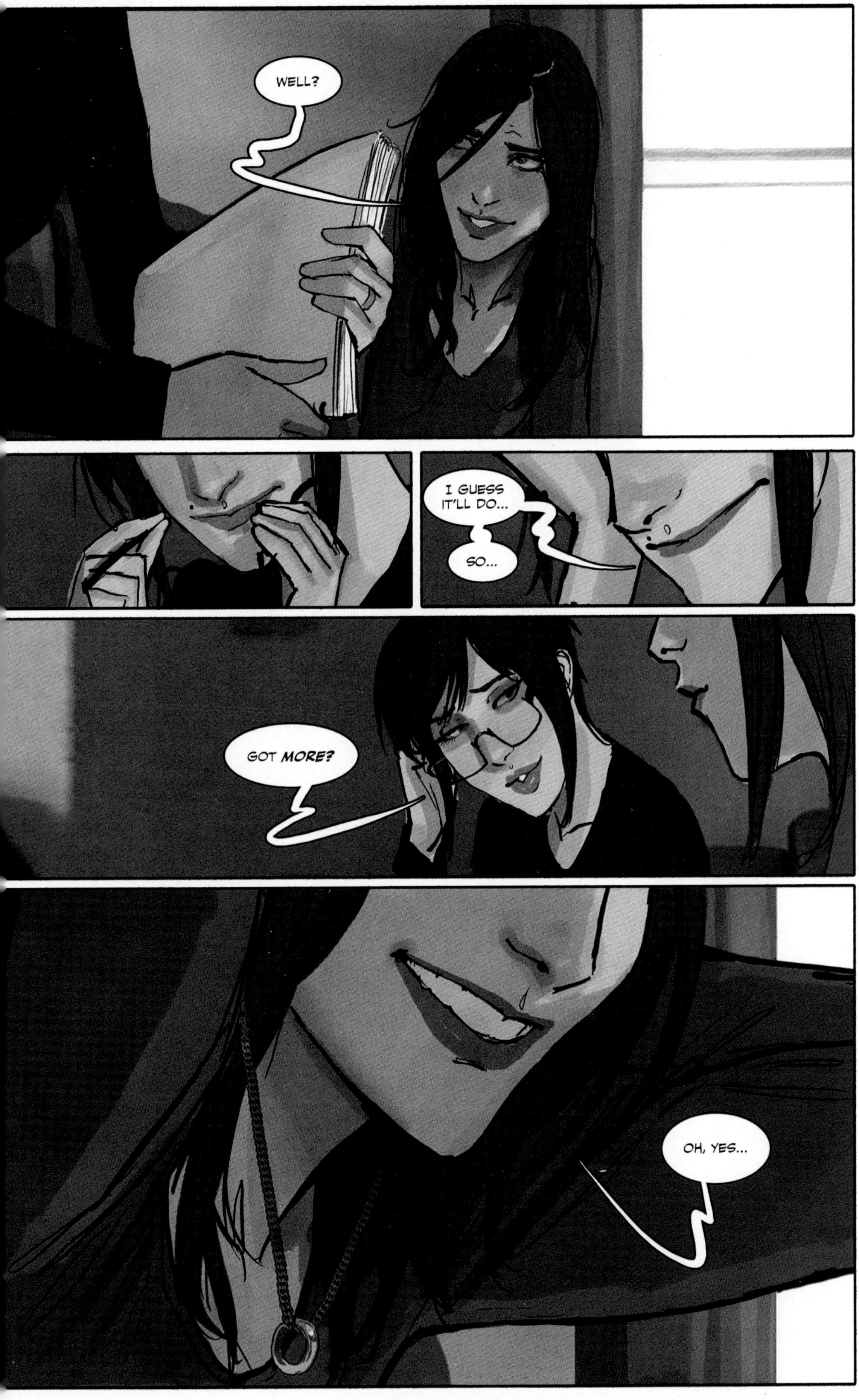
WELL?
I GUESS IT'LL DO...
SO...
GOT MORE?
OH, YES...

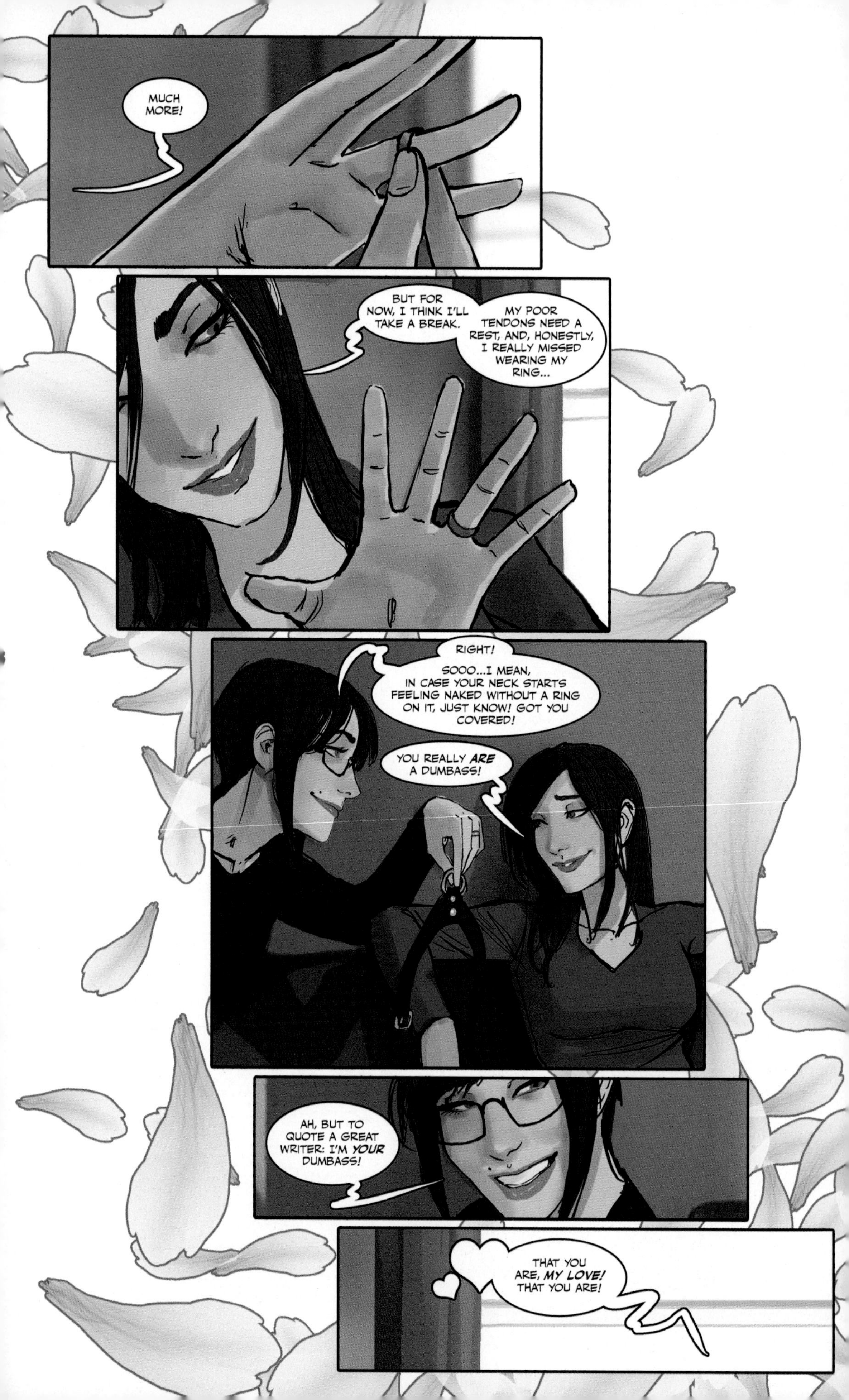
MUCH MORE!
BUT FOR NOW, I THINK I'LL TAKE A BREAK.
MY POOR TENDONS NEED A REST, AND, HONESTLY, I REALLY MISSED WEARING MY RING...
RIGHT!
SOOO...I MEAN, IN CASE YOUR NECK STARTS FEELING NAKED WITHOUT A RING ON IT, JUST KNOW! GOT YOU COVERED!
YOU REALLY *ARE* A DUMBASS!
AH, BUT TO QUOTE A GREAT WRITER: I'M *YOUR* DUMBASS!
THAT YOU ARE, *MY LOVE!* THAT YOU ARE!

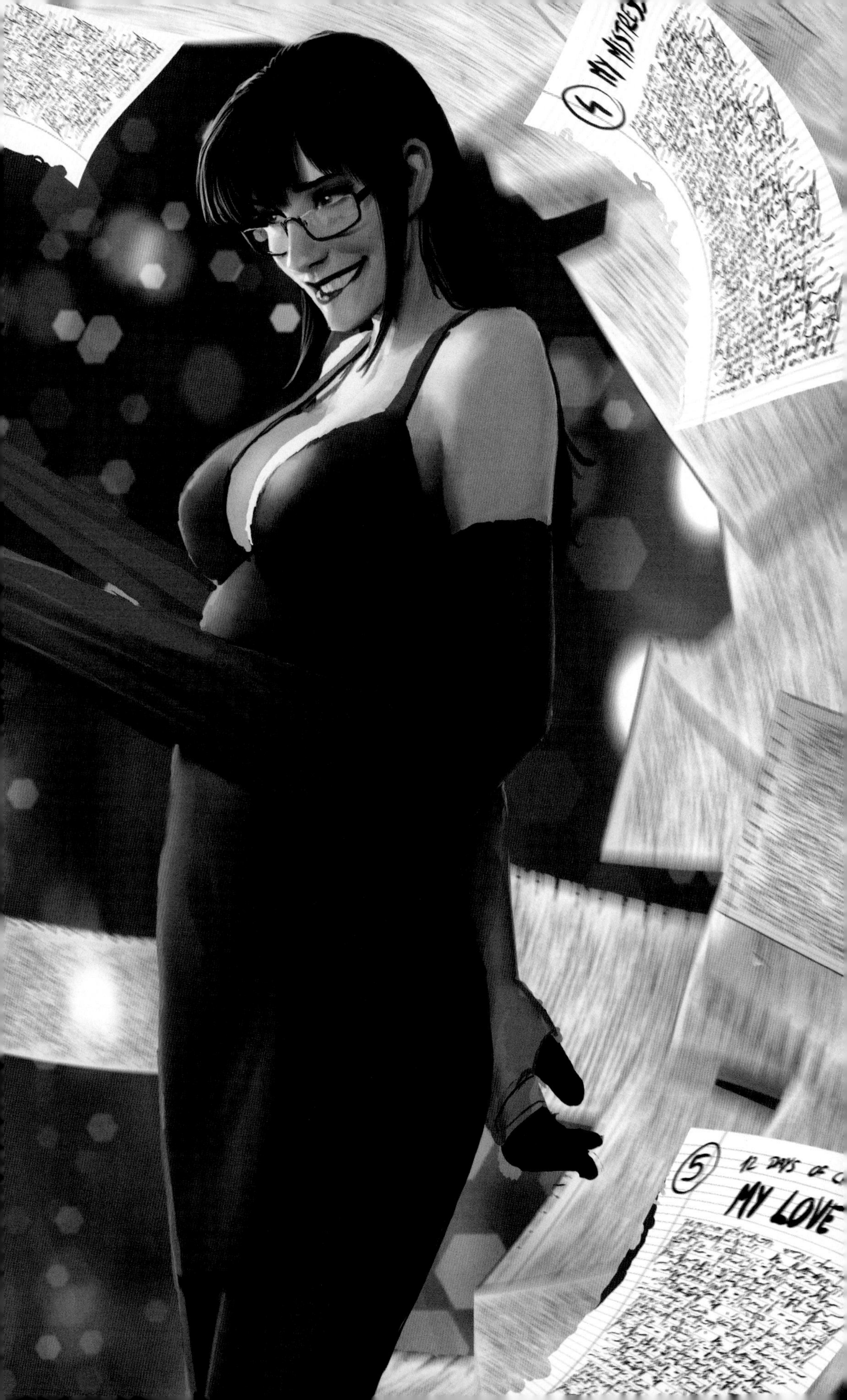

5
MY LOVE

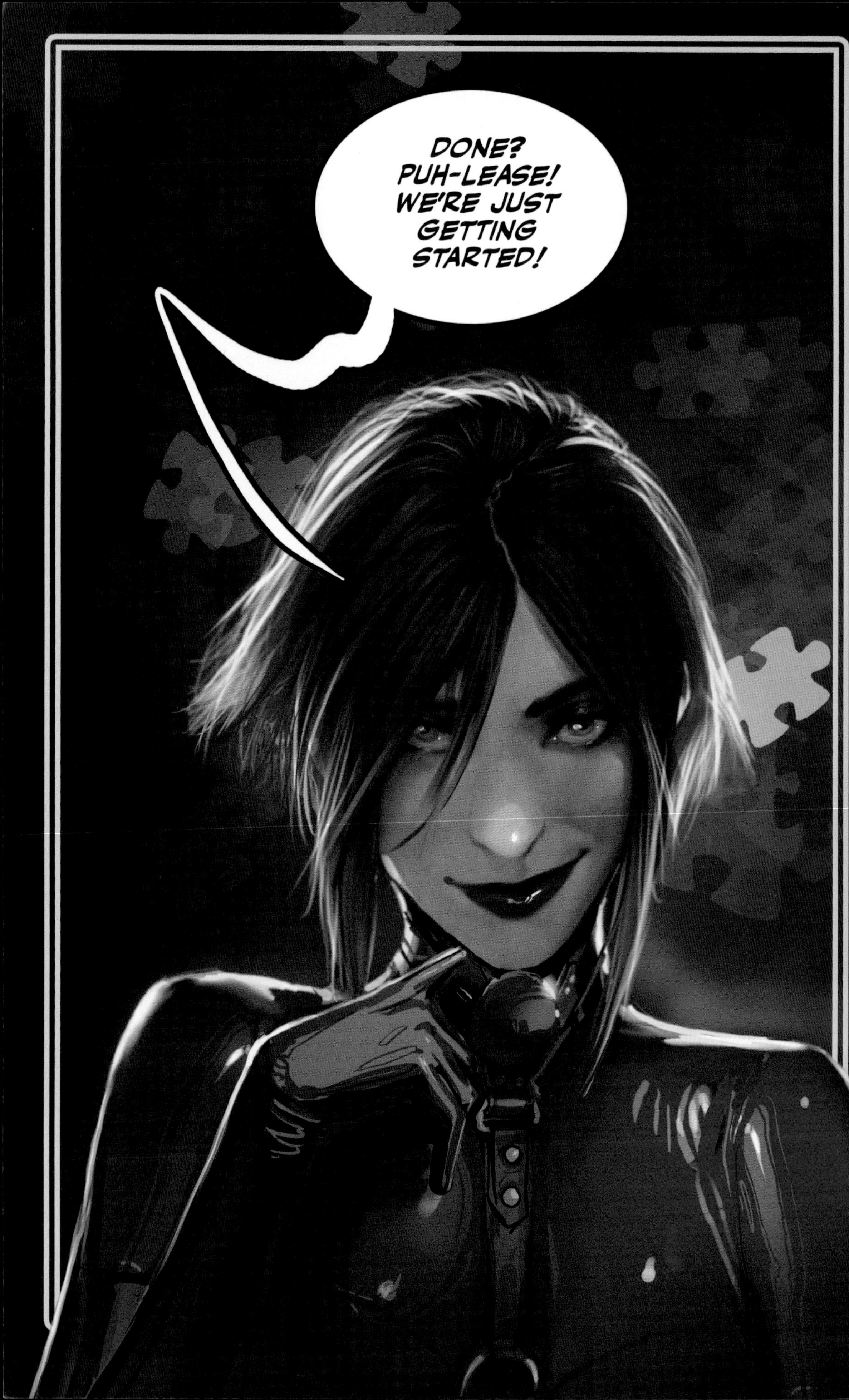
DONE? PUH-LEASE! WE'RE JUST GETTING STARTED!

WELL, HERE WE...

OKAY, NO, HONESTLY!?!?

HOW THE FUCK ARE WE EVEN HERE???

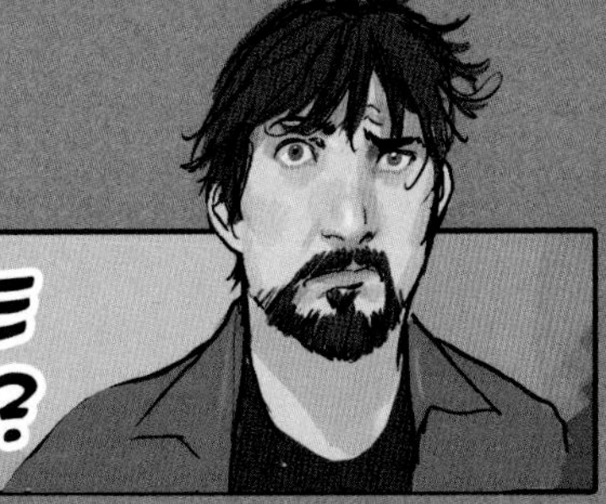

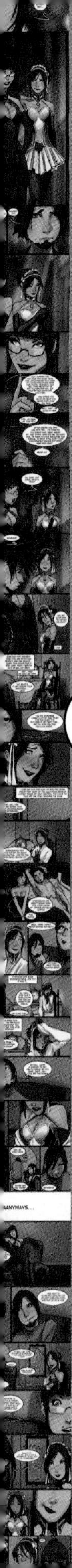

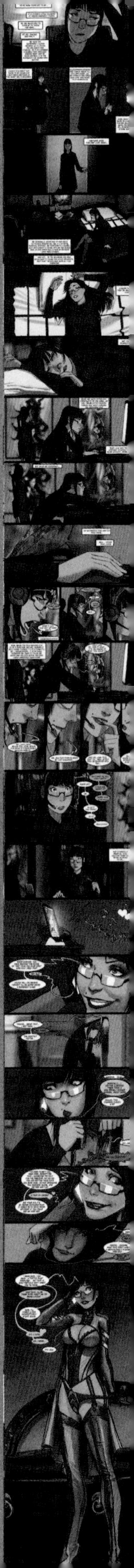

I MEAN, WOW. I STILL REMEMBER ABOUT FOUR YEARS AGO WHEN THE IDEA OF THE FINAL CLUB SCENE HIT ME. IT WAS DIFFERENT BACK THEN, BUT THE GIST OF IT WAS THERE. I STILL REMEMBER CHUCKLING THINKING, "YEAH, RIGHT...LIKE I'LL EVER TAKE THIS THAT FAR."

IT WOULD BE AN UNDERSTATEMENT TO SAY THAT I QUESTIONED MY ABILITY TO WRITE A ROMANCE. MY PREVIOUS EXPERIMENT AT WRITING BEING *RAVINE*, AN EPIC FANTASY, I HARDLY HAD ANY EXPERIENCE WITH THE GENRE.

SO THERE I WAS, SOMEWHERE AT THE END OF CHAPTER 1, THINKING..."ALIENS!"

YES, REALLY! I GENUINELY CONSIDERED AN ALIEN INVASION HAPPENING. THEY KIDNAP A BUNCH OF PEOPLE INCLUDING LISA, AND ALLY GOES ON A COSMIC ADVENTURE TO SAVE HER. SHE USES AN ALIEN DOMINANCE CROWN THAT ENABLES THE CONQUERING RACE TO CONTROL CIVILIZATIONS AND HER DOMME SPIRIT ENDS UP OVERPOWERING ALIEN CONQUERORS AND ENABLES HER TO RAISE AN ARMY...

AGAIN, ***YES! REALLY!***

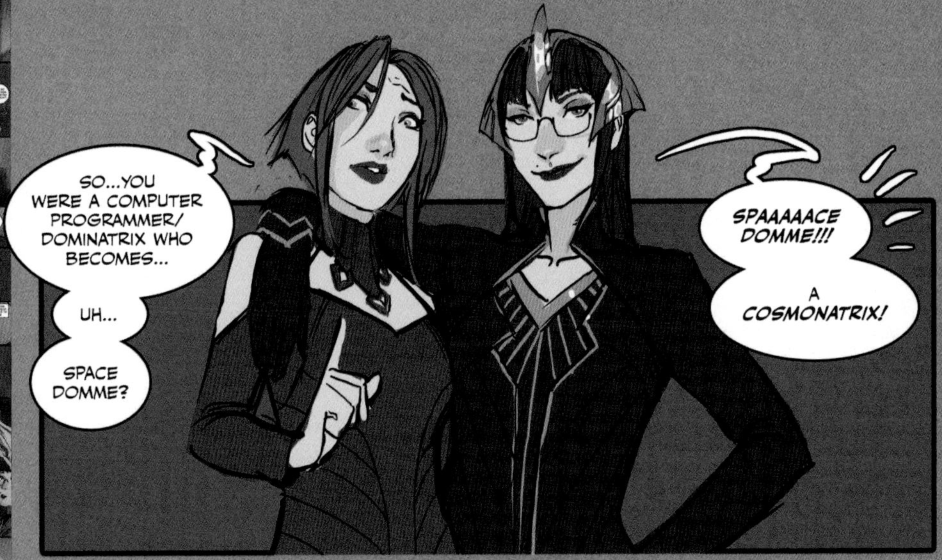
SO...YOU WERE A COMPUTER PROGRAMMER/ DOMINATRIX WHO BECOMES...
UH...
SPACE DOMME?
SPAAAAACE DOMME!!!
A COSMONATRIX!

IT WAS A CRAZY IDEA, BUT THE ALTERNATIVE SEEMED JUST AS CRAZY TO ME. BECAUSE THE OTHER OPTION WAS I WAS GOING TO WRITE A ROMANCE.

WRITING ABOUT BDSM WASN'T THE PROBLEM. LINDA AND I HAD OUR OWN LONG AND OFTEN HILARIOUS HISTORY WITH IT, AND WE HAD A BUNCH OF FRIENDS EAGER TO SHARE THEIR OWN DIFFERENT EXPERIENCES. NO, IT WAS THE ROMANCE PART THAT SCARED ME.

BUT...THEN I STARTED WRITING THE SECOND CHAPTER, AND CHARACTERS ONCE AGAIN DID WHAT THEY DID IN CHAPTER ONE. THEY CAME ALIVE. TURNS OUT IT WASN'T A FLUKE THE FIRST TIME.

ROMANCE AND SLICE-OF-LIFE GENRES ARE CHARACTER-POWERED STORIES. PLOT IS OFTEN SECONDARY. OVER TIME, I ADOPTED THE WRITING METHOD OF GETTING OUT OF MY CHARACTERS' WAYS. IF THEY OUTGREW MY PLANNED PLOT, I CHANGED THE PLOT, NOT THEM.

TRUST ME, EVEN PAST THE IDIOTIC ALIENS IDEA, THERE WERE MANY DISCARDED PLOTLINES THAT I PERSONALLY ***LOVED***. THEY PROVIDED ME WITH POWERFUL, EMOTIONAL, AND PLOT-DRIVING MOMENTS, BUT I HAD TO LISTEN TO MY CHARACTERS. IT WAS THEIR STORY TO TELL. THEIR REASONING, MOTIVATIONS AND EMOTIONAL STATES DICTATED THE PROGRESS. AND THEY TOOK US ALL DOWN SOME STRANGE PATHS.

AND HERE WE ARE NOW. FIRST STORY ARC COMPLETE. I SAY THE ***FIRST STORY ARC***, BECAUSE, AS IT TURNS OUT, WE'RE FAR FROM DONE.

DURING CHAPTER TWO, ANOTHER THING BECAME APPARENT. THIS WAS GOING TO GO FAR BEYOND JUST ***SUNSTONE***. THERE WERE RELEVANT THINGS TO BE SAID THROUGH SEVERAL STORIES. SEVERAL INTERTWINED RELATIONSHIPS...AND SO, I STARTED PLANTING THE SEEDS OF FUTURE ARCS.

(YOU PROBABLY PICKED UP ON AT LEAST SOME OF THEM.)

SPEAKING OF THESE FUTURE STORY ARCS...

SO, WITH THAT IN MIND WE TURN TO THE FUTURE. THE NEXT STORY ARC IS CALLED...

MERCY.

IT IS A STORY ABOUT ALAN AND ANNE. ABOUT THEIR STRANGE, COMPLICATED PAST AND THEIR STRANGER AND EXCITING FUTURE. WE WILL SEE ANNE'S COLLEGE DAYS, HER BECOMING AWARE AND DEALING WITH THE IDEA OF BEING BISEXUAL. HER FRIENDSHIP WITH CASSIE AND GROWING LOVE FOR THE ART OF TATTOOING. WE GET TO SEE HER MAKE MISTAKES AND LEARN FROM THEM... SOME QUITE HILARIOUS MISTAKES. (THERE IS A REASON SHE HAS A MASSIVE PHOENIX TATTOO ON HER BACK).

AT THE SAME TIME, WE WILL SEE ALAN AND ALLY'S FRIENDSHIP FORM THROUGH THEIR COLLEGE RELATIONSHIP AND ONWARDS.

MERCY IS A STORY OF PERSONAL GROWTH, OF TWO PEOPLE WHO HAD TO GROW UP ENOUGH TO BE READY FOR EACH OTHER.

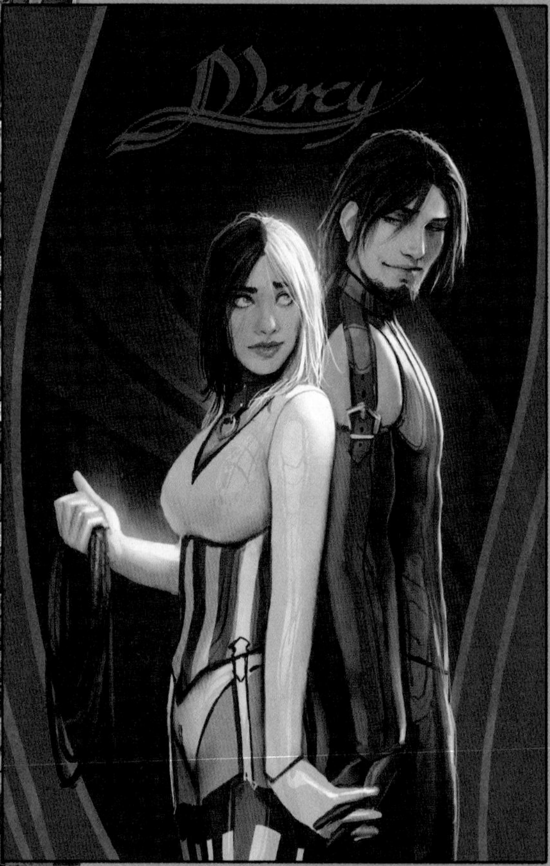
Mercy

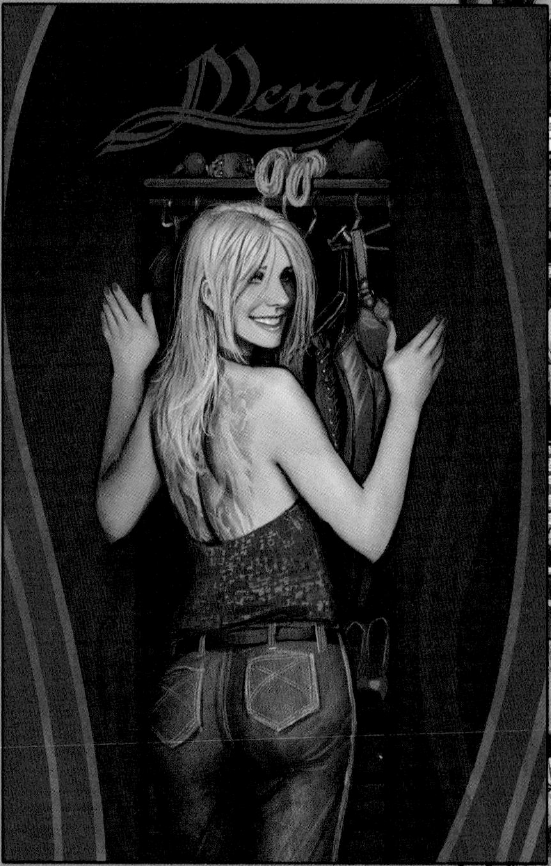
Mercy

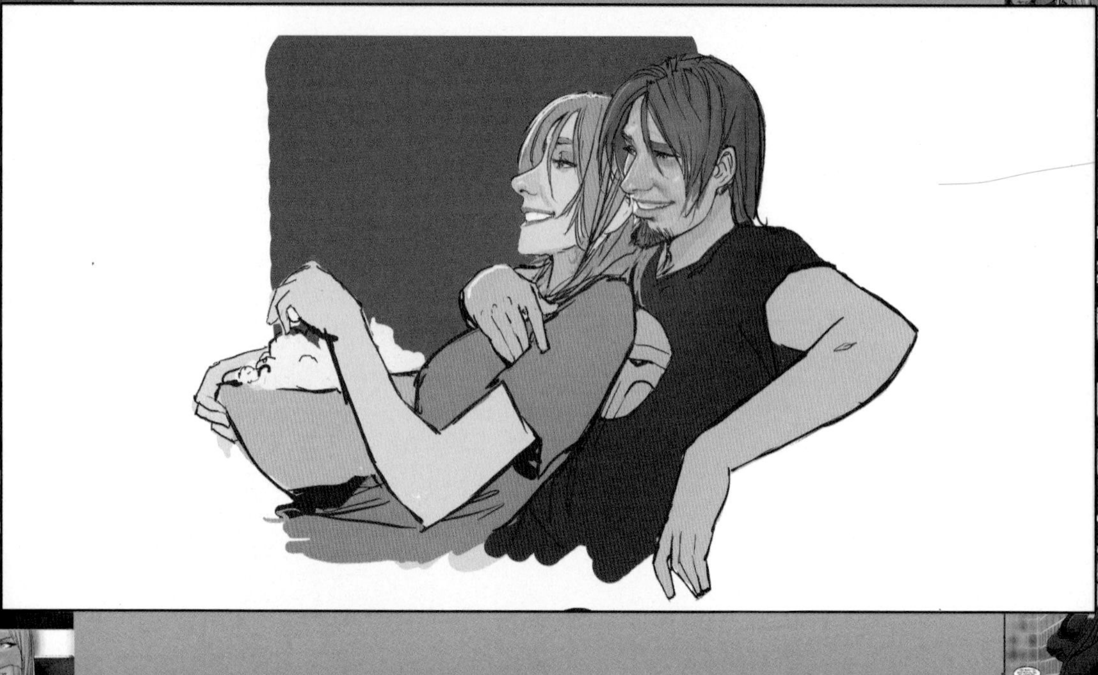

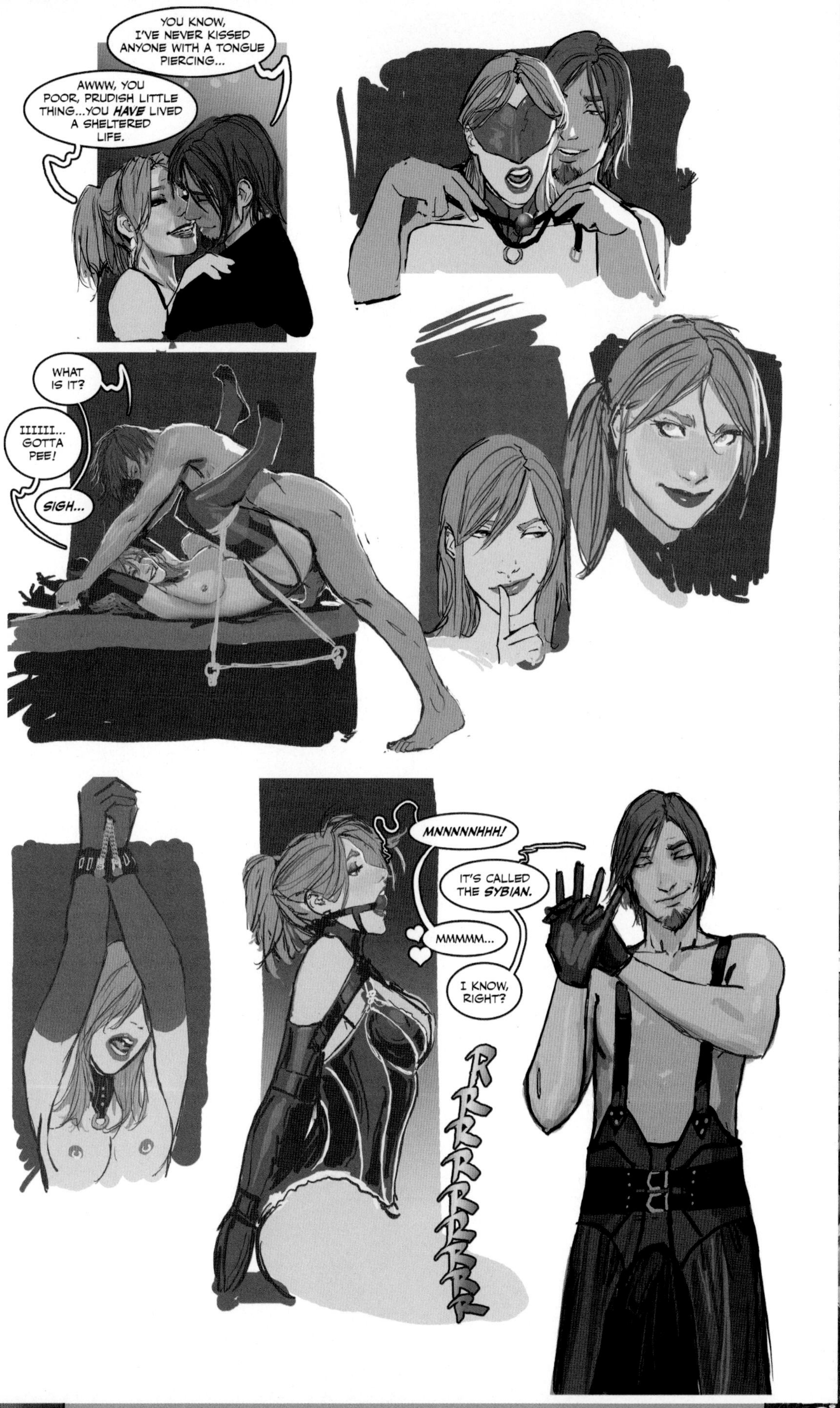
YOU KNOW, I'VE NEVER KISSED ANYONE WITH A TONGUE PIERCING...
AWWW, YOU POOR, PRUDISH LITTLE THING...YOU HAVE LIVED A SHELTERED LIFE.
WHAT IS IT?
IIIIII... GOTTA PEE!
SIGH...
MNNNNNHHH!
IT'S CALLED THE SYBIAN.
MMMMM...
I KNOW, RIGHT?
RRRRRRRR

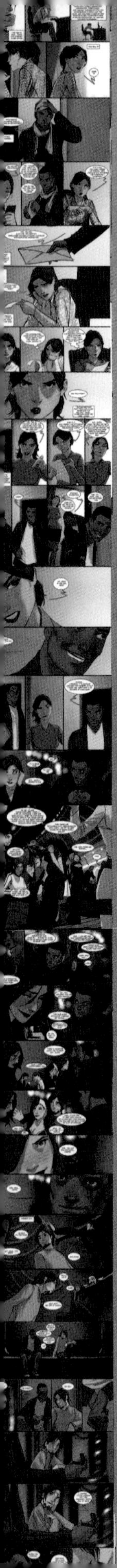

AFTER THAT, WE BEGIN THE THIRD STORY ARC...

JASPER.

THE STORY OF MARION AND JAMES. IN IT, WE WILL SEE IN DETAIL THE RISE AND FALL OF MARION AND ALAN FROM HER SIDE OF THINGS. FOLLOWING THAT, WE LEARN ABOUT THE AFTERMATH OF MARION DEALING WITH THE ADDICTIVE NATURE OF BDSM AS SHE SEEKS HELP FROM SEVERAL PSYCHIATRISTS. IN THE END, SHE FINDS THE RIGHT ONE, AND THIS PSYCHIATRIST ADVISES MARION THAT SHE CAN'T REALLY GO COLD TURKEY. IT WILL ONLY MAKE HER OBSESS ABOUT BDSM MORE. INSTEAD, SHE NEEDS TO REGAIN CONTROL AND BALANCE OVER HER SEX LIFE. EFFECTIVELY, SHE URGES MARION TO FIND HER ***DOMSPACE.***

MARION FINDS IT WITH JAMES, A CROSSDRESSER SHE KNEW FROM HER CRIMSON-FREQUENTING DAYS. COINCIDENTALLY, BACK THEN SHE WORKED HARD ON HOOKING UP JAMES AND ALLY.

(OH YES, IT'S THERE, MENTIONED AND EVEN SHOWN IN *SUNSTONE* CHAPTERS!)

THIS COUPLE HAS A STORY OF THEIR OWN AND ISSUES UNIQUE TO THEM.

AND THEN ...WELL...THERE IS MORE TO BE TOLD.

I WON'T SHARE TOO MUCH. BUT I GUESS THERE IS THE OBVIOUS THING COMING UP.

WE'VE GOT A LONG, FUN ROAD AHEAD OF US. THOSE OF YOU WHO ONLY READ IT IN PRINT ALSO HAVE A BIT OF A WAIT AHEAD OF YOU. HOPEFULLY IT WILL BE WORTH IT TO THOSE WHO FOLLOW THESE STORIES AS THEY APPEAR ONLINE. SEE YOU SOON.

-STJEPAN

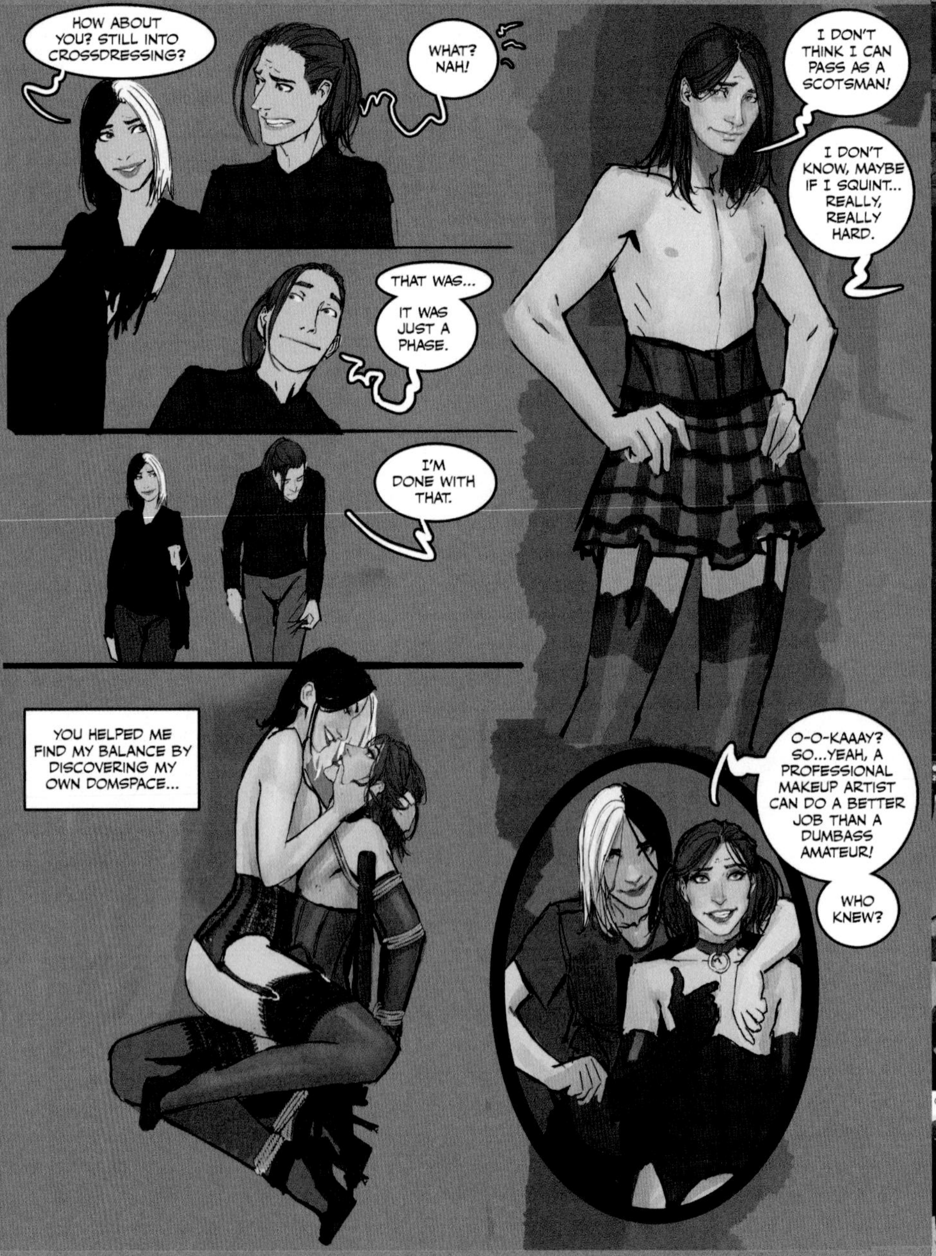
HOW ABOUT YOU? STILL INTO CROSSDRESSING?
WHAT? NAH!
THAT WAS...
IT WAS JUST A PHASE.
I'M DONE WITH THAT.
I DON'T THINK I CAN PASS AS A SCOTSMAN!
I DON'T KNOW, MAYBE IF I SQUINT... REALLY, REALLY HARD.
YOU HELPED ME FIND MY BALANCE BY DISCOVERING MY OWN DOMSPACE...
O-O-KAAAY? SO...YEAH, A PROFESSIONAL MAKEUP ARTIST CAN DO A BETTER JOB THAN A DUMBASS AMATEUR!
WHO KNEW?

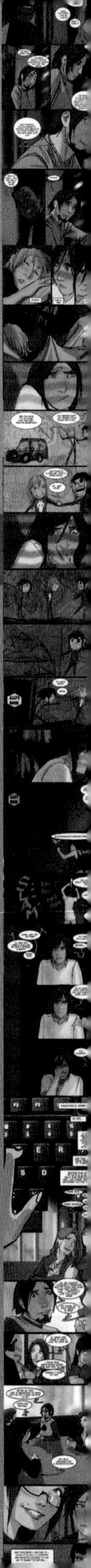

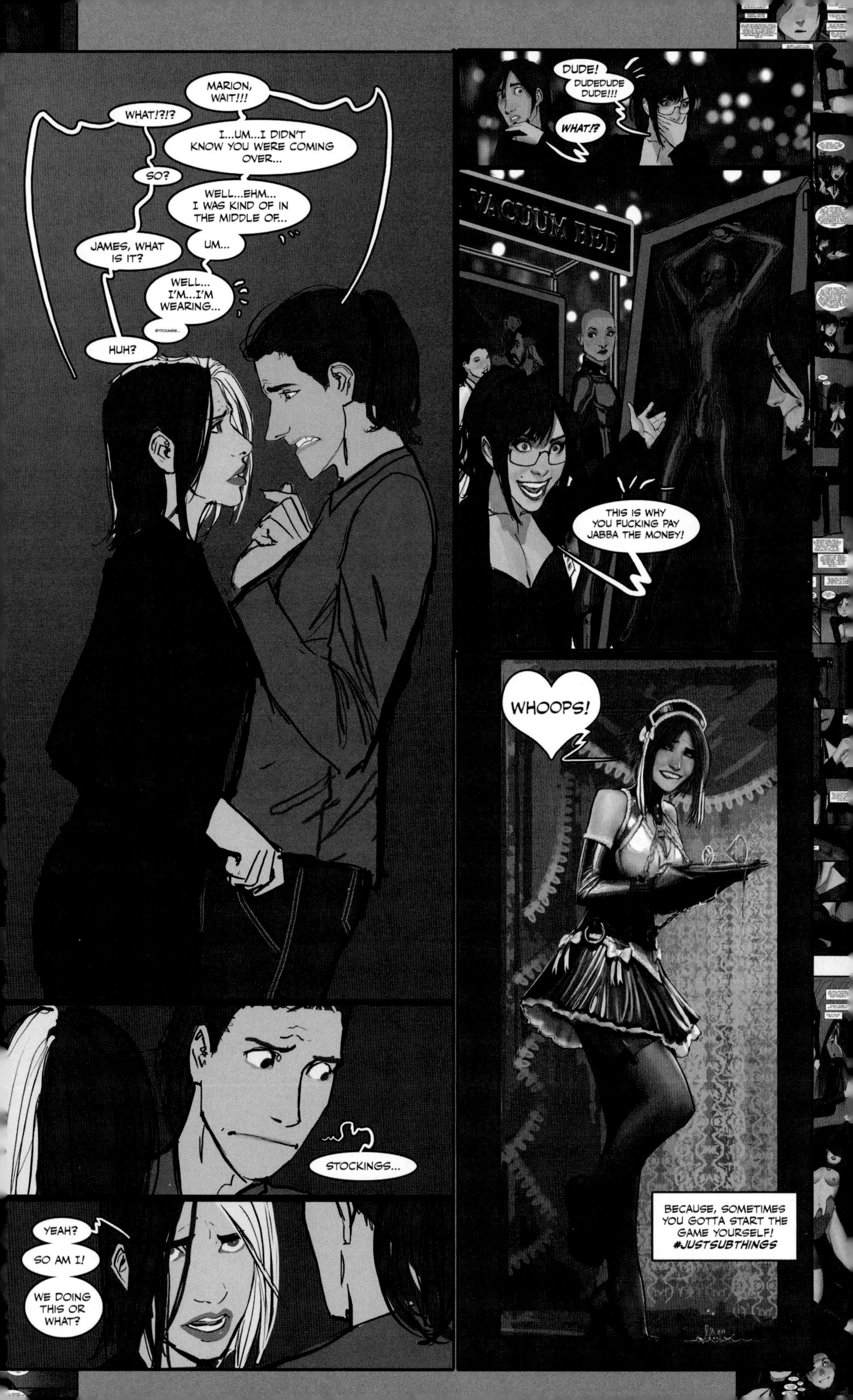
MARION, WAIT!!!
WHAT!?!?
I...UM...I DIDN'T KNOW YOU WERE COMING OVER...
SO?
WELL...EHM... I WAS KIND OF IN THE MIDDLE OF...
JAMES, WHAT IS IT?
UM...
WELL... I'M...I'M WEARING...
STOCKINGS...
HUH?
STOCKINGS...
YEAH?
SO AM I!
WE DOING THIS OR WHAT?
DUDE!
DUDEDUDE DUDE!!!
WHAT!?
VACUUM BED
THIS IS WHY YOU FUCKING PAY JABBA THE MONEY!
WHOOPS!
BECAUSE, SOMETIMES YOU GOTTA START THE GAME YOURSELF!
#JUSTSUBTHINGS

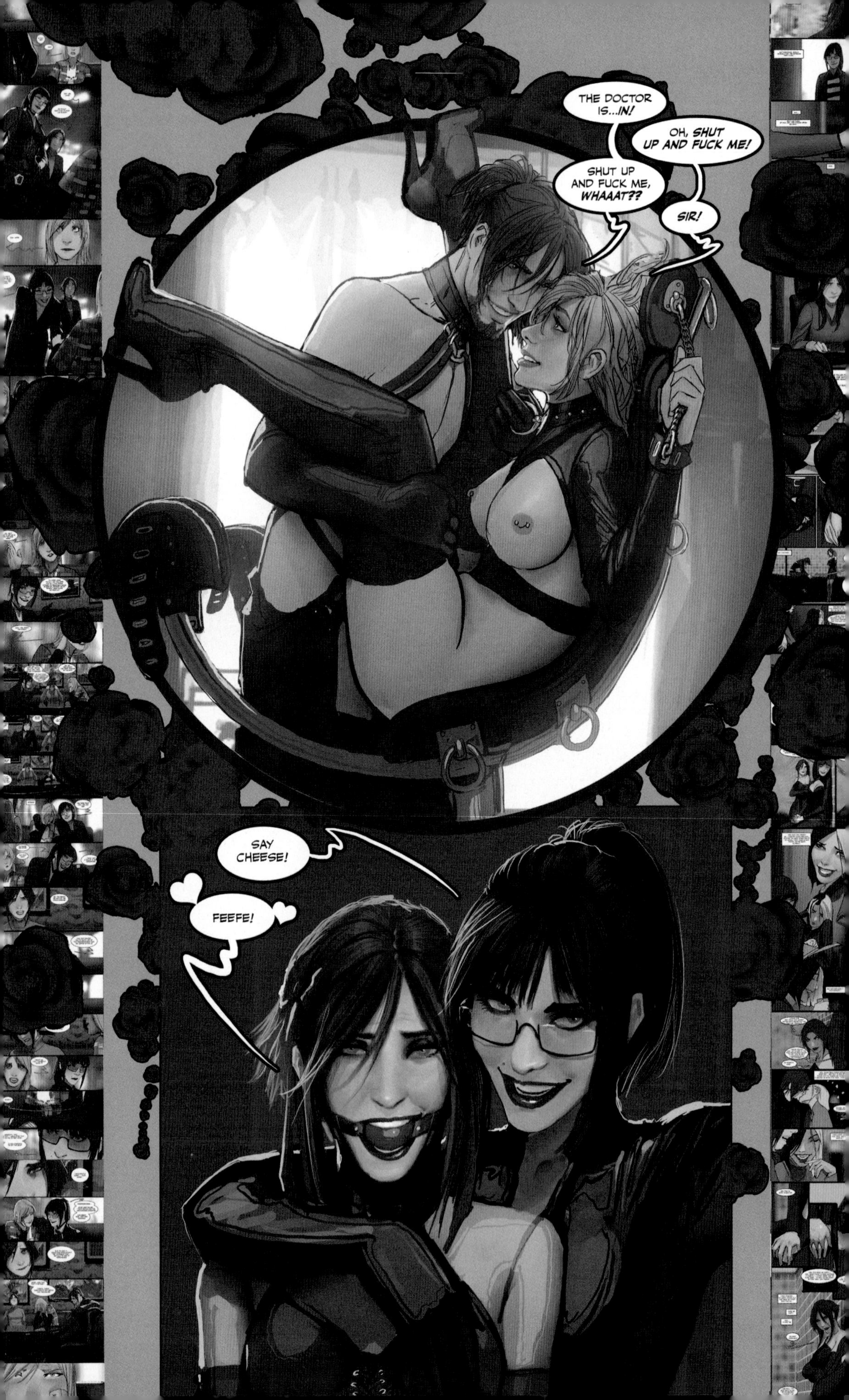
THE DOCTOR IS...IN!
OH, SHUT UP AND FUCK ME!
SHUT UP AND FUCK ME, WHAAAT??
SIR!
SAY CHEESE!
FEEFE!

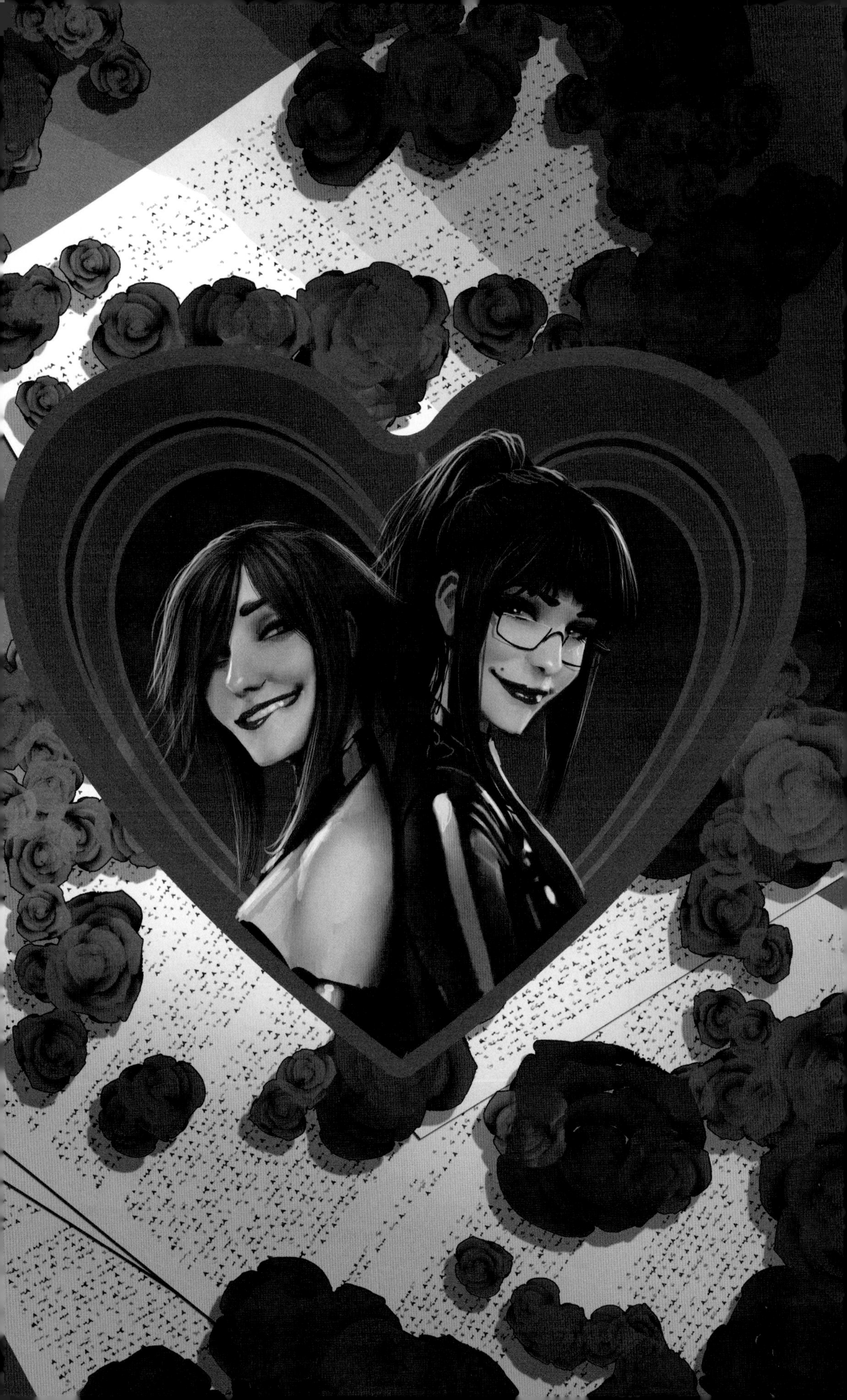

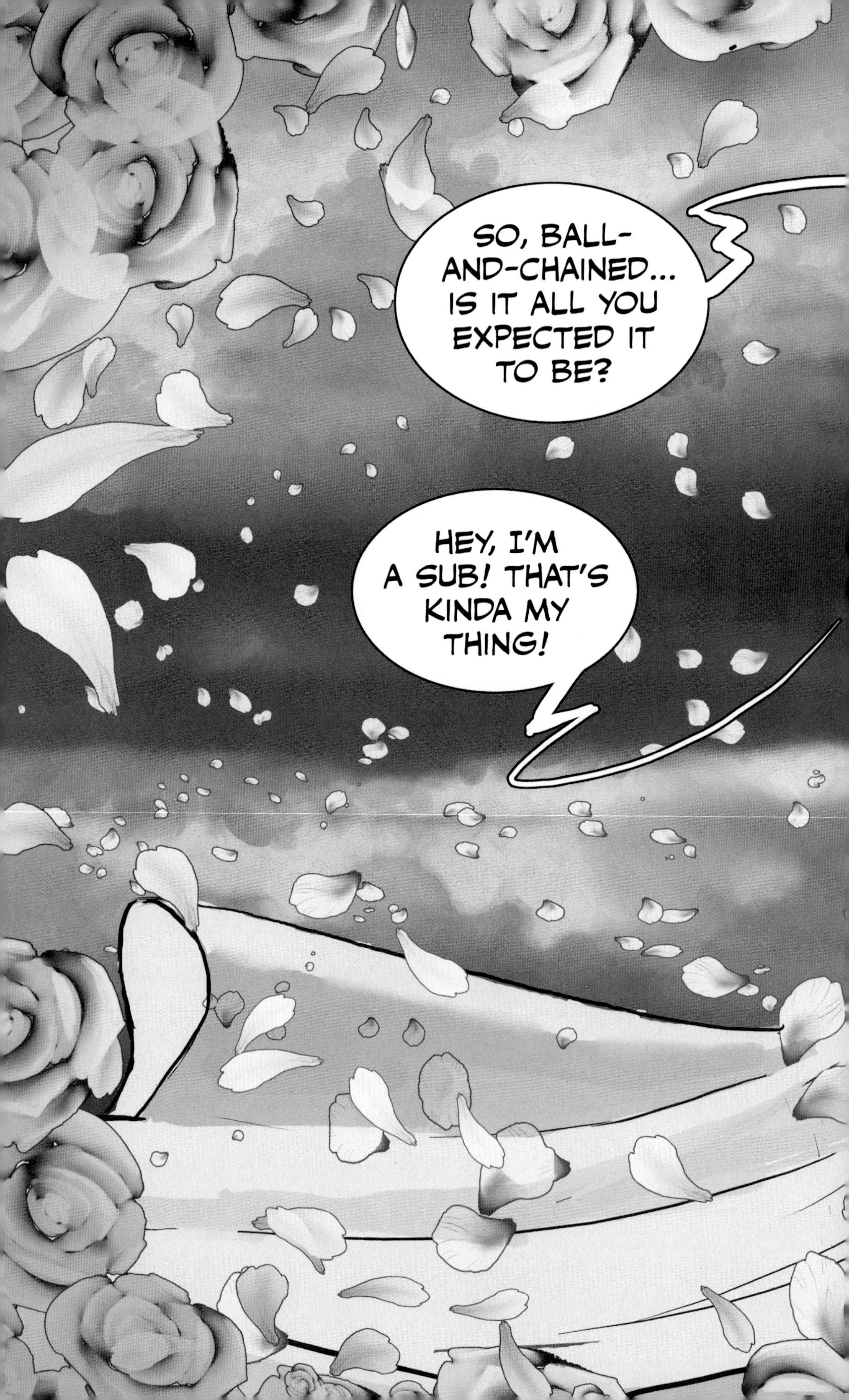
SO, BALL-AND-CHAINED... IS IT ALL YOU EXPECTED IT TO BE?
HEY, I'M A SUB! THAT'S KINDA MY THING!

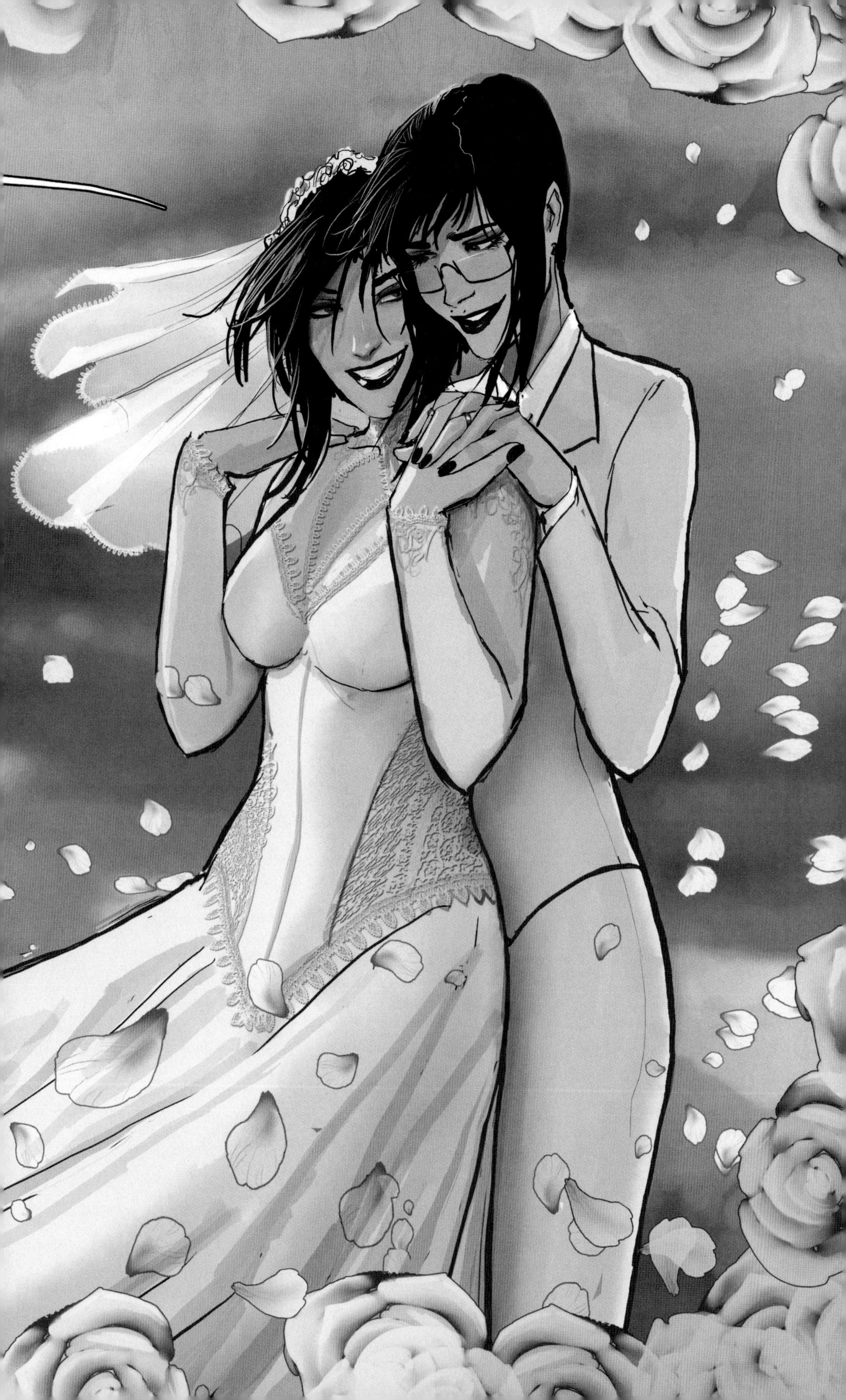

More volumes to be seduced by...

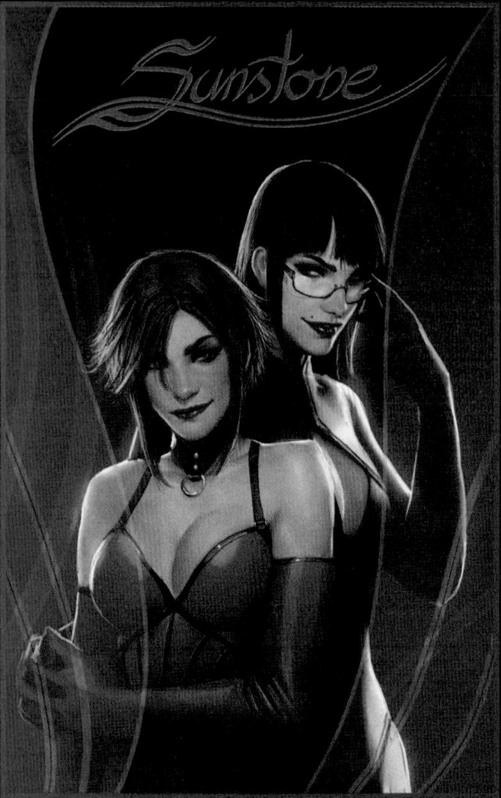
Sunstone

Volume 1

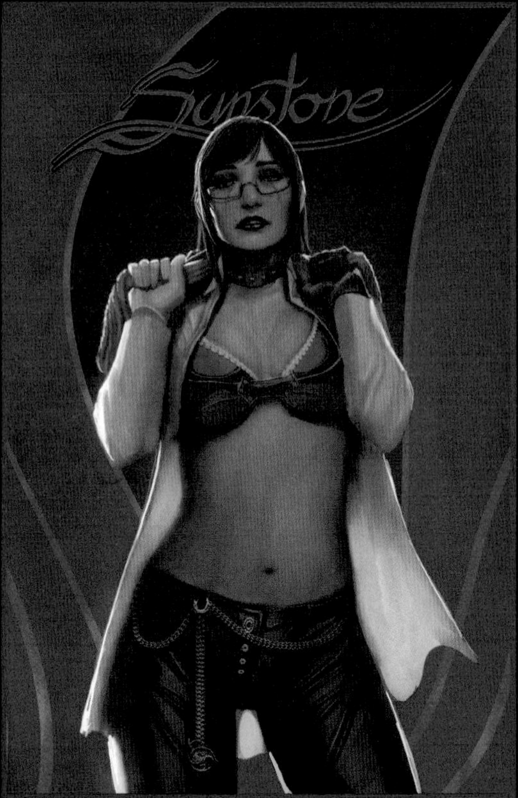
Sunstone

Volume 2

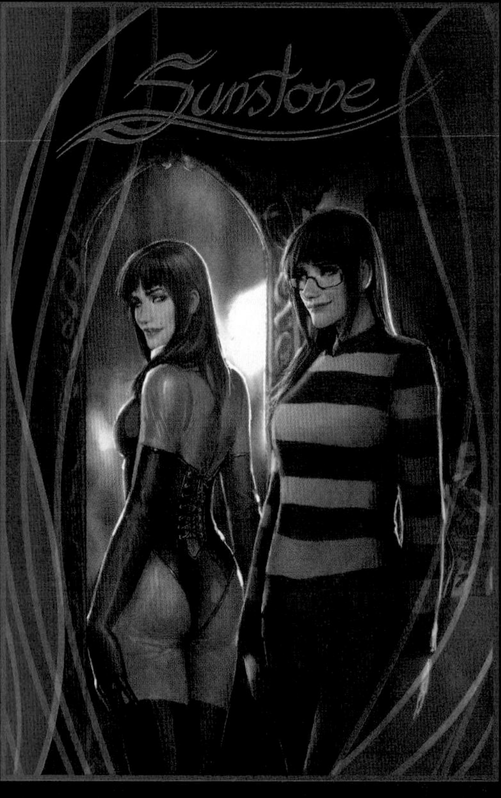
Sunstone

Volume 3

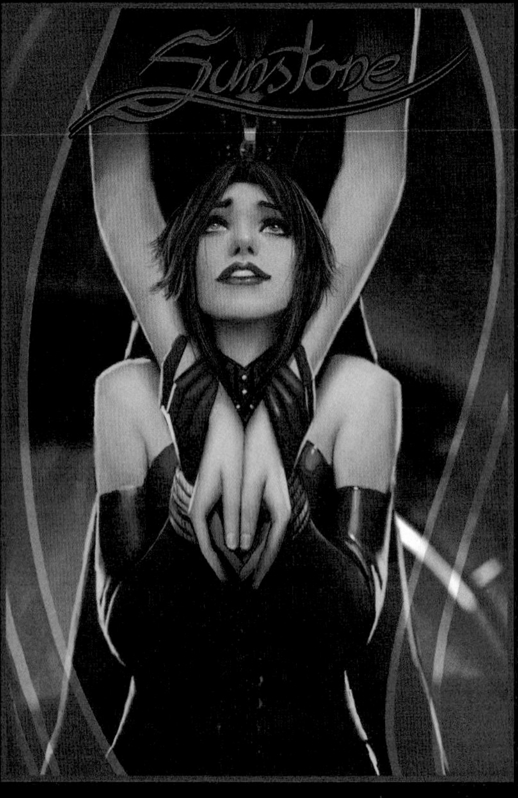
Sunstone

Volume 4

Available Now!

The Top Cow essentials checklist:

IXth Generation, Volume 1
(ISBN: 978-1-63215-323-4)

Aphrodite IX: Complete Series
(ISBN: 978-1-63215-368-5)

Artifacts Origins: First Born
(ISBN: 978-1-60706-506-7)

Broken Trinity, Volume 1
(ISBN: 978-1-60706-051-2)

Cyber Force: Rebirth, Volume 1
(ISBN: 978-1-60706-671-2)

The Darkness: Accursed, Volume 1
(ISBN: 978-1-58240-958-0)

The Darkness: Rebirth, Volume 1
(ISBN: 978-1-60706-585-2)

Death Vigil, Volume 1
(ISBN: 978-1-63215-278-7)

Eden's Fall
(ISBN: 978-1-5343-0065-1)

Impaler, Volume 1
(ISBN: 978-1-58240-757-9)

Mechanism, Volume 1
(ISBN: 978-1-5343-0032-3)

Postal, Volume 1
(ISBN: 978-1-63215-342-5)

Rising Stars Compendium
(ISBN: 978-1-63215-246-6)

Sunstone, Volume 1
(ISBN: 978-1-63215-212-1)

Symmetry, Volume 1
(ISBN: 978-1-63215-699-0)

The Tithe, Volume 1
(ISBN: 978-1-63215-324-1)

Think Tank, Volume 1
(ISBN: 978-1-60706-660-6)

Wanted
(ISBN: 978-1-58240-497-4)

Wildfire, Volume 1
(ISBN: 978-1-63215-024-0)

Witchblade: Redemption, Volume 1
(ISBN: 978-1-60706-193-9)

Witchblade: Rebirth, Volume 1
(ISBN: 978-1-60706-532-6)

Witchblade: Borne Again, Volume 1
(ISBN: 978-1-63215-025-7)

For more ISBN and ordering information on our latest collections go to:
www.topcow.com
Ask your retailer about our catalogue of collected editions,
digests, and hard covers or check the listings at:
Barnes and Noble, Amazon.com,
and other fine retailers.

To find your nearest comic shop go to:
www.comicshoplocator.com